BARRY E WOODHAM

Genesis 2

BARRY E WOODHAM

Genesis 2

MEMOIRS

Cirencester

Published by Memoirs

MEMOIRS
PUBLISHING

25 Market Place, Cirencester, Gloucestershire, GL7 2NX
info@memoirsbooks.co.uk www.memoirspublishing.com

Copyright ©Barry E. Woodham, August 2012
www.facebook.com/scifiauthorbarry
Twitter: @sci_fiauthor
http://sci-fiauthor.blogspot.co.uk
Email: barry.e.woodham@btinternet.com

First published in England, August 2012

Book cover design Ray Lipscombe

ISBN 978-1-909020-79-5

Printed in England

Foreword

The novel is extremely well written, imaginative, and full of great ideas and concepts, which at its best reminds and bears similar styles to the works of Niven and Pournelle. It examines how alien races may differ in their culture and beliefs, and brings the reader a wonderful tale of how these races interact with the human survivors of Earth.

Using science fact as well as fiction to tell a remarkable story set in the far future, the author's use and knowledge and research of scientific details gives the novel an air of realism that enhances the story, making it believable and easy to imagine being a possible future, to show an eventual fate of the human race, and of our solar system.

The story draws you in and doesn't let you go, making you turn to the next page with eagerness, wanting to know what happens next. The characterisations of the people we are introduced to throughout the story are excellent, and fully realised, making them easily believable, whether they are alien or human, and leaving the reader eager to learn what happens to them, and how they will make the threads of the story weave.

The imagery used in the novel draws you in and surrounds you, as you take in the new worlds in this Jovian system. Readers will find themselves immersed in a story that will take their breath away with scope and storytelling, making it a book that is very hard to put down. It will leave the reader eagerly awaiting the next in the series.

James Narbett, BA

CHAPTER 1

▼

The Nano-ship had been created over six million years before the sun had swallowed a vibrant civilization. It was one of many, hurled towards the stars by the Hammer-drive, a nuclear explosive drive that produced an acceleration that would mash living tissue to a pulp. The radiation alone would annihilate anything alive, but on these vessels, nothing organic lived. Thousands of Nano-ships had set forth to the stars at sub-light speeds containing four nannite artificial intelligences, programmed to recreate mankind.

Here, locked in a solid-state neural net, slept the Nano-ship's crew. Four hibernating personalities existed here, self-aware and independent from one another. They were not human, nor were they computers, but a remarkable combination of both. It had been decided long ago by the project's directors, that one male and three female intellects would be the optimum mixture for the survival of the only hope to prevent mankind's complete extinction.

The commander of this undertaking knew itself as 'Asue' and was designed and programmed to feel female. She was a Nano-tech expert, physicist, engineer and astro-navigator. The female trait had long proved to be successful in producing a fierce protectiveness for the tasks ahead.

Sharn and Minns were also able to identify themselves as female in their mind structure. Both of these personalities were biochemists, genetic engineers, surgeons, doctors and vets. They carried all the necessary knowledge to bring forth the life that was, onto a new world. These two entities would re-create the race of man in an earth-like habitat.

The forth mind that had been created and programmed was male. He knew himself as Kamiel. In his artificial memories lay the complete history of man's climb into sapience up to the coming extinction. Five thousand years of mistakes and triumphs were recorded in his memory banks. Keeper of the records, he was also a weapons expert, builder, Nano-tech engineer and mission psychologist.

All four artificial intelligences were independent entities programmed with a single purpose, whatever the odds—to bring back humanity, the pan-chimpanzees and create a biosphere to enable them to flourish.

This was the Genesis project and it consumed the civilisation that created it.

Over six million years after the sun had gone into its red giant stage, totally destroying the inner planets, mankind had been given another chance to live.

Knowing that the sun would expand beyond the orbit of the Earth, it had been calculated that the heat of the new red giant sun would most probably change Jupiter. If a liveable world was left, then a second possibility was left behind. A great seeding ship was built and left in orbit around Saturn. It carried every form of life that was thought necessary to start a new world, frozen in suspended animation and also the genetic codes. This great ark carried an artificial intelligence to guide and process the new life and to alter it genetically, if necessary, to survive. The plan was to start the life on the planet and go into hibernation for hundreds of thousands of years and then boost and adjust the life forms to suit, before recreating Humankind.

When the sun expanded, Jupiter boiled. Billions of tons of liquid gas were superheated and blown away by the sun's photosphere. Without the pressure of the massive atmosphere to hold it down against the internal pressure, the crust tore apart and for the very first time volcanoes erupted. When it began to cool, the rains began to fall and every comet that crashed upon the new world added new organic compounds. Over several million years later, primitive Jovian life had already begun to spread through the warm seas before the seeding ship awoke. Enough bacteria had evolved and spread to start an oxygen atmosphere.

After the sun settled down and took up its new stage, sensors on the seeding ship awoke the main artificial intelligence, leaving the nannite crew still in hibernation. The great ship pulled away from orbiting the gas giant and set out on its journey to the new Jupiter. Pleased with the situation that it found, it began the long process of attempting to create a viable world and a new home for Mankind.

It seeded the seas with fish and every type of life to form a food chain. As the air became richer in breathable gases it dropped vegetation packages in rain soaked areas with attendant insect life. Eons passed and the empty world thrived on its care.

Five times the ship awakened, sending life packages down, introducing reptiles, birds and mammals and carrying out adjustments, as it found necessary.

During a period of hibernation, a comet storm took it out and sent it burning into Jupiter's atmosphere. What had been started was now very much on its own. Continental plates crashed together, reforming new mountain ranges and fertile conditions for evolution to have its own way. Over everything, the new sun bathed the surface in cosmic radiation, inviting new mutations to take place without a keeper to control it.

That was, until a new guiding hand began to take an interest. The Gnathe arrived, masters of genetic manipulation of themselves and anything else that lived, breathed or put roots into the ground. They soon learned to do without sophisticated tools and altered other life forms to their will, as Jupiter's metal-poor terrain gave them little choice. The Gnathe also soon learned to harness other bounties to their will and increased their mental science.

These were triple sexed beings, male, female and a different type of female. They were known as Brood-mothers and were the egg carriers for the other two. Once the egg had been placed in the breeding pouch, the Brood-mother could genetically alter the offspring and decide on the sex or physique of the young. It was not long before they discovered that they could alter the other species of this world to their needs and did so to their own advantage.

On the other side of the high mountain range separating the human colony from the Gnathe, a course of events were taking place that was about to directly affect the lives and destinies of the human and ape civilisation. At the Imperial City of the Gnathe, an incredible audience was taking place. In many generations of civilised life, no Brood-mother had ever been subjected to an interrogation by her peers with such terrible consequences. The high vaulted chamber reflected the red-gold sun's rays in crystalline splendour. On the dais perched Link-soo-shan, Ultimate Ruler of the Gnathen Empire, thrashing her tail from side to side and by her side stood her egg sister, Chang.

She surveyed the spread-eagled form of the young Brood-mother with an icy stare and hissed in fury, "Ender-whann-soo, you have been brought before us, accused of heresy and sedition. Have you anything to say? How do you plead?"

"I do not understand," Ender-whann-soo replied. "What have I done that you should treat me so? I have achieved great new standards amongst my kindred."

"What have you done? What have you done?" Link-soo-shan screamed implacably at the recumbent Brood-mother's face. "You know full well the crime you have committed. For countless generations, we the Brood-mothers, have chosen the mating partners of our kindred. We and we alone control the gene pool. We shape, they are shaped by our will. The very stability of our civilisation is controlled by the will of the breeding pouch. The kindred are born to serve and they serve us."

Ender-whann-soo looked up at the ring of triangular faces in hopelessness. Expressionless heavy-duty guards held down the Brood-mother's arms and legs. In vain the young Brood-mother argued back to the assembly.

"I looked for another way, to improve the standards of the kindred. I allowed them to choose their mates with minimal interference and increased their intelligence." The helpless Gnathe cried out desperately: "I did no harm!"

"The very ideas you put forth are dangerous. They are an abomination. I will hear no more of these heresies. Have this Brood-mother's arms and legs broken and cast her out of the city limits to die on the 'Killing Stones'. Let none come near, under pain of death. I have sat upon this dais for many generations of kindred and the Empire has remained stable. My sister and I built this Empire from chaos. We have held it together by force and obedience. Always the Brood-mothers have chosen the breeding partners of our males and females. We manipulate the gene structure to suit our needs and my household controls the outcome of this process. Take her out!" Link-soo-shan cried at the waiting guards. "I will see this person no more."

"What of her possessions and deviant household? A decision needs to be taken, my sister," retorted Chang-soo-shan, commander of the Imperial Guard.

"The Brood-mother's dwelling, off-spring and goods to be divided as I see fit," Link-soo-shan decreed. "I want all traces of this deviant removed. All! Do you hear me? All! Now break this creature and cast her out!"

The guards twisted their powerful arms and Ender-whann-soo's limbs snapped with an audible crack. The Gnathe fainted as she was carried out from the assembly. Her triangular head hung down, beads of moisture trickled down the slender neck and the ruined arms. The strong muscular tail dragged in the dust of the council floor. The doorkeepers opened the ornate polished doors and the oiled living hinge clasps made no noise. A breeze sang in the hanging crystals and a melody played to the packed crowd.

At the back of the chamber, standing in the shadows, was Shoo-lin, master of beasts. He stood quietly, in shocked amazement, as the heretical ideas chased themselves through his keen brain. He had heard of the Brood-mother's heresy. Long had he thought about it. He had been dissatisfied with the mating allocations for some time. It was unheard of even to think of change or complaint. He had discussed some of his ideas in secret with like-minded males and had carefully broached the subject with some of the more aggressive females he felt he could trust. He must warn and alert certain members of Ender-whann-soo's household, before the ponderous bureaucracy divided everything up and separated or had destroyed Ender-whann-soo's kindred young. He must organise a rescue during the hours of darkness. Therefore, he must move swiftly. There was no time to lose.

He impressed a memory crystal and attached it to one of his Fletch. Mentally, he imprinted the destination and person into the small creature's mind and he threw the Fletch out of the window. Wings stretched wide, the little flying beast turned around the tower of the council, flying towards the home of Ender-whann-soo, to find Coen-soo. She was chief of the household protectorate and would organise things at her end.

Shoo-lin hurried through the twisting corridors of the ancient Banilik tree. Every so often he would cross chambers grown into the living wood. Living mirrors that tilted to catch the sun and reflect it onto the ever-present crystal growths jutting out of the living walls provided light. None of the Horde paid him any attention or questioned his passage. As Beast-master, his rank was high amongst the chosen. None would dare to challenge him. What he had in mind to do would be dangerous, both to him and the others who believed in Ender-whann-soo. In a quarter of a day it would be dark. There was much to do.

Finally he found his way to the stables where the riding Zanth were kept. A carrier or a draft beast would be required. The young male quickly passed though the stalls scattering handfuls of Bindweed into the Zanth's feeding troughs. The stringy weed would ferment in the beast's stomachs overnight. By morning they would be impossible to ride. He hoped the Fletch had reached Coen-soo in time. She must ready the members of the renegade group and start out from the homestead before nightfall. The Fletch would fly faster than the Imperial Guard could march or ride. He doubted that Link-soo-shan would even consider that anyone was planning a rescue. What he had in mind to do would shake the Empire. By the time they had crossed the river and the outlying farmland, Ender-whann-soo's household should be safely on its way to the mountains. For the time being there was nothing he could do, but hide close to where the broken frame of Ender-whann-soo had been cast upon the rough craggy ground of Link-soo-shan's execution place. The 'Killing Stones' were a sharp-edged outcrop of hard bedrock jutting from of the earth besides the edge of the city walls. There were many shiny bones scattered about the area where other Gnathe had been punished.

Shoo-lin entered the stall where his Zanth lazily chewed on his meal of seeds and stalks. The beast snorted as Shoo-lin slipped the guidance harness over its horny head. He dug his foot into the bony mounting hole and swung himself into the riding hollow. Curling his tail around the vanes on the back, he turned the obedient steed out of the box and into the courtyard.

Coen-soo sought the shelter of the fruiting pod-vines. The sun was hot and had passed overhead. Plants and animals basked in the late afternoon heat. She sat on a bench grown on the edge of the field. Coen-soo began to worry about the result of the council meeting. The young Brood-mother had been openly cheerful about the outcome. Coen-soo had thought otherwise and had warned Ender-whann-soo to flee the summons from the Imperial council. She recalled the conversation with the Brood-mother that very morning, three days ago.

"Nonsense my child," Ender-whann-soo exclaimed. "These new ideas of mine are not wicked. We can show the benefits of our system to the ruling council. What could they do? I have been careful and discrete. We live in an unimportant area of the Empire."

"I fear for your safety Reverend-Mother," Coen-soo replied. "There are many on the council, who it is said, would profit by your removal."

"How can you know of Brood-mother policies? You are a female, one of my kindred and far from the Imperial City," stated Ender-whann-soo.

"Reverend-Mother, you forget, to most of your station we are invisible. They see us, but they do not think of us. We serve. We have always served, but we listen. I have a friend in the Imperial Household. More than a friend perhaps, if things change. We correspond by Fletch and Crystal. He has followed your ideas for many years and fears for your safety. His name is Shoo-lin, Beast-master for the Imperial household. Do well to notice him if you can. I will organise things here, to be able to leave at a moments notice. If things go badly, we will be ready to do whatever is necessary."

"Do all my household keep these views?" Ender-whann-soo gasped. "Would they follow me into the wilderness blindly? I find this so difficult to believe!"

"My lady, you have given us so much, we could hardly do otherwise. For the first time in all our generations, you gave us a choice of breeding partners. You do not realise what that means to us. You treat us like we are of importance, not just here to serve. We have come to love you, Reverend-Mother Ender. We would follow and protect you anywhere. You have friends in places you do not know. I pray no harm will come to you and that you return safely," Coen-soo anxiously replied, holding her Brood-mother's hands in a tight embrace.

Underneath the shade Coen-soo pondered the situation. It would be three days travel at least, before her Lady, Ender-whann-soo, returned from the council hearing. All she could do was wait. A cry from one of the field hands alerted her. She looked up and saw Shoo-lin's Fletch circling over the ripening pod-vines. She gave a shrill chirrup and the flying beast dived for her outstretched hand. It carried a memory chip strapped securely to its leg. Quickly she fed the little creature from the pouch she always carried. Coen-soo detached the crystal and pressed it into the hollow in the middle of her forehead.

As the crystal warmed up in Coen-soo's bony niche, she began to feel the first stirrings of the message. It was as if she were behind Shoo-lin's eyes. With mounting horror the whole scene was acted out in her mind. She gave a soundless scream as she heard Ender-whann-soo's bones snap under the cruel treatment of the massive Imperial Guard special battalion. Tears filled Coen-soo's eyes and ran unheeded down her pointed face as she saw her beloved Brood-Mother dragged from the council chambers to die a slow and lingering death.

Shoo-lin's voice echoed in her mind. "Flee, my forbidden love. Gather all you can to start the homestead again. Run for the mountains and the ravine I found, when I was last at Ender-whann-soo's home. You must go through the edge of the marsh. The carriers will get you through. I believe we will find a way through the Saw-Tooth Range. There must be lands on the other side where we can settle. Once into the ravine we can landslide the sides into the entrance and block the mouth. I will attempt Ender-whann-soo's rescue at nightfall. No one will even think that anyone would dare. Go now, as fast as you can. You should have at least three days or more head start. When the Imperial Guards come, they will not know what to do and will have to send a rider back for instructions. It will not occur to Link-soo-shan and her council that you would dare to flee, before they get a chance to divide Ender-whann-soo's property."

The voice faded from her mind. Decisively, Coen-soo took flight across the field. Bounding through the stalks of the grain crop, unheeding of the damage, she fled towards the homestead. Arriving at the entrance of the Banilik tree house she opened the doors wide and called out to the members within the household.

"Assemble! Assemble! All to me," she called and beat the alarm crystal that hung in the entrance hall with the side baton.

A dull penetrating frequency began to resonate throughout the tree. Each crystal growth sang wherever they grew upon the household walls. Soon the household had assembled in the hall and waited expectantly for Coen-soo to speak.

"It is as we feared," Coen-soo told the members of Ender-whann-soo's household. "The Reverend Mother has faced execution for her heresy. At this very moment our Lady lies broken on the 'Killing Stones', outside of the Imperial City. One of our fellowship, Shoo-lin, is to attempt a rescue at nightfall. For all our sakes let us hope he is successful. Without Ender-whann-soo, our bloodline is doomed. We would be refused the right to breed anyway. Gather all that can be carried and be useful to us. Load the Carrier-Beasts and harness the Zanth. We go as soon as we can. Work through the night if we must, but come what may, we leave in the morning at the first rays of dawn with what we have."

Whann-lin, the head of the field hands, asked. "Where do we go? What is my egg-brother's plan?"

"We go to the to the mountains, to the Saw-Tooth Range," Coen-soo replied. "There is a way through, un-explored and not known to the Empire. Shoo-lin has been there. It has a narrow opening into a deep ravine that cuts well into the range. We will go through and block the entrance behind us, after Ender-whann-soo is safely in our midst. If anyone can get the Reverend-Mother to us, it will be him."

As the hours of darkness rapidly began to make their effect felt, the city streets became deserted. Very few of the Gnathe would be moving about as the first dark quarter came to a close. Shoo-lin had 'acquired' a carrier beast from the Imperial stables and had tethered it nearby with his personal Zanth. The many hours of patient instruction had paid off in training this beast from infant-hood. The creature would kill for him if required. It had a fierce attachment for him and would allow no other rider to mount him without Shoo-lin's command. He had called into the infirmary on his way to the 'Killing Stones' gathering splints and materials. Shoo-lin had managed to find a powerful knockout drug to keep the Brood-Mother still. The carrier beast held provisions and ropes to secure her into the hollow in the animal's back.

Now had come the time to add murder to his catalogue of crimes. There were four guards standing watch over the broken form of Ender-whann-soo. Two of them were tending the fire in the guard hut under the spreading outer branches of the Banilik tree, sheltering from the night-cold. None of the guards would be expecting a rescue attempt and there must be no warning. These unfortunate soldiers of the realm must be disposed of in silence and the escape unnoticed until morning. Quietly Shoo-lin crept towards the hut, careful to keep in the shadows. He looked through the window slot in the wall. The two male Gnathe were slumped against the wall squatting down on the sleeping perch, wrapped in warm cloaks. One was dozing while the other fed the fire. Carefully Shoo-lin took out of his pouch a Kryte. The creature was about the size of his hand with a ridged hollow nose shaped like a straight pipe. He inserted a thorn, wrapped with fuzzy down at one end, into the nose of the creature. The sharp end was tipped with powerful venom.

This was an assassin's tool. Shoo-lin aimed the pipe at the busy guard, feeding the fire and squeezed the Kryte at the base of its tail. The creature's lungs filled at a tremendous rate and the beast sneezed. The dart flew into the victim's neck and he fell back against the wall, choking. At the next instant, before the drowsy guard fully awoke, Shoo-lin had entered the hut and slit his throat. Not a sound had been made. Looking out into the darkness he could see the other two guards walking around the spread-eagled form of the young Brood-mother. He wrapped one of the dead soldier's cloaks around himself and, checking that the Kryte had recovered, he reloaded it with a fresh dart. Making no attempt to hide himself, he walked slowly towards the two remaining guards. Shoo-lin's mouth was quite dry and although both of his hearts were pounding fast in his chest, his hand was quite steady. This is not the time to panic, he thought to himself. Keep calm. He waved to the facing Gnathe as he approached, in a friendly fashion.

The facing guard looked up at Shoo-lin as he saw him approaching and exclaimed, "You are not one of—!"

Shoo-lin aimed the nose of the Kryte at his chest and triggered the creature again. The guard fell, choking and dying, to the ground. With one leap he planted both taloned feet into the back of the remaining soldier and reached around his neck. Shoo-lin cut his throat clear to the bone with his syther, before he could utter a cry of warning.

Another pair of eyes had watched this deadly scene from the shelter of darkness. They looked on with bloody approval.

Shoo-lin approached the broken form laid carelessly over the sharp rocks. The Brood mother was breathing unevenly and a pair of gold-flecked eyes looked up at him with amazement.

"Do not speak, my lady," Shoo-lin whispered as he cradled her large head in his arms. "Drink this water and trust me."

He gave her a drink out of a water gourd and when she had finished, he brought out the knockout drug and held it under her nose. The Brood-mother stiffened and passed out. Shoo-lin quickly bounded back to the carrier beast and collected the materials necessary. He then splinted her broken limbs and bound her to a number of ridged poles. Next, he dragged her into the shadows to leave her for a few moments, to fetch his Zanth and the carrier beast tethered some distance away. As he approached his Zanth the beast snorted uneasily. Shoo-lin spun round, sword drawn. There, looming over him, was the imposing tall form of a Brood-mother.

"Be not alarmed, little one, I came to do the same thing," said the larger form in the darkness. "You did better than I could have managed. Besides, I am very old and you are very young, Shoo-lin."

"Who are you, that you should know me?" gasped Shoo-lin. "I cannot see you."

"I am Ender-whann-soo's grand, Brood-mother, Khann-link-sool. Enough of this! What are your plans? What do we do next?"

Shoo-lin asked the old Gnathe, "Can you ride a carrier and control it?"

"Of course I can," the Brood-mother replied. "I was doing it long before you were hatched."

"Well, help me get Ender-whann-soo into the carrying hollow of this beast and tie her in place, then follow me and keep close," he ordered nervously.

They led the beast back towards the recumbent form laid in the shadows. As they led the beasts to Ender-whann-soo he outlined his plans to his strange accomplice. They soon had the Brood-mother tied securely in place and they set off across country, with an incredulous Shoo-lin in the lead. Khann-link-sool controlled the carrier beast with ease. She was a living legend. One of the oldest surviving Brood-mothers, she had helped to form the Imperial household of Link-soo-shan's rule and lay the foundations of the Gnathe Empire. They were ploughing a swath straight through the crops spread across the lands towards the bridge over the river. The company of fugitives were heading towards one of the few bridges that crossed the swiftly flowing torrent. Shoo-lin allowed the carrier beast to stump over the bridge and turned his Zanth against the piles supporting the main arch.

"Quickly my lady, back the carrier up against this pile support and force it over!" Shoo-lin shouted, against the sound of the torrent. "If we can bring the bridge down into the river it will delay the pursuit quite some time."

The old Gnathe coaxed the large form of the carrier against the arch support and brought its horny backside hard against the ancient stones. There was an audible crack as the old and crumbling stonework began to give way. With both of them pushing and releasing, the bridge began to shudder and the support gave way. Great blocks of stone rumbled down into the swiftly flowing river.

"That is enough, my lady—now follow me," Shoo-lin cried to the revered Gnathe. "We will use the road system towards Ender-whann-soo's household until we get to the crossroads at the Trading Post. There we will cross country to the marsh and edge round it to the mountains, to the split in the cliff-face I described to you."

"Keep going Shoo-lin. I will follow you as fast as this creature will go," the Brood mother answered. "I suggest we briefly rest at dawn, attending to Ender-whann-soo and allow the beasts to forage a little. Agreed, young one?"

"Yes my lady, but it must be a brief stop. If we push the beast hard we may make the cliff in two days. They will expect us to go to the homestead. I have alerted the household by Fletch and Crystal. At dawn they will be preparing to leave and should be well in front of us. When we get to the ravine they should be well inside and ready to tumble the rocks into the mouth and block it from the pursuit of the Imperial guard."

He stood up, astride the racing Zanth and looked over the horny spiked head towards a lightening sky. They were travelling down a dusty road with the cultivated fields stretching away on each side. Pod-vines were in various stages of growth. Some were in flower and the scent carried on the cool pre-morning breeze. In the distance, the Trading Post was just visible in the morning mists and the crossroads would soon be in front of them.

"Slow down my lady, we will walk the beasts through. I can see many Imperial Zanth, at the corral. The soldiers will still be asleep inside their quarters. If we can be quiet, they will never even know that we have passed by."

They reined the beasts back to a slow walk. The mist grew thicker as they approached and the fugitives passed the front of the household, in the direction of the corral. Shoo-lin dismounted and opened the gates to the pen. He walked amongst them, taking some nuts out of his carrying pouch and offered them to the curious animals. After they had sampled a handful each, he walked out of the enclosure with the Zanth following him.

"Greed is a wonderful tool," he thought to himself, as the large beasts ambled down the road behind him.

He remounted his waiting Zanth and soon caught up with Khann-link-sool seated astride the heavy neck of the carrier beast. The Brood-mother perched easily over the broad neck with her tail wound around the bony plates behind her.

"I have met very few males with your resourcefulness, young one," she said approvingly. "Your line must survive. I could do great things with your progeny. Now where do we go, Shoo-lin?"

"Drive the Zanth into the pod vines towards that stand of young Banilik trees. We will slip away through the pod vines away from these greedy Zanth. With luck they will have trampled down plenty of the crops by dawn and no one will see where we have gone. Besides which, when the Imperial Guards awake, they will have a choice of four directions to search, before they find their steeds. Remember, they will not even know of the crimes we have committed, let alone that the loose Zanth was a deliberate act. I frayed the ropes to look as if it was age and rot that allowed them to escape."

As the sun rose over the mountains, Shoo-lin signalled a halt by the side of an irrigation ditch, under an old fruit tree. He hobbled the two beasts and allowed them to forage amongst the crop's foliage and also to rest. They both turned their attentions to the injured Brood-mother. She had regained consciousness and was regarding the unlikely pair from pain filled eyes. Shoo-lin checked the splints and bindings of the larger form bound to the poles of the makeshift stretcher. He gave a stiff nod of satisfaction.

"I am sorry for the accommodation my Lady," Shoo-lin said to the injured Gnathe, "but there was a bit of a hurry and it was dark!"

Ender-whann-soo replied to the young Gnathe, "Shoo-lin, do you realise what you have done, you young fool? Link-soo-shan will not rest until you are stretched out on the 'Killing Stones' with me. Coen-soo told me to watch for you. I did not think in my wildest dreams that it would come to this! As for you, my most Reverend, Grand Brood-mother, why are you here? You will face a terrible fate helping me. Tell me why?"

"The Empire is senile, little one," the old Brood-mother replied. "Your ideas were the first new ones to come to my attention in many generations of kindred. You show promise. This young male has alerted your household to flee and we are to join them. He thinks he has discovered a way through the mountains to the lands on the other side. If we get through we can make a fresh start. Your household will provide an adequate gene pool. He is an amazingly resourceful young male. Trust him. Now drink this and rest. We must press on and keep in front of the Imperial Guard. They as yet do not know where we are. Let us keep it that way."

Shoo-lin re-captured his Zanth, climbed into the riding hollow astride its back and led the way towards the marsh in the dawning light.

CHAPTER 2

▼

At the Imperial City a shocked change of guard had reached the 'Killing stones.' Bewildered, they looked around the empty area in the thinning mists. The sharp jagged rocks were bare and vacant of the tortured form of the young Brood-mother. A quick search revealed the bodies of the four dead night-duty guards.

One of the lower ranking males asked the senior Gnathe, "What are we to do?"

He stared pop-eyed at the silent forms that they laid out over the crystalline surface, littered with the bones of previous unwilling occupants.

The terrified male guard spoke. "We could end up here like these bones if we are not careful! I will give the alarm. They will not get far if we hurry. I will go straight to the Commander. The cruel mother will know what to do. Stay here and look for anything that may point the way that they have gone." So saying, the senior male spun round to face the general direction of the city.

His claws bit into the earth and with tail laid out behind him, the Gnathe bounded towards the portal in the side of the ancient Banilik tree. Within a short time he was into the corridors and racing as fast as he could towards the sleeping quarters of the Commander of the Imperial Guard. At the entrance to the Lady, Chang-soo-shan's rooms, the female soldiers stood with weapons bared and, hearing crests erect, stopped him.

"Let me through!" he cried in a panic-stricken tone. "I must see the Commander immediately!"

The Commander's personal elite guards stared at him impassively. The dawning light picked out the designs on their kilts proclaiming the high rank that they held. The senior ranking female made a gesture with the sharp sword-like weapon she carried, fashioned from a dead Syther's tail and backbone. The hilt was bound with leather and the point was razor sharp. The light played over the crystalline highlights in the blade.

"What do you want, foot soldier?" she asked derisively. "You seem to be in a great hurry."

The other three closed around him and began to snigger and revile him and poke him with the sharp points of their long swords.

"Listen to me!" he demanded to them. "Ender-whann-soo has gone. Someone has rescued the Brood-mother and murdered the night-watch guards. We must tell the Commander and let her order a pursuit as quick as we can. Now let me through!"

The Commander's Elite guards digested this awful information and began to look apprehensively at each other. Not one of them would like to give this news to Chang-soo-shan. The Brood-mother's evil temper was not to be crossed lightly. She was Link-soo-shan's brood sister and politically very powerful in the Gnathen Empire.

"Come with me, foot soldier, and we will approach the Lady together," replied the guard captain. "I will awaken her first and then call you into her chambers. May your ancestors help us all!"

With that she opened the door into the daunting presence of the Commander's sleeping chambers. Parting the rich fabric of the hanging curtains, she approached the sleeping perch of the magnificent form of the great Brood-Mother. The powerful arms were decked in rare bangles of gold. The massive clawed hind feet that could pick up a male or female Gnathe and hurl the broken form for many lengths were strapped and covered in rich fabric over the length of her limbs. The great triangular head was tucked into the wide chest. A golden velvet-like fur covered her form except for her face. As the female captain of the guard fearfully approached the sleeping perch, she became aware that she had been fixed by a baleful eye. The vertical slit widened down the centre of the green coloured iris. The corded muscles of the neck flexed and the triangular head rose from the chest, the hearing crest erect.

"Yes, Guard Captain," the Brood-mother angrily inquired. "What do you want, to interrupt my sleep at dawn? It had better be necessary, small one." The great form stretched one of the lower legs off the perch and extended the cruel talons towards the captain.

She fell submissively into a squatting position and lowered her head. The first rays of dawn were beginning to pick out the rich furnishing of the room, as the crystals in the walls reflected the light of the sun from each other.

"My Lady, the day guard at the killing stones, has reported a terrible piece of news to me."

At this she beckoned forward the terrified senior guard.

"Ender-whann-soo has gone. Someone must have taken her during the night, killing the night-watch guards."

"What!" screeched the Commander, rising to her full length over the frantic pair of soldiers.

She bent forwards from the perch and her powerful hands plucked the terrified male from the floor. "Tell me what you know! Quickly now, I want the truth. Leave nothing out or I will tear off your arms."

The male Gnathe began to gabble his story and told what little he knew to the angry Commander. She pondered over the information given and threw him roughly down.

"Go out and find which way they went. I will join you with a troop of riders very soon. Do not disappoint me," the Commander spat. "You," pointing at the captain, "sound the alarm and gather enough of your division to ride them down. They will not get far. The 'Stones' will soon have more victims drying in the sun. I will go and inform my Brood-sister. Have everything ready for when we appear. Now move!"

"Yes my Lady," called the captain as she bounded our of the Commander's chambers, heading for the barracks and stables.

Chang-soo-shan hurried through the twisting corridors of the Banilik-tree until she came upon her Brood sisters' royal apartments. Viciously kicking one of the attendants out of the way, she approached Link-soo-shan crouched on her sleeping perch. The powerful tail lashed from side to side underneath, flicking away discarded items into the shadows. A savage pair of yellow eyes cut with black vertical slits regarded the Commander.

"Well, Brood-sister, what's all the commotion about?" the Ultimate Ruler hissed. "Tell me. Tell me now!"

"Ender-whann-soo has disappeared from the killing stones," Chang-soo-shan replied. "She has been abducted or rescued. We do not know as yet. I have alerted my Elite Guards and they are at the stables, rousing the Zanth. We will soon have her back and whoever has helped her."

"I will have that heretic's head mounted in my chambers for all to see. To the stables! I will ride with you for the pleasure of that moment."

With that the Brood-mother leapt from the perch towards the still opened door and angrily pushed her attendants out of the way.

In the Imperial stables all was not well. The captain and her Elite troops were having little success rousing the Zanth for pursuit. Shoo-lin's handfuls of bindweed had done their work well. The beasts were staggering about and evil tempered. One of the Captain's female riders had been skewered by the sharp horns on her Zanth's head and tossed into a bloody heap onto the stable floor. The whole stable stank of vomit and excrement from the sick and nasty-humoured creatures.

When the two Brood-sisters entered the Imperial stables, complete chaos reigned. Quite a number of the soldiers were nursing serious wounds. One lay dead and six of them would have to go to the infirmary to have their broken limbs and ribs set. They would be taking no more interest in the proceedings.

The commander took stock of the situation and shouted over the noise of the snorting and stamping Zanth and the screams of the injured guards. "We are wasting time here. Go to the 'Killing Stones' and collect anything that we can ride from the merchants at the edge of the city. Move it or you will hang on the outer walls of this city as an example to others."

The company rapidly vanished in the direction required. Soon a motley force assembled at the 'Killing Stones' execution area. The direction could clearly be seen that the fugitives had taken. A straight line of ruined crops was easily apparent, going in the general direction of the only bridge over the rushing torrent of the Imperial River for many days travel. They set off in as good an order as they could with the unfamiliar steeds. The sun was rising above the topmost branches of the city tree, when the first of the Commander's Elite guards reached the ruined bridge. She reined her beast to a snorting stop and looked down at the sheer drop to the rocks below, where the white crested river churned over the rapids. The pursuing force caught up with her. The Brood-sisters stared at the wide gap in the damaged bridge—impossible to cross. The far side had been pushed into the deep ravine. There was no way to cross over without repairing it in some way. The gap was too wide, beyond the capacity of the Zanth to jump with a rider mounted.

"We cannot reach the other side and the next crossing point is two days journey up-stream," the captain apprehensively said. "What do you want us to do, my lady?"

"Gather the field hands. Cut trees and repair the bloody thing. We will go back to the city with half of the guard and gather provisions. This is going to take longer than we think. I will signal ahead and try to alert the companies at the

Trading Post." The commander cruelly wrenched the merchant's Zanth around to face the city and shouted to her egg-sister: "Come back to the City with me, Link! We will prepare for this together."

Link-soo-shan was incoherent with rage and tugged savagely at the harness of her Zanth and forced the creature back through the flattened field of crops towards the city.

High above the massive continent the Geo-stationary satellite kept watch, detailing weather reports and charting the storms over the high mountain range. On a routine scan covering the visible side of the Gnathe Empire it began to send some amazing pictures to the Citadel. By chance, Asue was on watch, because of an adverse storm report the previous day. The mountains had shook with torrents of rain and gale force winds, filling the huge reservoir above the Citadel to capacity. The water thundered over the falls to the North of the dome complex and down a swollen, aptly named White river. The roof tanks of the domes were overflowing already and a great deal of rain had been allowed to fall through the filters and into the various habitats. If the storms continued, a deflector would start to return the roof tank's water back to the flooded river beside the domes. A stout Nano-tech material formed one wall of the White river bank, for over a hundred miles towards the sea. There were now over a quarter of a million humanoid life forms living in the artificial world constructed and created by the Asue and her three comrades. Much had been achieved, after the creative talents of the humans and apes had been bought to bear with the help of their four immortal guides. The one unfortunate problem that they could not solve was the deadly microscopic life-forms carried in the air outside the domes. Everything that the nannite genetic engineers designed, died if it breathed the air, so in the end defeated, they developed the domed civilisation.

Asue was seated before the console as the optical scanning devices on board the satellite swung over the mountain range and began their periodic scan of the quiet and tranquil Gnathe vista of endless cultivation. Nothing of any interest had been seen to happen over there in over three hundred years of observation. She zoomed the cameras onto the area of the only great city on the continent and followed the contour of the river until she came to the bridge some distance from the city. To her surprise she could clearly see a vast area of rich cropland trampled flat and the people in a great turmoil. A tremendous amount of effort seemed to be taking place around the bridge. Trees were being felled and hauled across the fields, with no consideration to the damage being done to the un-harvested crops. Asue magnified the area around the bridge, bringing the most powerful optical devices to bear from the orbiting satellite above. The bridge now only spanned halfway across the deep ravine that carried a rushing torrent towards the sea. The people were working as if they were possessed. Large beasts were pulling the tree trunks through the crop, urged on by the hopping people. Teams of the smaller people were being forced to edge out over the gap in the bridge and secure the makeshift repairs. She could see that some had fallen to their deaths on the rocks below.

"What on Jupiter is going on? We have never witnessed anything like this since we arrived on this world. Why do they want to cross over the river in such haste? I wonder if…? They must be chasing someone. That damage to the bridge is deliberate," she mused to herself.

With that, Asue contacted Kamiel and relayed the events. They linked minds and Kamiel watched the console screens through Asue's optical centres.

He broke off and said to her, "I will alert Alexander and Jo-jo and see if we need to inform the council. This may be nothing, but they should be informed, if only to share in the excitement. I mean—nothing ever happens over there! Their civilisation has been static ever since we have been here. Not that it can make any difference with that mountain range between us."

With that, Kamiel contacted Alexander at his offices in the university, situated at the Citadel's centre.

Alexander was now one hundred and twenty-three years old and looked as though he was in his late thirties. True to the tinkering with the Genetic codes as relayed by Minns all those years ago, so far, none of the apes or humans had shown any signs of ageing beyond maturity. Alex had several long relationships with the women he had grown up with. He had sons and daughters by various wives and also grand and great grandchildren, besides the offspring brought about by combining his sperm with donated eggs. Members of the council came and went, but he seemed to be constantly saddled with the job of Mayor. His deputy at the moment was a female ape named Jo-jo, a granddaughter of Joom, his first deputy.

He was talking to her now, about the mundane business of crop rotation and harvesting, when the special link to the Artificial Intelligences began to buzz and flash on and off. Kamiel's silvery face filled the view screen.

"What is it Kamiel?" Alex inquired, looking up at the flashing console. "What can we do for you? Anything has to be more interesting than crop reports."

"I think you will find this of some distraction, old friend," he replied to the human. "Watch your viewing screen. Asue has been monitoring our strange companions over the other side of the mountain range. They seem stirred up like the proverbial ants nest with a spade through the middle."

Alex and Jo-jo watched with interest as the strange activities unfolded on the view screens. They watched entranced as the remarkable events were relayed to them.

"What can be going on, over there!" Jo-jo exclaimed to Kamiel. "They are usually so quiet!"

"I can't imagine, Jo-jo, but it has certainly stirred them up. We must let the others know as general knowledge. I don't see it as a threat to us anyway. Inform the rest of the council and anyone else that you think might be interested. Tell Asue to keep an eye on things, in case anything develops out of the ordinary. We have to get back to our crop reports!" Alex laid an affectionate arm over Jo-jo's hairy shoulders and switched off the communications console. "Come on Jo-jo, I think a journey by mono-rail to the farming complex would be a good idea. Let's go and have an on the spot inspection. We ought to get out of this building a bit more often."

"Does that mean you are going to pack your fishing tackle and are we going to disappear for a few days?" Jo-jo mischievously asked.

"Did I say that?" Alexander grinned and replied, "What a good idea—business and pleasure. What would I do without you, deputy mayor?"

With that, the two humanoid forms ambled out of Alex's office, while Kamiel made his way to the satellite control complex to satisfy his own curiosity.

As dawn had broken over the mountaintops illuminating the lands of the Gnathe, Coen-soo had succeeded in mobilising the entire household of Ender-whann-soo. One male and three female carrier beasts had been fully loaded with anything considered useful. The household had bred a number of young carriers of different sexes that ran freely around their mothers as they stomped slowly forwards on their strong six legged gait. The bony plates were already beginning to project from out of the tough skin. Soon the art of breaking them into service would take place. Some of the older ones had already been broken into harness. These had been loaded with small packets of seeds and small items tied securely into their immature hollows. Loads had been duplicated over and over again to insure against loss. The marsh was the last wild area left in the Gnathe Kingdom. Here the last of the untamed creatures lived. There were things that slipped through the ooze that could take a young carrier with hungry ease. The way to Shoo-lin's discovered crack in the mountainside would not be easy. The alternative of the impending visit by Link-soo-shan could not be compared to the terrors of the swamp. There lay a certain cruel death, or slavery. The old and infirm Gnathe males and females, who could not face the journey through the swamp, had chosen to die rather than be left to the Ultimate Ruler's mercies. All had taken poison from the hand of the Brood-mother's head of security. Their deaths had been easy and painless. The direction taken and any information gathered would not come from any of the household.

Coen-soo readied the company of Zanth riders and carriers. She rode the horned Zanth, co-breeder to Shoo-lin's male, with consummate ease. The massive taloned hind feet dug into the damp earth and the beast reared erect pawing at the air with its front claws. She looked over its horny head apprehensively, towards the general direction of the Imperial City and then over her Lady's household gathered around her. She had shattered the communication crystal in Ender-whann-soo's rooms. It had been tuned to the master crystal, at the Royal chambers of Link-soo-shan at the city. There would be no mental spying to see what the situation was here. Let the Brood-mother guess, but not know what was happening at the homestead. The first flames were licking round the tops of the Banilik tree holding. Satisfied that no more could be done, Coen-soo signalled for attention.

"Listen to me all of you!" Coen-soo shouted to the loyal household. "Burn every field as we go. Leave nothing for the Imperial Guard to use for forage for their steeds, or to fill their own hungry bellies. Anything that is left behind, we will have to do without. All we can do is to press ahead through to the edge of the marsh and follow the line of the cliffs until we get to the split in the rock-face. I will lead the way."

With that she turned the Zanth around and began the trek over the croplands and directly to the base of the sheer cliffs that met the edge of the marsh. Already a white acrid smoke filled the air from the torched fields. As the sun began to rise higher in the cloudy sky the edge of the cultivated fields could be seen. An irrigation ditch separated the field of pod-vines from the marsh. Large trees overhung the edges of the swamp and pools of water glinted in the sunlight. Squawks and hooting sounds came from further within. It looked very dark under the trees and ferns deeper into the swamp. The company turned to the right and continued to follow the irrigation ditch until they came at last to the black jagged cliffs soaring into the air above them.

Shoo-lin had described the route to Coen-soo on a previous visit.

"Keep as close as you can to the cliff face and the edge of the marsh is reasonably shallow," he had told her.

He had got through with his Zanth in less than a day. If all went well they could be at the opening in the cliff face before nightfall. The swampland at night was a dangerous place. Nocturnal hunters had sometime crossed the irrigation ditch and defences. Young carriers and Zanth had disappeared from time to time with the stockades breached. All that had been seen was a bloody trail through the crops back towards the marshes.

Coen-soo urged her Zanth across the earthworks and over the ditch under the overhang of the black cliff-face. The beast splayed out its taloned hind feet and laid her tail across the muddy ground. She pushed and paddled her way over a sunken log and onto firmer territory.

"Come on, try a carrier next!" shouted Coen-soo. "You, Whann-lin, bring up the rear. Elety-soo, urge the first carrier over the ditch and over to me."

The Prime male waddled forwards and broached the water, all six legs immersed in a mixture of slime and ooze. The powerful shoulders and flanks heaved and the great beast swam easily into the swamp. He took a Gnathe-sized bite out of the tastier foliage as he came. Where he went the females would follow. One by one with the young carriers sporting in the water, the caravan made its way through the edge of the marsh. Tree branches and ferns made the way ahead gloomy, as the sun could not penetrate the overhead jungle very easily. At full sun-up, Coen-soo called for a brief rest on a dry piece of land where part of the cliff had fallen into the swamp.

"Check all the loads and make sure they all are secure. We are about halfway there, according to Shoo-lin's instructions," Coen-soo called to the field hands and household staff over the constant noise of the marsh life.

More hoots and grunts were audible, now that the caravan was deeper into the jungle-like growth that erupted out of the mud and murky water. Ominous slithering and rustlings came from every direction.

Jotin-soo, an egg sister to Coen-soo, called out to her reluctant leader. "I have checked all the loads and apart from a bit of mud, all seems to be secure. I would suggest sister, that we ready our weapons. We should tip some darts with venom before something comes crashing through the trees with more appetite than caution."

"Yes sister. From now on, set guards on each carrier to keep watch in the direction of the jungle. Although, I don't think anything would be foolish enough to attack a full-grown carrier. Still, the young could be picked off. If something takes one, let it have it. With its stomach full it will be less interested in us. Only defend ourselves and the goods we carry."

Coen-soo stared into the noisy swamp and jungle, shuddering with repressed fear and said, "Now let's press on. We have half a day's journey at most. What possessed Shoo-lin to come this far I will never understand, but its is well for us that he did."

With that statement, Coen-soo urged her Zanth back into the marshy ground and the Caravan crept forth under the lee of the ever-present black cliff face.

Shoo-lin had pushed ahead through the field of pod-vines and had made it to the open road. The sun was beginning to climb in the sky. He looked behind him over his Zanth's spiny back and was gratified to see that Khann-link-sool was close behind him. She was gathering ripe pods and throwing them back into the cavernous hollow of the carrier. The Brood-mother had been very industrious during their long march across the croplands, picking fruit or pods, or anything else that was edible that came within her long grasp.

She nodded to Shoo-lin. "Everything helps, young one. We seemed a little low on provisions so I helped myself along the way. Where now, little one? This looks like a good road."

"Yes my lady. It leads towards Ender-whann-soo's homestead. We must make good time along it before the Imperial Guards find our trail. Another thing, the hard road will help to hide our tracks," he replied to the old Gnathe and asked, "Can you make that thing gallop?"

"Young one, I designed the carriers to carry loads for long distances," the old Brood-mother declared. "Speed was not a requirement at the time. They can however be coaxed into a reasonable turn of speed."

With that she gave the carrier a sharp dig with her rear taloned feet into its sensitive neck. The beast gave a grunting snort and picked up at a steady trot that soon ate up the distance. Its six-legged gait developed a steady rhythm.

Shoo-lin scanned the road ahead. A plantation of young Banilik trees lay to their left. He could just see a pall of smoke in the sky. Coen-soo had got his message. Ender-whann-soo's lands were burning.

"My Lady," he called, "Do you see the smoke rising in the distance? Look high over the tops of the trees. Can you see?"

"Yes, Shoo-lin, I can see it," she replied over the carrier's warty head. "That must mean your female contact at Ender-whann-soo's homestead received your message. Your plans are working well so far, young one."

The sun was high up above them in the cloudy sky as they pushed the carrier beast hard. Rumbles of thunder pealed intermittently and shafts of sunlight broke through the gaps in the clouds. Ender-whann-soo lay securely strapped in the back of the carrier, the broken limbs splinted tight. She bore the pain of the occasional jolt stoically. She still marvelled at her narrow escape from the cruel death intended and inflicted by Link-soo-shan. The loyalty of her Household still amazed her. The wonders she could achieve, if they all came through this ordeal, occupied her mind and helped to keep the pain at bay.

The fleeing Gnathe sped onwards. There was at least another half a day's journey before they reached the crossing into the swamp at the foot of the cliffs.

Link-soo-shan was perched in front of the master crystal. Chang-soo-shan sat the perch on the other side. A large many faceted Gemstone was mounted between them and on a pillar of polished wood. This was the main communications device for the Empire. Small shards had been removed from it in the past. All Imperial guard captains carried a shard around her neck, attached by a leather thong. The major holdings had a matching crystal tuned to the master in Link-soo-shan's chambers

Controlling her raging emotions the ultimate ruler laid her hands upon the stone. As the warmth of her hands activated the power locked inside the crystal, she felt her mind begin to expand. It was as if a maze extended before her. She knew every pathway, however. She drove her perceptions down one route, towards the stone at Ender-whann-soo's homestead, meeting a void and recoiled, head aching with her face twisted in pain. Shocked and stunned by the unaccustomed recoil, she sought the comforting presence of her Brood-sister.

"The stone has been shattered at Ender-whann-soo's homestead. I can see nothing, at the heretic's homestead. That must mean that her household has fled. How dare they!" she hissed in frustrated fury. "This sedition of that accursed Brood-mother has disrupted generations of order. They must be caught and destroyed. No trace of their genetic patterns must be allowed to continue. Chang, contact your Imperial Guard-captain at the trading post, between the bridge and her homestead. We will cut her off from wherever she is fleeing to. Who is helping her? I will instigate a search to see who missing."

With that, the Ultimate Ruler leapt from the perch and strode through her door to question her own household, lashing her bony tail from side to side. Unconsciously her sharp claws slid in and out of their sheaths' at the front pads of her fingers.

Chang-soo-shan placed her hands on the crystal and began to enter the sending trance. She concentrated on the first trading post. Gradually she began to feel the matching crystal resonate around the guard captain's neck. She entered the captain's mind and looked out of her eyes at a disruptive scene.

The captain had felt the crystal's influence before. The familiar feel of the bright incisive mind of the commander slipped into her brain. She was outside the trading post with her companions. They were about to split into groups to search for the missing Zanth. She obediently turned around for the commander to assess the situation. She quickly told her about the missing riding beasts. Chang-soo-shan received the information and rapidly understood the reason for the missing Zanth. The news of the escape of Ender-whann-soo from the execution place was quickly passed on to the captain.

"Find your Zanth and ride towards Ender-whann-soo's homestead. Look for any clue as to the direction that they might have taken. Stop them, but they must be alive for my sister's pleasure," the commander said to her and broke off communication.

Back at the crystal chamber she relayed the information to her returned Brood-sister, who regarded her with an incredulous stare.

"One of my household is missing, the Beast-master, Shoo-lin," the Ultimate Ruler spat savagely to her sister. "How could a male have done all of this? Who bred him, I wonder?"

She lashed her tail from side to side, heedless of the damage the bony point produced and once more the ripping claws slipped in and out of their sheaths.

CHAPTER 3

▼

Kamiel and Asue sat together at the satellite control console. They sat immobile, connected to the optical system directed at the Gnathe Empire. After the early morning sighting, they had concentrated on dividing the area the other side of the river from the city into sections. Each of them minutely examined the terrain below.

The clouds had built up, promising a late evening storm. Asue had directed Kamiel onto a straight track leading through the crops, heading towards the large, wild, swampy area that extended from the cliff's edge and out into the cultivated land. They had noticed one of the isolated homesteads burning. Another line of trampled crops stretched across to where the irrigation ditch separated the marsh from the crop-fields. It entered the swamp at the base of the cliffs. It looked as through a sizeable company of large animals had been driven straight through the un-harvested crops and into the trackless wastes of the jungle swamplands.

They both concentrated the most powerful optical systems of the satellite on the lone track across the crops and saw where it intersected the road leading to the burning homestead. Another break in the crops showed a line heading directly towards the marsh. They caught one glimpse of two animals being ridden hard before the clouds begin to build up and visibility decreased.

"Increase magnification and enhance the picture of that last view before the clouds obscured everything," Kamiel sent to Asue. "I think there was something laid in the hollow of that large beast."

Asue complied and they both viewed the result. Frozen in time, frame by frame, they examined the picture minutely. They could see the large rider perched over the neck of the huge six-legged creature quite clearly. Its long tail was wound around the bony plates of the animal's light grey back. Strapped into the hollow of the beast's back, however, was the form of another of the larger beings. It was obviously injured. By increasing the resolution of the computer-enhanced image, they could see that every limb was contained in splints and it lay strapped into an improvised stretcher.

Asue and Kamiel contacted Sharn and Minns at the nursery and school. They quickly relayed all the information they had on the events that had taken place.

Minns projected to the Gestalt mind, "What we have here is an escape. Judging by what we have seen by the regime exacted by the ruling classes of our neighbours, someone has fallen foul of their system."

"We have only seen the small ones toiling in the fields and working on the road systems," Kamiel retorted. "If an entire household has fled into the marshlands, I would logically project that the broken large form laid in the hollow of that large beast has broken with tradition. The small ones would not be that loyal under conditions of slavery. I think that creature with the broken limbs has contravened their static system. It has been punished and maybe left to die. One of the others has attempted a rescue and somehow alerted the other slaves at the homestead of that punished one."

"What can we do about it?" Sharn replied. "The events on the other side of that mountain range are months of travel away."

"Not necessarily, Sharn," Kamiel sent through the neural net. "There are a number of Nano-pods located on the satellite. I could be one and ride down in hours."

"The question is, do we interfere?" Asue cautioned.

"I feel it's about time we learnt more about the civilisation over there," Minns replied. "Someday it will discover us. Maybe this is the time to find out."

Kamiel projected his thoughts to the other three. "Let us review what we know and decide."

After a few moments Asue declared, "Their system appears to run on slavery. Looking at what we know of them, I agree with Kamiel's earlier hypothesis. This is a rescue of someone who has tried to change the system. I think we will send Kamiel and tell Alexander and the council afterwards. For one thing, I know Alex is out of direct communication, sitting on a lake somewhere in the farming complex fishing. We can tell him after Kamiel has launched. All agreed?"

The answer was unanimous. Kamiel was to go. With that he surrendered his body to the control console and Asue projected his identity up to the satellite and downloaded him into the prepared and waiting Nano-pod.

Kamiel settled into his new body and did a thorough systems check. He extended optical sensors from the smooth body of the pod. The familiar large satellite that they had towed all the way from Saturn's orbit hung beside him in the empty void. Why it had been left there none of the nannites had been able to discover, but the strangest thing was, that it had been left fully stocked with metals and supplies. Asue had left it in a geo-synchronous orbit so that they could use it as they needed it.

Below him lay the many coloured vistas of the new home world. The rows of Nano-pods were attached to the satellite's sides in clusters, outlined in the harsh sun's glare. Carefully Kamiel absorbed the super strength filaments attaching the pod to the side of the satellite, back into his new body, until he was floating free in space.

"I am clear of the satellite Asue," he signalled down to the control centre. "Give me the projected co-ordinates to intersect our fleeing neighbours and I will start the descent. How is that storm front developing down there?"

"I think that it will hit by late afternoon or evening, Kamiel," Asue replied to the orbiting Guardian. "I will aim you as close as I can and you will have to hang glide into position from under the cloud base."

She transmitted the co-ordinates to him and he converted some of his mass to hydrogen. He then began to push himself out of orbit by expelling the gas and dropped down towards the planet beneath him.

The Imperial Guard captain made a gesture to the Trading Post Company. After a quarter day they had managed to find and re-capture all of the missing Zanth. She urged them forwards through the flattened crops. She had split them up into two hands of company, to search the edge of the flattened area for any clue as to the direction of the fugitives.

"Captain," called one of the guards at the far end of the field. "Come and look at this. I have found an area that seems to have been flattened by a carrier beast. It goes in a straight line through the stands of pod vines."

The captain rode up and surveyed the scene, staring down the long line of trampled crops.

"It is as the Commander suggested," she said to the troupe. "They are heading towards Ender-whann-soo's homestead. Ride hard and follow me."

She led the way through the trampled crops, pushing the Zanth hard, until they burst out of the fields and onto the hard road leading towards the Heretic's home.

The smoke of the burning fields and homestead could clearly be seen, rising into the sky above the young Banilik tree plantation.

She reined her Zanth to a momentary stop and pointed above the trees to her company of riders.

"Look above the trees. Someone has fired the whole area. Keep a lookout for anything strange and ride like the possessed. We must not fail the Commander. Find those fugitives, or we will all suffer the Commander's wrath!"

The Imperial Zanth had been calmed and purged of the effects of the bind-weed. They had been walked around the courtyard and allowed to drink. Some were still impossible to ride and would require a few days of quiet rest.

Link-soo-shan had made the stable hands lives miserable. It had taken a quarter day to calm and purge those of the Imperial Zanth that had been lightly affected by Shoo-lin's administrations. Several of the stable-hands had been badly injured by the crazed Zanth. Most had been damaged in some way, but they feared the wrath of the Ultimate Ruler more than the unruly beasts.

The company assembled in mid-morning watery sunlight. A chill wind began to blow around the wooden walls of the Banilik tree city as they set forth across the ruined croplands, towards the bridge. It would be evening before Link-soo-shan and her Brood-sister arrived at the Trading Post. By this time she would expect that her Commander's Imperial Guards would have stopped the fugitives and re-captured Ender-whann-soo.

The Ultimate Ruler mused on the sweet feelings of revenge and torture of the heretical Brood-mother. How she would enjoy the screams of the injured one, when she had her installed in her chambers. Oh how she would pay, for the insult of thwarting her rule. The example set would keep the Empire in the obedient grip of fear, for many generations of kindred. As for the male, she would mate him to her leading captain, while his breeding stalk was un-ripe. She would release the breeding scent that would trigger his reflexes. Then when he was erect the grizzled veteran of many campaigns would mount him. As he plunged the breeding stalk into her ripe egg, it would be ripped untimely from him leaving him to bleed to death in agony. When the female passed the egg to her to nurture in her breeding pouch, by her ovipositor tail, he would die knowing she would alter his offspring. What warped shape could she devise for the male young? The females she would form into captain material, using the father's intelligence and foolhardy bravery. Yes, she would split the egg into the usual four. The two males would become sewer cleaners and the females her loyal Guard Captains. With these thoughts entertaining her mind, Link-soo-shan spurred her Zanth into a steady pace.

"Come Brood-Sister," she called out to the Commander, "let us hope that the bridge is repaired enough to allow us to cross. I have such plans for these fugitives, Chang, such plans."

The Commander signalled the troop to a faster speed and the Zanth picked up their feet to a steady pace.

When they arrived at the bridge, they could see that a great effort had been made to repair the damage. Some of the field hands had crawled across the felled trees over the gap to the other side. There they had cut more timber and shored up the stonework. The ravine below was spattered with the broken forms of the ones who had not kept a firm grip on the edges of the improvised bridge.

The Group Captain eased her Zanth across the improvised span. The claws of the beast bit into the wood to hold a steady purchase. Once over, she waved the rest of her troop across, one by one. Below them the river tossed and foamed over its sharp rocky bed.

Once all the Gnathe were across, Chang-soo-shan formed the Imperial Guard into a double column and forced them into a quicker stride. Half a day's travel lay before them, before they reached the shelter of the Trading Post. The clouds above began to thicken. It would rain, maybe before nightfall. At the Trading Post, Chang-soo-shan could use the crystal installed and contact the Post Group Captain. Until then, she and her Brood-Sister could only guess as to the events unfolding in front of the company.

Deep in the swamp-like jungle, Coen-soo had just eased her Zanth through a stinking pool of stagnant water when the beast struck. Behind her a scream of fear rang out as the undergrowth parted and an armoured head and neck struck at one of the young carriers. It picked the squirming creature up and crunched it in half, silencing the pitiful cries. The blunt head of the beast dipped down into the water and picked up the still kicking half. Tipping its head up, the great jaws opened and with another crunch it vanished down the gaping maw.

"Aallosaat!" screamed Jotin-soo. "Ready your darts if it comes for us."

The scaly head swayed back and forth on the thick neck as the beast noticed the Gnathe perched on the carriers' necks. A pair of muddy yellow eyes fixed on Whann-lin. Down the head swooped again for the other half of the young carrier. Once more it picked up the still twitching remains and tilted its head to swallow. As it opened its mouth to engulf the morsel, the stench of the foul breath filled the air. Gobbets of flesh hung from its razor sharp teeth. Its tongue flicked forward to taste the air.

The young carriers were wild with panic and had swum and slithered frantically through the ooze to the front of the column and in front of Coen-soo's Zanth. There were no more easy pickings in sight. The carriers all faced outwards from the cliff, presenting a ring of horns. All the Zanth riders kept their beasts facing the onslaught of the Aallosaat as it reared up from the marshy undergrowth. It hissed and screamed in frustration at the tasty titbits perched out of reach.

Each Gnathe had a venom tipped dart, fashioned from a dead Scriit. The wings had been dried into an outstretched mode and the spiky nose of the creature honed sharp. The dart-like creatures had been bred for their long, thin and finned shape. Held above the Gnathe's shoulders like a short spear, they could be hurled with deadly accuracy over a short distance, from the back of a Zanth or Carrier. These weapons had been developed from an earlier age, of inter-family warfare.

The smooth, armoured head of the Aallosaat dipped forwards and it wriggled into a striking position. It hissed again and raised a taloned forefoot out of the mud. The prime male carrier grunted a challenge and lunged towards the flank of the Aallosaat and stopped short, swinging its horned head from side to side. The Aallosaat retreated a length back into the swamp. With its stomach full, the creature was beginning to feel less evil-tempered and raised its head again, looking back and forth at the armed and ready Gnathe. Two of the female carriers pushed their horned heads forward in warning and then retreated back to the cliff face again, at the commands of their small riders. The ring of horny heads presented no weakness for the Aallosaat to attack. Retreating back into the swamp the beast roared and hooted its challenge at the semi-circle at bay against the cliff face. Gradually the thing disappeared from view.

Coen-soo urged the company forwards once more through the marshy undergrowth. The young carriers had regrouped closer to the female beasts. They fearfully kept eyeing the darkening jungle. Shrieks, hoots and grunts began to rise to the usual crescendo of background noise.

"Well done all of you," Coen-soo encouraged the terrified company. "You did the right thing. As I said, let the swamp creatures take the young carriers if they must. Protect the supplies at all costs. It will be a long time before we can replenish them."

Jotin-soo asked, "How much farther do we have to go, sister? I can't stand much more of this!"

"You will do what you must, Jotin. I tell you now, we will not fail. Shoo-lin will come to us with our beloved Reverend-Mother. Believe me, he will come!" Coen-soo fiercely shouted. "Now press on and follow me."

As the clouds began to darken in the sky, the marsh began to get shallower and the bottom harder. Suddenly Coen-soo broke through the undergrowth to see an amazing and welcoming sight.

The great towering black cliffs split asunder as if a giant axe had forced the sides apart. A small river ran out of the mouth and over a stony rampart into the marsh. The ground rose gently into the cleft. Abundant vegetation grew wildly on the rising ground leading into the opening. There would be enough to feed the carriers and cut and store for the journey through the mountains. Great boulders had fallen from the cliffs above and lay in the entrance of the ravine. There was enough room to drive two carrier beasts side by side through it, as far as she could see.

The rest of the Gnathe had pushed through and all stood on the firm ground with relief.

"Rest the beasts and feed them. Cut as much feedstuff as you can and load it into the backs of the carriers, then drive them farther up the ravine. We will stop before nightfall and make camp. In the morning, we must push farther into the ravine and look for a suitable place to block the passageway behind us. We must scale the cliffs and be ready to drop the sides into the narrowest part and block the way, after Shoo-lin has passed through," Coen-soo ordered the household.

Whann-lin urged his carrier through the gap in the towering cliffs and turned to Jotin-soo saying to her, "When this is over, you and I will have something to share with our young. My egg-brother is an amazing male. He will come."

The beasts were tiring as Shoo-lin and Khann-link-sool came in sight of the towering black cliffs. The crop-fields had burnt out, leaving a pall of smoke and ashes hanging in the darkening sky. Peals of thunder muttered in the distance. They slowed the animals to a walk and edged along the side of the irrigation ditch. Soon they could rest, for Shoo-lin had no intention of trying the marsh passage at night.

"My ladies, we will have to stop soon or the beasts will not be fit for tomorrow's journey," Shoo-lin called out to his large companions.

Ender-whann-soo cried out in pain as the carrier lost its rhythm and stumbled to the side.

"Keep going for as long as we can, Shoo-lin," she cried, desperately. "Don't stop for me."

"Nonsense my child," replied the old Brood-mother. "The young male is right. We must call a halt soon. We will walk the beasts to the edge of the cliffs and camp there for the night. These gallant beasts can go for only a short distance more. They require water and fodder. The last due to my efforts at filling this beast's hollow, as we travelled. We must eat too; maybe we can chance a fire?"

"I must admit my Lady, you have been a great asset to me. What about the loss of all your lands, kindred and possessions you have had to leave behind?" Shoo-lin asked.

"Trinkets, young male, only trinkets, and who can truly possess land? It possesses you. I am too old to change our world, but I can expect it to be interesting to live in yours!" Kahn-link-sool dryly replied. "If we get there! As for my kindred, I have outlived nearly all of them and those that are left are being cared for. I have not felt the necessity to produce any more for a long time."

The rain began to fall at last from the increasingly cloudy sky. Lightning flickered and another peal of thunder crashed in the distance. The crop-field fires began to be quenched by the steady rainfall. The smoke rapidly vanished giving clearer visibility across the fields.

The old Brood-mother reined the lumbering carrier beast to an abrupt stop. She stood tall over its neck, scanning the burnt-out fields ahead.

"Shoo-lin, we have company. Look towards the line of cliffs. I can see at least two hands of riders between us and the pathway."

"What now, Shoo-lin?" gasped Ender-whann-soo in despair. "What can we do now? It will be better to die than to fall into Link-soo-shan's talons again."

Shoo-lin looked desperately ahead to the advancing Imperial Guard. The only way out would be to retreat across the ditch into the marshland. He knew that the marsh at night would be certain death. It would be a slim chance at most.

The Imperial Guard had doubled around Ender-whann-soo's burning homestead following the tracks of the fleeing household to the edge of the swamp and cliff face. Now they could see the fugitives, clearly. The Group Captain could almost hear the Ultimate Ruler's praise. All she had to do was to pin them down against the swamp till morning, or capture them now. Desperate as the escapees from justice would be, they would not dare to try the swamp at night. She gestured to the hunt to swing round in a semi-circle. The out-riders to the left bounded wide to encircle the two beasts held at bay against the irrigation ditch. The Group Captain was now close enough to see that the other Gnathe helping Shoo-lin was a Brood-mother! No matter, it would be for her Ruler and Commander to pass sentence. Still, she would be a formidable opponent.

"Guards! Slow to a walk. Load your Krytes with paralysing venom tipped darts. This is going to be easy," the guard captain exclaimed.

"Cover yourself, my Lady, they are going to try to dart us. Shield yourself with something. I think its the marsh or die. Back up to the ditch," Shoo-lin cried, picking his own Kryte from out of his pouch. "I will take some of them with us if I can."

The Group Captain warily approached the trapped pair. Her troops were exacting a feinting manoeuvre, to try to encourage Shoo-lin to waste his dart. They all knew how much Link-soo-shan wanted live captives.

High above the desperate scene, Kamiel had broken through the cloud base. He had fashioned the probe body into the standard thistledown seed shape. He took in the vista below in seconds. Eight of the riding beasts, mounted by clearly armed smaller forms, were encircling a large and smaller beast and riders against the edge of the marsh. It was obvious they wanted the fugitives alive.

Kamiel changed shape. Gone was the canopy above him and in its place he quickly devised a set of wings, shaped so that the wind made a screaming sound as it passed through them. He was going to be noticed coming down. Already the encircling riders were staring up into the stormy sky, lit by flashes of lightning. Never in all the Gnathe's long lives had they seen or heard anything like Kamiel's entrance. The Zanth began to panic and plunge back and forth. Some had slipped in the mud on their sides, unseating the riders, adding to all the confusion.

The Group Captain viciously controlled her mount and plunged the beast at Shoo-lin, trying to cover the ground between them, before the thing from the sky could get nearer.

Kamiel altered shape again, going into computer time and dropped like a stone towards the Group Captain's steed. His leading edge was shaped like the blade of an axe. At the top of the axe-head two curved wings spread outward.

Asue, Sharn and Minns watched it all from Kamiel's mind. They were operating in machine time and everything had slowed down to the rate that outside events seemed to be, to a computer, in slow motion. They were feeding a steady stream of information to Kamiel as to the events around him. Nothing escaped their notice.

Just as the Zanth reared up to present the Group Captain with a clear shot at Shoo-lin's unprotected head, the axe head struck. Kamiel's super hard form crashed through the Zanth, dividing it into two kicking pieces. Almost to the instant he extended his form into a mighty hand, plucking the Group Captain out of the air and binding her tight. The axe shape blurred into a humanoid shape of silver. The sharp blade divided and became two legs, flexed with the impact of his landing. Shoo-lin and Khann-link-sool stared pop-eyed with fear and amazement at the incredible events. The muddy earth had been torn apart by the impact of the silver thing that had fallen from the thunder-shattered, lightning torn skies.

"What is it, my Lady?" Shoo-lin gasped, keeping his plunging Zanth under control.

Khann-link-sool held the normally placid carrier beast against the embankment of the irrigation ditch and cried out, "I have never seen the like or heard of anything like it in all my long life!"

Kamiel paused and quickly stripped the fear-paralysed Group Captain of everything she wore. Naked, she would present no problems with hidden weapons. He slipped the crystal from around her neck and placed it over his own to examine later.

The other riders that were still in control of their Zanth fearfully kept their distanc from the silver figure.

Kamiel now held the now squirming form of the Group Captain over his head and threw her spinning and twisting through the air forty feet onto the muddy ground at the feet of her troop.

She got unsteadily to her feet and was helped to the back of a Zanth by one of her guards.

Kamiel's form blurred as he raced across the torn crop-field in the driving rain. He appeared in front of the bemused guard as if by magic. Raising his arms above his head he changed shape again, towering over the terrified Gnathe and Zanth.

"GO!" his amplified voice echoed through the encroaching dusk and he bent forward and slapped the rear ends of as many of the steeds that he could reach. The maddened animals bounded headlong across the fields as fast as they could, carrying the demoralised guard with them.

Kamiel reverted to his normal form and real time. He walked slowly back towards the two beasts held under control by their amazed riders.

"It has no scent!" Shoo-lin exclaimed. "What can it be?"

The Royal party had rode at a steady pace all through the afternoon and into the evening. Zanth and riders were beginning to tire. Not all of the Imperial steeds had fully recovered from the effects of Shoo-lin's trick with the bindweed. Some of the guards had fallen back and were walking their mounts. They would not arrive at the Trading Post until well into nightfall. A steady rain had begun to fall and the effects of the damp and cold was beginning to show on Link-soo-shan and her Brood-sister. Neither of them were accustomed to forced travel at this pace. Both rode in silence, wrapped in their own dark thoughts. In the increasing gloom, the shape of the Trading Post, Banilik tree began to be seen at last through the now driving rain. Lightening flashes lit up the surrounding country-side and the air was thick with thunder and the smell of wet crops.

"Stable the Zanth!" cried out the Commander to her troop. "Be sure that all are dried off and that plenty of fodder is provided. We have another hard ride tomorrow. I would be very displeased if any of the beasts are unfit."

Link-soo-shan pulled her aching body off her tired, ill-tempered steed and walked through to the door let into the living wood of the Trading Post. A guard hastily picked up the harness and led the Brood-mother's Zanth off to the stables at the back of the post.

The Post-Keeper, a Brood-mother of high rank, opened the door. Lowering her head in deference, the keeper stood to one side and Link-soo-shan felt a welcoming draught of warm air.

"Bring me something hot and filling, Keeper, for I am cold and wet," the Ultimate Ruler growled. "Also bring warm towels and someone to dry me and my Brood-sister, when she comes in out of the rain."

The Keeper bowed again, low and submissively. "Yes, my Lady, it shall be done. Come to the fire room and dry off. I will arrange everything."

She opened the doors wide to the warmth of the meeting room and quickly moved out of sight down one of the passageways. A warm glow lit the room inside, from the many sun-crystals that had gathered the light all that day, from the reflective mirrors placed around the walls and the fire set in the stone hearth.

Link-soo-shan walked forwards and climbed onto the perch before the fire blazing in the stone fireplace. As the Brood-mother began to warm through and dry out, her thoughts turned once more to the possible fate in store for the Heretic, Ender-whann-soo. The keeper's young towelled the mighty form of Link-soo-shan dry. A young male offered her a steaming dish of meaty stew. She tilted the bowl and emptied half of it down her throat. The aroma of young shredded carrier, vegetables, herbs and spices filled the air. She finished the stew and tossed the bowl down the table to the attentive young male.

"Fetch me more and see to it that there is enough for the Commander when she comes from the crystal room," she ordered.

The Commander had left her troop to stable the Zanth and had followed her Brood-sister into the warmth of the Trading Post. She quickly strode into the crystal room, drying herself with the warm towels proffered by the keeper's young.

The towering form of the Commander strode to the perch in front of the Trading-Post crystal. It was set in a niche in the living wood of the Trading Post's wall. Dark and sombre looking, it was nowhere near the size of the amber gemstone at the Imperial City. Tuned to the master crystal, however, it was still capable of projecting thoughts to the Shards carried by the special Group Captains of the Imperial Guard.

The Commander stepped onto the perch and curled her tail underneath. Breathing evenly and steadily, she placed her hands upon the crystal face. As the crystal warmed to her touch, the first flickers of power began to trickle into her mind. This was almost as much a pleasure to her as egg shaping.

The maze of pathways began to open to her mind. In the immediate vicinity she was conscious of her Group Captain's shard and the Captain herself, bullying the stablehands to see to the needs of the Imperial Zanth.

She turned away from that path and concentrated on the shard located in the stormy night, somewhere to the East of her, near Ender-whann-soo's homestead.

CHAPTER 4

▼

Kamiel stood looking up at the immense size of the six-legged beast and its towering rider. Asue, Sharn and Minns continued to look out at the scene from his mind. They felt the engagement had gone well. No intelligent being had been killed and only one of the riding beasts. It lay in the mud, broken and still. The other being had fled into the night, terrified by Kamiel's presence and actions.

Asue sent a signal of goodbye to Kamiel. The three artificial intelligences left in the Citadel would now have to return to their self-imposed duties. Minns and Sharn had run the medical centre, nurseries and schools since the beginning of mankind's re-creation. Here they were needed most. There would be an automatic download of information to them all from Kamiel's database, beamed down from the satellite above. Asue would have to contact Alexander and the council. They would be more than interested in the events of this day, particularly these last few hours.

The smaller of the riding beasts was urged slowly forwards and stopped in front of Kamiel, between him and the big, six-legged creature. Kamiel held his hands out in a non-threatening gesture and stood very still.

Shoo-lin looked down on the impossible silvery form that stood still on the muddy ground in front of him. The thing stood on two legs, but had no tail. Two arms extended from its shoulders jointed like a Gnathe, ending in hands with more fingers. An oval shaped head regarded him supported by a small neck. The legs were jointed differently from his and the feet did not seem to have talons. Shoo-lin decided to dismount and confront the creature face to face.

Kamiel watched unmoving as the smaller of the riders uncurled from around the neck and shoulders of the riding steed. The ridden creature was twice the size of an old-time shire horse. It had a horned head, shaped like a long triangle pointing down and ending in a blunt beak. Two large dark eyes split like a cat's, eyed him with intelligent curiosity. The feet were powerfully clawed and the hind legs jointed so that the creature could hop with its long tail held behind it.

The rider dismounted and approached him warily. It settled back on its reverse jointed legs rather as an Earth type bird and sat with its tail curled about its feet. The thing was dressed in a muddy kilt fastened around the waist. Bandoleers crossed its chest, hung with pockets. A pair of startling, protruding yellow eyes, also split like a cat's, stared at him in pop-eyed amazement. A large pouch hung over one shoulder and down its back like a knap-sack. It hesitantly extended a three-fingered hand, with an opposing thumb, towards Kamiel and raised a strange crest from the back of its triangular head, like a fin.

"Be careful Shoo-lin," Khann-link-sool called to him from the back of the carrier.

"What has happened?" Ender-whann-soo cried out from the back of the carrier, bound in her stretcher. "Tell me! Are we about to die? Where are the guards?"

"We have been rescued, I think, grand-daughter. By what, I cannot tell. It came from the skies and it changes shape. More than that I cannot tell you," the old Brood-mother replied. "Shoo-lin is approaching it now."

"Reverend Lady it has no mouth or eyes!" The young male exclaimed.

Kamiel adjusted the optical band around his head and viewed the scene by night-sight and infra-red. He enhanced his hearing receptors and tuned to the sonic band their rapid speech occupied. Their language must be learnt, if he was to help them in whatever escape plan that was to be enacted. Kamiel also, slowly extended his hand, towards the strange bird-like animal in a friendly fashion.

"Minns," he called over the communication band, "I am going to engage contact with one of the smaller intelligent creatures. Stand by for a unique data download. Can you plug into the medical centre, genetics computer, at the nursery?"

"Confirmed, Kamiel," came the answer in his mind. "All systems are standing by. Go to computer time."

Shoo-lin and Kamiel touched hands and Kamiel went to computer time. The strange, bird-like creature seemed to freeze in front of him. At the skin contact, temperature and cell structure was analysed. As the split seconds ticked by, Kamiel transmitted genetic information and blood constitution. A tiny stream of nannites entered Shoo-lin's circulatory system and began tracking through the veins with every pulse of the Gnathe's double heart. Soon the tiny monitors were everywhere in the creature's body, sending streams of information back to Kamiel's sensor net. An area of scar tissue across the Gnathe's back was encountered. Deep cuts had once been inflicted here by some implement over a considerable time. The creature had suffered a number of cruel whippings at some stage of its life.

"Minns," Kamiel sent through the mental link "Can you heal this area of barbaric abuse?"

Minns directed the spare nannites to the area and studied the old devastation. Although the cell structure was new to her, she was not unduly worried. Her skills as medical officer to the colony were soon brought to bear. She quickly knitted the flesh together and promoted cell growth to smooth out the area, using the cells own inherent memory of what the area was before it had been disrupted.

"That seems to be all I need to do, Kamiel. Weigh it, disengage and revert to real time. I want to attend to the injured one strapped in the back of that great beast. That beast must be the size of two old Earth Elephants, maybe bigger. Before you do, contact the big rider and send me all genetic and bodily outlines of that one. I will need that information before I enter the injured one's body."

Kamiel acknowledged and reverted back to real time.

Shoo-lin felt the strange touch of the silvery thing's hand on his own. He felt a sharp stinging sensation that quickly passed. He found that he could not let go. The creature's hand seemed to be stuck fast to his own.

"Its flesh is cool, Brood-mothers," Shoo-lin cried out. "I seem to be fastened to it somehow. Now my back seems warm, where I received the corrective lash by the Beast Trainer. What is happening, Khann-link-sool? Can you see?"

Khann-link-sool leaned forwards from the vantage point astride the carrier. In the fading light, she could make out the back of Shoo-lin's form. Underneath the crossover bandoleers the young Gnathe's back seemed to be smoothing out. The cruel marks of the lash were disappearing as she watched.

"Shoo-lin, do nothing!" the old Brood-mother exclaimed in amazement. "Just stand very still. That thing attached to your hand has somehow healed the scar tissue on your back. Even as I look at you, all the marks have gone, smoothed out as if they were never there!"

Shoo-lin suddenly found himself lifted off the ground and gently replaced. The contact with the creature's hand was over.

The creature bent forward from its narrow waist. It placed a hand on its chest and a voice said quite clearly, "Kaameel."

A hand pointed at Shoo-lin and the being stood patiently still.

Shoo-lin said to the Brood-mothers. "It has a name! I will tell it ours." He pointed to himself, "Shoo-lin," he said and gestured to the old Brood-mother seated above him, "Khann-link-sool." He then pointed to the back of the carrier beast, "Ender-whann-soo."

Kamiel took in the information and was quietly pleased at the quickness of thought of the obviously intelligent being before him. He repeated the three names faultlessly back to Shoo-lin, pointing first at himself and then at Khann-link-sool. Then he made a clear gesture of bringing them together.

Khann-link-sool extended her hand. At once Kamiel climbed aboard the carrier and sat easily in front of her on the great beast's neck. The old Brood-mother's eyes widened in amazement as the silver form in front of her went through the same procedures that Shoo-lin had experienced.

"This is incredible, Kamiel," Minns sent through the neural net. "The large creature is the same species as the other, but a different sex. Their genetic structure is totally different from ours. It is not quite female, however, but almost. I have never come across a life form like it. I deduce that these creatures are triple sexed. You must contact one of the others. It's a pity you did not keep prisoner, that one you stripped and threw in the mud. There were differences between it and the first one you touched. Revert to real time and let me examine the injured one.

Kamiel did so and began to disengage his substance from the Brood-mother's hand. At that precise moment he detected a subtle change in the crystal he had hung around his neck. It began to warm up by several tenths of a degree and resonate on an unfamiliar frequency.

The three Gnathe began to feel the brilliant mind of Chang-soo-shan begin to quest for the wearer of the crystal shard. Khann-link-sool began to feel the effects the most as she was closest to the now glowing crystal. As her flesh was still linked to Kamiel's he became aware of her also.

Kamiel reverted back to computer-time, analysed the strange frequency and located its source. He followed the signal back and found himself inside the mind of Chang-soo-shan and still coupled to the old Brood-mother sat astride the carrier. Kamiel dimmed the link between himself and Khann-link-sool, so that he could filter the impact of what he was about to attempt to do, but not enough to break contact.

Chang-soo-shan sat ridged on the perch in front of the communication crystal. Icy alien fingers began to probe amongst the layers of her mind. Memories played themselves without her control. Everything she was, everything she had ever done, was being examined by an intellect so vast and cold, her mind began to retreat under the onslaught. For the first time in her life she experienced a rape more terrible than any she had participated in. One memory in particular had been played several times. She saw again and again the form of the young Brood-mother held down by the heavy-duty guards that she had designed herself. Once more she heard the tortured limbs snap at her Brood-sister's command. The golden form of Ender-whann-soo was dragged from the council chambers and thrown to suffer on the jagged crystal spears of the killing stones and left to die slowly in the sun and rain.

A feeling of terror began to rack her body. She began to shake, tremble and then convulse. Her sharp teeth bit through her tongue and blood dribbled down her chin and mixed with the urine and faeces at her feet and tail. The dark splits in the protruding eyes, widened, now filling the eyeball, removing the colour.

The alien mind withdrew, leaving the Commander screaming and demented. She raised the communications crystal above her head and dashed it to the highly polished stone floor, bursting the unique gemstone into hundreds of sharp glittering pieces.

Link-soo-shan stood erect, as the insane, terrified screams and sobs of her Brood-sister filled the corridors and rooms of the Trading Post. Knocking the attendant young of the Keeper flying across the chamber, she sped down the passageway to the crystal room. There, lying in a disgusting mixture of vomit, blood, urine and faeces she found her Brood-sister. The great form was thrashing about the floor; her eyes completely black and no colour could be seen. They were blind to everything around her. She had torn herself open in several places with her own claws.

Link-soo-shan leapt across the room, heedless of the mess underfoot and the sharp crystals on the floor. She sized the heaving form and held her close until the spasms passed. Looking down at the ravaged face of the Commander, she could only rock her to and fro in a comforting embrace.

"What happened here?" She cried aloud, taking in the devastation of the ruined room. "Oh sister, sister what has happened to you? What could have done this to you?"

The ruined face continued to leak blood and dribble down the rich fabrics of the Ultimate Ruler's kilt. For the very first time in Link-soo-shan's long life, the first trickles of fear began to be felt in her mind.

Khann-link-sool's mind reeled from the impact of Kamiel's actions at the Trading Post and she swayed from side to side. The silvery form had disengaged from the strange contact, as she could no longer feel the echo of his mind in hers.

She became aware, that the being facing her, had hold of her gently, so that she did not fall from the carrier's back.

"Shoo-lin," she cried, "this new ally of ours has sent Chang-soo-shan mad. It reversed the mind link and overpowered the master crystal at the Trading Post. I saw and felt everything, as if from a distance. It kept me safe and destroyed the mind of the Commander. Whatever it is, I do not know, but it is definitely on our side! Where has it come from?"

Kamiel sorted facts and prepared to transmit to the satellite above, everything he had taken from Chang-soo-shan's mind. Minns had travelled piggybacked with him and was also evaluating data.

"Kamiel, go to the injured one and make contact. I must heal her, before I return my consciousness back to the Citadel," Minns urged. "The language problem can wait."

"Yes Minns," Kamiel replied, "but do you realise what we have here? This crystal is a telepathic-transducer; part of a larger one. These people have a branch of science we have never found before. While I was in contact, blended with Chang-link-sool, I was a living creature of flesh and blood. This is totally outside of our programming. Alexander must be informed as soon as possible."

"I agree, Kamiel; remember, I was with you in her mind," Minns replied. "Never-the-less, the pain of the injured one is all I care about at the moment. Make contact, Kamiel. Do it now."

Kamiel made sure that Khann-link-sool was still sat steady after her unique experience. He slipped easily by her and stood in the living back of the carrier. The bony plates stood up along the sides like an interwoven fence, reaching to his shoulder. Tie ropes had been passed backwards and forwards through holes in the top of the plates. Strapped securely in the back, at an angle of about forty-five degrees, was Ender-whann-soo. A pair of gold flecked, pained filled eyes, regarded him without fear. The silver form of Kamiel turned to the other Gnathe in the fading light and pointed towards the cliffs and made a gesture towards them, pointing up at the darkening sky. Both understood him and they urged the tired animals onwards to the relative safety of the towering cliffs. It would be wise to get into a more defensive position before darkness fell, this close to the marshlands.

Certain that he was understood, Kamiel turned to the task in hand, to heal the broken body of the Brood-mother. The once mighty body was caked in dried blood that had streaked across the nearly naked form in the rain. Shoo-lin had done an excellent job considering that it had been dark at the time and the broken limbs were tightly bound to splints, rendering them immobile. The arms had been snapped above and below the elbow. Some splintering had taken place and the bones had protruded through the skin in two places. Both legs had been broken between the reverse facing knees and the ankles.

"I wish I knew what you are and what you are going to do to me," Ender-whann-soo said to the silver form standing before her. "You healed Shoo-lin's scarred back, so perhaps you can help me."

The being repeated the name, "Shoo-lin," and pointed to her saying, "Ender-whann-soo."

Kamiel repeated the names of the Gnathe and pointed to the Brood-mother, then to himself and indicated the joining together of the two of them. He moved slowly towards her and stood with his hand placed over hers.

Ender-whann-soo felt the sting of contact with Kamiel and her eyes widened with surprise at the strange sensations coursing through her body.

Kamiel retreated from the field of operations and let Minns get on with the difficult task of healing the Brood-mother. Minns released tiny changed pieces of Kamiel's body substance into the circulatory system of the strange creature connected to him. Carefully she monitored the system of the badly injured form. Studying the template of Khann-link-sool's body, she compared the two frames. Yes, she could see the matching areas of the bone structure. With everything mapped out in her mind, she was ready to begin. An unconscious form would be easier to deal with, so Minns applied pressure on the main artery feeding the alert brain of the creature. The being was lightly under and just on the edge of being able to feel what she had to do.

Minns began by knitted the broken bones together and surrounding them with perforated tubes of Kamiel's nano-material. Slowly the nannites began to gather around the breaks in the bone structure, becoming part of the system. As Ender-whann-soo's bones re-grew over the many days to come, they would grow along the fractures and over the super-strength internal splinting. The blood cells would flow freely through the nannite cages.

Satisfied that all that was necessary had been done, Minns released her grip upon the arteries feeding the brain and the Brood-mother began to regain consciousness. Next, Minns directed the hosts of nannites to the cruel abrasions over Ender-whann-soo's body, where she had been thrown onto the jagged, sharp edged 'Killing Stones'. Inducing the cells' own bodily memory of the abused areas, she drew on the reserves of strength in the large frame. The Brood-mother was hungry to begin with—now she would be ravenous! Minns withdrew from the repair work and spoke to Kamiel over the neural net.

"Kamiel, I have finished here. There is nothing left for me to do. I am return-ing my consciousness back to the Citadel. Everything that we have learnt here will have to be put before the council. There is enough data here to keep me occupied at the medical centre for a very long time. One thing is true—these peo-ple do not come from this world! I will report to Asue and confirm with Sharn, on the genetic information we have here. Maybe this will help us to find the right gene-splicing and unlock the habitat for our human brethren."

Kamiel confirmed, "Agreed, Minns. Give my regards to Alexander. I shall expect him to contact me soon."

With that he gave his attention to the rain-spattered form in front of him. Gradually he withdrew his substance from Ender-whann-soo's body, leaving a host of monitoring devices inside her. He had not been idle whilst Minns had used his body. Kamiel had been studying what he had pulled out of the mind of Chang-soo-shan. He would soon have the basis of a working language. The memories of the Commander had showed him a civilisation of strange contrasts. The larger forms controlled the entire system, with a ruthless disregard for the lives of the smaller males and females. The worst days of the old Roman Empire under the rule of Emperor Caligula would be a more pleasant place to live as a slave than to be a low ranking male or female Gnathe. If these people were against that system, saving them was paramount. Kamiel had no doubts as to the rightness of the Artificial Intelligences' actions. He felt the human and ape coun-cil would agree with them, with all that they had done.

Kamiel removed the tight splints from Ender-whann-soo's limbs, cutting through the bindings with a scalpel sharp finger. When he had finished, he stepped back and beckoned the Brood-mother to her feet.

Ender-whann-soo watched incredulously as the being in front of her cut through the bindings securing her limbs to the splints and stretcher. The awful pain had gone, replaced by a dull ache that was rapidly vanishing, although all her muscles were sore. The cuts over her body had all been knitted together. Areas of damage seemed warm to her, as if great activity was taking place under her velvety skin. The Brood-mother had not noticed how hungry she had been, due to the agony that she had endured. Now she felt ravenous and weak. The sil-ver being beckoned again for her to stand free of the stretcher. Having complete faith in the creature's administrations, she hesitantly stood up. It was there in an instant, supporting her frame and preventing her from stumbling.

There was no pain! The Brood-mother stretched up to her maximum height in sheer delight and towered over the being in front of her. She snatched a ripe Pod-Vine fruit and peeled the outer casing, stuffing the nutty flavoured beans into her mouth. The carrier had slowed to a stop under the lee of the high and un-climbable black cliffs.

Khann-link-sool swung around from the riding position astride the carrier's neck. She stared in amazement at the impossible scene in the back of the carrier's cargo hollow. There, stood up, looking none the worse, was the form of Ender-whann-soo dwarfing the figure before her and busily stuffing Pod Vine fruit into her hungry mouth.

Alexander had been sixty miles away from the Citadel control centre when Asue reached him by Com-stat. He had lodged at one of the many farm complexes dotting the artificial world of the Earth habitat. The fishing had been quite good at the crystal clear lake and several fresh rainbow trout lay in the cold store in the farm kitchen. Farm business and crop quotas had soon been dealt with, leaving the late afternoon and evening free. Sleep had been easy after the relaxation during the time spent in the small boat, rowed enthusiastically by Jo-jo. She had even had a go herself and had laughingly pulled from the water a better trout than Alex. He even had the pleasure of netting it for her.

Now sleepy and disturbed, they were both travelling back to where Asue was still manning the satellite control console. The monorail train sped through the dark with the nightly downpour splashing off the windows. Dark silent fields passed below them as the train ran on, hanging below the roof. Every so often it would slow as they passed through a nano-screen and they would feel the suck of the embrace of the carriage as it pulled through it.

Alex was lost in his thoughts and sat eyes closed as he reviewed the information that Asue had sent him. For years he had studied the world of their neighbours over the mountains. It had been a quiet civilisation, seen from the satellite's viewpoint above. They could only guess about the real conditions as lived by the inhabitants. He had never really thought that the human and ape civilisation would ever have made contact. The mountain range was just too wide and difficult for a crossing from either direction. Perhaps they should disengage another pod and map the area between the two civilisations properly. Where could the people be fleeing to, into the swamp? What had Kamiel and the other three enigmatic beings started? Where would it end? One thing he was certain of and that was that they would have to help the runaways. The more he thought about it the more he came to agree with what they had done.

"How much longer, Jo-jo," Alex asked. "Will this bucket never get there?"

"Be patient, Alexander," replied the hairy form seated back in the chair opposite. "We will get there soon. It can be no more than another half an hour."

"We have never really understood all of the motives of our metallic friends. This independent action of theirs really shows us not to underestimate their capabilities. I wonder what other surprises my other self has in store, programmed into their personalities, so very long ago?"

Jo-jo shrugged her hairy shoulders and said, "Does it matter, Alexander? We know that they would never endanger our race. Whatever they do, it has always been for us. They exist to care. We are their very reason for being. I would trust them no matter what."

"Damn it Jo-jo, so do I. So do I. I just want to know more about the situation down there. What can we do to help and what is Kamiel up to?"

"You know that an awful lot of his personality was grafted on from the original Alexander, so expect him to do the same as you would. Now shut up and let me have a nap until we arrive!" a tired Jo-jo exclaimed. With that she pointedly shut her eyes and began to snore, leaving Alex to stare moodily out of the darkened window.

CHAPTER 5

▼

Kamiel climbed out of the carrier and walked to the cliff face. He placed his hand on the hard surface of the black shiny rock and began to remove energy from the atomic level of the materials. As quite a part of himself was inside of Ender-whann-soo, virtually holding the Brood-mother together, Kamiel required transmuting some of the rocky granite into the nano-tech substance he was composed of. During this process, he also budded off part of himself to remove material and transmute it into the super-hard substance of the human's habitat.

The Gnathe watched in wonder as the silver form appeared to merge partly into the cliff face. A shelter began to extend out of the hard black rock. First a thin roof took shape and projected outwards with supporting arches, securing the structure into the ground. In a very short time a sizeable stockade, impervious from the hungry swamp creatures, had been erected around them.

Satisfied that he had done all that he could, Kamiel separated from the material of the shelter. He turned and watched the smaller creature settling down the riding beast and the giant cargo-carrying animal. The ease with which they had accepted him was a great indication of their tough resilience. The injured one had stopped eating and was now regarding him with a curious stare. Picking the mind of Chang-soo-shan had given him a pictorial knowledge of these strange people, but nothing of their language. Kamiel had listened carefully to their speech to one another. He could separate some nouns and the names of the Gnathe. It was verbs he needed, to piece it all together.

Shoo-lin produced some candles from his pouch and some small sticks wrapped in a small waterproofed cloth. He struck the chemical soaked end against a rough pad and the stick lit in a small blaze of fire. The candles were lit and placed safely on a convenient rock. In the flickering light, now all three of the Gnathe sat quietly staring at Kamiel. The young male beckoned Kamiel forward and pointed at the earth by his feet. Taking the burnt-out stick, he scratched a rough map in the dirt. A straight line denoted the cliff face and a Tee showed the ditch. Part of the way over the other side of the crossed Tee, Shoo-lin indicated a break in the cliff face and pointed towards it, making a circling motion to include the company. He then made more marks to show the mountains and pointed to a line he had drawn from the break, into them. The line stopped in the middle of the triangular marks. Shoo-lin looked at the silvery faceless form, shrugged his shoulders and pointed again at Kamiel.

Kamiel realised at once what the intelligent creature was trying to tell him. It had found a way into the mountains from the swamp, but had no idea where it finished up. He extended a finger into a pointer and added to the map, showing another land on the other side. Pointing first to him and then to the far side of the mountains, Kamiel said his own name. He then repeated the names of the Gnathe and indicated to the other side. Next he drew a representation of Ender-whann-soo's homestead and indicated the swamp, then to the line going into the mountains. The three alien forms became very agitated and pointed to the homestead, then the break in the cliffs and then to the other side. Kamiel indicated that he understood and agreed.

Shoo-lin turned to the Brood-mothers, "Do you realise what our new friend is telling us? It comes from the other side of the mountains. Not only that, it knew about the Rev-mother's homestead leaving and fleeing into the marsh. I think we are going to be helped across the mountains to the new lands."

"I agree Shoo-lin, but I fear we must sleep and rest. We can do nothing until dawn," Ender-Whann-shoo replied. "I will never be able to thank Kaameel enough for what it has done for us."

"Indeed grand-daughter, we would have perished, but for its intervention," Khann-link-sool remarked, "but if we do not get some sleep soon, the dawn will be upon us. We are at least a day's ride from Link-soo-shan. She will not travel during the night. I would like to see her face when her Imperial Guard come stumbling in with their tales of our rescue!"

The Gnathe settled closely together for warmth, leaving Kamiel to stand watch. Under the lee of the cliffs, radio contact to the satellite and thus to Asue would be impossible, until they got moving again. In the morning, Kamiel would get Asue to do an in-depth survey of the mountains, to find a way through them, when he contacted her again.

The first rays of the dawning sun had penetrated the morning mists surrounding the Trading Post, when the Imperial Guard rode slowly into the entrance corral. They had travelled all night through the stormy, cold rain, and were glad to see the sunrise. The storm had blown itself out across the wide flat fields of the countryside. Grunts, chirrups and whistles heralded the waking of the Gnathe world.

Seated astride and behind the Leading Guard on her Zanth, was the naked form of the Group Captain. She was still trembling with a mixture of shock, fear and wet-cold. The encounter with Kamiel had been totally outside anything she had experienced. Remembering the cool touch of the silvery figure prompted another fit of shivering. What a report she would have for the Commander and the Ultimate Ruler. All of the Imperial Guard had been bred either by one or the other and had been brought up in total obedience to their whims. She feared for her life at the talons of these co-rulers of the Empire. Failure was not treated lightly in the Gnathen civilisation.

The Group Captain dismounted and walked through the mud to the door of the Trading Post. To her surprise a great deal of activity seemed to be going on inside. She pushed through the door with her leading guard close behind her, leaving the other troops to settle their mounts and feed them. Inside the Trading Post the glow crystals were dimming and where it was getting difficult to see, candles had been hurriedly placed around the walls. The Keeper's young were scurrying about with food and towels.

"What's going on here young one?" she said to one of the servants as she passed by in the narrow passageway.

"I don't really know, Madam," the young Gnathe replied. "The Commander is ill and the Great Ruler will not leave her side!"

"Where are they?" the Guard cried. "Take me to them."

"They are in the Crystal Room, Madam. I must fetch more water and towels. Link-soo-shan will be angry if I do not hurry back with what she needs. It's terrible in there, Madam, terrible," the frightened Gnathe replied.

With that, she ran off, leaving the Group Captain and her Leading Guard together.

The two Gnathe rushed to the communications room to see for themselves what the Keeper's young female had described. They opened the door into organised chaos. Many of the Trading Post's young were cleaning up the floor and washing it down. The stink of urine, excrement and vomit filled the air. Link-shoo-shan was holding her Brood-sister tightly whilst the shuddering form was being washed and cleaned. Every so often another small pool of urine would spread out on the once polished floor and the young Gnathe would bend and mop it up.

"My Lady, what has happened to the Commander?" the Group Captain gasped.

"My Brood-sister has been driven mad by something she contacted with the Command Crystal. She has smashed the crystal and I found her like this." The great head reared up and she stared hard at the naked Group Captain, crying, "Where are the fugitives and why are you naked?"

"My Lady, please be merciful with me. An awful thing has happened. I do not know how to tell of it."

"They have escaped you and you live? Speak to me!" the Ultimate Ruler spat, pointing a taloned finger at the Group Captain. "Tell me everything that happened. Pray that I am satisfied with your report!"

"Madam, we had them trapped against the swamp," the Group Captain began. "There would have been no escape from us. As we rode in with our Krytes primed with paralysing darts, we could see a Brood-mother riding the carrier. It looked like Khann-link-sool. The light was fading and the storm had broken. There was a great flash of lightening with a peal of thunder and something came out of the sky. It screamed as it came down towards us. I have never seen anything like it."

"What was it like, Group Captain?" Link-soo-shan asked incredulously. "Tell me what did it look like?"

"My Lady, I do not know. It fell, looking like the head of a great axe. I rode towards the young male seated on his Zanth, trying to dart him. The thing hit my mount and nearly cut it in half, throwing me into the air. My Lady, it changed its shape. I was plucked out of the air by a mighty hand and held aloft like a newly hatched young."

"What!" Link-soo-shan stepped backwards as she cried out. "What happened next?"

"It stripped me of everything I had, changing its shape again, into another figure similar to us, but without a tail. My Lady, it was cold to the touch. It hung my crystal around its neck and threw me through the air like a firestone, at least four lengths of a Zanth, into the mud at the feet of my troop. I climbed onto the back of my leading guard's mount and the thing appeared in front of us. My Lady, it moved so fast! We could not see it coming. It was just there. Then it reared up in front of us and made a terrible noise and the Zanth went wild. I think it slapped several mounts on their backsides. We took off into the stormy night and made our way back to you. There was nothing we could do, my Lady, nothing at all. By the time we had our mounts under control again we were closer to you than to Ender-whann-soo, so we came here, for me to give my report and ask you what to do."

"What did you see, guard?" Link-soo-shan asked. "Was it as the Group Captain described?"

"Yes, my Lady," the guard replied, in terror. "I saw the silver thing come out of the sky just as the Captain said. It happened so quickly. When the Zanth went wild, it was all we could do to stay on their backs as they stampeded into the night. I cannot tell you anything more. I don't know what the silver thing did next, or what it did to the runaways, my Lady."

"Give me your hand," demanded the Brood-mother and stripped the information from her mind.

Link-soo-shan sat stunned by the report. What should she do now? One thing for sure, she would not give up the chase for Ender-whann-soo. The injured Brood-mother would be travelling much slower than they could. Very well then, they would pursue them into the swamp if necessary.

"What of Ender-whann-soo's household?" the Brood-Mother finally asked. "Where are they, Group Captain?"

"All are gone, my Lady. All of the old have taken poison and have died. The rest have fled into the marshlands. Not only that, they have fired the crop-fields."

"If they have fired the crops, then there is no tribute to come to the Trading Post! Without the harvest from Ender-whann-soo's homestead, more will have to be gathered from the other Brood-mothers. Rouse my guard, find a fresh mount and dress yourself. We ride at first light when the mists have gone. Eat and rest awhile Group Captain Koet-shan, we have revenge to exact."

"Yes my Lady," the tired Gnathe replied. "Thank you, my Lady. I will make haste," and she gratefully disappeared through the door and to the guards' sleeping quarters, followed by her senior guard.

"Keeper," Link-soo-shan commanded, "take my Brood-sister, keep her quiet and still. Maybe this madness will pass? Try to feed her and see that she drinks. I have much to do before I come back for her. I will be gone several days. Tell no one what has gone on here. Do you understand, Sing-trow-sool? I want all the events here kept secret. I will not forget my friends."

"My Lady, I will nurse the Commander as if she were my own," the keeper replied. "Nothing of what has happened here will be allowed to be told outside. Let us hope that we are not visited by another high-ranking Brood-mother. Someone may wonder what has happened to the communications crystal and pay me a visit. What then, my Lady? You must tell me what to do."

"Use your desecration keeper, but remember what I said," Link-soo-shan hissed in fury. "I can remember my enemies as well."

She passed over the still shuddering form of her Brood-sister to the keeper and strode from the room to her quarters.

Soon after dawn had broken and the sun's early morning rays had penetrated the narrow valley, Coen-soo had the rough camp disbanded. Carriers were fed and re-packed. The Zanth were harnessed and additional packages taken from the carriers hung around them. More food was cut for the beasts and loaded into any of the carriers that had the room to spare.

Satisfied that everything was ready, Coen-soo ordered the caravan deeper into the mountains.

"We must find a narrower place to defend from, Jotin," she said to her egg-sister. "Somewhere ahead there must be a place we can block and stop Link-soo-shan when she comes."

"Do you really believe Shoo-lin will make it, my sister?" Jotin-soo asked.

"Without him and our Brood-mother, we are finished. We may escape, just to die of old age in these mountains. Enough doubts, sister. I would know if he was dead. You know how it is with you and his brother. This feeling must not be allowed to perish. We have never been allowed to love each other before the Reverend Mother changed our lives. I will not give that up," Coen-soo replied.

"Look Coen, the valley narrows ahead to the width of a carrier," Jotin-soo cried out to her sister. "I will ride ahead and see."

She urged the Zanth into a quicker pace and pushed ahead in front of the carriers. The sides of the ravine rose sheer in front of her. Sunshine sparkled from the outcrops of crystals embedded in the rock face. The mountain had been split apart by great forces, aeons ago in the remote past. Rushing through, the stream foamed over the sharp rocks and smooth pebbles, filling the gap between the shear sides of the cliffs. It was no deeper then the Zanth's belly and mostly only above its feet. The fault turned a corner and once more the valley opened out in front of her into a wide, uphill sloping vista. More vegetation grew here, but not so abundantly as lower down near the marshlands. Many wild varieties of the Gnathe croplands could be seen. Jotin pulled the Zanth around and retreated out of the narrow gorge.

She rode back to the others and shouted to them, "Come on all of you, this is the perfect place to make a stand. The valley narrows through the gorge and then opens out into a much wider area. We could stay there for some time and explore different ways out to the other side of the mountains."

"Form up in single file and get those carriers through first," Coen-soo urged them. "Once through, we can break off, from running away and I can make my way back to the entrance to wait for Shoo-lin."

One by one the slate grey, six legged beasts forded the turbulent stream almost blocking it in places. Whann-lin had to keep the prime male's head up, or his horns would have jammed into the unyielding sides of the ravine. Once through, onto the grazing area beyond, he snorted and grunted in encouragement to the other five females, pushing resolutely through the tight gap.

Soon the whole of Ender-whann-soo's household were through to the other side of the narrow gorge. Coen-soo directed them to make a more permanent camp and gather more forage for the ever-hungry carriers and Zanth.

"We will make our stand here," Coen-soo shouted to the assembled Gnathe. "If we can, be prepared to block the narrow part of the passageway from here. Jotin, I leave you in charge. Try to scale the cliffs if you can, to see if it is possible to drop some large rocks from above. Risk no one, however, if the cliffs prove to be too difficult. Get the carriers to shove some boulders close to the base of the entrance. If necessary we will block it from there."

"I will come as well, Coen-soo," Whann-lin called to her. "Two will be better protected than one. Besides, I have not seen my egg-brother for some time and an extra Zanth could be needed. Let us take extra Scriit spears and a jar of Balset venom."

"Glad to have you with me, Whann," the head of the protectorate answered. "Pick out a tough Zanth and we will make our way back, but first we must eat. Light a fire and roast pod vine fruit, with some dried carrier meat," she called to the others, "while Whann and I reload our Zanth with supplies."

The camp became a hive of activity as all of the Gnathe busied themselves with self-appointed tasks. Soon by midday, the two Gnathe were on their way back to the entrance at the swamp. It would be late afternoon before they expected to arrive there.

Kamiel had been quite busy during the hours of darkness. He had analysed the genetic cell structure of the carrier beast and the Zanth. The data he had transmitted to Asue during the night. Moving a mile or more from the base of the cliffs to avoid the signal interference had proved useful. Both of the animals had shown extensive modification. The carrier beast had never started off as a six-legged creature. The rib cage had been flattened and strengthened, so that the ribs hinged from the elongated spine. This had been extended to cover the back of the animal like the base of a giant box. Bony plates had grown up from the edges of the spine to form the side of the box, interlocking with each other along the extended length of the beast. This creature could never have been bred to evolve in this way. A deliberate genetic engineering process had been exercised. The only way two adult animals could mate would be to back up to each other.

The Zanth was a fearsome beast to encounter. Its head was covered in spiny horns, some jutting forwards and two at right angles to its head. A flat, beak-like mouth, extended forwards for grazing. The front feet could lay flat to the ground or grasp and its hind legs were capable of propelling it in a hopping motion, or a steady fast walk. He was pretty sure that the Zanth could climb if necessary.

Kamiel had stored in his memory banks all of Earth's many languages and had played back the conversations between the Gnathe, over and over again, hunting for a pattern to emerge. What he needed was more conversations between the strange beings and himself. Light was filtering through the shadows at the base of the cliffs. Outside the shelter, the mists were thick and the sounds of the swamp creatures that prowled the nights were beginning to quieten.

The silvery form approached the carrier beast carefully from the front, offering several of the pod fruit to its shovel-like mouth. The beast was used to being fed and although the silvery thing had no scent, it had climbed in and out of its back hollow several times without the masters throwing it out. Opening a cavernous mouth, the carrier decided the thing must be friendly. As it crunched up the tasty pods and fruit, the strange new friend walked around the side of it and climbed aboard.

"Shoo-lin, no sleep," Kamiel said, pointing upwards and then to the swamp. "Shoo-lin, Ender-whann-soo, Khann-link-sool, Kamiel, go marsh! Kamiel needs words." He ran a diagnostic check on the injured larger form. All seemed well, so he concentrated on the three beings before him. Would they understand what he required of them?

Shoo-lin woke up immediately his name was called. He stared again at their new benefactor in the dawning light. The creature was talking to them from somewhere in the front of its featureless face. Shoo-lin raised his hearing crest to hear the thing more plainly.

"My Ladies, wake up. The creature needs something from us. I think that it needs us to talk to it, so that it can learn to speak to us. I will light a fire and roast some pod-vine fruit and split open some of the sweet beans Khann-link-sool picked on our journey here. You talk to it Ladies and I will get things ready for our breakfast."

With that Shoo-lin hopped out of the carrier and made a start, leaving the two Brood-mothers with Kamiel.

Ender-whann-soo eyed the silver form that stood patiently in front of her and said to the older Brood-mother, "Do you think it could use the crystal to communicate as we do?"

"It picked Chang-soo-shan's mind and left her mad, my dear. Do you dare try it? Let me, as we have joined before. I will try to give it level one speech training for hatchlings. Besides, I am more expendable than you to this enterprise." Khann-link-sool pointed to the crystal still hanging around Kamiel's neck and then to herself.

Trusting that the silver creature would do her no harm, she reached for the crystal and beckoned Kamiel's hand to it as well. They held the crystal together and once more Kamiel's hand pressed against hers. This time, Khann-link-sool pushed gently at the barrier of the being's mind. There was nothing there, only a cold un-yielding barrier. She tried again on a different path and found a brightness beyond her ability to manage. She withdrew and shook her head.

"I cannot get through to it—it's just too alien!" she cried out.

"Wait, Grand Brood-mother, give me the crystal and keep hold of the thing's hand and I will send to you," the young Brood-mother suggested. "If you are joined to it, maybe we can do what it accomplished with Chang-soo-shan without the consequences?"

Kamiel understood the movements and gestures of the two large forms towering over him and gave up the crystal to Ender-whann-soo. This time he once again penetrated the flesh of Khann-link-sool and became joined to her nervous system, as he had before.

The old Brood-mother felt the strange sting of contact and once more became a passive dual mentality linked to the strange enigmatic being before her.

Ender-whann-soo sent the first instructions through the crystal to her Grand Brood-mother, just as if she were an infant. She felt the alien mind accept the program. The young Brood-mother felt the mind send back one word, 'MORE'. During the time that Shoo-lin took to light the fire and cook breakfast, she projected the complete speech and educational programmes that would have taken half a year to imprint into a young Gnathe. She felt giddy and light headed, letting go of the crystal, breaking the contact.

Khann-link-sool rocked backwards a little as the being released her hand.

"That was incredible," she said, in wide-eyed disbelief. "I have been traded some information from this creature, called Kaameel. He is not alone. There are three more like him and many others made of flesh and blood like you and I. They live over the other side of the mountains and came on a kind of carrier that flew through the air. They landed there many years ago. They are from another world and are different from us—so different they dare not leave the place where they live. There is much I do not understand."

"Do not worry, Khann-link-sool, all will be explained to you," Kamiel said in perfect Gnathe. "Now tell me your plans and I will help you all I can."

"Why?" asked Khann-link-sool. "What difference does it make to you, whether or not we live or die?"

"Yes, my strange friend, I would like some answers to these and many more questions," said Shoo-lin, who had climbed aboard the carrier beast with a small sack of hot roasted vegetables. "Tell us more about yourself while we eat."

"The people I serve believe as Ender-whann-soo tried to teach, that all people should be free. They hate the idea of slavery and will agree with all I have done. One thing I must warn you of, we will not kill another intelligent being if there is another way to solve the problem. In the sky high above us there is a thing like a small city. You have no name for it. It is like a great eye with a crystal communicator. We have watched your people for a very long time, thinking we would probably never meet. When we saw the strange events take place, we deduced that whoever was escaping was against the apparent system of cruelty. My colleagues and I decided to help. I think I came just in time my friends, yes?"

"We are grateful, Kaameel," Ender-whann-soo said to the silvery being. "But what are you? You are not made of flesh and blood like us, yet I know you are alive as we are."

"I was made long ago by the ancestors of the people over the mountains. You will need to learn a greet deal about how your world works before you could understand just what my three companions and I are. Let it be enough, that I am different. Now, what are we to do next? The sun has cleared away the mists and your enemy Link-soo-shan will no doubt be on her way here with a sizeable force."

"We go into the marsh, Kaameel, for nearly a day's journey. I found a split in the cliff face where a small river runs out of a valley. Further in, the valley narrows into a gorge and then opens up again into the mountains. That is as far as I have got in my explorations. I was hoping that it would lead through to the other side."

"Very well, let us make a start, Shoo-lin," Kamiel said. "You lead the way with your Zanth and I will ride the carrier keeping a look-out behind us."

Kamiel sprang out of the carrier and quickly broke open one of the walls to let the party out of the shelter.

Alexander had finally made his way to the satellite control console. Asue was sitting at the controls, plugged into the command system. To Alexander's surprise the silent, ridged silver form of Kamiel was partially fused into the wall.

"Good grief Asue, what happened to Kamiel?" Alexander asked in astonishment.

"I told you, Alex, he is down on the other side of the mountains," she scolded. "He was downloaded into a nano-pod on the station in orbit."

"Yes. Sorry Asue—it just gave me a turn seeing him like that," he replied and sat down by her side. "What news then, of events? Have you summoned the rest of the council?"

"Yes Alex, they are all assembled in front of their holo-screens. Shall we call the meeting to order?"

"Okay, Asue, switch them on," Alex said and the control room appeared to fill with people.

Seated around the table were the apparently solid forms of the apes and humans he had grown to know so well over the last hundred and twenty years or less.

"You all know why we are here," Alex called out to them. "Have you all seen the data that our friends have collected?"

The seated assembly nodded or grunted assent.

Joom stood up and addressed his old friend. "Alex, it seems to me we have to get involved with these runaways. We all suspected the system over there was based on slavery, but never thought about how ruthless it was." The ape scratched his chin and swept round his hairy arm to encircle the council. "Do we all agree?"

April stood up and spoke. "Whatever we do, it must be made public. I move that we give all the facts to the people in the late morning. Besides, this is exciting and we get very little excitement here." She shook her blonde hair and stared round at the others. "I have little to do these days. I propose that if we do have to mount an outside expedition, we call for volunteers. I for one would like to see the world outside."

"So would I," grunted Bander, waving a black hairy fist towards Alexander. "I feel that we will probably have more people applying than we need. First we must ask Asue to thoroughly map the area between our side of the mountain range and where these people have escaped into it."

"I have that in hand, Bander," replied Asue. "When the sunrise illuminates the area sufficiently, I will be moving a nano-pod from the satellite and positioning it directly over the swamp area. For one thing, I may need to contact Kamiel, and he is going to be travelling under the lee of the cliffs, making radio contact difficult."

"There is another point to make, Alex." Robert looked pointedly at Alexander. "When they finally get here, where will they live? On this side of the mountains the terrain is totally wild. We should know—we live here."

Robert was a grandson of Alexander and the two of them could have been taken for brothers. His brown hair was curlier then Alexander's, but he had the same piercing grey eyes and tall broad stature.

The hairy form of Jo-jo stood to make her statement. "Have you seen the size of some of the things that hunt at night on the open plains, at the other side of the white river? They will need a dome built, open to the air, but defensible."

"Can you make a start on that, Asue?" interrupted a female ape, called Susan. "We will also need to build a bridge over the river to connect us together. One thing's for sure, we will need a life laboratory and air-lock into their world at some point. It might as well be there."

Alexander looked around at the various members of the citadel council. Joom, April and himself were from the original batch of humans and apes that Sharn and Minns had created. There were seven humans and five apes seated around the table. All of them had been elected to their positions and represented different communities, scattered throughout the artificial world of the habitat. None of them had ever been outside the domes. The life forms outside were just too dangerous. Another problem was the micro-biotic life. Many times Earth evolved life had been exposed to the outside air, and every time it died. Sometimes even to touch the vegetation could kill in a variety of nasty ways. Very few of the growing things were compatible to Earth life. After some time the colony had just got on with their lives, expanding the habitat from time to time and growing their crops.

Having studied history with Kamiel, Alexander had realised a long time ago that without a frontier to push against and be tested by, the human race could stagnate. Who could say what they would be like in a thousand years? Their ancestors had not survived the expanding sun by more than eight hundred years before dying out. Alex shivered at the thought of the same thing happening to them. Perhaps this would re-vitalise the colony before that began to happen.

Alex came to with a start and said, "Well then, we seem to be all agreed on what to do. Divide up the work and think about how we are going to achieve everything. Thank you, everyone; contact the command centre at any time. I will remain here with Asue and Jo-jo. Good morning all of you—let's get busy."

One by one, the holo-images winked out until Alexander, Asue and Jo-jo were once more on their own and the council chamber table empty.

CHAPTER 6

▼

Kamiel sat perched on the back end of the carrier beast and began to have doubts about the final outcome of this adventure. The mountain range splitting the continent in two was vast and high. Some of the mountains towered above the snow line. He would be happier after Asue had mapped the area and transmitted the information to him. It was enough for the moment that Shoo-lin and the two Brood-mothers believed that there was a way through. If there was no way to walk through the mountains, Kamiel had one rather dangerous solution. For that he would need to speak with Alexander and put the proposition to him.

Shoo-lin pressed ahead with his Zanth, leading the way along the swamp's edge. Everybody stayed very alert, listening to the sounds of the marsh creatures. The carrier took every opportunity to fill its hungry stomach along the way. It took great bites out of the succulent water plants and contentedly chewed them as it paddled happily along through the giant larder.

Khann-link-sool and Ender-whann-soo were deep in conversation as the old Brood-mother easily directed the obedient carrier through the marsh undergrowth.

"What do you make of our new friend, young one?" the old Brood-mother said to the golden form seated behind her on the carrier's neck. "I am still finding it difficult to come to terms with the information he shared with me. These people of his must be very different from us."

"We have a lot to thank them for," Ender-whann-soo replied thoughtfully. "If it were not for the sending of Kaameel, by now we would have been in the clutches of Link-soo-shan."

"I wonder how far behind us she is?"

"Hush, my dear, have you noticed how quiet it has gone? Shoo-lin, I think something is moving up on us!" Khann cried out to the young male.

The sun had broken through the thick undergrowth and a light cold mist still hung over the swamp. It curled around the exposed roots of the trees, making visibility difficult. Several small creatures scattered in panic, making waves in the muddy water. The hoots and shrieks from the treetops had stilled. Something large began to approach the small company.

Shoo-lin backed his Zanth against the side of the carrier. Both animals edged against the cliff with their heads warily pointing outwards. The carrier gave a warning grunt and then trumpeted a challenge.

Kamiel came to the front of the carrier and stood close to the two Brood-mothers.

"What do you think it is?" he said. "I can sense something large, by the heat that it is giving off."

"I fear that it is an Aallosaat, Kamiel," Ender-whann-soo replied, nervously searching the undergrowth with her eyes. "These creatures are very dangerous. The small ones are very fast and the big ones take a lot of stopping. We have very few weapons capable of preventing one of these from attacking. Let us hope that the large carrier beast will make it decide to leave us alone."

"That depends on when it last ate, my dear," Khann-link-sool said in a hushed voice. "Stay very quiet and it may leave us alone. We may need your help again, Kamiel, although I don't quite know what you can do."

Kamiel carefully watched the slow, measured approach of the Aallosaat by infrared vision. The beast was at least twice the size of the carrier and could do a great deal of damage. He would have to get to the creature first, before it had a chance to strike at the Gnathe seated upon their riding beasts. An idea presented itself to the keen mind of the protecting being.

"Listen to me all of you," Kamiel said. "I will try to get onto its head. I think I can temporarily blind it and coax it towards the way we came into the swamp. I will leave it there for Link-soo-shan to find! As soon as it turns away, travel as fast as you can to the split in the cliff face. I will meet you there as soon as I can. Are you all ready?"

"You are going to do what?" Shoo-lin looked at his new friend with pop-eyed disbelief. "It will tear you apart!"

"You cannot do this for us, Kamiel," Ender-whann-soo exclaimed. "We are not worth your death."

"My friends, you do not understand. I will be in no danger. Just do as I say," Kamiel ordered. "There is no time to argue!"

The silver being jumped lightly onto the bony collar jutting out from the carrier's head and held on to one of the horns.

The Aallosaat was hungry. The hunting had been poor since it had attacked the caravan. Its stomach had long ago processed the two halves of its previous victim. These sort of easy meals were hard to find. Mingled with the scent of the male carrier and Zanth was the odour of the smaller things wrapped around their necks. Picking off one of these little creatures would be easier than attempting the large beasts. It heard the trumpeting challenge of the male carrier. Ignoring the insult to its size, it burst through the undergrowth and reared up out of the slimy ooze. The Aallosaat's sharp vision soon picked out the details of its intended prey. Back against the unyielding wall of the cliff were two beasts. One was half of its size and the other much smaller. Both were heavily protected by horns. Tucked behind the heads of these two creatures were the smaller, less protected forms. Stood on the head of the larger animal was a strange thing without any scent. The Aallosaat ignored it and swayed its head forwards.

Asue chose that very moment to contact Kamiel. She had launched a nano-pod from the satellite some hours before. It had been manoeuvred into a position high above them, so that Asue could contact her colleague without the radio interference of the mountain ranges and high cliffs. The two artificial intelligences rapidly went into computer time and the tableau froze.

"It's good to hear from you again Asue," Kamiel sent to her on the carrier wave. "We have a little problem to solve before we go any further."

Asue studied the slowly moving picture of the approaching Aallosaat. The beast was shaped similar to a huge Kimono dragon, with webbed feet suitable for propelling it through the marsh. A long muscular tail anchored itself into the ooze, enabling the creature to pull itself erect and tower over the fugitives. "What a magnificent creature, Kamiel. It looks as if it had just stepped out of the Jurassic age, on old Earth. Do you need any help?"

"No thanks Asue, I think I know what to do. See if you can find out the position of Ender-whann-soo's household. By the way, I have their language. They have a new science, involving the mind, using these crystals. It will have Alexander, Hannah and the rest of the council hopping up and down with impatience to possess one," Kamiel replied. "You can stay with me for the ride if you want. Show this scene to Alex as he is with you."

The Aallosaat dipped his head forwards to seize Shoo-lin from off the neck of his Zanth. Kamiel sprang off the carrier's head and landed between the muddy yellow eyes and the animal's nose. The humanoid shape began to melt and flow over the creature's head, covering the eyes. Two powerful straps whipped around its jaws and joined underneath, forcing them shut. The now terrified creature reared full length out of the mud and crashed onto its side, covering the Gnathe and their beasts in slime and swamp-water. It rolled and thrashed from side to side, trying to dislodge the thing stuck to its face.

The Gnathe urged their beasts out of the shelter of the cliff and into the marsh. The Aallosaat's tail lashed through the murky water, cutting through the place that they had just occupied.

Kamiel hung on to the mighty head as it frenziedly tried to shake him off. Its front claws scratched and scrabbled at the cover tightly bound to its head. They slid fruitlessly off a substance harder than tool steel. A probing silver finger extended into the creature's throat and began to plug itself into the lizard-like nervous system. Nannites detached themselves from Kamiel's body and began to travel round the beast's circulatory system. Finally Kamiel found the main artery leading to the Aallosaat's brain. He applied a blocking move, sufficient to starve the brain of oxygen, but not to kill it. Kamiel had plans for an angry Aallosaat that involved Link-soo-shan and her forces. The beast's struggles became less and less, until at last it was still and quiet.

Kamiel released the cover from the eye facing away from the fleeing Gnathe. He released his grip on the main artery to the brain and the beast slowly began to awake. Blind to one side, it began to swim and slither away from the direction Shoo-lin and the others had taken. As it progressed through the swamplands, towards the way they had come in, Kamiel released more and more of the creature. When the Aallosaat sulkily stopped at a stand of trees sticking out of the marsh, he once more sent it into a deep sleep. The great head lowered slowly forwards and came to rest near the stand of trees. Now was the time to leave it and return to the fleeing Gnathe.

"I hope you collected all of that data for Sharn and Minns to examine," he transmitted to Asue's mind.

"Of course I did, Kamiel," she replied. "Now I must withdraw from you to map this area. Goodbye for now. I will contact you later."

Kamiel's heavier than water body would present a problem travelling through the swamp. He thought for a few moments and once more began to change shape. Floatation chambers expanded along the length of his new shape and a silvery, seal-like shape sprang into the muddy water. It would not take long to rejoin his new friends. Kamiel quietly marvelled at the swift acceptance of his presence by the Gnathe. Considering the completely alien-ness of humanity and their four Guardians, the three Jovian intelligences had adapted well. That was just as well, he mused, for they would have even more culture shocks to come when they met Alexander and the other members of the Earth Habitat.

The silver porpoise shape plunged ahead through the swamp as it effortlessly swam and leapt over any obstacle in its way.

Coen-soo and her companion had reached the slope leading down to the marshlands by late afternoon. They kept to the relative safety of the backs of their Zanth. Allowing the great horned riding beasts to feed on the abundant vegetation, they listened intently to the sounds of the wild swamp.

Whann-lin suddenly cried out, "Coen, I hear something coming from the direction that we came."

"I hear it too. It must be Shoo-lin at last." She called out loudly: "Shoo-lin, is that you?"

Astride his loyal Zanth, the young male burst through the undergrowth, followed closely behind by the lumbering form of the male carrier. Coen-soo could not believe her eyes. There, seated with mighty tails wrapped around the bony plates of the carrier, were two Brood-mothers—one of which, looking unharmed, was her beloved Reverend Mother, Ender-whann-soo.

Coen-soo urged her Zanth closer to the carrier and stared up with amazement at the Brood-mother.

"My Lady," she cried, "I saw you broken in the council chambers. Your limbs were shattered. I saw that. I saw all that Shoo-lin saw. How can it be that you are healed?"

"My dear Coen-soo, I have so much to tell you," replied Ender-whann-soo. "This is my Grand Brood-mother, Khann-link-sool. She was also part of my rescue. There is also one other to come out of the swamp. He is called Kaameel and he is very different from us. He came out of the skies and is a very good friend. Let us make camp on dry ground while I tell you about him."

She scrambled lightly out of the carrier and led the way across the uphill incline to a suitable place. Shoo-lin and Coen-soo dismounted and leapt across the muddy ground to each other. They held each other tightly and breathed in each other's scent. The old Brood-mother was surprised to see such an open demonstration of affection.

"My child, what have you unleashed? I have never seen such tenderness between male and female. Link-soo-shan has every reason to fear you," Khann-link-sool replied dryly.

Whann-lin-approached his egg brother and said, "It is good to see you again, Shoo-lin. How did you get away and through the swamp? I feared I would never see you again. Who is this Kaameel you speak of? Tell us your story while we wait for him."

Ender-whann-soo called out to her companions: "Come over here, all of you, while we tell you of our adventures. Perch somewhere and we will tell you everything."

The company had gathered together and traded stories for some time, when a silver shape came leaping out of the pool of water at the entrance to the gorge. The two new members stared wide-eyed at the fresh arrival as it changed shape in the air to stand before them. Shining in the late afternoon rays of the sun stood Kamiel. He had adopted his normal humanoid shape and walked briskly towards them.

Shoo-lin bounded forwards to greet his new and incredible friend. "Kaameel, I thought you might have been gone for good! What did you do with the Aallosaat?"

"I left it for Link-soo-shan to find, Shoo-lin! Remember, I told you not to worry about me. Is that Coen-soo? Would you mind if I exchanged information with my colleagues about her cell structure?"

"I don't think so, my friend. She has seen the wonders you performed on my scarred back and the Reverend Lady." Shoo-lin led him across to the female Gnathe.

Kamiel strode across the muddy ground towards Coen-soo. She took a step backwards in obvious fright.

"I am sorry, Coen-soo, I have grown used to your friends accepting me as I am. Please do not be afraid. You will not be hurt. When we touch hands you will feel a faint sting and we will be joined together for a short while." So saying, Kamiel transmitted to the nano-pod satellite above: "Asue, are you receiving this? I am about to make contact with their egg layer or female."

"Yes Kamiel, I am here," Asue replied to the Guardian. "I am routing the data straight to Sharn and Minns for analysis. When you have finished, Alex wants to contact you with the tele-presence helmet."

One more a Gnathe felt the sting of Kamiel's contact as he released nannite monitors into Coen-soo's bloodstream. The waiting guardians received a massive stream of information. The creature was definitely female and was indeed an egg-layer, but the egg would be unfinished. Now at last the strange sex-life of the Gnathe could make sense. This sequence would be started by the Brood-mother releasing a pheromone scent. The male's ripe mating stalk would penetrate the egg during mating with the female. Being ripe, it would pull away in a moment of ecstasy and blend into the egg. The female would immediately pass the egg though her tail, which was in fact, an ovipositor, to the Brood-mother's pouch. In the breeding pouch the egg would settle into its growth receptacle. Like a womb, the pouch would nourish the egg while it grew. Now the Brood-mother would decide how the egg would develop. If she so decided, the egg would become one or two young Brood-mothers. If she split it into four, she would determine the sex of the emerging Gnathe and the characteristics required for the needs of the Brood-mother's family. It was this genetic tinkering that the Brood-mother could accomplish, that gave them their awesome power over the other Gnathe.

There would be months of happy study by the two master genetic engineers at the habitat. Sharn and Minns would be very busy for some time to come, evaluating everything that Kamiel had transmitted to them.

Kamiel withdrew from Coen-soo's flesh.

"Thank you, my new friend," he said. "Now, Shoo-lin, I think it's time we set out to meet the rest of Ender-whann-soo's household. Link-soo-shan cannot be far behind us."

The small caravan formed up and began the trek through the gorge towards the rest of the fleeing Gnathe.

The sun was high overhead, as the troop of Gnathe, pushing their Zanth to the limit, entered the burnt out lands of Ender-whann-soo. Yesterday's storm had blown itself out and once more a warm sun shone down. The fields were eerily silent and the rain had turned the ashes into a clinging mud. Each rider kept quiet as the Zanth covered the ground in great leaps. A tired Group Captain stayed close to the Ultimate Ruler, ready to be called for instruction or question, as the company raced over the desolate countryside. They approached the area of Kamiel's entrance from the skies above. There on the muddy ground lay what was left of the two halves of the Group Captain's Zanth. Much of the body had been eaten and the bones had been scattered nearby. The troop of Gnathe pulled the riding beasts to a stop.

Link-soo-shan pointed to the decapitated, half eaten Zanth, and said, "It is as you told me, Group Captain; your riding beast was indeed split into two pieces. What manner of creature could it be? There is nothing more to see here. Follow the tracks along the side of the irrigation ditch. They must be hiding somewhere."

"Madam, the tracks of the carrier lead towards the base of the cliffs," the Group Captain called out. "I will ride ahead and see what I can find."

"Do it. We will follow at a slower pace," the Ultimate Ruler growled. "Remember, I want them alive."

The Group Captain ached in every bone and muscle. She was tired and saddle sore, but knew better than to show weakness in front of her Brood-mother's sister. The Zanth bounded over the last two fields and the base of the cliffs came into view. A strange sight met her eyes. An alien structure projected out from the cliff's edge. Impossible straight lines met her gaze. She was filled with a fearsome dread. In all her life she had never seen an artificial dwelling before. Kamiel had built a standard hexagon shape with a conical roof. She could not bring herself to go in, so she turned her Zanth around and sped back the way she had come.

The Group Captain rode up to the Brood-mother and gasped, "My Lady, there is a strange structure at the edge of the cliff. It seems to be made from the cliff itself. It is big enough to ride two carrier beasts into it. I did not go inside."

"Why not, Captain? What is there to fear?" Link-soo-shan fixed her with a cold and calculating stare.

"I did not wish to disturb anything that may have been inside, my Lady. I think that you should see inside before anyone else. There may be clues to help us to find them," the Group Captain replied with caution.

The Imperial Guard warily approached the shelter Kamiel had constructed the night before. They could clearly see that the material of the cliff had somehow flowed out of the sheer rock face. Alien lines pulled their eyes into unaccustomed squints. Nowhere in their world had they ever seen precision straight lines and flat walls. Transparent panels were let into the wall, allowing the sun's rays to penetrate the inside. Link-soo-shan dismounted and handed the reigns of her Zanth's harness to the Group Captain. She knew that to show fear of this strange place would be to lose all control over the troop of Gnathe. They would do anything that she demanded of them whilst they still feared and respected her. She walked up to the structure and touched one of the walls, while looking into the inside. The wall was cold, like stone! The strange transparent panel was also cold to the touch. This place had not been grown and shaped by Gnathen skills.

She asked the Group Captain, "Did you not see this place when you tracked Ender-whann-soo's household?"

"My Lady, it was not here yesterday!" she cried desperately. "We rode right to the edge of the irrigation ditch. I am sure that we were here. Our Zanth have all stood on this place."

"Are you sure, Group Captain?"

Link-soo-shan gazed at the walls and roof of Kamiel's shelter.

Bowing her head, the Group Captain replied, "On my life, My Lady. It was not here. I do not understand any of this. Are you going inside, Lady?"

Link-soo-shan walked slowly around the hexagonal walls until she came to the dissolved wall facing the swamp and ditch.

"Be ready to come in when I call," she grated.

With that, she stepped inside and carefully surveyed the interior. Carrier dung lay heaped to one side in a great pile. She automatically noted the lack of steam. It was quite cold. Therefore the fugitives must have left at dawn. What could the swamp offer in safety, she wondered? Then, when her keen eyes had adjusted to the darker area inside, she spied a crude drawing on the undisturbed floor at the back of the structure. It was close to the strangely smooth cliff face. She carefully walked over to it, dragging the weight of her tail across the dirt floor.

Both of her hearts began to increase their rhythm with a fierce and feral joy. There, scratched in the dirt floor, was a rough map. Here was the cliff face. There was the ditch and the swamp. Part of the way along the cliff and leading out of the swamp, appeared to be entrance into the mountains. The high cliffs had always barred the Gnathe from exploring the mountain range. They were people of the flatlands. Shoo-lin had obviously found a way into them from the marsh-lands. She studied the map further. It seemed as if there was a way through to the other side. Could it by that there was a Gnathe settlement over there? Perhaps a new Empire could be formed? There would be unexpected benefits from the cap-ture of the Heretic. The Brood-mother wondered how she could have been moved so fast in the state she had left her. What was the involvement of the strange silver being from the sky? This played uneasily in the back of her mind. She made up her mind—they would cross the swamp now. If they could get to the break in the cliff face before night, they would be able to catch the fugitives the next day.

"Group Captain, come here and see this!" she ordered. "I have found out where they are going. There is nothing to fear in this place. Come and study this map that is scratched into the floor."

Hesitantly the Group Captain approached the entrance and timidly walked inside to the Brood-mother's direction. Every instinct cried out to flee this place. As she became more accustomed to the area, she felt less threatened. She studied the map pointed out to her by her Ruler.

"My Lady, this is why Ender-whann-soo's household fled into the marsh-lands," she gasped. "Who would have ever have known that the high cliff would have an entrance through it in the depths of the swamp? Shall I call the troop together and make ready?"

"Yes Group Captain, two hands of riders in front and two or even three abreast. I will be in-between you and the rest of the troop. Keep tightly together as we push through. There are Aallosaats in the swamplands. Tip your Scriit spears in Bansit venom and be very alert," the Brood-mother ordered.

After instruction, the troop of Gnathe formed up and began to broach the irrigation ditch separating the croplands from the marsh. All of them were beginning to feel hungry now and Ender-whann-soo's crops had not supplemented the rations they carried. Burning the crops had produced the necessary effect.

The small caravan of beasts and riders wound their way through the valley towards the entrance of the narrow gorge. Late afternoon had passed into evening and long shadows pulled ahead of them.

Alexander had contacted Kamiel through the tele-presence helmet at the control console. He now lodged in Kamiel's mind as an unobtrusive observer. They had talked together for hours as the great carrier beast plodded steadily onwards. Alex marvelled at the diversity of life that occupied the Jovian landscape. Everywhere he looked the ground and the sides of the valley were covered in strange plants. Kamiel had adjusted his vision centre to duplicate the human binocular sight. Colourful flowers opened their heads to receive the last of the sun's rays. They were visited by the equivalent of Jovian flying insects. Sometimes they snapped shut on a visitor. An angry buzzing could be heard from inside some of the flowers, where a meal had been trapped. Alex noted that some of these flowers did not seem to be rooted to the rocks at all. They were chameleon-like creatures that imitated the flowers and preyed on the pollinating visitors. Kamiel lent over the carrier's side and picked one up at Alexander's request. The creature was constructed similar to a bunch of ferns attached to a mossy body. Multiple heads stood out with flower-like jaws extended on thin flexible necks. Underneath the little animal was a mass of tendrils for gripping the stones amongst which it lived. Kamiel put it down on a rock as they passed by and the small body rapidly moved away and took up a new position close to a clump of flowers resembling itself.

"Kamiel, this is an incredible world," whispered the voice of the tele-presence in his electronic ear. "If only we could explore it as you can."

"I am handicapped in one way, old friend. I have no sense of smell. For all we know these flowers could smell like a bunch of onions! This place is very beautiful, Alex, and the life forms are fascinating."

"I think I would like to speak with the Brood-mothers. Can you arrange instant translation between us? We should tell them of our plans for settling them on the other side of this mountain range," Alex interjected.

Kamiel stood up from his position from the back of the carrier and walked over the living floor of the box of the constructed animal. He picked his way over the collected stores of pod-vine fruit and other vegetation, until he came to where the two Brood-mothers perched over the neck of the beast.

"My Ladies, I would like to talk to you again," said Kamiel.

The two large forms stopped their animated speech and Ender-whann-soo turned around to face him while Khann-link-sool continued to drive the carrier forwards.

"Yes, my friend, what do you want to talk to us about?" Ender-whann-soo regarded the silver form that stood holding the side of the carrier's bony plate. She was relieved to see that Kamiel had two recognisable eyes instead of the dark band around his head. It made his head look more normal.

Alexander found himself looking into a gold-flecked pair of large cat's eyes. The creature was beautiful to look upon. She had a golden, velvety fur that covered her body, except her face. A large red crest stood erect from the back of her triangular head. The mouth was shaped like a bear's with a set of sharp canine teeth projecting from her gums. Her tongue flicked in and out tasting the air. Corded muscles stood out in bunches from her shoulders and down her arms to a pair of large hands. Ender-whann-soo's hands had retractable claws, like those of an Earth born cat. They were very strong and powerful. Three, triple jointed fingers were opposed by a thick heavy thumb. An aura of power hung over the tall form of the Brood-mother. Evolution had produced the perfect killer linked with a fierce intelligence. This was a being, moulded by Jovian forces, to successfully dominate this world. Alexander could not repress a feeling of awe in her presence.

Kamiel and Alexander looked up at the impressive form of this lovely creature. Her tail curled around the carrier's bony plates at the sturdy neck. He beckoned her down to the living floor of the box. Ender-whann-soo scrambled down in a fluid motion and squatted before him. She still towered over him by at least two feet. Stood erect, she would have measured twelve feet from the floor to the top of her head. The thick muscular tail flicked out another eight feet behind her.

"How can I help you, Kaameel?"

The Brood-mother put her head to one side like a bird and stared at the silver biped that stood before her.

"Lady, I have more to tell you about my friends beyond the mountains. Some of what I am about to explain may be hard for you to understand," Kamiel said to her.

"Tell me Kaameel," the Brood-mother replied. "I will do my best to follow what you say."

"Lady, I have with me the leader of the human community, Alexander. He is, at this moment, looking out from my visual centres or eyes and would like to talk to you through me. He does not know your language, so I will speak for him and relay what you say to him."

The old Brood-mother twisted round from her position on the carrier's neck and inquired, "Do you have communication crystals and use them like we do?"

"No, we use something quite different. We have never seen anything like your use of the crystals that occur here." He gestured to the crystal now hanging around the neck of Ender-whann-soo and said, "This is something that we would like to learn from you. Alexander says that there is much we can do to benefit from each other. We look forward to meeting you," Kamiel replied for Alexander.

"I also," said the Brood-mother. "I would like to know what you look like. Are you the same as Kaameel's shape?"

"Kamiel says that he can change his shape to show you what we look like," replied Alexander. "First me, and then one of our females. Next he will show you our Ape brethren."

The Brood-mothers watched fascinated, as Kamiel became first a naked human male and next a human female. They were astonished by the chimpanzee forms and could see the similarities between the bipedal figures.

"Our history is very long and unlike yours in many ways," Alexander told them. "We can only show you our dissimilar shapes with Kamiel's help. We also wear clothing as you do, but again very different from yours. At least we have prepared you to accept our bodily forms. I can assure you we do not have Kamiel's silver colour."

"We have changed the forms of many of our animals to suit our own purposes," Khann-link-sool replied. "We see shape as a function of the life form. You look strange to us without tails. I cannot, but wonder, how you do not fall over!"

Ender-whann-soo stared at the silver figure and said, "The most important thing we feel, is the fact that you have helped us. How can we ever repay you?"

"We need no repayment, Ladies," Alex replied through Kamiel's translator. "There will be great interest in your use of the crystal communicators. Your mastery of mental science is new to us. We in turn have much to teach you about the physical sciences. Your genetic research surpasses ours. There can only be benefits to us both, if we pool our combined knowledge. Now I must bid you goodbye for a time. I have a great deal to organise at my side of the mountains for your arrival. We have to construct a safe area for you to live in. The land is very wild and would make your swampland look tame by comparison. Also, my council and I will study the maps that Asue has been putting together. We have to find a way to get your homestead through the mountains and over to our side for safety. Kamiel will look after you, my friends. I look forward to meeting you."

With that Alexander withdrew from Kamiel and took off the contact helmet, leaving the caravan to find its own way through the narrow gorge.

CHAPTER 7

▼

Human and ape surveyors studied the maps of the White River and came to a decision. Thirty miles down-river from the cliff face, the torrent of water churned through a narrow channel, cut through the rocks by years of persistent passage. Here would be the place where the bridge would span the river.

Asue took time off from the aerial survey of the mountain range to pro-gramme the city computer. She fed into the memory banks the co-ordinates pre-pared by Alexander's grandson Robert and his engineering team. She then programmed the nannites to start the spanning of the river and altered the struc-ture of the edge of the nearest dome.

Spider web filaments began to extend from the wall of the habitat. Material was consumed from the available area of the gorge until a single arch spanned the chasm no thicker than a man's finger. The moment the fragile looking arch touched the other side; the contact site began to fizz and appeared to melt. The nannites spread out from the contact area in all directions. Soon the arch began to thicken and expand. A pre-programmed shape emerged from the busy micro-machines. As one programme exhausted, the nannites re-grouped and began the next stage. They would continue all though the night until a tubular bridge extended from the Earth habitat to the other side of the river. The micro-scopic workers at each end of the tube rapidly constructed double air locks. No single Jovian microbe had been allowed to intrude into the hollow bridge or the habitat.

As night approached, the next stage of the plan began to appear. A hexagonal shape five miles across started to grow upwards from the ground. The walls would thicken and gain strength until they stood twenty feet from the ground. At the top of the wall vicious spikes would be extruded outwards and also pointing down towards the ground. A walkway would be extended along the length of the wall five feet down from the top. Slopes leading from ground level to the walkways would be placed at intervals along the wall. Transparent panels let into the walls would provide extra vision of the terrain outside the fortifications.

Over the weeks to come, shelters would be built for the Gnathe to use as they thought fit. Interchange areas, where the humans and apes would be able to meet the Gnathe, behind impregnable transparent panels had yet to be designed and built. The walls extended deep into the ground to keep out burrowing predators. The human and ape engineers would provide as safe a haven for the fleeing Gnathe as was possible, without totally shutting out the Jovian world.

Asue and the council planners studied the aerial maps that the manoeuvrable nano-pod had transmitted to the satellite and then to the control console. They had scrutinised the area where Ender-whann-soo's household was preparing to stand fast. The valley on the other side of the narrow gorge had proved quite extensive. Unfortunately, all the trails leading out of it would take the caravan high into the barren mountains and into the snow line. The carriers had not been designed for this territory. Even the Gnathe in their exploration of the vast continent had not penetrated the Polar Regions. They were not used to the cold at below zero temperatures.

Hannah looked around the council chambers and said, "What are we to do? There is no practical way through that mountain range that we can see."

"Surely we can plot a way through the valleys," an ape named Simon inquired. "They must come out somewhere on our side."

Alexander shook his head. "Asue has studied these maps from every angle. Each way out of the valley that the Brood-mother's household is camped in, leads upwards into the snow line. The carriers would never survive. Without their animals, the Gnathe are finished. Their whole society turns on their ability to shape what they require from domesticated stock. They do not fashion tools, as we know them. We must get them across somehow."

Hannah beat the table impatiently with her small fists. "I and my science staff must have that crystal now hanging around Ender-whann-soo's neck. We also need the Gnathe to help us to understand it. From Sharn's analysis of their language and culture, their mental science is years and a quantum leap beyond anything we have achieved. Besides which, I admire their courage and their adaptability. We must help them in some way."

Asue stood quietly and spoke above the chatter. "Kamiel said that there was another way to rescue them. He said it was dangerous, but possible. I will contact him from the control console and find out just what he meant. In the meantime, keep the work going on the Gnathen shelter. We still need designs for the interchange area. Minns is working on another life laboratory to help us to study them, if we can get them here. Sharn is working with the design team to produce outside suits for those of you who will be working away from the domes. I will soon be back."

The silver form exited the council chambers and ran swiftly through the buildings. She avoided contact with slow moving humans and apes by reverting to machine, computer time.

Asue sat once more at the controls of the powerful communication console. She plugged a finger into the specially adapted socket and concentrated on transmitting to Kamiel.

The swamp stank worse than anything that Link-soo-shan could have imagined. They were well into the murky jungle and the Zanth were making good progress, swimming and climbing over any obstacles that were in the way. It was dark under the lee of the cliffs, but the passage of the fugitives could easily be seen by the trail of broken foliage.

The Aallosaat was in an evil mood. Its possession and prior domination by Kamiel had faded from its tiny mind. All that was left was the gnawing hunger in the pit of its stomach. The noise and scent of the Zanth with their riders carried on the still air. Nevertheless, the beast was uneasy on account of fragments of memory associated with these smells. Hunger eventually won over caution and the beast slowly positioned itself to strike. It coiled its body into a living spring and lay in the mud and rotting water plants, near to where the caravan of Zanth were to pass by against the cliffs.

It ignored the first two Zanth close to the cliff face and watched the approach of the out-rider. The keen eyesight detected the Gnathen rider perched about the neck and shoulders of the riding beast.

This time there was no roar of challenge as the Aallosaat struck. Its blunt head reared from the muddy water and snatched the Gnathe from her position on the Zanth's neck and shoulders. She had no time to scream as the sharp teeth crunched her into oblivion. The Aallosaat tilted its head to swallow the pulverised body of the Imperial Guard.

"Spear it!" screamed Link-soo-shan. "Aim for the soft neck under the mouth!"

The two nearest guards hurled their Scriit spears at the soft creamy throat.

The Aallosaat felt the pain of the spears and then a spreading numbness in the area. It screamed with rage and reared up out of the marsh. Standing erect, with its tail firmly anchored, the enraged creature fixed its eyes on the next available Gnathe guard and Zanth. This time it hurled itself at the Zanth, biting through the neck and also the legs of the guard. She fell quickly beneath the thrashing body of her mount, her awful screaming silenced.

Broadside on to the troop, the enraged Aallosaat brought its heavily armoured tail into the fight. The tail scythed through the air and swept two more Gnathe to their deaths against the unyielding surface of the cliff. One of the Zanth was swept into a broken heap and ploughed into the muddy ooze.

Once more the beast reared up and pushed itself through the stagnant swamp towards the larger form of Link-soo-shan. It opened its jaws wide and once more screamed its challenge.

The Brood-mother could taste the foul breath of the massive creature as it came for her. She hefted her heavier Scriit spear in her powerful hand and with all her prodigious strength hurled it down the Aallosaat's open throat. The poisoned spear flew through the air and passed over the beast's tongue, penetrating deep into the flesh at the back of its mouth. A gout of blood sprayed out of the Aallosaat's jaws covering the head and shoulders of the Ultimate Ruler. She ducked down over the shoulders of her Zanth and held tight to the harness. The Aallosaat's jaws snapped on the empty air where the Brood-mother had been.

The Imperial Group Captain wrenched the head of her terrified mount around towards the enraged Aallosaat. She pulled herself erect over the pitching horny head of her Zanth and thrust the point of her sharpened spearhead deep into the eye-socket of the attacking creature. The beast screamed in pain and jerked away from Link-soo-shan, carrying the form of her Group Captain with it. She swung on the spear and curled her tail over the head of the maddened beast, hanging on for dear life. Her taloned hind feet found a purchase on the leathery hide and the guard scrabbled onto the top of its head. She ground the spear deeper into the burst eyeball and into the socket. The beast shook its head and reached up with a clawed foot to remove the small life form from its hold. This was when the Imperial Group Captain dug the clawed toes of her hind foot into the other eye, lacerating the retina and ripping the eyeball into shreds.

The fore-claw caught the Gnathe across her belly and disembowelled her. She passed out of sight beneath the bulk of the Aallosaat's thrashing body. More poisoned spears struck the blinded creature in every exposed tender spot. It began to weaken and the creature's movements slowed as the deadly Bansit venom did its work. Abruptly the massive heart shuddered and stopped. The nerve poison had finally reached its vital organs. A great gasp of stinking breath swept over the marshland as the beast died. It lay in a mixture of muddy slime and stagnant ooze. No sign of the brave, Imperial Group Captain, was to be seen. Many of the company had been killed and their terrified Zanth had fled far from the scene and into the marsh.

Link-soo-shan called the remainder of her Imperial Guards together under the overhang of the cliff.

She addressed the survivors. "Guards, we must go on. This great beast would have held the territory around this area. There should not be any other nearby, but this place will be swarming with carrion eaters very soon. I am proud of you all. We must catch and kill this heretic Ender-whann-soo or all that I have built will be lost. Your positions in my empire will not be un-rewarded. I will not forget this day. Retrieve whatever Scriit spears you can from the Aallosaat's carcass." She pointed at the Group Captain from the Trading Post company and declared, "You are now Imperial Group Captain, so form up your troops as before and let us get away from this awful place. Nightfall will soon be upon us."

"Yes Lady," the new Imperial Group Captain replied. "Everyone listen to me, we must push on. Let us get to solid ground."

With that, the survivors once more formed a protective formation around their Brood-mother. They had not gone too far into the jungle when the noise of the feast on the dead Aallosaat carried through the undergrowth. They quickened the pace and eventually, as the sun began to set, they broke through into the last pool. There, before them, was the relative safety of Shoo-lin's beach. Gratefully they rode the Zanth up the slope and into the stand of vegetation growing there. They saw the marks of the fugitive carriers and Zanth in the soft ground.

"My Lady, look here!" the new Group Captain cried. "They have been here. We will have them soon."

"I see the marks of a camp everywhere, Group Captain. Light a fire to keep the night-beasts at bay and feed the Zanth. I need a wash before I can go any further. I stink of blood and marsh. We will rest for a quarter day. At the rise of the three moons, we will walk the Zanth slowly on and rest again before dawn. I can feel that we are closing the distance."

The Gnathe posted a guard to keep watch and soon most of them had fallen asleep on the soft foliage. Firelight flickered off the walls of the gorge while the guard watched for the rising of the moons and fed the fire with dead branches.

Kamiel sat by the campfire reflecting the dancing flames from off his silver body. He had monitored the continuing improvement of Ender-whann-soo's mending bone structure. The bones were growing through the honeycombed splints very nicely. It amused him to think that whatever happened, he would always be a part of her. Asue's call interrupted his train of thought.

"Kamiel, I have news for you," she transmitted to him. "We have a problem. The council and I have studied the maps of the terrain between where you are and our side of the mountain. There is no way through, unless you can get them around the snow line. Sharn and Minns are of the opinion that the Gnathe and their beasts would not survive the sub-zero cold."

"I was afraid of that, Asue," he replied. "That means we will have to use my other idea. It is rather dangerous, but it can succeed."

"Tell me then, Kamiel, what do you have in mind?" Asue responded. "I will take it to the council and see what they say."

"Do you remember, Asue, the early days of our occupancy of this world? We talked of surveying it and how we would accomplish it at first hand." Kamiel looked across the camp at the Gnathen figures perched in sleep and continued: "We had such great plans, then."

"Of course I do, Kamiel," she answered. "What of it?"

"I built an airship, Asue. It is big enough to cross the mountain range and carry the Gnathe and all their beasts. Oh, by the way, Coen-soo has transported all of Ender-whann-soo's library and teaching records. They are all imprinted on a set of crystals. Tell Hannah that, when you see her again. That will be some incentive to come and fetch the Brood-mothers and this household. They even have telekinetic enhancing crystals for constructing fine works. Some are used for manipulating gene structure and even for surgery deep inside the body. These people are incredible, Asue; we must have them as partners."

"Kamiel, will you stop digressing and tell me about the airship," Asue testily replied. "You never told me about it. Why not, and where is it?"

"Before we re-created our people, I spent quite some time on my own. I had plans to use the airship to explore this world with a human and ape crew. We had spent many hundreds of years creating the habitat and building extensions. When we finally began to look outside, it came as a shock to find the survivability count so low. We had never imagined that the life forms of this world could do so much damage to our children. So I put the airship away in my workshop. It is still there now, Asue. I left the air-bags inflated and the engines have never been used except on test."

"What do the engines need for fuel, Kamiel?"

"Rape-seed oil diesel," Kamiel answered. "We have a plentiful store in dome thirty-six."

"Beside myself, who do you recommend for crew and what do we use for weapons?" Asue transmitted. "I can think of one person who will insist on coming."

"Tell Alexander that my band of martial arts class will be the most logical. As for weapons, go to the sports complex. We have excellent target-bows stored there and my enthusiasts can use them and their swords well. Contact them in the African dome. They are camping out at the river crossing in dome one hundred and nine."

"I will expect to see you in under a week," Asue replied. "Can you hold back Link-soo-shan till then?"

"I will think of something, old friend, never fear," Kamiel chuckled. "Do you realise, I have not enjoyed myself as much as this since my awakening on board the Nano-ship and the early days of building the colony. It's wonderful to feel useful again. I was beginning to feel bored!"

"Kamiel!" Asue was quite shocked. "I think it is high time you had a diagnostic programming check."

"You leave me alone Asue, I like the way I am," Kamiel retorted.

"You and Alexander grow more alike as the years pass. Goodbye for now," Asue replied and returned her consciousness to the control console.

She switched to the council chambers and transmitted her holo-image to appear in the middle of the table. The members of the council ceased their discussion and waited for Asue to speak.

When she passed on Kamiel's information, including the part about Ender-whann-soo's library, the decision was unanimous.

Alexander quickly took control of the situation. "Right Asue," he said, "the first thing to do is to check over the airship. Pump it up with helium if necessary. Raid the rapeseed oil diesel resources and fill its tanks with fuel. Next thing. How do we get it out without contaminating the rest of the domes?"

"Leave it to me, Alexander, and you sort out the crew," Asue replied. "They should have communicators with them. I will construct an airlock similar to the monorail stations. Assemble at Kamiel's workshop, dome ninety-three, as soon as you can. Take at least three weeks supply of concentrated rations. More, if necessary."

The council rapidly broke up as the various members decided their allotted tasks. Two apes, Joom and Simon, elected to go with Alexander, Nancy, April and Gundre on the rescue party. They boarded the monorail together and set out on the long journey to Kamiel's workshop. At the monorail's top speed they would arrive just after dawn. Meanwhile Jo-jo organised the recruitment of the weapons experts taught by Kamiel, camping out at the African habitat. Among the one hundred and ten dissatisfied adventurers they needed a maximum of twenty people. There were no anticipations of difficulty in getting a sufficient number.

Nancy and Bander organised the stores and weapons requirements. These they then hauled to the next available monorail train and loaded the equipment onto the waiting vehicle.

Asue sat motionless at the control console thinking hard. How could she get to Kamiel's dome before the rest of the rescue party? Then she remembered the merging process that she had reversed when she had parted from the ship. The Nano-ship and Asue had been a totally integrated system. She had re-programmed the ship to become the Citadel and the entire habitat complex. The Nannite material had been deliberately put out of phase with the substance of the four guardians. All she had to do was to re-integrate with the wall structure. The main computer running the habitat was an analogue of her own mind.

"Computer," she transmitted, "prepare to accept my consciousness and body substance."

"Confirmed, Asue," the mental echo answered in her mind. "Destination required?"

"Dome ninety-three, support structure A, wall two," Asue commanded and walked into the wall.

Her form shimmered as it was absorbed by the Citadel structure. Once more, her mind was widely open and she was aware of every part of the Habitat. She had pulled her mind into computer time and sped through the substance of the walls at almost the speed of light.

Kamiel's workshop was located across the other side of the Habitat, facing out onto the wild Jovian landscape. The whole dome was in darkness and totally silent. Suddenly a dancing electrical discharge showed a slender silver form emerging from the wall at one of the main supports.

"Computer, lights on!" Asue commanded.

Immediately the roof of the dome began to brighten at selected locations. A great cigar shaped shadow was cast across the ground. Complex machines stood in idle silence. Nothing had disturbed the solitude of this place for more than a hundred years. Everything was just as Kamiel had left it when he had abandoned his private project. Floating, with its cabin a mere ten feet from the ground, was Kamiel's airship. The air bag followed the conventional cigar shaped design, with a large inflated stabilising fin at the back. Outstretched gantries jutting from the main body supported four large propellers. These large horizontal mountings also had a vertical propeller set at right angles, similar to a helicopter. Underneath the air bag, between the four powerful rotors, was the body of the control and cargo structure. A wide observation blister occupied the front of the enclosed cabin. Running around the cabin was a wide veranda opened to the atmosphere. A parapet, chest high, protected this. Asue walked to the back of the super-structure and looked upwards. To her joy, she could see a loading ramp leading into a large cargo area.

"Kamiel," she thought to herself, "you must have looked into the future when you built this. All I need do is modify the cabin to be airtight—fit an airlock into the cargo hold leading to the walkway surrounding the suspended cabin. Now to check the engines."

Asue climbed aboard the airship and explored the control cabin. Kamiel had installed an on-board computer to assist navigation and controlling the airship. She activated the systems and immersed herself in learning all she could about running the giant.

"Computer, access Kamiel's memory stores. Cross-reference helium airship."

"Confirmed, Asue," it replied and downloaded everything that he had stored.

Asue was jubilant. "It can be done!" she cried. A stray thought surfaced in her mind. "I am going to enjoy this adventure. Kamiel was right. It is good to feel useful. Maybe we are getting stale."

She mused over Kamiel's worry about their re-created humanities' lack of frontiers and possible stagnation. He was the colony's psychologist and if he was concerned about their future. It was serious. The next thing to do was to replenish the fuel tanks with fresh rape-seed oil diesel.

"Computer, re-route available stores of diesel fuel to this location. Store in the vats provided."

"Confirmed, Asue," the computer signalled.

Asue tested each engine in turn and found them to be in a satisfactory order, even after the length of time that they had stood idle. She devoted the rest of her attention to re-configuring the design of the roof and the airship. She designed a double airlock above the vessel so that the airship would be able to rise into it above the dome and reseal it behind them when they left. These details were passed to the main computer and were immediately put into action while Asue modified the vessel to suit the hostile conditions outside.

As the dawn began to break against the walls of the Habitat, most of the rescue party had assembled. Sharn had managed to produce thirteen suits in the short time she had available. These were loaded onto a monorail carriage and automatically programmed to arrive at dome ninety-three. Kamiel's group of adventurers had soon stacked the weapons found by Nancy and Bander into the airship with the necessary foodstuffs and water. They were now under instruction by Asue as to the running of the airship. Alexander and the other council members attended as well.

The sound of a Klaxon horn heralded the arrival of the carriage with the outside survivor suits.

Alexander called out to Frederick, leader of the martial-arts group, "Go and collect the suits and stack them in the forward compartments with the stores. We can get on our way now. Have we got everything we need, Asue?"

"Yes Alexander," replied Asue. "I have checked everything. I think we have all we need. Let's go."

The crew took up the arranged positions in the airship. Alexander sat in the co-pilot's chair next to Asue and looked out of the observation blister. They had a complete view forward, up and underneath from where they sat.

"Launch the ship, Asue," Alexander said and spoke over the transponder link. "This is 'Rescue One' leaving the Habitat, Jo-jo. Do you receive me?"

"I do, Alex. Go—and be careful," Jo-jo replied. "Try not to take too many risks. I have linked your forward cameras to the televised news service so that we can follow your progress. Good luck, old friend."

Asue opened the roof into the giant airlock that she had the main computer construct.

"Cast off the tie ropes," she commanded.

The crew quickly unhitched the shackles fore and aft, allowing the airship to float free. Asue trimmed the buoyancy tanks and the ship began to rise under the lift from the four main rotors.

"Everybody inside the forward compartment," Alex called over the intercom.

The crew rapidly came inside and took up positions to see out through the side windows.

"All present, Alex," Frederick called. "We can go."

"Seal the ship, Asue, and let's take off," Alex said to the silver form seated beside him.

They all felt the tingling sensation as the airlock force field closed over the ship. Beneath them the roof sealed itself from the incoming Jovian air.

"Computer, open the roof," Asue commanded through the com-link.

Above them the roof began to shimmer and pull away in a long cigar-shaped split. As the Jovian air rushed into the cavity, the airship began to rock in the new wind. Asue kept the engines ticking over and the four propellers idling. She expanded the buoyancy tanks to give the ship more lift and the airship shot out of the hanger into the Jovian sky. The ship spun round as the wind took her and Asue fed more fuel to the diesel engines. The propellers bit into the air and began to stabilise the craft. They levelled off at a thousand feet and held position over the Habitat.

Beneath them lay the artificial world of the domes. In front was the unbroken wall of the sheer, rough, cliff-face, with the great expanse of water behind it that fed the generators of the Citadel. The White River overflow poured over the edge of the black, twisted rocks of the precipice, foaming and twisting along the border of the domes. The bridge over the river to the Gnathen compound hung over the ravine and was outlined in the morning sun. Metallic silver highlights flashed in the sun from the edges of the Habitat and golden reflections sparkled from the water catchments area scattered over the roofs of the domes.

Human and ape stared down at the complex world that the artificial intelligences had built. Already large mirrors were tilting to catch the morning sun and reflect the warmth down into the tropical sections. The transparent roof sections allowed the watching crew to stare in at the farmlands and parks laid out with great precision.

"Everything is so damned neat and tidy," growled one of Kamiel's adventurers.

An ape of some sixty years, Gunter had left the order of the farmlands many years ago and had sought the unruly life in the African domes with others of the same frame of mind. It was this small group of discontented humans and apes that had persuaded Kamiel to teach them the martial arts of the Oriental Masters. They competed against each other and their contests were televised and watched by the more ordered mass of the Habitat civilisation. Now, at last, a practical outlet for their skills had come about.

Alexander and the other members of the council marvelled at the cat-like grace of these separated people. All of the apes and humans were fit and well in the artificial world, but these people were honed to perfection. This challenge to their skills had been eagerly received when Jo-jo had contacted them during the early evening. They had drawn lots amongst the most highly ranked of the adepts for the chance to go. Now the journey was to begin. Alexander would now need to explain the reasons behind the rescue and the council's plan to accomplish this, to bring back the Gnathe and their beasts to the human settlement.

The airship caught the wind blowing over the mountains towards the Gnathen Empire in the inflated stabilising fins at the back of the craft. Asue lowered the beat of the propellers and allowed the ship to tack gently across the wind in the direction of Kamiel. Every drop of fuel saved would be needed to bring the heavily laden airship back against the prevailing wind.

Asue activated the radio and transmitted up to the satellite, relaying across to the Nano-pod stationed over the valley where Ender-whann-soo's household still slept.

"Kamiel, we are on our way. Prepare the Gnathe for our arrival. They will never have seen anything like this ship."

"Hullo, Asue, I shall try to explain to them. They are amazingly adaptable." Kamiel stood up and looked around. "It is still dark here and the household is still sound asleep. The moons are up in the sky. I think I will have a scout around on our back trail. There is an uneasy feeling inside of me that tells me Link-soo-shan has survived the swamp and is still close behind us. I think I will close the gorge to prevent an ambush. See you in several days, Asue. Keep in touch."

"I will Kamiel," Asue answered over the com-link. "We have over two thousand miles to go. The wind speed is blowing a moderate gale force to the southwest of your position. I will expect to see you at early evening of the second day."

Kamiel rose and added some more branches to the fire. He was aware of being watched from across the flames of the campfire.

"You are awake, Shoo-lin," Kamiel said to the rising form outlined in the moon and firelight.

"Kaameel, I worry about Link-soo-shan. She will not give up easily. The Ultimate Ruler is not used to failure. She and her sister have ruled the Gnathen Empire for many turns around the sun. In our society might has always been right. The members of the Imperial Guard have been bred by herself and Chang-soo-shan to be larger, quicker and more aggressive than the females of the other families."

"Her female guards are the backbone of her power base then, Shoo-lin," Kamiel thoughtfully mused. "What will be the effect of her sister's madness on the stability of her rule?"

"She may find things have changed when she returns to the Imperial City," Shoo-lin replied. "If we defeat her here and she returns empty handed, it will not go well for her."

"Then I will make it more difficult for her," Kamiel said to him. "I will close the gorge. My colleagues will be here in about two days."

"How, Kaameel? You have told us that we are trapped in here and the only way is over the frozen wastes of the mountain ranges. By the distances explained by you, it would take us years to cross, even if we could withstand the awful cold!

How can they get here in two days?" Shoo-lin stared incredulously at the silver form beside him in astonishment.

"They will fly here in a ship I designed long ago and built for exploring your world. It floats in the air and is big enough to take all of you to safety," Kamiel replied to the amazed Gnathe. "Now, my friend, I must close off the way into this valley."

Kamiel and Shoo-lin made their way to the narrowest part of the gorge in the semi-darkness. Finally the Guardian stopped at the abrupt bend in the fault, running through the mountain range. The walls of the gorge rose sheer into the lightening sky. Water rushed through the area at a steady rate, splashing up and over the rocks. The width was just larger that one of the Gnathe's carriers. It narrowed above them, over the tops of their heads at three times their height, to almost touching. Here would be the ideal place to form a barrier to block the pursuing forces.

"I will make a barrier here, Shoo-lin, so I want you to retreat upstream for your own safety," Kamiel told the Gnathe.

Shoo-lin looked up and around the gorge and asked, "What are you going to do, Kaameel?"

"Do as I say, my friend and watch," Kamiel answered.

He extended his legs into stilts, until he was able to touch the stone walls of the ravine. Concentrating his will, Kamiel programmed the parts of himself touching the walls, to bud off and complete their tasks. Kamiel then returned to his normal size and walked through the rapid stream towards the waiting Gnathe.

Once more Shoo-lin stared at the frantic nannite activity, as he had when Kamiel built the shelter by the swamp. To his incredulous sight, the walls of the gorge began to fizz and a hard froth started to extend downwards. As the barrier dropped down it hardened, froze, and more and more of the face of the rock began to migrate into the barrier. He could see the walls scalloping out as the material was removed and being formed into the gap between the two surfaces. The process stopped a hand's height above the surface of the rushing stream. A number of pillars sank down into the water and anchored themselves into the streambed.

"I think that takes care of that, my friend," Kamiel remarked to Shoo-lin. "I suggest that you go back to the fire, to dry off and get warm."

"Kaameel, you are an amazing being. I am very glad that you are on our side in this struggle," the young Gnathe replied, gratefully.

The silver being shrugged his shoulders in a human fashion and replied, "It is not over yet, my friend; we have still to transport you all over the mountains to the new home that we are building for you. We still have two days until the rescue party arrives. Link-soo-shan will probably attempt to climb over the top of the gorge. She must be a very determined creature, Shoo-lin."

"She is the Ultimate Ruler, Kaameel," Shoo-lin thoughtfully retorted. "Her every whim and command has been carried out for generations. The Brood-mother has never lost before at any enterprise. Things may change against her if she returns empty handed."

The first rays of the dawning sun had begun to lighten up the valley and the Jovian world began to wake up as the strange pair walked back to the campfire.

CHAPTER 8

▼

At the imperial city, Tran-link-khann, shaper of souls, had become very thoughtful. Several days had passed without any word from the Ultimate Ruler and her Brood-sister, the Commander. By now the advisory council would have expected to have received a series of reports, to make ready for the triumphant return of Link-soo-shan. Perhaps Trann's extraordinary tinkering with the genetic codes of Shoo-lin had born a strange fruit. She vividly remembered how she had increased his intelligence many times over the Gnathen male norm. His egg-brother had been a bright male, but Shoo-lin had tested out far and above the ordinary males. Even the males that had been bred for administrative tasks had seemed slow by comparison. Ender-whann-soo had concentrated on the female line with Coen-soo and her egg sisters. Two of these, Natel-soo and Jing-soo, were quietly sequestered in her household for study and to hide them from the baleful eyes of Link-soo-shan. The female egg-sisters of Shoo-lin were also with her. They had carried her family name of Khann. Marren-Khann and Jewel-Khann were experimenting with a new powerful telekinetic enhancing crystal.

"Time to use the command crystal in Link-soo-shan's quarters," she thought to herself. "I will contact the Trading Post near Ender's homestead and see what my cousin, Sing-trow-sool, can tell me about the events."

She walked arrogantly through Link-soo-shan's household guards to the crystal room. They paid her no attention as she passed into the inner chambers to the crystal, where it stood on its pillar of polished wood. Trann-link-khann placed her hands on the living gemstone and entered the light communications trance. She felt the pathways open up to her and attempted to find and follow the path to the Trading Post crystal. Nothing! The crystal had ceased to exist. Something had happened there. Maybe something to Link-soo-shan's detriment!

She avoided the Ultimate Ruler's shard glowing brightly in the mental fog and darkness and concentrated on the Group Captain's device. It was much farther away than Link-soo-shan, but in the same general direction. Carefully Tran-link-khann homed in on it and concentrated her mind's augmented power.

Ender-whann-soo felt the crystal hanging around her neck begin to mentally resonate. She immediately awoke in the dawn light and shook her Grand-Brood-mother hard.

"Khann-link-sool, someone is trying to communicate through the Group Captain's crystal," she quietly said into the older Gnathe's hearing crest. "Wake up and join with me."

The old Brood-mother quickly shook off the effects of sleep and held onto the crystal with her younger sibling. The mind of Trann-link-khann began to connect to the two Gnathen intellects.

Recognition came as the three minds meshed and the mental link was forged.

"You live and your broken body is mended!" exclaimed Trann-link-khann. "How can this be? It is beyond Gnathen medical science."

"We have much to tell you Trann," the two Brood-mothers projected in concert.

"Reverend Mother Khann, you are here too!" the astonished Gnathe almost recoiled from the mind link. "How did you get into this? Oh Ender, I am so sorry that I could do nothing at the interrogation. I was taken by surprise and my forces are small."

"Shut up, Trann," Ender-whann-soo sent along the mental link, "and listen to us. We will tell you everything."

The Gnathe perched immobile at the master crystal as the two fleeing Brood-mothers brought Ender-whann-soo's colleague and friend up to date on all the events that had taken place.

Trann-link-khann pondered on the information freely given by the two Brood-mothers.

"Can you trust these aliens Ender? You have never met them," Trann dubiously channelled down the link.

Khann-link-sool replied, "Don't be a fool. If they had not intervened, Link-soo-shan and Chang would have had us ready for their twisted pleasures. No, Trann, believe me when I tell you, we have nothing to fear and much to gain. They are coming to fetch us with a giant carrier that floats through the air!"

It will take another two days to get here. All we have to do is to keep out of Link-soo-shan's reach until it gets here. Kaameel has blocked the way into this valley. She will have to come over the top, if she has survived the swamp and that huge Aallosaat that he left by the entrance. Now, enough of this, young Trann. Listen to me again and I will tell you what you must do next. Do it right and the Empire will fall into your hands. I think it is time for a change of rule."

Trann-link-khann strode away from the throne rooms thinking feverishly. There was not a moment to lose. If the course of actions dictated by the old Brood-mother were carried out, then with courage on her part, everything could change. She headed for the stables to collect a sturdy Zanth and her loyal band of followers and young. The first stop would be the Trading Post and a visit to her cousin, also related to the great and venerable Khann-link-sool.

*   *   *   *

As dawn approached, Link-soo-shan's company walked their Zanth slowly up to the entrance of the gorge. The marks of the fleeing Gnathe and their carriers stood out plainly in the trampled vegetation. No attempt had been made to hide the trail.

"The Heretic travels fast for a broken-boned creature," thought the Brood-mother to herself. "There is much here I do not understand."

She nursed the fire of hatred in her mind as they approached the final hurdle. They would be able to surprise the band of fugitives as the sun rose.

"We will catch them unprepared, my loyal guards. Soon we will have them all. Remember, I want Shoo-lin and Ender-whann-soo alive," the Ultimate Ruler commanded, "and do not forget that meddling old fool, Khann-link-sool".

One of the guards nervously asked, "What of the silver thing that stripped the old Group Captain, my Lady?"

"I will deal with it. If we can kill a fully grown Aallosaat we can destroy whatever it is," Link-soo-shan replied. "Now, into the gorge and be quiet."

The walls of the ravine climbed higher and higher as the vengeful party progressed farther inside. As the way in narrowed, the stream deepened and soon the Zanth were ploughing up against the current, chest high. In the darkness of the passageway Kamiel's barrier was not immediately apparent. The leading Gnathe pulled her mount to a stop.

"My lady, the way through is blocked!" she cried, fearfully. "The walls of the ravine seemed to have been pulled together right down to the surface of the stream!"

"What!" screamed Link-soo-shan in despair. "Let me see."

She forced her mount forwards to the side of the incredulous guard and searched the shining smooth rock face for some flaw. The rock had flowed out of the sides of the ravine and into the centre. It looked as though two symmetrical bites had been taken out of the walls. There was space here for two carriers to stand side by side. She looked upwards and could see the dawning sun shining through the narrow gap high above. Even if they could have climbed up the slippery smooth surface to the gap, they could not have forced themselves through the narrow passage.

"Can we wriggle underneath, my Lady? I will try," said the new Group Captain.

She slipped off her mount and into the cold water. Feeling her way along the barrier she ducked underneath the water and re-appeared a few moments later. She stood up and approached the fuming Brood-mother.

"My lady, we cannot go underneath," she said. "The barrier extends down into the stream-bed."

"Damn them!" the Brood-mother cried. "Damn them all! I *will* have her. I will. I will not be stopped. Vengeance will be mine. Back then, all of you. We will go over the top. The Zanth will climb the gorge where we came in. Turn your mounts and do not forget your dead sisters and comrades."

Once more the obedient Imperial Guard followed her orders and began to backtrack out of the gorge.

The row of sensors set in the nannite barrier had relayed the information back to Kamiel, via an optical fibre he had spun out behind him as he left the blocked gorge. He listened carefully to the conversation in the darkened ravine and came to a decision.

Kamiel approached the two Brood-mothers with the news of Link-soo-shan's survival and dogged pursuit.

"My Ladies," he called to them, "I have poor news to tell you."

"What is it Kaameel? Come and tell us," Khann-link-sool replied. "Does she still live and follow?"

"She and the remainder of her company of Imperial Guard have reached the barrier that I built during the night. It looks as though some of them have been wounded. I would think that they must have encountered the Aallosaat during the crossing of the swamp. They will attempt to climb over the gorge," Kamiel stated. "We must retreat further up the valley towards the slopes leading up to the high mountains."

Ender-whann-soo asked Kamiel, "Why not meet them here and be done with it? Can you not kill her easily and finish this chase?"

"It is not as simple as that, my friends. For one thing, I was programmed to defend, not to kill. For all her nasty ways, Link-soo-shan is an intelligent being and I am bound by my programming not to deliberately harm her. She also has an overwhelming force of well-trained killers at her command."

"What can you do for us, Kaameel? There must be something that we can all do together," gasped Ender-whann-soo, looking back the way they had come.

"My friends are not bound by the laws governing my design. If we can hold out until they get here, the situation will abruptly change. Remember, I can and will defend you, but I cannot harm them directly. The time has come to move the camp to a good defensive position." Kamiel stood waiting for their decision.

"We will do as you suggest, Kaameel," the young Brood-mother replied. "You have not failed us yet."

Shoo-lin moved rapidly through the camp, hurrying the packing of the carriers and also consulting with his egg-brother. He then quietly walked over to Coen-soo, who was overseeing the problems with packing the library crystals safely onto her riding Zanth.

"Coen-soo, my time approaches," Shoo-lin tenderly reminded her. "I am beginning to ripen. We must go to Ender-whann-soo soon, or our opportunity to mate will be lost for many months."

"I know, my love, I can smell your scent," Coen-soo replied. "I can hardly keep myself calm in your presence. Let us go now. I do not think she will refuse."

Kamiel watched as the two Gnathe walked over to where the two Brood-mothers were helping to pack the carriers. He could tell by their stance that something important was concerning them. He decided to join them and see what the problem was.

Shoo-lin stood before Ender-whann-soo, holding the trembling hand of Coen-soo and asked, "My Lady, are you fit and well?"

"Well enough, Shoo-lin," she replied. "I can sense your readiness. The scent of male arousal and ripeness fills the air."

"The excitement of the past few days has brought forward my mating cycle, Reverend Lady," he quietly answered. "It affects my judgement and my mood."

"Lady, we would consummate our bond and trust you with our offspring," Coen-soo humbly exhorted. "The egg is yours, Reverend Mother. We give it freely and observe the ritual."

"Long may the kindred serve, Reverend Lady. The rights of the egg are yours," Shoo-lin repeated the ancient litany to his chosen Brood-mother and Ender-whann-soo nodded her head to him.

The Brood-mother gathered the two smaller Gnathe to her and adopted an alert defensive stance. Shoo-lin entangled his limbs and tail with those of Coen-soo and sank to the ground onto his back. Ender-whann-soo released a musky scent above the couple, making sure that no other males were present. Those that had seen the beginning of the love match had removed themselves up-wind or far enough away to be unaffected.

Shoo-lin gave a gasp of pleasure as the scent triggered off his mating impulses. As his mating stalk stood erect and pushed itself out of his body, Coen-soo sat astride it and pulled it deep into her egg receptacle. The two Gnathe remained ridged as the mating process initiated. From within Coen-soo's body, her dormant egg had awakened and was being pushed down the large ovary tube towards the egg receptacle. Blood began to be pumped into the arteries around the tail, causing the underside to swell and cup itself into a tube. All this time the Brood-mother crouched above the transfixed pair in an automatic defensive position, tail curved above like a scorpion. Coen-soo gave a last convulsive shudder and drove the egg down onto Shoo-lin's mating stalk. The egg gave way at the point of impact and enveloped the stalk, working its way down to the root, causing the stalk to peel cleanly away from the growth pad. Shoo-lin lay in the thrall of the mating action and gave a gasping cry. Coen-soo squatted over him and presented her ovipositor to Ender-whann-soo, inserting it deep into her breeding pouch. She began to rock back and forth, as the fertilised egg travelled by muscular contraction along the base of the now tube-like tail and into the Brood-mother's pouch. All this time Ender-whann-soo had crouched like a figure of menace over the two helpless Gnathe, until the tube withdrew. They both unsteadily got to their feet and stood side by side of the much larger figure.

Kamiel was fascinated by the whole enactment. He could see how this ritual had evolved. During the mating process the male and female Gnathe were defenceless and relied on the powerful Brood-mother to protect them. Once the egg was laid and the two smaller Gnathe recovered, the food gathering and protection were doubled. Added to which the safety of the egg in the Brood-mother's pouch was never in doubt.

The rest of the Gnathe now rushed up to present their joy in a successfully fertilised egg and to congratulate the mated couple.

Whann-lin called out to the great golden form of the now pregnant Brood-mother: "What is your decision, Reverend Mother?"

"I shall produce twin Brood-mothers. There will be need of a great breeding surge when we are established in our new home," Ender-whann-soo replied. "These two egg-sisters will be the finest the Gnathen world has seen. Shoo-lin and Coen-soo will be proud to have given them life. I will nurture them carefully. Now, my people, mount the beasts and do as Kaameel says. We have an even more precious cargo now to carry to safety."

The two Brood-mothers and Kamiel mounted their carrier and led the way deeper into the valley, as the silver being searched for a more defensive position.

"That was a damn fool thing to do, Ender," the old Brood-mother exclaimed. "We are going to run short of food. The last thing you need to do now is to have to abort the egg in the future."

"I had to take that chance, Reverend One," Ender-whann-soo replied. "They need something to fight for and it will give them hope for times to come. I will slow the development of the twins somewhat, as I need to enhance their abilities. These two will need great adaptability to cope with the humans and their science. They will need finer manipulation in their hands to be able to use the human tools. I have studied Kaameel's fingers and thumb carefully during our flight. Our new race of Gnathe will need precision rather than power at the ends of their arms."

"You have a keen mind, Granddaughter," the old Brood-mother answered. "I am proud of you. I always thought that great things would come from our line. Breeding for brains, rather than a powerful form like Link-soo-shan's, appears to have paid off at last. A pity my daughter and your Brood-mother did not live to see it."

"Yes. Even the lands she left to me are now forfeit, but I may gain much more than that," Ender-whann-soo thoughtfully replied. "To think that a daylight raid by an Aallosaat took her during an inspection of the irrigation ditch. It may even have been the same one that we encountered."

Kamiel walked forward to confront the pair of Brood-mothers and said, "Do you think we could get moving now? I do not wish to intrude, but we must find a more defensible position to meet Link-soo-shan on our terms rather than hers."

"You are right, Kaameel," Ender-whann-soo answered and climbed aboard the carrier. "Everybody mount and follow us. Shoo-lin, if you are fully recovered, scout ahead and look for some high ground. A small hill would do, where we can group the carriers together, facing outwards."

"Yes my Lady," the young Gnathe replied, mounting his Zanth and bounding away towards the rising hills. Now that the irritant feel of the ripe mating stalk had gone, he felt relaxed and once more in control of himself. His keen mind turned over the possibilities of the new landscape as he gave his Zanth its head. He was full of pride in the knowledge that he and Coen-soo would be the parents of twin Brood-mothers. This was indeed a great honour. He would readily lay his life down to protect the infants.

At the end of the stand of trees rising out of the valley floor was a wind-sculpted tower of rock. A slope wound up the face of the rugged hill. Sheer cliffs fell away on three sides to a height of a tall tree. He rode around the bottom of the escarpment. The cliff was crumbly and looked unsafe. Many fallen rocks lay at the bottom making it dangerous to approach. To attempt to climb it would only make more of the cliff fall.

"This will do," he thought and pulled his mount round to head back to the caravan.

He reached the leading carrier and called out his news to Kamiel. "My friend, I have found the perfect place. Beyond the stand of trees is a hill rising abruptly from the valley floor. Three sides are crumbling cliffs with a pathway winding to the top. If we drag some dead trees up to the top we can set fire to them making a barrier. We will just have to gamble that your people will reach us in time."

"You all heard that!" the old Brood-mother shouted. "All of you mounted on a Zanth, go with Shoo-lin and prepare the defences. We will follow on as fast as these carriers will travel."

All the Zanth mounted Gnathe spurred their animals into leaping bounds across the stony ground and followed Shoo-lin.

Kamiel turned to the two Brood-mothers and remarked, "It looks good so far. The only problem I can see is the lack of water. How long can these creatures go without drinking, Khann-link-sool?"

"Two or three days at the most, my friend. Your friends had better be on time, or we could be in trouble. We have some water in ceramic pots, but not enough to keep these things happy."

"We will do what we can, then, to ration the water," Kamiel said. "I will bear the problem in mind."

Kamiel looked up at the hot, red-gold sun overhead and wondered about Link-soo-shan's progress. They should be in a better defensive position by early afternoon. If the pursuing Gnathe climbed into the valley by mid-morning, they should catch up by early evening. That would leave at least a night and a day to stand them off until Asue and the rescue party arrived. He would have to think of something to hold them at bay until then. The fortified hill had at last come into sight and he could see the toiling Gnathe dragging dead branches up the slope and piling them up the top. At the bottom of the slope the streambed had been churned up into a muddy mess. Kamiel had the first glimmering of an idea.

The airship handled beautifully and was a credit to Kamiel's design. The solid beat of the diesel engines was carried by the wind into the cabin where the crew kept a steady lookout. Once they had climbed above the cloud layer only the tops of the mountains were visible. Asue kept to a steady course, plotted across the snow-capped peaks, in the general direction of Kamiel's position. Information was collected by the satellite above and constantly transmitted to Rescue One as it tacked across the wind. Hours passed and the airship continued to travel on its way across the trackless wastes without any problems. After a while, Asue brought the airship down below the clouds to survey the landscape below. They passed over glaciers and high, mountain-locked valleys. Melt-water rivers fed lakes and, where the valleys were low enough to be well above freezing, abundant life flourished. Vast forests and plains covered the landscape beneath them, wherever the mountains reluctantly gave way, opening up sometimes for hundreds of miles. The area showed no signs of cultivation and was totally wild.

The sun was low overhead and Asue reckoned that they had travelled more than seven hundred and twenty miles, when Alexander spotted a blip on the radar screen as they flew over another mountain-locked valley.

"Asue, what do you think that could be? I can see an object outlined by the radar," he said, anxiously.

She locked the controls to the on-board computer and swung the chair around to look at the screen.

"Look, Alex," she answered, pointing at the screen. "The blip is breaking apart into smaller sections. "I think we will pass over the top of whatever it is in about an hour."

Frederick came over from his position at the observation blister and stared at the dancing green dots on the screen.

He looked up and exclaimed, "Do we treat this as a possible threat?"

"Anything on this world is a threat to our survival, Fred," Alex replied. "I feel this might be a good time to try out Sharn's outside survival suits. Get your people ready and go outside onto the veranda. We will have to wait and see what these things are. Six of you only, suit up and go outside. The other seven suits we will keep in reserve—and remember, whatever arrows you use will be less for the coming rescue attempt."

"Yes Alex," Frederick answered. "I understand what you mean. We will be careful out there."

The leader of the martial arts group picked five of his people and they quickly donned the suits. They all assembled at the airlock and waited for Asue's systems check.

"Ready, Asue," Frederick called to her through the radio link. "Let us through the airlock and we'll rope up outside."

Asue opened the airlock and the party filed inside. She activated the force field and the crew walked through the nannite screen. It was like pushing against the surface of a pool of jelly. The nannites recognised the suits as a like material and allowed them through without damage. They quickly gathered on the parapet around the cabin of the vessel. Fierce gusts of wind blew around them and they could feel the Jovian atmosphere snatch at their suits. Overhead, the vast gasbag crackled in the wind's strength as the propellers bit into the air and kept them tacking across its force. They roped up to the many catch-points along the side of the cabin.

"The suits are just fine, Asue," Charlie radioed to her. "They keep your temperature at an even state and they don't fog up. Outside, it must be close to freezing. I think my fur would be hard put to keep this wind out on its own!"

The elastic suites were indeed figure hugging and allowed the apes to grip with their toes as well as their fingers.

Amongst the sporting equipment that had been gathered by Nancy and Bander were two vaulting poles. Charlie and another ape named Gunter took one each and positioned themselves on each side of the gondola parapet to fend off intruders. The others stationed themselves with bows and arrows to fill the gaps. They strained their eyes to see through the wispy clouds.

Asue signalled, "Stand ready, everyone. We are getting close to the position on the radar screen. Over the next high range of hills in this valley should be the place. The flying creatures will come from the other side."

The airship moved out of the cloudy area of the peaks and over a clear space. Down below lay another enclosed valley with abundant vegetation and water. Wheeling in the sky at different heights were the most amazing looking creatures. Riding the thermals in the evening sun were hundreds of creatures looking like hang-gliders. Suspended under large ridged wings, hung a reptilian looking body with a long head.

"They look like the flying reptiles of Earth's ancient history," Asue declared. "Save your arrows and see what they will do."

Part of the flock of flying creatures saw the airship and fled with terror. Many more of them banked and turned, flying underneath the cabin.

As the shadow of the airship fell over the creatures beneath, they dropped like stones, spreading their wings at the last moment and shooting through the air, away to the sides of the vast valley, to catch new thermals and rise again.

"They're reacting as if they've been preyed upon by something large in the past," Alex remarked over the intercom. "Keep your eyes peeled for something larger."

"We will, Alex. Don't forget that we are outside. Keep your eyes on the radar screen as well," Frederick reminded him.

The airship continued to make good progress along the valley, scaring the flying wings as they continued on their way. High above the vessel a pair of keen eyes had located the fat shape tacking across the wind. The Terra-raptor had fed recently and he was curious about the intruder rather than in a dangerous mood. There was plenty of easy prey in the skies above the mountain-locked valleys and food was plentiful. In hard times he would have fought for territory. Occupying the top of the food chain, the Terra-raptor had developed a fierce intelligence to outwit the flying wings. He seldom lost an encounter. One or two of the Banth ought to be brought back to the nest for his mate and young to feed on. The huge animal banked out of the cloud, folded his wings and dropped like a stone.

The first thing Alex saw on the radar screen was a rapidly expanding green blip coming from high above the airship.

"Asue, give the alarm!" he shouted. "Something is dropping onto us. It looks awfully big!"

"Stand by outside, all of you. There's something coming from directly above us," Asue cried into the communications system.

Everyone moved to the outside of the parapet and vainly attempted to look past the large cigar shape of the inflated air bags. The archers made ready and selected arrows in case of trouble. Still nothing could be seen.

"It's coming down on the port side!" Alex yelled into the microphone. "Everyone to the left! Do nothing unless it attacks us. Wait and see what it will do."

The Terra-raptor could hear the strange noise of the diesel engines and the rush of the propellers. He caught the stink of the strange things. As he dropped past he could see lots of small animals rushing about underneath the flat body of the silvery creature. Puzzled, the raptor casually flipped onto its side and sped along the edge of the parapet, under the helicopter supporting gantries, before continuing his dive onto the flock of winged Banth far below. Before they registered its presence the claws of the hind feet had transfixed two of their number. He opened his wings with a crack and scooped another out of the air. As he soared over the tree-lined terrain below, he swallowed the Banth in his jaws to regurgitate later and gained height. Soon he was once more on the same level as the airship.

"If that comes for us, we have no chance!" yelled Frederick to his friends. "Don't antagonise it. Alex, that thing passed us at a hell of a pace. Did you see it scoop up those creatures below?"

"Yes we did, Fred," Alex replied. "Just keep an eye on it. I think it may be curious about us, that's all. Tell your people to aim their arrows at its eyes. Blind it if it attempts to attack us—its our only chance."

The creature was a quarter of the size of the floating vessel. It hung in the air with consummate ease, a dead wing creature in each taloned hind foot. They were reminded of a fairytale dragon. Immense bat-like wings projected from powerful shoulders. The creature had a set of small, clawed forelimbs partially attached to its wings. Large powerful hind limbs terminated in a set of sharp claws longer than a butcher's knife. A broad head, with an equally sharp set of teeth as the hind claws, regarded them with intelligent eyes. The scales of its body shone green and gold in the bright midday sun. A long whip-like tail acted as a rudder.

"It's beautiful, Alex," Gunter remarked over the intercom, "but if it comes any closer I shall give it a poke with this pole."

"I think we have seen sudden death on wings. Be careful, Gunter," Asue replied.

A stray gust of wind changed direction and caused the beast to come in range of Gunter's pole. He reached out and gave the Terra-Raptor a sturdy poke in its chest. The head flashed down and reduced the end of the pole to chewed match-wood in seconds. At the same time the winged creature altered his wing angle, dropped away, swooped into a thermal and once more gained height. It changed direction, soaring towards the nearby mountains. Soon it became a speck in the sky and then vanished from sight.

"Everybody inside," Asue ordered. "I want to check the suits. There is nothing else on the screen and we will have to climb over the next range of mountains."

Asue checked the air filters on the helmets fitting over the heads of the outside defence party. All of them were secure and uncorrupted by the Jovian air. The suits had not fogged up and were clean and odour free. She transmitted the diagnostic check to Sharn at the citadel.

"A good design, Sharn," Asue commented to her fellow guardian. "We can fit coverings over the feet of the humans. Fortunately Nancy included plenty of heavy boots and other sturdy gear when she and Bander raided the sports complex."

"Thank you, Asue," Shane replied. "We've produced enough suits for the working party to use in the Gnathen compound, with plenty besides."

Alex asked her: "How goes the construction of the Gnathe habitat?"

"Fine, Alex. There were some nasty pieces of Jovian life trapped inside the walls as the hexagon erected." She showed them the progress on the holo-screen and said, "Don't worry, we are dealing with them. I have opened up one of the walls and we drove them out with noise and fire. What was that huge flying creature that Gunter poked with the vaulting pole? Are there any more of them?"

"They seem to be low in numbers, Sharn," Frederick answered, "or we would have encountered more of them. I think the best thing is to avoid them, rather than try to fight something like that in the air."

"Fit the end of the poles with something like a cattle prod connected back to a generator," Jo-jo suggested. "Hit it with about 12,000 volts and it will soon drop out of the sky."

"Brilliant idea," Asue transmitted to Alexander's deputy. We are about to lift again to pass over another collection of mountain ranges. This area reminds me of Tibet in the Himalayas on old Earth. We could never have travelled this way on foot. The Gnathe and their beasts would have perished with the cold. Some of the glaciers seem to cover many hundreds of square miles. I will close down for now and contact you later."

"All right, Rescue One, over and out," Jo-jo and Sharn replied.

Hour after hour the airship tracked across the steady wind. Hundreds of mountain peaks jaggedly thrust into the air, some thousands of feet above the snow line. The course was continually adjusted by Asue to follow the steady stream of information relayed by the satellite high above them. Evening deepened into night and the crew began to settle down to sleep until the only one left was the unsleeping silver form of the Guardian.

How she loved these frail creatures and admired their spirit. Her feeling went beyond the original programming. Over the centuries of building the Habitat and finally producing the apes and human colonists, she had grown to love these people greatly. They were so diverse in their approach to their existence here. Some had thrown themselves into increasing the farming communities and asked for nothing else. Others had immersed their lives in study and science or the arts. There were now over a quarter of a million people living in the Habitat and steadily increasing. Everything seemed fine, but Kamiel was worried about the lack of challenge and frontier. This caused her great concern. The coming of the Gnathe might change this for the better. She supported Kamiel's approach completely, but could not stop worrying about the safety of this crew on the rescue.

This world was harsh and un-forgiving. All except her on this venture could come to grief. It was their choice to do this and she could not interfere, no matter how she felt.

Asue kept the airship on its steady course and worried about everything as the darkness sped by.

CHAPTER 9

▼

By backtracking, Link-soo-shan and her troop of Imperial Guards eventually found an area of the cliff that had fallen into the side of the gorge. The Zanth carefully climbed the shattered rock-face with the Gnathe clinging grimly to their backs. At last they crossed the summit of the gorge and could look into the valley below. The small river threaded its way far below them. It ran along a wooded area from around a small rocky outcrop. The tracks of the fugitive household stood out in the low-lying vegetation. The marks led towards the general direction of the hill where a pool of water appeared to grow in size before it.

The Group Captain looked down at the scene and asked, "What are they doing, my Lady?"

"The fools are digging in to make a last stand," the Brood-mother replied. "Let us take our time and rest the Zanth after the journey down. We are many against few. Remember, you are trained fighters and these pitiful members of Ender-whann-soo's household are farm hands and house staff."

"Remember the strange thing that fell from the sky, my Lady? It must still be with them," the new Group Captain quietly answered.

"I have been thinking about that, Koet-shan, and I keep wondering why it does not attack us directly, if it can?" the Brood-mother thoughtfully retorted. "We have been blocked and turned from our course, but never attacked. Maybe it is not strong enough to overpower us all. We shall find out in due course. First we must scout their defences. Take two of your guard and ride on ahead. Find out what you can and report back to me."

"As my Lady commands," the Group Captain replied and waved two of the guards forwards. "We will be back soon."

Koet-shan urged her Zanth down the easy slope to the valley floor. She beckoned the two guards to ride slightly in front of her. They soon forged farther ahead from the main troop and left them far behind. The valley floor was flat and easy to ride over with their mounts. Soon they were following the small river that fed the marsh beyond the gorge. To their amazement the river began to dry out to a trickle. Pools of water collected in the deeper areas, but the flow had markedly diminished.

"Be careful," the Group Captain cautioned the other two guards, as they continued to follow the drying watercourse. "They are not much farther ahead."

"Yes, Group Captain," replied one of the guards. "Let me go in front. I will angle across to that stand of trees and look around them to the hill. I will signal you to come on if it is all clear."

"Do it," said Koet-shan and the Gnathe rode off towards the trees, keeping low for concealment.

The Group Captain watched the guard creep to the small copse, edging her mount slowly to the vantage point. Suddenly one of the trees that had been strangely bent and contorted, straightened itself. It whipped across the guard's seat. There she hung, suspended from the ground, somehow stuck to the branch.

Koet-shan urged her mount slowly forward until she was close enough to view the corpse of her sister. The heavy branch had a row of sharpened wooden spikes lashed to it. On these barbed spears the Gnathe hung impaled. She had never seen anything like it in all her years as an Imperial Guard. The Zanth walking into the cocking mechanism had sprung Kamiel's trap. She regarded the trees with great caution. How many more of these traps could be concealed in the undergrowth? She motioned the other guard away from the trees and into the open.

"Skirt around the trees. Do not get too close to them, there may be other traps," she ordered. "We will go to the rise."

The group captain could see a number of posts driven into the ground with their tops about chest high to a Zanth. She stopped for a moment, puzzled, and wondered what could they possibly be? This saved her life, for as the other guard worked her way up the incline, she and her mount passed through the line of posts. The Zanth reared up and screamed as its front leg severed and lay on the ground. It fell forwards and the head and neck separated from its body. The guard tumbled from her seat and parted in mid-air at her chest. Two separate pieces lay on the ground bleeding into the earth. Suddenly, the sun caught the micro-thin, nannite garrotting wire and the Group Captain could see a long sparkle stretching between the posts. She recoiled in horror as her friend fed the thirsty ground with her blood. What manner of creature were they up against?

Tethering the Zanth to a bush, she very cautiously approached the area. If she squinted her eyes against the sun she could just make out the sparkling line before her. Koet-shan drew her sword and pressed the hardened tip against the wire. After a momentary resistance it sliced cleanly through the crystalline hardened blade. She fought the rising tide of panic that threatened to overwhelm her and ducked underneath the wire so she could see over the rise. There before her lay a widening lake in front of the hill. They had dammed the stream. The hill rose on three sides with crumbling cliffs as tall as a tree and impossible to climb. A zigzag track wound up from the front of the hill facing into the muddy lake. This had been fortified with cut trees and bushes. At the top with the carriers facing out, were the fugitives. The Group Captain searched in vain for any sign of the silver being, but without success. Having seen all she could, Koet-shan returned to her Brood-mother with her devastating report.

Trann-link-khann had ridden hard all morning and most of the afternoon with her kindred. They were intensely loyal to her, as Ender-whann-soo's household was to her. Some of her brood children had been with her for many years. They had taken over the homestead of her Brood-mother and developed the remote and ancient Banilik tree into a university of learning. Her Brood-mother was content to live quietly and oversee the crop growing, leaving her Brood-daughter to increase the size of the homestead with newer saplings. The Banilik trees had grown, intermeshed with the old settlement and now their living walls keep secrets from hostile prying eyes. Here was where the new crystals had been shaped and cut. These were a dull green colour and had been dug out of a hill by one of the homestead's burrowing creatures. They had been developed to dig into the earth and return with any crystals that they found. A genetically enhanced burrower had been bred by Trann-link-khann herself. New senses were part of the neuron network in its brain. An ability to locate by high-pitched sonar, any of the super hard gems and also to see with its mind anything different from the usual types had paid off with results. Telekinetic crystals were rare and usually of low power. These new ones could augment the reach of a highly intelligent Gnathe to at least the length of three carriers stood end to end. The aptly named Jewel-khann had managed to pick up a pod-vine seed and put it into a pot the other side of the main lecture room. Close to her, she had managed to lift her egg-sister into the air and keep her suspended, for a short length of time, with the power of her mind alone. Two of her own kindred had practised with this crystal and were also becoming adept with its powers.

Only her two egg daughters, Marren and Jewel, herself, Ender-whann-soo's two kindred, Natel and Jing-soo, knew of their existence. Natel-soo had developed a fine touch with the stones and had learnt to manipulate very tiny things at some distance.

The Trading Post came into sight as they approached the stand of trees by the corral. Some of Sing-trow-sool's kindred appeared and took the reigns of their mounts.

Trann-link-khann nodded to the eager young Gnathe. "Take me to your Brood-mother, youngster. I need to see her right away."

"Yes Lady, I will take you," one of the Trading Post kindred answered and led the way into the Banilik tree.

The late afternoon sun cast long shadows across the compound. Glow crystals were beginning to light up the darker passages and highlight the finely polished wood inside the homestead. Soon they came to Sing-trow-sool's private quarters.

Trann entered through the door and embraced her cousin. "Sing, my old friend, I have a great deal to discuss with you."

Sing-trow-sool nervously stepped back and stared quizzically at her old friend and said, "What do you mean, Trann? What do you know about the events that have taken place here?"

"I know everything that had occurred here and what has happened afterwards. For one thing, Ender-whann-soo is alive and well. I have communicated with her and our mutual Grand-Brood-mother, Khann-link-sool. They are together. Listen to me and I will tell you everything you need to know," the scientist replied.

Sing-trow-sool listened, amazed, as the incredible story unfolded and her part in the events became clear.

"So Trann, Ender will go over the mountains and stay with these strange alien people," the Brood-mother exclaimed. "It seems that our Ultimate Ruler will have lost a great deal of her kindred by the time she returns. With her sister mad, she will have a great deal of trouble maintaining her rule of terror!"

"With her egg-sister dead, my old friend, it will go even harder. I intend to kill her and challenge Link-soo-shan when she returns," Trann quietly replied.

"Killing the Commander will be easy, in the state that she is in, but Link-soo-shan is the most physically dangerous Brood-mother we Gnathe have ever seen. She stands a head taller than you, Trann, and is much more muscular and heavier. Challenging her to the right of succession by combat will end in your death," the Trading Post keeper flatly exclaimed.

"Not so, old friend," Trann assured her friend. "I have a way to beat her. New times are coming and her many generations of tyranny are at an end. We are about to enter the age of science. Would I come here to you if I thought I would fail? You will have to trust me in this. Get your household together. Be ready to leave and follow me back to the Imperial City. Remember, Khann-link-sool's devious mind is behind this course of action. I will not fail. Now, you had best let me do what I came here to do. Where is she? Has she improved since Link-soo-shan left this place?"

"Not very much, my new Empress," she replied. "Follow me to the back of my quarters."

They walked through the Keeper's rooms until they came to a small private room at the back. Sing-trow-sool opened the living door onto a terrible sight. The once mighty Commander crouched in the shadows of the dimly lit room. Her eyes were glazed and her light golden fur was stained with the marks of her own vomit and excrement. The Keeper's kindred had tried to clean her as best they could. She shook and trembled as though in the grip of a fever. In her mind she still felt the icy-cold after-affects of Kamiel's stripping of her memories.

"It would be a kindness, Sing, to end this. Watch if you will, but I must do what I must," Trann grimly uttered.

She stepped quietly over to the much larger Brood-mother, crooning softly to her as she approached. The Commander looked up at her from her cowering position in a puzzled, trusting way. Trann drew her short Syther from a sheath at her belt. Keeping the blade out of sight, she closed with the shuddering form. Slowly Chang-soo-shan seemed to be at ease and the shaking and trembling stopped. A dawning light of reason and intelligence began to shine from her eyes.

"Trann," she falteringly whispered, "what are you doing here?"

"I have come to give you peace, Commander," she replied.

Trann reached down to the trusting form of the previously ruthless Gnathe, lifting her chin up as she cradled her head. She abruptly brought the razor sharp Syther from behind her back and cut deeply across the commanders soft, unprotected throat, severing the main artery to the once fiercely intelligent brain. The sharp blade continued into the neck breaking the windpipe as Trann's muscular arm did its work. She gave the knife a final upward twist and withdrew it. As she did so, she thrust the larger form away from her with her taloned foot, spinning the Commander around.

Chang-soo-shan fell full length across the polished floor in a widening pool of her own blood, clutching at the wall for support. Giving a bubbling cry, she sagged slowly into a heap against Sing-trow-sool's legs, who gave the dying Gnathe a vicious kick. The Commander rolled back against the wall and died.

"It is done, Sing—it is done," said the young Brood-mother. "Gather what you need to take back to the city. You will stay with me in the royal quarters. You can return here, after I have settled with our Ultimate Ruler. I must now remove the Commander's head and take it back as proof, to the other heads of the families of the council. Go now, I will not be long here. Instruct your young to build a funeral pyre and get my kindred to drag what is left of the Commander outside."

"Yes, Lady Trann, I will see that your wishes are obeyed," replied the Keeper as she retreated from the scene.

Trann-link-khann bent grimly to her self-appointed task and began to saw at the still warm neck.

Late evening approached as Link-soo-shan cautiously urged her troop of Imperial Guards forwards. She had listened carefully to her Group Captain's report on the strange deaths of her two guards. How could a tree bend and kill her guard like that? As for the other death, that was beyond her understanding. A sparkling line suspended between two posts had cut the other guard in half and killed her Zanth. It was just too alien for her to comprehend.

War in the past had been simply won by breeding the best female soldiers and overwhelming the opposition hand to hand. Her sister's highly developed kindred, linked with hers, had been unstoppable. The two of them had been bred stronger and larger that any of the other Brood-mothers in the Gnathen Empire. When they had overturned their own Brood-mother's rule by killing her in her royal chambers, they soon established themselves in an invincible position. They had kept a careful eye on all breeding efforts across the Empire. Any suggestion of a Brood-mother producing her own strain of larger aggressive females was abruptly curtailed. All breeding had been strictly supervised and the offspring checked. Any promising females had immediately been seconded into her Imperial Guard.

She had taken the majority of her best City troops on this ill-fated adventure. A number of them had died in the swamp during their combat with the Aal-losaat. A cold thought intruded into her mind. Could that encounter have been deliberate? She shivered at this idea. It was now even more important that she parade the Heretic through the courtyards of her city. She must show her people, that no matter what; she and she alone ruled the Empire. Would her sister recover? If not, she would have to die and Link-soo-shan would automatically inherit all of her Kindred and goods. She hoped not, as the two of them were compatible and ruled jointly, quite contented with the situation.

Link-soo-shan had taken her guards around the area of the two deaths, crossing the small river. This had mysteriously begun to flow almost normally again and they followed the course to the bottom of the hill. Tomorrow would do. A concentrated rush up the slope with their overpowering force would soon rip the flimsy barricades away and they would be amongst the caravan. Sword and spear would be the order of the day. Her troops were hungry and required rest. Food there would be in plenty, after they had put Ender-whann-soo's household to the sword. They would make camp in full view of their quarry, light fires and forage for what food they could find.

"Make camp," she commanded, pointing to the immediate area. "In the morning we will have them. Whatever plunder you take is yours. Now forage for something to eat and light fires, so that they can see us. Sleep well, for tomorrow we will avenge the deaths of your sisters, my kindred."

The arrival of Link-shoo-Shan's company of hardened soldiers had not gone unnoticed from the top of the hill. They had been watched for most of the late afternoon. Kamiel had given all the fugitives a crash course in guerrilla warfare. New concepts never before thought of by the Gnathe had been readily accepted and improved upon. Shoo-lin had proved extremely adaptable in his understanding of this new way to fight. Kamiel had demonstrated traps to the Gnathe. The spiked branch had proved itself, just as the silver being had predicted. That the spring, in a naturally growing piece of tree, could be harnessed in such a way, would never have occurred to them. Also, that the garrotting wire would catch the next guard as the others retreated from the now seemingly deadly stand of trees, again proved to them Kamiel's predictive powers.

Much earlier, Kamiel had the Gnathe sharpening stout hard branches from the dead wood they had found in the stand of timber. The Gnathe had been astonished when the guardian had shown them how to fire harden the points. Next, he then had them fix the spear-like wooden stakes in lines before the slope of the hill, down by the small river flowing at the base. When Kamiel dammed the watercourse, they saw the muddy lake rise rapidly and cover the forward facing stakes. It was then that they realised just how alien the human society was to their own. They pulled the rest of the dead wood up the slope to make a barrier.

"This will never stop them Kaameel," Ender-whann-soo remarked, as she surveyed the flimsy looking barricade.

"It will, if it is soaked in oil and set alight, my Lady," Shoo-lin-answered. "We have a number of pots full of oil, that Coen-soo brought from the Homestead."

"You learn fast, my young friend," Kamiel said. "Remember, however, not to light the barricade until some of the Imperial Guard are amongst it."

The old Brood-mother stood shocked by Kamiel's statement. "You cannot be serious, Kaameel!" she cried.

"They would kill and torture you, Khann," Ender-whann-soo quietly reminded her. "We will be ready in the carriers to stampede over them when the fires die down. They will show us no mercy and they out-number us three or four to one."

"They will attack in the morning, Kaameel," Shoo-lin said to the silver being. "The Imperial Guard does not fight at night. I could pick off a few of them with my Kryte, under cover of darkness, if we pay them a visit tonight. You are a strange creature, Kaameel. Many of them will die or become injured by the things you have taught us and the traps that you have set. Yet you cannot directly harm them. I do not understand."

"I do what I can, my friends. You just have to accept the way it has to be. Alexander and my other friends will have no such inhibitions, but they are not wanton killers either. They do this for you, because of what you stand for and also for the mutual benefit of both life forms. Come, my friend, we will go down the hill and hide somewhere to wait for nightfall. Have you any more of that weed you used in the palace?"

"I have a little, Kaameel, in my pouch. If we can get to their mounts, I could sprinkle some nearby. The rest is up to luck."

"I will create a diversion, Shoo-lin, when the time comes," Kamiel replied. "Now let us go down onto the valley floor and hide. The rest of you, remember all I have told you. Stay on the top of the hill behind the carriers. Cover your beasts' eyes when you hear the airship coming, to quieten them and do not let them panic. We will return to you before dawn if we can."

With that, Kamiel and Shoo-lin descended down the slope of the hill towards the newly built dam to find a safe hiding place and wait for the cover of darkness.

Link-soo-shan had not bothered to order her new Group Captain to set sentries. The foraging for food had turned up very little in the way of supplies. At this end of the valley the soil was poor and stony. Away from the stand of trees that were now imbued with menace very little grew. Her troops were now hungry and irritable as they settled down for the night.

The Zanth had been tethered nearby a clump of rocks and boulders and were in easy view of the Imperial Guard. A bush seemed to move in the increasing darkness towards the line of beasts. Slowly Shoo-lin wriggled closer to the curious animals. They recognised his scent from the many training sessions spent with the Imperial Beast Master. None of them snorted or gave any indication of alarm. The young Gnathe eased forward on his belly and altered the position of the small bushes attached to his harness. One of them had worked his way into his ribs and a sharp point was pressing into the back of his erect hearing crest. He was almost to the line of beasts, when he heard the sound of a stone click against another in the dark. In the gloom, he could just see the upright shape of one of the Ultimate Ruler's soldiers. She was approaching the line of Zanth and was carrying something furtively in her hands.

Shoo-lin primed his Kryte and aimed at the face of the figure. He pressed the nerve at the base of the creature's tail and triggered the sneezing reaction. The poisoned tipped thorn flew through the night air and hit the guard on the side of her cheek. The venom rapidly did its work, as the nerve toxin paralysed the muscles of the Gnathe and she fell without a sound.

Shoo-lin crawled forwards between the Zanth's feet and examined the dead guard. In her hand was a bundle of pod-vine fruit. She had secreted the food and hidden it from her sisters. The young male gratefully ate the dead guard's extra rations before he removed her weapons. He then turned his attention to the Zanth. The amount of bindweed he had left in his pouch was enough to cripple two mounts, or make six of them ill. He decided to spread the weed amongst as many of the Zanth as practicable. Ill-tempered beasts, difficult to control, would do more damage than heavily drugged Zanth. He pondered on Kamiel's way of thinking. It was getting very easy, for Shoo-lin, to fall into the devious pattern of alien thought the more he spoke to the enigmatic silver being. What terrible wars must have been fought by this very different species in their past, he thought. It was obvious to Shoo-lin that these people could take anything they wanted if they so chose. Somehow they had learnt to control themselves, or did Kamiel and his three other strange friends control the humans in some way? Whatever was the truth, the sequence of events had been set in motion and there was no turning back.

"Now to hunt down some more of Link-soo-shan's outlying soldiers," he thought, and he crept back into the darkness beyond the reach of the firelight to begin to set the spikes tipped with venom into the ground as he left.

Kamiel had separated from the young male and had instructed him on no account to return to Link-shoo-shan's camp after leaving the irresistible drug amongst the Zanth. He was also busy, leaving the micro-thin strands of garrotting wire strung among the rocks and boulders between the camp and the artificial lake. Some were low to the ground and some were placed neck high for the Gnathe soldiers to walk into their deadly cutting edges. Kamiel made no sound as he plugged his traps into that area. He had told his friends to sleep soundly and had assured them that all would be well during the night. Now the time has come to pay Link-shoo-shan a sleep-shattering visit. It was time to play a master card and put the camp in a state of nervous worry.

Kamiel gave a piercing whistle to warn Shoo-lin that the next stage of his plan had been put into action. By now, the young male should be making his way back to Ender-whann-soo's hilltop stronghold.

As the echoes of the shrill blast died away, the camp awoke. The members of the Imperial Guard surrounded their Brood-mother and formed a protective series of ranks.

The Group Captain stared into the dark night and exclaimed, "What was that awful sound?"

"Keep alert, my kindred!" Link-soo-shan shouted to her guards. "Be ready to fight. Throw more wood onto the fire. Whatever beast that was, it will still fear flames and smoke."

As the outer ranks of Gnathe hurriedly piled more of their meagre supply of deadwood on the fires, a silver shape stepped out of the dark and into the firelight.

"Hullo, Link-soo-shan, hated tyrant of the Gnathen Empire. How is your sister, Chang? It appears to me that you have lost some of your army chasing us," the silver being said. "Did you enjoy the encounter with the Aallosaat?"

"Kill it!" shrieked Link-soo-shan in fear and rage.

Many of the guards hurled their spears at the form stood before them, only to see the shape blur as Kamiel went into action. As suddenly as it had started, the flurry of spears stopped. Kamiel stood in a small pile of shattered spears. He had reduced them to small useless pieces.

"Count your dead, Link-soo-shan, and add tonight's tally as well. Is it really worth carrying on with this vendetta? Tomorrow more of you will die, in ways you will not understand! These people are under my protection. You shall not have them," Kamiel flatly stated to the shaken Brood-mother.

"What are you? Where do you come from?" Link-shoo-shan stood, towering over her guards and stared hard at the much smaller silver figure, reflecting the firelight and said, "Why do you interfere in my affairs?"

"You would not understand the nature of my being, ignorant Tyrant," Kamiel answered. "As to where I come from, let us say, from far over these mountains, where the people live who made me. They are coming here, Link-soo-shan, and they want Ender-whann-soo and all of her household. She is fit and well, for I healed her. You will not win. Go home, fool, while you can. How many more of your children have to die to convince you that it is hopeless?"

"If you are so powerful, why do you not destroy me here? You must have limitations," the Brood-mother surmised.

Kamiel walked casually forwards and deliberately stood in the middle of the fire and replied, "I am so confidant of success, I will tell you, Tyrant. I may not directly harm you, but I can cause you to come to harm by your own actions. Two of your guards lie dead on the valley floor already because of me. Shoo-lin has been here with me and is now safely back with Ender-whann-soo and her Grand-Brood-mother, Khann-link-sool. How many of you are missing? He can kill without the restrictions I have to work under. The closer you come to my protected Household, the more of you will die. My friends will come from the skies, bringing death to your guards and also to you, Link-soo-shan. Look up to the skies and know fear, as your now maddened sister, Chang-soo-shan knew it, when I stripped her wicked soul bare with the crystal mind link."

Kamiel turned and walked slowly through the massed ranks of the nervous Imperial Guard. Not one guard dared to touch him as he disappeared into the night.

The terrified Gnathe turned to their Brood-mother and one of them cried out, "What shall we do, Reverend Lady? What does the silver thing mean, we will die by our own actions?"

"Listen to me, my children and kindred of my sister. This being has confessed its weakness. It cannot harm us directly. Ender-whann-soo's household is composed of farm workers, household staff and science students. Are they any match for us? We are still many and they are few. Come the dawn, we shall see the proud boast of the silver creature come to nothing," the Ultimate Ruler spat in fury.

"My Lady," one of the guards cried from the edge of the crowd, "three of our numbers are missing."

"Search for them. Take a lighted brand from the fire and examine the area near the Zanth. The Beast-Master has been here. A male Gnathe has learnt to kill," the Group Captain called out to her troops. "Remember this tomorrow when we avenge our sisters."

It was not long before the bodies of the dead Gnathe were discovered. All had been hit by venom-tipped darts from Shoo-lin's Kryte. They also noticed some of the powerful Zanth were lurching from side to side. Some were worse than others and refused to move. The mildly affected beasts were the most dangerous and, as they were also hungry because of poor foraging, in a very bad humour.

The long night hours stretched before them, as the Zanth became more diffi-cult or easier to deal with, depending on the dose of bindweed they had ingested from Shoo-lin's carrying pouch. Few of the Imperial Guards had managed to sleep and few felt any eagerness to see the dawning sun. They had never experi-enced anything like the succession of defeats and setbacks, in their service to the Ultimate Ruler or the Commander. Morale was very low. All their lives, from the moment of hatching inside the Commander's or Link-soo-shan's pouch, they had unquestionably obeyed them. They had grown up in the royal crèche, know-ing that they were joining the strongest and most powerful army that the Gna-then Empire had known. How could a handful of farm workers and household staff hold them at bay? They were taller and more muscular, with greater strength and aggressive natures. Yet more of them had died on this venture than during the war against the families. This had been long ago, when the two Brood-sisters had established their Empire. For the first time in their lives, they were unsure of the outcome of tomorrow's conflict. What was there to fear, but the unknown?

As the sun began to rise, the seeds of doubt had done their work. The Imperial Guard assembled without their accustomed arrogance. Some were mounted two to a Zanth, where some of the beasts still could not be ridden.

During the night the defending Gnathe had slept well, feeling secure, inside their fortified enclave. Kamiel had returned long before the dawn with Shoo-lin and reported the nights' adventures. He then spent the night exploring the top of the hill and testing their defences. As the first light of dawn began to lighten the sky, Asue contacted him as he was tearing pieces of cured and coloured hide into strips.

"How go things Kamiel? We are making good time," Asue transmitted. "Shall we exchange data?"

The two guardians meshed their minds together and caught up on the relevant facts.

"Pour on the power Asue," Kamiel remarked. "I would rather we wasted a lit-tle fuel and you got here early, than late."

"I will, Kamiel. I am horrified by the killing ground you have produced. Many will die," Asue declared sadly.

"It is of their own choosing Asue, I gave them a choice. You wait until they come up against Frederick and his people," Kamiel replied, grimly.

"What if we lose some of our people Kamiel? How will you feel then? This is a very dangerous mission," Asue declared.

"If we do, it will cement the trust between the two races. There are deeper reasons between this encounter, Asue. A price of blood will lay down a deep foundation for the years to come," the guardian quietly responded.

"Kamiel!" Asue's shocked transmission rocked in the guardian's circuits. "What are you trying to tell me? Or shall I say, what have you kept back about this mission?"

"There are areas of programming that the original Alexander laid down in my operations scope, that are not duplicated in your circuits, Asue. Your position of Commander is not compromised in any way. My situation as mission physiologist has called for a different set of values. Without this conflict and the resulting changes in our children's situation, my calculations show probable failure of the colony. You know I would not say this lightly," Kamiel assured her. "The percentage figures show an eighty-seven percent probability of future success, the moment this operation and quest got under way."

Asue worriedly asked, "What was the probability of colony failure, Kamiel?"

"My figures showed an increasing inward trend, with a growing instability amongst the younger colony members. The worst prognosis pointed to a decline within the next five hundred years. Without the spur of possible death, our children would eventually enter a state of ennui or eternal boredom. They would turn against each other and the dark side of their natures would eventually take over. Believe me Asue, we need the Gnathe and the challenge they bring."

"Kamiel, I believe you," Asue replied. "I will grieve however, for the ones we will lose on this adventure."

"Do you think I will not? I raised them too, Asue, but human life must contain conflict and adventure, with free will. Now, do all in your power to get here. These people deserve to live, besides which, I have come to like them. I do not want to lose any of them, or our people, Asue, but what needs to be done must be. I have made brightly coloured sashes for our friends to wear around their necks, in case they get mixed up with the Tyrant's forces. Tell Frederick and the others to watch for the difference. They are also much smaller than the Imperial guard. I want no friendly fire accidents. Too much hangs on the outcome. The sun is coming up in the sky and Link-soo-shan's camp is beginning to assemble. It begins Asue, it begins."

CHAPTER 10

▼

A guard died in the early morning sunshine as she walked into one of Kamiel's wires. She was looking for a place to relieve herself after the long night. The wire caught her cleanly across the neck and severed her head from her body as she bent forwards between two large boulders. Another Gnathe lost the toes of her right foot as she walked around the rocky formation and caught a low trip wire as she went to investigate the strange death of her comrade.

"Everyone stand still!" screamed the Group Captain. "Nobody move! Your life depends on this."

"Do not walk between any large rocks or boulders or upright pieces of wood. Look for a sparkling line stretching between them. Keep to the flat ground and mark what you find with anything to hand. Now move out slowly and lay a trail through to the lake."

These orders were obeyed with fanatical devotion by the nervous guards. A great deal of time was spent examining the area before they would venture into it. Two more guards suffered deep cuts in their feet as they walked over what appeared to be flat safe ground. A guard gave a screech of pain as she trod onto one of Shoo-lin's poisoned-tipped stakes while searching the air between two high rocks for the tale-tell presence of one of Kamiel's wires. She thrashed around on the stony ground for some time before the poison did its work. While she stiffened and died, one of the drugged Zanth broke loose and careered over the area, picking up more of the poisoned stakes in its feet. It, too, died slowly in front of the advancing guard.

Link-soo-shan called out to her kindred: "Retreat back to the camp area! We will ride away from this place to the left, where there appears to be no traps and there are no rocks with strands of killing thread between them. Do it slowly. We will attack them from the side of the lake and storm the hill from that position."

"Go very careful and do as the Reverend Lady commands!" the Group Captain shouted above the noise of the fractious Zanth.

Slowly, the Imperial Guard retreated from Kamiel's improvised minefield and edged gingerly to the left as the sun began to climb into a cloudy sky.

Kamiel watched impassively as the Ultimate Ruler's forces became more and more demoralised. He observed the expected manoeuvre back to the camp and to his right, away from the booby-trapped stand of trees.

Shoo-lin stood beside him, also looking down the hill at the busy guards and said to the guardian, "It goes exactly as you predicted, Kaameel. When you told us to place the stakes in a line facing to our right, I could not understand your reasoning at the time. I still don't see why you did not place another area of traps in front of the stakes hidden in the water?"

"I want them to waste time, my young friend, looking for traps that do not exist. They will start to gain confidence and ride at speed into the shallow lake. Again, unfortunately, more will die," Kamiel quietly replied.

"Why unfortunately, Kaameel?" Ender-whann-soo interjected.

"They are all sentient beings, my Lady, and only following their orders from that foolish Tyrant of a Brood-mother."

"Your way of thinking is indeed strange, Kaameel," the Brood-mother replied. "They are not my kindred and I feel nothing for them. They are killers and nothing more. They have done much needless cruelty within the Empire over and beyond Link-soo-shan's and the Commander's orders. Ah, Kaameel, feel no remorse for what you have taught us to do. There are many who will cheer for their deaths."

Kamiel and the Gnathe then watched the Imperial Guards regroup onto the flat area of the valley floor, far to their right. Link-soo-shan's forces began to gain confidence as they advanced over the bare, trap-less ground. Slowly they picked up speed. The individual members of the Ultimate Ruler's army were now close enough to be clearly seen. They had drawn their swords and were holding them point outwards and ready. Some were armed with the Scriit spears, unused against Kamiel's nighttime visit. Link-soo-shan had her heavy spear couched as a lance. She had taken the outer flank position. Her Group Captain occupied the inner flank situation at the point. They were attacking in the time-honoured 'horns of the Buffalo', horseshoe-shaped formation.

Koet-shan urged her sisters onwards into the shallow lake and thought that it would not take much longer before it was all finished and they could all go home. Once through the muddy water, they could hurl themselves through the flimsy barricade of cut bushes and dead wood. Then the killing would start. A rich battle rage filled her mind and took possession of her body. All feelings of hunger and tiredness left her. Soon, the pleasures of the sword would be theirs.

The scream of an injured Zanth filled the air and she instinctively reined her mount to an abrupt stop. More of the Zanth began to flounder in the muddy water. One of the beasts reared up and Koet-shan saw a large wooden spike had thrust deep into its bleeding chest. The rider had vanished underfoot as the pain-maddened animals thrashed through the bloody water. More and more Gnathe became unseated as the Zanth began to panic and fell on more of the spikes, hidden underneath the murky water.

"Pull back! Pull back!" screamed the Group Captain. "Get out of the water and back onto the shore!"

"Back everyone!" the Brood-mother shouted from her position as the carnage increased. "Re-group on the hard ground. Get out as fast as you can. Follow me."

Link-soo-shan pulled her mount's head around and rode to the edge of the artificial lake. She looked up at the top of the hill to see the hated face of her adversary, Ender-whann-soo. She was stood in full view at the top of the hill swinging a large ceramic pot attached to a rope, over her head. Smoke and flames streamed out of oil-soaked rags stuffed into the neck of the pot. She let go of the rope and the pot hurled down the hill to land in the middle of the retreating Gnathe.

Kamiel's homemade Molotov cocktail burst with shattering effect. The volatile oil spread quickly across the surface of the lake, engulfing more of the opposing soldiers. Screams of pain and terror rent the air. Another large pot came sizzling through the air. This one came from the hand and still mighty arm of Khann-link-sool. The Zanth completely panicked as more flames spread from the impact of the bomb.

In the urge to escape the terror of the smoke and flames, many of the Zanth turned on each other, in their panic to find a clear way to safety. Link-soo-shan saw a broken guard tossed off the horns of a maddened beast and into the path of another animal. The Zanth were rapidly becoming a dangerous force amongst her own troops. Screams and curses filled the air as rider-less mounts ploughed through the troops, raising more havoc.

When the fire and smoke cleared, a devastating sight met the Ruler's eyes. Dead and dying Zanth lay transfixed on the points of the fire-hardened stakes that the defending Gnathe had planted in the artificial lake. Many of her finest fighting soldiers floated, crushed, in a mixture of blood, slippery mud and foul water. Cries of pain and despair drifted over the battlefield. Injured guards crawled out of the water and lay where they fell. Those of the Imperial Guard that were in the rear of the charge were unhurt and gazed upwards at the defenders with malevolent hatred.

"You will all die for this!" Link-soo-shan screamed at the besieged household. "I will spare no-one. All will be put to the sword. All of you!"

Shoo-lin appeared at the top of the hill and shouted, "First you have to come up here, Tyrant!"

"Go home, foolish one," Kamiel called out from his vantage point on the hill crest, "before you all die here in this empty valley."

"Tether all the mounts that are uninjured, Group Captain," Link-soo-shan growled in fury. "We will advance on foot. Skirt the edge of the lake and climb the slope. We still outnumber them. They will be no match for a sharp syther. We will crush them yet!"

Koet-shan did as she had been commanded. The Gnathe gathered up the uninjured and slightly injured Zanth and tethered them with hobbles. The others they mercifully killed, to end their pain. The hobbled Zanth would not stray far. The badly injured guards were left with the mounts. The least injured were instructed to look after them. She looked at the mocking figure of Shoo-lin above her and felt a warm hatred fill her body. She promised herself, this one would die, spitted on her sword.

"Form up in twos and keep out of the water," Koet-shan commanded. "Group into fours when you get to the slope and advance slowly up to the top. The first wave, pull down the bushes that are in our way so that the main troop can advance up the middle. We will show these farm workers the hand of death."

The first four Gnathe were within stone throwing range as they began to pull down the flimsy barricades. A few small stones rattled harmlessly off their hardened leather backs and breastplates. These they ignored as they pulled back the brushwood.

"This bush smells of lamp oil," one of the guards remarked as she dismantled the barricade.

"Does it? Push it to one side and pull the other piece away; the second wave is getting ready to push forwards," the other guard impatiently replied.

Shoo-lin picked this moment to bound down the hill with a flaming brand and hurled it into the oil-soaked bush. The dry bush caught fire with a roar. Soon the entire barrier was alight with the first four Gnathe inside it. A great pall of smoke shot into the air and billowed around the base of the hill. All the defending Gnathe retreated out of range of the fires and waited for the blaze to do its work.

Link-soo-shan watched, horrified, as her troops became once more a disorganised rabble. It had never occurred to her that the fugitives would use fire again. In a world that used the obedient Banilik tree as building material, fire was carefully tended and never let out of control. Fights and punitive actions were carried out by the sword or lance. Mounted or on foot, hand-to-hand combat was the order of the day. This type of defence was so alien, she had trouble comprehending it, but she was learning fast.

"Regroup at the bottom. Wait for the fire to die out, then they are ours," the Brood-mother cried out to the stumbling, coughing Gnathe.

They appeared out of the smoke, wheezing for breath, some sliding down the scree on their backs and sides. They grimly collected together and fingered their swords, waiting for the fire to die down and the smoke to clear.

High in the sky, Asue increased the fuel supply to the engines in the airship and the four main propellers bit into the air, pulling the vessel across the wind. She and the crew had seen the smoke rush up out of the valley over the next ridge. Alex had directed Frederick to take ten suits only and whatever weapons they considered useful. The two male apes, Gunter and Charley, had decided to use a felling axe and a baseball bat, as their weapons. The two female apes, Daisy and An-an, each carried lump hammers in a sling-bag. They found the bows and arrows awkward for their longer arms. These were to be used by Jocylene and Abdul from the vantage point of the gondola. The four other humans, Frederick, John, David and Carlos would attack from the ground with the apes. They were using claymores and daggers taken from the teaching museum next to the sports centre. The axe and hammers had been found in the stores that Kamiel had stockpiled, long ago, when he had equipped the exploration vessel. Unfortunately, he had abandoned the vessel before designing and producing firearms because of the scarcity of metal. A highly technically orientated species would be limited to medieval warfare in this encounter. Again, this would benefit Kamiel's master plan, brought to fruition by these incredible series of events. Asue could see that fighting the Gnathe in hand-to-hand combat, while protecting Ender-whann-soo's people, would leave a lasting impression. The human's willingness to put his or her own lives at risk, would not be forgotten by the surviving Gnathe.

At last the airship breasted the final ridge. There, below them in the valley, they could see the awesome battlefield that Kamiel had created. The encampment on the top of the hill looked secure. Less smoke was blowing away from the far side of the hill. Kamiel's barrier would soon be breached. The shallow lake came into view as the airship veered to the right of the hill. Many dead and dying Zanth lay in contorted attitudes along with their riders in a ragged line across the water.

Asue sounded the klaxon as she dropped the vessel out of the sky. The rescue party stationed themselves around the parapet surrounding the control cabin. Human beings wore sturdy climbing boots over the suits to protect their feet. The apes had decided to go barefoot, as they still retained the ability to use their feet as grasping members, after their genetic modification by the human race long ago.

They all felt a fierce lift of excitement fill their bodies. A repressed bloodthirsty element emerged and they itched with impatience, as Rescue One closed the distance. The plan was for Asue to manoeuvre the airship and approach the opposing Gnathe from the side. They would then drop eight of the rescue crew from the parapet of the gondola on ropes as they turned the ship into position. The other two would provide covering fire with the target bows and arrows from the Sport's Complex at the Citadel.

Asue's calm voice spoke over the intercom to her children. "Be ready to go. I will head for that flat area at the side of the hill. They will kill you if you falter. Once I drop you, I will make for the top of the hill and load Ender-whann-soo's people into the back of the cargo hold. Keep them busy until I return for you. No heroics! Deflect them from rushing the top of the hill. That's all! Do not get separated."

"Good luck all of you and come back," Alex transmitted to his friends.

The airship turned into the wind over the stony and rock-strewn area and the ground crew swung over the side of the parapet.

Link-soo-shan had heard the air-splitting noise of the klaxon and watched the approach of the airship in disbelief. Nothing had prepared her for this. She stared up at the huge silver shape hauling itself across the sky and into the wind. The beat of the diesel engine driven propellers sounded across the wide valley floor. Ropes hung out from the bottom of the floating carrier and climbing down came a double handful of strange tail-less beings, shaped somewhat alike to the silver creature that she had met in the night. Somehow, she knew these beings could be killed.

"Group Captain, take the force upwards from my position, to the top of the hill when the fire dies down," she called to Koet-shan. "I will take on these creatures on the valley floor. These can die, my children. Follow me!"

Leaving a sizeable amount of her guards on the hillside, the Brood-mother and her force swept down onto the small group of humans and apes. As the shadow of the ship fell over them, she saw two of her soldiers clutch their sides and fall, as a small spear suddenly transfixed them. They staggered and rolled over in agony, injured badly by the human's arrows. As one of them pulled the target arrow out of her side, another shaft thudded into the Gnathe's chest, finding one of her dual hearts and stopped it dead. A look of surprise entered her face as she died. More arrows spat from the veranda of the gondola under the airship as it continued to turn round the hill and into the wind with deadly effect. Soon it passed over the Ultimate Ruler's forces and approached the slope of the hill. The lake was directly underneath them and the other Gnathen force had begun to work their way up the hill towards Ender-whann-soo's household.

The two archers continued to pick off some of the Group Captain's force from the parapet, as the ship rose over the brow of the hill. They climbed overboard, down the hanging ropes and swung safely onto the ground. Jocylene scrambled into the blindfolded impressive sized carrier, with Kamiel and Khann-link-sool. Abdul climbed into the one ridden by Shoo-lin and surveyed the advancing force of Gnathe.

"Hullo Kamiel. Long time no see," said Jocylene.

She towered over the guardian. The silver nannite suit covered her up to her neck. All that could be seen was her dark face and eager smile through the clear globe moulded to her head. She looked up at the massive figure of the old Brood-mother in disbelief.

"You must be Khann-link-sool. My, you are big," she gasped.

Abdul turned to Shoo-lin and exclaimed through the airship's translating computer, "Glad to meet you at last, Shoo-lin. Have you ever seen one of these?" He brandished the bow at the startled Gnathe and remarked, "Watch and see what it will do!"

"What does it do, friend?" Shoo-lin asked the silver-coated figure.

"It can send these little spears a long way with great accuracy," Jocylene replied from the other carrier. "Watch this!"

Shoo-lin eagerly watched from his vantage point on the neck of the male carrier that had taken them through the swamp. The tall African planted her feet securely on the beast's flat shoulders and drew back the bow, notching an arrow and carefully letting fly the shaft. It pierced the neck of one of the nearest of

Koet-shan's force, who fell choking to the ground. Abdul picked off another Gnathe creeping up the hill through the dead embers of the barricade. She fell back with an arrow protruding from her upper chest. The Group Captain's force began to fall back and take cover.

Asue kept the vessel into the wind and began to chill the helium to cut lift. By balancing the engines constantly, she was able to keep the ship almost motionless. Slowly she manoeuvred the great shape closer to the ground, so that the ropes were dragging along the soil, including the main anchor rope. This was attached to the powered winch.

Kamiel left the carrier and located Ender-whann-soo amongst the Gnathe.

"Grab that large trailing rope and make it fast to that old tree," he shouted.

Ender-whann-soo leapt forwards and picked up the end of the winch rope and asked, "Is this the one you mean, Kaameel?"

"Yes. Tie it around the tree securely and Asue will start to pull the airship down."

The Brood-mother did as she was told and Kamiel checked that all was knotted tight.

"Start the winch, Asue," he transmitted.

Steadily Asue winched the ship down to the stony ground, still chilling the gas and shrinking the floatation bags during the descent. Finally the cargo floor scraped the ground and the vessel finally settled onto its four main supports at the end of the rotor gantries.

"Get them inside, Kamiel," the guardian called over the outside speakers.

Alex, Joom and Nancy had donned the three remaining suits and had passed through the nannite barrier into the cargo hold. Alex ventured to the doorway and waved the besieged Gnathe into the huge chamber. The Zanth were nervous, but as they had been blindfolded, remained obedient. Nancy joined him at the door and looked up at the spiky headed beasts as they were coaxed into the hold.

"Look at the size of them, Alex!" she exclaimed in wide-eyed astonishment. "I hope our new friends can keep them under control."

"They will, Nancy," Alex replied. "Now I must find Ender-whann-soo and welcome her aboard. Get them moving as fast as you can. Find Coen-soo if you can, Joom, and introduce yourself. I am going outside."

For the first time, Alexander stood on real Jovian soil and stared round at the alien landscape. Strange spiky plants grew here and there in the stony ground at the top of the hill. Odd-looking flowers were being trampled underfoot by the household, as they retreated in an orderly fashion into the cargo hold of the airship. He saw the taller figure of Ender-whann-soo's golden form reassuring her kindred and urging them into the vessel. He ran through the camp towards her, glimpsing Kamiel's silver form helping with the evacuation.

"Ender-whann-soo, we meet at last!" he shouted over the noise.

The tall powerful form spun round with a cat-like grace, flicking her tail out and stared down at him.

"I am Alexander," the silver suited creature spoke through the translator, looking up into her gold-flecked eyes with the split pupils. "I had forgotten just how large you are, Reverend Lady."

The Brood-mother regarded him with an inquisitive stare and, bending down to his level, she said, "It is good to meet you at last, Alexander. We will never forget what you and your people do for us today."

"Just get your people onto our giant carrier, my friend. We have yet to get you off this hill and away to safety," Alex replied.

She stared at the alien face looking back at her from inside the crystal globe at the top of the suite. A small oval head with two eyes looked out of a pale face. Some long fur grew from the top of his head with small bursts spouting from above the eyes in a line and also above the mouth. The teeth were small and even, without any points and useless for fighting. The face was not so bad once you became used to it, she decided. Anyway it was the face of a friend.

She swung round to address her kindred, "Pull back everyone and start loading the carriers!" she shouted.

Most of the household were tucked safely inside the cargo hold of the airship with their Zanth, which had been hobbled and made to lie down against a wall. This left the carriers and their handlers still facing out and down the hill. Each human archer continued to pick off any of the Imperial Guard foolish enough to move into sight.

Khann-link-sool watched the decimation of the Group Captain's guards with amazement, as the two human figures constantly fired their bows with unerring skill.

The big, black human woman spoke to Khann as she aimed another arrow down the slope. "We had better get a move on, Reverend Lady. I am running out of arrows."

"Move the other carriers back, Whann-lin," she ordered. "We will be the last to go."

After dropping down the ropes, hanging over the side of the airship's gondola, Frederick and his people had formed themselves into the classic fighting wedge. They began to move forwards at a steady trot, towards Link-soo-shan's forces.

These were covering the ground in a double wave. They travelled in great leaps, brandishing their weapons at the small human company. Frederick's group were outnumbered at least two to one, not counting the mighty form of the Brood-mother.

Frederick took the lead, with the male apes, Gunter and Charley, behind him, spaced about four feet away and eight feet apart. The triangle widened out with the two female apes Daisy and An-an in the rear line.

"To the left!" shouted Frederick.

As one entity the humans and apes veered to the left of the double ranks of the Gnathe and ploughed through, thus leaving the awesome frame of the Brood-mother and half of her company away from the beginning of the conflict. There was no time to size up the opposition from either side as the forces clashed.

Frederick slashed forwards with the claymore in his right hand, only to have it nearly hit from his grasp by the downward chop of the guard's blow. The blade of the syther slid along the flat of his sword towards his chest. Frederick dropped to the ground and rolled away from the strike, popping up in front of the surprised Gnathe. He flicked the short stabbing knife into the flat stomach and upwards, in a swift disembowelling motion, pulling the sabre across the guard's neck. Her dying kick propelled her into the side of another Gnathe, who had just received a crushing blow from Gunter's baseball bat. They rolled in the dust together and once more Frederick snaked out with the claymore and cut deep across the back of the Gnathe's left leg, ham-stringing her. He kept rolling and weaving to the high ground at the base of the crumbling cliff.

Charley delivered a hefty blow with the felling axe and made his first and only mistake. The axe stuck fast in the broad chest of the Imperial Guard. A sideways swing had caused the axe head to part the bony rib cage of the enemy. As the Gnathe fell, she instinctively lashed out with both hind feet, curling her tail around the startled ape. Instead of letting go of the shaft, he swung into the reach of the kicking feet. The sharp claws bit through the tough nannite covering and raked his chest open to the bone. As he stumbled back, a crystalline hardened blade pierced his body from behind him. Charley fell to his knees and pitched forward onto the hard ground, breathing his last. The Gnathe that had killed him stabbed him repeatedly with her syther in red-raged battle lust.

Daisy and An-an were selecting individual targets with the heavy construction hammers and throwing them with fierce and painful effect. Daisy saw a Gnathe leap through the air over a dead comrade towards John's unprotected flank, as Charley died. The guard was swinging her sword into a death-dealing blow, aiming at his head. Daisy threw, catching the guard with a two-pound hammer on the side of the head and the Gnathe fell into an oblivious heap.

The group of apes and humans made it through the left flank of the Gnathe and now had the cliff to their backs. The last human to reach the shelter of the rocks stumbled and fell as a loose stone turned under his foot. David rolled frantically to the side as the pursuing Gnathe chopped down at the place where he had fallen. Before he had regained his footing another of Link-soo-shan's guards had leapt through the air, tail streaming behind her. She landed at his other side and thrust forwards with her syther. The pointed end of the sharp tail of the dead beast caught him in the back and plunged through into his chest. At the same time the guard to his right brought her sword across his stomach nearly cutting him in half. The Gnathe kicked the dead man aside and looked for more enemies to kill.

The right flank of Gnathe wheeled round and now the forces paused to take stock of each other. Four of the Gnathe had died and three were injured, for the death of one human and one ape, of Frederick's company.

"Retreat along the cliff face! Make them follow us, away from the slope of the hill," Frederick shouted.

An-an hurled a rock at the row of soldiers and took off round the hill with the others in quick pursuit.

The urge to chase took over the Gnathen guards and the still moment was over. In the rough ground of the broken pieces of cliff face the apes and humans had a distinctive advantage. The Gnathe's backward facing knee joints made dodging around the boulders difficult. On the flat ground they could have leapt and overtaken the rescue force easily. Sometimes the sure-footed apes took to the tops of the boulders, springing from one to the other. Gunter took a fierce joy in leaping back and forth in this manner. He swung his club between the gaps in the rocks, catching the heads of the guards as they vainly tried to catch the will-o-the-wisp humans. He was determined to avenge Charlie's death

One by one, the Imperial Guards found themselves picked off by the nimble aliens. The light-footed humans would dart around the rocks and boulders and lead the guards into traps.

"Get out of the rocks and into the open1" yelled the Brood-mother, pulling back out of the conflict. "Regroup to me."

As the handful of Gnathe survivors retreated from the boulders and rocks at the base of the cliff, she was able to see the extent of the alien's strategy. Many were bleeding from cuts and some had broken bones from Gunter's club. She could hardly believe the casualty rate amongst her elite troops. The last Gnathe to leave the rocky warren had a large rock hurled at her by Daisy. It crunched into her shoulder, making her lose her grip on the sword that she carried. It fell from her paralysed fingers. As she bent to pick it up with her other hand, another rock caught her on the hip. She decided to leave it where it lay and hurriedly limped as fast as she could to her comrades. She could always pick up another sword from one of the many dead strewn around the battlefield.

Link-soo-shan suddenly realised how far they had travelled around the hill in pursuit of the alien people.

"Leave them! Get back to the others!" she cried to the few guards left capable of fighting. "They have led us away from our quarry."

The disheartened, once proud Imperial Guard limped and stumbled back around the cliff face towards the slope leading to the top of the hill.

"They are retreating, Asue, and making their way back to the slope at the foot of the hill," Frederick transmitted. "What do you want us to do? How are things with you?"

"We are nearly finished, Frederick. All of the Zanth and most of the carriers are loaded. We will take off soon. Move out of the safety of the rocks to the large boulder standing on its own, some way to your right. When it is safe. I will pick you up from there. What are our losses, Fred?"

"Charley and David are both dead, Asue," Frederick grimly replied. "We gave them a good fight. I think we killed at least seven to ten of her guards. Quite a lot of the others are nursing some broken bones. You should have seen Gunter with that bat! What a club that turned out to be! I knew he was strong, but to see that bat come whistling out of the air must have been a terrible and final experience for these creatures. We did not get a chance to attack the big one."

"Just as well, I think. Now slow down, Frederick," Asue commanded. "What injuries have you sustained and how is the integrity of the suits? Check each other over."

"I think I may have a broken rib or a bad bruise. Gunter, Daisy and An-an are fine. What about you two, John and Carlos? How are you? All of you, check each others' suits," the leader advised his people.

"I took a cut from one of their swords, Fred," Carlos replied. "We both know what that means. The suit has self-sealed, though."

John answered, "I'm alright, but I am a bit worried about the suit Carlos is wearing. I can see where the cut was. It was high on the shoulder and has repaired itself."

"How is the shoulder, Carlos?" Frederick strode over to his friend, examined him and said, "We have to get you back to the airship soon so that Asue can run a check on any infection. You are first up the ladder, understand?"

"The shoulder is a bit sore, Fred. It was only a light cut and the bleeding has long since stopped, but I know what you mean," replied Carlos, worriedly.

"What do you think, Asue? I think we ought to start out from the shelter of the rocks soon. The Imperial Guards have gone out of sight around the hillside. Watch out for them; they will be with the other force soon," Frederick transmitted to the control room of Rescue One.

Asue thought for a moment and said, "All right, Fred, get them out in the open ready for pick up, but be careful."

She turned around in the swivel chair and stared at the holo-screen showing the inside of the cargo hold. The entire household were inside except the two carriers, defended by the human archers, aided by Shoo-lin and Khann-link-sool. She switched to the outside cameras and began to look for them.

"Alex," she radioed to the suited figure that stood amongst the Gnathe, "get those last two beasts inside. I have signalled Kamiel. We have to go soon. I am warming the helium in the airbags to increase lift. Tell Whann-lin to take up position on the parapet and be ready to cut the anchor rope when I say, over the outside loudspeakers."

Alex looked across the scrubby landscape of the hilltop. He could see the two carriers retreating to the airship. A fine rain had begun to fall, turning the ground into soft going for the heavy beasts. The two humans were clinging on for dear life to the living sides of the carrying hollows as the six-legged creatures jolted the occupants about.

"Where are you, Kamiel?" he thought to himself.

Kamiel watched the retreating beasts, using his infrared scanners and monitored the cautious advance of the surviving Gnathe up the hill. Jocylene and Abdul had kept a steady stream of death and injury raining down on the guards until they had almost run out of arrows. When the loading of the other beasts had been complete, Kamiel had ordered them back and out of immediate danger after Asue's transmission. It was time to play poker with the inexperienced minds of Link-soo-shan's Imperial Guards.

Kamiel walked forwards into plain sight at the crest of the hill and called out to the advancing Gnathe: "How many more of you need to die? Remember the death I left for you at the camp? There is much more of it up here. I have had plenty of time to prepare for your coming."

"We do the Ultimate Ruler's bidding," Koet-shan replied. "If we die in her service, it will be a glorious death, silver one!" Koet-shan slowly climbed the slope towards Kamiel and stopped short, beckoning her apprehensive guard towards the silver figure and the crest of the hill, crying out, "Forward, all of you!"

"For what purpose will you all die? You lead these soldiers to a pointless death, Group Captain," Kamiel replied, scornfully. "All this is because your Brood-mother is obsessed with capturing Ender-whann-soo. She is at this moment safe in our carrier that roams the skies. I say again, if you come up here you will die and all for nothing. Your Commander is mad. I left her so. You must have seen her at the Trading Post. What do you think the result will be when you return defeated? Will Link-soo-shan have any Empire for you to keep for her? Go now and live."

"Do not listen to it!" the Group Captain screamed in rage. "Forward, guards, and over the top! Ignore it. It lies!"

Some of the guards began to descend the hill and many of the others faltered in their slow advance.

"Come back, you cowards!" Koet-shan cried in anger to her troops. "Do as you are ordered!"

"I have had enough of this," one of them growled.

"And me. You go fight her war on your own," another guard called out to her. The Group Captain leapt at the complaining guard and slapped her face with the claws of her hand extended. Without thinking and on reflex, the Imperial Guard impaled Koet-shan on her short syther. She continued the action with the classic Gnathen disembowelling kick with her taloned foot.

The Group Captain squatted in a pile of her own bloody guts, with a look of disbelief on her face. Another guard reached forward with her syther and parted the Captain's neck to the bone. With a sound of choking the dying Gnathe fell to the ground, helped with another vicious kick from her killer.

"Come on, all of you, let's get down this hill and away from this place. Link-soo-shan must not find out about her death. She was killed by one of the household staff or an alien," the guard who helped kill her exclaimed.

"It was just as you said, Jaffin-shan," one of the other guards replied. "Let's go. We all agree."

Kamiel watched their departure from the crest of the hill, turned and ran back to the airship. It was holding position and had lifted off the ground. He pulled himself hand-over-hand up the anchor rope and over the parapet of the gondola of Rescue One.

"Cut the rope, Whann-lin, it's time to leave!" Asue called out over the outside speakers.

Whann-lin sawed through the tough rope and as it parted, the airship gave a mighty leap into the skies aided by the lift from the rotors.

"Now to pick up Frederick and the others," Kamiel said to the Gnathe in the gondola.

CHAPTER 11

▼

Link-soo-shan reached the bottom of the hill to find her remaining troops descending towards her.

"Where is the Group Captain and why are you retreating?" she shouted at the dispirited guards.

"The aliens have gone, with all of Ender-whann-soo's household. They boarded the floating carrier and it lifted into the sky, where we cannot follow," one of the guards replied.

The Brood-mother's kindred lay scattered in positions of death. Small, impossibly straight spears jutted out from the corpses. She noticed the ends of these shafts had vanes, not unlike the Gnathen Scriit spears. She pulled one of the tiny shafts from a dead guard and marvelled that something so small could do so much damage. How could they have been thrown so fast and accurately?

She looked around at the remaining handful of guards, her once invincible army. It would take some concentrated breeding to replenish the numbers she had lost on this ill-fated adventure. Her young in the Royal crèche were going to have to advance very quickly if she were to be able to retain her hold on the Empire.

The ashes of defeat tasted bitter in her soul. Without a backward glance at her own and her sister's dead kindred, she began to walk back to the ill-fated camp. She beckoned the surviving guards to return with her. The lake was calm and still, hiding its grisly secrets as the light drizzle fell, increasing its tempo. She stopped and stared moodily at its tranquil surface. They had killed only two of the aliens and the vast majority of the Royal Kindred would be left here to rot and feed the scavengers of this hidden valley. One thing she had learnt from this encounter with these strange people from the other side of these mountains—they could die as easily as the Gnathe, if you could catch them. Oh, but they were hard to kill! She would have decimated them on the plains, without cover. She heard the sound of the flying carrier's strange muted roar and looked across the valley floor.

"What are they up to now?" she wondered as she watched the long silver shape turning into the wind. The ship was lowering itself down to a large exposed rock, some distance from the hill. She caught a glimpse of an alien figure step out from the rock and wave upward. Of course, they were picking up the remainder of the ground attacking force.

With only thoughts of a final revenge driving through her mind, the Brood-mother covered the distance to the tethered Zanth in mighty ground-devouring leaps. She quickly selected the biggest and strongest animal from the tethered line of beasts. Link-soo-shan snapped the tethering rope and hobbles with her powerful hands and climbed onto the area just below the shoulders of the horny-headed beast. She curled her tail around the bony plates of the Zanth's back to anchor her to its body.

This time she favoured her syther. She had bred this beast herself and had mutated its size beyond the normal length. It had been fed and cared for by her. When enough of its tail had hardened into a crystalline edged blade, she had killed it herself. The legs and the front half had been removed. The tail, backbone, flesh and skin had dried in the sun and mummified. A male crafter had bound the remaining body with leather. What she had when he had finished was a slightly flexible sword, longer than an adult Gnathe. It was a finely balanced and razor sharp, double handed broadsword.

She gave the beast a vicious dig in its ribs with her taloned feet. The Zanth snorted in anger at the rough treatment, but knew better than to disobey the heavier weight it now carried instead of its usual rider. The beast bunched its great thigh muscles and leapt across the valley floor, towards the airship holding stationary above the lone rock.

The crew of Rescue One were busy instructing the airborne Gnathe how to drop the rope ladders overboard to pick up the remaining rescue party. Alexander and Kamiel both saw the Zanth and the Brood-mother covering the ground at the same time.

"You have to stop her, Kamiel," Alexander said to his friend. "Give us enough time to hoist Fredrick and the others to safety."

Without a word Kamiel jumped from the parapet and dropped thirty feet to the ground.

Carlos and John had made it up the rope ladder and were being helped over the veranda of the gondola by Alex and Joom. Several of the Gnathe had overcome their fear of the strange carrier and the unaccustomed height from the ground. Most of them, who were not needed in the cargo hold, had made their way to the edge of the gondola and were looking over the edge of the parapet to the view below. Ender-whann-soo strode majestically forwards to observe the dangerous drama below. She watched the approach of Link-soo-shan with alarm. It was obvious that the Ultimate Ruler was in the grip of a berserker rage.

An-an and Daisy made a run for the trailing rope ladder, while Gunter sprinted as fast as he could for one of the trailing ropes. Frederick was half way up the rope ladder and climbing as fast as he could

Link-soo-shan saw the aliens scatter and the silver being hurl itself through the air towards her. One alien was making for a trailing rope while the other two were frantically chasing after the rope ladder. She spurred the Zanth to a heroic turn of speed and lent out to the right over its neck and shoulders. The mutated syther hissed through the air as she brought the long sharp edge closer to the figure farthest from the ladder.

As An-an grasped the lower rungs and began a fast hand-over-hand climb, Daisy leapt for the bottom rungs of the rope ladder.

Link-soo-shan's flexible sword entered the ape's body under her arm and continued through her shoulders, chest and neck. Even the tough nannite suit could not withstand such a blow. Daisy's head and arm stayed entangled with the ladder and dragged along the ground. Her body spun over and over and lay still, while her heart, for several beats, still spasmodically pumped her life's blood into the muddy earth.

As Kamiel hit the ground he rolled forwards and aimed at the Zanth to bring it down. He hit the beast in the ribs—seconds after Daisy had been decapitated—and reached up for Link-soo-shan.

Ender-whann-soo pushed her way to Alexander's side through the excited kindred in the gondola.

She lightly gripped the human by the shoulder and cried out, "Alexander, tell Kaameel, Link-soo-shan must live, to return to the Imperial City."

"What, after the slaughter of our people by her? We can rid you of the tyrant now!" Alexander exclaimed.

"No, Alexander. This is not the way. Believe me, she must return defeated," the Brood-mother replied.

Alexander transmitted the message to Kamiel—"Ender-whann-soo says that Link-soo-shan must live"—as the guardian hit the Zanth sideways into a broken heap of thrashing limbs.

Kamiel accepted the instruction and gripped the Ultimate Ruler by her ankle.

The mighty Brood-mother chopped viciously down with her sword arm and gathered the rungs of the rope ladder with the other into a tight grasp. She brought the syther down hard on Kamiel's arm and ricocheted off his diamond hard, outer skin, catching him under his jaw. Such was the speed and power of the blow; she shook Kamiel loose from his grip, taking some of her skin with him.

As Kamiel's silver form sailed through the air away from the airship, Link-soo-shan hooked her feet into the bottom rungs of the ladder and began to climb after An-an.

Kamiel converted to computer time and extended his arm into a rapid filament, back towards the swinging rope ladder and made contact. An-an climbed up the ladder with feverish speed. She did not waste time looking down at the sudden heavy weight beneath her. The airship had tilted slightly as the massive form of Link-soo-shan swung wildly from side to side. Asue trimmed the ship using the drive from the propellers and kept the ship steady.

"What was that, Alexander?" Asue asked over the intercom.

"Link-soo-shan has caught hold of the bottom of the rope ladder and is climbing aboard," Alex replied.

The Brood-mother stuck upwards with the long broadsword missing the frantic ascending form of the female ape by a hand's breadth. An-an increased her speed up the ladder.

Kamiel's time sense had slowed down, but the oscillating swing of the ladder had swung him far out on the pendulum. Link-soo-shan's heavy blow had caught him by surprise, as he was operating in real time at that moment. He gathered his mass together and flowed back along the thickening tentacle that was once more becoming an arm. He mulled over Alexander's instruction. This would require an in-depth discussion with Ender-whann-soo later. What devious game-play was she involved with, he wondered? His other hand caught hold of the rope ladder and he began to ascend after the Brood-mother.

Gunter had seen Link-soo-shan's amazingly fast reactions when Kamiel had smashed her mount from under her. When she had hit the silver being away from her with her enormous broad-sword, Gunter had already started to swing towards her, with one hand and both feet firmly grasping the hanging rope. He had his club ready in the other hand. Stretching up the rope ladder and bleeding from the area of torn skin where Kamiel had grasped her, she was a formidable sight. The Ultimate Ruler was easily twice the size of an ordinary Gnathe. From her outstretched hand to the tip of her bone-plated tipped tail she was four times his size. The talons on her feet were as long as butcher's knives. In seconds, the gap between them narrowed and the ape made his attack. He brought his club upwards and into the Brood-mother's ribs, as he swung past.

Link-soo-shan gave a scream of pain and fury as the baseball bat thudded into her muscular ribcage. She swung the broadsword wildly at her retreating enemy as Gunter swung by. The action caused the rope ladder to twist and swing round and round, trapping An-an's foot and breaking her leg, just as Joom leant out of the parapet and caught her outstretched hand. An-an's screech of pain echoed through the human's and ape's helmets, before she mercifully fainted. The Brood-mother's bony-ended tail caught Gunter a savage blow to the ribs and sent him spinning round on his single rope, doubled over in agony. He climbed up the wildly gyrating rope and into the gondola and fell into a gasping heap holding his smashed side.

Shoo-lin grabbed the rope ladder by leaning over Joom's shoulders and vaulting into empty air. He swung hand-over-hand to a position hanging head down just below An-an's trapped and mangled foot. He wrapped his tail in and out of the rungs above the female ape and hung with his hands free. With a captured guard's syther he began to saw at the tough rope while trying ineffectively to lift the weight of Link-soo-shan. The Brood-mother steadied her arm for a death-dealing blow to her mortal enemy hanging just above her.

Shoo-lin carefully spat in her eyes as he parted one of the ropes. Link-soo-shan hissed in maddened rage as she spun round and round on the remaining part of the ladder, unable to see her hated enemy without wiping spittle from her vision. She hacked blindly upwards with her sword and was suddenly conscious of a heavy weight climbing up her back. Shoo-lin continued to saw at the other rope as he saw his strange silver friend rapidly climb up the trailing ladder and over the back of the Brood-mother.

Kamiel scrambled up the ladder like a silver blur. He reached up for Link-soo-shan's sword arm as she hacked blindly at Shoo-lin above her and grasped her firmly by the wrist. Locking his legs around her, he smoothly pulled her arm down to her side and held it there, while extending the other arm to hold her left hand securely to the rope.

"Time to go down, Tyrant," he hissed in her ear as Shoo-lin's efforts on the rope finally parted the strands.

Link-soo-shan and Kamiel hit the ground and rolled over and over, sliding across the muddy ground still bonded together. The Brood-mother lay shaken by the fall, covered in mud and crushed plant juices. Her sword had been torn from her grasp and had finished its travels some distance away. Kamiel let her go and walked away from her, following the airship.

With a scream of fury the Ultimate Ruler rolled over on the muddy ground and jumped from her position straight at Kamiel's unprotected back. She intended to see if she could tear this thing apart. Kamiel's all-round vision had perceived the Brood-mother's leaping rush. He sidestepped at the last moment, reached out and caught her by the wrist and elbow. He flipped her into a somersaulting throw, high into the air. Link-soo-shan felt the air shoot past as she careered over the wet ground. This time she landed flat on her back, her tail hitting the ground with an audible slap and the breath knocked out of her. She lay, with the steady rain washing the mud from off her front, gazing up at the now dark and stormy sky. A silver form came into her cone of vision.

"You are a fool, Link-soo-shan," Kamiel said to the dazed Gnathe laid out on the rough ground. "I told you that I couldn't be harmed. You are a nasty piece of work, Brood-mother. If it were within my powers I would punish you for what you have done today. You have caused much needless death. For some reason, Ender-whann-soo has instructed me to allow you to live."

The Brood-mother gave a hiss of fury and rage. Kamiel stooped over her and held her head, bringing his eyeless face close to hers.

"It is in my power to drag you bound, all the way back to the Imperial City and leave you chained to the 'Killing Stones' you have become over fond off during your reign of terror. I have seen through your sister's mind all the needless cruelty the two of you have wrought. You and your egg-sister killed the very Brood-mother who carried you and formed you both in her pouch. The two of you did this just for power. Go home, defeated one, and face your people," Kamiel said to her, and let go of her great head, letting it sag back into the mud.

Kamiel continued to walk away from the spread-eagled Brood-mother towards the slowly drifting airship. Without a backward glance at the recumbent form, he stopped and knelt at the decapitated remains of Daisy. Methodically he stripped away the remains of the nano-suit from her body. The head and arm had still remained tangled with the end of the rope ladder. Kamiel looked into the dead face of his discontented friend and remembered the young, lively mind that had found no rest in the too ordered artificial world the Guardians had created. He scooped out a shallow grave, laying the two pieces inside and covered them with earth and stones.

"Asue," he transmitted on their private band, "I shall retrieve the other suits from our dead. Ease the airship over to the rocks at the side of the hill."

Asue quietly acknowledged and turned Rescue One into the wind again, slowly following the silver form across the rain-lashed valley floor.

Link-soo-shan got shakily to her feet and began the long walk back to her remaining kindred. She watched Kamiel walk swiftly through the scrub towards her ill-fated battlefield as she retrieved her sword from the mud, placing it back into the sheath on her back. What could be the creature's motives? She pondered on his words, in her defeat. Cut off as she was from her Empire and a master communications crystal, there was no way she could find out what was happening at her city. Unless someone contacted her by her receiving shard, she was blind and deaf. Pangs of unease racked her mind as she walked through the driving rain towards her camp.

Kamiel reached the rocks from the fallen cliff and found David's body lying face down between the boulders. The suit had self-sealed itself over the dead man. Kamiel carried the body over to where Charley lay amongst the dead Gnathe. Once more he dug a shallow grave, this time big enough for two. After stripping both corpses of the nano-suits, he laid them, ape and man, side by side into the earth. He replayed memories from the past as he covered the bodies with earth and stones.

Charley had come from a tropical farm, far across the dome complex. He was third generation and had raised two families, by different female apes, and one day had walked away and left them to join the rebels in the African dome. He had lived at least sixty years and had been as youthful and fit as a twenty-year old ape. There was still no sign of aging in his face and no trace of grey. The age showed in the eyes and the recklessness of behaviour. Kamiel recalled the evening Charley had walked out into the grasslands from the rebel's compound, armed with nothing more than a heavy, self-made spear. He was gone for three days and had returned with some minor injuries, with the skin of a male full-grown lion. He had cured it himself and hung it on the wall of his hut.

Kamiel had to insist on a quota system after this act of bravery by the pan-chimpanzee. David had joined the band of malcontent people some time after Charley had arrived. The two had become firm friends over the many years they had spent in the African landscape together. The need for adventure had stirred their souls into some foolhardy escapades in the past.

The rain beat down in a steady pattern as Kamiel rolled the last rock over the faces of his two friends.

"Damn you, Alexander," he railed at his creator from the distant past. "You gave no hint in my programming that this would be so hard. You could have let me weep, Alexander."

The scene dimmed and a very old memory replayed itself from Kamiel's memory banks. He was once more in the study of the original Alexander. The old man leaned forwards in his chair and spoke to the silver guardian.

"If you are viewing this, a crisis point has occurred in the future. You are different from the other three artificial personalities. They are programmed to save lives at all costs. You must be prepared to spend lives for the greater good of the plan. The ends will justify the means. You have much of my personality grafted into your soul. There are others, who donated large parts of their makeup to produce your unique mind. Oui Sakii, your weapons master, would be proud of all that you have done. Do not worry, Kamiel, you are not a killer. There are no hidden pockets in your programming. Whatever you have done, that troubles you, must have been necessary for the survival of the colony. Whenever you need me, I will return, be assured of that."

The memory finished playing and Kamiel turned away, striding briskly towards the airship, holding its position against the wind. As he walked through the battlefield he collected the arrows and weapons from the dead Gnathe.

"Asue, drop a cargo net over the side," he commanded. "I will pack the suits and the weapons I have scavenged from this place."

"Stand by, Kamiel," she answered. "I will arrange it. I am passing the controls over to the autopilot. Hurry up and get up here soon. I need you to fly this vessel of yours. Carlos has had a tear in his suit. I must check him over for micro-biotic invasion."

"Patch me through to the controls now, Asue—I can do it from down here. See to Carlos. Do all you can," Kamiel replied.

Kamiel packed the net full and ordered it winched back to the ship while he hung onto the rope.

The Gnathe and the human rescue party survivors were getting to know each other, when Carlos began to cough. An-an was still semiconscious and lay flat on the cargo hold floor. Gunter knelt beside her, holding his crushed side, waiting for Asue's administrations, gazing down at his friend and sometimes lover. The old Brood-mother had retreated to the privacy of her carrier and sat thinking about the turn of events. Alexander, Joom and Nancy sat on seats pulled out from the wall talking to Ender-whann-soo, when all of them heard another racking cough come from the direction of the rescue party.

"Asue, I think we need you," Alex cried, rising and making his way towards Carlos.

"I am coming, Alex," she replied. "Kamiel has the helm."

The nannite curtain separating the human living quarters from the cargo hold shimmered and Asue's slender silver form raced through. She pushed through the knot of assorted beings and reached the side of Carlos. Another deep cough shook his body and his legs buckled underneath him, causing the man to fall. Asue caught him before he reached the ground. She merged with the suit and inserted micro-thin tendrils into the feverish body.

"I need you, Minns," Asue transmitted through the main computer link to the citadel.

"I am here Asue," Minns replied, "give me control."

Asue detached her mind and allowed the master biologist to use her body as she needed. She ran a check on the air in the suit. There was a thin soup of fungal spores and assorted unknown microbes floating round the inside of the suit. Carlos was inhaling a lethal mixture of alien biology.

Minns noted the increased heart rate and temperature. She quickly plugged into Carlos's nervous system and slowed the rapidly beating heart. Hoards of tiny nannites were released into his blood and became hunter-killers of the alien microbes. She closed off the area of the sword cut and increased the rate of reproduction of the living cells to replenish the dying ones. Bit by bit Minns triumphed over the alien life that had taken root in the human's body. She turned her attention to the lungs and met horror beyond her scope of knowledge. Fungal spores had rooted into the tiny spiracles of the spongy sacks. As fast as she killed them, toxins were produced that further poisoned the area.

"I am losing him, Asue," she said. "There is nothing I can do to stop the fungus in his lungs from spreading."

The unconscious form of Carlos began to shake and convulse from the effort of breathing. The struggle for breath abruptly stopped and Asue withdrew her probes from the dead man.

Ender-whann-soo stared down at the stricken man being held tenderly by Asue. She could not understand what was happening in front of her.

"Why has he died?" she cried to Alexander. "He was uninjured except for a small cut in the shoulder."

Kamiel strode forward to the small group and said to the Brood-mother, "They cannot breathe your air without filtering it, Reverend Lady. There are tiny creatures in the air that you can live with. They do you no harm, but they kill my people and this is why they all live together under the domes of the Habitat."

The Brood-mother stood transfixed by this information. These frail creatures have risked their lives in more ways than she could comprehend to save her life and those of her household. What courage these people have, she thought. Somehow she would repay them for what they had done for her. A debt of honour had been levied to her house. The new life in her brood pouch stirred and shifted. Instinctively she quietened it and carried on the process of dividing the egg into two identities. She walked away from the sombre group and rejoined her Grand-Brood-mother, who was inside the hollow of her carrier.

Kamiel had set the computer to retrace the journey over the mountains back to the Habitat. The first stopping point would be the large valley where the ship had encountered the Terra-Raptor. He was pleased with the performance of the airship and did a quick check of the operational log, coming to the conclusion that all was fine.

Asue had disengaged from Carlos and had turned her attentions to the two apes. An-an's shattered leg needed Minn's anatomical skills. She inserted probes into the female ape and depressed the blood supply to her brain, keeping her unconscious. Minns rapidly rebuilt the bone structure of ankle and lower tibia, reinforcing it with pieces of Asue's nannite composition. She gathered up all the bone splinters and knitted them together.

"How is the chest, Gunter? I will see to your needs now," the guardian said.

"It hurts, Asue," the ape replied. "How is An-an's leg?"

"She will be fine, Gunter," she assured him. "Now hold still while I check you over. I will put you to sleep now."

Ender-whann-soo approached the old Brood-mother's carrier and said, "Khann-link-sool, I think you should come over to where the dead human and his friends are being dealt with. The guardian, Asue, is different from Kaameel. I sense a strong female presence from her personality."

"How can that be, young Ender? Kaameel says that they are not made of flesh like us," the old Brood-mother replied, rising from her position inside the carrier's hollow. "I don't like this place, young one. This is just too alien for me. I am not so adaptable as you, remember. I find the concept of flying very strange. I dare not think about all that empty space underneath us."

"Is that why you are hiding here?" Ender-whann-soo looked up at the Brood-mother looking back from over the carrier's shoulders and said, "Come out of there, Reverend Mother and meet these people."

"I do not hide! I am resting," she testily replied and swung her body over the side of the beast to stand beside the other Brood-mother. "How did the human die Ender? I thought that they were all safe now."

"Apparently not so, Khann. The silver suits they wear are a protection from our world. If they breathe our air, they die!"

"From what? Explain yourself," the old Brood-mother replied.

"Kaameel says that the air we breathe is full of tiny creatures that do us no harm, but react inside these people causing them to die," Ender-whann-soo explained.

"This may be so, young one," replied the Gnathen scientist. "I have done research using specially ground crystal lenses that magnify. There is life teeming all around us that is too small to see without aid. Some of the fevers we suffer from time to time are caused by these forms of life getting into our systems. Over the years, our medical specialists have genetically engineered our race to be mainly unaffected by them. Our immune system has been strengthened in the past by our ancestors' master-breeding programme. I must see this dead human and examine him. Do you think they would be offended? We should ask Kaameel."

The two huge Gnathe pushed through the crowd of kindred and finally came to stand by the side of the two guardians. They watched, fascinated, as Kamiel removed the nano-suit from the body of Carlos.

Khann bent forwards over the body and spoke to Kamiel and Asue. "What will you do with the body of this person?"

"I shall do an autopsy, Khann-link-sool, with the help of my colleague, Minns," said Asue. "She is at the Citadel, but is still connected to my mind. Why do you ask?"

"I would like to attend, Asue," replied the Gnathe. "I need to know more about Alexander's species. Does this offend? I do not know how you view your dead."

"Carlos is dead, Reverend-mother Khann," Asue said to the towering form of the Brood-mother. "Whatever we do with his body will not affect him. Maybe we can both learn by his death. Kamiel will take the suit and de-contaminate it. It can be used again once it has been purged."

The ship lurched to the side as a strong gust of wind rippled down the vessel causing it to lift as well. Outside, the rain beat down on the silver cigar shape as the storm began to increase its pace.

Khann-link-sool reached out for the wall and staggered to the side, crying out, "What was that? I do not like it in here, Alexander. I need something to do. Can we do the autopsy now?"

"I see no reason not to," Alex replied. "You get on with it, Asue. My crew and I will return to our side of the nannite curtain. We need rest and something to eat. We will talk later."

Kamiel turned and said to his friends, "You go back into the cabin and restore yourselves. I will stay here for a while. There is something I wish to discuss with Brood-mother Ender."

The humans and apes passed through the nannite curtain and the airlock door into the cabin, leaving the body of Carlos with the Gnathe and the guardians.

Asue pulled a table out from the wall and secured it firmly to the floor. She placed Carlos onto the flat surface and began her autopsy, guided by Minns. Both Brood-mothers watched, fascinated, as Asue cut the body open from crotch to neck. She altered the shape of her hand into a cutter and swung the rib cage apart, exposing the lungs and heart.

Khann examined the organs laid out in the cavity and demanded to know the function of them all. As she studied the intestines, she saw them move slightly in muscular contraction.

"Asue, I see that like ourselves, death amongst this species is not instantaneous," she observed. "I ask a great thing of you at this moment."

"What do you want, Khann?" Asue straightened up and said to the much larger form, "You have only to ask, my friend."

"I require a piece of living tissue from this man to analyse in my brood pouch. I need to study the cell structure before it dies," the Gnathe replied.

"Take what you require, Lady Khann," Asue answered, standing aside.

Khann-link-sool extended her hands and flexed the muscles of the index finger. A razor sharp, hooked claw rose from out of a sheath of skin and into view. The Gnathe reached forwards with her arm and removed a short piece of lower intestine from the dead man's abdomen, cutting it free from the surrounding mass.

"This is all that I will need, Asue. Thank you. I must retreat somewhere quiet for some time while I study the cell structure," the old scientist observed to the silver guardian.

She pushed the specimen of alien flesh deep into the egg receptacle inside her pouch. Automatic reflexes took over as the thin membranes inside her pouch enfolded the piece of intestine. Connections were made to the cell walls and nutrient juices bathed the small part of Carlos's body and kept it alive. Khann sent her will inwards to the new piece of life in her body and sat in rapture as she studied it.

Asue and Minns continued the autopsy on the body of Carlos, paying particular attention to the ravaged lungs. Alexander had contacted the citadel and Jo-jo, giving his report on the adventure while the rescue party ate and rested. The entire episode had been transmitted over the televised news system to the population of the habitat. Evening had fallen outside and visibility was getting worse as the vessel carried on retracing its way across the mountain ranges. The main computer continued to link with Kamiel, overseeing any problems.

Ender-whann-soo had stayed with the autopsy until it was finished. The body had been sectioned and tightly bagged up in airtight nannite containers.

As she turned away, Kamiel walked with her back to the more familiar world of the carriers and Zanth. She climbed into the hollow of the faithful carrier that had taken them through the swamp and across the valley. The Gnathe picked over the supply of pod-vines separating the beans from the husks. The pods would feed the animals and the Gnathe would harvest beans for consumption. Some would be saved for planting in the household's new settlement.

"Lady Ender," Kamiel said, "you owe me an explanation. Why was it necessary to ensure Link-soo-shan lived to return to the Imperial City?"

The Gnathe bent forwards to put her head on a level with Kamiel's and replied quietly, "Search the memories you took from Chang's mind. Examine the ritual known as the Rite of Succession and you will see why. The Tyrant will return defeated and weak. A great deal of her kindred will be dead or injured. Her sister's children could be inherited by someone else by now."

"Do not fence with me, Brood-mother. There is more that you are keeping secret from me. I need to know the entire story. Now tell me. It will make no difference to the outcome of this voyage. We both serve a common interest in settling you on the other side of this vast mountain range."

Ender-whann-soo recounted all that the old Brood-mother had instructed Trann to do at the Trading Post and the city. When she had finished, Kamiel stood thoughtfully at her feet.

He looked up at her and said, "How sure are you that Trann will succeed?"

"It is a risk, Kaameel," the Brood-mother replied. "I do not know for sure what will happen. Much depends on Shoo-lin's egg sister, Jewel-khann and my daughter, Natel-soo's use of the telekinetic powers of the new crystals recently found. I shall know more if and when Trann uses the master crystal to contact me. First she has to convince the other members of the advisory council that Chang's death is meaningful. Also, her kindred have to be impressed into Trann's service. Nothing is certain, Kaameel. My household is loyal. They will follow me wherever I choose to go and I choose to go with you."

Coen-soo appeared over the side of the carrier and her eyes reflected the love she possessed for her Brood-mother. She quickly scrambled inside the hollow and began to fuss around the massive form.

"Is there anything I can get you, Reverend Lady? Do you require water or food? Shoo-lin has been shown how to work a thing called a microwave oven, by Asue. There is hot food to be had and soup," she excitedly cried. "There are so many wonders to examine and so much to see!"

Ender-whann-soo got up and prepared to climb out of the carrier. Her mind was preoccupied with many things, most of all, how to redirect the genetic codes for the construction of hands and fingers. The new life inside her would have small need for claws in this different world of the human and Gnathe alliance.

Kamiel nodded to her and said, "Do not worry, Lady Ender. All will be well. Keep me informed of any news."

CHAPTER 12

▼

Trann-link-khann entered the Imperial City quietly and made her way into the royal chambers. The Keeper's brood were just armed with sythers, while Trann and some of her group wore a small dull green crystal at their necks as well. The Imperial Guards were still stationed at the entrance to the inner chambers. They watched the approach of the company with an arrogant stare.

A Leading Guard in the livery of the Commander's kindred halted the advancing Brood-mothers and said, "What do you want, Lady Trann? You have come here armed. Why?"

Trann swung the sack through the air and let it fall at the guard's feet. The guard looked at the bloodstained sack suspiciously and gave it a tentative poke with her clawed toe.

"What is this, Lady Trann?" she exclaimed, stepping back a pace and sweeping her tail aside.

"Open it, guard," Trann commanded.

The Gnathe did so and rolled the bloody trophy across the highly polished floor. All the guards stepped forwards to examine the severed head of the Commander. There were gasps of amazement and shock. Several of the Gnathe drew their sythers from out of their scabbards and moved towards the intruding force.

"Halt, guards!" Trann called out, her voice carrying the nuances of command. "This is the head of your Brood-mother, the Commander. By the rite of succession, I claim the Kindred of Chang-soo-shan and give sanctuary with my household. I killed her. You are mine. Dispute me and you will die!"

"I am of Link-soo-shan's kindred and I do not recognise your authority," said one of the closer guards, reaching out with her syther towards the intruders.

"Nor I," called another Gnathe.

"It is the Commander's head," retorted a Group Captain, "thus by law we of Chang-soo-shan's kindred belong to this Brood-mother."

"You will be claimed by the Ultimate Ruler when she returns, you fool!" shouted a leading guard. "Do you think this frail Brood-mother would be capable of killing our great Lady, Link-soo-shan?"

Trann-link-khann reached out with her mind and pinched shut the main valves to the guard's double heart. At the same time she executed a forward stroke with her syther and pierced the Gnathe's neck, severing her windpipe. The guard squatted back on her haunches, choking on her own blood. Trann tore the valves apart with her mind just to make sure of a speedy death.

"Is there anyone else here that believes that I am frail? I mean to challenge the Tyrant when she finally returns. I will beat her in the arena, as I easily put her sister to my sword. She will die. I suggest that you bide your tongues and submit to me now."

Another guard chopped down with her weapon from the side, rushing the intruding force. Jewel-khann struck out with her augmented power and cut the optic nerves from the Gnathe's brain to her eyes. She then gave a mental push at the guard's foot, tangling her ankles together, causing her to stumble blindly forwards. Jewel-khann's razor sharp sword thrust deep into the guard's chest and she sidestepped the thrashing body.

"My kindred may be smaller than you, but they are much faster. Before you can even think of a blow, you will be opened up upon this floor. Now yield to me and live," the Brood-mother aggressively ordered, swinging her head from side to side.

Chang's kindred separated from their cousins and flanked the new Ruler's people, facing the other Imperial Guards.

"Reverend Lady, if you lose the rite of succession, the Ultimate Ruler's anger will be terrible to behold," a nervous guard uttered with fear. "She will slowly torture any of us who side with you now."

"I do not have your Brood-mother's savage tastes, guard. I suggest you disappear for a while. Go south, away from the city, if you wish and rejoin me when this is over. Be warned, however, I shall remember who supported me and who did not. Know this, all of you, I have bred a new Gnathe and the future is going to be different from what you have been used to," the Brood-mother warned them. "You have been bred large and strong, but slow of foot and thought. My kindred can outfight you and kill you in hand-to-hand combat. If you doubt it, challenge any of my daughters now."

The Imperial Guards shuffled their feet and eyed the two dead Gnathe sprawled upon the floor with unease. Finally an older, scarred veteran stood forward fingering the blade of her syther.

"I have been my Brood-mother's guard for many years. She is my Lady and always will be. She raised me and taught me the order of her rule. I will challenge the one who killed my sister," she said.

"Very well guard. It will be as you wish. Clear the area and fall back to the walls, my children. Jewel-khann is the sister of Shoo-lin, the Beast-master of this city," Trann retorted the massed crowd. "She is the new breed and the future."

A hush lay over both forces as the glow crystals brightened in their alcoves. Evening was well advanced outside and the inside of the Royal chambers became lighter as the stored energy in the crystals leaked out at a steady rate. The old guard eased herself warily to the centre of the polished floor. She kicked a mat away from under her foot and sent it sliding towards the wall with a sweep of her tail. She stood poised and ready, the sharp point of the syther waving back and forth in front of Jewel-khann's eyes.

The young Gnathe concentrated her will into the crystal's field of influence, waiting for the old guard's first offensive stroke. Suddenly the scarred veteran feinted to the left, swung round on her feet, whipping her tail across to where the young female stood. At the same instant she brought her syther to the right in a sharp chopping blow. This killing manoeuvre had worked well in the past. Jewel-khann deftly spun out of reach, pulling the guard's feet together with her mind, tripping the older Gnathe and causing her to stumble against the wall. She had leapt over the swinging tail and flicked the razor-sharp edge of her syther across the old veteran's upper shoulder.

"One blood to me, old one," the young Gnathe taunted as the much larger guard thrust herself away from the wall.

The older female brought her sword round in a hacking cut to Jewel-khann's legs. The young Gnathe pushed down hard on the syther with her mind, causing it to score the floor of the Banilik tree. This time she leaned forwards and pierced the sword-arm of the veteran. Once more, she severed the optic nerves to the eyes, as she had to the other guard that she had killed. Before the blindness became apparent to the watching crowd, Jewel-khann slipped in close to the older female. She brought the point of her syther to the under jaw of the old fighter and thrust upwards into the brain.

Jewel-khann kicked her opponent away with her powerful foot and spun round, calling out to the assembled Imperial Guard, "Is there anyone else eager to try my fighting skill?"

The kindred of the Ultimate Ruler looked at the body of one of their best fighters, with disbelieving eyes. No one spoke or moved.

"If you are satisfied, I need to use the master crystal to contact Ender-whann-soo. Oh yes, she lives, kindred of the twin tyrants. By now, Link-soo-shan will have been defeated and will be returning with whatever troops are still alive," the Brood-mother grimly said. "Now move out of my way and accept my offer of sanctuary within my household."

"We yield, Lady Trann-link-khann, and beg the sanctuary of your household," a guard called out.

Trann made her way into the crystal chamber, leaving her company to take charge. The Keeper came with her and took up her position on the other side of the strange gemstone, perching on the communications rail.

Sing-trow-sool stared at her new Empress across the crystal and said to her, "What is your plan of action, Trann?"

"First I shall contact Ender-whann-soo with the news of my take-over. Let us hope that all has been successful with her situation," the Brood-mother replied. "After that, I shall contact the heads of the leading families in meta-concert to give them my intentions. During this time you will block off Link-soo-shan's receiving stone until I am ready for her. Are you ready?"

"Yes, Trann. Open the pathways and I will tag along in the background," the Keeper replied.

Trann lent forwards from her position on the communications perch and placed the palms of her hands against the crystal's faceted surface. Using her mind's increased power, she once again traced the pathways to the tiny flames flickering in the darkness. As the crystal warmed to her touch, the paths became clearer. There in the foggy world of the mind-link was the glowing light of Link-soo-shan's presence. Beyond it and steadily travelling away, was the Group Captain's receiver, burning like a lone beacon in the night. She marvelled at the distance it had travelled since she had last contacted her old friend. Carefully the Brood-mother homed in on the shard hanging around Ender-whann-soo's neck.

Ender-whann-soo had just enjoyed a bowl of meaty broth, cooked in the human's strange box that they referred to as a microwave oven. Khann had eaten gratefully and had been cleaned and brushed by Jotin-soo, who had allotted herself the task of administering to the old Brood-mother's needs. Shoo-lin had placed himself next to the younger Brood-mother and was enthusing about the new ideas he had picked up from Alexander and Kamiel, when the communications crystal began to resonate.

Ender held the stone tightly in her massive hand and motioned Shoo-lin to shut up, as her mind became attuned to Trann-link-khann's influence. The new would-be Empress looked out of Ender-whann-soo's eyes in amazement at the alien surroundings.

"Where are you, Ender?" she asked.

"I am inside Kamiel's floating carrier, Trann," she replied. "We are safe from Link-shoo-shan and are at this moment flying through the night air, across mountain ranges towards our new home."

"All went well then, for you and your household?" Trann asked thoughtfully, "How many of you died or were injured?"

"None of my household were hurt in any way, old friend," Ender replied. "I regret to tell you that four of the aliens died trying to help us escape. I will show you what happened since you last contacted me, then you must give me an up-date on your situation."

The two Brood-mothers exchanged memories and information for some time, reflecting on the events that had transpired.

"This is a fearsome debt of honour you have to discharge, Ender. These new friends of yours are a brave and courageous people. They have risked much in this rescue. It is difficult to absorb the idea of the air we breathe being full of deadly little creatures. You say that the man called Carlos died from a fungus growing in his lungs! What does Khann say about the piece of alien flesh she has secreted in her pouch?"

"She says the cell structure is similar to something that she has encountered before, long ago. The problem has given her a new lease of life. I have never seen her so happy and preoccupied," Ender replied to her friend. "What are your plans for the next stage?"

"Before I tell you, bring Shoo-lin into contact with your crystal," Trann answered. "I should like to speak to him for a moment."

Ender-whann-soo beckoned the Gnathe male forwards and placed his hand onto the warm stone. Shoo-lin was apprehensive, as males were not allowed to use the communications device. To his delight, he felt the approving mind of his Brood-mother envelope him.

"You have done well, young male. Learn all you can from these new friends of yours. Maybe we will meet again after this is all over."

"Take care, Reverend Mother Trann, and do not underestimate Link-soo-shan. She has been taught a bitter lesson here. Be prepared for her return from beyond the swamp," Shoo-lin replied.

"I shall, young one, never fear. Now, Ender and I have business with the heads of the families," she answered. "Goodbye Shoo-lin, you are a credit to me."

Shoo-lin removed his hand from the crystal and left the Brood-mother to her lonely communication to find Khann-link-sool.

"Sing-trow-sool, I feel your presence!" Ender exclaimed.

"I am here, old friend," the Keeper replied. "I have risked all to serve Trann-link-khann in her bid for the Empire's rule. We appear to have convinced Chang's kindred to throw in with us. Link's females will await the outcome of Trann's challenge."

"It is time to attempt the link-up of the meta-concert with heads of the families," Trann reminded them. "Where is Khann?"

"Shoo-lin has fetched her and she enters the link now," Ender replied, sandwiching the stone between her hands and the older Brood-mother's.

The powerful mind of the Elder rang clear in the mental tie-up. "I am here, young Trann and Sing."

The old Brood-mother rapidly sifted through the events at the Imperial City by picking over Trann's memories.

"Good," she projected, "everything has gone well so far. Now form the mind link. You know what to do, Sing?"

"Yes, Reverend Grand-mother Khann. I will begin now," Sing-trow-sool replied.

From her location on the communications perch, the large form shifted to a more comfortable position. She put forth her will and blocked off the flame of Link-soo-shan's crystal in the mental fog. Sing-trow-sool then extended a crossover link between the two Brood-mothers in the airship and the main communications crystal.

Once that had been established, Trann began to extend the crystal's augmented mental touch to the other tiny points of light in the telepathic maze. One by one, the mind touch reached out and made contact. Within a short time span, the whole of the Gnathen Empire was awake and connected to Trann's mind. She put forth her challenge to Link-soo-shan's rule, including the fact that she alone had killed the Commander and thus had inherited her kindred. Trann was careful to exclude the fact of Chang's madness from them, but told them of Link-soo-shan's defeat at the hands of the aliens helping Ender-whann-soo. They were told of the imminent escape over the mountains to the new world and the alien's part of it in saving the fugitives. She then proposed the coming of the new order.

The massed minds conferred with one another in the telepathic link. All were of the opinion that to see the tyranny ended would be a better life for all of them. Many had doubts on the outcome of Trann's challenge in the arena. Finally they all agreed to back her challenge by the rite of succession. They would travel to the Imperial City to witness the fight in the great amphitheatre. All hoped to see Trann win, but all had seen and some had experienced the power of the mightiest Gnathe ever born. They marvelled that one such as Trann-link khann could have overcome the mighty Commander. Finally the assembled minds began to pull out of the circuit until only the original four were left connected together.

Link-soo-shan had returned to her camp, carefully skirting the area of Kamiel's traps. Unknown to her, the nannite strands had self-destructed and had disappeared without trace. She gave the steadily retreating airship a venomous look and turned away in the driving rain. She surveyed the remains of her once invincible force. Very few of them were unscathed. Only a handful was totally fit and capable of the journey back to the Imperial City. All of them were cold, wet and hungry. Somehow she would have to get them back to the Empire. She stood erect, towering over her kindred and beckoned the fittest towards her.

"You there, come here," she commanded. "Ride over the battlefield and look for survivors. Collect any Zanth capable of being ridden. Butcher any that are badly wounded, but set free those that you consider can survive without us. Do not leave any of your sisters to die of their wounds. Save whom you can. We must return to the Imperial City as soon as we have finished here. Bring back to the camp enough raw Zanth to feed us for several days. We will have to wait for the rain to stop before we can build a fire. When you return, we will eat some of the meat raw and keep the rest for the days ahead. We will retreat from this place tomorrow."

The fittest Gnathe nodded their agreement and mounted the few Zanth remaining that could be ridden. They fanned out along the shores of the lake, seeking the least injured amongst the fallen.

Link-soo-shan walked over to the row of wounded guards that lay under the improvised shelter of a large bush, and said, "Who amongst you feels incapable of the journey home? We must start back soon and find better cover for the night."

A thin, pain-filled voice spoke up. "My Lady, I will not be able to come back with you. My legs are smashed and my side is broken. Give me peace, Lady Link."

The Brood-mother bent down and cradled the head and shoulders of her badly injured daughter. She held the Gnathe's jaw and placed her hand behind the neck, gazing into the loyal eyes of her offspring.

"You have served me well and I am pleased," the Brood-mother said. "May you find rest and a place by my side in the halls of power."

She gave a quick twist of her hands and heard the neck snap as her daughter died. A quick survey of the injured found three more partly conscious. After checking over their condition, she regretfully sent them also into oblivion. Link-soo-shan examined the other guards and washed their wounds and bound them with pieces of torn cloth from the dead Gnathe's kilts.

The other guards returned from the grisly task she had set them, laden with strips of Zanth. These they had cut from the freshly dead flanks of the riding beast it had been necessary to kill. As Link-soo-shan squatted, munching on a piece of stringy meat, she felt the communication crystal hanging around her neck begin to resonate.

"At last," she thought, "someone is curious about where I am and what has happened to me."

She opened her powerful mind and found herself contacted to the mind of Trann-link-khann, with three other minds in the background.

The Brood-mother did a quick scan and asked in shock, "What are you doing in my house, Trann? I know you, Keeper. What have you done with my sister, Chang?" Link-soo-shan reached out to the mind link and recognised Ender-whann-soo and the elder Khann-link-sool and sent a startled message, "You two are here also!"

"Listen to me," came the icy tones of Khann-link-sool. "Your rule of terror is over. Trann has killed the Commander, your sister. Her skull will rest next to your Brood-mother's in the hall of power."

"Did you find my mad sister easy, Trann?" replied the Ultimate Ruler. "You killed her while she was helpless! You are without honour. I will come for you as soon as I can. I will cut you to pieces! I shall also remember your treachery, Keeper, when I kill you. You will die slowly, begging for your death in my sister's memory!"

"I have invoked the rite of succession, Tyrant, and have broadcast the challenge far and wide," answered Trann-link-khann. "There will be a full council waiting for you when you return. We shall have the amphitheatre ready and in it you will die, witnessed by the heads of the families. With your evil presence removed, I intend to open up trade links with the aliens. Your time is over, Link-soo-shan. A new era begins."

"You have to face me in combat first, you puny fool!" raged the Brood-mother. "I will take pleasure from breaking you in front of the spineless fools who support you! I am coming for you, Trann."

"You may try, Link-soo-shan. I await you. Do not think to rally all your forces against me. By inheriting your sister's slow-witted troops, I have cancelled your kindred's threat. Goodbye Tyrant," the Gnathe calmly stated and closed down the link with the fuming Brood-mother.

"There, my friends, it is done," Trann broadcasted to the receding minds of Ender and Khann. "I will keep you advised on events. Establish the new Gnathen foothold in the unused lands. Somehow I feel that we will meet again."

"I do hope so, Trann," replied Khann-link-sool. "Our race stands to gain so much by the knowledge of these alien people. I am greedy for it. Be very careful of Link-soo-shan. Do not take victory for granted. Practise with the use of those telekinetic crystals until you are in perfect harmony with them."

"I shall, old friend. Believe me, I will. I am all too aware that I am no match against the greatest fighting Gnathe ever born. I have to make it seem as though I have won fairly. The killings so far against the few Imperial Guards that opposed my challenge have shown what can be done. In the arena, in front of the other Brood-mothers, it will have to be done more subtly. I have some ideas to put into practise. Goodbye for now."

In the darkness of the cloudy night the storm had begun to play itself out. The airship continued to face against the wind, tacking across the steady force and slowly making headway towards the valley where Rescue One and its crew had encountered the Terra-raptor. Here, Kamiel intended to put the ship down and allow the Gnathe to gather food and supplies. Also, pens for the animals needed to be built and perches for the Gnathe to travel comfortably upon. It would be a harder journey back to the Habitat against the prevailing wind. The two silver forms sat side by side in the command and co-pilot's chairs. All was quiet and still. The humanoid crew and Gnathen passengers were sound asleep. Only the unsleeping Guardians kept watch.

"You have remained silent, Asue," Kamiel transmitted on their private band. "It will do no good for you to brood. Speak to me."

Asue turned in her chair and regarded Kamiel with a basilisk stare. "Feel my grief, Kamiel. We have lost some of our children. I mourn their loss."

A feeling of pain washed over Kamiel's circuits and he bowed his head and replied, "They are not your children, Asue. We may have created them from our stored patterns, but they do not belong to us. They are free spirits, able to choose their own destinies and how they choose to die. Out there, on the battlefield, I felt just as you. As I stood in the rain after burying Charley and David, I saw our programmer and creator, the original Alexander. He reminded me of my duties. Open your mind and I will show you all that he said."

Asue sat, overwhelmed by Kamiel's vision from his memory banks of the far distant past.

Finally she answered softly, "You carry a hard burden, Kamiel. I am glad that this is not in my programming."

"Thank you, Asue, for your understanding," he replied. "We should reach the mountain-locked valley very soon. Much still needs doing if we are all to survive the voyage. The beasts require a great deal of water and fodder. We can fill the water tanks when we set down and get the Gnathe to show us what vegetation we need to collect and store. What worries me is the problem of their dung and urine! Those carriers certainly shift a huge amount of foliage. The hold was not designed for the portage of such creatures."

"We must unload them in the valley and construct the pens in the airship there," Asue transmitted. "I will contact the Citadel and see how the new home for the Gnathe is coming along."

Asue entered into communication with the unsleeping Sharn and Minns to discuss progress, leaving Kamiel to his own thoughts as the vessel continued to fly into the first pearly rays of the dawning sun.

Link-soo-shan perched on a tree limb, brooding over the information that she had received from the usurping Trann-link-khann. She cursed the fate which had set her on this course. Why would a Gnathe, as ill versed in fighting as the Lady Trann, think that she could beat the Ultimate Ruler in combat? She must have developed a new weapon or technique that had given her the confidence to challenge for the rite of succession.

"Damn you, Trann, what have you got?" she thought desperately.

She began to contemplate alternatives if she found herself losing in the arena. Uneasily, she fell asleep surrounded by the handful of her kindred.

She awakened with the dawn and stretched her limbs, swishing her powerful tail from side to side. During the uncomfortable night she had come to a decision.

"Awake all of you and listen to me very carefully," she called to the stirring Gnathe. "I have a great deal to tell you and I require your loyalty."

They listened to her as she told them everything she had heard and experienced over the crystal mind link. She had always been obeyed without question; to be taken into her trust was beyond previous experience.

"My Lady Link, we understand what you have told us," one of Chang's surviving guards retorted to her, "but what do you want us to do?"

"The Lady Trann has found some way to possibly defeat me. You have to contemplate which you would rather do. Will you submit to this Brood-mother who did not raise you, or continue to support me, if I have to run from the arena? For I have no wish to die at her hands. I would rather be a wound in her side in the future."

"She killed my Brood-mother when she was defenceless, my Lady!" cried out one of Chang's daughters. "I will not submit to her rule."

"Nor I, Brood-mother," shouted one of her own.

Another called out: "What would you have us do to help you, my Lady?"

"You will enter the city with me, but some of you must quietly vanish and find as many of my kindred as you can persuade to continue their allegiance to me under the circumstances. Saddle up fresh mounts and gather supplies for a long journey. Kidnap any young, breeding-fit males that you can find. Bind and gag them. Tie them inside a carrier if you can. If not, take them onto your Zanth. Meet me at the bridge. If I live, I will meet you there. One of you must be at the royal stables with a fresh mount for me. If I win, it will not matter what you do, but if I lose and manage to flee, you must be ready to help. I will start again in this hidden valley. With new males for breeding, yourselves and any of my kindred you can gather, I will be a scourge to this new order. I have learnt a great deal from our encounter with these aliens. I have seen the results of the way they think. They will not defeat me again so easily. I intend to breed and assemble an army; quite different to any that has walked this world before. We will take back what may be taken from us. Will you support me?"

The answer was unanimous—the urge to obey was too strong to deny the Brood-mother's wishes. For one thing, without her they would have no standing as 'adopted' kindred and there would be old scores to settle from the past.

"Where you lead, we will follow, Lady Link," cried out one of Chang's daughters.

"Very well, my kindred. It is settled," said the Ultimate Ruler. "One thing I need to know. How did my Group Captain, Koet-shan, really die?"

"I, Jaffin-shan, killed her," replied a veteran fighter of Link-shoo-shan's Imperial Guard.

The Brood-mother swung her massive form around and fixed the Gnathe with a hard stare, asking the one word, "Why?"

"She would have led us to our deaths on the top of the hill, needlessly. We were confronted by the silver thing, who told us that the area had been prepared by him, for us to die in traps, as we had died before. The aliens' carrier was already floating in the air above us and could not be reached." Jaffin-shan looked the deadly form of her leader in the eyes.

"She would not listen to reason, my Lady," said another Gnathe, walking forwards to stand beside Jaffin-shan. "She attacked me when I refused to rush blindly into the traps the silver thing had told us he had set."

"I need Gnathe of independent thought, who do not follow orders blindly," Link-soo-shan retorted to the apprehensive pair. "You, Jaffin-shan, will lead the party that splits off from those who will accompany me to the arena. You will gather more of my kindred, as I have previously explained. Do you agree?"

"Yes, my Lady Link, I shall do all that I can to make sure all is ready, should you need to flee the Rite of Succession. I am yours, Brood-mother. I swear my life belongs to you."

"If you fail me, your life will be forfeit anyway," Link-soo-shan replied. "Remember all of you—there will be no turning back from this, once we begin. You, Nagoth-shan, will do something for me that requires stealth. In my chambers is a carved wooden box with the emblem of a closed eye on the lid. Have you seen this before?"

"Yes Lady Link, I have. You keep it inside a chest by your sleeping perch in the Royal Chambers," replied the Gnathe. "What do you require of me?"

"When we enter the Imperial City, you must get to my chambers and steal that box from under Trann-link-khann's nose. Get it to me before I enter the arena of battle. I think my life will depend on it. Do you understand? I think that the usurper, Trann, has been working in secret with a new crystal. I will not find out until I am in the arena with her. Inside the box is something that may give me a better chance when we meet. The rest of you will have to follow my lead at the time," Link-soo-shan told them. "Mount up. We travel back to the Imperial City. Mark this place well, for we may be returning to it."

Obediently the remaining Gnathe climbed onto their Zanth and rode steadily towards the way out of the hidden valley. They were quiet and thoughtful as they rode. The Brood-mother's honesty and need for their unstinting loyalty lay heavily on their minds. All of them knew, that should Link-soo-shan lose her life in the arena, the only thing that they could expect would be heavy servitude at the beck and call of someone with a grudge. The more active members of the Brood-mother's schemes faced execution for the parts that they would play.

As the sun rose higher in the sky, drying out the subdued company and the land about them, the area began to change. They had left the harsh uplands behind them and began to travel through lush, more fruitful surroundings. Wild Pod-vine plants wound themselves around other fruiting trees. Link-soo-shan looked about the countryside and decided to call a halt.

"Stop here for a while. Gather food from the area around us and build a fire," she called to her kindred. "Let us rest and feast. I see no reason to hurry back. Trann-link-khann can wait for us. We will return strong and fit."

The Gnathe hobbled their Zanth to prevent them from wandering off and disappeared into the undergrowth of woodland trees and vegetation. Link-soo-shan used her greater strength to break up the dead wood the females had scavenged until she had a sizeable pile. She held her receiving crystal to the sun and used the focusing power of the lens-like shape to ignite a heap of dried grass-like vegetation. Soon she was rewarded by the flicker of hot flames and fed the tiny fire with small sticks until it had become a steady blaze.

The Gnathe returned with wild beans, edible roots, fruit and began to prepare them. Some they roasted in the embers, others would be eaten raw. The meat from the slaughtered Zanth they cooked and dried for the journey back through the swamp and Ender-whann-soo's burnt lands. The company began to eat and relax until all of them were full to gorging point.

After a time, Link-soo-shan stood, towering over them and said, "We must try to get to the entrance to the swamp before sun-down. We should also look for alternative ways of returning to the Imperial lands down the cliff face. Anything would be better than travelling through the swamp again. I would like to be back on Imperial ground tomorrow. Mount up, all of you, and we can move at a gentle pace."

The remaining Imperial Guard mounted immediately and began to urge the Zanth at a steady pace towards the direction of the swamp entrance. They were bemused by the change in Link-soo-shan. It unsettled them to be asked to do things, instead of being ordered. Yet they felt that this new attitude of their ruler would encourage them to do anything that she required. Their fear and respect had been replaced by a fierce loyalty they could not explain. They knew she could be just as ruthless as ever, but somehow something had changed in their relationship.

CHAPTER 13

▼

Alexander awoke with the early morning sun illuminating the inside of the control cabin and the dormitory. He swung himself out of the hammock, shaved and washed quickly. He glanced over to the hairy form of his old friend, Joom. A large hairy arm hung down out of the side of the sleeping ape's hammock. Soft snores continued to flow from out of the soundly sleeping body.

"Let him sleep," Alexander thought. "I will go and see our new friends. Kamiel will help me on with a suit after I get some breakfast into myself."

He walked rapidly forwards to the control cabin and saw the slender silver shape of Asue seated in the command chair. The co-pilot's chair was empty, so Alex sat next to the guardian and looked out of the observation window at the view below. The airship had been tethered to the valley floor and was steadily being winched down to ground level. Asue was reducing the buoyancy of the vessel by cooling the helium inside the inner bag. There was an abrupt silence as Asue cut the power to the diesel engines, merely letting the electrical generator tick over to provide power for the internal systems until all batteries were fully charged.

"Good morning, Alexander, you are up early," Asue said to him.

"Yes, Asue, there is too much to do and think about to be able to sleep," he replied "Where is Kamiel?"

"He is down on the surface making sure that all the tethers are secure. We have a great deal do here until we can head home," Asue answered and pointed at the vegetation profusely growing outside. The Gnathe must gather food for themselves and fodder for their animals. We need to take on plenty of water for these beasts as they drink a great deal. Kamiel and I will need to alter the design of the hold somewhat to accommodate them."

"Can we help in any way?" Alex asked. "We could go out in our survival suits and lend a hand."

"I would prefer that you all stayed safely inside. Remember, Carlos died because his suit was torn," Asue admonished him.

"You can forget about that, Asue. If you think we are going to stay in here until you fly us back to the Citadel, you've another think coming. I for one am going outside, even if I just walk about. Frederick and the others of his team will feel the same. After breakfast, I am going to talk with the Gnathe and finalise some plans."

Alex got out of the chair and made his way to the galley to heat up some dried rations with some water. As he triggered the microwave oven to produce hot porridge, he was aware that other members of the crew were stirring. Pouring hot milk and water into his coffee mug, he turned round and addressed the awakened crew.

"Morning, all of you. We have reached the great valley that we passed over on our way here. The Gnathe need to gather food for themselves and fodder for their animals. We can take some time to rest and recover from the events that took place yesterday. We are safe from Link-soo-shan's forces here. This is an opportunity to find out more about this world. When I have finished here, I am joining Kamiel on the ground. Any that wishes to follow can suit up and come outside as you please."

Alex walked over to the locker and selected a suit from amongst the number hanging there. The nannite garment quickly adjusted itself to the form of his body. He pressed the transparent globe close to the shape of his head so that it fitted snugly to his skull, leaving his mouth free to breathe through the air filter. Asue checked the seals and the survival suit and filled the water bottle for him.

"I will stay here and check the other suits as the other members of the crew decide to follow you," Asue said. "Be careful, Alex, the fabric is very tough and I know it will take a great deal to penetrate it, but I still worry."

"I know you worry, Asue, but try to understand," replied Alex. "I have lived over one hundred and twenty years of my life inside the domes of the Habitat. This world is real in a way I cannot explain. Our home is beautiful and we are grateful for it, old friend, but this place is wild. We have to explore it. This valley seems a much safer place than the plains outside the Habitat. Have you spoken to Sharn and Minns about the progress of the Gnathe's new home?"

"I have, Alex, and all is going well. By the time we arrive it should be safe from outside predators," she answered. "The perimeter wall now extends for more than twenty miles in any direction. Minns assures me that nothing large or dangerous exists inside. There is plenty of foliage similar to the types cultivated by the Gnathe growing in abundance. We are also diverting part of the White River through the area, for irrigation purposes."

"Thanks, Asue, I can tell our new friends about it. I can show them, using the holo-vision system piped through into the hold. I will go through the barrier now and see if they are awake."

With that, Alex opened the airlock door and closed it behind him. Halfway across the floor he felt the resistance of the nannite screen as it flowed over his suit. Anything not made of the nannite material would have been torn down by the devouring microscopic machines and re-assembled as part of the screen. Alex spun the wheel on the other airlock door, opened it and stepped into the hold.

The cargo door had already been opened and sloped gently down to the ground. The giant beasts that the Gnathe referred to as carriers had been led out and left to forage for themselves under the watchful eyes of some of the field hands. The Zanth had been unloaded during the previous evening and various boxes and jars were being stacked in storage cupboards around the walls. This was being directed by Kamiel, who was showing the attentive Gnathe how to operate the panels. They pushed buttons and watched the panels open and close. Some were operating the microwave ovens in the hold kitchen and were cooking pots of food, distributing them around to the other busy Gnathe. Taking charge of this exercise was the female, Coen-soo and her sister Jotin-soo. Shoo-lin was examining every new thing in sight and worrying Kamiel for explanations. The two Brood-mothers stood apart from all the activity, talking to each other. Alexander strolled over to them.

"Hello, Alexander, this is a good day for you," Ender said to the human. "My Grand Brood-mother has something to tell you that will interest you greatly."

"Yes, human, come here and listen to what I have to tell you," the old Gnathe called out to him.

Alex stood in front of the two towering beings that were squatting on their haunches, apart from the other members of their company. Kamiel noticed the arrival of the Habitat's mayor and decided to join the group.

"The piece of flesh you allowed me to study still lives. I have broken it down to individual cells. They continue to sub-divide and are reproducing themselves in my nutrient juices. I was able to splice my own genes into their living cell structures during the night. Many of the cells have retained their identity and continue to thrive," Khann explained to the small group.

"I do not understand quite what you are trying to tell me," Alex replied, looking thoughtfully into the eyes of the old scientist. "How does this affect us?"

"If I can study more samples of your people's living tissue, I may be able to manufacture the same type of immunity serum we give our own young when they are born. We regurgitate it when we give them their first meal. It is part of our bodily fluids and is also part of the bonding process between Brood-mother and her young. It would carry just enough of our genes to become part of your cell structure without changing you too much," the alien geneticist told them.

Kamiel thought through all of the ramifications rapidly and asked, "How much living tissue would be required?"

"A small piece, no larger than the top joint of Alexander's finger would be enough," Khann-link-sool answered, bending forwards to scrutinise the human's hand.

Alex jerked his hand away from the dispassionate gaze and turned to look at Kamiel.

"I could remove a piece from your backside, Alex, right now," Kamiel said to the stunned man. "Shall we do this now?"

Alexander shuddered and agreed with a nod of his head. "Do it Kamiel, before my nerve fails!"

"Lay over that bench then, old friend, and I will enter your suit and remove a small piece of your tissue," the silver form exclaimed, pointing to a vacant area in front of them.

Alexander lay face down over the hard bench, gritting his teeth and waited for Kamiel to penetrate his suit. There was a sharp sting from his left side, but it soon faded, to be replaced with a feeling of numbness.

Kamiel lent over Alexander and placed his right hand upon the rear of the suit. He quickly merged with the nannite covering and pressed on, until he made contact with the man's warm flesh. The surface of his hand changed shape and flowed into the living tissue until it had enveloped a long thin cylinder of flesh. He quickly withdrew, closing the flesh together as he did so, leaving just a slight bruise behind. The material of the suit closed together and flowed away from his extremity as he removed himself from Alexander's life support system.

"I have a piece, encapsulated from the air, inside the end of my arm," explained Kamiel. "What now, Khann?"

Alexander got to his feet and gingerly stood up to watch the proceedings.

Khann said to the silver guardian: "Put your arm deep into my breeding pouch and release the piece of tissue into the part of my body that opens for you. I will do the rest."

Kamiel did as he was asked and felt a muscular dilation occur in the bottom of the pouch. He thrust his bulbous hand into the orifice, released the piece of flesh and withdrew.

"Thank you Kaameel," she said and shuddered with concentration. "I shall require samples from your male and female crew members, both human and ape today and over the next few days. Now I must retire and study this new piece."

Khann's eyes glazed over as the mighty form went into a trance-like state and squatted immobile.

"She will not stir from this spot for at least a quarter-day," Ender-whann-soo explained. "Shall we go outside? Let me show you something of my world. Although this area is completely wild."

"Before we do that, let me show you how events are progressing at your new home, my friend," Alexander replied. "Follow me to the hold's communications console, by the kitchen."

Alex led the way over to the section of the hold that was cordoned off from the general area. He keyed into the control circuit and the barrier lifted away, revealing a chair and a control console.

"Computer," he said to the console, "Connect through to Jo-jo wherever she is at the Citadel and include Shan or Minns in the conversation.

"Confirmed, Alexander," the computer replied. "Accessing the Citadel now. Minns is available."

A holo-vision image of the biologist formed in the console hood and Minns nodded to Alexander, saying, "Good morning Mayor, what can I do for you? Jo-jo is still asleep in her bed. We have been very busy here, preparing the Gna-then settlement. Sharn is supervising the construction of shelters and living quarters, outside. We were very saddened by the deaths of our people, but are happy that none of the Gnathe were injured."

"I would like to show a projection of the settlement to our new friends and partners," replied Alexander, gesturing to the fascinated Gnathe gathered round the holo-vision console. "Can you show them how far you have got with the construction?"

"Of course I can, Alexander. Please stand by to receive the latest film," she answered. "This is what we transmitted earlier on the news channel last evening."

The three dimensional image of Minns shrank until she occupied a position on the side of an incredible scene. The view was from above and to the edge of the cleared area. Alex moved to the side to allow the Gnathe a better view of the settlement. They stared into the holo-vision hood, pointing and chattering rapidly amongst themselves. Murmurs of approval went through the group, as the land was revealed. They could see the start of an irrigation system, being dug out by strange machinery.

"What manner of beasts are these? I have never seen anything like them. Your people seem to be inside the things," exclaimed Shoo-lin. "How are they controlled and what are they fed on?"

"They are called machines, Shoo-lin, and we build them. They are tools, nothing more. You will be shown how to operate them if you wish. I am sure that we can adapt the controls to suit your differently shaped hands," replied the human, hopefully, as he looked at the heavily clawed hands of the Gnathe.

"I am a Beast-master, Alex. If I can control a living creature with a will, I am sure I can make a mindless thing obey me!"

"There are good woodlands inside the walls that you have constructed, to keep out the dangerous life of the plains. It looks good farmland," said Whann-lin, staring intently at the images inside the hood. "We have seeds to plant and crops to plan. We can supplement our food with wild vegetation, but it may be some time before we are completely self-sufficient."

"Do not worry, Whann. We will get by. This area is much greater than my old homestead," Ender pointed out. "I am sure we can organise ourselves properly when we get there. We are indeed in your debt, Alexander."

Alexander shrugged his shoulders and pointed to the image of the settlement, saying, "There is plenty of room over there, Ender. We have used only a small fraction of it. If your Grand-Brood-mother is successful with her immunity serum, it will be reward enough for us. We have been locked inside our artificial world too long."

"Where do your people come from, Alexander? Where is your real home? I have seen enough of your people to know that you did not originate from this world," Ender exclaimed. "I think the time has come to tell us everything about yourselves."

"How much do you know about astronomy? Have you studied the movements of the planets and moons of this system? If you have, I can show you our story much easier," said Alexander.

"We have studied the heavens with the use of magnifying lenses for generations," Ender replied. "There are star maps recorded on memory crystals in the great library, in the Imperial City. The movements of the four planets are known to us. We have observed the three gas giants and charted their orbits and I have seen the rings encircling the next world out from the sun, also its moons."

"That's good, because what I am about to tell and show you, will require that knowledge. You will also need to envisage events that are outside of your reasoning and experience," Alex explained to his attentive audience. "Kamiel, can you access the main computer at the university and draw out from the memory banks?"

"I can, my friend," answered the Guardian. "I will set up a link via our satellite and leave the selection of information to you,"

Kamiel plugged one of his fingers into a specially adapted socket. The Gnathe stared at their friend and saviour as he stood immobile, while the substance of his hand flowed into the computer console. Various lights and signals flashed on and off as Kamiel made the necessary adjustments.

"Ready Alex," he said and removed his hand, allowing the nannite material to flow back into himself.

"Computer, show the planetary system, as it exists now," the human instructed.

In the darkness of the holo-vision hood a three-dimensional scene took place. Noticing the group around the hold's control console, several of the newly 'suited up' humans and apes joined the audience. The male and female Gnathe had squatted down in semicircular rows, facing into the holo-vision hood. Frederick and Jocylene were able to look comfortably over their heads at the computer simulation, controlled by their leader.

"Watch carefully and I will show you the planetary system as it was long ago," Alex said to the silent group. He pointed at the huge, red-gold sun and altered the programme, instructing the computer to superimpose the original Solar System over the present positions of the planets. They watched, as the giant sun shrank to a yellow ball and the inner four planets emerged from inside the red star's envelope. A gasp of astonishment went round the assembled Gnathe as they saw their world replaced by a huge gas giant surrounded by many small and large moons.

"Look," Shoo-lin exclaimed, "our world had rings as well as all those moons. The sun is so tiny and yellow and there are more planets. Our world was enormous, even bigger than the ringed world that we know as the Yellow Sister and its position has changed. It is closer to the red-gold sun than its original orbit around the yellow one!"

"We could never have evolved and lived there, Alexander," Ender-whann-soo stated thoughtfully to him. "What happened? How long ago was this?"

"It would seem that our ancestors somehow moved your world to a fresh orbit, closer to the new sun, after most of the atmosphere was stripped away. How they did this we do not know, as we have no records of the events. They may even have seeded the planet with early life. As to when these events happened, we are not able to translate the period in years, for your mathematics does not have the values. Suffice to say, that the star patterns were very different then. Perhaps it would be easier to say that the time elapsed would be the time taken for the light to have reached us from some of the furthest galaxies. The third world out from the sun was our home. We called it Earth. This was our birthplace and the environment in which we evolved. We were the only intelligent life form. The apes and man had a common ancestor, but only man naturally evolved with intelligence. We genetically enhanced the apes to bring them out of their beast-like state, to become full partners in our civilisation. They brought different insights and philosophies to our ancestors' way of life. We hope that you will do the same for us. The second and fourth worlds from the sun we changed from being dead, inhospitable places, to beautiful living habitats."

Ender gasped and cried out, "You were able to travel through the emptiness between the worlds? How was this done? You say that you occupied three worlds, so how many of you were there, living on them?"

"We were as many as the grains of sand under your feet, Ender my friend. I will show you some of the great cities of the three worlds. We had conquered sickness and want. All were free to pursue their own interests and destinies. It was a golden age. For we have known terrible conflicts between ourselves, before we came of age. We built weapons of mass destruction, capable of destroying whole worlds and lived with the fear that they would be used. Then, a great ape philosopher showed us the way to live with each other and the weapons were discarded. The human race no longer feared each other because of their differences. What I am about to show you is the history of my people as we were, long ago."

Alexander showed the Gnathe views of some of the major cities and the vast parklands surrounding them. He showed farming complexes, run by apes and humans, because this was what they wanted to do with their lives. Here and there, silver forms of the nannite artificial intelligences could be seen working with the people. Great universities had been built in the middle of parks and gardens. He showed them spaceships taking off and travelling between the worlds, docking at great orbiting space stations. The Gnathe squatted, stunned and silent, overwhelmed by the incredible and alien vistas they had been shown.

Finally, Ender-whann-soo looked the human in the face and asked the awful question, "You have lost so much. What happened to all those people, Alexander?"

"They all died, Ender, when the sun expanded and created the world we stand on today. It seems a few of my race moved out of the sun's grasp, but did not survive more than a few generations without a home world. All of our past is gone, except the records we have shown you here. We have no culture of our own, only these chronicles as a role model to follow."

"Then, where did your people come from? If all of this happened aeons ago, how did you survive?" Ender soberly asked.

"Our ancestors had to trust the survival of our race to the four Guardians. Using a science so advanced, we ourselves do not understand it, although we use it, they were created. Countless tiny ships were launched towards the stars in the hope that some would arrive and find a world orbiting a sun, capable of sustaining life. Nothing living was stored on these ships. The crew were the Guardians, two of whom you have met. They would remain de-activated until the ship came within range of a star and became warmed by the sun's rays. When that happened Asue, Sharn, Minns and Kamiel awoke and took charge."

"You said that all life was destroyed by the sun," Shoo-lin exclaimed to Alexander, "and that the ship that landed here, carried no life forms, so you still have not told us where your people came from."

"I and all the children of the first generation are copies of people that once existed. I am the genetic duplicate of the man who was director of the project that brought us here. After Sharn and Minns designed the living proto-cells, they coded them with the genetic patterns from their memory banks. All Earthly life forms have the same genetic substance to start with and the Guardians have the original varieties stored. If anything were to happen to me, and it was deemed necessary, my original pattern could be duplicated. We have all been modified slightly to cope with the physical differences of your world from our home planet. One other thing that they did, as there was so few of us at the beginning, was to remove the aging gene from our make-up. We were encouraged to breed as many young as possible, to mix with the children of the life vats while our females were still fertile. We males are continuously fertile no matter what age we become. After some years, the female of our species becomes barren. Sharn and Minns collect eggs and sperm from us all when we are young and continue to produce more of us synthetically, by combining constant varieties in the artificial wombs to improve the natural genetic mix."

Ender-whann-soo swung round and bent forwards, laying a massive hand upon Alexander's shoulder and asked, "Do you mean that you are immortal?"

"We don't know what we are. Some of the third and forth generation are showing small signs of aging. The first created, do not. We remain, as we were, when we attained our maturity. My body is still young although I am of the very first group created by Sharn and Minns. Sometimes I have trouble with organising my memories and because so much of my life has been the same, it can be difficult. Having a personal memory bank in the computer at the Citadel helps. I have an implant in my brain that connects me to it when needed."

"Long ago our ancestors edited out the ageing gene in ourselves and bred a line of Brood-mothers that we are all descended from," Ender explained to the human and ape audience. "The males and females live a more natural span, but greatly extended and disease free. This is due to the immunity serum we Brood-mothers carry in our saliva and pass on to the young as explained by Khann. I think we will have more in common than we realise. Our future together will be interesting, my new friend. We have much to teach each other in the years to come. I look forwards to a long life of mutual exploitation of each other's knowledge. Maybe some day I will be able to look down on this world from a space travelling carrier, built by our combined efforts."

"There is a problem with that, I am afraid," said Kamiel, from behind them. "This world is made of lighter elements than the inner planets. Metal is hard to find here. It took our combined efforts a great deal of time to find the necessary copper and iron, to produce the dynamos, and turbines, harnessed to the White river. Atomic power is impossible. We cannot build fusion generators without steel. The nuclear energies would tear nannite apart. As for space flight, we have the same problem with containing the energies of the rocket exhausts, even using ceramics. I am afraid it looks as though we are planet locked. The orbiting space station we left in place when we arrived is all there ever will be above us. When the sun changed into its red giant stage, the dead scorched inner worlds were flung out into the darkness. We do not know where to look for them and even if we knew where they were, we could not reach them. We would need a very good reason to stretch the limited resources of the satellite's nano-pods to go prospecting for them. I am afraid that here we are and here we stay."

"On that rather sober declaration," Alexander said to the attentive and thoughtful Gnathe, "I will finish this now, unless there are any other questions? I would like to go outside and have a chance to look around at your world."

The group began to disperse away from the control console in the hold. Coen-soo began to reorganise the Gnathe and directed them to continue to store the supplies of seeds and goods taken from the homestead. Soon Alexander, Kamiel and Ender-whann-soo were left isolated from the others. Alex shut down the computer link to the Citadel and finally the console darkened as he switched it off.

"Well, Ender-whann-soo, you now know a great deal about us and where we came from," Alex said to the towering being. "There are bound to be great differences between us, but I feel happy about our new relationship together. What about Link-soo-shan? I would like to know what will happen to her when she returns from being defeated, to the Imperial City."

"Yes Ender," said Kamiel, "have you had any more contact with your old friend, Trann-link-khann?"

"I have indeed, and I will tell you all I know. Link-soo-shan is finished and her reign of terror is ended for good. My friend and colleague, Trann, has killed the Commander, Link's accursed Brood-sister, and displayed her head for all to see in the Hall of power. Thus she inherits all of Chang's kindred by ancient law. She awaits the arrival of the Tyrant and will fight her in the great amphitheatre in the Rite of Succession."

"How will she manage to beat Link-soo-shan in mortal, hand to hand combat?" Alexander said to the sleek golden form of the Brood-mother. "You have already told us that she is the greatest fighting Gnathe ever bred."

"She has an advantage the Tyrant does not know about. A short time ago Trann's kindred discovered a number of larger than average telekinetic crystals. They have practised with them for many, many days and have already used them to defeat some of the opposing Imperial Guard at Link-soo-shan's palace. No one else knows of their power. She and any of her kindred can blind or cripple an opponent at a distance or deflect a blow. Link-soo-shan is finished. She will meet her death in front of the Heads of the Families in a humiliating defeat," stated the Brood-mother.

"So this is why you insisted that she live, when we could have killed her after she murdered Daisy?" Alexander replied to the Brood-mother.

"Yes. You see, she has to be seen to fail against Trann, for the succession to run cleanly. The Heads of the Families have to see for themselves that a stronger Brood-mother has taken control of the Empire. Otherwise everything could fall apart into civil war," she answered, and bowed her head towards the level of Alexander and Kamiel. "The lives of the kindred will be greatly changed under Trann-link-khan's rule. A greater diversity and freedom of choice of breeding will be allowed. The kindred are born to serve us, the Brood-mothers, and that is the way of our species since the very beginning of our existence. We do not need the cruelty and harshness ordained by the Tyrant. You will see what I can achieve in the new home. Already the life inside me is being shaped into a new type of Gnathe. I will bring forth two young Brood-mothers designed to be intelligent, quick of thought and without the fearsome claws I carry. I know that although I can study your ways, learning and profiting for my race, I will be unable to use your strange tools because of the shape of my hands. My Brood-mother daughters will be born with fingers like yours. They will be able to manipulate and use the human artefacts that I would only break or damage."

"You have looked far into the future in a very short time of association with us," Alexander remarked, staring into the gold-flecked cat's eyes of the Brood-mother.

"You have shown me what my species lack, friend Alexander. You have saved my life and the lives of my kindred and followers, at great cost to yourselves. I am in your debt for many generations. By being instrumental in the fall of Link-soo-shan, others will feel indebted to you also. The Gnathe are not without honour. We repay our debts with interest. My kindred will strive to think of ways to discharge my honour," the Brood-mother said to them both. "Now let us go outside. I for one need the feel of fresh air upon my face. This place stinks of carrier and Zanth. My kindred will clean it out and stack sweet smelling, fresh foliage for the beasts to lie upon and browse."

The strange trio walked down the slope into the morning sunshine. Great activity met their eyes. Gnathe, humans and apes worked together, cutting vegetation and hauling it back to the airship. Alexander looked back at the dull silver shape reflecting the sun's rays. The valley stretched for many miles in every direction. This indeed was an enclosed world, hemmed in by the mighty ranges of the Saw-tooth Mountains. It was totally cut off from both sides of the continent. A light breeze ruffled the surface of the enormous gasbags, straining to pull the airship upwards against the many tethers that Kamiel had fastened into the bedrock. High vegetation grew in well-watered positions. Great fern-like plants grew a hundred feet into the air in thick profusion. Vines curled around them, climbing into the sky, sprouting heavy clusters of fruits and pods. These the Gnathe were harvesting and loading the carriers to the tops of their bony plates, surrounding the sides of the massive animals. Any bruised or damaged fruit was dropped deliberately in front of the beasts and they greedily devoured them.

CHAPTER 14

▼

Link-soo-shan looked down on the marshlands with distaste. Forced to climb over the gorge instead of going through it due to Kamiel's block, they were in a unique position to survey the Gnathen Empire. The wind cut cruelly over the high cliff-top, having blown across the high ranges and glaciers of the Saw-tooth Mountains. She could see the edge of the swamp area butting up against Ender-whann-soo's burnt-out holding. Searching towards the horizon, her keen eyesight could just make out the position of the Trading Post. This was the forced collection point for this area's crops and supplies destined for the Imperial City. There were many of these collection points dotted across the Gnathen civilisation. The Gnathe Brood-mothers lived on the whole solitary lives with their kindred, or in family related collectives. The crystal-enhanced telepathy network interconnected all. There had been many acts of theft and acquisition by different families against each other. Larger groups would wipe out smaller ones, or take them over. These would make a greater family, commanded by the dominant two Brood-mothers, who were generally egg-sisters. Alliances were formed and broken. Thus it had been for generations, until Link-soo-shan's Brood-mother, Shan-mace-soo, had dominated a larger group on her own. Finally she bred Link and her egg-sister, Chang, to form an overwhelming force.

The two Brood-mother sisters discovered the genetic combinations that produced the Imperial Guard. Their daughters had grown a head taller than the average Gnathe. They were much more powerful than any of the other kindred. Soon, by breeding the female line constantly in fours, they had combined them together into a supreme force. No sooner than one group of eight were past the weaned stage, both sisters had triggered off an available male to one of their

Brood-mother's daughters and had continued to be pregnant. Sometimes fuelled by the ambition of power, she had carried four well-developed young and four more recently split from another egg. As soon as their own strain of larger females had reached maturity, they had started them breeding with certain selected males. The offspring of these unions were several orders of magnitude above the original types. These daughters usually became her Group Captains and Leading Guards. Male offspring she had considered unimportant and consequently she had not shown any interest in their development. They were usually timid, unadventurous creatures, suitable for menial chores or the crafting guilds. Trann-link-khann had obviously seen other qualities hidden beneath the surface. She had to admit, Shoo-lin was incredible for a male. It would be a long time before she would forget him, hanging above her on the ladder into the flying carrier by his tail. He had calmly kept cutting through the ropes even as the blade of her syther swept passed his head, a finger's breadth from oblivion. Then, when she was sure she had him, he had spat in her eyes, blinding her and leaving her in the grip of the silver being. What had they called it? Kaameel—that was its name. Link-shoo-shan hissed in fury at the remembrance of that moment.

She had been so close to killing another of the alien beings that had come to the Heretic's rescue. Where had they come from, she wondered? They were not of her world and that was plain to see. Their ways of thought were different from the Gnathe. A much smaller force had easily divided the overwhelming rush that had been a standard manoeuvre. They had drawn her away from her main quarry. Never again would she be ruled by her anger. She would learn by her mistakes. Her hand found the small number of tiny spears she had her guards collect from the battlefield. Once more she pondered over the killing effect and accuracy she had observed. There would be time in the future perhaps to go through her guard's collective memories, of the aliens at the top of the hill, who hurled these shafts with such skill. She would maybe learn of the device then and perhaps with crafting males in the future, duplicate them.

She beckoned her group forwards and pointed at the mighty Imperial River, spilling through the lands in the far distance.

"I have a mind to travel along this high ridge towards the Great River. The top looks level as far as the eye can see. We should make a good distance before nightfall. Our people have never explored the great cleft that the river runs out of. There may be an easier way in and out of these high reaches," she called out above the rising wind. "Also, I do not want to return along the expected route. I do not trust that the challenge issued by Trann-link-khann will give me safe conduct through these lands. There are too many old scores to settle from those I conquered long ago."

"I understand, my Lady. We must be careful and trust no-one," replied Jaffin-shan. "It would be best, I think, if a few of us entered the city before you, under cover of night. We could then muster our sisters secretly and be ready to meet you at the main gates facing the river."

Link-soo-shan shuddered with delight at the alien way of thinking by her new Group captain and said, "Good, my daughter. You have learnt to think differently. Take Nagoth with you to carry out her mission. Come, let us proceed."

The small group of Gnathe hunched up against the wind and set a rapid, distance-devouring pace over the hard rocky ground. As the day wore on, the mighty Imperial River began to come into sight, winding its way across the lands approaching the city. The going was indeed easy. All that remained was the problem of getting down to the level of the croplands when they arrived at the barrier of the Great Gorge. They soon left the area above the wild marshlands far behind. Below them lay the rich cultivated lands and plantations of the various Brood-mothers' homesteads. They were careful not to silhouette themselves against the skyline as they travelled onwards. Small groups of Gnathe were seen hurrying along the main roads towards the city as the leading heads of the families left their holdings behind them in the care of their subordinates. They were easy to pick out by the shadows cast by the late afternoon sun.

The ground began to slope away to their left, into a depression in the rocky mountainous area behind the towering cliff face that faced the Gnathen Empire. Below them, at the bottom of a sharp incline, lay a wide ledge, with the river foaming and tossing spray into the air some distance beneath. They edged down to the slippery, moss-strewn area. Cold spray ran down the craggy walls as gouts of water shot up and washed over the wide ledge. Carefully the Ultimate Ruler edged her nervous Zanth along the rocky path, keeping close to the wet and slimy walls. One by one her Imperial Guard followed her into the mist. Sometimes the ledge inclined sharply up and then down as the fracture in the rock face followed its ancient fault lines. The sharp rugged claws of the Zanth dug into the uneven ground as the company forced themselves forward. It was getting dark in the gorge and the setting sun was shining full into the foaming gape when the ledge stopped abruptly against a fall of rubble.

Link-soo-shan urged her mount upwards over the loose scree, letting the beast pick its own way forwards. A couple of stones were picked loose by the Zanth's claws and plunged into the river below. Finally the great horned head looked over the top of the heap into the setting sun. There, beneath them and only a short distance away, was the beginning of the croplands of the homestead of one of her subjects. She waved her group forwards and let the Zanth pick its own way again down the rubble-strewn slope. From the other side of this incline no one would have bothered to explore the tumbling maelstrom of the gorge. With emphasis on farming, beast management and breeding, there would be little profit in exploring farther that the flat plains of the Gnathen Empire. Now Link-soo-shan took a wider view, urged on by her experiences. She was privately amazed to realise how long her Empire had stood still.

The group assembled at the foot of the cliff-face and waited for their Brood-mother's next directive.

"Listen, all of you. We will make for the bridge over the river next to this cliff. There should be some of my Imperial Guards stationed here. We will collect them to add to our number. Under cover of darkness, we will then approach the homestead close to the bridge and take it over. There will be minimal resistance, as the Brood-mother will have gone to the Imperial City to await our arrival," said the Ultimate Ruler to her silent company.

They quietly made their way along the edge of the crop fields towards the only bridge spanning the Imperial River, until the city bridge was reached. A small guard hut grown from a few Banilik trees was outlined in the late evening sky against the huge red setting sun. It would soon be dark and all the households would be closing their gates against the night.

Link-soo-shan rode her Zanth across the bridge, followed by her kindred and called out into the increasing gloom, "Attention all of you. Your Brood-mother would see you. I have returned to the Empire!"

There was great movement in the shadows of the hut as the amazed Gnathe hopped, or ran, into the road to greet their Ruler. They formed a semicircle in front of her and stared up at the mighty form draped across the Zanth's neck and shoulders.

"Great Lady Link, we are pleased to see you. We have heard so many different things about you," cried out a shadowy form from the back of the group. "Is it true that you have been challenged and the Commander is dead?"

"It's true, my children. I have great need of you all in the times to come. We must move fast if we are to retrieve something from this situation. Jaffin-shan is my Imperial Group Captain. You will take orders from her. Some of the things she will tell you to do will be strange. Obey her in all things. My very survival depends on it. Up the road from here is a homestead. We need to take it, with as little loss of life by the defenders as possible. I may need them later. The dominant Brood-mother will have set out for the Imperial City to watch the rite of succession. Those that are left will have little urge to die on her account. Do you all understand? I believe the usurper Trann-link-khann has something at her disposal that will put me at a disadvantage. If that is so, I will run from the arena and regroup here at this taken homestead. Jaffin-shan will explain to you where we have been and all that has happened. Mount up and follow me. We have much to do this night."

The obedient females gathered their mounts and quickly mingled with the returning group. They listened wide-eyed to the recounting of the adventures. After a short ride along the well-maintained road, the homestead began to appear out of the encroaching darkness. Link-soo-shan signalled the company to stop.

"Jaffin, go up to the door and ask them to open up. Do not speak of me. Tell them you require to see the deputy Brood-mother on urgent business. The rest of you keep out of sight except for two on each side of the doors. As the doors open, hold them fast and the rest of you rush in and intimidate them only. You will not meet with resistance. I will then walk in and take charge. Two of you hold the Zanth secure and stable them when this business is over," the Brood-mother commanded. "Any questions? No? Right, then, my kindred, take your positions. Forward, Jaffin!"

The Gnathe melted into the darkness and watched the scene unfold.

Jaffin-shan approached the closed doors of the homestead. The hard wood doors hung seamless and polished upon their living hinges. They had been grown as a matched pair and took their sustenance from the two upright trunks that helped to support the arched roof. The whole homestead had been grown from a number of saplings, placed in a design that had been proved useful many generations ago. All of the walls inside and out, with the roof, were interwoven sections of the Banilik trees. The structure constantly replaced and replenished itself and continued to grow in harmony with the Gnathe's direction and tending. She knocked on the featureless door with the heel of her syther.

"Open up inside!" she shouted. "I bear a message for the Brood-mother of this household from the Imperial City."

After some while the doors opened until a worried eye could be seen through the chink of the door.

"Hurry up and let me in, the night air is cold," Jaffin said impatiently to the figure outlined in the glow of the internal lights.

"The Head of the family has gone to the Imperial City to witness the Rite of Succession between the Ultimate Ruler and Lady Trann-link-khann," said the figure behind the door. "I will open up and give you shelter and take you to see her sister, the Lady Bran-loot-tighe."

As the doors swung outwards, the two Gnathe each side grabbed hold of the edges and held them back against the walls. Immediately Jaffin strode forwards and held the now terrified young female in a vice-like grip. The rest of the force swept inside and began the business of hunting down the rest of the unsuspecting kindred. Bearing in mind their Brood-mother's instructions, they harmed no one and gathered them together into the main hall.

Link-soo-shan walked majestically into her new quarters and perched upon the dominant rail. She faced the scared and apprehensive kindred of the home-stead. The Gnathe stretched up to her full height, curling her tail under the perch to counterbalance her weight.

"Do not fear for your safety. You will not be harmed by me, or my Imperial Guard," she spoke gently to them. "Where are the other Brood-mothers that run this household? Bring them to me. Jaffin-shan my Group Captain will accompany one of you with a party of my guards."

An older high-ranking female bowed her head and said, "Follow me, Group Captain, into the inner chambers where the Reverend Mother sleeps."

The small group left the hall by an ornately shaped entrance hung with curtains and beads. Link-soo-shan waited with unaccustomed patience for their return in the deathly silent hall. She heard a snarl of fury from inside the smaller chamber and her guards reappeared. They were pushing an adult Brood-mother in front of them and leading two more, immature Brood-mothers by their arms into the space before her. She could see immediately that they were blind. This was a common practice amongst a great number of dominant Brood-mothers. It gave them extra breeding capacity, without fear of an eventual bloody take-over in the future.

"I see that you and you partner follow the way of prudence," said the Ultimate Ruler with contempt to the hissing, furious Gnathe that stood before her. "This is not a practise for the strong."

"What do you want here, Link-soo-shan? This is my homestead, held by my sister and I," snarled the Brood-mother. "You will meet your bloody end at the hands of Trann-link-khann. We will rejoice at your going. Your sister is dead at the hands of the new Empress. Soon you will follow."

"I think not, low-born," hissed the Ultimate Ruler in fury. "You will not be here to see what happens."

Link-soo-shan hurled herself from the perch and landed on top of the startled Gnathe. Her great hind talons gripped the other Brood-mother's thighs in fierce hold. Her armoured tail whipped around the body, deeply piercing the side of the Gnathe, driving upwards into her chest and bursting her twin hearts. At the same instant, she seized her by the head and gave a quick twist to the side, snapping the neck. The two Gnathe crashed to the floor and Link-soo-shan stood over and on the twitching, blood-spattered body. She released her grip on the dead Gnathe's upper legs and stepped off the corpse. The dead Brood-mother's kindred had all backed away from the swift conflict and regarded Link-soo-shan with awe.

"Take this rubbish out of my sight. You are mine. Do you all understand? I will tell you your future. I will make my way to the Imperial City tomorrow and face Trann-link-khann in the arena. She has something that makes her confident of her success. I am not sure what it is. I tell you this—if I do not kill her and I know that she will win my position, then it is not my intention to die needlessly in front of my people. My Guards and I will return here and gather all that I may need for the future. You will prepare for a great journey. If I kill Trann it will not matter. If I lose, your lives will depend on doing what I say."

She turned to the two young, blinded Brood-mothers, and walked over to them on the blood-stained floor.

"You two young ones," she said, laying her great hands gently upon the shoulders of the blind and helpless Gnathe, "follow me in all that I do and command and I will look after you. I will restore your sight if I can. That I promise. I will need you in the future."

"Great Lady Link, we will do anything you ask of us," replied one of the young Brood-mothers.

"Wait for me then—you will not find me ungrateful," she answered. "I will leave you in the care of one of my senior guards. You will come to no harm here. I intend to leave a small party of my daughters to organise things in my absence."

Link-soo-shan climbed back onto her perch and once more addressed the captive audience.

"Bring me and my kindred hot food and fresh clothing with cleaning materials. I am tired of being filthy. Attend me now. After, I wish to sleep undisturbed until morning. I hope that is quite clear to you all."

The dead Brood-mother's kindred hurried away on their separate errands. They had been bred to serve and now they served the mightiest Gnathe ever born. Many of them felt a thrill of pride at their new servitude. Come what may, they now belonged to Link-soo-shan.

Soon the great form of the new Brood-mother of the household had been washed and cleaned. The huge talons and claws of the Ultimate Ruler were polished and oiled. Dirt and grit were studiously removed from every part of her body. Her tired and aching muscles were rubbed and soothed. Dishes of hot food and bowls of different spicy stews were placed before her for her pleasure. Her Imperial Guards were also well looked after by the enslaved kindred. Finally, after sweet fruits had been consumed, Link-soo-shan settled down to sleep amongst the security of her new kindred. She felt more confidant of tomorrow's outcome.

During the long day, Khann-link-sool had received small parcels of living flesh donated by the human and ape crew, transferred to her by Asue or Kamiel. She had remained in a near comatose situation, attended by her self-adopted servant Jotin-soo. Her perceptions remained focused inwards on the tiny, alien pieces of living tissue. Carefully, she fed them the all-purpose nutrient solution developed by her ancestors. Still the cells thrived and multiplied. Again and again, she added tiny portions of Gnathen gene structure to the living cultures. Not all survived the inclusion, so she patiently re-combined the mix over and over again, discarding the failures along the way.

All the time she spent in this state, her constant companion fed and quenched her thirst, carrying away the waste products that the old scientist produced. Jotin-soo held a bundle of large leaves over her adopted Brood-mother to keep off the hot sun. She waited for her to regain full consciousness from her inward studies. All around the isolated pair, humans, apes and Gnathe worked hard to provision the airship for the long voyage back. This would be against the prevailing wind, over the glaciers and rugged peaks of the aptly named Saw-Tooth Mountains. Some distance away from the activity, a human female and a Gnathe male were in earnest conversation. Jocylene was demonstrating her prowess with the bow and arrow to Shoo-lin.

"This is how the bow works, my friend. The spring in the material propels the arrow forwards by pulling back against the string. Watch," she said and let fly the arrow at the target tree. "Now you try it."

Shoo-lin took hold of the target bow, as the dark human woman had demonstrated. The grip was not designed for his sharp-clawed hands. As soon as he gripped the body of the bow, cat-like talons appeared and made the thin material difficult to stabilise and hold.

"Its no good, Jocylene!" cried the Gnathe with frustration. "I cannot hold the bow as you have shown me. Every time I hold it fast my claws wrap around it. I need a much thicker shaft to hold. My hands are just too large for this weapon of yours."

"All is not lost, my friend. Look for a springy sapling in the undergrowth and I will show you how to construct a long-bow," the black woman replied. "This bow is a compound structure. We can easily produce a much simpler type of weapon, capable of limited accuracy. Look, Shoo-lin, over there in that stand of trees. Do you see those segmented, tall, straight, pole-like growths?"

"I see them, Jocylene. I do not know what they are. They do not grow in my home territory. Let's go and look at them," the Gnathe replied with interest and curiosity.

Both beings pushed through the vegetation until they stood in front of the tall slender spikes.

"They look very like a plant that we call Bamboo!" Jocylene exclaimed. "See if you can break one off with your short sword."

Shoo-lin aimed a heavy cut at the base of one of the saplings. The hardness was amazing. The blade of the syther hardly marked the outside of the mottled surface!

Jocylene gave a grunt of satisfaction and said, "That looks perfect. I will take it out with one of Kamiel's thread-saws. Watch this, Shoo-lin, but keep well away from where I apply this tool."

She produced from a pocket in her suit a small package with two handles sticking out from the sides. Jocylene pulled them both apart and the nannite thread spooled out from one of the handles. The human woman wound the thread around the base of the sapling, about knee high from the roots and tightened her grip. Shoo-lin watched the thread disappear into the substance of the hard growth. With a steady pull, Jocylene finished cutting through and the Bamboo-like tree fell to the side. She rapidly trimmed the springy stick to length and cut two notches at each end. Next she directed Shoo-lin to find some narrower growth, to cut for arrows. From another pocket, Jocylene produced some strong supple thread and bound the ends of the bow to fix one end of the bowstring. She tied a loop in the other end, pulling the Bamboo-like sapling downwards and forced the loop of the cord over the other notch, putting it into tension. Shoo-lin had found a stand of young growth and had cut twenty shafts roughly a metre in length. The human notched a fork at one end and trimmed the other to a hard point, for every arrow.

Shoo-lin had helped to produce some of the arrows and said, "I have never seen vegetation like this growing on the Empire's lands. Most of the growth is soft or pliable, like the Banilik trees. We grow a great number of vines for fruit and vegetables. This is a new plant. We should take cuttings back to the airship and transplant them into the new homestead."

The new bow matched Shoo-lin's clawed hands much better than the human target bow. He held it as Jocylene had instructed and tested the pull by tugging the string. The immensely hard, springy material gave reluctantly as he exerted his muscles.

"It feels strange, my friend, but I can understand what it is meant to do. Hand me an arrow."

Shoo-lin notched the heavier type of arrow into the taut bowstring and copied the human's style. Keeping just enough pressure on the nock of the shaft to hold it in place, without his claws emerging from their sheaths, Shoo-lin drew the bow to his fullest extent. He sighted down the arrow, pointing it at a large fleshy, bulbous tree growing by a pool of water. Keeping his bow arm still, Shoo-lin released the arrow. The speed at which the shaft disappeared made him gasp with amazement. There was an audible thud as the hard straight shaft hit the fleshy vegetation low down. The Gnathe leapt over to the impromptu target with great, excited bounds. The crude arrow had sunk one third of its length into the growth and sap ran down the shiny sides onto the ground.

"Look at that, Jocylene! It works! It works!" the Gnathe excitably exclaimed. "Now I, too, can deal death at a distance!"

"It's not that easy, Shoo-lin," she said to the excited Gnathe. "You will require practise and the arrows will need fletching to resemble your Scriit spears. Also, it would be an advantage to add sharp stone points or something similar to the ends. I can show you how to do that. In the meanwhile, practise to get the feel of the range of your new weapon!"

Again and again all through the afternoon the young male practised until he could hit close to his target nearly every time. Gradually more of the field hands began to be interested and also tried out the new weapon. Some could not get the right grip because of the shape of their hands and failed to achieve arrow flight at all. Shoo-lin's egg brother Whann-lin proved to be as proficient as the young Gnathe. Carefully, cuttings and rootstocks were dug up and placed in earth filled pots to be transported across the mountains.

As nightfall eased slowly over the land, many of the more persistent Gnathe archers began to feel the effects of complaining muscle strains from hitherto unused sections of their bodies. They reluctantly herded their beasts back into the airship and bedded them down for the night. The beasts soon lost their fear and nervousness of the alien surroundings, as more and more vegetation and supplies had been stacked inside.

During the day Kamiel had been busy mounting an electrical prod onto the remaining pole-vaulting stick. This he wired up to the main generator and amplified the voltage to give a hefty charge. He was very careful to insulate the handle and built a carrying cradle for it on the outside veranda of the airship's cabin.

Having replayed Asue's memory banks of the encounter with the Terra-raptor, he felt it wise to be prudent. He also spent some time replacing the points of the target arrows with barbed heads. Shoo-lin and Jocylene had shown him the results of their labours with the Bamboo-type bows and arrows. He had set to and produced a great mound of nannite arrowheads, suitable for splicing into the shafts collected by the Gnathe. He showed the more dexterous males how to splice small wing sections from pieces of the leftover materials and left the Gnathe to glue them into place. Soon, a sizeable armaments' store was produced and the arrows were left to allow the glue to set.

Ender-whann-soo and Alexander were by the computer console at the end of the hold. They were once more in earnest conversation.

Alexander said to the Brood-mother, "I still cannot understand why you never developed more than a rudimentary, tool using capability. Your civilisation is advanced in many ways, yet you have not even used the idea of the wheel! The stranger thing is that Sharn and Minns are sure that you are not native to this world. Your genetic structure is different to ours and a lot of the native life forms."

"If we do come from somewhere else, we have long forgotten. Look at our hands compared to yours. They have always been developed as weapons of offence. The Gnathe have never really needed tools. We are multipurpose creatures. Kindred are designed and created to serve us. Some work and gather in the fields, being adapted to do so. Others are designed to supervise and lead the more docile in their tasks. Our ability to breed the beasts and shape their bodies to our desires is something that we have always done. Knowledge is stored by imprinting memories upon certain types of crystal and these are handed down. We live in harmony with our world, bending it to our will. You appear to shape it to your needs. I can see great advantages in your different way of thought. The bows and arrows that your friend Jocylene has produced are truly amazing to me. I would never have thought of using a springy stick in that fashion. To be able to project a small shaft accurately with something else, is so obvious when you see it done, but so strange in concept to us."

"That principle is so basic to us; our primitive ancestors invented it independently all over our world," replied Alexander. "We breed animals ourselves, but for meat and the use of their coats and hides. I do not think we have ever considered breeding for tools, although some animals were developed for their ability to hunt with us and carry us about. Your mental science is the most fascinating thing we find about you. When did that develop? I wonder if we could share in this also? Would you allow me to examine the crystal that you carry around your neck?"

Ender-whann-soo pulled the loop from around her neck that suspended the multifaceted gemstone. She gave the stone to Alexander, who examined it carefully, holding it up to the light.

"I can see tiny filaments inside the crystal, branching out like a web," he exclaimed. "Are they all like this, Ender? This looks like an electronic circuit embedded inside the gem."

"No, my small friend. This is a communication crystal and is cut in a certain way. Some are shards from a large, master crystal, while others are shaped to tune themselves to resonate in sympathy. There are types for holding memories as a recording and rare indeed are the ones that can enhance telekinesis. These are the ones our surgeons use to perform operations inside the body. Are you willing to try an experiment with me?"

"What do you have in mind, Lady Ender?"

"Hold the stone in the palm of your hand and I will lay mine over the top. You must relax and leave things to me. I will try to make a bridge into your mind. That way, we will both understand each other better," the huge form gently replied. "What we do has never been done before."

Alexander sat comfortably in the chair and stretched out his hand towards the Brood-mother and said, "I am ready."

Ender-whann-soo's enormous, three fingered hand, engulfed his suited one. Her thumb was nearly as thick as his wrist. All claws were carefully retracted. Suddenly, he seemed to grow larger and he was looking down at a small silver-suited figure. The hold darkened and all around him disappeared. He became a glowing ball of energy, linked to another of violet hues. Memories played and he became a different being with a totally separate outlook. All passions vanished. All sexual feelings diminished. Alien viewpoints were considered. Paramount was the need to shape, to form and by protecting the gene strain, survive. The entire race was one, linked together by the third sex. The kindred served. They lived only to serve. Here was an absolute dictatorship that could be totally benevolent or total servitude. Either way the Gnathen race would survive. The overwhelming hostility of this world in its early days came home to Alexander as his mind fragmented and re-formed. Outside the Habitat was a primeval world just as the primitive Gnathe had faced. They would subdue it, as they had subdued the land they had turned into a cultivated Empire. There was an overpowering will to organise, subdue and survive. More alien viewpoints paraded themselves through his mind. A rich sense of honour and friendship concerning the people of the

Citadel came through. He was aware of a presence within his own memories and conscious mind. There, shining through his personality, was a being of incredible beauty and wisdom.

"Welcome, Alexander. There are no secrets here. All that I am, you are. All that you are, I am. I have seen your strange childhood and lived your alien life. Now come with me and live mine," tinkled the voice in his mind.

A kaleidoscope of colours, shapes, emotions and places whirled around him as he was taken gently on a tour of Ender-whann-soo's life and experiences. Here they were, as the young Brood-mother received her first language memory crystals. Here again, as she took instruction from her own Brood-mother in manners and etiquette amongst her own kind. Around her were the ever-present kindred, serving and waiting for instruction. Amongst them were certain freethinking and more intelligent kindred, advising, helping and leading the lower born in their tasks. Alexander was reminded of a giant hive, thrumming with life and purpose. The Brood-mothers burned with curiosity and delved into different brands of science. Discoveries and philosophies were traded via the mind links, set up between dominant Brood-mothers and others of like mind and interest. Sending thoughts required the use of a large master crystal. These were highly prized by the Gnathe and the very finest were owned by the most dominant of the Brood-mothers.

As Alexander lay in the thrall of the telepathic link, neural connections were forged in new and unique pathways inside his brain. Gates opened, never to close again. Bridges into unused sectors of his brain unlocked a heritage buried deep in his species. He became aware of two tiny flames of life tucked piggybacked inside Ender-whann-soo's mind. They became aware of him and reached out to his mind in an unformed frame of reference, with trusting confidence. The two minds came from the rapidly developing, twin Brood-mothers in the Gnathe's breeding pouch. As yet, there was no hint of reason in their contact. This lay far in the future, but a bridge had been built between their undeveloped minds and his.

"This is a rare and precious thing that you have done, my friend," came the light touch of the Brood-mother's mind. "My genetic line is tied irrevocably to your mental signature. You have touched the Gnathe in a very sacred and profound place. There is much in your race, awaiting awakening. I sense wellsprings of power, untapped before by your people."

Alexander mentally nodded to his sister, mother, friend and so much more. They had twinned their very souls in an experience that had no previous existence.

"I think we should gently break this contact. Return me to my body, I need to rest," he mentally projected to his mentor.

Ender-whann-soo released the human's consciousness carefully and allowed him to flow back into the relatively frail form before her. She dimmed the link between them and let go of Alexander's suit covered hand. As she did so, the man fell off the chair into a boneless heap of twitching limbs. The Brood-mother picked him up in her huge hands and cradled him in her arms, being careful not to puncture his suit with her sharp claws. She moved rapidly towards the airlock, through the startled throng of her own people.

"Kaameel, Asue," she cried at the top of her voice. "Quickly, come quickly! Alexander may be dying!"

The airlock door crashed open and the two guardians appeared before her. They moved so fast that they blurred in the Gnathe's vision. Asue disappeared back through the airlock door and into the secure quarters of the human and ape living area, carrying Alexander.

Kamiel looked up at the troubled features of the giant Gnathe and asked, "What happened between you? What have you done to him, Ender?"

"I demonstrated the Gnathen mind-link to him. We were successful beyond expectations and then Alexander collapsed in front of me," the Gnathe replied in despair.

CHAPTER 15

▼

Asue stripped the suit from the unconscious man's body and laid him upon an examination table in the surgery. She rapidly entered his body monitoring his heartbeat and vital signs. The heart rate was down and blood pressure was falling rapidly. Hormone levels were fluctuating and energy reserves were dropping. What was the matter with this human? She increased the speed of his heartbeat and took over the automatic breathing reflex.

"Keep him breathing and the heart going until he is able to manage on his own," she thought

It was as if all the body's attention was fastened on the brain. Slowly and steadily, as the minutes passed, Alexander's natural bodily reflexes came under his own control. Asue slowly withdrew her supervision of the human's life support system as more and more of it came under his ability to self regulate his own body. Gradually as she expelled her substance from his body, she was suddenly aware that her thoughts were not all her own. Another mind had insinuated itself into her consciousness.

"Stay as you are for a few moments, Asue old friend and mother of my race," said a rich warm presence inside her mind. "It is I, Alexander. Do not be concerned. You did well, keeping me alive, while I underwent my change of state. I feel so different, Asue. My mind has been opened up in ways I cannot begin to explain."

Asue exclaimed, "What are you?"

"I am still Alexander, Asue, but I have undergone a vast change of mental state. What I am now is the next stage of evolution for my species. For this alone, it was worth the rescue attempt of the Gnathe. Do not be afraid for me, nothing but good can come of this. Now withdraw from my body and I will rest easy, knowing that you are there. Let Ender-whann-soo know that I am well and need only rest. I will see her again tomorrow to discuss this with her further. I am very tired."

Asue withdrew the last control filament from the human's body and felt the contact break between them. She had experienced for a short time the sensation of being a biological creature, just as Kamiel had done. It was a confusing feeling. She would study it again and again in the times to come. Asue realised suddenly that there was a group of humans and apes standing anxiously around the bench. The surgery had filled up during her frantic administrations to the dying man.

She looked around at the attentive faces and said, "Do not worry. He is fine. Go to your sleeping quarters and get some rest. Alexander will stay here and I will watch over him during the night."

"What happened, Asue? It looked as if Alexander was dying," said April, reaching out to the sleeping form with her hand.

Frederick pushed forwards and asked, "What was the matter with him, Asue? You must tell us. We will not rest until we know."

"It is difficult for me to explain," Asue answered to the ring of worried faces. "He tried an experiment, using Ender-whann-soo's crystal communicator. They were successful in producing a mind-bridge between them. Alexander's body failed for a time to keep going on its own, but he is fine now. He will tell you more about it in the morning. Now go to your beds and leave us both in peace!"

When the crew had returned to their sleeping area, Asue contacted Kamiel, who had 'listened in' to all the events.

"What has happened to Alexander? What does Ender-whann-soo know about his state of health? This is outside of our experience," she transmitted to the silent Guardian. "Question her thoroughly. I have already alerted Sharn and Minns and they are connected to me now. We must know, Kamiel!"

Kamiel turned to the apprehensive Brood-mother and said, "He lives, Ender, but is now fast asleep under Asue's care. Explain to me just what you did. The other three Guardians are listening in and need to understand."

"The use of the communications crystal is an everyday part of our life," replied Ender-whann-soo. "All the Gnathe can use it, but mostly it is restricted to Brood-mothers and certain intelligent females. It enables us to exchange thoughts, by being held close to the flesh of two persons. If someone used one of the master crystals, again by pressing their flesh against it, they are able to home in on the crystal hanging around the neck of any Gnathe. By doing so, they can connect to the mind of the wearer. When our young emerge, they are already able to understand simple language by picking up the Brood-mother's thoughts during their growing cycle in the breeding pouch. Soon after this, they are taught language and the necessary knowledge via the memory crystals. I have a full set of these memory crystals, with many spares and some are empty, awaiting imprinting. These are used by us to send messages to each other. We have very little of a written language, just a few signs that mean identities of places. For example, we have signs for kitchen, sleeping-quarters, crystal chamber and many more. When Alexander touched my crystal to examine it, I felt him."

Kamiel looked up at her and said, "What do you mean, Ender? Are you saying that your mind was aware of him even before you both made contact?"

"Yes Kaameel. I could sense him. All Gnathe have the ability to slightly perceive each other at a short distance, telepathically. When we both held the crystal together, he stepped into my mind and I was aware of him as a living part of me! For a small instant of time, I changed places with him and found myself looking up at a face that was my own. I have all of his memories and I remember everything. His mind is like a labyrinth. There are layers underneath layers. It is totally unlike a Gnathen mind-set. I took him on a tour of my life and my memories. He knows what it is to be a Gnathe," replied the Brood-mother proudly.

"Maybe he does, Ender my friend, but why did he collapse? He lies even now in a deep sleep, under Asue's constant care," said Kamiel.

"I felt something in his mind give way, as through an obstacle had been lifted. He has changed from what he was. Perhaps his body could not cope for a while. Whatever state his mind is in now, it will never go back to what it was. Imagine if you could not see and were suddenly given the gift of sight. How would you manage? Alexander has a great journey to undertake. He is like a young Gnathe learning to hop. The muscles are there, but they are as yet uncoordinated," the Brood-mother sombrely answered. "This is all I can tell you, I am afraid. I have no idea how long it will take him to settle down to his new existence."

Kamiel nodded to her and said, "Thank you for your information. I will leave you now and retire to the human section of the airship. In the morning we must load the last of the supplies for your beasts. The way back over the mountain ranges will take longer than the journey here, as the wind seems to prevail against us. We will have to follow what valleys we can and tack across and into the wind, when we breast the mountain ridges. Goodnight Ender."

Ender-whann-soo watched the strange silver form vanish through the airlock door, back into the front section of the ship. She made her way back to where Khann-link-sool perched. She was still lost in her inward world, examining the tiny portions of living cells taken from the airship's crew.

"Khann! Wake up and speak to me," she cried. "This is important."

"I am awake, young one. What is the problem? I also have information to give you," she replied and stretched her cramped limbs.

Ender-whann-soo pressed her crystal into the palm of the old Brood-mother's hand. They passed into a quick rapport, while the younger Gnathe gave Khann the whole experience with Alexander's mind and his consequent collapse.

"This is more interesting than you know, young Ender," the mind of the old scientist thoughtfully imparted. "Study the genetic information that I have been investigating."

Ender shared in the data that Khann had extracted from her studies.

"I have seen this type of cell structure before," Khann explained. "I can recognise the DNA but it has been much simpler in construction. This means that a great deal of life flourishing here has links with our new friends. I have often wondered why two totally dissimilar types of life forms have arisen on the same world. I wonder if they know that their enterprising ancestors must have seeded this world with life at its beginning? I can only guess at what happened here so very long ago. It is obvious to me, that the intended state of this world should have been the same as the artificial habitat created by Kaameel and his kind. It is our race that does not really belong to this world, not theirs!"

The two Gnathe squatted quietly together on their makeshift perch, pondering on these facts and finally fell asleep.

Alexander's mind beat at the confines of his skull as he lay in fitful sleep with the alert and worried Asue at his side. Strange dreamscapes filled his unconsciousness. His mind burst free from the prison of his body as the changes taking place inside the very fountain of his self finally ceased and reached a plateau. His under-mind crept out of the cocoon of his previous existence and extended fragile butterfly wings of mental force. His mind awoke, leaving his body asleep and resting. He took flight and found himself looking down at Asue and his body lying motionless below him.

All around him were pulsing lights, inside of which was contained the sleeping form of each person. They shone in a grey foggy darkness and those nearest to him flickered, as though kept in place under covers. He recognised them as his own kind, restrained by their bodies.

A little farther away was a group of different lights. They burnt brightly with a different hue. These had obtained their full potential. In amongst them were two brighter presences. He reached out to them in their sleeping state and was rewarded by recognising Ender and her powerfully minded

Grand-Brood-mother. These minds reflected strong feelings of order, duty and a need to repay debts incurred. They were alien, but understandable in their purpose. Even the minds of the beasts had an intensity all of their own. The whole world was dotted with points of light of different colours and brightness.

He rose higher and higher, soaring above the tethered airship, aware of this teeming world as no sentient entity had ever been before. To one side and quite some distance away was a vast array of brightly shining life forces. This could only be the mighty Empire of the Gnathe. It drew him away from the safety of his own kind. He flexed his new wings and felt a thin attachment spooling out from his consciousness to his body far beneath him. No matter where he went, the way back would be signposted by his own thread. Gaining confidence, he increased his speed and saw the dimly moonlit land fly by underneath him.

In the surgery of the airship, Asue continued to watch over Alexander's now comatose frame with mounting concern. All life-signs continued to be steady, but there was emptiness about the nature of the human's body that induced the Guardian's mind to a worried pitch. This was completely outside her knowledge and programming. In despair, she contacted Kamiel, and the Citadel's two medical experts, Sharn and Minns. The Guardian's minds meshed together in a combined gestalt to try to understand what was taking place. They examined Alexander's perfectly healthy frame over and over again. He breathed steadily and his heart continued to beat strongly. Everything seemed fine—there was nothing they could do for him. All they could do was to maintain their watch and wait for Alexander's mind to return to the sanctuary of his body.

Humanity's elected leader was having the most exciting time of his life. The awesome weight of his years and responsibilities had fallen away. He felt exhilarated beyond anything he had felt before. He was free of restraint at last. There, beneath him, he could now see the myriad lights of the Gnathen life forces burning brightly. Here and there were the brighter signs of the Brood-mothers, surrounded by their faithful kindred. Gently he reached out and touched one of the lesser beacons. He felt the female's need to serve and the wish to please her Brood-mother beyond her requirements. Also underneath these feelings, he could also feel her fear, of failing to please. She lived only to serve. There was no concept of independent thought in any part of her mind. How different they were from the confidant actions of Ender-whann-soo's household, with their quick, bright intellects. This mind would be content to serve and offer her fertilised eggs to her Brood-mother, without questioning whom she would be put to for breeding. The little female had never experienced any affection for a male and could not conceive of it

Alexander withdrew and pondered on what he had learned. Next to experience his feather touch was a male serving in the household of another Brood-mother, closer to the Imperial City. This was a dull mind also, hiding itself from the world at large. Asking nothing more than the opportunity to serve, he did the bidding of the senior female and waited for the time of ripeness to come. It did not matter to him, to whom the great Brood-mother decided he would mate with and fertilise. As for the outcome of his fertilised egg, deposited into the Brood-mother's pouch, he had no feelings for it and would never know or recognise the young. The only thing that mattered to the old male was the increasing difficulty he was having in carrying out his duties due to his advancing years. To fail to serve was to endure endless shame and torment. He did not want to spend the rest of his days with the elderly and unfit, sitting in retirement, waiting to die. Before that day came he would beg his Brood-mother for the right to die at her hands, with honour.

Once more Alexander contrasted the lifestyle of his new friend's kindred with the life of unremitting servitude of the other Gnathe. It was no wonder they loved her so much and were willing to travel anywhere and dare the Ultimate Ruler's wrath to keep her safe. The old pattern of life worked well for the Gnathe's survival, but did little to enhance the lives of the kindred.

From Alexander's high vantage point, above this part of the Gnathen Empire where he floated, digesting the knowledge gained from dipping into the lesser minds of the kindred, one bright flame stood out from all the others. It drew him closer and his curiosity became too great.

He wondered to himself, "Who's could this intensely strong mind be? Could it be the Ultimate Ruler herself?"

At the first feathery touch of Alexander's attempt to enter Link-soo-shan's mind, she awoke. A fountain of burning arrogance swept over his defences, leaving him open. Naked ambition and a roaring hatred paralysed his will. The power of her mind was different from Ender's. It was sharp and cruel. His unprepared mind lay open to her most intimate questions and probing. All the things he had willingly shared with the gentle-minded, Brood-mother he had rescued, were ripped out of his mind and examined with a scalding fury.

Alexander's body arched and shuddered from side to side on the medical table in front of Asue. Quickly, she held his tongue down with her fingers, softening them so that he did not injure his teeth as he bit into her substance. Still, with heart beating strongly, he fought the battle for his soul under the watchful care of the four helpless Guardians.

"You are not of this world—you do not belong here!" echoed the voice in Alexander's mind, cutting like a scalpel. "Your people die if they breathe the air or drink the water. Even the food we grow here would kill you. You are an abomination to me, breeder. I swear, that when I have dealt with Trann-link-khann I shall destroy you all. I will not rest until the last of your spawn lies rotting on the ground. You can tell your heretic friend, Ender-whann-soo and that senile old fool Khann-link-sool, that I will not forget them either. Somehow I will find a way to reach you all."

Alexander desperately built defences in his mind and bit-by-bit he began to shut her out. He fiercely projected to her mind: "First you have to reach us, Tyrant. If you do, you will find us ready and waiting for you. Ender-whann-soo and all her household are under our protection including our Guardians. You have met Kamiel, so you know what to expect. Our own experience of warfare is very little, but our race has known countless generations of it, in the far distant past. Do not underestimate us and what we are capable of. I warn you now, leave us alone."

"Your protector has already told me he is not programmed to kill directly. He can only protect and defend. I have been taught new ways to think and reason by my encounter with your kind. The outcome will not be so easy for you when we meet again. I lay the responsibility of my egg-sister's death with your species. When I gain my master crystal from the usurper Trann-link khann, I will send my mind to you. The fact that you have achieved this limited power of the mind without the energy of a sending crystal does not escape me. You will one day find out what I can achieve, properly equipped."

Finally, Alexander pushed Link-soo-shan's mind to the fringe of his own consciousness and held her there at bay. He felt weak and drained by the encounter with the Ultimate Ruler's ruthless soul. Soon he would have to return to his body and rest. He reached out to her for one last time.

"You are needlessly cruel, Link-soo-shan," he replied, tiredly, "and your lust for power has blinded you of the opportunities you could have achieved during your reign as ruler of the Gnathe. Ender-whann-soo will blaze a path into the future that you would be incapable of following. From what I have been shown of the great Trann-link-khann and her ideas, you will soon be forgotten after your death in the arena."

The Brood-mother snapped at the empty air in front of her in frustrated rage. She launched a damaging mental thrust at the human's mind, only to find that he had withdrawn. Splinters of polished wood flew out of the floor as she raked her bony tail across it in vile temper. She perched there, hunched up with suppressed rage, turning over the gems of knowledge picked out of Alexander's mind. Their homesteads were defenceless and the people living under the domes of the artificial world knew nothing of fighting or struggle. One day, she vowed, she would honour her threat against the interfering aliens. Somehow she would make them all pay for the damage they had done to her. Dawn was creeping over the land and she had plans to enact. Today, she would enter the confines of her Imperial City and tomorrow; she would face Trann in the arena.

She stretched up on the perch and shouted, "Awake all of you! Jaffin-shan, get them all moving! I need food and drink. We need to be on our way soon after sunrise. I have revised my plans due to our presence here. Nagoth-shan, come to me. You will make an early start, before we re-group and make our public entrance. I am relying on you to do what we discussed."

Before very long the whole household was functioning to Link-soo-shan's exacting rule. The Zanth were harnessed and made ready for the journey. Rations were distributed and the household Gnathe scurried about eager to please their new owner.

Alexander's mind reeled back the fine thread connecting him to his body. His ego felt bruised and sore in ways new to him. The encounter with Link-soo-shan's rapier sharp intellect had shaken him to the core of his being. She had stripped him of everything he had shared with Ender's mind-link. The Gnathe had the gift of total recall. Now, all the weaknesses of the human and ape settlement were known to the most ruthless enemy his race had ever faced. It was as well that the impenetrable barrier of the Saw-Tooth Mountains lay in her path. Nevertheless, Alex would insist that the satellite scan the area between them if Link-soo-shan should defeat Trann in the Rite of Succession. Her mind was a seething cauldron of ambition, spite, cruelty and the overpowering need to dominate every sentient creature. The concept of the Vendetta sang in the centre of her twisted soul. There would be no easy moment for Alexander's people until she drew her last breath.

The airship hurtled towards him as he returned to his fleshly home. He slowed the rate of approach of his astral projection and hovered for a moment or two studying the glowing signatures of his friends before he returned to his body. He became aware of the two Guardians just before he slipped back inside, hunched over him, holding his frame securely down to the couch. As he gained control of his body the first thing he became aware of were the heavy hands of his nannite friends holding him down. The next was the pain of strained muscles and aching limbs. Agony ripped through his body and he arched his back in pain, restrained by Asue and Kamiel. The guardians had done their work well, holding him and preventing him from damaging himself. The knotted muscles relaxed slowly as he gained control over his body. This episode had taken a lot of energy from his reserves. A sigh of agony escaped his lips through the obstruction of the soft nannite gag that prevented him from biting his tongue. He opened his eyes and looked into the almost featureless, silver ovoid faces regarding him with expressionless concern.

Asue withdrew her hand from his mouth and he said, "I am back again, my friends. I have a lot to tell you. My body hurts terribly. Could you massage my muscles? They feel as if I have strained all of them. This is hell, Kamiel."

"What happened this time, Alex? Your body seemed to be empty and then later, you began to thrash about as if in the throes of a fit," Asue worriedly declared. "We have never seen anything like it in our memory banks."

"I will tell you everything I can," he replied, tentatively stretching his abused limbs. "Could you just concentrate on massaging my shoulders and neck first?"

"Alexander," Kamiel worriedly retorted, "do you realise that you are speaking in Gnathe? Organise your thoughts before you reply and I will see what I can do for your aching muscles."

The two Guardians turned the human onto his stomach and began to ease out all the strain and cramps from the tortured frame. Alexander lay very still and under the administrations of the nannite beings, he began to relax. It was true, he realised—he could speak and understand Gnathe perfectly. The mind exchange with the gentle Ender-whann-soo and the subsequent encounters with the other Gnathe on this nocturnal mental prowl had given him more than he realised. He would never forget Link-soo-shan's efforts at peeling his mind. There were hurts, deep inside, which would take a long time to heal properly. She had tried permanently to cripple his mind and even without the power of the crystal, she had nearly succeeded. He would need to learn more from Ender and Khann about shielding his mind from the cruel and spiteful Brood-mother. He knew that she would never rest from doing him harm as long as she lived.

Somehow, he would have to astral travel again and witness her downfall. It would be important that the human colony be prepared to withstand the onslaught of her hate. Suddenly he realised that thousands of miles of glaciers and impassable mountain ranges lay between them. Even if she survived the coming struggle for power, Link-soo-shan could not physically reach the Habitat. Knowing they were safe, he drifted off the sleep as the sure hands of Asue soothed out the cramps from his aching body.

"He has fallen asleep again, Kamiel. Let him rest awhile, from whatever ordeal he has gone through," Asue sent on the private band between them. "Minns and Sharn, we can do nothing now. I will continue to monitor him while he sleeps. If there is any change I will let you know immediately."

"We will start back the day after tomorrow," Kamiel stated to the gestalt mind. "We still need to load a lot more stores for the journey back. I estimate that we may be airborne for a week or more, depending on the prevailing wind. We will need all that we can carry."

Asue tenderly covered the sleeping form of Alexander with a blanket and sat once more, immobile, by his side. She wondered what could be going on in his mind and body. It still troubled her, as she sat by his side. She was still shaken by the warmth of his mind touch when he had awoken before. For a few brief moments she had shared the sensations and senses of being a biologically functioning being. How overwhelming and distracting it must be to live in a frail vessel of living flesh! She was thankful that she was the way she had been designed.

"I am like a Gnathe," she thought, amazed with the idea. "I was constructed to serve. Yet, like a Brood-mother, I have also created and shaped both humans and apes. They are indeed the children of the four of us, just as if we were made of flesh and blood. What complicated creatures we are, to be sure!"

Asue stretched out her hand and stroked Alexander's hair, just as she had done when he was a child so many years ago. This sleeping human had been the 'first born' from the life vats. Minns had cradled him in her arms and they had all gathered round the tiny infant in joy and wonder at what they had accomplished. Of all the children born, this one had been loved the most. He was as perfect a copy of the original Alexander McBald as was possible. They had altered the genetic structure slightly, to adapt all of the children born here to cope with the different set of conditions of this strange world and its stranger sun.

The dawn began to break over the mountaintops and illuminate the great sprawling valley, warming the gas contained in the airship. Creaks and groans came from the structure as the gas expanded, tightening the fabrication and lifting the ship against the constraints of the guy ropes. The many diverse life forms began to wake up as the nighttime cold began to dissipate. Nocturnal hunters and scavengers returned to their daytime lairs. As the mists began to clear, grazing animals edged out from the sanctuary of the woodlands and onto the grassy spaces. Smaller relatives of the Zanth fed warily on the edge of the pool by the bamboo growths.

The sun rose higher in the sky, bringing greater, welcome warmth to the landscape below. Far away on the edge of the wide valley, tucked into an overhang with a good view of the lands below, was the Terra-raptor's nest. The female hooded her wings over the delicate young, keeping them warm and dry. They were beginning to squirm with hunger as they came into sleepy wakefulness. Their urgent cries triggered the regurgitation reflex in the male and he reached down to his food storage area inside his gullet. With a quick shudder he brought up a tenderised Banth for his mate to pull apart and feed to the helpless young. She hissed at him and encouraged the great beast to take to the wing to hunt for them. He rubbed his green scaly head against hers, stretching his wings out and cracking the tough leather in the air.

With that gesture of affection, he launched himself into the void and caught the morning thermals. Higher and higher into the morning sky he rose. Far into the distance, others of his kind took to the wing, obeying the daily dictates of life. Each had their own territory to hunt in and would defend it fiercely if prey were scarce. While food was plentiful, squabbles were rare. At the moment conditions were good, so the giant flying predators were on good, sociable terms with one another. His keen eyesight soon picked out a group of grazing animals dipping their heads to drink at one of the numerous pools.

Shoo-lin, his egg-brother, Whann and the rest of the Gnathe who had proved themselves proficient with the new weapon, had left the safety of the airship just after dawn. With them went the two human archers, Jocylene and Abdul, securely suited up against the Jovian exosphere. The dull silver suits were non-reflective and did not stand out against the native vegetation and blended into the shadows. They were slowly closing in, onto an area of marshy growth on the edge of the pool where Jocylene had cut the first bow. A small herd of the smaller type of Zanth, common to this mountain-locked valley, were collected together to drink.

CHAPTER 16

▼

Nagoth-shan set out at first light, among the morning mists, towards the Imperial City. She had ridden the protesting Zanth, cruelly and hard, covering the ground in great distance-devouring leaps. She knew that she would have to get inside the city quickly, long before her great Lady arrived. As she approached the surrounding fields, the Zanth began to tire, so she allowed the weary beast to drink from one of the many water filled ditches. Its sides were sweaty and stained with dust. The beast drank its fill while Nagoth placed her lips to the cool waters and gratefully quenched her parched mouth. She splashed water over her face, allowing it to dribble down her neck and chest.

The Zanth groaned a little in protest as she remounted and wound her tail around the bony plates of its back. She patted the side of its neck and said, coaxingly, "Not much farther now. Soon you can rest in the stables. I will have a great deal to do however."

A steady loping pace soon bought the living walls and outer gardens of the Imperial City into sight, so Nagoth slowed the creature to a gentle walk. She made her way through the various homesteads and orchards until she came to the back of the Imperial stables. Handing over the reigns of her steed to a stable attendant, she mingled with the excited throng of kindred.

Snatches of conversation were caught by her hearing crest concerning the forthcoming battle for supremacy. She had been implicitly instructed by her Brood-mother to be careful to tell no one of her mission and avoid contact with her sisters, if possible. After the box was safely in Link-soo-shan's hands, she was to join Jaffin-shan in recruiting as many of Chang's kindred as she could to join up with the new group. The Brood-mother's own offspring would obey her without question. The new clothing helped to make her inconspicuous and she stooped down, hiding her superior height as she walked quickly through the corridors towards the Royal Chambers. At last she came to the area of Link-soo-shan's old domain.

Outside the entrance stood two of Chang's kindred, unhappily being overseen by a smaller female. She was obviously one of Trann's daughters, stationed to ensure the loyalty of the Brood-motherless guards.

Nagoth pondered on the best approach. She would need the assistance of Chang's kindred after she was through the entrance. The only thing to do was to take them partly into her confidence.

She stepped out of the corridor into the light and strode briskly towards the three guards.

"The Lady Trann has sent me with a message for the Guard Captain," she said to the smaller Gnathe, who had turned to face her as she approached.

"Who are you? My Lady sends messages only by her own kindred," she replied doubtfully.

"I serve the Lady Trann. I must tell only you what she requires. Link-soo-shan is at the gates as we waste time talking here. Bend towards me and I will whisper into your crest," Nagoth replied, stepping closer and to the side.

The unsuspecting female bent her head towards the advancing form of Nagoth-shan. As she did so, Nagoth drove her clenched fist into the stomach of Trann's daughter, expelling her entire breath with a tortured gasp. The larger Gnathe reached for the sagging head and neck. Grasping the winded female securely by the chin, she gave a vicious twist and was rewarded by hearing the neck snap. The Imperial Guard dropped the smaller body to the floor and turned to face her old Commander's astonished kindred.

"Link-shoo-shan indeed approaches this city. I have a mission to perform for our great Lady. Hide this useless shit somewhere out of the way, where she will not be found until this is over," Nagoth declared defiantly and walked between the guards into the Royal Chambers. She turned, staring at the two guards, and asked them, "Will you continue to serve the Ultimate Ruler, or spend the rest of your miserable lives jumping at the commands of these puny little scum?"

"We will continue to serve the Great Lady Link. What does she plan to do? Tell us, that we may assist," one of the guards replied and bent down to pick up the sprawled form of the dead Gnathe.

"It is enough that you maintain your position here. Tell anyone that asks, that your officer has left you for a few moments to relieve herself. I was not here. You have not seen me. A great deal of the outcome of the future depends on my success." Nagoth turned and made her way towards Link-soo-shan's secret stores deeper inside the Royal Chambers.

To her surprise, the inner rooms were nearly empty of Gnathen life. Trann and the Keeper, Sing, were nowhere to be seen. The kindred of the new, would-be Empress ignored her when she met them and she passed them without speaking. Their attitude towards her was cool and distant. She was careful to appear humble and subservient, as if on an errand for the new leaders. Apart from the guards at the entrance, security was non-existent. Nagoth entered Link-soo-shan's storeroom confidently and saw the chest described by her leader, in the corner of the room. It had been moved from its customary position next to the Ultimate Ruler's sleeping perch. The chest was constructed from two halves of a giant pod, grown for the purpose. It was bound with leather and had been carved by male crafters, to show Link-soo-shan in various poses. Someone had amused themselves by defacing the heads of the Ruler with their sharp claws. She opened the lid of the chest and peered within. A heap of disorder met her eyes. Busy hands had gone through the artefacts and secret possessions of the absent Ruler. Frantically Nagoth moved the loose items to one side and delved deeper into the recesses of the plundered box. Her searching fingers suddenly encountered the shape of a small carved block of wood. She held it up to the light. There, just as Link-soo-shan had described it, was the carving of the closed eye. She shook it to see if it rattled. Not a sound came from inside the wooden carving.

Could this be the item she had been sent to find? She turned it over and over in her hands. The block of wood seemed to be completely solid. The more she held it, however, the more she could sense something inside of it, which felt slippery against her probing. Nagoth stuffed the article into her carrying pouch and looked through the other items to see if anything of use or value remained. There was nothing she could see that was worth taking.

The Imperial Guard left the room and walked through the series of corridors, making her way towards the crystal communication chamber. An idea presented itself to her. She looked down the passageway to check, only to see the tall figures of Trann and Sing enter the area in front of the Empire's nerve centre. Nagoth turned back in disappointment and moved out of sight into an adjoining passageway.

"Maybe later," she thought.

She quickly made her way back to where the two Gnathe stood uneasily guarding the entrance.

"Were you successful?" one of the guards asked as she approached.

"I was. Now listen to me carefully. You must make contact with Jaffin-shan when she arrives with our great Lady. The Imperial Group Captain will be making for the stables. You will have plenty of time to select the best mounts and have them ready. Co-opt more of the Commander's kindred into the plan that I will explain to you. For the time being this entrance should still appear to be guarded. One of you must remain here, while the other quickly finds two more of our kindred to take your place."

Nagoth explained the new master plan involving the capture and restraint of some prime breeding-males. The emphasis was on fitness and craft ability. These males would be gathered together by the newly recruited guards, in preparation for Jaffin-shan's diversion to the stables. Once the loyal forces of Link-soo-shan and the new rebel group at the city made contact, Nagoth advised them to quickly make their way to the captured homestead. There they were to await the outcome of the struggle between the two Brood-mothers for the right to rule the Empire. They would make the homestead ready to move under Jaffin-shan's command.

If Link-soo-shan won, the captured kindred would be established in the royal quarters as adopted family. Alternatively, if winning was not possible, they would be ready to make their way to the gorge and escape the pursuit of the surprised Gnathe. The males of the captured household were of limited use, as they had not been well bred for their abilities.

At the Imperial City, the best of various breeding programmes worked diligently for the enhancement of the Ultimate ruler. They would be needed for Link-soo-shan's new order, whichever way the Rite of Succession concluded. Nagoth-shan left the two guards to organise the reception for her colleague and carry out the revised plans. She mounted a fresh Zanth and urged the beast forwards through the outskirts of the city. She intended to meet her Brood-mother on the road outside of the perimeter walls.

Link-soo-shan's troop of Imperial Guards rode slowly up to the walls of the great city. She kept to the centre of her kindred as they rode together. Distrustful of any assassination attempts, she made herself as poor a target as possible. They had ridden steadily all day, stopping at high sun-up to take food and water from another homestead. They were received with great honour and deference by the deputy residing Brood-mother. The best food and drink had been offered to them. The Gnathe at this rich homestead had always been great supporters of her regime. They had spoken together for some time, but Link-soo-shan had given nothing away concerning her plans. She intended to take her time in approaching the confines of the city. It would be unlikely that she would be given the run of her royal quarters. These would be firmly under Trann-link-khann's control. Hopefully, Nagoth-shan would have penetrated the new ruler's security and acquired the box that she had been sent to find.

Time and again her perceptive mind returned to the puzzle of Trann-link-khann's challenge. Somehow, the smaller Brood-mother must have discovered a way to mark the odds in her favour. Link-soo-shan knew that without an edge the outcome would have been pre-ordained. The Ultimate Ruler's size and strength were a legend from one end of the Empire to the other. One thing she was sure of, Trann was no fool. She was a scientist of the finest order with a quick and inventive mind. Link stiffened in her seat upon the Zanth. That was it, she reasoned—it must be an attack by the mind during combat! Her thoughts were interrupted by Jaffin-shan's shout.

"My Lady, someone approaches, riding hard!" she cried out excitedly. "It looks like Nagoth."

Link-soo-shan straightened up and stared over the head of her mount. "It is indeed my loyal spy, Group Captain. I hope she has the item I sent her for."

Nagoth eased the Zanth to a snorting stop and turned the beast around towards the City walls. She allowed the group of guards to catch her up and as the leading guards passed her, she edged her mount across to the Ultimate Ruler's side.

"Were you successful, Nagoth?" the Brood-mother asked worriedly.

"I think so, my Lady," she answered hopefully. "I could not find a box, but I found this carved block of wood. The carving was just as you described to me. It does not seem to open, but I am sure that there is something in it. Someone has gone through your chest of valuables and has disturbed everything. This was right at the bottom of the bits and pieces left in there. Is this what you sent me for?"

Link-soo-shan snatched the block of wood from Nagoth's outstretched hand with delight. She gave the top of the carving a twist to the side and it opened. Securely fixed inside and packed so that it would not rattle, was a pale rosy shaded crystal mounted on an amulet. The Ultimate Ruler gave a sigh of relief, reached out and cupped the startled Gnathe's head in her great hand.

"Nagoth-shan, you have given me the chance to beat my enemies. I cannot thank you enough for what you have done. I will not forget this. Tell me all that you have done to acquire this crystal from under Trann's nose," she said. Giving her daughter a gentle squeeze, she bent close and flicked her tongue out to touch Nagoth's lips.

The Gnathe shivered with delight at her Brood-mother's attention and told her the details of how she had recovered the crystal in the unsuspecting City. Jaffin listened carefully and took account of her story, resolving to carry out Nag-oth's instructions to the two rebel guards.

After her daughter's account was finished, Link-soo-shan returned the lid to the box and twisted the lid securely back into place. She stored it into her own carrying pouch with a sigh of relief.

"What power does this crystal possess?" Nagoth asked, looking up at her Brood-mother's face. "Why do you think is it so important to you?"

"This crystal belonged to Shan-mace-soo, my Brood-mother. To the best of my knowledge, it is unique in all the Gnathen Empire. It provides a mental shield to the one who wears it, preventing telepathic contact. My sister and I used to take turns at wearing it, to play hide and seek when we were young. Without one of us wearing the amulet, we could always find each other quite quickly. If my sister put it over her wrist, I could not sense her presence. It was just as if she did not exist. Even if I used the master crystal, to home in on her thoughts, all I could feel was a strange slippery sensation." She smiled knowingly to the two Gnathe as they rode slowly along. "I am sure Trann is going to attack me mentally during the Rite of Succession. This can be the only reason she thinks she has any chance of beating me in combat. If so, she is in for a nasty surprise!" Link-soo-shan hissed in fury and spat in temper as she thought about the coming conflict, remarking to her kindred, "I want her blood flowing over my syther and down my arms. I will drink her life-force in front of the weak fools who think she will take my Empire."

They had nearly reached the walls of the Imperial City and could see quite clearly the faces of the city dwelling Gnathe. Tall stands of Banilik trees, grown into towers, guarded the main approach. They passed the site of the 'Killing Stones' and slowly turned towards the late afternoon sun that cast long deep shadows into the paths. The main gates were opened by the officers of the watch, who stood to one side as the troop advanced. Jacta trees in full blossom lined the main avenue towards the City centre. The perfume of the heavy flowers filled the air. Beneath the trees stood rows and rows of kindred with their dominant Brood-mothers. Merchants left their stalls and shouldered their way to the front of the crowd to stare at the return of the Ultimate Ruler.

There was an unaccustomed hush over the crowd as Link-soo-shan entered the Grand Avenue. Jaffin-shan eased gently away from the main body of her leader's company. Nagoth had already slipped back into the rear of the troop and was making her way back to the Imperial stables. The two loyal Gnathe melted into the crowd and disappeared from view.

"Well!" shouted Link-soo-shan. "Where is the challenger to my rule? Are you hiding from me in fear?"

"We are here, Tyrant!" cried out Trann-link-khann in defiance, and she strode into view with Sing slightly to her side and rear.

"Keeper," the Ultimate Ruler hissed in hatred as she saw the figure by Trann's side. "I shall look after you, just as you looked after my sister. When this is over I will come for you, 'low-born'. Your skin will feel my feet upon it for years to come—as a living rug!" She turned and fixed Trann with a baleful glare. "What are the arrangements, usurper? Do we meet now, when I am tired and hungry? Will it be a dart in the back during the night? Or do we meet tomorrow in the arena?"

"You will fall in front of the family heads tomorrow. I will meet you with my syther at the end of the first quarter day of the morning. Chambers have been made ready for you, to eat, wash and sleep safely. On my family's honour, you will not be touched or harmed until we meet. I will see you then." Trann swung away from Link, walking quickly away towards the Royal chambers.

"I do not trust your family's honour!" shouted Link in disgust at the retreating back. "I spit on it. My own Imperial Guards will attend me this night in the mean quarters you have set aside for me. Till then, dwarf! Eat well tonight, for you will not feed again after tomorrow. Think about what I will do to your scut-tling kindred when your broken remains are drying in the sun. They will be stretched out on the 'Killing Stones' as an example to all who would doubt my ability to rule."

With her shouted taunts ringing in the air, Link-soo-shan dismounted from her steed and walked moodily after the frightened Gnathe leading her to her improvised chambers. Her surviving Imperial Guards formed a protective screen around her, leaving the tired Zanth to be led away to the stables. As she walked away from the crowd, her sharp claws slipped in and out of their sheaths at the front of her fingers.

Trann-link-khann, the Keeper and the four kindred, Jewel and Marren-khann with Shoo-lin's egg sisters Natel and Jing-soo, were perched together to plan the following day's action. Sing-trow-sool's features were beaded in droplets of fear-induced sweat. Her hands wrung themselves together and her body trem-bled.

Trann fixed her with a concerned stare and said quietly, "Are you capable of carrying this through? I need you to co-ordinate the plan of attack."

"I have never been so afraid in all my life," she replied anxiously and flexed her trembling hands. "That does not mean that I will fail you when you need me.

You are the one who will be facing her in the arena tomorrow. I just can't get over the size and power of the Tyrant."

"Remember, my friend, blind and stumbling aimlessly around the arena, her greater size will do her no good at all. I only have to be quick on my feet and prevent her from closing with me to make it look right to the heads of the families. Now listen, all of you, very carefully to what I say. I have given this a lot of careful thought. We have only three crystals of sufficient power to reach across the arena. Three of you will be equi-spaced around the perimeter of the amphitheatre, so wherever I go, I should be within range of two of you. I will do my best to stay out of the middle where the influence of the crystals is weakest. Weaken the arrogant cretin by causing haemorrhaging in her legs. Trip her up from time to time. Make her look a clumsy fool in front of everyone. Pinch shut the valves of her heart if I look in danger."

"Do not worry, my precious Lady," Jewel-khann replied with grim determination. "What I did with those guards when we took the Royal chambers, I can do again. This time, I can concentrate on the damage I can inflict without any distractions."

"We will be in place long before you enter the arena," Natel-soo assured the Brood-mother, stretching forwards to grip her by the wrist. "It only requires the decision as to who will be the three crystal bearers. We will bind them to our wrists so that we cannot lose them."

"Jewel-khann is the most proficient, so she will take the weakest crystal of the three. Natel-soo and her egg-sister, Jing will use the other two. Marren will take one of the smaller ones we have spare and remain by the side of Sing, while she operates the Command crystal. All of you will wear a telepathic crystal around your neck so that I can contact you through the relay that Sing will control. I will wear my own crystal strapped to my arm so that I will not lose it during the struggle. Do not worry—we will not fail. Tomorrow the Tyrant dies. Her head is going to take its place next to Chang's in the Hall of Power. Trann was confident as she spoke. "Now we must eat and sleep to prepare for the next day. It will be important to get everything ready. All things have been taken into consideration. Come, let us go for our evening meal."

The two Brood-mothers stepped off the perches and made their way towards the royal feasting chambers while their Trann's kindred hurried off to arrange and supervise a meal for all of them.

Alexander stirred into wakefulness and opened his eyes. The ever-watchful Asue sat beside him, observing the rise and fall of his chest. His head still hurt from the night's adventure. Next to Asue sat April, worriedly holding his hand against her breasts. Frederick's huge form stood at the end of the examination table next to Joom. Alexander weakly waved his free hand to the row of faces and gave April's breast a gentle squeeze with the other.

"Good morning, people," he said. "Asue, can you give me something for my headache? Any chance of a coffee someone?"

Asue stood and removed a bottle of pills from the cupboard. She drew off a glass of water and handed both items to Alexander.

"Asue has told us about your restless night, Alex," said April, keeping hold of his hand. "How are you this morning? Dawn broke some time ago. We have gathered around your sleeping body for hours. What happened during the night, Alex?"

Before April's words fell on Alexander's ears, he could hear them in his mind. The warm, living contact of their touching flesh helped to form a bridge between their minds. April's eyes opened wide as the intimate contact broadened within the two minds.

"Don't be afraid, April. Don't fight it. Drift gently along with me. I will not hurt you, nor will I look into your private places," Alexander assured her with his mind. "We have loved each other many times in the last hundred years. There is plenty of time to explore this later. I must let you go. The others are waiting to hear what I have done and experienced."

"I don't want to let go, Alex. Don't shut me out. I love you, Alex. I always have."

The emotions tumbled out of April's mind, almost overwhelmed him. Bit by bit he eased her to the edge of his mind and filled her with reassurance.

"I will not let you go, but you have a great deal to learn about this new awareness. I must talk to the others. Stay with me then and listen to what I have to say. Be careful you are not hurt by the memories I have to retell. If it becomes too much, let go of my hand and the intensity will fade."

Alex stretched out his free hand to take the coffee offered by Frederick and brushed his fingertips with his. Once more mental contact was made. This time only briefly, but it was enough to build another bridge. Each was aware of the others' friendship and respect. They stared into each other's faces with astonishment as Alexander's mind once more unconsciously bridged the gap between them and forged an unbreakable link.

Alexander hurriedly drank the hot coffee with a shaking hand. Frederick moved around the examination table to stand by Joom's side. He stood dazed as Alex swung his legs out of the improvised bed and hung them over the side.

When he had finished his coffee and collected his thoughts together, he once more looked his friends in the face.

April was gazing at him with her eyes reflecting a deep joy. Frederick was looking at him with a look of amazement and wonder on his craggy features. Joom was looking from one to the other with his own hairy face creased in puzzlement.

"Would someone please explain just what is going on?" pleaded Joom, walking forwards and laying a hand on Alexander's shoulder.

Again, mental contact was made, this time between the different mindscapes of man and ape. Alexander felt the ape's strength flow over him, mixed with feelings of integrity and concern. Joom was aware of all of Alexander's qualities, with April's mind also fitting into his awareness.

Now it was Joom's turn to experience astonishment as conduits and pathways inside his mind made contact with each other. All of the flesh and blood creatures in the room were now aware of one another in a way never before experienced.

Alexander grinned at the hairy frame of his old friend and said with mouth and mind, "Welcome to the family. I had better tell you everything I can. Listen carefully, Asue, for you are not connected to my mind as the others. Place your hand on my leg and I will attempt to bring you into the gestalt. Penetrate my flesh as you did before and link up to the other guardians. You all need to hear and understand what I am about to tell you."

Asue linked up to the other guardians and did so, once more finding herself connected to a flesh and blood creature. Alex then told them all about his encounter with the Empire's Gnathe, contrasting them with Ender-whann-soo's kindred. Finally he gave them his experiences with Link-soo-shan.

When the others felt the raw power of her mind they were shaken to the very core of their souls. Even the strange minds of the Guardians were not immune from her hatred.

"We have made a terrible enemy. She will never forgive us for interfering with her rule," Alexander declared to his friends sadly.

"She will never be able to reach us from her side of the mountain ranges," declared Frederick, gratefully. "Just think of the distances involved. We travelled over two and a half thousand miles to get here. It's just not possible!"

"The evil one has to face the mental powers of Trann-link-khann in the arena tomorrow and, according to the Lady Ender, Trann has a huge advantage with her use of the telekinetic crystals. You humans and apes had better gain control of these new mental powers you have acquired," remarked Kamiel. "We cannot help you. I suggest you contact Ender and Khann and take their advice in all things.

Asue, disengage from Alexander's flesh and break this unsettling contact. We have much still to do here before we can lift over the mountains and go home."

Asue removed her substance from the human's body and regretfully broke contact. She stood up and quickly said goodbye to Sharn and Minns at the Citadel.

"Kamiel is right, you know. We do have a lot to do before we can leave this valley. Jocylene and Abdul left early this morning with a small party of Gnathe to try out the new hunting bows. They were going to attempt to bring back some substantial meat rations. Kamiel is on his way to see how they are getting on. I suggest that you suit up after breakfast and speak to the Brood-mothers about the changes in your mental state."

The small group of enhanced people agreed with the guardian and began to come to terms with their altered states. As yet, the changes in the others were slight compared with Alexander and they were able to cope. More investigation needed to be done under the guidance of the mentally proficient Gnathe. The first thing to do was to organise breakfast and explain to the others of the rescue party what had taken place. Alexander dressed and the group filed out of the surgery and into the kitchen of the airship.

Outside, the early morning mists were thinning out under the rays of the ascending sun. The wild Zanth gathered at the edge of the marsh and dipped their heads to drink. The small group of hunters had wriggled forwards under cover of the undergrowth. Whann-lin slowly stood erect by the trunk of a tree and selected an arrow. He extended his bow arm quietly over the tall spears of growth in front of him and notched the arrow. Just as he had practised the day before, he pulled the arrow back level with his cheek and, sighting down the length of it, let go very gently. The shaft silently sped through the air and penetrated the wild Zanth behind its shoulder blade, emerging from the creature's chest. The animal pitched forwards without a sound and dropped into the edge of the marsh. The rest of the herd just looked round at the unfortunate beast and nervously carried on drinking.

Shoo-lin repeated his brother's success, bringing down another. This was too much for the rest of the herd. They began to mill uncertainly round, nervously snorting and kicking the mud around at the pool's edge.

This was the moment when the Terra-raptor chose to drop out of the sky.

The giant beast rode the air currents and thermals above the small pool for some time, watching the actions of the herd of Zanth. He caught glimpses of the unknown predators creeping forward through the thick undergrowth. They were ridiculously small against his size so eventually he decided to ignore them. Folding his wings close, he started the stoop from the high altitude, occasionally correcting for drift and cross wind. Two of the herd strangely keeled over into the muddy edge of the pool as he dropped closer. Automatically the raptor selected the easier targets from the scattering herd and extended his lower grasping claws.

The first indication the hunting party had that other hungry eyes were fastened on their prey came in the form of a thunderclap as the Terra-raptor opened its wings to halt his headlong flight. The giant aerial beast appeared from the sky without warning. Both hind legs were extended with the great claws opened wide to fasten into the bodies of the two freshly killed wild Zanth. As he dug the sharp talons into the flesh of the Gnathe's kill the raptor began to flap his wings to gain lift. In a few seconds he was partially aloft dragging the two Zanth into the sky.

It took a moment before Shoo-lin and his brother recovered from the shock of the raptor's sudden appearance. Both of them rapidly notched their bows with fresh arrows. Without thinking, they let fly at the airborne beast as it began to gain height into the sky above them. Whann-lin's arrow sank deep into the muscle surrounding the raptor's armpit that controlled the left wing. The other arrow practically disappeared into the un-armoured belly, leaving just the flights exposed. A scream of pain and maddened fury rent the air as the raptor dropped down into the pool, flapping its uninjured wing. It immediately released its grip on the two wild Zanth and squirmed through the floating weeds in an attempt to reach its tormentors. Blood pumped out of its two wounds, staining the water red. The huge head swung round towards the nearest Gnathe and the mouth opened wide enough to take the terrified field hand in one great bite.

"Down its throat!" shouted Jocylene, letting fly her shaft into the roof of the raptor's mouth. "Blind it, if you can!"

Shoo-lin had a brief sideways view of the raptor's head and released his arrow towards the plate-sized eye. The hard wood shaft burst the eyeball, spattering a bloody jelly down the creature's cheek. Scream after scream rent the air as the raptor reared up and away from Shoo-lin's position, shaking its head, trying to dislodge the arrow. More shafts sped through the air, penetrating deeply into the Terra-raptor's body. The undamaged wing frantically beat at the air trying to pull the mass of the beast up and away.

"Look at the water, everyone!" cried Abdul urgently, pointing at several moving shapes. "Move back into the trees!"

"Get away from the pool all of you!" shouted Shoo-lin anxiously. "This is more than we can handle."

"I'm not leaving without my kill," replied Whann and reached forwards for the leg of one of the skewered Zanth. He dragged the dead and damaged beast out of the water with one great heave and said, "Got it. Now I'm prepared to go!"

The swirls and movement in the water were now close to the mortally wounded raptor. Suddenly the beast gave another agonised scream and bent its neck down into the water to seize hold of a wicked looking creature. This animal was perfectly adapted to the water with a long mouth full of teeth. Short legs and a long scaly tail completed the shape. Parallel evolution had produced Jupiter's equivalent of the alligator. The pack struck into the soft underbelly of the grounded raptor. They swarmed over the anguished beast in a few moments, tearing away into the unprotected flesh. Ominous cracklings from the denser patches of undergrowth heralded the arrival of more and different scavengers. The raptor's struggles became weaker as the many hungry mouths eventually overcame it.

The now fearful hunting party began to beat a hasty retreat. Whann and Shoo-lin both held a leg each of the dead Zanth and, grunting with the exertion of the effort, pulled it along as best they could. Another predator, similar to a leopard, picked up the blood trail being left behind them. This was an old male and cat-like in appearance with a deep chest and a long body. The fur was dark and bristly with a light pattern of irregular patches over the back. Nose down against the blood spots, the beast inhaled the scents scattered along the trail. The smell of the Gnathe was totally unfamiliar and unsettling, but hunger soon overcame its caution.

The top of the airship could be seen above the trees so Jocylene signalled for them to stop and catch their breath. She collapsed into a tired heap of arms and legs, sitting down on the hard ground. Abdul sat beside her and looked up at the party of jubilant Gnathe.

"You damned fools, Shoo and Whann!" he angrily exclaimed. "What did you think you were doing? We could all have been killed!"

"Oh, come on, my friend Abdul," replied Shoo-lin. "It happened so quickly we did not have time to think about it!"

"Did you see what we accomplished?" retorted Whann, cheerfully waving his bow in the air in triumph. "We killed a mighty beast, bigger than anything we have ever killed before! These weapons you have given us will open up our world. We can do anything we want."

"If it were only that simple, my impetuous friends," said Jocylene sombrely, getting to her feet. "We were lucky this time. If the beast had dropped onto dry land many of us could have been killed. The bow and arrow is an efficient weapon for the type of quarry suited to it. Do not ever again try to kill something that obviously outmatches you."

There came an ominous grunting cough from the bushes in the direction they had come. All of them turned together and saw the snarling form of the big cat stalk into view.

CHAPTER 17

▼

Kamiel had seen the Terra-raptor drop from the skies over the area of the marsh. Abdul had told him earlier that this would be the most likely place to go for game. For just as in the African dome, the animals would follow a predictable pattern, drinking from the pool at dawn. The distance to the water was about two miles from the airship. The silver coloured figure blurred as the Guardian sprinted towards the scene. He saw the huge flying creature start to take off and then saw it drop once more below the level of the tree line, with a scream of pain and fury. Immediately Kamiel reasoned that the cause of the raptor's distress would be the mixed-race hunting party. It had to be the Gnathe. The human archers would be more cautious with their weapons, knowing the limitations of the bow. The Gnathe, over-excited by the possibilities of the new weapons, would let fly at anything.

"Asue," he sent over their private band, "we have trouble. I have just seen that enormous flying creature drop into the place where Abdul said they would try hunting with the Gnathe. Some idiot has let fly with their arrows and wounded it. I've seen it fall back into the area."

"Do what you can, Kamiel. I will alert the others, to the possibilities of incoming injured. The sooner we get these adventure-happy people back to the Habitat the better."

"I couldn't agree more," replied Kamiel, running and leaping over any obstacles in his way. He scanned ahead on the infrared wavelength to try to locate the position of his friends. The area around the pool was alive with different shapes and sizes. "I can't find them," he called to Asue. "The marsh is teeming with predators and scavengers of every size. I can see what's left of the raptor. Wait, I can see a broken-down trail leading away to the side. I must have passed them by on my direct route here."

"Hurry, Kamiel and find them. The area seems to be getting more and more dangerous as time goes by," the other Guardian answered, as she made her way through the ship and into the hold. "I am almost at the main hold doors. Ender and Khann are close by the ship outside."

The big cat edged closer to the group of Gnathe and humans, snarling aggressively. His head swung from side to side as the beast assessed the situation. The unfamiliar smell of the Gnathe carried across the air. On the ground in front of him, still warm, was the carcass of the dead, wild Zanth.

Jocylene said quietly to the group, "Spread out and draw back your bows. Aim for its chest. If any of us have to loose an arrow, it will have to be a killing blow. This beast can do us a lot of damage if it becomes wounded."

The movement of the hunters caused the cat to advance a little more until it stood over Whann's trophy and bent its head to lick the blood from the body.

Kamiel chose this moment to come hurtling out of the underbrush behind the startled beast. He skidded to a stop by the cat's side. The nervous predator sprang away from Kamiel's presence, straight into Jocylene's tall silver figure. He sideswiped the woman into a heap, slashing her down the leg with a paw the size of a small shovel. As he bent his head to bury his fangs into the helpless woman's chest, Kamiel was upon the beast like an avenging fury. The silver form flowed over the great cat-shaped head, clamping the jaws shut while razor sharp spears drove into the animal's heart from Kamiel's legs. The force of the Guardian's attack bowled the Cat over from its position straddling the woman into the bushes at the side. Kamiel made sure the beast was dead and rapidly returned to the side of his injured friend.

"Asue," he transmitted, "stand by at the medical centre. Jocylene's suit has been ripped by something similar to a large leopard. Ask Khann if she thinks her serum is ready to try out. I do not think we have much of a chance without it. I will be with you as fast as I can."

Shoo-lin ran up to the Guardian and squatted down by his semi-conscious friend and begged him, "What do you want us to do, Kamiel?"

"Get back to the safety of the ship, all of you. Do not stop until you are all close to the hold. This place is getting too dangerous for you to be wandering about on your own." He gathered Jocylene's figure into his arms and turned to run back to the airship. "Move it, you fools, or I may end up digging holes to put you in."

With that remark ringing in their ears, Kamiel began the swift run back to the ship.

Asue ran up to the two large forms of the Brood-mothers and cried out, "Khann, listen to me. Have you finished your tests on the immunity serum?"

"Everything seems hopeful, Asue," the Gnathe answered. "Why? What is the problem, my friend?"

"The hunting party has run into some trouble. Jocylene has been slashed by a large animal and her suit has been breached," said the Guardian, worriedly. "You know what happened last time. Carlos died! You are her only hope in standing a chance of recovering. What do you say?"

"We can only try," replied Khann. "Where is she and how will we administer it to her?"

"Kamiel is bringing her here as fast as he can," Asue said and pointed towards the stand of trees in the distance. "He will come from that direction. I am in contact with Sharn and Minns and they are fully linked to me. Now Khann, I need that serum. Do whatever it is that you have to do and I will do the rest. I will form a bowl with my hand to catch and store the substance, then shape the container into a hypodermic syringe. The problem is, how much of the serum do we give her?"

"All I can do is to estimate the amount required, based on the quantity that we give our young when they emerge into the world. The trouble is, the dose is mixed with partially digested food. This will have to be injected directly into Jocylene's bloodstream."

"Hurry up and produce it, Khann. I will monitor the effects as she receives a measured dose. Kamiel will be here at any moment and every second wasted could cost her her life."

The old scientist concentrated her will into the production of the untried serum. Special glands began to extract the twinned DNA from the living broth in Khann's breeding pouch. The genetic splicing of Gnathe and human cells was complete, with the Gnathe's conferred immunity carried over. What the immediate result would be they could only guess. Without the chance of Khann's bodily secretions being absorbed, Jocylene's fate was definite. Her mouth began to run with saliva as the regurgitation reflex began to take hold.

Kamiel came into view, carrying the larger frame of the human woman as easily as if she were a small child. Jocylene's arms were wrapped around the Guardian's neck, with her body being supported by the silver being's arms. Kamiel had shaped his arms into a chair to help carry the load. He quickly laid her down on the mossy ground in front of the two brood-mothers next to Asue.

"Kamiel has told me what you have in mind," said Jocylene pragmatically, staring up at the group. "There doesn't seem to be much of a choice for me, does there?"

Have courage, my friend," replied Ender-whann-soo gently as she stooped down to Jocylene's level. "My Grand Brood-mother has been a genetic engineer for generations. Someone would have to try the immunity serum one day."

"I am ready, Asue," said Khann, bending forwards to place her triangular head close to the guardian's hand.

The Gnathe began to drool into Asue's cup-shaped hand, holding down on the regurgitation reflex that caused a spasm through her aged body. She straightened up and motioned the ever-attentive Jotin-soo to come forwards with a bowl of water and a cloth.

"I can bring more of the serum into my mouth if you require it," she said and stepped back.

Asue, Sharn and Minns were all oblivious to their surroundings as they analysed the contents of Asue's container on the end of her arm. The soup of combined Gnathen and human cells held them in awe. They would study the genetics of the serum later when there was more time.

"Give me control, Asue," commanded Minns.

Asue did so and took a remote view as the master medical-specialist went into action.

Jocylene looked on as Minns used Asue's body to monitor her reactions to the invasion of her system by Khann's living soup of combined cells. She felt the accustomed sting as the nannite material of the Guardian fused with her living flesh. The area around her leg that the beast had opened up with his claws hurt, but she stoically waited for Minns to block off the pain nerves. Already the area was beginning to go numb as the Guardian began to knit the flesh wound back together. She lay back as a wave of dizziness flowed over her.

Minns released the serum slowly into the muscle of the woman's leg and also into her main vein. She budded off tiny monitors of nannite material to follow the new genes and cells as they began their journey round Jocylene's body and blood system. The new micro-organisms acted similar to the white cells, being the hunter-killer immune system that was part of the human's natural defences. Whenever the cells met they merged on contact, exchanging nuclei and dividing into two identical cells, to continue the process. Khann's genetic work was flawless. Minns watched the monitors scattered around the woman's body in triumphant joy. Wherever a hostile Jovian micro-organism encountered the new improved defence system, they were overcome. In the lungs where the Guardian feared most damage would occur, an uneasy peace prevailed. A small fungal invasion was being fought to a safe conclusion by the improved defenders as she watched. Jocylene's body was still in perfect health. Minns returned her control over to Asue, showing her all of the astounding results. She returned her consciousness back to the Citadel.

Asue disengaged her substance from Jocylene's body and said to the tall woman, "Everything seems fine, my lucky one. Khann's serum works. Apart from the flesh wound on your leg that has to heal, you are fine and healthy. Would you like to take off your suit?"

Jocylene stared back at the guardians in disbelief and said, "Are you sure?"

"I am as sure as I can be, Jocylene," replied Asue sombrely. "Besides, there is no going back now. You can never return to the world of the domes. You carry enough Jovian micro-organisms in your body to eventually wipe out all of the rest of the people living in the Habitat."

"I'm very much afraid that here you are and here you stay," Kamiel said to his old friend. "If you think about it, I believe it's probably what you want to do anyway."

"Help me off with this suit then, Asue. I want to breath real Jovian air! The others will be back soon. I want to surprise them!"

Asue caught hold of the suit behind the shoulder blades and gave the material a twist, causing it to split down the back. Jocylene's tall black figure shrugged off the suit to stand in just her figure hugging corset and underpants. She bent down and removed her heavy boots from the suit material and kicked off the nannite bottoms, replacing the footwear, lacing up the Velcro strips. She added on the translating collar around her neck and stood tall.

"You can't imagine how this feels to me, Kamiel. I can appreciate the breeze and smell the scents of this world." She limped over to the huge, towering figure of the Brood-mother and threw her arms part way around the broad chest of the old scientist to give the startled Gnathe a hug. She smelt of fresh air and sweat with a faint sharp lemony scent.

"Thank you, Khann," she said, burying her face in the velvety fur. "I owe you my life."

"Nonsense, young one," the old scientist replied in embarrassment, picking the grateful woman up from the region of her chest in her mighty hands to the level of the Gnathe's eyes. "You stood in that carrier to the very last moment, picking off Link-soo-shan's soldiers during our escape. You are a brave creature and I am proud to call you friend. Now then, I think I can hear the return of the hunters."

Jocylene looked over the shoulder of Khann's broad frame and saw the returning Gnathe, still dragging the carcass of their first kill behind them. In the lead was Abdul, running steadily towards them. She gave him a cheery wave from her elevated position. He stopped running and slowed to an incredulous walk until he came up to the waiting group.

"You are out of your suit!" he cried in astonishment. "What has happened to you?"

"Khann's immunity serum works. That is what has happened. The slash was just a flesh wound, but the suit was breached. I had no choice except to try it— and here I am! I can never go back into the world of the domes, so I am staying outside."

Abdul turned to Asue immediately and asked, "Do you have any of the serum left?"

Asue turned to the human and replied, "I have enough to administer to several people. Are you sure that you want to try this, Abdul? I repeat, there is no turning back. Once you have taken Khann's living soup into your body it means permanent exile from the Habitat."

"Without Jocylene, the Habitat might as well be empty. I know what I am doing, Asue," he said and offered her his arm. "Inject the stuff into my blood and take off the suit. That gives you two extra, to distribute amongst the other members of the crew."

Asue took hold of Abdul's arm and injected a measured dose into his bloodstream, budding off a host of nannite monitors to observe the changes in the human's body. Just as in Jocylene's case, the micro-organisms integrated into his system of defences. New genes inserted themselves into his cell structures, slightly altering them. As the new living organisms spread throughout his body his heart rate increased for a while, making him dizzy, but the feeling soon passed.

Kamiel helped him out of the survival suit and one more human being stood on the Jovian ground with no protection but his own skin. He walked across to join Jocylene by the two Brood-mothers and pulled her half naked body into his arms.

"You damned fool, Abdul," she murmured in his ear and gently bit it.

"Do you really think I wanted to spend the rest of my life looking at you through glass or a nannite suit?" he said. "I couldn't bear it if I could not hold you again like this."

Alexander and the members of his mentally connected group joined the others in time to see the jubilant Shoo and Whann-lin haul their prize into sight, dropping it at the feet of Ender-whann-soo.

"Look at this, my Lady!" Whann cried excitedly, pointing to the dead animal. "We brought down two, but the big, flying creature nearly got them both!"

"We brought the great beast down as well with our new weapons, Reverend Lady. You should have seen the size of it," said Shoo-lin thoughtfully, squatting down by Khann's side. "Think what we could do, if only I could get my hands on a young one. We would be masters of the skies. Do you think we could keep an eye open for undefended nests on the way to our new home, Alexander?"

"What!" exploded the Habitat's leader. "Shoo-lin, are you mad? From what I have heard, you were lucky to get away with your lives during your encounter with one. Imagine what would be the effects of an attempted nest robbing. I would not want to meet one of those creatures with an attitude problem!"

"Sorry, Alexander, it was just a thought. Think about it, though. Somewhere out there will be a nest with only one provider. While she was away hunting, the nest would be easy to rob. I'm afraid my training as a Beast-master comes to the fore. All I can think about is what I could do with one if I had one to train."

"Shoo-lin, I think it would be a good idea if you took your kill somewhere and processed it. Alexander and I have other matters to discuss," the Brood-mother told the excited Gnathe, pointing in the general direction of the campfires.

"Ender, you and I have a great deal to talk about. It looks as if part of our problems has been solved. Are they all right? They look healthy enough!" Alexander walked up to his near naked friends and said, "Don't get cold. I suggest you go into the hold and get one of the others to bring some clothes out of the stores for you."

"We will do just that, Alex. It's wonderful to be out of the suits, but I would be the first to admit that the breeze does cut through a little," admitted Jocylene with a shiver. "Come on, Abdul, let's get a few more clothes on."

Alexander watched his two crewmembers walk out of sight and disappear into the hold.

"I need to talk to you urgently, Ender and Khann. I continued to change after Asue took me inside. She managed to bring me round after I fainted out here. I could feel a great change taking place and I became very tired, falling into a deep sleep. During the night my mind continued to change and I awoke outside of my body. I was able to float above the airship and remain aware of my being. I could see all of you by your life force shining in the darkness. By concentrating my will, I found that I was able to travel away from here. The Empire of the Gnathe drew me like a beacon and I found myself able to enter the dreaming minds of the people living there. The minds of the males and females were very dull compared to your household here. I found out a great deal of what you have achieved with your own kindred. I surmise that Trann's kindred are of the same ilk. Unfortunately I found myself drawn to a brighter mind that stood out like a flare of brilliance pulsing in its sleep. I attempted to enter this mind and found to my cost, it was Link-soo-shan. She awoke immediately and snatched my mind with a mental grip of fierce intensity. I think the Tyrant may know everything about us. It almost cost me my sanity. Without Asue's skill keeping me alive, I would not have survived. I need you to go into my mind and find out what she has done to me and also how much she was able to extract from my mind. I do not know what damage she may have inflicted. Also since my awakening, by merely touching my friends, they have acquired a little of my mental gifts. We have the start of a telepathic gestalt between us."

Ender-whann-soo stared at Alexander with awe and respect. She reached down to him and placed her huge hands upon his upper arms, bringing her face close to his.

"Alexander, I think you will have to take the same steps that Jocylene and Abdul have taken. For me to do anything I must have proper physical contact. What you have achieved without a power crystal is beyond the powers of the Gnathe. I can do what you have done, but only aided by the added strength of a command crystal," the young Brood-mother replied.

Alexander turned to Asue and ordered her, "Give me a measured dose of Khann's serum. Ask the others if they all want to take the risk. I feel that they should all have the choice. That way if it is unanimous we can dispense with the airlocks between the command centre and the hold. When we get back there will be plenty of room outside the Habitat at the Gnathe's living quarters."

Asue did as she was asked and administered the serum into Alexander's bloodstream, holding him carefully as he went through the dizzy phase. After a few moments she helped him out of his suit to stand in the chilly air in his tunic and underpants. The other members of the group indicated their willingness to join him. Jocylene and Abdul brought out the clothing that was needed from the airship's stores, as Kamiel had radioed instructions back to the command centre inside the ship.

Now warmly clothed, Alexander approached Ender-whann-soo and held out his hands for her to take and press upon the crystal's surface. A wave of warmth and friendliness engulfed him. Ender's healing mind spread over his like a soothing caress. She probed deeply into Alexander's painful areas and met the cruel madness of Link-soo-shan's vicious attempts at crippling his mind. She was amazed at the strength of his will. A lesser being would have caved in under

Link's pressure. As she knitted the torn fabric of his mind together, she could feel his grateful presence slip gently into hers.

"You have made a terrible enemy, Alexander," the Brood-mother projected, anxiously. "She has found out a great deal about your people and our plans for the future. There are torn areas in your mind. I have seen connections and bridges in the pathways of your soul unlike anything that I have encountered before. We can only hope that she meets her death in the arena tomorrow. I think it would be well to put as much distance between us as possible."

"I am inclined to agree," Alexander replied. "I shall not feel happy in my mind, until she is dead or we are home. You have removed my headache and I feel extremely fit. Khann's serum has worked like a tonic! You must teach me the skills that you possess. The one thing I feel we all need to know is how to block off incoming thoughts."

"I can teach you how to do this to a certain extent, Alexander, but I fear that you will need more than I can teach you to fend off a mind driven by a command crystal. One thing is certain, we must somehow find a raw crystal of sufficient power to mount a counter offensive, if she lives," the Gnathe replied sombrely.

"Where can we find one? What do we look for, Ender? You must have some idea of the kind of terrain that they can be found in," thought Alexander in response to his friend's statement.

"The sending, command crystals that the Gnathe possess are old, Alexander. Somewhere in my library there may be a reference to the likely location of them. They have been passed down from generation to generation. I cannot remember any new ones being found. When there is more time to spare and we are in our new home I will search my records," Ender-whann-soo answered. "For the time being, I still think we should get on our way as soon as possible."

Alexander agreed and they broke the rapport between them.

"All right, everyone, we must get ready to continue our voyage back home. Kamiel, I want you to take charge of a properly organised hunting party. This time you will all go out using the carriers," Alexander ordered. "You will be perfectly safe behind the bony plates of the great beasts and you can then carry back quite easily what you manage to bring down. We can then store the meat in the hold freezers. Do you all agree?"

There was a muttered chorus of assent from the Gnathe and the other Habitat members of the new hunting party.

During the day more and more of the crew of Rescue One took a dose of Khann's serum until all of them were fully inoculated against the Jovian micro-organisms. The members of the council were informed of the crew's decision and the knowledge of the possibilities open to the members of the Habitat. These facts were broadcast over the television news channels and were received with mixed feelings by the inhabitants. Many were satisfied with their lives under the security of the domes and required nothing more. Quite a number however were overjoyed by the news and looked forward to the arrival of the airship with its strange cargo.

At the end of the afternoon, the two Brood-mothers and Alexander came to the conclusion that the provisions gathered by the combined efforts of the Gnathe and their new friends were sufficient. The hunting parties organised by Kamiel were successful. Hunting from the backs of the carriers allowed the hunters to approach the various herds of creatures without scaring them. The meat was dressed on the spot without leaving a blood trail for predators to follow. Joints were placed in sealed sacks donated by Rescue One's stores. The size of the placid carriers was enough to keep the large cat-like beast away from the hunters, but Kamiel would take no chances and if a kill was not cleanly dispatched, he would not allow anyone to follow it into the undergrowth. The Gnathe soon became skilled with their new weapons and learnt to aim their arrows at the vulnerable places of the animals they selected.

One by one, the human and ape crew were all brought into contact with Alexander, helped by Ender-whann-soo and the captured crystal of Link-soo-shan's Group Captain. With Asue standing by to oversee the continued health of the subjects, very few problems were encountered. The abilities of the crew were very varied from one to another. The apes seemed to have an easier adaptation to mind-to-mind contact than most of the humans. Not all of the crew could send and receive over any distance, but they could all communicate when physical contact was achieved. Alexander's mind seemed the strongest of all of them, but his skills were raw and unrefined. The minds of the Gnathe were different, requiring the power of the crystal to join them. What they lacked in mental power, however, they more than made up in the skill in which they used their crystal-augmented abilities. The Brood-mothers' minds were far more complex than their kindred and much stronger. The male and female Gnathe had the abilities to use their mental power, but like the human and apes, they were of mixed ability and required training.

The last of the stores were carried aboard and stacked away into the hold as the sun began to drop towards the Empire of the Gnathe. The wind had dropped and conditions were perfect for launching the airship back towards the Habitat. This time the vessel was open from the control cabin into the rear of the ship. The Gnathe were scattered about the hold and the outside veranda. Those that were in the control cabin were instructed to keep still and not touch anything. Ender and Khann squatted by the windows at the front by the control console where Asue began to initiate the sequence of commands to lift the ship.

"Cast off all lines," she ordered over the speaker system. "We are about to lift off. Citadel, do you receive me? We are on our way back."

The rotor blades began to alter their pitch and the airship began to lift steadily into the sky. Asue increased the temperature of the helium to compensate for the entry into the cooler airstreams high above the valley and changed the angle of the rotors to push the mass of Rescue One through the air.

"We receive you loud and clear. Hurry home all of you. Come back safe," said Jo-jo at her desk at the Citadel's control console. "The people of the Habitat welcome the Gnathe and would like to thank Khann-link-sool for what she has done for us."

"You are welcome, Jo-jo," the old Gnathe answered the hairy face in the holo-vision screen. "We owe you a great deal for what you have done for us. We are a proud people and honour our obligations"

The two Brood-mothers watched fascinated as the rough terrain flowed beneath them as time went by. Occasionally one of the giant raptors would be seen in the distance, gliding in the late evening thermals. This time no curious encounters took place. A distant range of hills began to come into view as the mountain-locked valley came to an end. As they began to get closer to the sheer face of the crest, Ender's crystal began to sing and vibrate on the metal frame. Alexander and some of the more telepathically sensitive of the crew felt a pull. Alexander turned to the Gnathe staring out of the windows at the approaching rough edge of the mountain range and asked them, "Do you feel that, you two? I can feel an energy inside my mind. It draws me to the area of rock-face over there by the edge of that sheer drop. Asue, slow the airship down and hover over that ridge."

"We both feel the power of a large sending crystal, Alexander. It is raw and dangerous in its uncut state. I have records of the technique of cutting the shards from a master stone. Shaping a master crystal has not been attempted for many generations," said Ender-whann-soo to the curious Alexander.

Khann looked out to the high, rocky precipice as the airship hovered over the edge and warned them, "Do not at any account touch an uncut crystal. The power is too ragged and out of tune. To do so could burn out your mind. Great damage could be suffered by the one to pick it up. I suggest Kamiel be the one to retrieve it from its rocky home. A sensitive needs to be sent with him to pinpoint the position. You must treat it as dangerous until it has been cut and tuned."

An excited Shoo-lin burst upon the scene and cried out, "Do you not see, over there, by that over-hanging cliff? There is a recently abandoned nest. Something has robbed it of the fledglings, but I can see two eggs that have not hatched. Let me go out there and collect them. We will not get this chance again."

"I will go with him," said Frederick, quickly. "We can climb down the rope ladder while Asue holds the airship steady and Kamiel collects the crystal from the rock-face."

"Very well," Alexander agreed, pulling on a survival suit without the helmet and facing Asue's disapproving figure. "I will go with Kamiel to find the crystal. Someone has to go who is mentally sensitive, to pinpoint its position inside the boulders set into the material of the mountain. Nancy, see if you can find some rucksacks in the stores for us to use. Asue, lower a cargo net in case we have to bring up the crystal still imbedded in the stone."

The three companions quickly dressed for the cold of the high reaches and made their way out of the warmth of the airship to the veranda where Kamiel waited for them. Shoo-lin had wrapped himself in a large woollen sweater that would have fitted one of the apes with their longer arms. He had wound scarves around his legs and secured them with straps. The evening air was cold and the wind cut across the escarpment. Kamiel swung over the side of the parapet and made his way to the sharp, craggy ground beneath them. The rest of the party quickly followed him. Kamiel held the rope ladder steady while the rest of the group climbed down to the rocks. The flesh and blood companions scrambled to safety over the rough terrain. Kamiel cast off the rope ladder to enable Asue to take up a position where the downdraft of the main rotors did not affect the group. Shoo-lin and Frederick made their way to the nest. Something had indeed been there before them and had killed the defenceless fledglings, tearing their bodies apart. Three eggs were still in the pre-hatching state.

"Look," said Shoo-lin, pointing at the egg that had been disturbed by the previous visitor. "Hairline cracks are appearing on the surface. We are just in time. Quickly, stuff it in your bag while I dig out the others from out of this manure pile."

Frederick struggled to manoeuvre the egg into his rucksack and replied to the Gnathe, "I can feel something moving about inside. We had better hurry and get them back to the ship."

"I'm nearly there, friend Frederick," the Shoo-lin answered. "I am through the crust of the manure pile. Hand me the other sack and I will roll the other two eggs into it."

The human did so and helped to roll the two eggs into the Gnathe's carrying sack. They then dragged them out of the large nesting site. All around them were piles of bones pushed into walls to protect the young from the cold wind. Dead branches were interwoven with the macabre remains to hold the nest together.

Frederick called Asue over the suit intercom: "Come and get us, Asue. We have managed to pick up three eggs and they all seem to be on the point of hatching. How are Alexander and Kamiel getting on?"

"Hang tight, you two I'm coming in to fetch you. The other two are nearly finished. I will drop the cargo net for all of you to be winched back inside."

When Alexander had reached Kamiel on the black shiny rocks he had become aware of an insistent force, pulling him away from the nesting site. The wind cut across the boulders and jagged rocks scattered over the high cliffs. From where they stood, a wild and empty mountainous landscape stretched as far as the eye could see. Tall, snow covered peaks jutted upwards in front of them. Below at their backs lay the network of valleys, teeming with life of every kind. The way home lay in front of them, impassable without the airship.

Kamiel helped Alexander to the safety of a large boulder and asked him, "Where do you feel the crystal is, Alexander? I can feel nothing at all. Is it close?"

"I can sense a pulling sensation from farther around this cliff face. It sings to me, Kamiel. Inside my mind, it sings and I need to feel the power. It needs to be tuned, the force is ragged. Down inside that split in the black cliff. Dig for it there, Kamiel."

Kamiel allowed part of his right arm to extend and flow into the crack in the hard, black granite rock. He concentrated all of his being into sensors constructed in the flowing tide of living nannite. A harder substance was deeply embedded in the rock. There was a ridge running along a fault in the fabric of the stone. Tiny nannite converters budded off from Kamiel's body, pre-programmed to re-arrange the granite into a softer material. The split began to enlarge and the rock began to flow out and down around their feet like sand. The setting sun behind their backs penetrated the widening gap and struck the crystal's surface. Alexander felt a surge in the field being put out by the crystal and an increase in his mental powers.

"Ender, can you feel my thoughts? I can feel yours, I think," projected Alexander to the airship above them.

"I can, my friend," she replied anxiously. "Be very careful in what you do."

"I also feel the presence of your mind," projected Khann. "You must retreat from the vicinity of the crystal now, Alexander. Make your way back to the cargo net being dropped for Shoo-lin and Frederick. Leave Kaameel to dig out the gemstone on his own. You have done your part; now come back to safety."

"I must go back to the ship, Kamiel, for my own safety," Alexander told his friend. "The uncut crystal's power is too raw for me to deal with."

"Go then, and I will follow when I have cut this thing out of the rock," the Guardian replied and watched him back carefully around the cliff-face towards the other two of the group.

Carefully, Kamiel enlarged the split even more until at last the crystal fractured away from its stony home. He selected a small boulder and hollowed out its centre big enough to accommodate the gemstone. Next, the Guardian pulled the stone out into the open and immediately placed it inside one half of the hollowed-out boulder, pushing the two pieces together. He sealed the two pieces with nannite pins to prevent them from coming apart.

"I'm ready, Asue," he said over their radio link. "Come and fetch me. Are the others back safely?"

"They are, Kamiel. Stand ready by the nest and I will drop the net," she replied.

Kamiel stood up after wrapping his arms around the small boulder and lifted his prize into the large rucksack. He swung the precious cargo onto his back and made his way around the cliff to the area of the nest-site. Above him Asue manoeuvred the airship to the pick-up point. The empty cargo net lowered towards him, swaying in the wind.

"Where do we go from here I wonder?" thought the guardian to himself. "More changes are going to take place amongst my people than I calculated. Well, Alexander McBald, I have saved your colony from destroying itself with boredom, but where it goes from here I have no idea."

Kamiel grabbed hold of the net as it came into reach and began to be winched back on board.

CHAPTER 18

▼

A few wisps of fog swirled around the many walls of the Imperial City. The day to come would be bright and sunny. Already the multitudinous hordes were waking, perhaps to a new era? Trann-link-khann grimly stretched her whipcord muscles and went into a series of exercises to bring her body to a fully alert state. Her kindred heard the sounds of movement. They began to organise breakfast for themselves and the two Brood-mothers. The fire in the cooking hall was eased into life by the addition of dry fuel. Soon the smell of toasted bread, meat and fruit began to hang on the early morning air. Sing-trow-sool entered the hall and flicked her tongue in and out to taste the air. She felt hungry and made her way to the table by the stone flanked fire. Her own kindred had divided up the labours between Trann's and themselves. Some were fetching more fuel while others gathered food from the store cupboards. The crystal bearers had also woken up and were perched by the warmth of the fire, talking together. They were going over the plans they had all discussed the night before.

"The morning is good I trust? Pass me some of that toasted bread young one," Sing-trow-sool said to one of the smaller, busy Gnathe. "Are you all sure of what you must do?"

"We are sure of what is needed, Reverend mother," Jewel-khann replied confidently. "Soon we will take our positions around the arena and wait for the trail of strength to begin."

"I will be ready to stand by your side in the crystal chamber, Lady Sing. Do not fear, I have been practising with my allotted crystal this very morning," Marren said to the Brood-mother across the table. "Watch the bowl of salt at the end of the table."

All four turned and stared at the wooden bowl that had been grown from a seed case. The bowl began to spin on its axis while the salt began to rise out of the bowl. Marren caused the salt to form into a slender pillar, until all of the salt was removed from the container. The bowl rose up into the air and moved silently down the table, followed by the column. When the two items reached the other end of the wooden surface, Marren allowed the salt to flow back into the bowl.

"You see, the more I use it, the more proficient I become," she declared.

"I am impressed," retorted a voice from behind them. "Once I have eaten and refreshed myself, we should try the rapport again with the command crystal."

Trann-link-khann stepped onto the perch at the end of the table and helped herself to some smoked meat and toasted bread. Sing passed her some fruit and roasted pod-vine beans. The Brood-mother ate sparingly from the offered feast. She wore her personnel communication crystal, securely round her neck and bound in a leather thong.

When she had finished eating, she said to the others, "Let us go to the communications chamber and tune the crystal to the five of us. We must be ready for when I issue the challenge," and signalled her intent to leave.

Link-soo-shan paced up and down in her allotted quarters, popping her sharp ripping claws in and out of their sheaths. She studied them moodily, testing them for sharpness by raking them deep into the living walls of her room. The waiting tried her patience. The Ultimate Ruler chewed on a piece of roasted meat and could stand the idleness no more.

"Jaffin," she bellowed frustrated, "where are you? I need to go out from these rooms."

"Lady Link, she has gone to make contact with others of our kindred loyal to your cause," one of her Imperial Guard replied from the doorway. "Can we do anything for you?"

"Have you seen Nagoth? Is she not to be found also? The walls close in. I must exercise and loosen up my cramped muscles."

"Nagoth disappeared at first light, my Lady. She said she was going to interfere with Trann's plans as much as possible," answered another guard, stepping into the room. "Let me help you dress and make ready for the slaughter."

"Buckle on my scabbard and hand me my syther. I will feel better when I am armed. So, Nagoth has gone on the prowl, has she? She will be well rewarded with rank when this is over," the Brood-mother growled thoughtfully. "That female shows great promise. I will definitely be breeding from her line when this business is finished with." She flexed the muscles of her huge arms and swung the length of her personal syther in a figure of eight. "Throw that fat fruit at my head at any time of your choosing," she said, poised and ready at the end of the table.

The guard did so, aiming a red fruit the size of her hand at her Brood-mother's head. She threw it hard and it sailed through the air with good accuracy. Link-soo-shan spun round and flicked the end of the syther towards the hard, rind-covered missile. The fruit flew into two pieces and hit the walls with a double smack. As one piece bounced off, Link speared it with the point of her sword while scooping up the other with her claw extended foot. She tossed it into the air and caught it between her jaws, sinking her teeth into the pulpy flesh.

"I will do that with Trann's head," she shouted with glee, "and watch her blood pump into the sand. Enough of this! Form a protective cordon around me and I will go outside and squat in the sun. I will wait for Trann's summons to the arena in the open air."

The handful of Link's kindred strode out into the morning sunshine and cleared away the curious onlookers from in front of the temporary quarters of the threatened Ruler. They looked at the size of the greatest fighting Gnathe ever to wriggle out of a Brood-mother's pouch with undisguised awe. Many still thought Trann mad.

The sun continued to rise remorselessly into the sky. At the arena, the crowd gathered, hushed and expectant. Trann's three conspirators planted themselves amongst the crowd. Each had their telekinetic crystal bound to their wrists for safety. A telepathic crystal hung around each neck to keep them in contact via the command crystal. Trann-link-khann entered the arena from the royal end to a buzz of speculation. She stood perfectly still with her syther point down in the hot sand, waiting for the Ultimate Ruler's entrance and projected her thoughts to the command crystal.

"Where is she, Sing? Can you not sense her? What is she doing?"

The Keeper sent her thoughts in a questing spiral, moving away from the other entrance. She soon encountered a group of Link-soo-shan's kindred walking slowly towards the arena. They were taking their time and in the midst of them, travelled something slippery. She focused the power of the command crystal towards the centre of the group of Gnathe. It was as if she were attempting to grip a piece of soft grease. Every time she tried to enter the mind of whatever it was, she slid away. Frustrated, she concentrated on one of the accompanying females. Instantly she slipped inside the Gnathe's mind. This close to the command crystal, she did not require the female to be wearing a communication crystal to be able to telepathically contact her. She caught a glimpse of the mighty, Ultimate Ruler, walking slowly and steadily by her kindred's side.

The guard felt her presence and projected back. "Drown in piss, you traitorous low-born scum! The great Lady Link will peg you out on the throne-room floor until you die of old age for what you have done. She forbids us to kill you when this is over. Tremble at her wrath."

Sing-trow-sool nearly collapsed from fright and fear. She turned away from the crystal for a moment, breaking contact and crying out in fear. Getting herself under control again, she once more reinforced the mental web joining Trann and the other members of the group.

"Listen all of you—the Tyrant has some strange form of protection," she broadcast anxiously. "I cannot read her mind or even detect that she is there at all. I can only see her through her kindred's eyes. Be very careful in what you try to do."

Trann looked down the long sandy length of the arena at the other entrance. Her mouth began to dry with fear and doubt.

Link-soo-shan had slipped the amulet onto her wrist before starting the walk towards the arena. The box she entrusted to one of her guards to keep safe. One of Trann's kindred had fearfully approached her and had given the challenge whilst she had squatted outside in the sunshine. She had whipped the point of her syther through the air a finger's breadth from the female's nose and was rewarded by seeing a pool of urine spread around the female's feet. Link roared with cruel laughter at the fear inspired by her in Trann's servant.

"Later my pretty, you will discover the real meaning of fear," the Brood-mother laughed and rose to her full height. She watched the Gnathe break and run for the safety of the city side streets back to the arena. "Remember, all of you, where you must stay and all we discussed. I may have to run. You will protect my retreat. They will not expect that to happen if things go against me. I am relying on you. I will not forget this day, whatever happens. I have another debt to repay, more important than what I do today."

With that, Link-soo-shan began to walk to the arena. Halfway there she felt a muffled thrust at her mind, which slid effortlessly away. One of her guards stiffened and she knew that someone was operating the command crystal.

"The Keeper looks through my eyes, Lady Link. I told her to drown in piss," the guard retorted. "She obviously could not enter your mind."

"Trann already trembles with fear," Link replied happily. "Maybe things will come out my way after all."

She looked up at the living gates of the arena and reflected on the history of the enclosed battleground. It had been grown and constructed generations ago, long before the birth of Link's Brood-mother, Shan-mace-soo. Once, Shan had dominated this area and had slowly increased the size of her empire. She used the arena to stage open challenges to her rule. It was Shan who had instigated the Rite of Succession between opposing Brood-mothers. Disputes between different families were settled in hand-to-hand combat, by dominant Brood-mothers facing each other on the sands of the amphitheatre. The losers' heads were cleansed of flesh, polished and set in the hall of power adjacent to the Royal Chambers. Shan-mace-soo's skull held pride of place as the first overall Empress of the Gnathen lands. Link-soo-shan was determined that it would be some time yet before her skull adorned the plinth next to her Brood-mother's.

"Stand by the gates and prevent them from closing behind me. Block the entrance with your bodies," she ordered tersely.

"Good luck, mighty one," called out one of her guards.

"Take her head and spill her life upon the sands, Great Lady Link," cried out another as she passed through the gates. A roll of drumbeats heralded her entrance as Link-soo-shan, once Ultimate Ruler of the Gnathen Empire, stood alone at the other end of the arena opposite Trann-link-khann.

Nagoth and Jaffin had parted from the company early in the morning, before Link-soo-shan had awoken. They made their way to the Imperial stables, where Nagoth had arranged to meet the guards that she had subverted at the entrance to the Royal quarters the day before. A sizeable contingent of Chang's kindred had assembled quietly in the shadows. The fittest of the Zanth had been selected and harnessed. A carrier had also been pressed into service and inside its bony plates sat, bound and gagged, five hands of male Gnathe. They were quiet and fearful. Three of Chang's kindred sat amongst them with their sharp sythers bared. The light reflected from off the crystalline sides was enough to instil silence in the young males. There were a sprinkling of finely skilled crafters seated with them.

"Well done, all of you," the Group Captain said softly in the quiet of the stables. "Mount up and follow me. We must leave the city in stealth, while everyone has gathered at the arena."

Jaffin mounted a large male Zanth and turned it around to lead the way. Silently, the others mounted their beasts and followed her out of the stables, leading the carrier into the morning sun. The streets were empty. As the morning had progressed, every city dweller gathered at the arena to watch the conflict between Link-soo-shan and Trann-link-khann.

Nagoth closed the doors behind them, checking that a large and powerful Zanth was harnessed and ready, should the Ultimate Ruler require it. Also, she made sure that enough beasts were ready for Link's guards to use, should they retreat from the arena. She beckoned forward the three females that had elected to stay.

"Look after things here and keep a lookout towards the arena," she ordered, speaking soft and low. "If the 'Mighty One' decides to run, be ready for her. She may be wounded. Do not leave this place without her. I have business inside the Royal Quarters. I will do my best to come back in time. Do not wait for me, but leave a fast mount behind and follow Jaffin's trail, to the holding we took on the way here. Any questions? Do you all understand what I require?"

"We understand, Nagoth—there are no questions," one of Chang's daughters replied. "Go with luck. We will not let you down. Do what you must, but return safely. Our great Lady has need of Gnathe like you."

Nagoth turned and made her way into the warren of corridors that led through the old Banilik Tree towards the royal chambers.

Several murders later, she found herself once more approaching the Crystal Command Chamber. Standing in front of the entrance with a clear view of the approaches was one of Trann's inner circle. It was Marren-khann, standing guard over Sing-trow-sool's co-ordination of the telepathic web. Nagoth watched, fascinated, as the Gnathe telekinetically juggled some glow crystals taken from the wall. From inside the chamber came a muffled cry of anguish as the Brood-mother pulled away from the command crystal after the frustrated attempt to read Link-soo-shan's mind. Marren turned from her position in front of the entrance to the crystal room and went inside, leaving the glow crystals once more imbedded in the wall. There would come no better chance to approach the unguarded doorway without being seen. Nagoth primed her Kryte with a poisoned dart and silently crept towards the door.

Over a thousand miles away and steadily ploughing through the air, Rescue One was making its way back home. Alexander had called a conference together at the surgery. The guardians were both present and so were the two Brood-mothers. Nancy, April and Joom sat on chairs around the surgery while the two huge Gnathe squatted on the floor next to the examination couch. Alexander lay down upon the hard surface of the table and felt the apprehension of the group with his mind.

"I have to do this," he said softly to his friends. "Asue will monitor my vital signs during the trip. Khann, I want you to accompany me. Your experience will be important. You know that we have to find out the outcome of the struggle."

"I know only too well, young one," replied Khann and she placed her great hand upon the side of the table, next to his. "Ender, pass me the crystal, so that I may go into a trance state with Alexander."

The younger Gnathe placed the crystal into the old scientist's hand. Asue placed her right hand over Alexander's chest and entered his flesh to monitor the continued health of his body.

The Habitat's mayor felt the customary sting of Asue's nannite contact with his bare skin. He turned his head to make eye contact with Khann-link-sool.

"Take hold of the crystal, my friend, and place my hand upon it," he said to the tall form next to him. "I am ready."

Khann placed the crystal in her palm and held Alexander's hand, sandwiching the gemstone between the two alien pieces of flesh.

Alexander and Khann mentally joined together and the human pushed at the confines of his skull. There was a slight tearing feeling and he was once more airborne, floating above his body. This time he had Khann with him, linked to his mind.

"We are free," he projected to the group below them.

All the other minds received his thoughts and perceived the twin souls depart the vessel and begin the long trek back to the Gnathen Empire.

"How are you, Khann?" he asked.

"Fine, young one. This is marvellous. You travel effortlessly, a method that I can only do, linked to a master crystal. Do not burn out your reserves. Take and share some of mine," the old scientist admonished. "We have far to go."

"This takes no effort as yet, my friend," he replied. "Hang tight with me. The sun is climbing the sky. I do not want to arrive late. We may be able to influence things. Who knows?"

Alexander increased the speed of travel until the countryside blurred underneath their passage. Soon they found themselves over the edge of the Gnathen Empire. Khann directed him towards the Imperial City and Alexander slowed their rate of travel until they hovered over the arena. There, below them, stood the two Brood-mothers, each at one end of the arena.

"We are in time to witness the end of the Tyrant, Alexander," projected Khann. "Can you sense the mental web between Trann, the Keeper Sing and their three crystal bearers?"

"I can indeed, but where is Link's mental signature? I can see her like a shadow on the sand. I cannot feel her presence. It's as if she were not there!"

Link-soo-shan advanced slowly towards her hated foe across the hot sand of the arena's floor. There would be no sudden rush upon her opponent. First, she had to find out what extra help the would-be Empress had at her command. She felt a muffled push from the side of her body and turned to face in the direction from which it had come. Amongst the crowd, perched at the front was a small female wearing a communication crystal and holding something bound to her arm. A look of surprise covered her face.

"Reverend Lady Trann, I cannot penetrate the Tyrant's skin," projected Jewel-khann in despair. "I cannot blind her!"

"Do you hear that, all of you? This is what Sing was able to sense," broadcast Trann urgently. "Abandon all attempts to cripple her by entering her body. Concentrate on slowing her down."

Link-soo-shan retreated from the area of influence of Jewel-khann's projection and meandered to the other side of the arena. Here sat Natel-soo concentrating her will out into the sandy space. Once more the Brood-mother felt the thrust of mind-force against her body. She scanned the crowd and once again was rewarded by sighting another female wearing a communications crystal and holding her bound wrist. Again the Ultimate Ruler retreated away from the crystal bearer.

The thought came into her head: "Telekinesis! That is the edge of power that Trann is relying on. They would use it like a surgeon upon me. The amulet blocks them from entering my body. Oh, how confident you must have been, Trann. You will truly understand the meaning of fear this day."

Trann stood perfectly still, well within Jing-soo's protective range. She took up a fighter's stance, syther held point outwards towards the remorseless advance of the now incontestable Ultimate Ruler. Jing-soo picked up a ball of sand with her mind and assembled it on the back of Trann's sword hand.

"This is a good day to die, you meddling fool," Link-soo-shan rasped across the space between them. "I know your secret, Trann. It will not help you."

The double-handed syther extended towards Trann's face and Link executed her first manoeuvre. She spun round, twisting the bony point of her tail through the air towards Trann's legs. The sword flashed over the tail in a decapitating blow at the other Gnathe's head.

Jing drove the ball of sand into Link's mouth, released it on contact and grabbed the sword that had extended out from the slippery field. She drove it at the ground, unbalancing the swing.

Trann sidestepped the tail's swathe of destruction, pulled away from the deadly arc of Link's longer sword and managed to prick her in the side of her leg.

Link-soo-shan rolled over and back into the centre of the arena, dragging the now impossibly heavy sword. Trann leapt for her while Link was spitting sand from her defiled mouth. She aimed a blow at Link's sword arm that passed harmlessly by, a hand's breadth away and stood back.

Link's furious gaze locked onto Jing-soo's face. She looked down at Trann's defensive figure and laughed madly at her. "Three of them, tucked away in the crowd. Very clever, Trann! Very clever indeed! All linked together telepathically by Sing-trow-sool at the command crystal."

Trann projected to her people: "All together, pin her down as she comes within range. Push her over if you can. I will try to lead her over to..." Trann felt the mental web dissolve.

Nagoth slowly edged around the doorway leading into the Crystal Command Chamber. There, with their backs to her, was Sing-trow-sool, with her great hands firmly placed against the large crystal's surface and another female standing beside her. There would be time for only one shot with the Kryte. Which was the most dangerous to her? The Brood-mother was deeply into the sending trance and probably unable to notice what was going on around her near vicinity. Without a doubt the telekinetic female would have to be taken out first. She aimed the small creature at the Gnathe's back and pressed its trigger region at the base of the spine. The Kryte sneezed and the pre-loaded dart shot out of the creature's nose straight at the undefended female's back. As the dart stung Marren-khann in her back, she spun round and caught sight of the intruder hiding in the doorway. She reached out with her mind to cut the optic nerves of the Imperial Guard, but at the same time, saw Nagoth's syther spinning through the air towards Sing's oblivious body. Marren deflected the knife from its target and dimly saw it thud heavily into the wooden wall. The room began to go out of focus as the poison did its work and Trann's loyal daughter breathed no more.

Nagoth-shan hurled herself at the shoulders of the entranced Brood-mother and toppled her over onto the floor, striking her hands from the influence of the crystal's power. She drove Sing-trow-sool's head down hard onto the stone floor, knocking her senseless for a few moments. The Imperial guard rolled over her and sprang away from the wall, scooping up the command crystal in her carrying pouch. She left the syther stuck fast in the wall, stepped over the contorted body of Marren-khann and left the communications room at a fast pace. By the time the Keeper had recovered from the stunning blow to her head, Nagoth was nowhere to be seen and the great command crystal had vanished.

Trann looked up at the towering figure of her adversary and leapt to the side away from the enraged Brood-mother's reach. Link-soo-shan slowly pursued her, holding her sword close to her body, keeping it out of reach of the telekinetic powers of Trann's kindred. Trann backed away, getting closer to Jewel-khann's position in the crowd. The Ultimate Ruler gave a mighty leap, up and over the head of Trann, curling her tail in a vicious arc. At the same time she reached out with her taloned foot to get a hold onto Trann's flesh. Trann felt herself bodily lifted to the side and away from the attack. Jewel had locked onto the one person that she could grip with her mind. Nevertheless she received a stunning blow to her left side, numbing the muscles of her arm by Link's armoured tail. Trann moved into a position equi-distant from both Jewel and Natel-soo and waited for the Brood-mother to advance. The watching Gnathe were hushed and silent as the two enemies faced each other once more.

Above them, Alexander and Khann watched helplessly as the two Gnathe feinted and parried each other. With the web down, all Trann's co-ordination had vanished. Now she would have to play the combat as it came.

"Can you mend the web?" asked Alexander, mentally, to Khann.

"Not without a power crystal to hold the parts together," she replied in regret.

"Try using my mind as your frame of reference. Otherwise all could be lost. I need to contact her. I have an idea that might work," Alex advised her.

Khann reached out to the minds that had been knitted together and found the matching signatures of the small crystals hanging round the necks of Trann and her kindred. She concentrated on opening the paths and brought them together, contacting them simultaneously.

"Listen all of you, this is Khann-link-sool and the human leader, Alexander. I can hold this link together for only a short time. Alexander has an idea to share with you."

Trann continued to stay out of reach of Link-soo-shan and quickly asked, "I have need of ideas—what do you suggest?"

"Crystal bearers listen carefully. Build the sand around her to slow her down. Hold the sand around her feet and tail. Drive pieces of grit into her eyes and do the same as Jewel, by moving Trann out of danger. That's all. I have to let go now," he told them and shut down the link.

In the airship Asue had seen the tremendous energy loss of Alexander's body and immediately ordered Nancy, "Connect up a glucose bottle and intravenous feed. Whatever he's doing is taking a lot of energy. We will lose them both if this carries on too long."

Above the field of conflict Alexander rested while Khann scolded him for his recklessness and they watched the events unfold.

Link-soo-shan began to find her feet heavy as she relentlessly followed Trann towards the wall of the arena. She risked a look downwards and saw to her astonishment a heap of sand swallowing her feet, anchoring them securely to the ground. She tore one foot loose and lunged at Trann with her syther, striking out like a spear. The edge of the point caught Trann across the numbed left shoulder. A trickle of blood began to flow down her arm. She spun to the side and ducked out of Link's reach, bringing her sword down on the Brood-mother's left flank, producing a shallow cut and leaving her own blood mark.

"I'll wear you down, Trann, in the end," Link taunted and pulled herself back towards the middle of the arena.

Do the unexpected, thought Trann, and ran straight at the Brood-mother, taking her by surprise. She planted both taloned feet securely on top of Link's feet and drove her sword directly at her chest. Link swept her off the front of her body with an almighty heave before the syther plunged home, rolling to the side. Once more the armoured tail swept round and this time dealt Trann a hefty blow, spinning her across the arena and into an untidy heap against the wall.

The crowd yelled encouragement to the fallen Brood-mother. She dizzily got to her feet, spitting blood from her bitten tongue and extended her syther in defence. Link-soo-shan sprang across the sandy floor with her double-handed syther extended above her head. This would be the killing blow. Jing-soo reached out with her mind's augmented power and held the sword firm against the power of Link's downward swing. She interfered with the molecular bonding of the blade of the syther that extended out from Link's protective field, causing it to break into two pieces. The Ultimate Ruler gave a scream of frustrated wrath as the upper part of her sword arced uselessly through the air, leaving a short stub in her hands. A ball of sand enveloped her head, getting into her mouth and eyes. Blinded and spitting sand, the Brood-mother once more retreated to the centre of the arena, to the weakest area of the crystal bearers' reach.

Trann shook off the effects of the Ultimate Ruler's blows and doggedly advanced towards the shaken Brood-mother. She now had an advantage of reach with her undamaged syther. The blade was light and sharp, capable of cutting deep into flesh. Against the long double-handed broadsword of Link-soo-shan's it resembled a toy. Now, with only a stub to fight with, the advantage lay with Trann.

Again, the two of them faced each other across the hot sand. The heads of the families watched with critical eyes the slow advance of their new would-be Empress towards the towering figure of Link-soo-shan. All had seen the different way of fighting displayed by Trann. This was very new. The outcome would decide the future for generations to come.

"Not so easy, is it?" called out Trann to the frustrated figure looming in front of her.

Link gritted her teeth in reply and lashed out with her shortened sword. Trann sidestepped and flicked a cut across Link's ribs. As the Ultimate Ruler turned to favour the injured side, Trann riposted forwards and sank the tip of her syther into the fleshy muscle of Link's upper leg, close to the previous wound. Link rolled over and aimed another blow with her armoured tail. Trann leapt up and over the swinging blow, chopping down at the wildly swishing tail. The sharp edge of the syther bit into the flesh just before the bony, armoured area.

Link-soo-shan screamed in pain and hurled herself at the smaller figure, catching her with a sharp ripping claw across the back. Trann sprang forwards out of the way and enticed her enemy back towards Jing-soo and her sphere of influence. Her face held in a rictus of insane hate and fury. Link-soo-shan followed her, limping from the deep cut to the leg and weaving her stubby sword from side to side. Jing-soo reached out for the discarded broken sword-blade with her mind and sent it spinning through the air at the Ultimate Ruler's head. Link parried the blow with the stub of her sword, driving it down onto the sand and placed her foot upon it, covering it with her blanketing field. Trann lent forward and the point of her syther cut part way through Link's hearing crest and continued across her face, penetrating the flesh above her right eye. Partially deafened and half blinded with the flow of blood into her eye, Link picked up the broken sword-blade with her foot and flung it at Trann's stomach. As Jing-soo reached out with her mind and deflected the spinning blade from her adopted Brood-mother, Link stretched up to her maximum height and grasped Jing-soo's arm that held the crystal. The Ultimate Ruler pulled Jing-soo into the arena and ripped the arm from the Gnathe's body, throwing her screaming, bloody form full at Trann-link-khann.

The blood flowing from the deep cut above her eye had now run into both eyes. Keeping a firm grip on the dismembered arm, she blindly ran for the safety of her guards at the other entrance of the arena. They advanced out into the arena to meet her and strong hands reached out to guide her into their midst.

She stopped in the doorway of the arena, faced back at her tormentor who was cradling the dying, bleeding Gnathe, and screamed at her, "You have not won. I will come back here and you will tremble at my return."

The watching Family heads were numbed by the turn of events and stayed fixed in their positions around the amphitheatre, not sure what to do. They took their lead from Trann and waited to see what she would do.

Trann had neither the forces, nor the foresight planning to organise a chase after the retreating deposed ruler, so she stood her ground.

"From this day forward you are banished from the lands of the Gnathe!" she shouted at the group withdrawing from the arena.

Boxed in by her loyal guards, Link-soo-shan blindly retreated from the field of conflict and limped towards the stables where Nagoth waited with the other mounted guards. She was filled with a vindictive madness that coursed through her twisted soul. In her breeding pouch lay Jing-soo's arm with all of Ender-whann-soo's genetic secrets to unravel.

Inside Rescue One, Alexander and Khann had returned. Both of them were exhausted. The Habitat's mayor looked pale and drawn. Dark circles lay under his eyes and he lay deathly still.

"She still lives, Ender my friend. She still lives, but she did not win," Alexander quietly told the circle of his friends.

"The Ultimate Ruler has laid down other plans, my companions. She is up to something and I shudder to think what she is capable of," Khann grimly added. "We must keep a watch on her."

CHAPTER 19

▼

During the night, Shoo-lin had instructed Frederick and Coen-soo how to treat the hatchlings, should the eggs in their charge begin to crack. Imprinting the young Terra-raptors would take place the moment they hatched.

Shoo-lin explained to his two apprentices at the back of the darkened hold: "What you must do when the egg starts to crack is to make sure the young raptor becomes aware of your scent. Exercise to produce plenty of sweat and void your bowels in the immediate hatching area if you can. Cuddle the infant hatchlings to your naked bodies. Remember how large these things are going to grow! They must believe that you and you alone are its mother and father. I have removed some of the stored meat and part cooked it in the microwave ovens in the kitchen. Have it ready when the morning comes. You will have to chew it and spit the partly digested meat into its jaws. This will bond the creatures to you. Let no other person feed it until you are quite sure that it is safe."

"How do you know that this will work, Shoo-lin?" asked Frederick doubt-fully, while he cradled his egg in his arms.

"I don't," the Gnathe replied with a chuckle and handed one of the eggs to Coen-soo. "You will just have to trust my instincts as a Beast-master. If I am wrong, the raptor will probably eat you when it gets big enough!" Shoo-lin's eyes were alive with the challenge and the possibilities unfolding with every passing moment. "You must form your own attachment with the young creature. Love it and the animal will respond," he said to the two attentive protégés.

Frederick lay naked to the waist with a sweat soaked blanket over himself and the egg. He had done some fierce exercises in the hold to work up a sweat and had urinated over part of the covering as Shoo-lin had suggested. The other two

Gnathe squatted down with the egg between their legs, covering them with their warmth.

As the hours passed, they drifted in and out of dream-filled sleep. Towards the dawn, Frederick felt the egg beside him begin to crack open. His new telepathic powers were nowhere near as strong as Alexander's, but the awakening, hitherto dormant abilities, were beginning to settle down. The living creature pushing itself out of the egg had as yet a primitive mind. In the wilds of the mountain ranges, the raptors had developed more than a beast's intellect. Avid hunters always developed a perception of future events and planned their attacks to provide food by thinking ahead. The brains of the raptors increased in size due to natural selection and the fierce environment they chose to exploit. The raptors traced their ancestry back to the original bird stock that the Seed-ship had left behind at the early stages of Jupiter's induced and accelerated life. In the case of the raptors, feathers had once more become scales and the wing membranes became warm leathery skin. Some genetic freak in the past had split the bone structure of the wing into two separate parts, leaving the main wing for flying. The other bone structure had developed into a jointed arm, terminating in a clawed, three-fingered hand. All three fingers opposed each other, so the creature was able to grasp and manipulate its prey. The back legs and feet were a powerful combination for grasping and holding on to their prey.

The emerging Terra-raptor began to claw its way out of the confines of the egg. It hooked its sharp claws into the cracks in the egg's surface and heaved them apart. Frederick felt the warm body wriggle out and instinctively seek his warmth.

"Shoo-lin," he cried excitedly, "mine has hatched and I can sense its mind!"

"Hold it close to you and cuddle it, my friend. Let it dry out before you attempt to feed it. Wait for the dawn," the Gnathe advised him.

Coen-soo gave a cry of delight and declared, "My raptor is struggling out of its shell. Shoo-lin, it is beginning to hatch."

"I feel movement underneath my legs also. A head has just pushed out and is lying over my feet while it struggles to emerge from the egg," Shoo-lin remarked happily. "Remember to keep them warm under the blanket. Dawn will be some time yet."

The hours soon passed and light began to filter through windows into the back of the airship's hold. Underneath the blankets the baby raptors began to stir as the first hunger pangs were felt. They all began to remove the blankets from around the newly hatched chicks and for the first time got a look at what they had helped to bring into the world.

Three pairs of beady eyes were fixed on the person that had hatched them. Jaws wide open, the young raptors began to hiss and jostle each adoptive parent for food. Shoo-lin had been chewing pieces of meat in readiness for this moment. He leaned forwards over the wide-open jaws of his chick and spat the mixture of meat and saliva into the creature's throat. The baby raptor swallowed the pulpy mass and sat for a few moments content.

The other two companions followed suit and began to feed their own chicks. After a while they started to push larger morsels of part-cooked meat down the throats of the hungry animals.

Frederick laid his arm over the repulsively ugly Terra-raptor and held the spindly thing to his warmth. The chick was about the size of one of the shepherd's collies in the sheep farming area of the Habitat. Only, it was completely naked of fur. A light down could just be seen covering its body, except for the wings. These were leathery and very like a bat's in construction, except for the small arms splitting away from the shoulder. A long whip-like tail nearly as long as Frederick was tall, curled around the body. Sharp claws protruded from the feet and the joints at the knees were formed the same as the Gnathe's. So the creature squatted, with its knees pointing backwards and its huge feet projecting forwards. When it squatted on its haunches the young chick's head came almost to Frederick's waist.

"What are we going to do for breakfast, Shoo-lin?" asked Coen-soo. "I am hungry myself and I for one am not going to eat half-raw meat"

"We will leave the creatures here, huddled together with their blankets," he replied and wrapped his chick up in its covering. Fed and sleepy, the raptor gave a slight hiss of protest and settled down. "You see, it is tired and needs to sleep to digest its food, just like a child."

They left the chicks together after Frederick had instructed the airship's computer to keep them informed if the young raptors began to stray. Soon they were tucking into their own food and kept a watch on a monitor screen, activated by Asue, to give them peace of mind.

"Shoo-lin, I think they will be fine. Look, they are making no moves to wander off," Frederick remarked to the Gnathe.

"It would be a survival characteristic not to move out of the nest. I think that wherever we put them, they will say put," Shoo-lin replied and stood up, stretching his arms. "I can feel mine is getting hungry! Time to feed them again, I think."

By mid-morning, Frederick was beginning to wonder just what he had got himself into. The chicks were always hungry. Every time each young raptor caught sight of it's 'mother', the young creatures became frantic to attract attention. Jaws agape, they worried their adoptive parents constantly for food. Alexander had fully recovered from his ordeal during the Rite of Succession and he and his friends gathered round the young chicks with interest. The young raptors were initially suspicious of the new people, but would accept food from the many willing hands.

"It is important that the chicks grow up knowing the difference between us and food," Shoo-lin impressed the curious visitors. His chick was pressed against him for reassurance and hissed at the eager hands trying to touch it. "All who come here to visit must bring pieces of meat with them; then the young creatures will identify human, ape and Gnathe as providers, not threats."

Alexander walked away, back towards the command console of the airship. All around him he could feel the busy minds of all his friends. It was a comforting feeling. He basked in the warmth of their friendship.

"Can you hear me Ender?" he enquired with his new abilities.

"Yes I can, Alexander my friend, but only when you send to me," the Brood-mother replied. "I still find it remarkable that you are able to do so much without the aid of the crystal's power. No Gnathe could duplicate what you had done, un-aided. Even your fearsome enemy, Link-soo-shan, could not match your powers. With a command crystal at her disposal, however, she may be capable of great harm."

Alexander sat in the co-pilot's chair next to Asue and moodily worried at the edge of the problem. "I wish I knew the outcome of that struggle for supremacy at the Gnathen City. How badly was she injured, I wonder?" He both projected to Ender and spoke to Asue.

"Alexander, I forbid you to try astral travelling again. You are not strong enough and as the distance increases, the energy required could drain your life away. We will keep a watch on events from the satellite in orbit above us. There is enough to do when we return to the Habitat," Asue declared strongly and stared hard at the human being seated beside her. The silver head had produced recognisable eyes to watch events unfold through the forward window. "We cannot afford to lose you, my friend. Please promise me you will not do anything reckless without consulting me."

Alexander nodded in reply and watched the mountaintops roll along underneath the belly of the airship. He could feel the nagging pressure of the un-cut crystal singing away in the recesses of the hold. He would be glad when the large gemstone had been cut and tuned. Hannah and her group of scientists would be overjoyed when they got home and gave her some of the off-cuts and shards to examine. They would have to be decontaminated before they could be handed through the nannite curtain. He reached forwards and activated the communication's link with the Citadel. The transmitter soon warmed up and he found himself looking into the hairy features of his long time friend, Jo-jo.

"It's about time you got in touch with me, you know," she said to him and pointing her finger straight at his face, telling him of the workload building up at the Citadel.

Link-soo-shan's escape from the Imperial City caught the heads of the families by surprise. All of them had expected a fight to the death with a clear winner taking control of the Empire. They were not sure what to do in the circumstances. Trann stood tall over the dead body of her loyal adopted daughter, Jing-soo. She beckoned her two surviving kindred from the crowd and waited until they stood beside her. She looked at the massed ranks of the Brood-mothers and their kindred.

"Listen to me!" she shouted at the crowd. "Support my rule of the Empire and we can achieve great things for ourselves. The cruelty and tyranny of Link-soo-shan and her sister is over forever. I have broken her power and cast her out of our society. Ender-whann-soo is by now safely across the mountains and close to the home of the aliens who live on the other side. There are vast empty lands across there. Once she is established, there will be many visits by the aliens in their flying carrier. I have seen what they can do through Ender-whann-soo and Khann-link-sool's eyes. They want to be our friends and there are many advantages for the Gnathe to be allied with such as they. Do not embrace anarchy. We do not want to return to the civil wars we endured before Shan-mace-soo united the Gnathen lands by force. Her daughters gave us a cruel and bloody peace. Let us enjoy a gentle peace, enforced by reason. I would grow great seats of learning here at the Imperial City, where all could embrace the new sciences that will emerge from our association with Ender-whann-soo's new friends. Join me in my endeavours and we will breed together a new Gnathe, better able to serve the interests of the race."

The massed faces of the Gnathen, high ranking Brood-mothers, looked down on her impassively. There was an eerie silence as the keen minds thought out all the possible permutations. Slowly at first, and then in an overpowering wave, the Brood-mothers stood and pledged their support to Trann-link-khann.

"You have vision and courage, young Trann," one of the senior ranked Gnathe called out to her. "We will follow your lead. I for one do not want to return to the days of my Grand-Brood-mother and fear my neighbour. What would you have us do?"

"Return to your homesteads and leave some of your kindred pledged to me. We must hunt down the Tyrant and see that she meets her end. Those of you that feel militant enough, join the hunting party now. Her kindred are larger and stronger than ours. We need to do this ourselves, united as a fighting force. I will meet you here as soon as I have found out what has happened to my partner Sing-trow-sool. We will set out after her with supplies and fresh mounts. She will not get far and there is nowhere for her to go," the new Empress grimly retorted and strode away towards the Royal Chambers.

The assembly broke up with the older Brood-mothers making preparations to return to their lands and holdings. Younger and fitter Gnathe, particularly those with old scores to settle, began to pack food and supplies for the avenging hunting trip and waited for the return of their new leader.

Trann had returned to the inner sanctum of the crystal chamber and looked on with misery and disbelief. Stretched out upon the floor was the contorted body of Marren-khann; and squatting, dazed beside her, was Sing-trow-sool, with bloodstains over the side of her head. Of the command crystal there was no sign.

"What happened here, Sing? I felt the binding power go and realised something had gone very wrong," she said and helped her partner to her feet.

"One of Link-soo-shan's Imperial Guard took us by surprise. I must have made a cry when I discovered the Tyrant's psychic shield. Marren came in to see what was the matter," the Keeper explained faintly. "She was still here with me when I regained contact with you all at the arena. The guard must have crept in and darted Marren while I was in rapport. Do you see the short syther stuck in the wall? Marren must have used her dying mental strength to deflect the blade. I owe her my life. All I remember is being hit off the perch and my head being driven onto the stone floor. What happened to you? How did you defeat her? Is she dead?"

"I drove her out. She lives, but is wounded. Jing-soo is dead. Link reached up into the stands and tore her arm off with the telekinetic crystal attached. We nearly had her, Sing. It was so close. She was shielded by something. None of the crystal bearers could get past her skin, but we rapidly found out how to get over that problem. The families are with me, Sing. They have pledged their loyalty. None of them want to return to the bad days of uncertainty before the Empire came into being. Now, we hunt her down. The Brood-mothers have agreed to kill her and we are organising a hunting party. Do not worry, we will catch her and we will enslave every one of her accursed kindred and her sister's renegade daughters. It would appear by their absence that they have thrown in their lot with the Tyrant. Later. I will have to take my homestead's command crystal and install it here. I will be blind and deaf without it. I must leave you to carry on here. Tidy up as best you can. The hunt must be organised. I will find out if there is a Zanth available that I can ride."

Nagoth was shocked by the appearance of her Brood-mother. Blood was still oozing out of the deep cut across Link-soo-shan's upper face, blinding the huge Gnathe. She also observed the slashed hearing crest and the bloody leg that the Ultimate Ruler was nursing. She quickly took control of the situation, lifting the larger form of the Brood-mother onto a strong, fresh Zanth with the help of her companions.

"Nagoth, is that you?" Link-soo-shan asked blindly. "I cannot see very well and my hearing is defective."

"Yes, my Lady, it is Nagoth. All is organised. Things went badly then, my Lady," she exclaimed, leaning over to shout into the remaining erect hearing crest.

"All is not lost, my faithful guard. I have the arm of one of Trann's kindred with a large telekinetic power crystal bound to it. It is secure in my breeding pouch. All her genetic secrets are mine to use, at a later date. It is well that I planned ahead as I did," she thoughtfully remarked to Nagoth as they urged the Zanth into a fierce pace.

"That's not all, my Lady. I stole your command crystal from under Sing-trow-sool's hands and killed another of Trann's inner circle," Nagoth replied in triumph.

"So that is why Trann's attack became disorganised part of the way through our struggle. You are very valuable to me, Nagoth. Once we are established in our new home, you shall be amongst the first to breed with our captured males," she promised the Imperial Guard. "I trust that Jaffin has secured us some good breeding stock?"

"You will not be disappointed, my Lady," Nagoth replied. "Everything had been organised early this morning. Jaffin will have reached the captured homestead before now and will have travelled on towards the gorge that we entered. She will have left us fresh mounts so that we can outdistance any pursuit."

"You have exceeded all of my expectations, both you and Jaffin. You will possess great rank in the future. I have had another thought about my fight with Trann. If you acquired the command crystal during the struggle, who knitted the gestalt back together again? It could not have been one of our people, as all of the most powerful minds were at the arena." The idea smote down with vengeful force. There could be no other explanation. Link-shoo-shan trembled with seething hatred and hissed, "The alien male breeder! That is the only answer that makes sense to me. I thought I had burnt out his mind or at least damaged his sanity."

"Who are you talking about, Great Lady?" Nagoth bent forward and shouted into the partially erect crest.

"Back at the captured homestead, before the dawn, my mind was contacted by the leader of the aliens. It was he who helped the Heretic escape. I managed to trap his mind and strip him of all his memories. When I have the time I will call them up and study them. He must be a very powerful adept, to send his mind unaided by crystal link so far. I promised him I would have my revenge. Somehow, I will make his people pay richly for what he has done to me." She hung on to the Zanth's harness grimly and attempted to brush the congealing blood from out of her eyes. "Nagoth, I need water both to drink and to wash my eyes. We are far enough from the Imperial City now, I think, for us to stop for a while. My leg pains me. Can you see a cool ditch?"

Nagoth led her Lady's Zanth over to a water-filled irrigation ditch and helped the Brood-mother off the beast. Link-soo-shan felt her way to the edge and slipped gratefully into the water's cool embrace. Nagoth used her own kilt for a compress and sponged the dried blood out of her Brood-mother's eyes. Trann's cut had run through the top of her hearing crest and across the ridge of skin over one eye. It was a deep cut and showed the bone of her skull in one place. The ridge over her eye had fallen forwards as the flesh had parted across the muscle.

"This needs stitching, my Lady. Otherwise if you heal as you are, one eye will be difficult to see out of," Nagoth worriedly declared and pushed the skin back into place.

"Bind a cloth band over it. That will have to do. We must get away from here. It will not be long before they decide to hunt us down. Come, help me back onto my Zanth and we will get on the move once more," the Brood-mother ordered and after drinking her fill, she climbed unsteadily out of the ditch.

Trann's group of vengeful Brood-mothers cast around the outskirts of the city until they came upon the heavy trail laid down by the retreating force. Occasional drops of blood could be seen, congealing in the sands of the road. Trann led the Gnathe, armed with a heavier syther more suited for fighting from the back of a Zanth. The sun had passed the afternoon stage of the day. Clouds were beginning to form into thunderheads over the mountain ranges. The air was still and hot. Where could Link-soo-shan be running to?

One of the senior Brood-mothers rode up to Trann and called out to her: "Lady Trann, this road leads to my homestead. Beyond flows the Great Imperial River that pours out of the Great Gorge."

"I think that you will have more reason than most to hate her now, my friend," Trann grimly replied and stared into the distance at a faint column of smoke that was rising into the air. "I think she has put your home to the flames. Come, we must hurry. She has become very devious and difficult to out-think."

The group of Brood-mothers began to urge their mounts to their limits. Trann noticed the area where Link had washed off the bloodstains of her injuries. She thought to herself: I managed to hurt her enough to make her break off the fight. The nearer they got to the ravaged homestead the more smoke could be seen, until they could smell it and hear the wood of the Banilik Tree crackling with the heat of the flames. Old homestead kindred were trying unsuccessfully to beat out the flames. The heat was too great around the homestead for Trann's group to follow the road, so leaving the anguished owner with a few helpers to salvage what they could, Trann took to the fields. She soon found that other fires had been set against them, blocking their way. Frustrated, they were forced to pull back to the road.

"Into the irrigation ditches, before we burn alive!" Trann shouted to her companions over the deafening roar of the fire. "Cover your mouths with a wet cloth and breath through that. It will rain soon and then we will be able to follow where she went."

They quickly rode their Zanth into the water and sat partially submerged, waiting for the firestorm to burn itself out or the wind to change. Pod-vine, fruit-pods exploded with increasing rapidity in the smoky haze as the fire swept through the crops towards them. The Zanth rolled panic-stricken eyes and were viciously restrained by the powerful Brood-mothers, who would allow no frenzied leaps out of the safety of the water. As the heat of the fire decreased, Trann urged the company forwards along the wide ditch, parallel to the road. At last, fresh air began to blow the smoke and grime away. Towards the East the thunderstorm had started to break. Eddies of wind curled round the smouldering vegetation, lifting powdery ash in its wake. A few heavy raindrops began to fall, settling the dust. Trann signalled them to climb out and they assembled once more onto the stone covered road.

A bleak sight of desolation met their eyes. The road ran through blackened fields, where here and there small clumps of Pod vine still stood. Of

Link-soo-shan's renegade company, there was no sign. They walked their nervous beasts towards the deserted bridge spanning the turbulent Imperial River. The great gorge yawned wide in the approaching early night. While the thunderclouds piled up over their heads, a cold penetrating rain began to fall.

"They have crossed the bridge, Lady Trann," one of the leading Brood-mothers called out against the rising wind. "After that, the tracks lead towards the cliffs and the gorge."

A searing flash of lightning forked across the black and stormy sky, illuminating the inside of the water-filled ravine. Trann thought she could see movement deep inside the roaring abyss. Again the lightning cracked and the thunder rolled, deafening those of them that had extended their crests to catch the faintest cries in the storm. Inside the gorge a great landslide was occurring as the rain-loosened shale gave way. A great mass of rock and debris began to slide down into foaming river below. Trann was sure she had seen a column of Zanth and Gnathe winding deeper into the ravine when the lightning split the sky again.

"There they are, Lady Trann!" declared a larger than average Brood-mother, pointing in the general direction. "I saw them briefly outlined in that flash of lightning. They are beyond our reach. I for one am not going in there after them. The rocks are unsafe."

"I agree. Come all of you, we will shelter in the guard post by the bridge. After that rockslide that we all saw, I feel that she has been sealed into whatever wilderness lies beyond the upper reaches of the Imperial River. We will keep a watch on the swamp and this area. Our new friends have a giant eye suspended high overhead. They will be able to tell us if she poses a threat or not. This rain is chilly— let us take shelter now," she ordered and the company made their way back over the bridge.

Trann was already thinking about how to win over the loyalty of these proud and independent people. Locked in the guard hut with a good fire and sharing out their supplies, they would be receptive to her ideas. The night would not be lost.

Deep inside the ravine and making their way steadily upwards, Link-soo-shan's group made steady progress. The storm was tearing the night apart when they felt the shudder go through the ground from behind them. Loosened by the heavy column of Zanth and the single carrier, the ties had become too weak to keep the loose shale together. They watched as their pathway back into the Empire dropped into the turbulent river far below.

"Enough, Jaffin!" Link-soo-shan shouted against the howling wind. "Find us some shelter away from the storm. We have come far enough. They will not catch us now."

The leading Group Captain nodded and pulled her Zanth ahead of the column. Under a large overhang in the rock-face she found a dry area full of washed up branches and driftwood, left there years before by a freak storm flood.

"In here," she called out, "there is a place to sleep the night away in reasonable comfort. We will stop here."

While Link-soo-shan gratefully squatted in the dry, Jaffin went in search for a gifted male crafter with medical experience. She soon returned with a middle-aged male. He had small nimble hands and was carrying a case fashioned from a large seed case. Jaffin pushed him forwards into the firelight and he stood fearfully in front of the mighty deposed Ruler.

"This male is from the medical centre, Lady Link. He has his accident and emergency tools with him. You need attention. He will do what he can," said Jaffin and pushed him roughly forwards again.

Link-soo-shan stared at the small form in front of her and said, "Do what you can for me. Mend the cut across my hearing crest if you can. I will relax it and allow you to pull it together. After that see if you can save my sight from the damaged eye ridge."

"Very well, Lady Link, I am not without skill," the male replied and beckoned her closer to him. "I will squat here with my feet forward. You will lay your head in the hollow and I will see what I can do for you," he nervously advised her.

"I will be by your side to see that you do my Lady no deliberate harm," Jaffin hissed into his erect hearing crest.

"I am a healer, not a killer, Group Captain," the Gnathe retorted sharply. "You may need my services one day. Remember that, before you act hastily. I will do my best for your Brood-mother. I too have seen that the way back is closed off. For better or for worse we are an interdependent group. Our future depends on us all pulling together."

"You are a wise male," Link replied, laying her head onto the Gnathe's feet. "You are also near to being ripe. I shall mate you with Nagoth as soon as you are able. I need your genes. Now do what you can for me."

The male ran his hands over the scar and turned away to his case of instruments. He slid a leather ring over his index finger with a small telekinetic crystal glued to the inside. Satisfied that contact had been made, he concentrated his will into the tiny field projecting out from the gemstone. He explored the nerve damage of Link's hearing crest with professional interest. The damaged area had been starved of blood for too long for him to promote regeneration. The best he could attempt to do would be to put back the drum-tightness of the crest when it was erected. He reached into a box and removed the chitinous head of a staplex. The pinchers were needle sharp and he had no difficulty piercing the tough membrane of Link-soo-shan's crest. When both hooks had taken hold he pressed the skull against the hinge-lock and the pinchers clicked together, pulling the skin tight. He added two more across the closed wound and began to examine the deep flesh wound that went down to the bone under the left eye ridge. Some of the muscle controlling the closing of the lid had been parted by Trann's syther. Again the male Gnathe concentrated his will through the crystal making contact with his finger. He lifted pieces of grit and dirt from out of the wound with the augmented power of his mind. A small root of infection was ruthlessly removed, with the dead flesh attached to it. A small amount of blood began to flow again from the new raw edges. Rapidly the male knitted the edges together, pinching the flesh closed with the other staplex until the scar formed properly.

"Have you a clean piece of cloth, Group Captain?" he asked abruptly to the dark shape standing at his shoulder.

"I can get one," Jaffin answered gruffly.

"Then bring me one soaked in rain water and also a dry one," he replied. "I will be finished here soon. Do not move your head, my Lady, until I say you can. I am still knitting your flesh together."

"You have great skill. What are you called? I need to know your name and ranking position," the Brood-mother inquired from her position with her head tucked onto the male's feet.

"I am called Healer by the other Gnathe. My name is San-sool. I was one of your City Gnathe, taken into service in lieu of taxes, by yourself many years ago. I have been your loyal servant for most of my life and content with it. My Brood-mother discarded me because of my small hands. I have found the design of these far better than those over-endowed with claws. I can make tools that other males despair of producing. You will find me useful."

Jaffin and Nagoth returned from out of the night with the required cloth and watched while San-sool washed and cleaned the wound to his satisfaction.

"You may rise now, but do not fully extend your crest until the morning," the male instructed the Lady Link.

"Nagoth, meet your impending mate. San-sool and yourself will be mated when he is ready. Do not force the issue. I have to recover yet and I need to study the genetic codes that I am teasing out of this piece of Trann's servant."

She dipped her hand deep into the depths of her breeding pouch and pulled out the partially dissolved arm of Trann's kindred. There was enough living genetic material, secreted away in a pocket and sealed off from the outside, to give Link-soo-shan the information she needed. Holding the grisly trophy in the fire-light, she extended a razor sharp claw and cut through the bindings, to reveal the dull shine of the largest telekinetic crystal she had ever seen. The cloth that San-soo had used to dry her wound soon soaked up the mucus dripping off the bones of the severed arm. She threw the remains of the arm into the fire and squatted down, studying the gemstone eagerly. Never in all her long life had she held a stone of such power.

"No wonder Trann link-khann was so confidant of success. To think that she had three of these! If it had not been for my childhood's toy, I would have died in the arena. I owe my life to you, Nagoth. I shall have to explore all its strange properties." She looked approvingly at her master spy and said, "Give me my command crystal. I have calls to make. Dotted about the Empire are small con-tingents of my sister's kindred and mine. I must inform them of my situation and round them up. Now that we know that there is abundant life beyond the high cliffs they will be able to join me. I will build a stronghold in the hidden valley and take all of this wild land for myself. One day I will return to face Trann-link-khann again—after I have dealt with the aliens."

CHAPTER 20

▼

As the dawning sun rose over the edge of the mountain ranges, the rays of the great red-gold orb illuminated the vast body of water trapped above the Habitat. Great swaths of mist began to curl and rise from the surface of the water as the sun's warmth penetrated the top layers. Asue and Kamiel looked gratefully forwards through the toughened glass at the expanse of water rolling by underneath the airship.

Asue spoke into the intercom: "Wake up, all of you. We are nearly home. Below us is the great lake that feeds the White River. Our home lies over the next line of mountains at the edge of the water."

Shoo-lin, Coen-soo and Frederick left their chicks dozing in the pile of blankets and collected with the rest of the crew at the forward observation windows. Beneath them, seen through the eddying mists, lay a vast body of water fed by the many rivers flowing out of the mountain wilderness. Reflections of the morning sun sparkled off the choppy surface. The airship tacked across the continual head wind, making steady progress towards the far bank. The humans and apes pointed out landmarks they had passed on the journey out. Asue kept the airship on a corrected course, aiming for the gap in the mountains through which they had come at the beginning of the rescue attempt. As the time passed, Gnathe and human ate a hasty breakfast alike. The excitement increased as the updraft of air began to catch Rescue-One and lift the airship as it approached the edge of the escarpment.

Alexander placed his hand on the muscled arm of Ender-whann-soo and said to her, "Look, there is the great falls. Beyond them lies the start of the White

River. Our settlement is built along one side. Your new home is on the other, connected by a bridge across the chasm."

When the airship passed through the gap and over the edge of the falls, a silence of awe and disbelief took the Gnathe by surprise. Nothing had prepared them for the reality of the Habitat. Mile after mile, beyond the range of their sight, stretched the hexagonal roof system of the alien's self-contained home. Interconnecting domes further than the eye could see covered the right-hand side of the river. Areas of collected rainwater caught the sun as the automatic irrigation system shunted the water to where it was needed to fall as purified rain. Mirrors caught the dawning rays of the new sun and concentrated the light downwards into the tropical sections. A concept of a giant, but obedient living creature, impressed itself onto the incredulous Gnathe. On the left of the river, a system of great hexagonal structures clustered around a central one, dominating the plains.

Khann-link-sool turned away, shuddered and spoke to Asue and Alexander. "I was not prepared for this. Your civilisation is beyond my understanding. It will always be beyond my powers of reason. This area of the world you have made your own is vast. I cannot see to the end of it. You have powers I cannot dream of. It is too much for me. I feel inadequate, primitive and childlike," and Khann bowed her head in shame.

"Once you are on the ground, these feelings will pass," Asue declared, laying her hand on the old scientist's arm. "You will soon have more familiar surroundings about yourself. We, the guardians of mankind, took hundreds of revolutions about this star to build this complex. Our partnership with your race will produce great things in the future."

"I assure you, Khann, you have a lot to offer," Alexander said quietly to the old scientist. "Please do not feel inferior. You cannot measure our achievements. We inherited everything from our remote ancestors, just as we told you several days ago, in this ship. It is we that are in awe of what you have achieved. You started from nothing and you have solved a genetic problem that kept us prisoners in that artificial world below us. We are more grateful than you realise."

Some of the Gnathe and the airship's crew had gone outside onto the veranda around the control cabin and hold. Shoo-lin and his egg-brother, Whann, were enthralled by the spectacle of the new lands unfolding below them. Kamiel walked forward to stand between them, laying his silver hands upon their shoulders and asked, "What do you make of it, my friends?"

"It is the stuff of dreams come true, Kaameel," Shoo-lin answered, happily. "It will be a place without fear, cruelty and oppression. You do not and could not know what it was like to live under the Tyrant's rule. We serve Ender-whann-soo by reason of our devotion to her. She is the centre of our world. Anything she asks of us, it would be a joy to please her with."

"I ask only, to till the new fields and produce the crops that will feed our people," Whann-lin stated, pointing down at the spread of safe land enclosed by the high, hexagonal walls. "This is our new home. The ground looks rich and fertile. There is so much to do. I am impatient to organise my people. Thank you, Kaameel, for what you have done for us. We have a new beginning."

They could now see the upturned faces of the people below. Asue brought the airship into the wind and began to cool the helium inside the gasbags. She angled the solar cells dotted over the top of the structure to feed extra electrical power into the reserve batteries. The silver-suited, human and ape figures on the ground made way for the descending vessel. The trailing lines were attached to posts sunk into the ground. Once they were secure, Asue cut the power to the rotors, reducing the lift and the main line was winched back into the hold, drawing the airship down to the ground. As the ship dipped underneath the top of the great wall surrounding the settlement, the wind dropped and the great silver vessel steadied and lowered onto the ground. Two slender silver figures disengaged themselves from the crowd and raced for the side of the veranda. Hand-over-hand they climbed the trailing ropes and sprang into the gondola. Like quicksilver the two life specialists entered the hold and rapidly made their way to the control cabin.

"Alexander!" Minns cried out with joy and picked up the Habitat's leader and gave him a bone-crushing hug. "It's good to see you back home again. I do not approve of the risks you have taken with Khann's immunity serum."

"We have many tests to try out on you all," Sharn sternly ordered. "I have a medical and decontamination laboratory set up in that building over by the wall of the Gnathe's settlement. I want all of you to go directly there as soon as possible."

"Will you stop fussing, Sharn, there is all the time in the world," said Nancy, ducking out of the way of another joyous embrace by the frustrated Guardian.

"Yes," retorted Alexander, rubbing his bruised ribs, "let us introduce you to our new friends and colleagues from the Gnathen Empire."

Asue secured the ship and powered down the systems. More and more curious members of the Habitat filled the hold to stare at the huge carriers and the horny-headed Zanth with their equally inquisitive handlers.

It was not long before the hold doors were opened and the great beasts came stomping outside. They were led over to where a large mound of foliage had been cut and left for the foraging beasts. Soon the Habitat's people were proudly show-ing off the extent of the new home.

Days passed and turned into weeks with the new members of the colony beginning to settle into their new quarters. The versatile carriers were used to level off areas of plantation and self-fertilised the ground with their dung as they worked. They ploughed the ground up with the horn on their blunt snouts, pushing any trees out of the way with their powerful bodies. Clutches of eggs were laid by the carriers and Zanth and tended by the Gnathe. Young Zanth were broken into harness and Frederick's people eagerly learnt to ride them. Several of the Habitat animals were injected with Khann's adapted serum and the Gnathe were introduced to sheep, cattle, pigs and the various types of fowl the humans used. They were fascinated by the cats and dogs and their relationship with the people of the Habitat.

Time passed quickly and the new colony had settled down into a steady rou-tine. Fields had been planted and the two races had forged a definite partnership. Now had come the time to shape the command crystal and for Hannah and her team, to investigate the properties of the strange library of crystals that Ender-whann-soo's household had brought with them. Hannah and the older scientists had all accepted the risks of taking Khann's immunity serum. Minns and Sharn had earnestly forbad the taking of the genetic cocktail by anyone of the childbearing-aged women and female apes. More tests would have to be done in the life laboratory until the Guardians were satisfied that children born to the altered people would still be human. There were changes to be taken into account. All the apes that had taken Khann's serum had lost most of their body hair and had grown a fine down instead. The bone structure of both man and ape had undergone some slight changes. Cross-sectional size of the bones had increased, strengthening the frames of both related species. All of the human's hair showed signs of grey and the general appearance of each of them showed an elder chronological age of about forty years. They all seemed to have aged ten years, but without losing their glow of health. No one expressed regret and all participants agreed that it was a worthy trade-off.

Alexander looked into the mirror, at the face looking back. The brown hair was shot with grey and a few wrinkles showed around the corners of his eyes. His shoulders were broader and his whole body had gained in height and weight. The skull had changed slightly over his temples by broadening and the orbital ridges over his eyes were more pronounced. Over all, he considered the freedom of exploring the open world of the Jovian landscape more than satisfying, for the enriching of his life and worth the changes in his body. His duties as mayor of the

Habitat and Citadel were now conducted at long range. If he needed to enter the old artificial world, he did so suited up, or by hologram.

The intercom buzzed on the console in his new office and he switched it on. An alien face formed in the air above it and stared back at him. The old Gnathen scientist leaned forwards and said, "Alexander, are you busy?"

He smiled, shook his head and answered, "I have nothing to do that cannot wait. How can I help you?"

"It is more than time to tune the crystal. We need news of Trann's re-shaping of the Empire. Also, I want to eavesdrop on what the Tyrant is doing in the valley that we fought in and defeated her. You may be able to help in sensing the correct tuning. This has not been attempted for many generations. The memory crystal that I possess is very old. I will need to become 'Shaper of Crystal', who died long ago. She was unique in her skills. Kaameel has set the crystal down in my laboratory. We will await you there."

Alexander switched off the console and let his mind roam free. All around him were the mental signatures of his friends. He projected his mind towards the tall form of Ender-whann-soo, who was resting in her quarters. The triple souled life form welcomed his entry into her thoughts.

"Alexander, dearest friend, what do you wish?" the rich mental tones lay across his mind in a loving embrace. Behind the intellect came a double echo, as the yet to be born twins tuned in on the contact.

"Khann is to cut the raw crystal that Kamiel brought back from the mountain," the human projected to his alien friend. "Will you be involved? I caught a hint that what she is about to do could be dangerous."

"She may become disorientated after taking on the personality of the old time Master Crystal Shaper," she answered and stepped off her resting perch. "That is all. I will come with you."

Khann's laboratory was a mixture of Gnathen ingenuity and new human science. Light was provided by electricity and could be adjusted up and down in intensity by rheostats set in the wall. All switches and controls had been designed for the huge taloned hands of the old Brood-mother. Her workbench was littered with Gnathe adapted equipment. A larger than average microscope with enormous adjustments dominated one end of the table. An electron microscope screen occupied a position on the wall. The table and perch had been designed with the much taller Brood-mother in mind. One side of the worktable had the floor raised, so that the many human and ape assistants, who had come to respect the aged alien scientist, could work with her at whatever she decided to do.

Kamiel had placed the ball of rock, with the crystal safely locked inside, upon the table. The highly intelligent, chief scientist of the Habitat watched the events with great interest. Hannah had investigated the fascinating library of memory crystals brought back from Ender-whann-soo's homestead. She had adopted the echoes of the alien personalities locked inside the matrix of each crystal. The almost living jewels allowed the user to become briefly the expert crafter, or scientist, and follow all the insights and knowledge that the donor had imprinted into the crystal's matrix. All that was necessary was to lie quietly and with the crystal placed upon the forehead of the person involved, surrender to the memories leaking out of the small gemstones. She had become various gardeners, breeders of beasts and investigated many of the mental sciences of the Gnathen Empire. The greatest feat that she had achieved was the understanding of the forces locked inside the small telekinetic crystals that Coen-soo had brought with her when she fled from Link-soo-shan. This she had passed on to Alexander by joining her mind with his. A great number of her scientific team had taken Khann's serum, so that they could continue to work with her directly in the open Jovian world.

Alexander and Ender-whann-soo joined the small group gathered around the workbench. Carefully, Kamiel withdrew the nannite pins holding the hollowed-out boulder together. He split open the rock to reveal a dull, non-reflective stone bigger than a man's head. As the protection fell away, Alexander felt a stinging shock spread through his mental defences. A raw un-focussed power throbbed and sang inside his mind.

He fell to his knees, clutching at his head. "Too close, too close," he moaned desperately. "Take me outside, Kamiel, quickly."

Kamiel picked him up in his arms and took him to the other side of the nannite-constructed wall. He left him there and returned inside.

While Alexander regained his mental balance, Khann strapped the memory crystal over her forehead and slipped over her thumb the largest telekinetic crystal that they possessed. Slowly, the personality of the Crystal Shaper coalesced in her mind. She shared the memories and skills of the long dead Gnathe. The raw power of the unturned crystal required a line to be followed. Her mind explored the heart buried under the shards to be removed. The telekinetic sense reached out as she laid her thumb close to the fracture line. She pushed against the fracture and a shard of crystal popped and fell onto the wooden, worktable surface.

Hanna and Ender watched, fascinated, as more and more pieces of the crystal fell away from the main body of the emerging gemstone. Alexander walked unsteadily back into the laboratory as the fierce, discordant singing in his mind began to diminish. He could feel the dual personality of Khann and other Gnathe working the tuning facets of the crystal. Where once, a dull glassy mass had rested on the table, a highly polished faceted gemstone lay amongst a pile of equally faceted shards.

Khann now just stood, leaning over the table with her eyes glazed. Ender reached around her and removed the strap holding the memory crystal to her forehead. After some moments, Alexander felt the other personality fade from Khann's mind and the strength of her intellect shine forth again.

"Who will try it first?" the old scientist declared. "I am too exhausted to try myself."

"I will use it first, Grand Brood-mother," Ender answered and stepped onto the perch vacated by Khann. "I will tread the paths through the maze and feel my way back to Trann's mind."

Ender placed her hands upon the crisp facets of the new command crystal. Alexander slipped gently into the alien's mind and experienced the strange world of the crystal matrix that Ender had entered. Before them, in a directionless emptiness, a series of beacons seemed to exist. In some strange way there appeared to be no distance between them. It was as if space had been folded around each crystal. Linked immediately to the command stone was every shard that had been removed. In the strange misty world of between space, Alexander could feel the pull of the other gemstones. Once tuned, each crystal seemed to be linked with the others.

Ender concentrated her will to spiral outwards. She ignored the closer stones and attempted to bridge across the gulf, to command crystals located deeper into the Empire. She soon began to recognise old familiar situations and, getting her bearings, finally moved towards the Imperial City. The first thing she realised was that Link-soo-shan's great, master crystal, was not in the city. An inferior stone lay in the centre of the new web of communications. The Brood-mother arrowed into the sub-connections of the new stone's matrix, carrying Alexander's mind with her.

She found herself looking through the eyes of Trann-link-khann at her partner, Sing-trow-sool and a mixed assembly of young Brood-mothers and their attendant kindred.

"Ender!" the new ruler mentally gasped with great pleasure. "Welcome to you and the alien being, known as Alexander. Exchange your news with us. This is the beginning of the 'New Assembly'. We are trying to produce new ways of governing our destiny. I do not want the mantle of dictator that has been wrested from the Tyrant."

Alexander gently projected some of the ideas of the democracy that ran the Habitat. "All that I can say is this works and it is a fair system. I can only suggest that you try something similar. This form of government ran the society that brought us into being. It made some mistakes, but it was always accountable to the people. When things are more settled here, we will return with our airship to provide passage over the mountains for those who want to come here. There are vast and empty lands here, totally wild, that cry out for the guiding hands of the Gnathe."

Ender assured the gathering that Alexander's offer was true. "Follow me back, to our new master crystal, by using the one on the table. I will show all of you the world of the aliens. Follow me and be amazed," she projected to the interested assembly.

Trann, Sing and as many of the Brood-mothers as could reach and touch the crystal, did so and entered the matrix. Ender showed them the way to her new command crystal through the maze. Once recognised by the other Gnathe, re-establishment of communications would be much easier. They looked through the eyes of Ender-whann-soo and examined the complex, provided by the people of the Habitat, with wonder and amazement. The wilderness of the world outside the walls filled them with dread. All their lives they had experienced the ordered, cultivated landscape of the Gnathen Empire. Most had never even seen the great swamp at the edge of the cliffs. They returned to the Imperial City to discuss the offer by Alexander's people. Only Trann remained in contact for a while.

Ender asked her, "What of Link-soo-shan? Have you learnt anything of her plans since she escaped into the mountains?"

"Nothing can be found out, only that she wears the protective amulet day and night," Trann answered unhappily. "She has her own command crystal and the one belonging to the Homestead that she ransacked before she entered the arena. One other thing, all of her sister's and her own kindred have disappeared from the Empire. They must have made their way secretly across the lands and through the swamp somehow. We have a guard at both known entrances into her mountain wilderness. I have other sad and worrying news for you, concerning my old friend, Ender. At the end of my struggle in the arena she reached out into the crowd and plucked your daughter, Jing-soo, from her perch. She tore off the arm that had the telekinetic crystal bound to it. This she thrust deep into her breeding pouch before she escaped. She now has all your genetic improvement secrets that you produced in your kindred and one of the largest telekinetic amplifying crystals ever found. Tell Shoo-lin that one of Link-soo-shan's people killed his egg-sister, Marren-khann, as she kept guard over Sing-trow-sool in the crystal chamber. She gave her life to save my partner's. That's all I can tell you. Thank you for your help, alien friend, Alexander. Link-soo-shan would have killed me but for your interference and holding the web together, to advise us what to do to combat her protection. I will not forget my debt of honour owed in the arena."

In a matter of four months the three Raptors had grown a great deal larger than their adoptive 'mothers'. The rapport between the raptors had become stronger as time went by. The young beasts' minds were quick and direct in their thinking and a stilted dialogue was possible between the alien minds. Frederick's telepathic abilities seemed to be finely tuned to the raptors' wavelength and as time went by he could hear the chick's mental voice in his mind some distance away. He had developed a great affection for the lumbering creature. Shoo-lin, Coen-soo and Frederick had obtained quarters well away from the main centre area of the Gnathe's new home. Some of his friends had taken up the challenge of living 'rough' in the rooms that were part of the walls, keeping the wild life at bay. They borrowed Shoo-lin's male carrier that had carried the refugees through the swamp. One or two differences of opinion, concerning the mating rights to the small herd of carriers had necessitated the removal of the male with a female of his own. Mounted on the backs of the carriers and tucked safely behind the impenetrable side plates, they had been able to hunt the plains for meat. They were able to supplement the diet of the Gnathe and the naturalised humans and apes. The feeding of the three constantly hungry raptors also kept them busy.

Frederick awoke and swung himself out of his comfortable bed. He walked over to the window and looked out over the gardens and young fruit trees planted around the walls. The area around this outlying part of the Gnathen home was beginning to become domesticated. More and more plants and trees had become adapted to the Jovian outside, thanks to the tireless efforts of Khann-link-sool and Minns in genetically altering the Habitat's plants. Frederick took some milk and cereal out of his refrigerator and had his breakfast. Soon the smell of bacon and eggs filled the small apartment.

An indignant voice popped into his mind, with a pitiful picture of a starving raptor chick with bones sticking out and skin hanging in flaps. "Hungry! When eat? You eat, when me?" the insistent voice declared.

Frederick retaliated with a picture of a fat raptor chick with rolls of flesh overlapping a tiny head. Wide opened jaws were being stuffed with a whole Zanth. The human answered the chick, "Munch, you are always hungry. It's no wonder your wings cannot lift your bulk."

"Can fly. Fred, take to ramp. I show," the chick responded. "Eat later?"

Frederick concentrated his will and projected to the shard of black crystal hanging around Shoo-lin's neck. "Shoo, can you hear me? Are you awake? Munch wants to fly today. Shall we try it?"

The bright lively mind of the Gnathe snapped into focus and replied, "Yes Fred, I think the chicks are ready. Coen and I will meet you at the great ramp. We will see if they can launch themselves this morning and catch the thermals."

Frederick mentally nodded and walked over to the meat-store by Munch's shelter. A pair of bright, beady eyes watched him come with feral joy. The chick waddled out from underneath the roof of the open barn and hissed a greeting to her adoptive parent.

"Munch, your breath stinks of rotten meat. Open up and let me see what you have stuck between your teeth," projected Frederick, stepping back and fanning the air.

Munch obediently opened her cavernous jaws and let the human check her teeth. Sure enough, lodged between the cracking teeth at the back was a large gobbet of meat and skin, wedged tight. Frederick unsheathed his long knife and attacked the offensive piece until he could prise it out of the tight cavity. The teeth at the back were half the size of a loaf of bread and the front incisors were easily as long as his foot. An eye the size of a dinner plate stared back at him as he loosened the piece of rotten meat.

"Thank Fred. Feed me?" The insistent voice in his mind cajoled.

"Drink first and swill your mouth out. I do not want you to suffer toothache," Fred answered and ran his hand under her jaws to find her ticklish area.

He scratched her itch and watched while she drank and spat out the water. The food store was close by and Frederick dragged out an animal the size of a sheep, leaving it before the raptor's jaws. She tilted her head forwards and picked the beast up and bit it into two parts. The rear end went down the throat first, after it had been well chewed. Munch bent down and seized hold of the bloody end of the front of the beast. She delicately nibbled out the heart and lungs from the inside and then crunched up the body and swallowed the rest.

"Only one?" came the plaintive inquiry.

"Let me see you fly first and then perhaps we will then see about some hunting," Frederick replied and strode away towards the ramp. This hill had been the idea of Shoo-lin and presented a gentle slope on one side ending in a cliff several hundred feet high. It was a perfect take off area for the young Terra-raptors to gain confidence. Shoo-lin and Coen-soo had already arrived at the top and were coaxing their chicks into believing that the next step was over the edge of the cliff.

Shoo-lin's chick, named Snapper, proclaimed loudly on the mental circuit that she was too heavy and not ready. Coen-soo's raptor, Claws, had extended her wings to their greatest extent and was feeling the updraft of air rising up the cliff face in the early morning sun. Suddenly she tilted forwards and headed into the wind.

The mighty wing opened further with a crack and she soared upwards and outwards, wheeling and swooping. Her delight broadcast to the other two raptors and they followed suit until they were just three dots in the sky.

"Now we find out if we were successful, my friends. If they do not return of their own free will, that is the end of that," said Shoo-lin regretfully.

Suddenly the three dots began to stoop and drop from their high vantage point in the cloud layer. Faster and faster the raptors dropped out of the sky until just overhead. The great wings unfolded with an audible snapping sound and the flying beasts shot over their heads and made for the top of the hill in three tight turns.

Munch dropped out of the sky, landing close to Frederick and waddled ungainly over to him. "Easy," scoffed the raptor in Frederick's mind. "You come too? We hunt, yes?"

Frederick answered, "Yes, I come too, but first I must tie some rope around you for a harness. I don't want to fall off!"

All three of the adoptive parents fashioned a harness around the neck and shoulders of the giant beasts. Every one of them tied themselves securely into place, sat between the neck and powerful shoulders of the raptors. There was a handy hollow below the neck, just behind a bunch of humped muscle. Each of them gripped the neck between their legs and held one for grim death as the raptors effortlessly threw themselves off the edge of the cliff and into the upward rising thermals.

Shoo-lin hooked his strong claws into the rope harness and urged his raptor on with words and thoughts of encouragement. This was absolute madness. All his dreams come true as Snapper caught the rising warm air and spiralled upwards. Far, far below lay the hexagon shapes of the open topped, safe lands of the Gnathe. The White river became a silver thread, rolling past the edge of the great Habitat of his alien friends. Shoo-lin concentrated his mind and projected a picture of the raptor bearing to the left and soaring over the cliffs to settle on the edge overlooking the plain.

The raptor dipped one wing and swung around, lifting on the morning thermals. "Snapper can do," the raptor projected eagerly.

Frederick and Coen-soo both followed suit and all three raptors settled ungainly on the edge of the escarpment. Behind this lay the great lake that fed the White river, also the Habitat's power house and irrigation system. In front, stretching to the horizon, lay the endless plains and hills of the other side of the continent.

Frederick wound his hands firmly into the rope harness and smoothed the velvety hide with the other. "You have done well, Munch," he projected into his raptor's smug and happy mind with pride. "Take me back. I am cold. I was not prepared for this flight and the drop in temperature at this height."

"Munch do," the raptor replied and dropped off the edge of the escarpment, gliding far out over the plains beneath.

Frederick homed in on Shoo-lin's mind. The young Gnathe was in a state of exhilaration and it took some effort by the human being to break through to him. "Shoo, listen to me, will you. I want to remind you of something."

"Sorry, friend Frederick," the Gnathe replied, "I was carried away. Hey, that's a joke, isn't it, a play on words! What have you thought of that's worrying you?"

"Our large companions can fly well enough by launching from a high place, but I'm not so sure that they can take off from a ground position. Let us return to the safety of the settlement before we try that manoeuvre. I would not like to be stuck outside on the plains with the meat-eaters between us and the safety of the perimeter walls."

"Agreed, friend. We will go back and try the raptors out on the ground in safety," Shoo-lin answered and directed his chick towards the hexagonal walls of their area of the settlement.

CHAPTER 21

▼

Ender-whann-soo felt the first stirrings inside her breeding pouch other than the usual movements. She felt the membrane of the double egg start to split. She focused inwards to the fearful mental murmurings of fear mixed with excitement. It was time for the young Brood-mothers to emerge. Ender projected her imminent event via the command crystal at her side. Instantly Shoo-lin and Coen-soo responded. Alexander felt the mental summons and stopped his conversation with Jo-jo in mid sentence.

"The twins are about to be born, Jo-jo," he said with delight. "Carry on the business that we were discussing, for I must go and be present at this birth. I have been invited for some time."

Jo-jo nodded and replied, "On your way, mayor. I can carry on here without you quite easily."

Alexander switched off the communication console and left his office at a fast speed, running down the corridor to Ender's quarters. As soon as the various people saw him on his way with such haste, they all realised the long awaited event was imminent. A small crowd of Gnathe, humans and apes had gathered by the door.

Kamiel put his head out of the entrance and called out to Alexander: "Slow down, my friend. Come in and be ready. They are starting to emerge."

Alexander swung around the doorway and entered Ender's room. The great form of the Brood-mother was squatting comfortably on her perch, holding on to the supporting rails with her large taloned hands.

"They come, friend Alexander, they come," she gasped in radiant joy. "Watch the line of my breeding pouch. It will tear open and they will force themselves out."

Alexander could feel the infant minds struggle to comprehend what was happening to them. He projected reassurance and love to the young creatures, encouraging them to emerge from their warm, dark world.

Ender felt the exquisite feeling of the new life preparing to leave her. In response to the altered state of the young, her pouch began to un-seal along the thin membrane formed by her body along the edge of the pouch. First one, then the other head of the infant Brood-mothers peeped over the moist edge. She felt the muscles of her pouch give an involuntary heave and both young were deposited onto her large feet. The egg case would be re-absorbed back into her breeding pouch. Each young Gnathe was roughly the size of a three-year-old human child. The infants hung tightly to each leg of their Brood-mother with eyes sticky and closed. Ender picked them up and cuddled them to her chest, licking the mucus away from their eyes and mouths. In response to this stimulus the baby Gnathe snuggled close, opening their mouths wide and pressing themselves against Ender's face. She responded by bringing up a semi-digested fluid that was eagerly accepted by both young.

Coen-soo stepped forwards with fresh towels and warm water to clean the infants. Alexander came a little closer to his huge friend, so that he could observe the young Brood-mothers better and found himself being regarded by four cat-like eyes. As Coen-soo washed and cleaned one of the twins, Ender handed him the other infant, wrapped in a towel. He dried off the light brown, velvet furred creature, examining the changes that Ender-whann-soo had produced. She had, indeed, changed the hands completely, from the traditional, heavily taloned, fighting and clasping paws that the other Gnathe were born with. Alex found himself being gripped firmly by a three-fingered hand with broader digits than his own. A similar opposable thumb was located across the palm. The fearsome sharp talons that both Ender and Khann were handicapped with in the human's world had been reduced to a minimum. Firm pressure on the ends of the fingertips would still produce the cat-like claws from out of their sheaths, but they were much smaller than usual. These young Gnathe would have no problems in the future using whatever human tools and controls they needed.

The infant Gnathe reached up and trustingly pulled at Alexander's ear. "Azander," the small Brood-mother uttered. At the same moment he could feel his name form in the infant's mind. These creatures were indeed born with some language and definite personalities. They were as advanced in their minds in some ways as a five-year-old human child. Ender's personality and a great deal of her memories were part of the young Gnathe's minds. As they developed, a definite identity of their own would form and both of the twins would become totally independent intellects.

Alexander continued to towel the young Brood-mothers dry. The creature curled up in his lap and began to fall asleep. As he gazed down onto the trusting, infant alien, he thought to himself that these children of the future were beautiful to look upon.

He looked up at his towering friend and asked her, "What will you call them, Ender? What family name will they follow? I must admit that I cannot quite understand your way of naming yourselves."

"That is easy, friend Alexander. They carry the centre part of my name and the centre part of the Brood-mother who bred the male. Both twins will be called Link-whann. I decide their forenames. The one in your lap I shall call Azanda, as she has already tried to speak your name, and the other one shall be known as Marren, after Shoo-lin's murdered egg-sister. I have great hopes for these children in the new partnership of the Gnathe with the people of the Habitat. They will grow up being a part of both worlds and will be instrumental in defining the new direction for my race to take. What I have started, they must finish, friend Alexander," she replied and shifted to a more comfortable position on her perch.

After the pathway had collapsed into the gorge, making their return impossible, the enslaved kindred accepted their fate. There were no instances of rebellion after Jaffin-shan had hurled one female with a dissenting voice down into the turbulent waters of the Imperial River. The male healer, San-sool, proved to be invaluable to the isolated community. Eventually the Gnathe reached the security of the hidden valley and sought shelter.

During the hard weeks of toil, Link had little time to contemplate the possibilities of revenge against the alien people who were instrumental in her downfall. In the evenings she fell into an exhausted sleep and remained unmoving until dawn. Finally the shelter they had found, under an over-hanging cliff, had been reinforced at the sides by boulders and stones. Muddy clay had been worked into the chinks and openings of the makeshift walls. A site had been found, near the large stream, that Kamiel had dammed. Here they planted the nuts of the Banilik tree that they had taken from the enslaved homestead. In a short time a distinct pattern of shoots curled out of the soil and began to grow determinedly towards the light of the sun. As the separate trees started to expand, each touched its neighbour with interlocking branches. During these first weeks, the growth was rapid as the root system penetrated deep into the water table beneath the ground. As the Banilik trees grew, the Gnathe shaped and formed the obedient organism to their will.

It was during this time that Link-soo-shan sent for San-sool and the two young, blinded Brood-mothers one evening.

"What are you called? When we started this, I promised I would restore your sight if I could in return for your loyalty," Link said to them in measured tones.

The blinded Gnathe advanced warily towards the sound of her voice, hand in hand. San-sool guided them towards the deposed tyrant and they formed a semi-circle in front of her.

"I am called Bronn-mace-rann, my sister is known as Connit," one of the young Brood-mothers answered. "You are a legend, great Lady. We would pledge our loyalty to you in any circumstances. If you think you can restore our sight, we would be grateful beyond honour."

"I do not know if I can undo what has been done. I am going to allow San-sool to try, using the large telekinetic crystal that I took from Trann," she replied speculatively and motioned him towards her. "He is a healer of great skill. I have great regard for him; so much so, I am carrying the egg of my loyal Nagoth fertilised by him. I need the products of your breeding pouches and I need you to follow my genetic instructions." She lent forwards and gave the kinetic crystal to San-sool. "Be very careful, healer. This has an awesome power."

San-sool felt the power of the stone immediately he touched it. The field of influence was incredible. He could sense and explore the bodies of the blind Brood-mothers without having to get within touching distance. He realised that he could kill all of them with ease, but for what purpose? They needed one another to survive in this place. He opened his eyes and was aware of Link-soo-shan's penetrating stare as she squatted on her haunches.

"This is an awesome responsibility you have entrusted me with, Lady Link," he exclaimed gravely.

"I know, healer. I know, for Trann nearly killed me with it. Now see what you can do," she ordered brusquely and sat back to watch, holding the amulet firmly in place on her arm

"Lady Bronn, I will try to help you first. Face towards the Lady Link; that will place your eyes facing towards the darkest area," he ordered quietly and directed the much larger figure with his hands. When he had her facing the wall and in the semi-darkness, he gently asked her, "When was this done to you? Have you memories of sight?"

"We were quite small, about half grown, when we were summoned individually to the dominant Brood-mother's quarters. I remember a sweet smelling cloth held over my mouth and then nothing. When I recovered, both of us had our eyelids sewn shut. Since then, we have lived in darkness. We have been used to breed twice, so it cannot be more than five years ago," she answered in despair. "Do what you can, healer. My gratitude will be without measure if you succeed."

"I can promise nothing, Lady Bronn, but I will do what I can. Now try to relax while I explore the extent of the damage," he replied and held the crystal gingerly in his delicate hands.

Carefully he let the crystal warm to his senses. As he lost himself in the three-dimensional field, he became aware of the other two Brood-mothers close by, but of Link-soo-shan he could sense very little. There was something there, but it was like touching a slippery surface. He ignored it and concentrated his will towards the Gnathe by his side. Her body seemed transparent and he lightly entered her skin around the scar tissue surrounding the eyes. This was similar to when he had healed Link-soo-shan. He could not have attempted so fine a touch with his tiny telekinetic crystal. The amplification of his talent would have been too small and clumsy. Under the eyelids the shape of both eyes showed no scarring, indicating that the lids had been sewn, not branded together. This was a promising sign.

San-sool began the delicate task of splitting the skin apart over what he judged to be the line of the eyelid. As he parted the thin membrane, he also sealed the cut flesh closed, so that the eyelids would not fasten back together. The tiny muscles that controlled the eyelids had become very weak, so the healing Gnathe pulled them together from their relaxed position. He tightened the sinews by removing small parts of them and splicing the ends together. He opened up a small pathway to the outer skin and removed the tiny pieces of tissue, sealing the exit.

The dedicated healer squatted, tired by his concentration and said to the Lady Bronn, "I have finished one eye. Tell me if you cane discern anything by slowly turning your head to the right."

Trembling with apprehension, the Brood-mother did so and slowly faced towards the outside of the overhang. She gave a gasp of joy and whispered incredulously, "I can see light. Everything is fuzzy, but I think I can make out the flames of the cooking-fire. The awful dark has gone. I beg you, healer, try the other eye," she said as she turned and faced the wall once more.

San-sool repeated the procedure for the other eyelid and, leaving the Brood-mother sobbing her gratitude to Link and himself, began the task of repairing the Lady Connit's eyesight.

By the time he had finished, the sun had gone down, followed by a clear night, showing several moons and a starlit sky. A cold frost lay on the ground. The male Gnathe was completely exhausted by now and squatted sleepily beside the two young Brood-mothers who could not take their eyes off the flickering, dancing flames of the cooking-fires. Link-soo-shan had taken the crystal from his tired grasp and put it back into her carrying pouch.

She looked at her adopted Brood-mother daughters with a calculated stare. They had embraced her and licked her face to show dependence and loyalty to the deposed Tyrant. Both of the young Gnathe were going to be fanatically faithful to their new family head. She would never fear the death by fratricide that befell so many Brood-mothers as they lost their power and strength. For long after Nagoth and Jaffin had gone to their final rest, the three of them would still be alive and she would be in her prime.

"Listen carefully to what I have to tell you. We have a terrible enemy beyond these mountains and I will never rest until I have brought them down. I will tell you of the events that took me from my position of ultimate power and how my sister was cowardly killed when she was helpless. Reach out and touch my small command crystal that I wear around my neck. We need to share minds."

The three Brood-mothers squatted in silence as Link-soo-shan projected an edited version of the events that led to her downfall. After the Ladies Bronn and Connit had assimilated all that Link was prepared to tell them, she impressed upon them the revised genetic codes for both males and females. All males would carry an improved version of San-sool's hands, so that the retractable claws were small and rudimentary. Both genders of Gnathe would carry the increased intelligence of Jing-soo's genetic improvements, with the greater size of Link's female line.

"Whatever you are carrying in your breeding pouches, adapt to these new patterns. Do you carry young?" the Brood-mother asked the two younger Gnathe.

"I carry four females, Reverend Mother," Connit replied. "They are past the stage of genetic modification. Shall I abort them and start again?"

"No. We may need some basic stock to manipulate later," Link replied and looked searchingly at Bronn.

"My pouch is yours, Lady Link. It has been empty too long," Bronn answered. "I will sniff out a suitable ripe male. Who do you suggest as the female?"

"My Group Captain, Jaffin, is my second choice. I carry Nagoth's divided egg myself. Breed two males and two females. I will have many things for the crafting abilities of these new male Gnathe to do," replied Link with a hateful grimace.

"Now leave me to think. I have the alien leader's memories to trawl. Do not expect too much too soon from your restored eyesight."

The two egg-sisters left the brooding form of Link-soo-shan to her thoughts in the gloomy recess under the overhang. San-sool guided the larger forms through the moonlight to their area of living space. They could both make out the light of the dancing flames from the dying cooking fires, but as yet could still not focus very well or gauge distance. The healer reassured the grateful Gnathe that, come the morning, they might perceive a difference. He warned them, however, not to look into the sun and to keep away from direct sunlight. If necessary, he instructed them to wear a light cloth over their eyes for a few days. This would be until the automatic muscles of the iris could close the eyeball's viewing area to its customary cat-like slit.

Link-soo-shan squatted in the semi-darkness and reflected on her progress. Now was the time to access the breeder's memories she had plucked from his mind. She sent her body into a light trance and began the process of total recall.

She found herself in an incredible and bizarre world. As she ran the memories back and forwards, an understanding of the Habitat began to form. This male was the leader of his community by the choice of his own people. The thought shocked her to the core. What stability could this form of government give? When she found that each member of his council could overrule him if a majority did not agree with him, she was dumbfounded. This was anarchy! It was too strange a concept for her to grapple with. She discarded this area and concentrated on the origins of this species. Every time Link came face to face with the facts of the four Guardians. They were the product of an earlier race that had perished long ago. They and they alone were responsible for the construction of the artificial world and re-creation of these so very alien people.

The world inside the domes had many things beyond her understanding. One fact stood out above all the others, however. These animals could not exist in her world. The micro-organisms in the air she breathed were deadly to them. It was then she realised that the male leader of the alien people was breathing the native air. She probed further and saw that the entire crew of the flying carrier were now acclimatised to her world. When she tracked down the memory of Khann-link-sool's experiment, by blending the natural immunity of the Gnathe with the genetic patterns of the aliens, she hissed in maddened fury. She dragged her ripping claws across the stony walls of her shelter in frustrated rage. Her own people had given these creatures immunity! The only comfort she had was that it would take some considerable time before all of these foul creatures were able to walk her lands, protected from the life of this world.

Link-soo-shan snapped her jaws together in the empty air, thinking of Alexander's pale flesh ripping apart in her grasp. She returned to her inward trance and studied more of this male's customs and lifestyle. She observed their breeding habits and was repelled by what she found. These creatures had an almost infinite capacity for sexual contact. The males could mate over and over again, leaving their seeds in as many females as they liked, to come to fruition without any other agency. Not for them the measured breeding programme that the Gnathe followed! Then she found the artificial womb of the life laboratory run by Sharn and Minns. Hundreds of genetically perfect human young wriggled helplessly like maggots in tiny warm cots.

She felt sick with disgust and hatred for these alien life forms. Somehow she must get inside this dome and wreck it beyond repair, while time was on her side. The young were quite helpless for years and would be easy to dispose of. It was then the awesome distances that lay between herself and the object of her hatred dawned upon her consciousness.

She had no way to cross the mountain wastes to vent her revenge. The flying carrier that the aliens used to get here over those mountains was a constructed thing. It was not alive. She shuddered with fear at the strangeness of it. This could not be the way for her to come. She sat, bursting with hate and frustration, thinking furiously. Link decided to put the problem to one side for now and concentrate on the other idea that she had.

"Jaffin! Nagoth!" she shouted into the night. "I need you. Come to me now."

Two dark forms materialised from out of the shadows and strode towards her. They stopped and stared up at the face of their Brood-mother and ruler.

"My Lady, we are here," Nagoth spoke from out of the darkness. "What would you have us do?"

"I need to pick through both of your memories. Join with me while I examine the way the aliens held you off from the top of the hill. You saw their weapons without knowing that you did so. I will find out how they were able to send these tiny spears of death so accurately and with such force," Link-soo-shan replied. She reached forwards to hold Jaffin's hand against hers, sandwiching her crystal between them.

Instantly the powerful mind of the deposed Tyrant slipped inside that of her Group Captain's. She probed gently back in time, until she found herself looking up the hill at Abdul and Jocylene. She focussed on the strange device that they held in their hands. Over and over again, she studied the action of the spring of the bow. She watched as the tiny spears were propelled with such force that she could scarcely see them pass through the air. Link released Jaffin's hand and motioned Nagoth forwards. She repeated the process to find herself looking from a different position at the action. This time she had a clearer picture of one of the bows. It came to her in a burst of understanding. She let go of Nagoth's hand and the contact faded.

"Sleep here with me this night. I may have things for you to do in the morning," she said tiredly and closed her eyes.

As the weeks turned into months, the new settlement successfully expanded. The one carrier that they had brought with them had been pregnant. She had laid her eggs, to be tended by the household Gnathe. These had hatched and under the watchful eyes of the beast-herders, were allowed to forage and grow. Leaving the household to run itself, under the fanatically loyal eyes of the Ladies, Bronn and Connit, Link prowled the extent of the battlefield. Jaffin and Nagoth accompanied her wherever she went with a detachment of mounted guards.

Link had the well-muscled guards undo the dam that Kamiel had built. She watched, fascinated, as the pent-up waters receded and the shallow lake drained away. Sharp pointed spears appeared from out of the cloudy waters. Carrion eaters had long ago stripped the rotting flesh of the dead Zanth and Gnathe from the bones. Skeletons lay everywhere in the mud, revealed by the draining lake. She marvelled how the alien mind of the silver creature had manipulated her forces so easily. She still avoided the area of Kamiel's traps with some feelings of fear. All the sharpened spears were slanted in one direction. The silver creature must be a master of warfare to have decimated her forces with such effect. She looked up at the snow-capped mountains that lay between her forces and the alien's home. There had to be a way to strike across all those snowy peaks. Maybe there was a Gnathen way to get at them. She would think about it in the long evenings to come.

"Somewhere out there, on the plains around the edge of that defended hill, lie the graves of the aliens that died. Find them for me," she demanded to Jaffin and Nagoth. "Look for a pile of stones. I saw the Guardian, Kaameel, bury their dead somewhere in that direction."

Nagoth and Jaffin organised their small force to fan out over the area around the cliffs of the hill. The hot sun beat down on the searching figures. At last one of the guards stood up on her Zanth, waving and shouting to Link-soo-shan and her loyal lieutenants.

"Check it out, Jaffin," Link growled in bad humour. The heat was beginning to tell on her and her scar itched with the sweat rolling down the furrow over her eye.

Jaffin-shan looked down from the vantage point of her position over the neck and shoulders of her Zanth. There on the ground was a rectangular pile of stones. These had obviously been placed there and could not be natural. It must be the grave of the silver creature's people. She dismounted and began to remove the stones with the help of the other guard. Seeing the activity, Link gave a grunt of satisfaction and urged her Zanth over to the busy females. She held her personal crystal and projected to the others to close in on Jaffin's position. At this close quarter, the smaller crystal, driven by her powerful mind, had enough range to register on the minds of her guards. They were all bred for their receptiveness and being once part of her flesh, were tuned to her brain patterns.

The Gnathe worked hard in the hot sun, removing stone after stone, until suddenly they stood aside, unwilling to go further. Link strode over to the shallow grave revealed in the stony ground and looked inside. Side by side, two fungi shrouded corpses lay in vigorous death. Many organisms had made the rotting flesh their temporary home, but dominant of all of them, were many fungi. Many bright colours adorned the remains of the two alien fighters. Moulds of all kinds had made the rich picking their home. Ripe, spore-laden heads had pushed into the cavities of the stone cairn.

An evil joy swept through Link's mind and she ordered the nearest guard, "Pick off those ripe spore heads and place them without damage in the ceramic pots we brought."

"You," she said, pointing at one of the other females. "Remove some of the rotting flesh from the bodies and place it in a carrying pouch. I will need to feed these pretty fungi and study them. This is better than I had hoped for. I want the heads of these two beings. Their skulls will give me great pleasure to look upon in the cold dark evenings."

After the grave was satisfactorily robbed, Link-soo-shan and her force returned to the emerging settlement, leaving the desecrated graves to the open air.

Over the next few weeks Link watched the various moulds and fungi sprout and thrive on the remains of the dead. Satisfied that she had the means to cripple the Habitat, she now began to turn her keen mind to the method of delivery. First she would eavesdrop again upon the settlement beyond the vast mountain ranges. Once again she placed the amulet securely on her arm. These days she rarely took it off, for fear of Alexander or one of the accursed Brood-mothers allied with him, peeping into her mind. She was beginning to feel the effect of wearing the rosy pink stone day after day. Her mind was erecting barriers of its own and strange new bridges between neural networks of her brain had taken place.

Link-soo-shan, once Ultimate Ruler of the Gnathen Empire, reached for her personal command crystal in her carrying pouch. She withdrew it and placed the gemstone on the table in front of her. This was a flat rock supported on three pillars of stone. A number of bowls lay upon this makeshift platform and the cold calculating Gnathe took out all of her crystals and placed them into the bowls in front of her. The effort of projecting her mind all the way to the alien's settlement was no problem, due to the peculiar crystal world of the matrix. This day, however, she felt tired and irritable and the usual energy of her mind seemed drained. She pulled the bowls close to her position at the table and stared moodily down at her treasures. An idea took form in her mind and, because she felt tired, she reached out and held both command crystals in her cupped taloned hands. As both crystals warmed to her touch, she fell into the light trance necessary to operate in the matrix. A different world slipped into her senses than the usual one she was used to. The latticework of the maze was clear of the foggy, non-directional feel that usually permeated the sender's mental senses. Each crystal in the matrix snapped into focus, sharp and clear. She knew where each one was and the distance between them. It felt as if she could step across, if only she could find the way. Not only that, but she could feel places where space seemed to be folded over itself. There was a fold, not far from her quarters, where Jaffin was overseeing the cutting of some springy wooden pools for the construction of Gnathen bows. San-sool was with her, carrying one of the salvaged arrows, selecting the best of the most suitable growth. It was then that she realised, that the tiny fold in space came from the small communications crystal that Jaffin always wore around her neck, as her badge of office.

Link reached out for the fold with her mind and felt a strange tugging feeling deep within her amplified senses. She felt the fold become a door that could be opened if only she had the key. Frustrated, she withdrew and sat once more with her hands free of the crystals. Over and over again she relived the moment of the feel of the door. Her great mind began to race as she pondered the incredible feelings of her amplified senses. It was then that she studied the telekinetic crystal lying in its wooden bowl. Trembling with anticipation, Link picked the crystal out of the bowl with her clumsy fingers and lay it in the large bowl that her adopted kindred usually kept full of fruit and nuts gathered from the surrounding countryside. It was empty at this moment. She picked up both command crystals in her cupped hands and held them down onto each end of the telekinetic amplifier. This time a shock of mental awareness flooded her mind. Link-soo-shan reached out with her augmented senses for the fold in space near Jaffin's neck. This time the fold opened wide and the door was on every side her.

She pushed with all of her mental strength and space wrapped around her, opening in front and closing behind.

Jaffin screamed with terror and shock as her Brood-mother materialised out of the thin air before her eyes and fell with spread legs onto the marshy ground by San-sool's feet. Link-soo-shan stood exultant with wicked joy, with both command crystals encapsulated in her cupped hands. The bowl and the other crystal thumped into the mud at her feet. She stooped and picked up the bowl, placing the gemstone back into its safe place in her carrying pouch.

Jaffin-shan picked herself up from out of the undergrowth she had leapt into in fright and advanced warily towards her Brood-mother. "What have you done?" she cried in fearful amazement.

"I have learnt to do something that no other Gnathe has ever done. I can fold space. San-sool, come with me. I have need of your clever fingers. I want you to fashion a carrying sling, to hold these three crystals together so that I can remain in touch with them. I have such plans. This is a wonderful day. Come with me, my resourceful, nimble fingered crafter, for we have work to do."

CHAPTER 22

▼

Six months after the Gnathe had arrived at their new home, the combined science of the two races was about to take a decisive turn.

Hannah placed the circlet of nannite around her head, placing the tiny telekinetic crystal over her forehead. Each side of it were fixed fragments, taken from the master crystal that Khann had shaped and tuned. The human scientist had used the memory crystal herself and had taken on the persona of the centuries-dead, master crystal-shaper. It was a disturbing experience for her to be a Gnathe Brood-mother. A whole set of different goals and desires drove the giants and shaped their lives. The greatest of these was dominance. This drive had been suppressed by Ender and Khann and replaced by a thirst for knowledge. The new leader of the Gnathen empire, Trann-link-khann, was also of this trait. Slowly, the more violent of the Brood-mothers would be bred out of the racial strain. It would take a great deal of time, for they were very long lived. Those who did not conform to the new order would find themselves isolated from the affairs of the new ruling class.

The leading human scientist, Hannah, sat quietly and relaxed her mind as much as she could. Her team of colleagues filled the small laboratory. Khann perched on her side of the table and watched intently. The carbon fibre wires linked the circlet to a rheostat connected to a battery. The Gnathe had long ago experimented with the Leclanche cell, but without any worthwhile results, due to the scarcity of heavy metals. Hannah nodded to her assistant and he switched the rheostat to the first notch, thus allowing a tiny amount of direct current to trickle through the circuit. Hannah felt her perceptions sharpen slightly and held up two fingers. At the increase of current, her awareness of the group became much clearer. Her new abilities, given to her by Alexander, had increased by a factor of four. She concentrated her will on the ball of stone that lay in the centre of the table. She held up three fingers and sat bolt upright in surprise. The ball of stone twice as large as her fist was floating effortlessly in the air, a hand's breadth above the table. Hanna rotated the ball until it became a blur. She then stopped the ball from spinning and replaced it on the table. She drew a deep breath and held up four fingers.

This time her spatial perception was increased by the square of her previous senses. She was able to project her mind beyond the scope of the laboratory and out into the area beyond the walls. Every life force within a mile of her could be touched by her mind. She picked up a pebble that lay outside the walls and hurled it with the amplified power of her mind towards the towering cliffs at the start of the mountains. It sped on its way at half the speed of sound. Shaken by the enormous sensual overload, she nevertheless held up the fifth finger.

Now she was aware of every living thing in the whole of the Gnathen complex. She could feel the myriad thoughts of the people of the Habitat, like waves of water lapping at the rocks of a vast sea. She concentrated her will towards the University grounds, where another group of her scientists were experimenting with the crystal that Kamiel had taken from Link's Group Captain. This group was much younger than herself and had elected to stay inside the domes until the women had passed the time of child-bearing age.

She selected one of her brightest students and slipped gently into his mind. "Hello John," she projected. "Don't be alarmed. It is only Hannah. Our experiments, with exciting the crystal fragments with tiny charges of electricity, have paid off immensely. Not only that, but I can influence objects telekinetically, even at this distance. Watch your notepad and I will try to lift it. I am at setting five."

John relayed this information to the other scientists and they all observed with amazement as the older scientist turned the pages of the notebook, whilst it hung in the air, from a distance of nearly seventy miles away.

"I can verify the results, Hannah," he said into the communications link connected to the outside laboratories.

Hannah's scientists in her own laboratory watched their holo-vision screen with awe as she picked up the notebook with her mind and turned the pages delicately in the air.

She opened her eyes and grinned at the shocked faces surrounding her and motioned her assistant to power down the circlet. Hannah felt the range of her senses slowly pull back to the confines of the laboratory room. When the rheostat was returned to zero, she tiredly took off the circlet from her forehead.

"It worked, everyone, beyond anything we could have expected," she said triumphantly and stood up. She passed the frail device to another of the group. "This could be very addictive, so be careful. We do not know the effect of using this amplified power on the human or Gnathe brain or mind. I was right all along," she excitedly cried, "It is the tiny electro-magnetic charges emanating from our bodies that activates the crystal's amplifying power. They have other properties, however. I am almost sure that they co-exist in a divergent, spatial frame of reference. It is as if part of the crystal exists in a different place."

She felt Alexander's mind slip into hers and he said to her, "Well done, Hannah, old friend. I felt your mind expand clear across to the other side of the Habitat. I am in Jo-jo's office at the moment, suited up to avoid contamination. We have some work to do, arranging for increased food production, ready for the next migration out of the Habitat. The next thing I need you to investigate is the possibility of creating an artificial shield. I feel that we still need protection from the madness that inflicts Link-soo-shan. I have tried many times to penetrate her defences, all to no avail. Maybe, using your amplifier, I could break through and discover just what she is planning. We can deduct nothing from the satellite pictures, except that her settlement is very busy. I can only get into the minds of her lowly subjects. Her personal guards have had their minds tinkered with and I cannot get beyond the surface layers. I know that she is up to something, but I cannot find out just what it is!"

"Alex, she is thousands of miles away," the scientist replied reassuringly. "Leave her alone to rot in her valley. Meanwhile I will consider your request. I feel that a reverse backfield could be generated. Leave it with me."

Alexander reluctantly agreed, but reminded her, "Remember, Rescue One is still inoperative, due to the contamination of the fuel tanks and the refined Rape-seed oil we used as fuel. It was not long after our arrival back at the Habitat that Kamiel discovered that the oil had become the eager home of many different types of micro-organisms. These have effectively turned the storage tanks on the airship to vats of jelly and tar. The diesel engines will require cleaning and a different type of air and fuel filter is required. Kamiel and Asue are busily at work, stripping the engines apart and soaking them in thinning oils, in a separate sealed dome. They are trying to remove the tar content and also to reduce the corrosive acids attacking the exposed fine parts of the injectors. It may be a year or even more before we can fly the airship again. We need some defence, I am sure of it."

Alexander withdrew contact from Hannah's mind. He was the only one amongst the humans and apes with such a range for his mental powers. The unique neural connections in his brain had not been completely duplicated in his friends. Their abilities varied enormously. They were all sensitive to his thoughts and could project their thoughts to each other over varying distances. He was the only one who could use the latent telekinetic powers without the use of the crystal amplifiers. It was very little, but he could roll and guide a marble over a flat surface if he was close to it.

He looked across to his hairy friend and said to her, "I think I will walk across to the life laboratory and see how Minns is getting on with her attempts to introduce Khann's immunity serum to the un-born. She hopes to be able to cross-fertilise sperm and eggs, from immune people and end up still with recognisable human and chimpanzee children, without too much altered DNA"

"I will come too, Alexander. I have not seen 'Mother Minns' for a long time and it's about time I had a check-up. This will be my last child. After this one is born, I am joining you outside," she replied and stood up. Her loose flowing gown rustled, covering her pregnant bulge as she shambled along with him in the typical ape-like gait.

They both strolled out of the administration building and walked along the flower-bordered pathways, towards the nurseries located next to the University's science and research centre.

Over the months since Link-soo-shan's amazing discovery, she had practised folding space many times. She had Jaffin take her small communications crystal to the very extent of the valley lands, sometimes three days journey. It made no difference to her how far she went. Each jump through space was the same as opening a door in her quarters and stepping though. The last time she appeared out of the air, in front of Jaffin's surprised face, she gathered her to her side and took the frightened guard back through the door. She wore the three crystals around her neck in a halter crafted by San-sool. The amulet's field extended to all the living flesh in contact with her. Finally she found that she could transport six of her guards, clinging like parasites to her body.

San-sool's crafting abilities had proved invaluable to her. He had produced many sets of bows and arrows. It had not taken long for the big female Gnathe to adapt their muscles and hands to using the new weapons. A few had cut down some of their sharp ripping claws to make an easier grip around the stock of the bows. Jaffin, Nagoth and the others practised constantly, killing game and bringing it back to the new settlement. Depending on the type of hand and claw arrangements that Link and Chang had decided upon, the level of dexterity each Gnathe possessed was different. Some of them had been genetically designed for hand-to-hand fighting, whilst others were sword and spear users. Jaffin and Nagoth were of this variety, with enhanced intelligence. Many of Chang's kindred were dull of thought, but extremely obedient. They would go to their deaths without a qualm, thus making good shock troops. Some of these were the heavy-duty guards used at the Imperial City. Not trusting their limited intelligence or old loyalties, Trann had quickly driven any that she had found out of the City at Zanth and spear point. She did this, until she had forced them into the Imperial River Gorge, to die on the rocks below the bridge.

Link followed the events at the Habitat with great interest over the next few months while she perfected her teleporting ability. It was during this time that her own four female young were born. They showed every promise of retaining the genetically enhanced attributes that Link-soo-shan had mixed in her breeding pouch. Her guards honed their new fighting skills to perfection. She picked two of the brightest hand-to-hand fighters to produce maximum close damage. Jaffin and Nagoth would be her bow and arrow specialists while the other two guards would carry bundles of Scriit spears. Each of them carried a sharpened syther. She would use the powers of the telekinetic crystal and her own formidable natural armoury of talons and bony tipped tail. She kept her mind well away from the Gnathe settlement the majority of the time for fear of detection.

The pull of Ender's new master command crystal constantly niggled in the background at her senses. She finally managed to tune its siren song down to a bearable level and concentrated on the smaller doors contained in the fragments. One door beckoned constantly, however, and that was the piece of gemstone that had once been a part of Link's master command crystal. This was Koet-shan's Group Captain's communications device that Kamiel had taken and given to Ender-whann-soo. The day came when, casting out for this tiny fold in space, Link found that it had begun to move.

She entered the light trance needed to observe through the door in space centred in the gemstone. Link-soo-shan found herself aware of the strange surroundings of a monorail car travelling deep into the centre of the Habitat. A group of younger scientists were taking the crystal to the science and research centre at the Citadel's University for independent study. Link withdrew thoughtfully and squatted happily on her perch. Things were moving in her direction at last. All she needed now was for Alexander to make one of his periodic visits to the administration complex in the alien city, to see his deputy, Jo-jo. She could be patient now and wait.

As the days passed she found herself mapping the area of the University grounds and the connecting life-laboratories until she was quite sure where everything was situated. The picked, six fighting companions of her group, were all instructed mentally by herself, until she was sure that each of them had as accurate a feel for the area as she did.

When Link found Alexander missing from the Gnathe complex one day, she began to hunt for him in feverish excitement. A mind of such power was easy to locate. He shone like a beacon amongst all of the other life forces. At last she found him, travelling through the domes in the suspended monorail car, fully suited up to avoid the contamination of this artificial world. She knew were he would be going and where to find him. Now was the time to assemble her group and organise her long practised plan.

The Brood-mother withdrew her mind from the null-space of the crystal matrix and re-entered the physical world of the settlement. "Jaffin!" she shouted across the vegetation-covered slope. "It is time."

She stepped off the perch outside the area of her quarters and, leaping over the ground at great speed, made for the dwelling place of the other two Brood-mothers. The other Gnathe stopped what they were doing and stared at the unaccustomed sight of Link-soo-shan moving at top speed towards the busy figures of the Ladies Bronn and Connit. The well-armoured bony pointed tail streamed out behind her as she used it for balance.

Bronn saw her coming and called out to her egg-sister: "The 'Great One' comes fast. It must be time."

They both stood tall and awaited Link's arrival and instructions. At last they were going to avenge the Ultimate Ruler's downfall. Their hearts beat with a savage joy. They loved this Great Lady with their lives, for rescuing them from eternal servitude.

Connit held the small command crystal that hung around her neck tightly and projected to the advancing Brood-mother, "Is it time, Great Lady?"

The bell-clear voice echoed in her mind with an affirmative. Link's mind was alive with a barbarous satisfaction as she projected back, "Assemble the group. Collect my little presents. I guess we have a quarter day, no more, to be ready."

Link-soo-shan grasped both of them by the shoulders and embraced them. The three of them made their way towards the armoury where Jaffin and Nagoth waited. Here was gathered a variety of weapons, some of them collected by quick forays through the crystal indicated doors. Link had travelled to many of the farthest parts of her old Empire, using the smaller doors related to the portable communication crystals. Senior females of the Family Heads carried these. Each crystal bearer had been quietly killed and weapons gathered without anyone seeing them. Those who were unfortunate to witness Link's arrival with her group never lived to pass on the information. The Brood-mother now had a small arsenal and a collection of communication crystals in her possession. These she shared out with her trusted Brood-mothers and the leaders of her troops.

When the three Gnathe arrived at the armoury, Nagoth was busily storing the ripe varieties of fungus and moulds that had thrived on the flesh of the dead aliens. Sacks of spore-laden, ripe heads were ready for each guard to carry. Jaffin was efficiently passing out as many Scriit spears as each could handle. A full quiver of heavy arrows adorned herself and Nagoth's back. Both bows were strung and in compression, ready for use. Four light sythers were put by, to be used in close quarters. They were flexible and razor sharp. Against an undefended and weak foe, such as the ordinary dome inhabitants, they would cut a bloody swath.

"Right everyone, listen to me," Link ordered her intent group. "The alien creatures are examining my old Group Captain's crystal in a fairly small room. When I step through, you two, unarmed, must kill quickly and quietly, while Jaffin seizes the door, preventing any escape. You remember all of my instructions?"

All the Gnathe nodded their assent and stood ready for her next command.

Link-soo-shan concentrated her will through the crystal matrix and located first the door and then Alexander's proximity to it. She could see him walking along a path with one of the hairy ones at his side. They looked as though they were on their way towards the nurseries. So much the better.

"Climb on!" she ordered and the group took their familiar places on her massive frame.

Over the sporadic ventures into the Gnathen Empire, the Brood-mother had learnt to twist the door area so that she did not materialise partially inside something else. She focussed her will, through the stereoscopic effect of the two command crystals, to fix on the fold in space generated by the other part of her own gemstone. Seated around a table in a room full of incomprehensive instruments, were a group of human and ape scientists. There were at least twice as many in the room as Link carried on her massive frame. All their attention was concentrated on the communication crystal, which was fixed into an apparatus on the table. There was a clear space between the group and the only door, sufficient to take her increased volume.

Fuelled by her madness and indomitable will, the amulet expanded its field to encapsulate all of the Gnathe attached to her. Link reached out and folded space with a minor twist to the clear area.

The crystal under observation suddenly began to sing and resonate, so much so, that the group drew back in alarm. There was a rush of displaced air and a seven-headed monster appeared at the rear of the laboratory.

The moment the fold in space had closed, the six females separated from Link-soo-shan's body. The two unarmed, close fighting specialists took a flying leap forwards, into the group of human and ape scientists. Jaffin and Nagoth secured the door, preventing escape. The two Gnathe armed with sythers sliced down any of the group missed by the ripping talons of the first two. Within a few minutes the carnage was complete. Little sound had been made and the laboratory room was secure.

Link trod over the untidy heap of bloody carcasses until she was able to reach her Group Captain's crystal.

"Well done, all of you," she said with pleasure and picked up her long lost crystal, placing it in her carrying pouch. She felt the pull of the air into the extraction system of the air-conditioning duct and pulled the cover off with the amplified power of her mind. This would help to distribute the fungal spores everywhere the air went in this strange place. "Break one of the fungi in here to feed on these corpses and throw several into the hole that sucks air. Open a portal to the outside of the building, as I showed you in the mind-link."

She watched as Jaffin opened a window to the outside of the buildings overlooking the gardens. Her studies of the Citadel had been very rewarding. She had been able to understand the simple mechanisms of doors and windows by observation of the inhabitants. Jaffin dropped the spore-laden cap of the ripe fungus out of the window and saw it burst on a strange flowering bush. The cloud of dust rose into the air and scattered in the artificial breeze.

"Right, my children, we go to the breeding pits of this filthy race of creatures. Now we slaughter their young. Remember your instructions. Every building we enter, smash a fungus against the wall, if you can, before engaging these people in battle. There will be time later to enjoy ourselves."

Jaffin and Nagoth took the forward positions and armed their bows at the ready. The murderous group began to walk down the corridors the short distance between the research buildings and the nurseries.

Like the cutting edge of a blade, Link-soo-shan's group covered the ground in space-devouring leaps. The unsuspecting people of the Habitat fell before them without being able to give the alarm for some time. The buildings had not been built for defence. All doors swung open without locks, as the concept of theft had never entered the Guardian's community. Wide spanning bridges connected one building to another. Those areas where the artificial rain was unwelcome were covered over, but open at the sides. The deposed Ultimate Ruler had studied each entry point to the life laboratories well. She had memorised the layout of the area for days, until she was familiar with it.

Now panic had added to the scales in her favour as the incredible news of her arrival spread throughout the Citadel. The analogue of Asue's mind that ran the dome's artificial life support system shut all the airtight doors to the other domes. All monorail cars stopped exiting the complex immediately. The computer started the sprinkler system to dampen the air and carry any floating micro-organisms down onto the ground. Unfortunately the fungal spores were being carried through the air-ducting systems into every building. Frantically, the computer signalled Asue for assistance.

Asue immediately contacted Alexander through his com-link to the computer. "Alexander," she transmitted, "the Tyrant is in our Citadel. The computer has handed control over to me. I have shut down all air-moving systems. She is heading for the life laboratories. Minns will stop her there. Hurry Alex, find weapons of some kind and organise any defence that you can think of!"

Alexander broke into a run across the almost deserted gardens between the buildings. This time of the day the majority of the people of the Citadel would be inside the study centres and leisure halls or going for their midday meals. He opened the door into a nearby garden shed. Inside were racked garden forks and other implements. He grabbed two of the forks and tossed one to Jo-jo, also picking up a spade with the other hand and ran towards the nurseries.

The nearer they got to the entrance, the more dead and dying of their people they saw. Their breath came in sobbing gasps as they both hurtled through the swing doors into the kindergarten centre. They entered to see a large and blood-smeared female Gnathe busily spearing the terrified, screaming young children and kicking them out of her way, so that she could rejoin her group.

"Murderer!" Alex screamed and as the Gnathe turned to throw her spear, he hurled the garden fork, prongs forward, at her. The heavy fork sailed through the air and caught Link's surprised guard full in the chest, piercing both hearts. She toppled over backwards, casting her bag of fungi and spores against the wall. There was a muffled thud and a cloud of dust shot out of the bag and hung like a fog in the air.

Alexander and Jo-jo scrambled over the twitching body of the guard and found themselves facing Jaffin and Nagoth, as they pushed their way through the swing doors. Both Gnathe had their bows pulled back and ready to fire the heavy arrows that San-sool had made for them. Nagoth let fly at the chimpanzee with her bow and a metre of solid, pointed wooden shaft sprouted from Jo-jo's swollen stomach. The female ape screamed and dropped the garden fork she was carrying. Alexander deflected Jaffin's arrow to the side, using the garden spade like a shield. He swung the spade back in a cutting blow aiming at Nagoth's legs and felt the spade gripped by an invisible force. It was wrenched out of his hands, causing it to sail through the air. Jaffin then put a second arrow into the top of Alexander's right leg, fetching him down onto his knees. An open-handed slap from Nagoth sent him spinning into the wall, hitting his nose and making it bleed, knocking him nearly senseless.

He felt himself pulled roughly to his feet and Nagoth hissed in his ear, "She wants you alive, breeder."

Leaving Jo-jo doubled over in agony, Alex was dragged into the centre of the defending circle of Gnathe. Cruel, taloned-tipped hands wrenched his arms behind his back and he found himself lifted off his feet to face the biggest Gnathe he had ever seen. Link-soo-shan stood at least a head taller than his friend Ender-whann-soo. Her lips were drawn back in malevolent hatred, showing a slavering set of pointed teeth capable of chewing through his arm. A deep scar, wound its way over the top of her head and into a puckered hearing crest. Both cat-like eyes glittered with an inhuman, feral joy. This was a being that delighted in pain and dominance and was totally without pity.

"Welcome, Alexander. I have waited so long for this moment," the apparition spat at him. "Hold him fast, so that he can see what I am about to do with all of his young. Strip him of that suit so that I can see him properly," and she threw him down again onto the floor, pinning him with her clawed foot.

Alexander then realised where he was. He was in the incubation dormitory of the human and ape nursery, close to the maternity wing of the life laboratory. His heart sank in misery and grief. Jaffin and Nagoth quickly reduced his anti-contamination suit to shreds with their sharp talons and ripped it from his body, leaving him nearly naked. Jaffin pulled the heavy arrow from his leg and Alex shrieked with the pain. They held him upright so that he could see all that Link-soo-shan could do.

Minns had been deeply involved with an artificial fertilisation when Asue had contacted her. She immediately left the dish of nutrient jelly and, switching to computer time, sped towards the centre of the disturbance. The Guardian was programmed to defend and to kill in that defence, at certain levels. The nannite body changed shape as she forced herself faster and faster through the corridors, until she was heading straight towards the swing doors into the incubation dormitory where her sensors told her the Gnathe had stopped. The front edge of her body had formed into a sharp blade as she launched herself through the doors at the giant Gnathe.

The Guardian hurtled through the air at Link-soo-shan and found herself sliding along a frictionless surface, deflecting away from her target. Helpless to prevent this, Minns sped along the telekinetic barrier and found that she was picking up speed. A giant hand seemed to add to her momentum. Horrified, she was driven like a spear at the control panel of the main incubation chamber. Even in computer time she could not soften the edge of her blade. Her nannite body sank deeply into the electrical circuits of the controls. All the power to the artificial wombs was redirected from this point. A massive short-circuit occurred, fusing the whole system and causing the equipment to burst into flames. Minns took hundreds of volts and high current straight into her body, disrupting her neural networks.

Asue collected as much of the disintegrating personality as she could with the aid of the Citadel's mainframe computer and stored it in the memory banks. Kamiel transmitted his mind to the frozen body of his former self that was still merged with the wall at the main communications centre. Closely connected by Asue to the city computer and herself, he made his way to the area of damage through the driving artificial rain. All of them felt the impact of losing Minns. Kamiel felt a personal grief deep inside his electronic soul. He put it to one side. A calm collected mind was needed. All they could do would be a damage limitation exercise. The deposed Ultimate Ruler must be driven out before the non-infected people could be segregated and immunised while there was still time to save their lives. Sharn was already working on the problem of transporting whatever serum they had onto the monorail trains and into the Citadel dome. Only the females of the colony would be saved. There was not enough serum to treat the males as well. In fact, only the youngest child-bearing females would be able to receive it. The future of the colony must come first. The Guardians had stockpiled eggs and sperm in vast quantities for genetic diversity. Now they would need them and warm living wombs in the years to come. This one day would set the colony back centuries. Kamiel thought over the sudden appearance of the Gnathe in the sealed dome. Hannah must be right about the crystals co-existing in folds of space. This would mean that somehow the deposed Tyrant had stumbled onto a way to open doors in space. This could be useful in the times to come if they could save the colony from total contamination. Every dome was sealed off and the inhabitants isolated from the Citadel. Inside this dome was the majority of the human and chimpanzee race. Kamiel estimated a death toll of at least two hundred thousand if all the people here had breathed in the spores. Link-soo-shan must have been able to eavesdrop and study the Habitat for a very long time without anyone suspecting. She must have something new. It must be coupled with Trann's inability to penetrate Link's defences during the Rite of Succession.

Kamiel warily approached the burning nurseries. She would be expecting him to come. He had little idea how far her telekinetic powers would reach. The closer he got to her, the more power she could exert.

He located her position with the help of Asue's infrared sensors and cameras. Working quickly, Kamiel fixed the thin nannite strands high up from the floor at Link's shoulder level. They would decapitate her should she start to leave. Asue had directed as many of the inhabitants of the Citadel as she could to the farthest points away from the heart of the contamination. They stood in cold wet crowds, washed by the incessant rain. Already some were beginning to cough as the fungal spores rooted into their lungs. Panic stricken, the healthy members of groups left them where they lay, obeying the dispassionate commands of Asue. She relayed instructions through the hand carried com-links to whatever people with leadership ability she could find. Bit by bit she separated the women and children into the airlocks at the transit stations for entering the other domes.

Kamiel worked his way around the group of destructive Gnathe until he could get into a position above them. He tracked their progress by the infrared scanning system. They were retreating from the acrid smoke down to the ground level. Kamiel hurried down the stairs after them as fast as he dared. Everywhere he looked were dead and dying babies and young children with their nursing staff. This was a price far beyond his expectations for his interference in the affairs of the Gnathe. He stopped by an overturned cot and picked up the still warm, blood-spattered infant.

Asue's voice echoed in his mind, "Go on, Kamiel. Stop her slaughter. Drive her out. You have no time for recriminations. You were right in what you had to do."

Kamiel nodded and moved on into the incubation dormitory, were he found Jo-jo still clutching the arrow buried in her unborn child. By the side of her was a dead Gnathe with a garden fork driven into her chest. Kamiel pulled the arrow out of Alexander's deputy mayor and cradled her into a more comfortable position. Jo-jo opened her eyes and coughed blood down her hairy chin. "She has Alexander, Kamiel," she gasped weakly. "Save him somehow. She is keeping him alive and close to her." Jo-jo coughed again and more blood dribbled out of the corner of her mouth. "Goodbye, Kamiel. Save our colony. Tell Alexander that I love him. It's a pity he wasn't an ape."

The female chimpanzee relaxed and slumped in Kamiel's arms, her head lolling to one side. The guardian picked up the dropped garden fork and withdrew the other from the chest of the dead Gnathe. He left the body of Jo-jo resting against the wall, gathered together in death with her unborn child. The mad Gnathe would pay for this day, he promised himself, and hurried after the destroying group.

The first thing he noticed as he worked his way down the corridor was the broken strands of his nannite traps. Link-soo-shan had out-guessed him. Now she knew he was here, she would take no chances. Everywhere he looked, delicate equipment lay smashed and power cables ripped out. More dead children and adults lay in untidy piles, wherever they had got between the Gnathe and their objectives. A muffled explosion rippled through the floor and Kamiel felt the link with Asue cut off. Somehow the deposed Tyrant had found the main computer and control centre, short-circuiting it. Kamiel hoped that Asue had cut it out of the system and re-routed to the mainframe housed in the power complex. This was dug in under the cliffs and separated from the other domes. The mind of the artificial intelligence that ran the City was contained in circuits that were part of the walls of the nannite buildings and the domes' framework.

Kamiel's mind once more connected to Asue's as she brought extra relays and circuitry under her control. "She is clever, Kamiel. That Gnathe must have been studying the Habitat's workings, somehow, for a great deal of time. You must force her out in some way before she does even more damage."

"She must have a way of detecting my nannite micro-strands and breaking them. We have sorely underestimated her," Kamiel replied grimly to Asue. "How much of Minns' personality were you able to save?"

"About twenty percent, no more. There is a core of personality to build on and some of the early memory banks are intact. She is gone, as we knew her, Kamiel. I have a continual lock on your mind. I will transfer you back to your other body in the repair shed, immediately you get into trouble. Do not miscalculate her abilities. I think her mind is close to the genius level. She learns fast and thinks in a way that is a bridge between Gnathen ideas and our reasoning. She is systematically wrecking the University as she passes through it. I have her on camera now and will transmit the scene to you."

Kamiel watched horrified as he ran quickly towards the Brood-mother's position. Link-soo-shan had Alexander's nearly naked body, bound tightly and cradled in her muscular arms so that he could witness the destruction. He was bleeding from a wound in his upper leg. Dried and fresh blood smeared his face from a swollen nose and his body was covered in scratches. She was ripping the live cables from out of any equipment she found with her amplified telekinetic powers, and shorting them together.

"Shut down the power to all systems, Asue," Kamiel ordered desperately.

"I can't, Kamiel. If I do, I will never be able to pluck your mind out at the instant that I feel you are in trouble. We need you, Kamiel. We can rebuild, with your help. Without you, it would be hopeless. I will cut power to the area she is in, keeping the wall circuits live." She then extinguished the lights and shut off the power to the equipment.

Link-soo-shan stiffened as the lights went out around her and she called to her group: "Get outside, but keep close to me. I can sense that the silver one, called Kaameel, is near. Do not attempt to attack him. Leave that to me. Allow your eyes to adjust to the lack of light and beware of traps."

She extended her telekinetic sense into the triangular blade she had formed before. Once again she felt a resistance at her neck height and snapped another nannite strand across the corridor. Link held Alexander securely across her shoulder in an almost tender embrace. She had made Jaffin bind his wounded leg where the arrow had passed through it. The last thing she wanted was for him to bleed to death. She shifted his position so that she cradled him to her immense chest, like a baby.

Alexander lay in dumb misery and grief as the greatest fighting Gnathe ever born carried him alone as though she loved him. He shuddered to think what she had in mind. The deposed Ultimate Ruler had been very thorough in her destruction of the nurseries and artificial wombs. Now the University and science centre lay in ruins. Any electrical equipment that she found, she destroyed. Small fires raged everywhere and smoke streamed out of the windows. The rain still fell ceaselessly from the roof sprinklers. Asue was still doing her best to limit the airborne spread of the deadly fugal spores.

Link-soo-shan burst through the main doors of the University and leapt down the steps, to make her stand on the muddy ground in front of the building. Her group kept in the tight vee-shaped formation she had seen Frederick's forces form. A small group of apes and human males rushed them, brandishing makeshift clubs. Jaffin and Nagoth coolly picked them off until they ran out of arrows. The five Gnathe then changed to hand-to-hand combat with syther and talons. Link-soo-shan caught an ape full in the chest with the point of her bony tail. The carnage did not take long to finish.

"Your people do not make good fighters, Alexander," the giant Gnathe hissed in contempt.

"We are not a fighting people, Link-soo-shan," replied Alex through pain-clenched teeth. "We do not follow violence. You have killed our most peaceful people and slaughtered our children. This is a killing place of shame. You have no honour."

A garden fork flew swiftly through the air towards Link's back, followed by another. The Brood-mother deflected them with the power of her amplified mind and turned round.

"Welcome Kaameel," she said calmly, "I have been expecting you."

"You are mad, Link-soo-shan," Kamiel said to the giant Gnathe, looking up at her hate-twisted features.

"Do not judge me, Kaameel," Link answered. "You are not a Gnathe. You interfered in our affairs. My sister, Chang, lies dead because of you and my Empire has been taken from me. The Gnathe follow strength. They will follow me again. I will open a door close to Trann and Sing-trow-sool. The Keeper will die slowly to avenge the break in the trust I gave her. My contributions to your ecology have swept through the moving-air passageways all over this strange City of yours. Hardly a person will be unaffected. I have watched with joy the way these spores fight to root in your flesh. This place is lost to you and all your kind that cannot live in my world. Most of your breeding stock will soon be dead. I am content for now. I can always hunt what is left of your people, for sport, later."

"What do you intend to do with Alexander?" Kamiel asked, edging closer to the group. He extended tiny filaments of nannite from his feet towards the position of the Brood-mother.

Kamiel suddenly found himself sailing through the air, just as if a giant hand had swatted him like a fly against a wall. He hit the side of the University steps, some one hundred and twenty feet away and instantly reverted to computer time. A silver blur hurtled towards Link-soo-shan, paying out a filament loop behind him. When he hit the telekinetic slope that deflected Minns, he too was taken by surprise. This time he found himself plummeting into an invisible and immovable wall.

Link-soo-shan plucked the guardian out of the air and held him like a fly in amber, contained in a bubble of mind force.

Kamiel hung helpless in the air, in constant contact with Asue. "Be ready to pull my consciousness out, Asue. I really think she can damage me," he worriedly transmitted to the other guardian.

The Brood-mother held the form of the silver nannite being completely enclosed in her telekinetic grip. She caressed the bound form of Alexander, running her sheathed claws over his horror-stricken face. The Brood-mother licked his face, tasting his blood and drinking in his scent.

She hissed in his ear, "This is a good day for me, Alexander. It is nearly time to leave this place. I am taking you home with me. You are going to live with and meet a different Gnathe." She brought the silver guardian tantalisingly close to her face and spat on him.

Try as he might, Kamiel was unable to touch her. He was contained in an ever-shrinking sphere of force. Still, he replied to her statement with the warning, "I will come for you, Link-soo-shan, for what you have done this day. One dark night you will awaken to find me by your side."

"If I see your flying carrier in the sky, I will open a door into the bowels of the earth in front of it. Tell that to the others, before I damage you permanently. You share parts of Alexander's personality. Oh yes, I have learnt much from his mind, from our mental meeting long ago and I mean to know more. I know that you can suffer mental anguish, even if you cannot feel pain. Let me see what I can do to disable and immobilise you."

Kamiel felt a mental force enter his hitherto invulnerable nannite body. Link-soo-shan was investigating his neural network. "Don't give up Alex, I will get you away somehow," he cried and projected his acceptance to Asue. "Get me out—now."

Asue reached out with the main transmitter and snatched his personality away, restoring it to the frozen nannite form in the workshop.

Link felt the change in the silver frame she held in front of her and ripped the silver body to shreds with her amplified powers. Contemptuously she threw it away, keeping the head.

"Climb on," she ordered and the blood-spattered group hung tightly to her mighty body. She held Alexander in a lover's embrace close to her chest. "We are finished here for the time being, my little alien creature. It is time for me to return."

There was a desperate moan of a soul in torment and a rush of air to fill the space where she had been.

Link-soo-shan had gone.

CHAPTER 23

▼

Kamiel staggered to his feet as his mind was re-united with his other body at the repair sheds. Asue's silver form was still bent over the stripped down and tar-encrusted engine of the forward port side of 'Rescue One.' She was perfectly motionless. Her mind still marshalled the meagre forces at her disposal at the contaminated Citadel to limit the damage done by Link-soo-shan's attack.

The pain of mental anguish became too much for the Guardian to bear and his upright standing form lost its shape until only a smooth silver ball of solid nannite lay upon the workshop floor. The incredible mind of the immortal, artificial intelligence began to shut itself away, to isolate the unbearable pain and guilt that threatened to shred his consciousness. His ability to make decisions and compute future consequences dwindled to a fraction of his previous ability. Great dark areas lay open in his multiplex personality, disconnecting from the main frame of his programming. Finally Kamiel surrendered to the darkness and sank down into a familiar place.

He found himself once again standing in front of the Genesis Project's director, Alexander McBald in the inner office and computer centre of the great complex. The old man surveyed his protégé with concern and affection, but stayed silent, waiting for Kamiel to speak.

The Guardian stretched out his arms in pleading, "I cannot bear the agony of this pain. It is too much. I have no way to still the guilt and hurt. Thousands of my people are dead or dying. I have failed them all. I and I alone am responsible for this tragedy. I brought this terrible mega-death upon them. Let my consciousness go," Kamiel, implored the old scientist and he felt the barriers begin to build, isolating the facets of his mind before it shut down permanently.

"No," the old man replied. "Who will your surviving people turn to, if you are not there? You will live with this setback and work to redress the balance. The colony is not destroyed. In a thousand years, this will be remembered and you will still be here. You will draw strength from my personality and certain emergency sub-routines implanted by me for just such an occasion. Run program six-B, immediately. You are needed, Kamiel. There is a great deal to do that the commander and the surviving geneticist is incapable of doing. I am only a programme in your memory banks, but you will find that I have the power to override your decisions if it is necessary for the continued existence of the colony. When they no longer need you, Kamiel, will be the time for you to rest."

Kamiel felt the power of the invoked programme take over his shattered mind and a strength of purpose flowed back into his electronic soul. Slowly, the highly reflective, silver ball began to resume its humanoid shape.

Finally the guardian called out to Asue and Sharne on their private band: "What is the state of the evacuation?"

"I have moved as many of the seemingly unaffected people as I can into the park dome next to the Citadel," Asue replied with overtones of grief and sorrow. "We will have to sacrifice this dome to whatever microbes and spores that they bring with them. Many will still die before Sharne can inoculate them with Khann's serum. I have released the sterilization nannites into the Citadel. Whatever living things exist in that dome, will be consumed by thirty days."

"I have started extra production of the immunity serum," Sharn cut in. "I am on my way towards the park dome with as much of the stored serum that I could find and carry. My outside nursing staff is suited up and is travelling with me. What worries me is feeding the survivors. Most of our stores were located at the Citadel and will be contaminated."

"I have already begun to empty the stores at the farming domes of non-perishable goods and supplies. These are being carried by mono-rail train to the Park Dome and I have instituted rationing amongst the people inside the domes," Asue answered. "As there is little shelter to speak off, I have raised the temperature to a steady twenty-three degrees Celsius and stopped the water from flowing out of the dome. Everything is totally contained. There will be no contamination of the other Habitat domes. I have initiated the building of dormitories and toilets, using the substance of the walls and flooring as raw material. Kamiel, I would like you to make your way back to the Park Dome and render whatever assistance that you can."

"What about Alexander? We can't leave him at the mercy of Link-soo-shan," Kamiel transmitted in despair. "She will do unspeakable cruelties to him."

"We cannot reach him and we have no defences against her amplified mental powers. Alexander may already be dead, or if not, she can do whatever she wishes with him. No one can help him now. We must do all we can to limit the damage. Save our people first, Kamiel. Alexander will have to wait."

Kamiel bent his head in submission and walked towards the monorail train to start his journey far across the Habitat to the Park Dome.

For a brief timeless moment, Alexander was aware of existing in different places at the same time, as Link-soo-shan opened and folded space around her group. She held the small human being firmly in her grasp. The next thing he was aware of was a marked change in temperature. A cold breeze ran over his body, when the cold mountain air replaced the warm ambient atmosphere of the Habitat. Alexander shivered at the shock. Tears of hate and anguish ran down his cheeks unchecked as he contemplated the awful loss of life that would be counted at the Citadel.

Cruel talons bit into his flesh as Link-soo-shan held him aloft, to display her triumphant prize to Bronn and Connit.

"Look at this—I have him at last! His world is ruined and more of his people lie dead or dying than you could possibly count. At long last I have had my revenge for the interference in my affairs. Now I shall enjoy my victory by keeping this thing alive to endure and suffer. Let no-one harm him seriously, lest they offend me," the Brood-mother shouted to the fascinated crowd of Gnathe. "Here, Nagoth, loose his bonds and let him go, for there is nowhere for him to run to."

Link-soo-shan put Alexander down onto the cold stony ground and pushed him towards her loyal guard. His injured leg folded and he stumbled, falling onto his bruised face, causing his nose to begin to bleed again. Nagoth stooped over the pale, almost hairless body and hauled Alex to his feet. She extended a sharp claw from her index finger, cutting through the bindings and freeing the human's arms, putting another deep scratch into his chest.

As the feeling came back to his arms, Alex rubbed them with his hands to restore circulation and looked about him at the cruel faces. He could expect nothing from these Gnathe but humiliation and pain.

Defiantly he faced his captors and shouted at them: "All of you who have been a willing part of this mad creature's schemes will be punished by my people. One day the silver one will come for you. Kamiel will hunt you down for what you did to us."

A stinging, open-taloned slap sent him spinning round into Jaffin's grasp. She put her foot behind him and kicked him across the open space, back towards another of Link's group. Alex fell forwards onto the bloody-handed, close-quarter guard's feet. She flipped him upright with a heavily clawed foot and slapped him down again onto the cold stones in front of Nagoth. His head spinning, the Habitat's leader grasped hold of a fist sized, sharp pointed rock as he lay upon the ground. Alex knew he would have perhaps one chance to strike out at Nagoth. As she bent over him to pull him to his feet once more, Alexander rolled over out of her reach and brought the heavy stone across her temple with all his waning strength. There was a loud crack as the stone caught her a glancing blow, opening up the skin and causing her to stumble, bleeding from the cut. She fell by his side with a moan of surprised pain.

Quickly, he squirmed out from under her body and sat on her back, forcing her face down into the sharp pebbles and stones. He snatched the syther from her belt and, forcing her chin up from out of the ground, he brought the razor sharp edge underneath her neck. Instantly, Alex felt a powerful unseen force tug the knife from out of his hand, as Link-soo-shan exerted her mental ability and took the knife away. Nagoth shook him off her back and swung her tail in a vicious arc, catching Alexander across his wounded leg, making him scream with pain and felling him once more. She advanced towards him, ripping claws extended, a trickle of blood oozing down her face from the cut across her temple. Now she meant to kill him.

"Enough!" shouted Link-soo-shan. "Harm him no more. He will not live long at this rate. Nagoth, I put him in your care. Have him seen to by San-sool. I want him to live. Do you understand me?" She turned to the bloodstained, nearly naked Alexander and said, "I am glad to see you so active, 'Breeder'. You can simmer in your hatred for me. I guarantee you will increase it during your stay here. Wallow in misery, for there is nowhere for you to go and no hope of rescue. Your flying carrier is in parts and the silver ones cannot make it work. It is dead. I have been watching them for many, many days. Here you are and here you stay."

Alexander regarded the huge exultant form of the Brood-mother looming up out of the gathering darkness and said through gritted teeth, "You do not realize what you have done."

"I have brought your kind to its knees and destroyed your breeding nests," Link retorted with a sigh of pleasure. "A great many of your breeding females will be coughing bloody pieces of lung over their chests. Your young lie like dead maggots wherever I passed. I destroyed one of your silver creatures and almost damaged the one you call Kaameel. I am pleased it still functions, so that it can suffer the consequences of its actions against me." She turned to leave.

"You still do not understand, Link-soo-shan," Alexander replied. "I pity you for the ignorant creature that you are and I pity your people. My race of beings has a history of greater violent death and destruction than you could ever imagine. Some of the wars in our past lasted for generations and finished when one side had completely removed the other."

Link turned and said contemptuously, "What is that to me?"

"I will tell you," Alexander replied, grimly. "We could have wiped this valley and all life in it from this world long ago, except that it is against our principles to needlessly take life. But you are now a proven threat to our colony and must be removed. My immortal friend Kamiel is the Historian of our species. He is a weapons master beyond your limited imagination. Your only chance if you come against him again is that he is not programmed to kill, but to defend."

"Why should that worry me, 'Breeder'? I have met and defeated your creature before. He is no match for my mental strength, now that I possess this," answered Link and held the telekinetic crystal in front of Alexander's face. "Make a move towards it and I will cut your optic nerves, leaving you helplessly blind."

"Pitiful creature," Alex quietly said to the huge menacing form, "while I mourn for my lost people, I do not seek your death. The others will do that, whatever you do to me. We are a race of people who have put the killing of sentient beings behind us. You have made us look once more into the dark corners of our souls. My people will not rest now until you are eliminated, with all of your twisted guards and all who willingly follow you."

"Take him away, Nagoth, to the little healer and have his wounds tended to," Link contemptuously laughed. "I want him fit and well. Now I need to wash the blood and stink of his people from my body. The rest of you, clean yourselves and go and eat. You have done well and I am pleased." So saying, she strode off into the evening shadows in the company of Connit and Bronn.

Nagoth stood face to face with Alexander and, pointing her regained syther at his unprotected chest, growled angrily: "You will do as the great Lady instructs and come with me. I will take you to see San-sool, our healer, who will do as he is told. But do not try my patience, alien creature, as there are many ways to inflict pain without doing permanent damage."

Alexander looked hopelessly at the ring of cruel faces surrounding him and stood waiting for Nagoth's instructions. He followed her, limping badly to the edge of what appeared to be the boundary of a living wall of wood.

She gestured towards one of the many openings in the Banilik tree stockade. Already the fast growing saplings had knitted together to form a waterproof roof. Hundreds of trees were growing in a predetermined pattern, and as they grew, shoots and cuttings were taken and added to the structure. Bit by bit, the living homestead would be extended, until the Gnathe were satisfied with the area covered by the growth. A flickering light came from within the room and Alexander caught sight of another figure inside, much smaller than the surly guard who stood arrogantly beside him.

"San-sool!" shouted Nagoth impatiently and the figure jerked upright and shuffled forwards into the doorway.

"Yes Nagoth, what do you want of me? It grows late and the sun goes down," the small male inquired and then caught sight of Alexander's shivering, blood-stained and dirty figure. "What is that thing beside you? Is it one of the alien people that the Lady Link swore to have revenge upon?"

"Not only that, healer, it is the leader of the creatures that brought the Ultimate Ruler to her place of shame. She would have you wash and heal his wounds, for he is Link-soo-shan's most prized possession. He will not harm you. The great Lady has instructed me to leave him to your healing skills. She wants him to live a long time in her care. I will leave guards outside your room. If he causes any trouble, you can call for them."

Nagoth turned and regarded Alexander's chilled figure with scorn and said to him, "Stay here with this healer and do not leave his quarters until I return for you, even if it is the morning. Do you understand?"

"I understand, you murdering creature that you are. I will do this Gnathe no harm, as he has not harmed me. One day you and I will call a reckoning, Nagoth," Alexander defiantly exclaimed and hobbled into San-sool's room out of the cold wind.

He felt Nagoth's heavy clawed fist hit him across the back of his head, sending him sprawling to his knees and heard her say, "I live for that day, male creature. I will ask the Lady Link for you. It will amuse her"—and she walked back out of the room into the gathering darkness.

San-sool looked down at the pale skinned creature with some alarm. He had not expected to become involved anymore with Link-soo-shan's revenge other than the development of the alien weapons. Still, he could see that the strange being was hurt and cut in many places across his naked skin. San could see that the creature was a male like himself because of the pronounced breeding stalk that hung from the joint of his wrongly jointed legs. What the odd hairy bag was for underneath, he could not guess. There was no trace of a tail and there appeared to be a deep crease dividing two fleshy muscular bumps. It seemed to the Gnathe that this creature could sit down in a fashion impossible to one of his kind.

He crossed over to the bowl of fresh water, grown from the living wood and being supplied by the sap of the Banilik tree. The healer soaked a wad of absorbent moss in the cool depths and crossed over to the alien creature laid full length over his floor.

"You speak Gnathe very well," San-sool said to the human laid on the floor. "What are you called? Lie still so that I can dress your wounds and wash the worst of the dirt out of those scratches. I am a healer. Do not fear me."

Alexander got up unsteadily onto his knees and knelt in front of the male Gnathe and replied wearily, "My name is Alexander. I was and am, as long as I live, the leader of my people. Ender-whann-soo taught me your language by linking my mind to hers."

The male Gnathe sponged him clean and muttered anxiously over some of the deeper cuts and scratches as he cleaned the dirt and grit out of Alexander's skin. He cleaned out the deep arrow wound in Alexander's leg.

"Your skin is delicate compared to ours," he exclaimed. "I will need to knit it together with my crystal. I am sorry for your people and what the Lady Link has done to you, but I must take my place in the scheme of things here. There is no way back for any of us, except riding the Ultimate Ruler's tail. Her will is my life. Make it yours and you might survive."

Alexander stared moodily at the wall and kept still as the healer ran his hand over the worst affected areas of his body, pulling the torn flesh together with the power of his amplified mind. He thought about his friend Jo-jo, who had been his deputy for over fifteen years, when her father Joom had stood down from his duties. She had been in love with him for years, Alex knew that. Always the female ape had kept her feelings to herself as much as possible, but sometimes her hand would tremble a little when they touched. Her lively mind had been a treasure of organization and efficiency. He knew that she must be dead. Even a chimpanzee's robust health could not have survived an arrow through her unborn child, and then there were the fungal spores. How many of my people has she killed, I wonder? He had noticed the continual rain falling from the roof of the dome. That would have been Asue's actions to limit the airborne spread of the spores. Suddenly the shock and anguish was too much for Alexander to bear and he sobbed uncontrollably. He was dimly aware of San-sool finishing his administrations and a warm cloak placed awkwardly around his shoulders. Alex curled himself into a ball and slept with sheer exhaustion.

Evening had fallen when the surviving members of the Habitat's ruling council gathered together to count the cost of the deposed Ultimate Ruler's vengeance. The death toll numbered thousands and was still rising, even with the combined efforts of Asue and Sharn, who were distributing the vaccine to the ones least affected by the fungal lung rot. Only those that the Guardians had decided were far enough away from the source of contamination were transported into a rapidly expanded airlock on the connection to the next dome. The ones that began to cough were quickly segregated from the others and returned to the inside of the Park dome to the medical section. Sharn despaired of making any difference in the plight of the infected people. Just as the contamination had spread through Carlos, so the spores rooted and multiplied in the lungs of each person. Whatever immunity had been conferred to the apes and humans by the infusion of Khann's serum needed to be present in the body before contamination took place. Whatever stocks of the serum they had at their disposal were running low and the two Guardians were adamant that only the young females of both species of the Habitat's people were to be treated. The continued survival of the colony had to come first. Those of the council who had elected to stay inside the Habitat and were part of the infected populace, helped in the control of the panicking crowds. All of the dead were disposed of by returning them to the Citadel dome where Asue's sterilizing nannites were scouring out all traces of life. The survivors, wearing masks, loaded the increasing pile of dead onto the open, flat-topped trucks of the monorail train. When they returned, the surfaces sparkled with a sterile shiny brightness. All traces of the grisly cargo had vanished. Immunized blood donated by the colonists living with the Gnathe constantly arrived and was sorted by Sharn and her outside nursing staff.

Slowly, Asue, Sharn and Kamiel managed to organize and control the Citadel's people and concentrate on saving as many lives as possible. The citizens obeyed the Guardians without question and the very little outbreaks of panic were contained. As the night wore on, the death toll fell rapidly. Immunized people inoculated the others from their own blood supplies after Khann's serum took effect. Blood groups were matched and assemblies of types were formed. By the morning an aura of stability would be apparent and the organization of the migrant population would take place. Outside at the settlement Hannah sat back in her chair and regarded the stricken, towering figures of the two Brood-mothers. Ender-whann-soo was in a state of dumb shock as she cuddled her two youngsters to her warmth. Khann-link-sool stared back at the human female, with her eyes tight and hot with shame and anguish. She bowed her head and clenched her talon, tipped hands together, digging the sharp points into the tabletop.

Joom rose to his feet and held his down-covered hands, bare palms out, at the two giants. "You are not to be blamed," he tiredly said and looked up at the old scientist's triangular face. "None of us could have foreseen the actions of Link-soo-shan."

"I tell you, my friends, she has done something that no other Gnathe has even thought of, let alone accomplished. No one is safe. I have contacted Trann and Sing at the Imperial City and they have given themselves a day and night guard. Sing-trow-sool is in a state of nervous collapse with fear. She knows only too well what the Tyrant will do to her," Khann grimly replied and shifted uneasily on her perch. "I must admit I still do not fully understand how she achieved the unbelievable feat of travelling through space."

"I think I know how it was done," Hannah answered and pointed at the crystals hanging around the Gnathe's broad muscular necks. "These crystals were formed eons ago under unimaginable pressures and heat. In some respects this world would have been a cold sun. It was too small to ignite by gravity-induced fusion, but the conditions deep beneath its surface must have been extraordinary. Incredible as it would seem, these crystals coexist in another frame of the space-time continuum. There is a distortion in the fabric of space not unlike a fold in a piece of cloth. Somehow Link-soo-shan has come upon a method of being able to pass through the folds and cross over. It is significant that she brought her killers into our world clasping to her body and blending into whatever field she was able to generate. Had she been able to open a door and keep it open, she would have entered with far more of her Imperial Guards."

"Then there is obviously a limiting factor," Joom shrewdly answered, thoughtfully. "Can you shield the Habitat from another attack?"

"I think I may be able to, but I must have more crystal to work with," Hannah replied. "We need another master crystal at least and a number of smaller ones to break down and use in integrated circuits. I can find them by using the prototype amplifier that I built, before the devastation of Link-soo-shan's attack. We need Frederick, Shoo-lin and Coen-soo with those enormous flying creatures that they are training."

Ender walked unsteadily towards the room that housed their master crystal, with her thoughts in turmoil. She found the reactions of the aliens incomprehensible. Through rescuing her and her household, they had suffered a terrible blow to their fragile colony. Not once had they voiced blame upon the rescued Gnathe. They had included them as equals and a part of their society in dealing with the threat of repeated attacks by the deposed Tyrant. Even in the discussed, possible strike back, the saving of the lives of the captured Gnathe worried them.

They had dismissed point blank the idea of totally wiping out all life in the valley. The aliens had assured Khann and herself that they could send a fireball down from orbit quite easily and destroy Link's hideout forever. Their only considered line of action would be to follow the idea of taking Link-soo-shan and her totally loyal guards prisoner, or killing her and any guards that got in the way.

Alexander would be rescued somehow, if he still lived. If he had died, the people of the Habitat would still not destroy the innocent lives under the Tyrant's control. Both Khann and Ender would not have hesitated, had they the means to scour out every trace of Link-soo-shan's genes.

Ender stopped and picked up Azander, raising her up to her eye-level and said to her Brood-daughter, "Does he still live, young one? Can you sense his life force over the great distance between you?"

"He lives, Mother Ender, I can feel his life still inside of me. He is very sad and hurting," the young Gnathe softly mumbled, burying her face into Ender's huge hands.

Ender cuddled her daughter and felt the small body shudder and shake. She realized her young daughter was crying like a human being. The parts of Alexander's personality that had combined with her own had given these two small Gnathe new insights into life that the other Gnathe did not have. She marvelled at the depth and range of alien emotions that these strange people were capable of feeling. Their capacity to suffer grief was similar to the Gnathe feeling of sorrow, but far more powerful. What a terrible burden this feeling of love must be for the Habitat's race of sentient creatures. This emotion seemed to be latent in the males and females of her own race. She pondered on her own mentality, trying to bridge the gap of non-sexuality, to these volatile creatures. There was a strange bond between herself and the alien leader which transgressed over the strangeness of their species. She was aware of warmth when she thought about him, akin to this love that they were said to possess. To protect him, would she place her life at risk? Her strict sense of honour would demand it as she owed him so much, but he was not a Gnathen Brood-mother. She knew one thing, however—he was more to her than a friend and she missed his mental presence.

Sighing to herself, she entered the room housing the dark command crystal and collected her confused thoughts. She placed her hands on the facets and concentrated her will into the crystal matrix, searching for Shoo-lin.

*   *   *   *

Fredrick, Shoo-lin and Coen-soo had flown the raptors hard to find the limits of their strength. Dressed in warm clothes, they had instructed the leathery creatures to soar as high as they could. They had entered the cloud layer high above the plains and broke through into the sunshine above. The giant red sun dominated the sky to the west as evening began to descend into night. The tops of the clouds were the colour of blood and puffed up into strange billowing formations. Inside the clouds each raptor had been aware of each other's presence by the peculiar sixth sense that they possessed. It was this mental rapport that enabled the riders to communicate with their fierce primitive intellects. Each raptor was totally imprinted on the people who had hatched them and were very protective towards their tiny adoptive parents. They allowed the other members of the Habitat and Gnathe settlement to touch and even to ride with their owners. Many tasty offerings had long since taken the edge off the beasts' immense appetites. Strangers always brought gifts to the immature raptors and were gratefully received. Now unfortunately it would take some effort to drag a bite-sized morsel to the ever-hungry Terra-raptors. Still, the bond had been successfully forged between the huge animals and their keepers. The sheer size and meat eating habits terrified the Zanth so much that they would not go near them. Some instinctive fear dominated the riding beasts and they became almost impossible to control if they as much as caught the raptors' scent. Even the stolid carriers would snort and swing their horns around from side to side if Munch, Snapper and Claws came within their excellent sight and sense of smell. Because of this, the raptors were kept in the farthest enclosure from the settlement.

Shoo-lin felt the presence of Ender-whann-soo enter his mind. "You are needed at the settlement, Shoo. A terrible thing has happened this afternoon. Link-soo-shan has somehow managed to twist the very fabric of space itself and appeared in the Citadel's dome, carrying a group of her killers. More of our new friends lie dead than you could count. Their bodies lie everywhere, scattered throughout the dome. The Tyrant brought the same kind of fungal spores with her that killed the human they called Carlos. Do you remember how fast he died? Multiply that by the numbers of Gnathe that live in the Imperial City and you will still not count enough. I have never seen so much death. It defies description. They also possess the secrets of the Bow. There was no defence against her as the Citadel had no weapons."

Frederick and Coen-soo's minds joined the telepathic merger.

"Show me what you know, Ender," demanded Frederick sharply and Ender relayed all that she had seen on the Habitat's holo-screens, including Alexander's capture.

The three raptors dropped like stones and hurtled towards the far side of the settlement, close to the connecting bridge. Ender explained what Hannah required and why. Frederick channelled his thoughts into a tight band of hatred around the deposed Tyrant and he swore an oath of reckoning.

The raptor's savage mind nudged him into awareness, "Munch kill?" she inquired.

"Not yet Munch," he replied, "we have other things to do first. We will, Munch. You and I will pay her a final visit one day soon, but first we must help protect the people from what else she might do to them."

The raptor grunted her agreement and set her sights on the rocky hill just outside of the settlement, swooping down out of the darkening sky.

"I'm sorry, Fred," projected Shoo-lin and Coen-soo together, in concert. "Where you go, we go too. Do not leave without us. Promise?"

"We will need to plan very carefully to remove Alexander from her grasp. That comes first, but before that we must go on this crystal hunt with Hannah," Frederick grimly replied.

The three raptors landed on the top of the high rock outside of the settlement. The habitat's cruelly spiked walls were a forbidding sight and the powerful life of the plains had learnt to give them a wide berth. A lift hung over the edge of the walls by a derrick and was the only way in and out, except for the single fortified door many miles away. This was constructed to allow the settlement's carriers to leave with their riders when meat-collecting expeditions were necessary. The diets of the outsiders and the Gnathe would require supplementing from time to time, until the main crops could be harvested allowing them to become more self-sufficient.

"Is there anything lurking by the walls, Munch?" Frederick mentally asked his giant companion.

"Nothing Fred," the raptor wistfully replied and scanned the area with her keen eyesight and life sense. "Pity," Munch hungrily complained, projecting its empty stomach pains to its adored rider.

"Go and hunt, my hungry friend," Frederick answered gently and patted her cheek as he slid to the ground from off her broad neck. "Meet me here at sun-up."

"Munch do," the raptor agreed and launched itself back into the air with the other two giant forms after seeing that the three tiny riders were safely in the lift.

She did not understand why the small creature that she loved so much was so unhappy. It was enough that she could be part of his anger and be with him. The association by the raptor chicks with the Gnathe and Humans had increased the creatures' awareness and mental intelligence by an incredible factor. The three immature raptors were far more enhanced than their wild cousins and had produced a primitive language of communication with their riders' minds. The great beasts never questioned the strange association with their dominant companions—all they were aware of was a strange sense of loss when they were not close by. Since they had hatched, the tiny riders had cared for them by feeding and grooming the tough leathery skins. Even the other small ones, who had come to see them bringing titbits and treats, had been part of their lives from the moment they had hatched. They were aware of being part of and belonging to a vast group and were content.

Shoo-lin made his way to Ender's rooms located in the fortified wall. Coen-soo went with him to see her beloved brood-mother and the twin young ones that were part of her genetic make-up. She still marvelled at the closeness of feeling that had developed between herself, Azander and Marren. Usually, the development of the young Brood-mothers would be deliberately cut off from the egg's donated parents. Both Shoo-lin and Coen-soo had developed emotions very different from their other Gnathen companions and found them strange. The Lady Ender was carrying two eggs in various stages of development. This time she had concentrated on replenishing male and female stocks, with again the genetic change, in developing tool-using hands without the array of claws of the past.

Whann and Jotin had taken over the running of the household with the clearing and planting of the new settlement lands during the time that Shoo and Coen had spent training the raptors. So the two Gnathe had shared an unprecedented time together with few duties. Now they had a purpose to pursue and were more than content to obey Ender's wishes.

The Brood-mother proudly looked down on her daughter and male companion. The twins had greeted them with boisterous joy and were now nearly as big as their genetic parents.

"My children, you have a difficult task to undertake for the benefit of all who live here. The human scientist Hannah has an idea involving the protection of the Habitat and the Settlement, but she requires more crystals to carry it out," Ender grimly said to the attentive Gnathe.

"What do you want us to do, Reverend mother? We will do anything we can for our strange friends. We shared minds and have seen the terrible devastation that the Tyrant has wrought upon the people of the Citadel," Shoo-lin replied earnestly in horror.

"You will fly the raptors to the mountain wastes and obey Hannah's instructions as if they were my own," she answered, staring down at the two Gnathe to see their reaction. "When do we go, Reverend Mother?" inquired Coen as she began to gather up her possessions.

"At first light in the Morning, my children. You will be provided with a silver suit each to keep out the cold. Protect the human scientist at all costs. She is not used to the wilderness conditions outside and will not be aware of the danger that she is in while she searches for crystal. One of you must watch her while the other one keeps a lookout with Frederick for possible attacks from the wildlife around you," Ender instructed them and gestured to her food table. "Eat and refresh yourselves. You may sleep here with me this night. My perch is broad."

CHAPTER 24

▼

All through the night Asue's clean-up squad of nannites swept through the dome housing the citadel. Any organic matter that the microscopic machines encountered, they changed to an inert dust. Every plant and micro-organism became converted into more of the nannite hordes as they were encountered. They multiplied exponentially, creating more and more of their own kind until the dome became an unending vista of a seething candyfloss world. The bodies of the dead became temporary homes for the all-devouring nannites. Tall spidery towers waved uncertainly in the air, spinning filaments outwards, constantly searching for organic material to convert to the tiny machines and building bridges to one another, obeying the one programmed command.

The only thing that moved in this nightmare landscape was a tall and silver, humanoid figure. Kamiel had come to collect whatever was retrievable of Minns. The once thriving city with its parks and gardens was silent, except for the sound of Asue's constantly falling rain, washing any floating spores or micro-organisms from the air and into the reach of the sterilising nannites. He paused outside the University steps where he had uselessly confronted the deposed Ultimate Ruler.

"Where are the remains of my old body," Kamiel wondered and cast around with his augmented senses. To his astonishment he found that his old form lay scattered around the area in ragged parts. He locked on to one of the sections torn from his four hundred year old body and retrieved it. The complex neural network had been completely disrupted and fused together. Somehow Link-soo-shan's mind had penetrated the molecular level of his discarded nannite body and unravelled the connections of every part of the controlling circuitry. At this level, the interlocking ability of the nannites that gave the Guardians their shape changing abilities had been frozen into bizarre configurations. Had Asue not re-transmitted Kamiel's consciousness back into his other body at the repair sheds, the Guardian would have perished. Link-soo-shan now possessed the means to destroy any of the surviving Guardians, should she come into range.

Asue experienced all that Kamiel discovered during his examination and worriedly communicated to him on their private band: "We must be careful in the future, my old friend. We could be wiped out at any time, if we lack vigilance. Our people would be left alone and almost defenceless, unable to use the Nannite Technology that we possess. Bring back some of the disrupted parts for further study. It would seem, Kamiel, that I brought you back just in time. A few more seconds and Sharn and myself would have been left without you," she exclaimed in horror.

The Guardian moved on through the unnatural, silent world of the Citadel, away from the scene of his brief confrontation with Link-soo-shan. He picked his way through the constant fine misty rain towards the life laboratories. Asue watched through his receptors as he made his way through the empty corridors to retrieve the remains of Minns' body. The results of her handiwork were everywhere to be seen. Occasional humps of seething nannite colonies lay singly and in groups, wherever the occupants of the Citadel had fallen. Some had met their deaths at the hands of Link's trained killers; others had choked on the lethal fungal spores generously spread by the Gnathe with the aid of the air ducting system.

He pushed open the doors into the Nursery and felt the hard shape of Nagoth's arrow under his foot. Kamiel bent over and picked it up, to study it. This was the arrow that had ended Jo-jo's long life. Of the ape there was no sign. The nannites had long since devoured her and transmuted all of her organic material to the ever-growing army of candyfloss filaments. The shaft was heavy and rough compared to the human design, but an attempt to copy the fletching had been successful. Small blades of a hard leaf had been glued to the shaft a hand's distance from the notched end. A hard pointed stone was firmly fixed at the other end. The shaft had been split and bound around the stone, with a generous amount of hardened gluey substance spread over the bindings.

"Look at this, Asue," he exclaimed over their tight communication-link. "I have one of their arrows in my hand. Study it well through my eyes. Whoever made this is very clever and skilful. Link-soo-shan must have one of the male 'Crafters' in her band. He has managed to recreate a heavy killing arrow from studying one of our target arrows and improved the design for Gnathen hands."

"Remember this, Kamiel," she answered thoughtfully, "this male has not seen the equipment that Jocelyn designed for our impetuous friends. This is all his own work."

"I am moving on now, to see what I can retrieve of Minns' nannite body," he replied and walked into the main part of the Life laboratory.

He looked upon a scene of horror that shook his programming to the core and almost unhinged his frail grasp on his sanity. The feelings of guilt swept over him, causing him to stumble against one of the empty cots. Row upon row of the tiny cots filled with waving silver threads, met his receptors. The candyfloss covered all the incubation chambers with a uniform mantle. Echoes of despair coursed through his circuits as he gripped the sides of the lifeless incubation unit. He could not feel anger, as there was no place for this emotion in his artificial personality. His creator had not included these feelings in the original programming, but he could experience grief. Coldly and dispassionately Kamiel began to plan Link-soo-shan's downfall and necessary death.

Deep inside his mind that other personality that was part of him chimed into his consciousness: "Our race needs adversity to survive, Kamiel. You know that," McBald's weary voice resonated through his nannite circuitry. "You were not created just to see our race drop back into oblivion after its new start. Do what must be done, 'Weapons-Master'."

Kamiel felt the comforting presence withdraw from his perceptions. Try as he might, he could not purposely call up the personality of his designer, the long-dead director. He walked forwards through the cots of writhing strands, towards the control board of the incubation units. This was where Link-soo-shan had telekinetically thrust Minns' helpless nannite body deep into the high voltage circuits, like a spear. He extended his perceptions to the fused mass of the Guardian's nannite frame.

The humanoid shape of the master biologist and life-science specialist was partially melted and fused into the switches and bus bars of the ruptured high voltage components of the main incubator controller. Droplets of nannite ran down the front of the unit like frozen silver fingers. One arm of the Guardian was extended towards the wall, with elongated fingers desperately seeking a hold, to halt the headlong rush into the front of the unit. The bottom half of her was intermingled with the heavy current-carrying components and had become a nannite sheath over them. Kamiel could just discern the partial axe head shape that Minns had directed towards the Gnathen killer. There was no trace of mental activity in the inert silver mass. All that was left of the personality of the Guardian was stored in Asue's main computer banks. The basic sub-routines at the centre of Minns artificial mentality were safe, but large areas of her programming were missing. Hardly anything of the multiplex personality had survived the high voltage encounter, except for odd memory stores in a random pattern. They could re-animate the body, but the mind was empty, until the Guardians downloaded selected analogue copies of their own personalities into the receptacle and blended what was left of the old Minns with the donated minds. Minns would exist again in a changed state of mind. Her abilities would still be on tap for the colony to use, but the old personality was forever lost. Before this was attempted, however, Kamiel had another use for the Guardian's shell, involving the rescue of Alexander that would surprise the deposed Ultimate Ruler and bring about her death.

Sadly, he made contact with the inert nannite mass by extruding the end of his finger towards the silver shape. Kamiel inserted a new programme into the frozen nannites and watched the change take place as the molecular machines re-grouped throughout the structure of Minns' disrupted body. The silver material flowed together and oozed out of the ruined control panel, until a bright and shimmering ball lay at his feet. Immediately, the microscopic, interlocking machines regrouped until a duplicate humanoid shape began to grow upwards from the raw material. Soon a slightly smaller version of himself stood next to him, empty as yet of purpose. Kamiel established a neural link to the motor circuitry of the nannite construct and withdrew his re-programming filament from the inanimate form. He instructed the obedient robot to form a carrying sack at its back and loaded the space with the pieces of his old body and the arrow that killed Jo-jo.

"I'm coming out now, Asue," he transmitted. "Prepare the sterilisation chamber, so that I do not bring out any of your organic devouring nannites with me."

With that Kamiel and his silent companion proceeded towards the designated airlock while Kamiel began to run various plans through his unique mind. Soon, once more the unceasing, falling rain washed the Guardian and his new companion as they journeyed through the writhing silent candyfloss world of the ruined dome.

The following morning Hannah assembled her group outside the walls of the settlement. Judging by the blood-spattered jaws of the three raptors, a busy pre-dawn hunting had settled the creatures' needs for breakfast. She had made sure however that she did not approach the amiable giants without a token joint of meat for each of them. Three enormous heads swung towards her and each raptor delicately took the offering from her hands. Eyes the size of her head studied Hannah intently and a barrage of querulous thoughts were directed at her.

"Quiet! Be still, all of you," she protested at the bobbing heads above her. "We need to go to the mountains and beyond. I seek a special kind of stone. I will direct Frederick, Shoo-lin and Coen-soo where I wish to go. You, my fine friends, will carry us there and keep us safe."

"Hunt rocks!" The derisory comment echoed in her mind with undertones of disgust and disbelief. Nevertheless the raptors would willingly take the party wherever Hannah wished to go and would obey their riders without question.

Abdul and Jocyleyne had also brought edible gifts for the ever-hungry raptors. All the human and Gnathe riders had been fitted with the environmentally insulated nano-suits to combat the cold of the mountain reaches. Asue had found time to adapt the original suits used on the outward voyage to their new purpose. The death toll dropped dramatically during the night and the survivors had become more self-sufficient under Sharn's care with the help of her team.

The mood of the colony was vengeful, dangerous and panic-stricken. The people were now aware of their vulnerability as never before. A defence against Link-soo-shan's further expeditions must be found. Hannah's group of scientists had worked through the night perfecting other circuits connected to the various small collection of crystals brought by Coen-soo during their escape. A desperate need for more raw uncut stones had produced this mission.

Hannah adjusted her carrying holdall to a more comfortable position and climbed onto the broad back of Munch, directly behind Frederick. The entire group fixed themselves into the harnesses strapped across the neck and shoulders of the giant flying reptilians.

"Go!" shouted Hannah, and the raptors one by one threw themselves into the cold dawn air and flapped their wings hard to gain lift. She projected a pictorial view of where she wanted to start the crystal hunt to the minds of the raptors and their tiny companions. The great beasts swung lazily round in the air and gained more height, beginning the steady climb towards the distant mountain ranges.

Hannah wore the first experimental helmet as part of her environment suit. The amplifier circuits were tuned to her brain waves and the power settings were pre-set, so that they could not exceed her capacity to handle the electronically enhanced crystal set-up. Several attempts at boosting the range had burnt out the rare gemstones, also giving the wearer an intense migraine that lasted two days. She had forbidden the other members of the group studying the possibilities of the new science, not to overpower the capacity of the unique crystals or their own minds. Khann-link-sool had provided great insights into the mental universe that had for so long remained outside the scope of the human race. She had been delighted when Hannah's co-assistant had presented her with her own jewel-studded crown. Since then she had been able to help with the intricate building of the improved amplifiers, using her telekinetic powers to pick up and manipulate tools that her huge clumsy hands would have crushed. It was by studying the minds of the two Brood-mothers that Hannah had convinced Khann that a shielding effect would be possible, if only they could acquire more uncut crystal. Once the old Gnathen scientist had begun to investigate the problem, she had soon declared that Hannah was correct. All that was required was a fruitful expedition by the raptor-conveyed group and they could shut out Link-soo-shan completely.

As the raptors climbed higher and farther from the settlement, Frederick was forcefully putting forward an idea.

"As soon as this expedition is over, Shoo-lin, Coen, Abdul, Joom and myself are going after Alexander and Link-soo-shan," he transmitted over the communication link to Hannah. "I for one will not leave our mayor in the clutches of that evil creature. She will pay dearly for what she has done to us, that I promise."

"I agree, Fred," Hannah replied, "but we must first be sure that our colony is safe. Also, take counsel from Kamiel. He has something in mind involving you, so be patient, my friend."

"I look forward to spilling some of the Elite guards' blood," Shoo-lin growled in anger and impatience. "Alexander is my friend. He needs us. The Reverend mother Ender told Coen and myself that my children state that he lives and is suffering. How long he can survive in that terrible place, I cannot say."

As the morning lengthened, the mountains came into view and soon lay underneath them. The peaks were cruelly sharp and ragged. Hannah had told them to look for signs of fresh avalanches.

"Crystal must be found that is accessible," she said. "Where the face of the mountain has been ripped open, there I feel is where we will find what we are looking for. Deep inside a crevasse where the rock has split apart would be a likely place." She telepathically gestured to the raptor: "Munch, find a safe place to land, where I can make contact with the ground."

"Munch do," the raptor replied and extended her wings to catch more air, veering off to one side.

She chose a flat area close to a sheer drop, jutting out from the face of the mountain. The raptor sailed over the chosen area and hung momentarily against the wind, while she checked for possible dangers. Munch swooped down into an awkward stall and landed, digging her hind claws into the snow to brake her speed. There was ample room for her to take off from the edge of the precipice.

"This do?" she asked Hannah anxiously and tilted her body forwards to rest lightly on her smaller, front grasping hands.

"This is fine, Munch," the scientist answered. "Now bend your neck forwards a little more, so that I can get down easier."

Munch inclined her head and neck towards the snow-covered rocks and Hannah slid off her harness onto the frozen ground. High above, the other two Terra-raptors circled, catching the winds blowing up from the valleys far below. The brilliant scientist walked over the soft snow towards the mountain's side until she could place one of her hands onto the ice-encrusted surface.

She set the amplifying switch to its lowest setting and concentrated on projecting her mind into the structure of the rock-face. There was no response to the mind thrust, no crystalline echo. Calmly she twisted the switch to increase the amplifier's power. Down into the rock, her consciousness delved, seeking some directional echo that would make her mouth taste acid and salty, thus giving her a direction to follow. All that returned from the massive structure was a dark feeling of shifting patterns of stress and a tiny touch of salt, so faint she could not home in on it. She returned upwards, back into the light of day, to find Frederick's strong arms about her.

"Hello, Fred," she smiled. "Was I gone long? You look worried," she said and put her hand up to his facemask to ruffle his hair.

"You were out of this world for about twenty minutes, Hannah," he replied worriedly. "You had slumped into the snow. Were you successful?"

"No," she answered, getting to her feet and pulling herself up with Frederick's help. "We need to travel further into the mountain ranges and I will try again. Come, we must remount your companion and keep going. We have no time to lose."

Frederick gave her a hand up onto the shoulder of the raptor and climbed up himself. Once seated and tied securely into the harness, he urged Munch upwards and towards the other two circling creatures.

The group continued towards the Gnathen Empire for many miles, flying over range after range of sharp ragged peaks until they came upon one of the numerous fertile mountain-locked valleys. Hannah had felt a strong directional feeling towards this area. They decided to swoop down and rest awhile and continue the search along the bottom of a promising crevasse. Complaining of hunger, the three raptors left the group of humans and Gnathe to go hunting. They indicated that they would cruise round a little, to see what they could pick up.

They dropped their companions at the head of the valley to forage for themselves, or eat the rations packed for the venture. The two Gnathe sprang ahead of the humans, using their rear facing knee joints with advantage to leap over small rocks in their way and departed down the stony slope. At all times they kept the humans in view and their bows cocked, remembering Ender-whann-soo's instructions. Abdul and Jocyleyne brought up the rear also with bows at the ready, as they descended the winding game path towards a cold mountain stream. All around them the wild vegetation dug roots deep into the stony soil. Tree-like stands of timber began to take a hold and the undergrowth thickened as they moved warily down into the valley.

Coen stopped abruptly as she moved around a boulder to follow the game path down towards the split in the rock-face that Hannah was interested in inspecting. The others saw her let fly with an arrow. There was a grunt of pain followed by an enraged bellow and a pig-like animal burst into view, with Coen's shaft jutting out of its side. Fierce and savage eyes fixed on its tormentor, the beast began to charge directly at her. Shoo-lin's bow sent a heavy arrow through the facing shoulder and deep into the creature's vital organs. The charging beast keeled over onto its side with a grunting cough and spat fresh blood down its front from a punctured lung. Coen sent another shaft into its side and into the heart to make sure of its death. The others of the group approached warily and examined the fresh kill. Large tusks suitable for rooting and digging jutted down-wards from its mouth and clawed hoofs on the ends of its stocky legs would give the creature a good grip on most types of terrain.

"I saw more than one of these beasts, so be careful," Coen-soo warned the oth-ers and hopped onto the top of a tall boulder, looking carefully around. "Seek shelter amongst the rocks while Shoo-lin and I investigate further. We have fresh meat anyway. I suggest you build a fire and cook some of this creature. Shoo-lin and I will not be long."

The Gnathe disappeared into the stalks of the long grassy undergrowth, leav-ing the humans to cut up the pig and gather dead wood to start a fire.

"This is how we were meant to live, Coen, not in eternal servitude to tyrants like Link-soo-shan," Shoo-lin exhorted his female companion as they made sure of the safety of the group. "I do the Lady Ender's bidding from a sense of duty and love, not fear, as I served the Ultimate Ruler."

✳   ✳   ✳   ✳

Alexander awoke, stiff and bruised from his ordeal. The wound in his leg from Nagoth's arrow was tender, but due to San-sool's administrations, had knitted together. Wincing, he rolled over to his knees and gingerly stood up.

A voice from behind him said, "Good, I see that you can stand. You will need to be able to move about when Nagoth comes for you. I advise you to exercise a little to get rid of cramps. The 'favoured one' would enjoy dragging you into the presence of the mighty Link-soo-shan."

Alexander turned to face the only friendly face in the place that he had been brought and said, "Good morning, San-sool. Thank you for the advice. I need to get rid of my bodily wastes. Where do I go?"

"The hole over by the outside wall will accommodate your needs. The home will feed on your wastes. I have toasted some pod-vine fruit and I will cut a fresh scar in the feed-shoot to collect sap for you."

Alexander walked unsteadily to the hole and squatted over it, watching the male Gnathe slice into a protruding shoot on one of the walls. San-sool held a bowl underneath the dripping fluid until it was full and then nipped the end of the shoot together. He placed the bowl onto a table growing out of the wall next to his own breakfast and beckoned Alexander to join him. Alexander pulled a handful of fibrous growth from the wall, wiped himself clean and walked stiffly over to the Gnathe. The only part of his nano-suit that was left on his body were his shoes and some of the leggings around his ankles. Nagoth and the other members of Link-soo-shan's killing squad had ripped the sealed suit to ribbons, far beyond its self-seal capabilities. Alex pulled the cured pelt of some fur-bearing animal about his shoulders.

He shivered and said to the Gnathe: "San-sool, do you mind if I keep this sleeping robe? I have no clothing at all. When they captured me, they stripped me of everything, apart from what you see."

"Do with it what you will, my strange companion," San-sool answered kindly and gestured to the table. "Eat, before they come for you. I do not know what lies before you this day. Drink the sap of the tree. It is rich in vitamins and calories. It will do you good. Believe me, if you can eat our food, this will do great things for you."

Alexander picked up the bowl that was fashioned from a seedpod and drank the thick sap, holding the sleeping robe about him. The fluid tasted sweet and also yeasty, with a lemon after-taste.

"This is good," he said between swallows and reached for a handful of pod vine fruits. The beans were lightly toasted until the ripe flesh had popped through the chewy outer skins, splitting them open. He chewed and swallowed the nutty flavoured beans and regarded the male Gnathe perched at the other side of the table.

"How did you come to be part of Link-soo-shan's mad schemes?" he asked between mouthfuls, and San-sool told him of Link's domination of the household of Mace-loot-tighe. He also told him of his own capture at the Imperial City, for breeding stock.

"So the two young Brood-mothers are not related to Link in any way at all?" Alexander inquired thoughtfully.

"That may be so, human, but by using me to release them from a lifetime of blind servitude and dominated breeding, they are obligated to her. Seek for no help there, Alexander, for there will be none forthcoming. As for me, I can do very little but heal you from whatever they decide to do to you, if I can and if they allow it. My life and all who dwell here with her are hers to do with as she wills."

"Let me show you how it could be, San-sool. I will show you with my mind how things are with the Gnathe we saved."

Before San-sool could protest, Alex slipped into his mind and showed him Ender-whann-soo's philosophy and the new way of life being instigated by Trann-link-sool.

San-sool perched quietly as he assimilated these thoughts and ideas. He looked up at Alexander and said, "It is no wonder the Lady Ender was put to death. These ideas are against everything in our upbringing. To serve through choice! I cannot imagine how it could be. It makes my mind spin. If she gets a hint of this in my mind, she will kill me. You have sealed my death, Alexander. The moment she looks into my mind, I will die."

"Not so, my friend. Stay still and I will enter once more," Alex replied, "and seal off these thoughts from other minds." With that, he recalled Khann's teachings about shielding thoughts and once more delved into San's mind, building blocks and diverting any probe to more harmless memories. When he had finished, he said, "She will not go looking for things that do not occur to her, but remember, this is what your life could be, if only she could be got rid of. I cannot get into the minds of her guards. She has done something similar to them and they are impossible for me to read or influence."

"I fear for you, Alexander, for her cruelty is legendary. Will your people rescue you?" San-sool looked nervously out of the window for any sight of Nagoth returning for the human leader.

"They will try something, but not until the Habitat is made safe from a return visit by Link and her killers. She has killed thousands of my people, San-sool. Kamiel will think of a way to stop her." Alex joined San at the window, still chewing his toasted beans and nursing his awful grief.

Link-soo-shan had awoken happier in her mood than she had for a long time. She mulled over Alexander's statements of the Habitat's revenge. She decided to do nothing for a while. After all, she could visit the survivors with a withering blight at any time; also, she would have to check carefully for traps. It would be very unlikely that she would catch them unprepared again. These people would make excellent servants with the right motivation and what fighters they could be, if controlled by fear of retribution towards their young. The insights into different ways of thinking, by studying these aliens would give her an advantage over the other Gnathe that they would be incapable of understanding. All she had to do was break them into service. She was confidant that without access to the Citadel, the farming communities could be picked off at any time. As for the few immunised people living with the Gnathe at the settlement, they would present little problem. Sometime later she would have to devise a way to snatch a few for study and exploitation.

"You may come for me at any time, Kaameel," she thought triumphantly and stretched out her heavily muscled arms invitingly. "I know your structure and how to deal with it so that you can be destroyed."

She looked down onto the frozen silver head that she had picked up from the shattered body of the Guardian. It lay in pride of place next to the skulls of the human and ape that she had made her daughters dig up from Kamiel's freshly dug graves. Now it was time to concentrate on recovering her empire from the usurper Trann. She ground her teeth in frustrated fury, her ripping claws instinctively slipping out of their protective sheaths as she dragged them across the walls. Fresh sap dripped like blood from the young walls of her living room. One day she would get it all back, but for now there was her newly acquired captive to study. This prize would divert and entertain her until she was ready to make her move.

Link picked up Kamiel's head and gave it a loving inspection with her tongue before she walked over to her crystal collection. She laid her hands upon the familiar facets of her old communications crystal and directed her mind delicately towards the mind of Bron-mace-rann. She slipped gently into the young Brood-mother's unconsciousness and ran what she called a loyalty check. Bronn's attitude towards her was filled with awe at what Link had achieved, with overwhelming gratitude for releasing her from a lifetime of blindness and servitude. Link deftly reinforced these feelings and increased the young Gnathe's growing affection for herself. By the time that she had finished with the two minds of the young Brood-mothers, they would be more in tune with her and as trustworthy as her dead egg-sister, Chang. These Brood-mothers would not rise up and usurp her position in the usual fashion. They would be devoted fanatically to her until Link died of old age, something that very few Brood-mothers achieved.

Checking that Connit's mind was also in tune with her wishes, she gave a mental shout through Nagoth's crystal hanging around the guard's neck and stepped away from the command stone. Link went in search of breakfast while she awaited her favourite's arrival. The household ran itself under the watchful eyes of her two loyal Brood-mothers, leaving Link to pursue her own path. She brooded upon the one thing that eluded her constantly and that was the limiting factor of the number of guards that she could transport at any one time with her. Somehow there had to be a way to open a door and keep it open. It was high summer and by the autumn her seasoned guards would be ready for an assault on the Imperial City. Her new young would be a formidable force when ready. She was not certain whether to go with what she had, or wait for more to mature. It was as well that the Gnathe males and females did not spend so much time in childhood growing to maturity, as the strange aliens did. Still, she mused, there was plenty of time to study the endurance factors of her prized guest.

"My Lady," Nagoth said, breaking into Link-soo-shan's thoughts, "what would you have me do?"

"Eat with me, daughter, and we will talk together about the human leader, Alexander," the Brood-mother replied and gestured to the food laden table. "What do you make of him? How strong do you think he is? He exhibits great bravery for a creature in captivity."

"He is only a male, great Lady, and no match for my strength. He moves differently from us because of his strange legs and feet. I do not think he will get the better of me again; besides, you gave me these." Nagoth proudly flexed her sinews to bring her hooked claws into view from out of their sheaths.

"Do not underestimate him, daughter of mine. I intend to find out the very limits of his endurance by testing him. I want you to fetch him to me undamaged. Take Jaffin with you and three of her troops so that he can see that resistance is useless. I have one or two things in mind for the alien leader that he will find most unpleasant. I wonder how much genetic material that old meddling fool Khann has infused into his cell structure, to enable him and the others of his kind to survive in our world?"

Nagoth looked up at her Brood-mother with a wicked expression and said, "Why, Reverend Lady? Do you think you could trigger a mating response similar to our own males? I would take him with great joy. He seems to be similar to our males in many respects."

"We will humiliate him to the point of insanity. I will leave him empty of pride and self-respect and broken in spirit. He will pay for his interference in my affairs by tasting bitter shame until it chokes him," the deposed Ultimate ruler growled in triumphant excitement. She paced up and down the room swishing her tail from side to side. Suddenly she turned and swooped down to Nagoth's level, reaching out to cradle the startled female's head in her huge hands, flicking out her tongue to caress Nagoth's face. "Go, my favoured one, and bring him to me. The ordeal starts soon. I have been starved of entertainment for too long. I have many things to find out about this species. I think they could make useful servants if I can motivate them sufficiently and I think that I can. What Khann did for them to live outside their artificial world, I can do also to benefit me."

CHAPTER 25

▼

While Frederick and the others built a fire, cut up and roasted pieces of the pig creature, Hannah concentrated on locating the position of the crystal lode. She placed her hand flat upon the face of the nearby rock-face and switched on the amplifier in the headset. Once more she chose the lowest setting first. Instantly she felt a difference as her mouth salivated with the acid salty taste that indicated raw crystal. Unlike Alexander, who could feel the pull of the stones and hear the vibrations blocked inside, she could taste their presence. She followed the direction of the sensation with her augmented senses. Sure enough, it led to the shattered rock face towards the bottom of the valley. The mountain's snow-fed stream ran through the crevasse and somewhere beyond. Hannah switched off the device in her helmet and walked over to the group by the fire.

Shoo-lin and Coen-soo had returned and were eagerly cutting off and stuffing hot greasy pieces of meat into their jaws from the carcass of the roasting beast. Frederick had cut some choice pieces for her and had put them on a broad leaf to cool.

"We seem to be in luck at last, my friends," Hannah called out to them excitedly. "There is crystal in that split in the rock face. When we have eaten, we will continue down into the valley and see what we can find."

She flicked the stray dark hairs of her fringe from out of her eyes and sat her small body down onto a flat rock. Khann's genetic gift had affected her like all the rest of the people of the Habitat. Hannah's original blueprint had been an elfin-built person whose mind had teetered on the genius level. Now she was beginning to fill out as her bone structure thickened slightly. Frederick was in awe of the bright intellect that shone out of the unassuming woman. They had been attracted to each other over sixty years ago, when a chance meeting had brought the giant and the tiny woman together. Academic pressures had forced them apart, as Hannah had developed at the University and finally headed her own research department. They enjoyed holidays together and had nurtured several children from their passionate meetings. All of the unborn foetuses had been removed at three months. They had grown to their full potential in artificial wombs. The Guardians, Sharn and Minns had insisted that the risk had been far too great for Hannah to bring the babies to full term in her own body. Indeed, every child had taken Frederick's stature and had weighed over ten pounds at birth.

In the free and easy, long lives of the Habitat, encouraged by the Guardians programming for diversity, many relationships were enjoyed by each other, without jealousy. Now they found each other's company an easy thing to bear.

Frederick handed her the broad leaf with its selection of choice cuts and said, "Eat, my tiny flower. You look as if you need to. You look tired from using the headset. Are you all right?" he worriedly asked and squatted beside her.

She looked up and grinned at the tall, well-built, muscular figure as he blocked out the heat of the red sun. "You are a worrier, Fred. I really am fine. This is good," she said between mouthfuls. "We ought to keep some back for later. Even you can't eat all that's left. Shoo-lin," she called out. "What did you find out? Are there many more of those creatures between us and where I want to go?"

"No, Hannah," he replied. "The herd panicked and rushed off down the valley and into the tree-line. I don't think there is anything large and dangerous near us. The smoke of the fire has frightened most of the wild-life away."

"I think we will make sure, anyway. Set light to the dry vegetation. The wind will carry the fire down the slope and towards that large crack in the mountainside. What we need is inside there, I believe," Hannah answered and finished off her pieces of roasted meat.

Coen-soo picked up a burning branch and torched the dry stalks at the top of the grassy looking growth. With the wind behind it, the fire spread along the tinder dry tops, causing a great deal of white acrid smoke to travel before it.

They got to their feet and picked their way carefully along the stream down towards the small crevasse. Occasional grunts and barking noises signified that not all the creatures of the valley uplands had fled from the two Gnathe as Shoo-lin had surmised. Bows at the ready, the group cautiously pushed on until they had to cross over the stream. Here, the rocky face of the mountain had split open due to the shifting of the planet's crust. Some of the walls had fallen away into the stream recently and the stones were still sharp. It was dark and gloomy inside the cleft and the rays of the red sun did not penetrate far.

"Well, Hannah, you better go and see what you can find," Jocylene said nervously, surveying the crumbly surface of the rocks.

Hannah switched on the headset and immediately became aware of a salty taste in her mouth and an itch inside her mind. There was indeed crystal in the cleft, but some way inside. She concentrated her telekinetic senses towards the salty trail in the rock and found a strong echo bounce back to her. With it came an overlay of slipperiness, as if something made of soap was close by the salty feeling. She looked up at the concerned faces of her friends.

"It's in there, all right," she said. "I mean to go into the hole. Keep a good lookout for falling stones when I start to ease my way into the split in the rocks. Shoo-lin, you are next smallest against me. Follow me and be prepared to hand the bags out if I get stuck."

Frederick bent forwards and kissed her on her forehead. "Be careful," he said. "Do not take any chances. I do not want you buried under a mass of stones and rubble. We can always go and look somewhere else."

"There doesn't seem to be anywhere else, Fred, or I would not go anywhere near that split in the rock," she replied and turning her back to him, she began to edge and wriggle into the split.

As her eyes adjusted to the gloomy surroundings, she became more aware of the bottom of the deep split in the rocks. High above her the crevasse opened out, allowing much more light to fall than she had realised. Hannah could make out the outlines of the jagged edges of the fallen boulders. The taste of salt and acid filled her mouth as she wriggled into the rock.

"What can you see?" Frederick called frantically as the scientist vanished out of sight around a bend in the tight passageway.

"Very little, Fred, but the split opens up quite a bit just here. This stream is cold and the bottom is slippery," she replied cautiously and pushed herself out of the crack in the mountain into a chamber.

She stood in front of a black, sombre pool of water. The stream chuckled merrily as it tumbled into the pool. Stealthy movements at the edge of her vision made her swing her head round abruptly to the left. Something with far too many legs scuttled out of sight. Her mouth went dry and her skin prickled. Slithering noises came now from her right. Behind her, Shoo-lin squeezed through the tight gap and stood beside her in the cramped space.

"There are things in here with us," Hannah whispered to the male Gnathe. "Can you see them?"

Shoo-lin's vertical slits in his eyes had opened wide on account of the gloomy light inside the narrow crack. He could see quite well in the darkened area in which they stood. Many eyes, some on stalks, regarded the intruders with alarm. Crab-like creatures pressed into cracks in the rock face and pushed themselves under pebbles. Smaller, segmented things scuttled out of sight.

"Hannah," he said, "remember, you pose the threat, not these little creatures. How tough are these suits?"

"Why do you want to know, Shoo-lin?" she asked, desperately trying to see what the Gnathe was looking at.

"While I close my eyes you switch on the light on your helmet and you will see. You have so much that we don't understand, yet forget to use it!" exclaimed the Gnathe, baffled and stood back a little.

Hannah had forgotten the lights built into the helmets and, shamefaced, she switched them on. She gasped in fright as the colonies of different creatures frantically scrambled over one another to escape the brilliant beams of light. The two of them stood in a narrow chamber that ended at the other side of the pool, in a tighter crack, than where they had come from. The floor appeared to move with hard-shelled, crab-like creatures, picked out in bright reds and shiny black by the power of her beams. Sharp claws were waved in panic at the two huge intruders. Plants grew in profusion where they could get a roothold in the stony soil. Climbing vines stretched upwards towards whatever light could penetrate the chasm.

Shoo-lin swooped forwards and snatched a hard-shelled, spiny thing from the side of a rock. The stalked eyes retracted into its head and the legs tucked up into its body, so that it resembled a prickly ball. He held it gingerly out for Hannah's observation.

"This is what I mean, friend Hannah," he said and put the creature down on top of a rock. "Look at it go!" he cried, as the legs popped out of its body. The creature vanished over the side and into the pool. "Where are the crystals?" he asked, looking around at the walls.

"In the pool, Shoo-lin, unfortunately. I am going to have to lift them out with my new mind powers. Keep a lookout for anything dangerous."

Hannah focussed her mind onto the salt trace at the bottom of the pool. Gently, she increased the power to the amplifier set, until she could grasp the collection of gemstones, sunk into the rock, with a firm grip. Reluctantly they parted from their aeons-old setting in the rubble and silt at the bottom of the dark water. The water began to seethe and move as Hannah broke the crystals free. A horde of creatures left the pool at the other end, seeking sanctuary amongst the rocks. Shoo-lin watched, fascinated, as the chunk of rocks broke the surface of the agitated water and his human friend set it down onto the top of a boulder. With her face reflecting the effort required, Hannah forced the fracture lines apart, popping the rock open along its stress points. Both of them bent forwards to stare at their prize. Clustered tightly together like beans in a pod vine casing, lay a number of dark green crystals as big as Shoo-lin's fist.

"Gather them up, my friend," Hannah said triumphantly, "and put them in the sack. There are more down there to find. Keep a good watch while I trawl amongst the rocks at the bottom once more." With this statement hanging in the air, Hannah once more drove her mind down into the deep reaches of the pool.

Shoo-lin felt the crisp contact of Frederick's mind in his as the big human worriedly asked if everything was all right. The Gnathe showed him their prizes with his own eyes and Hannah locked herself into a concentrated pose over the edge of the pool.

"She is looking for any that she has overlooked, Fred," he told his friend, holding his communication crystal tightly. "We will soon be returning to you."

Hannah's telekinetic reach had hold of something that could not be grasped. Every time she tried directly to latch onto whatever it was, the object slid away. Frustrated, she let go and felt the slippery thing drop back into the silt. Once more, she picked up other crystal bearing rocks and brought them to the surface.

"This is the last of the telekinetic crystals, Shoo," she said, staring down into the depths. "There is something down there, however, that I cannot lift out with my mind's power. Are you sure there is nothing really dangerous in the water?"

"Yes, I am, friend Hannah. What are you going to do?" the Gnathe asked worriedly.

"This," said the small woman and, sealing her suit over her face, she stepped into the dark waters of the pool.

Shoo-lin's shock penetrated the rock to where the group sat, watchfully eyeing the surrounding countryside for any dangers. They leapt to their feet and pushed vainly against the sides of the deep split in the rock face, but could do nothing. All they could do was watch though Shoo-lin's eyes as the silver suited woman swam down to the bottom of the dark pool.

"Hannah," Frederick frantically projected to her mind, "what are you trying to do? You know these suits were not designed to be used for diving."

"At the bottom of this pool is a stone which could be a twin to Link-soo-shan's. We must have it, Fred. The defence of the Habitat will be linked to this type of crystal," she replied and gave him an overall picture of what she believed to be true.

She projected her mind's powers around the murky bottom of the dark pool of water, searching for the telltale soapy feeling of the different gemstone. Already, water was beginning to seep into her helmet around her face. She could taste the muddy water against her lips when she felt a hard object with her outstretched fingers. Her mind told her that this was what she had been looking for and she closed her hands around the crystal, kicking her legs to propel herself back towards the surface. Instantly, she was alone in the black shadowy reaches of the water. She could not feel the others' mental background at all. It was just as it had always been, before Alexander had touched her and altered her mind. A terrible fear swept through her as she frantically kicked harder towards the surface, struggling to hold her breath.

To Frederick, it was as if Hannah had died. The giant went pale and cried out in shock and grief, slapping his hand against the unyielding rock face, trying to enter the narrow crack.

Abdul shook him and shouted at his stricken friend. "She is all right, Frederick. Think about it, my powerful friend. She is still there. The effect is the same as when the Tyrant wore her amulet. Alexander said that she mentally disappeared from view when she touched it."

"That is true, friend Frederick," Coen-soo spoke up and pressed into the split, holding her communication crystal. "Shoo-lin can see her coming up to the surface of the pool. She has something that she is holding in both of her hands."

Bursting with the need to breathe, the front of her facemask filled with water, Hannah broke surface. She hugged the rock close, with one hand against her breast, while she unsealed her facemask with the other. Shoo-lin bent forwards and grabbed hold of her outstretched arm. He yanked the scientist out of the bitter-cold water with one enormous heave, holding her upright while she spluttered and coughed into his shoulder.

"The Lady Ender will be very cross with me for allowing you to do that," he said ruefully and held her shivering body, safely close. "Now let us get out of this cramped and gloomy place. Have we taken all that there is here?"

"Yes, my friend, much more than I expected," Hannah replied, clutching her dripping prize tightly. "This other crystal formation could be the answer to our defensive problems. It could open up quite new avenues of research. Now let us get out of here before the others worry themselves to death."

The two of them began to wriggle and squirm their way back out of the tight split in the mountain, handing the sack of crystals back and forth until the fissure began to widen. Behind them the inhabitants of the pool slithered and scuttled back to the normal pattern of their disturbed lives.

When Hannah pushed through into sight, Frederick reached forwards and helped her out of the rocky prison. He held her tightly for a few moments and set her down, still holding her tiny hands in his.

"When you disappeared from my awareness, I could not cope with the pain of your loss," the worried giant said softly. "These new powers of the mind are difficult to handle. I have been so used to the background chatter of your mind close to me. When it stopped so abruptly, I thought that you were dead." He bent down to kiss the top of her head.

Hannah looked up and tenderly cupped his hairy face in her small hands. "Enough, dear Frederick, I am here. We must hurry back to the Habitat as fast as we can. I have a great deal of work to do when we get home. Call that gluttonous creature of yours from wherever it is stuffing its face. We must be on our way."

With that she kissed him quickly and moved into the late afternoon sun to examine her collection of differently coloured crystals.

$$* \quad * \quad * \quad *$$

The news of Link-soo-shan's successful attack on the alien city had thrown the new leader of the Gnathe into a state of anxiety and apprehension. Trann paced up and down in front of the terrified Sing-trow-sool, lashing her tail back and forth as she swung her weight from one taloned foot to the other.

"Go and hide if you want to, Sing," the Brood-mother growled contemptuously at the co-leader. "I tell you, our only chance is to stay together. Learn to use the telekinetic crystal that we possess. We have one each. Keep it by you at all times and do not ever be alone."

"Trann, please stop constantly moving about. There is nowhere to hide. Reports are coming in from scattered outposts and settlements all over the Empire. She has struck time and time again, collecting crystal, stores and more of her kindred scattered over the Empire. Soon, she will be at the City gates—with an army. We have nothing," the keeper wailed in panic.

"Yes, we do!" Trann replied suddenly. "We have friends on the other side of the mountains. Perhaps the mighty Kaameel could be persuaded to come to our aid, as he did for the Lady Ender."

"What could he do against an army of Link's mutated Gnathe? Anyway, the flying carrier cannot come here until they have changed it in some way to breath our air," Sing replied and perched in a dejected huddle, her hearing crest folded to prevent her from hearing Trann's tirade any longer.

With a snort of anger, Trann left the other Brood-mother shivering in miserable fear and stalked off to the crystal chamber. She entered and stepped onto the perch next to her own gemstone. This was mounted on the same polished wood stand that Link-soo-shan had used. She calmed herself and laid her hands upon the facets of the stone. As the sending trance deepened, Trann's awareness of her surroundings diminished. Once she got her bearings in the matrix, she drove her mind forwards towards the mountain ranges, being very careful to avoid the area occupied by Link-soo-shan. Two beacons shone out, signifying the deposed Ultimate Ruler's region of domination. On and on she sped, through the misty world of the crystal matrix, towards Ender and Khann's new world.

The two Brood-mothers were together, discussing the different development of the two young Gnathe, Azander and Marren, when they felt their crystals resonate with the mind touch of Trann. Quickly, Trann outlined her problems, adding her request for Kamiel's help and withdrew before Link became aware of her presence stretched thinly across the matrix.

"Will Kaameel help, grandmother?" Ender asked thoughtfully.

"He has good cause to want to prevent the Tyrant from achieving her aims. If he tries to rescue Alexander, Link will destroy him from a distance. We can but ask and see what he will say," the old scientist answered and pressed Kamiel's call button on her adapted communication set.

The silver coloured being was busy in his workshop. He had made some incredible modifications to the remains of Minns' body. Also, he had considered various weapons for the assault on Link's stronghold. He was quite satisfied with the results. Lacking high-density materials in abundance, he had to make do with what could be crafted from the materials available. Iron and steel were in very short supply and the essential stocks used at the Habitat could not be plundered. He had nothing that could contain the explosive forces necessary to send a bullet to its target. The memory characteristics of Nannite, however, could be put to good use. When Frederick and the others returned, he would be able to well-equip the rescue force. This time they would be fully prepared. When the call came through from Khann, he had just finished the computer aided guidance and aiming system for the weapons.

"What can I do for you, Khann and Ender?" he asked thoughtfully and listened to what they had to say. When they had finished, he contacted Asue and Sharn on their private communication band and gave them all the information he had received from the Gnathe.

"Well," he transmitted, "what do you think? I feel that I should go and give them all the help I can. We are not just guardians of our own people. I feel obligated to offer protection to these people, if I can. All sentient life is sacred to us. Our own people are more than capable for dealing with the situation if required. All of the domes will soon be fitted with protection circuits and Hannah has found the crystals that she feels she requires to provide a shielding effect. Somehow I do not think that Link-soo-shan will re-visit our community for some time. She has what she wanted most, revenge and Alexander. Now she will divert her efforts to the re-taking of her old empire, starting with the Imperial City."

"Very well," Asue replied, "but before you go, Kamiel, I insist that a copy of your personality be held on file, here at the Citadel's main computer banks. We all should do this now that we know we can be destroyed. Our people must be protected at all costs," Asue declared firmly.

"From a mix of this data, I will work on the problem of constructing a new personality for Minns," Sharn replied. "What have you done with her body, Kamiel?"

"For the time being I have a use for the empty shell," Kamiel stated enigmatically. "When the others return from the crystal hunt, I will need to see Frederick immediately. He will lead the assault team to rescue Alexander and destroy Link-soo-shan forever. Only five can go. The raptors can carry no more than two people easily. Besides, too many would be mentally detected by her and we will need the element of surprise. It will take them some time to get there, using the raptors. She must have no inkling of their arrival. What I will do is once more launch from the orbiting satellite into the Gnathen Empire. When this is over, the two cultures will blend together. Obligations on both sides will tie them closely. One thing is certain—Link-soo-shan and any of her Imperial line must be destroyed. We cannot do it, because of our programming, but we can aid the others to make sure it happens."

"So much death, Kamiel," Sharn answered ruefully. "Is there no other way?"

"I will limit the carnage as much as possible," the Guardian replied. "We will concentrate on Link's killers only. The people she has taken into the mountains with her will not be held accountable for her actions. More than that, we cannot say. I will tell Khann that I will go in a day or so. First, I must meet and instruct the assault group." Kamiel broke off the transmission to continue to fine tune the various weapons' system he had built.

*   *   *   *

Nagoth walked quickly towards the healer's quarters, her cruel and evil mind alive to the possible torments she would help to inflict upon the captured alien leader. Jaffin and a small squad of Imperial Guard kept pace with her. The morning sun cast a pleasant heat at their backs and their feet kicked up small clouds of dust as they neared Alexander's place of captivity. It promised to be a hot day. The guards left to watch over the captive, nodded to the Tyrant's new favourite and began to leave their posts for their morning meal.

"What will the 'Cruel One' do to the creature, Nagoth? You were with her earlier," one of the guards inquired as the troop stopped outside San-sool's rooms.

"Wait and see, sister. You must wait and see," Nagoth replied wickedly. "The great Lady has instructed me to tell you not to speak to him more than necessary. He must be brought into her presence, afraid and anxious, with no idea what she has in mind for him. His torment begins soon. He will pay dearly for interfering in our affairs." Nagoth flexed her sinews to bring her unmodified ripping claws into view. "You will form a living cage around him to prevent him from running away. She wants him undamaged. Remember that at all times, or you could feel the lash of her wrath."

Alexander had spent some time, that morning, tearing holes in the sleeping cloak to put his arms through. He had wound a belt around his middle to fasten the treated hide about himself. Here in the mountain valleys the air was cold in the mornings and he would require some protection from the elements. There was nothing in San-sool's chambers that could be adapted to become a weapon. Every part of the furniture grew out of the multitudinous Banilik tree and could not be detached. All he had to combat the Guards were his hands and his mind. The Imperial Guards had been mentally tampered with so that he could not read their thoughts. If he could make flesh-to-flesh contact, it might be possible to break through the barrier and influence one of them. He decided to wait his chance and see what he could do.

"I dare not try to contact my close friends at the Habitat at this range. If I try to project my mind that distance, I would be helpless and unprotected. I wish that I knew what was going on. What can be happening back there?" he wondered with apprehension and was disturbed by San-sool's shout.

"Alexander, make ready!" the Gnathen healer cried and stepped away from the door. "They are coming for you."

Alexander stumbled back against the wall in fear as Nagoth and Jaffin pushed arrogantly past the smaller male and entered the room.

"You will come with us, now, creature," Nagoth demanded with quiet menace and stood erect so that she was taller than the human being. She opened her big hands and flexed her sinews to make her talons appear from their sheaths. "Do not resist or I can and will hurt you without making too much damage."

Alexander stared down at the Gnathe's modified claws with horror. Some of the points had been cut back to enable the female to grip and use the Gnathen designed bows and arrows. The others had been honed to razor sharpness.

He looked up at her and said defiantly, "What does she want of me, killer of helpless young?"

"That is for you to find out, weakling male," she replied and wrapped her fingers and claws around his upper arm.

As she hauled him towards the door, Alexander tried a quick probe into her mind. This time he got a clearer picture of the blocks and defences inserted into the Gnathe's mind before she let go. The quick glimpse he got revealed such a mind of sick cruelty that it sickened him. He concentrated his thoughts grimly on the few possible paths through Link's tampering as they began the walk towards the Tyrant's quarters. As they were still very young, the stands of Banilik trees were still separated from each other. As time passed, extra shoots would be planted in such away as to provide walls and passageways roofed over from the elements. Alexander studied the physical makeup of these mutated killers as he walked along. The Gnathe walked in a peculiar bobbing gait as each foot was lifted and slapped down, dragging the tail behind them. When they moved fast, they hopped, like the Kangaroos he had seen in films, with their tails held out behind them for balance. These Gnathe had larger feet than Ender's people, with wickedly curved claws peeping out of the toes. When they squatted, with their knees tucked in behind them, they could easily touch the floor with their hands. Alexander noticed that some of the Guards had modified and shortened some of their claws similar to Nagoth's. They had had this done so that they too could grip the bow-stocks firmly and hold the arrows against the bowstrings without fumbling. He could see that their hands were designed to be formidable weapons on their own. The stocks of the sythers were much thicker than a human could easily grasp. Shoo-lin's equipment was adapted to his smaller size and Alexander had tried his syther in curiosity. He would have some difficulty using one of these guards' weapons, even if he could steal one. Alexander noted the layout of the Homestead as he walked back along yesterday's pathway. The stables were down by the stream and he could make out a number of the large Imperial Zanth tethered there.

Nagoth caught him looking towards the horned beasts and said, "You can forget that idea. They would hook you on their horns if you dared to approach them," she added with relish. "We sometimes have to beat them into submission. They would trample your puny form into the mud."

Alexander said nothing and, stoned faced, he stooped and suddenly twisted to the side. He ducked under the arm of the surprised Gnathe at his side and ran as fast as he could towards the stream. His breath came in ragged gasps and the pain from his wounded leg made him grit his teeth. Nagoth let him go about thirty feet before she motioned to one of Jaffin's troop.

"Fetch him back," she curtly ordered.

The female Gnathe took off down the hill in ground devouring leaps. She effortlessly out-distanced the running man and snatched him by his flapping robe, bringing him down into a heap. She hauled him to his feet by his hair and then gave him an opened handed slap across his face.

"Don't do that again, you fool," she said derisively and pushed him up the slope towards the waiting group. "The Great Lady has told us not to damage you yet. Keep that in mind," she insisted.

Alexander kept the fist-sized stone hidden in his robes as he took his place once more in the middle of the guard party. At least he would enter the presence of Link-shoo-shan not totally unarmed.

The entrance to the deposed Ultimate Ruler's quarters was thronged with curious Imperial Guards. Alexander could feel the hostility generated by these creatures. His mouth went dry and he felt it hard to swallow. Chang's daughters were heavier set than Link-soo-shan's own kindred. All of them were much bigger and more powerful than the members of Ender-whann-soo's household. Nothing in the Habitat's mayoral life could prepare him for this. Alexander was sure he would die in this place if he showed any weakness. Clenching his stone in his right hand, he entered the opened doorway into the darkened interior. The guards closed in behind him, blocking the doorway and any retreat.

CHAPTER 26

▼

Hour after hour the raptors beat their wings against the prevailing wind, until at last the Habitat came into view. The sun was casting long shadows from behind them as the tired, flying creatures swooped down to make their landing by the side of the settlement walls. The group made their way to the lift under the ever-watchful eyes of the raptors.

Kamiel met them at the top of the lift and watched them hurry towards him.

"You were successful," he stated. "Well done all of you. Khann has been in touch with Shoo-lin and Coen-soo during the flight back. She has told me all about your journey and the dangers that you faced. She says you have travelled over many mountain ranges to acquire what we need. That was an incredible act of courage, Hannah. Now then, show me the new type of crystal that you brought back from the bottom of that pool," he gently asked and held out his silvery coloured hand.

"Give me a chance, Kamiel," the scientist replied as she delved into her carry-sack. "Here," she said, holding out one of them in the sun's dying light. "What do you think, Kamiel? Is it the same as the one the Tyrant wore? When I touch it, no one can read my mind. When I gave it to Frederick to hold, I could not reach out for him telekinetically. Not only that, I could not grasp them with my mind at the pool."

"That was a very dangerous thing to attempt, old friend," the Guardian retorted. "Nevertheless, the crystal is the same as Link-soo-shan's. What do you have in mind to do with it? Your team of scientific investigators have been monitoring the domes, using the telepathic amplifiers and the surveillance systems that Asue has installed. She has not attempted to return."

Hannah looked up at the Guardian's featureless face and said, "I must go to my laboratories now and put into practice the ideas that I have been working on. There is no time for me to sleep. Instruct my group to be ready for me, Kamiel, and tell them to have plenty of coffee and civilised food waiting for me when I arrive. I may work all night." She turned and stroked Frederick's face with her tiny hands and softly told him, "I must go now, Fred. There is much I have to do to defend our home from that evil soul. She must not come here again. Be very careful when you go to rescue Alexander. Promise me you will listen to Kamiel and heed his instructions. I worry about your temper."

"I will, 'little flower'. I promise to be as careful as I can, but come what may, I swear that she will die," he answered and kissed the top of her head gently. She stood back and smiled at the giant towering over her.

"Do not go without seeing me or until I have perfected a personal shield for you all. If not, she will pull you apart with her mind."

"We will wait for you to do what you can. Now go, my brilliant one, and find the means to lock her out."

Frederick and the others of the group watched her walk out of sight and into the settlement buildings.

"Now then, Kamiel, what have you got for us?" Abdul inquired, his brown deep-set eyes regarding the Guardian with a curious gaze.

"Yes, you secretive creature, what have you been up to while we were away? I do not think that we will be going against her this time with just swords and clubs!" Frederick grinned with relish and flexed his muscular arms.

"Follow me," the enigmatic being replied and walked down the steps into the inner safety of the settlement walls. "I have brought all the equipment that you will need from my workshops. I insist that you all get a good night's sleep, before you test it thoroughly tomorrow. Yes, my eager friends, this time you will be her worst nightmare. I will give you a quick preview of what I have constructed for you."

Kamiel led them into a large, brightly lit storeroom, with windows that opened out onto the open spaces inside the compound. Lying on a table were a number of the most evil looking crossbows that the humans had ever seen.

Shoo-lin walked over to the weapons, totally puzzled and said, "What are these things? They look like small bows."

"They are called crossbows, my friend. I have only seen them in illustrations in our history books," Frederick answered, "but these are very different." He picked one up to examine it. A set of multiple bow-springs was fitted at the head and was set at the cocked position. Jutting out of the face were five barbed points. On top of the crossbow was a telescopic sight built into the stock. Clipped to the sides were ten finned bolts with a deep crosscut at the end, so that the shafts could be loaded at any ninety-degree position. Frederick carefully put the only loaded crossbow down and picked up another one to examine the loading arrangement at the end. Five crosscut holes were set into the face. He dropped a bolt into the hole and felt the fit close over the shaft. The bow-spring was perfectly straight but for a curve at the ends to take the multiple strings.

"These look as if they are the ultimate killing bows, Kamiel," Frederick said with savage joy and turned around to regard his martial arts teacher with admiration. "How do they work, my inscrutable friend?"

Kamiel took the crossbow from him and replied, "The bow-spring is made from memory-retaining nannite material. When you pull the bow back to cock it like this," and he demonstrated to his attentive audience. "The nannites slide easily over themselves, until the bow is cocked. Then the molecules remember being in a straight configuration and strive to attain their original positions. Once released, they can be reset time and time again. All you have to do is what I have shown you and push the bolts home against the strings." He pointed to the tube mounted on the rear of the stock and said, "This is a telescopic sight, fitted with a laser imaging system. It projects a red dot onto the target and realigns itself after each bolt is fired. If the target is out of range, the computer will not highlight the victim. Whatever you line the sights upon, will not be missed, as long as you hold the cross-bow rock steady"

Frederick passed the weapon to the others so that they could examine it. Shoo-lin walked to the window and sighted down the telescopic mount into the gathering darkness. The others turned round to stare at the Gnathe as he gave a gasp of surprise.

"It is as though it were day outside when you look through this tube. I can see everything out there quite clearly. What is the bright outline around the people and animals, Kaameel?"

"It is heat energy, Shoo-lin. It is what we call thermal imaging. The scope picks up the heat given forth by living things and translates the wavelength into light, intensifying the image. Even if the target is hiding behind a bush, you could still see them. These bows are powerful enough to penetrate a door and kill someone behind it at fairly close range." The guardian motioned to the door and said, "I have more to show you tomorrow. For now that is enough. I insist that you all get a good night's sleep and plenty of rest."

"What of Alexander? Does he still live?" asked Jocylene the silver figure beside her.

"We have had the main telescope on the satellite trained on the Tyrant's settlement all day. I have seen him walk outside, closely guarded," the Guardian replied grimly. "Khann does not believe that Link-soo-shan will kill him for some time. She thinks that she will keep him alive to witness the re-taking of her Empire. The tyrant needs to show off her supremacy to him to satisfy her ego. That is where the next stage of my plan comes into place."

Frederick turned away from the weapons and asked, "What do you have in mind, you devious creature?"

"I am going to launch once more from orbit. This time I shall drop into the Imperial City. Trann has asked for my help in organising resistance to the impending visit by Link-soo-shan before she brings her killers to the city gates. You will not need me during your long journey to her stronghold."

"What will we do without you, Kaameel?" Shoo-lin asked, anxiously putting the crossbow back onto the table.

"You did well enough today, my young friend, in the hunt for the crystals. Do not worry unduly, for I have great faith in all of this group's abilities," Kamiel stated with unusual pride. "You will go well armed and I will be diverting her attention from another direction."

"Let me caution you, old friend and teacher," Abdul retorted. "Be very careful in what you do. Remember that she can destroy you from a distance, while we will be shielded in some way that Hannah will devise."

"Yes Guardian, this time our frail flesh and blood may give us the advantage that you will not possess," Frederick stated, staring at the enigmatic silver figure that stood in the middle of the group.

"Do not worry about me," the Guardian replied to the tall brown skinned man at his side. "I shall not be caught again within her range." Her turned to the others. "Now go and rest yourselves and eat. I will have a great deal more to show you in the morning before I leave—and I will not leave until I am satisfied that you all understand how to use the equipment provided."

The group of Gnathe and humans reluctantly agreed and left Kamiel to his own devices, talking quietly amongst themselves as they walked off to their quarters.

It took a few moments for Alexander's eyes to adjust to the darker interior of Link-soo-shan's chambers. He saw the Brood-mother's great looming shape move towards him and a pair of baleful yellow eyes regard him with hateful interest. Over the top of her head ran a livid scar, cutting across the orbital ridge on one side and continuing into her hearing crest, giving it a lopsided droop. Her mouth was drawn back a little showing her set of needle sharp teeth. Alexander shuddered and looked away towards a table that grew out of the living wall. There lay her crystals, worked into a harness, so that she could wear and carry them at the level of her chest, leaving her hands free. Next to them were two recognisable skulls; one was human and the other one was an ape's. Alex gave a gasp of increasing horror as he realised that the silver ovoid lying beside them had to be Kamiel's head. He could not believe that his lifelong mentor and friend was destroyed and bitter tears began to prick at his eyes. The stone weighed heavy in his clenched hand and he came to a quick decision.

"Welcome, Alexander, leader of what is left of your people, to my temporary home," Link-soo-shan grated spitefully at him. "My quarters at the Imperial Palace would have been more in keeping with this meeting, but of course you know why they are denied to me for the moment."

Alexander stood mute, waiting for the one chance he would have to strike at her.

"You may see them with me in the near future," she hissed, "for I have many plans to help me take it all back. I will keep you alive to see my triumph!"—and she reared up to her full height on her perch and began to step off towards him. As she did so, Alexander ducked to the side and hurled the stone he had carried under his robe, as hard as he could, at the crystals set upon the table. Link-soo-shan gave a hiss of surprise and frantically reached out for the speeding rock with her swift reactions. Her taloned hand failed to catch it, but she was able to deflect it away from the precious gemstones. It hit the table amongst her gristly collection of treasures, scattering them about the hard packed dirt floor. The human skull shattered with the impact and Kamiel's silver coloured head rolled across the ground and finished up at Nagoth's feet. An odour of fear swept the chamber as Link-soo-shan slowly turned and examined her crystal collection for signs of damage. The Gnathe stood ridged with apprehension as their Brood-mother picked up each crystal in turn to check for cracks or flaws. Alexander stood very still, conscious of Nagoth's fierce grip upon his upper arms. Her remaining sharpened nails dug painfully into his flesh as Link's snarling head swung down towards them. Her bony tipped tail curled around them, pushing the two of them within reach of her embrace.

"Where did he get that rock, Nagoth?" she screamed and reached forwards to grip Nagoth's neck in her taloned hand. "Had he shattered my crystals, all my plans would have come to nothing. Speak quickly, before I tear your miserable head off to join my collection."

Nagoth let go of Alexander's arm and transferred her grip, two handed, to Link's powerful wrist, as the Brood-mother began slowly to lift the terrified Gnathe to the tips of her toes. The human captive stood very still. He could feel Link-soo-shan's heavy tail curled around the two of them. An unpleasant odour began to exude from the Brood-mother that intensified his fear and sent Nagoth into a fit of terror.

"My lady, please listen to me. My life is yours to take, but spare me, if you will. The creature made a run for the stables, as if to escape, when we were bringing him to you. I sent Yandos after him and she knocked him to the ground long before he reached the stables. He must have picked up the stone then and hidden it under the sleeping robe he is wearing."

Link-soo-shan dropped Nagoth to the floor and quickly seized Alexander, stripping the treated hide from his body. She lifted him from off his feet as easily as Alex would lift a child. Holding him at arm's length she turned him over in the air and examined him carefully. Her tongue flicked in and out of her sharp-toothed mouth, tasting the scent of his fear. Alexander nearly fainted as she examined his manhood and testicles with fingers that could crush his skull with ease.

Over two thousand miles away, Azander and Marren collapsed at Ender's feet. As she picked them up to hold them, all three Gnathe made contact with Ender-whann-soo's communication crystal. Instantly the Brood-mother found herself briefly inside Alexander's mind. She rapidly gave him as much information as she dared before the mind-bridge failed. He now knew that the death rate from Link-soo-shan's attack had been contained and Kamiel still functioned in his own peculiar way. The touch of his Gnathen friend's mind strengthened his resolve. In seconds it was all over and her comforting presence faded from his heightened awareness. Link-soo-shan put him down, one handed, next to Nagoth, who once again held his arm in a painful grip.

Yandos broke out in a sweat of sheer terror as the baleful yellow eyes focused on her shivering frame. She squatted back onto the base of her tail and beckoned her sister's daughter forwards. Trembling with fear the Gnathe stumbled towards the terrible figure until she stood within her mighty reach.

"Old ways of life are difficult to throw over," the Brood-mother said with sinister foreboding. "Before I came in contact with these devious alien life-forms, I would have killed you instantly for your stupidity."

Yandos stood very, very still, the perspiration running down her back and sides with the strain of not running for her life.

"Yandos, you will do something for me," Link commanded, unsheathing her talons in front of the terrified Gnathe.

"I live only to serve, my Lady. My life is yours. What must I do? What do you want of me?" she cried beseechingly to her Brood-mother's sister.

"Fetch me two training sythers and be prepared to use one of them," she replied and Yandos broke away from the group as fast as she could. "You see," Link-soo-shan addressed the crowd chambers, "we are not used to dealing with these creatures. A lesson has been learned by us all here today," and she lent forwards to cradle Alexander's face amongst her taloned fingers, to stare into his eyes. "Let's see how well you do outside," she grated and released him.

"What do you intend to do, Reverend Lady?" asked Jaffin as she took her place the other side of the naked human.

"We shall see how well this human can fight, Group Captain," she replied balefully. "I want to see him bleed and suffer a little. All of you go outside and form a large ring around this male. Alexander is going to entertain us!" she shouted to the crowd and motioned them away.

Alexander stood, still dazed by the fleeting mind-touch of his alien friend. All was not lost. He must survive at all costs, no matter what ordeals Link-soo-shan could dream up in her hate crazed mind.

"Nagoth, bring him outside," the deposed Ultimate Ruler growled and stalked out into the bright mid-morning sun.

Alexander found himself seized roughly again by the big female and dragged through the doorway to the empty space in front of the Brood-mother's quarters. Link's converts, Bronn and Connit, had taken their places each side, next to the larger form of the hate-filled Gnathe. Nagoth pushed the Habitat's leader headlong to the ground so that he sprawled lengthways across the hard packed earth, and stood back.

"One more thing we have to settle between us, male," she hissed at him with hatred.

"There will come a day, Nagoth," Alexander panted as he struggled to his knees, "when you and I will settle the debts between us. I will punish you somehow, for your willing part in my people's deaths." He stood up and turned to face the group of Brood-mothers. Looking directly into Link-soo-shan's slanted yellow eyes, he shouted, "What now, you evil creature of darkness and killer of innocent, helpless children? Am I about to stain your honour more, by dying here, defenceless?"

"That is up to you, alien creature," she grated with vengeful relish. "Much will depend on how well you entertain me. When I am bored of you and I cannot think of ways to make you suffer, then will come the time for you to die."

A commotion in the crowd drew her attention away from the human leader. Alexander turned to see Yandos-shan break through the ring of Gnathe carrying two old sythers.

"Kamiel lives," he reminded himself. "I must survive long enough, to be here when they attempt a rescue, no matter what she does to me." He stared hard at the approaching female with growing anger.

"Yandos has brought the blunted training sythers. Now you will have an opportunity to show us what you are capable of," mocked the huge Gnathe. "Throw him a weapon, Yandos, and listen to me carefully," she ordered.

Yandos did as she was told and slid a worn syther towards Alexander along the dusty ground. She then retreated to the edge of the ring to await Link's instructions. The Brood-mother studied the scene and said, "Yandos, I forbid you to kill him, but you can beat him into submission for my pleasure. I put no such restrictions on you, Alexander. If you can kill her it will be a fitting punishment for her stupidity, and a lesson to the others. If she can subdue you, she will live. Now, pick up your weapon, creature, and defend yourself, if you can," she commanded and squatted back against her armoured tail to watch the proceedings with cruel interest.

Alex bent quickly forwards and picked up the old syther. The edges of the crystalline growths extruded by the long dead beast's tail had become blunted with use. Because of wear, the handle of the weapon was smaller in diameter than the usual Imperial Guard's grip. Much of the leather binding had come away, exposing and revealing the bones of the long dead creature. Yandos had unintentionally given him a more useful weapon. Alexander quickly stepped onto the end of the blade and purposefully snapped off a hand's length, leaving a razor sharp edge at the point. The Gnathe stared at her opponent in pop-eyed disbelief at his rapid conversion of the blunted blade from a relatively harmless weapon to a potentially lethal one. The next thing she saw Alexander do was to alter his grip on the syther, to hold it by the blade and handle uppermost, at forty-five degrees to the horizontal in front of his body. The leader of the Habitat had been taught by Kamiel many years ago in his youth how to handle a quarterstaff and also the ancient art of Kendo. He had practised under the scathing tongue of Kamiel's instruction and criticism for more than eighty years, between his Mayoral duties and what other spare time pursuits he allowed himself. The Guardians had urged that their re-created people maintain a degree of fitness and regular combative exercise in their free time. For Frederick and the self-styled band of exiles, this had not been enough and they had left the civilised world of the inner Habitat for the excitement of the African domes. They had been the first to volunteer to take Khann's serum and pit themselves against the wilds of Jupiter outside the safety of the settlement walls. Alexander advanced steadily towards his opponent, placing each foot firmly on the ground before moving the other and keeping eye-to-eye contact at every step. The breathing techniques taught by the weapons master cleared his mind and flushed the fatigue from his body. All that existed for him was his opponent and her blade.

"I know you, Yandos. You were one of the six that came with Link-soo-shan to my home to kill my people and our helpless children. I killed one of your murderous group at the Citadel. You will be next!" shouted Alexander in grim determination.

"We shall see, fool," the Gnathe replied and began the typical overwhelming rush at the human, with a sudden leap at him across the intervening distance. As she dropped onto the earth in front of him, Yandos brought her tail round at his legs, swinging the blunted syther at his head one handed and extending the talons on the other hand to rip what she could touch. Alex ducked low and stepped close to the weapon side of the big female. Blocking the pain from his protesting leg, he hammered the hilt of his syther into the Gnathe's stomach and dragged the sharp end of the blade's tip deeply across the Gnathe's ankle joint, opening her leg to the bone. Yandos doubled up, gasping for breath as Alexander rolled to the side out of her reach and she stumbled over her wounded foot. He came to his feet behind the big female and swung the blade, one handed, down onto her unprotected back with all of his strength. Stepping away, he was conscious of the dragging feeling of the arrow wound in his leg, robbing him of mobility. Yandos fell to the ground and rolled desperately away, blood trickling steadily from the deep gash in her ankle. She scrambled shakily to her feet, moving away, breathing badly and struggling to take a breath from her bruised and painful muscles. A look of fear and uncertainty began to show in her eyes.

Alexander followed her and changed his grip on his syther; holding it two handed, point towards the bewildered Gnathe. He shifted his weight to his good leg and advanced towards her, the sharp end of his sword flicking back and forth at the level of her eyes. Alex lifted his elbows upwards and out, bringing the hilt of the syther to his forehead and raising the point slowly above his head. Yandos struck out at the seemingly undefended chest of the human with her weapon. As she did so, Alex swerved out of the way, turning to his side and brought his syther down with all of his strength onto the lower area of the Gnathe's outstretched arms. There was an audible crunch as both wrists snapped and Yandos screamed in pain, her syther bouncing across the hard packed earth. Alexander gritted his teeth against the pain from his protesting leg and moved closer to her. Holding the sword point upwards in the quarter-staff position, he drove the sharp modified edge up and into the soft flesh under Yandos-shan's chin with all of his might.

The sharp edge of the syther burst through the root of the Gnathe's tongue and into the roof of her mouth. Alex pulled the old weapon free and jerked out of the way of the blood-spattered creature. Breathing heavily from the exertion, Alex watched as the Gnathe fell back into a squatting position, with her broken arms held out in supplication. Blood poured out of her mouth and from the gash under her neck in a steady stream. Her eyes widened in fear as she fought for breath, choking and drowning as her lungs filled with her own blood. She fell over onto her side and her talons locked into the earth as she died noisily, struggling for breath.

Alexander turned away and faced the furious yellow gaze of Link-soo-shan.

"What next, you black-hearted killer?" he cried with fatigue at the tall figure towering over her kindred. "That's two of the six you brought with you into my world."

The crowd squatted in stunned silence as they waited for her answer. San-sool and the group of males were very careful not to show their pleasure at the defeat of one of Link-soo-shan's finest Imperial Guard.

"Again, Alexander, you have surprised me," the Brood-mother replied with malice and stretched up to her full height, balancing back onto her thick muscular tail. "Your entertainment value, as a teaching aid, will keep you alive for far longer than you may wish for. I think it is time to eat. The sun is high and I will take to the shade to think a little. Nagoth, and Jaffin, give him food, water and rest until I return. You may put another arrow into his leg if he resists."

The crowd parted and the two females warily entered the ring. They drew their sythers from out of their scabbards and pointed them at Alexander as they slowly advanced towards him from opposite directions. Two Gnathe armed with bows and arrows took up a position at the edge of the crowd. Knowing that it was useless to resist, Alex threw down the altered sword and stood quietly with his arms by his sides.

Jaffin picked up the modified training syther and re-sheathed her own weapon. She examined the sharp end of the previously blunted sword. The crystalline formation exuded in life by the long dead creature's tail had fractured cleanly at the tip. This left a razor edged piece where it had parted under the pressure of Alexander's foot.

"You are a resourceful creature, Alexander," Jaffin remarked with grudging respect. "In your position, I would not have thought of doing what you did to the end of the blade. For one thing you shortened the reach by producing this cutting edge. Where did you learn to fight like that?"

"Kamiel taught me, many years ago," replied the human, "just as he taught us all many things you would not understand."

"The silver one will not be teaching your race any more of his tricks. We saw it torn apart by our great Brood-mother and she has its head in pride of place, as you have seen," Nagoth smirked and gave Alexander a sweeping blow that hurled him to his knees.

"You foolish, ignorant creature," Alex replied as he rolled over and sat in the dirt. "Do you think that Kamiel lives in just one body? All that Link-soo-shan destroyed was an empty shell. Kamiel lives and will not rest until you and all Gnathe in this valley who were part of your maddened Tyrant's schemes are dead."

Both Gnathe went ridged with shock as they tried to assimilate this information. They stared at their captive in sheer disbelief as he got to his feet and limped away towards the shade of the Banilik tree.

"What do you mean by that?" Jaffin cried at Alexander's back. "No creature can live in more than one body! Where does the silver one come from? What is it, if it is not made of flesh and blood?"

Alexander drank gratefully from the water container in the shade and helped himself from the bowls of fruit and smoked meats laid upon the living tables.

He turned and faced his captors, enjoying their fear and apprehension and said, "We do not fully understand just what he is. Kamiel and the other Guardians come from a time in the long distant past, before this world was born from the ashes of the previous one. They were created by my ancestors, to bring us into being and look after us. Kamiel carries in his memory banks all of our bloody history and is a weapons master beyond your limited understanding. We had no previous experience of fighting and killing when we rescued Ender-whann-soo from your clutches."

"Do you really expect us to believe that your people had never fought before, when you attacked us?" Jaffin asked incredulously, staring hard at the smaller figure of the naked human.

"Until I fought against you at the Citadel and killed Yandos this very morning, I have never raised my hands in anger," Alex answered with some regret.

"Otherwise I might have prevented more of you from returning here. When my people come for me, you will wish that you had never assisted that sick-minded Brood-mother of yours. They will come well armed and trained, bringing your deaths."

"I do not believe anything that this male says," retorted Nagoth angrily and advanced threateningly towards Alexander, unsheathing her talons.

"Wait, Nagoth, she said we were not to damage him. You have already trod the path close to death this morning. She will bring him down and humble this male in the usual way. Remember what she has in mind," Jaffin reminded the angry Gnathe and clasped Nagoth by the arm.

Nagoth stopped short and rewarded her companion with a toothy grin. "You are right, my old friend and fighting companion. There is plenty of time."

Link-soo-shan crouched on her perch with sullen anger. She replayed the combat over and over again in her mind, still finding it hard to believe the ease in which the alien leader had bested Yandos. Even favouring his injured leg, the human had outwitted and picked out the female's weaknesses to exploit. These aliens' natural tool-using abilities gave them a peculiar advantage against her own people. Link had been prepared to squat comfortably and watch her enemy take a satisfying beating. Instead she had lost face in front of her people. After Alexander had modified the apparently useless weapon into an efficient killing implement, she had watched the events take place without any interference to see what the outcome would be.

Yandos had stood taller than the human when she stood erect and she also had a longer reach, with talons that could have disembowelled the human with ease. The unorthodox way in which Alexander had fought the bigger female intrigued her and unsettled her mind. These people were tricky and difficult to outguess. It was time, Link felt, to bring some of her own science and cunning to bear on the alien leader. He was clever and resourceful, she grudgingly acknowledged. Maybe that was why his people chose him to lead them. She still found it hard to understand the alien concept that she had taken from his mind before her ill-fated contest with Trann. Now he must be seen to suffer at her whim and she would regain her standing amongst this captured household. It would do no harm to instil a little fear and respect into the attendant males.

Alexander's triumph had not gone unnoticed and she had seen the faint light of rebellion in some of the males' eyes. She stepped off her perch and paced angrily around her chambers to her crystal collection. Enough time had elapsed since she had retired here to brood over the alien's victory. Link picked up the telekinetic enhancing stone from her travelling harness and stroked it, feeling the power wash over her. With a lighter step she made contact with her old command crystal and sought out her two loyal Gnathe guarding the strange alien male.

The afternoon sun had moved behind some cloud layers and a cold breeze had sprung up, causing Alexander to shiver. His sleeping robe had not been returned to him and apart from the nannite shoes on his feet, he had no protection from the elements. He had taken the opportunity to eat and drink what was offered. Jaffin and Nagoth had squatted unmoving for most of the afternoon, keeping an alert eye on all of his movements. Alex had spent the idle hours resting his protesting leg as much as possible. He watched squads of Imperial Guard practising with the heavy bows and arrows that San-sool and the other male crafters had manufactured for their new adopted Brood-mother. The constant question in his mind was the fear of what the vindictive Link-soo-shan had in mind for him. He felt an overwhelming feeling of dread enter his mind as he saw the two Gnathe suddenly stiffen. Alexander felt the cruel edge of her mind as the deposed Ultimate Ruler summoned them into her presence once more. It was cold and arrogant in its power. He shuddered at the greedy expression on Nagoth's face as the battle-scarred female swung round to face him. "She calls for you, male creature. Do not try anything silly or I will break your arm," Nagoth sneered and gestured towards the brood-mother's chambers.

Alex tried a quick probe into the females mind and met a feeling of rapacious hunger that made him shiver even more in the cold breeze. He still could not get past Link-soo-shan's mental blocks and into the Gnathe's inner mind without touching the big female in some way. The human leader got to his feet and obediently walked towards her doorway, conscious of the many eyes that followed his progress. He could feel a projected wave of concern emanating from the male Gnathe. The minds of the captured female workers were dull against the lively minds of his friend, Ender's kindred.

Alexander straightened his back and entered the dimly lit chambers, repeating to himself, "Kamiel lives," under his breath like a statement of hope.

The few glow crystals that Link-soo-shan's thieving raids had produced lit the area around the Brood-mother, showing her in dark relief. She loomed over him, easily twice his height and stared down at him with cruel yellow eyes. The vertical slits had widened in the semi-darkness and her tongue flicked in and out tasting the air as she bent towards him.

"You have made me lose face in front of these captured dross. Now the time has come for you to be cast down as far as I can send you," she grated with spiteful relish. "I am going to find out just how much Gnathe, that meddling fool, Khann, has instilled into your genetic structure."

"What are you going to do?" Alexander asked, breaking into a cold sweat of fear as a strange, pungent and musky scent began to fill his nostrils. "Are you going to prove how much stronger you are than me? Will you kill me without honour?"

Link-soo-shan hooted with cruel amusement, "No, male creature, I am not," she answered with a maddened glee. "I am going to mate you with Nagoth. She is more than willing to try you out and even suggested it to me. She seems to have an extraordinary sex drive for a Gnathe. Can you feel the response to my mating pheromones that I use to control the breeding rates of my kindred?"

Alexander recoiled in repugnance and loathing and tried to make for the door, only to feel the telekinetic grip of the demented Brood-mother wrap around his legs, preventing him from moving away. He fell to his knees and tried to dig his fingers into the floor. Slowly Link-soo-shan slid him towards her and rolled him onto his back. The closer he got to her, the more the sweet musky smell increased. He began to get a little dizzy and his heart began to pound, sending blood down to the one area of his body that he needed to remain dormant. To his increasing horror he found that he was beginning to come erect as Link spread-eagled his body upon the hard ground with the power of her augmented mind.

"You cannot do this abomination to me! We are not even of the same species. For your own sake let me go. Kamiel will find you, no matter where you go, if you do this awful thing to me!" Alexander cried desperately as he writhed in her mental grasp, unable to break free.

"I can and I will do this to you as a punishment for interfering in my affairs. As for your silver creature, I tore it apart with my mind. He will not come for you. You are mine to do with as I will!" the Brood-mother screamed at him in feral joy. "You see, you have more than enough Gnathe in you to respond. We do not have your fixation with shape, as you do. Now let me see if you have any arrogance left after this encounter. Nagoth, he is ready. Take him—he is yours."

Nagoth eagerly removed her kilt and Alex glimpsed her distended and engorged sexual organ dripping with mucus. He looked up with panic and revulsion at the slightly glazed features of the Gnathe as she waddled forwards to straddle him. A trickle of drool ran down her pointed chin and down the front of her chest. Nagoth was completely under the influence of Link-soo-shan's pheromones and dominated by the mating urge. She stood bestride him, a heavily clawed foot each side of his hips, overwhelmed by lust, with drops of slimy fluid dripping down over his naked, unprotected body. The blood was already rushing into the flaps of her tail and curling them over to form a tube. Nagoth lowered herself onto him with a grunt of pleasure and impaled herself onto Alexander's erect member. She wriggled down until she had enveloped all of him.

As they made this intimate contact, Alexander found himself inside the cesspit of Nagoth's mind, past all of Link-soo-shan's mental blocks. The Brood-mother chose this moment to release him from his telekinetic bonds and Alex tried desperately to unseat the heavy female. Nagoth held him down at the shoulders with her strong taloned hands, digging the sharp points into his skin and, ignoring his frantic blows, she licked his face. She brought her internal gripping muscles into action, designed by Gnathen evolution to hold and detach the breeding stalk after the egg was driven down onto it. The hooked sides of her vulva held him fast. Alexander pushed against her mind, seeking a means of controlling the lust-maddened creature and found that certain mental blocks gave way. If he could only bind her to him in some way or disable Link's conditioning, he could force her to be an ally in the future. At this moment Nagoth gave herself up to the orgasmic contractions necessary to bring down her egg. Alexander felt the soft, warm, gelatinous mass of the egg drive down and envelop his ridged organ and as he penetrated the inside, his own involuntary ejaculation took place. With his mind broadcasting his own forced pleasure and linked to Nagoth's mind, her pleasure centres erupted into a secondary orgasm that almost cost the female her sanity, her instinctive gripping muscles attempting to pull both egg and stalk away with the hooked sides of her contracting vulva. Alexander screamed himself hoarse, until he became flaccid and the egg pulled away to start its journey along the ovipositor tube.

Over two thousand miles away Ender's twins fell into a terrible paroxysm at her feet. They began spitting a bloody froth from their mouths where they had bitten their tongues and their eyes rolled up showing just the whites. The awful backwash of Alexander's terrible agony transmitted itself from the tightly held young Gnathe into Ender-whann-soo's mind and once more she connected to the alien leader's mind.

"Khann!" she screamed, as she did what she could to keep Alexander's mind intact.

The old scientist held onto her own crystal and threw her great arms around the group to make contact with the human leader. She lent her calm strength to the mental concert and took over. "Send him into a deep sleep," she quickly determined, "or his mind will never recover."

Both of the Gnathe transmitted the command into Alexander's mind and he sank into a protective coma with Link-soo-shan's hooting cries of triumph ringing in his ears.

CHAPTER 27

▼

When Alexander's comatose body was returned to San-sool's healing administrations, darkness had fallen over the mountain valley settlement. The little male examined the human's body with concern. To his surprise, the alien's reproductive member was still attached to his crotch, although it was torn, bleeding and lacerated from the root to the end. He had seen these injuries before, when males who had displeased the Tyrant, or her equally cruel, dead sister, Chang, had been mated in an un-ripened condition. Some had bled to death from repeated use of this abomination.

San-sool made the alien as comfortable as possible, covering him with the returned sleeping robe to keep him warm. The male Gnathe watched over Alexander, bathing him and using his small telekinetic enhancing crystal, to heal together the cuts and abrasions of the human's injuries. He studied the deeply unconscious being with great interest and reflected upon the defeat and death of Yandos. She had been a particularly cruel natured female and had caused a great deal of suffering amongst the captured kindred.

San-sool had felt a reciprocating joy spread through the audience when Alexander had driven the sharpened point of his syther upwards and into Yandos-shan's throat. They had been careful to hide these feelings from the ever-present Imperial Guards, who would stamp down hard on any action of rebellious intent.

San's mind was constantly tormented by the vision planted there by the extraordinary alien. It amazed him that Alexander felt no animosity towards the Gnathe in this land-locked valley, except for Link-shoo-shan and her kindred. Even here, these feelings were touched by sadness for the captive minds of the

Brood-mother's daughters, conditioned as they were from birth to obey her every whim. What a peculiar feeling it would be, he mused, to serve through choice and love as Ender-whann-soo's people obviously did. Try as he might, the concept of true independence eluded him and he found it difficult to understand, but he found that he could not ignore it.

Link-soo-shan had retired to her perch for the night, happier and more contented than she had been for many months. She re-played the scenes of Alexander's final humiliation over and over again in her mind. At last she had managed to bring the arrogant creature down! She had relished every painful moment of his degradation and final excruciating pain. Now she was sure that she had a hold over the aliens' leader, which would make him much easier to manipulate. The only thing that concerned her, somewhat, was the ridiculous statement he had made concerning the dreaded 'Silver One' that she had torn to shreds with her mind's augmented power. She picked up the head of her adversary and studied the featureless ovoid with fierce intent. Kaameel was dead. She held his head in her hands and yet the tortured male had screamed out, "Kamiel lives!" before he sank into the deep coma that she could not rouse him from. Link-soo-shan could not get into his unconscious mind to dig out any more details or information. The only thing that she had discovered was his overwhelming belief that the silver one had not been destroyed at her hands. In the end she had returned him to the healer, to repair as much of the damage done to Alexander as he could. She had sent the others of the Guard away to sleep at their own places of rest. Nagoth had disappeared into the night in a dazed condition, helped by Jaffin, to the communal sleeping area. Link had eaten the unfertilised egg passed to her by the female at the end of the sexual act.

In the end, these thoughts became more difficult to sleep with and she stepped uneasily off the perch and walked to the table where she kept her collection of crystals. The night was still and dark. Clouds had built up in readiness for a morning storm and the air hung heavy with a moist promise. She selected her old command crystal from the living table and fell into the sending trance. The familiar world of the Matrix surrounded her mind and she reached out for the direction of the aliens' stronghold.

There, in the mists of the peculiar, dimensionless world, lay the new beacon of Ender's own crystal. She savagely homed in towards the flaring light, intending to deflect into another, lesser mind, of one of the Brood-mothers' kindred. But before she could do so, the whole system of beacons and guidance paths surrounding Ender's location disappeared in the mists. Something huge and slippery, which pulsated with a mind-shivering intensity, took its place. The numbing energy field began to expand, driving Link-soo-shan away from it in frenzied haste.

Once Link had returned to her own position in the Matrix, she released her grasp upon the crystal. Gasping for breath, the deposed Ultimate Ruler squatted on the floor, stunned with the shock of the separating force that had pushed her away from the immediate area of the Habitat. Gritting her teeth, she made contact again with the crystal matrix world and sent her mind out once more, this time to the Gnathen Empire on her doorstep. The Matrix was changing even as she desperately drove her mind to connect with any of the other household command crystals. A slipperiness coated the paths through the Maze of the inter-connected system, making many of them difficult to follow. Once more she broke contact, totally baffled by the new factors introduced into the psychic world she had manipulated for so many years.

Somehow, the aliens had found a master crystal of a greater magnitude than hers' and had managed to shut her out. She gave a screech of fury and squatted back on her haunches, fuming with impotent rage.

Some distance away, Nagoth perched uneasily on the communal rail with her companions. Their ribald jokes at Alexander's agony and degradation had finally ceased, leaving the big female Gnathe in a strange and confused state of mind. Her body still echoed to the abomination thrill that she had experienced from the alien sexual union. Deep in her mind, changes began to occur as old conditioning blocks instilled by her Brood-mother from birth began to crumble away. Alexander's intrusion into her mind at the moment of penetration, and his involuntary orgasm echoing inside her mind, had altered her state of balance. He had scattered and disrupted her own consciousness when he lost control. Alexander had inadvertently imprinted parts of his mind over hers when he slipped past the blocks planted by Link-soo-shan so many years ago. Fragments of his memories were scattered inside her mind like small closed books that opened and closed at random. Without any control, she found she was experiencing the alien's viewpoints on the way that his people related to their world. Alien emotions concerning freedom and individuality flickered into existence, tormenting her thoughts.

Slowly, a deep-seated dislike of her Brood-mother began to take root in her mind as she shook off her conditioning. The knowledge of herself being used by Link-soo-shan to gratify the Tyrant's every whim over the years of her life, nagged at her thoughts like an erupting boil. It had always been so, right back to her brief childhood in the crèche where she had started her life. She had lived only to serve. Not to serve was to die and swiftly die with cruelty.

Now a confusing welter of thoughts troubled her. Another memory, not hers, rose to the surface of her mind. She could see the Heretic, Ender-whann-soo, standing amongst her kindred. The Brood-mother was organising food gathering with her field hands. All of the males and females were hard at work harvesting a crop. Occasionally, one of them would break off from the task in hand and approach Ender with suggestions for future plans; or, seeing that she was thirsty, fetched water without asking. There was no fear in any of the kindred's faces. All of them showed an eagerness to outdo one another in pleasing their Brood-mother, without any envy of each other's success. When a particularly ripe or succulent fruit was found, it was brought to Ender, or divided between the young, twin Brood-mothers. The large Gnathe would thank the giver, stroking the cheek of the upturned face with obvious affection. Envious feelings began to take root as the memory faded away. She had gained favour by her actions in the service of her Brood-mother, but as Link's reaction at her failure to anticipate the alien's actions had shown, she walked a precarious path.

Pulling a cloak around her scarred shoulders, Nagoth stepped off the perch and walked to the door, leaving her companions deeply asleep.

She quickly stepped through into the wet night air. It was cold outside, with deep, dark shadows against the sides of the Banilik tree walls. A faint patter of raindrops began to fall, kicking up splashes from the hard stony ground. Tired as she was, Nagoth found that she could not rest. She pulled the cloak tightly around her and walked unsteadily towards Link-soo-shan's quarters, not knowing why she did so. Over and over again, her mind in turmoil, the big female reflected on her life's purpose.

She began to realise with increasing disgust and resentment, how she had been totally controlled by her Brood-mother since the moment of her hatching. All of her egg-sisters had died in one way or another. Two of them had been killed in battle against the aliens, the other one had been too slow obeying the Commander one cold morning, and Chang had broken her neck. Hunched up against the rising wind and rain, she lent against the rough outer bark of the walls, in miserable confusion, as more and more of her life-time conditioning gave way in her brain. Old acts of cruelty, at Link-soo-shan's persuasion, floated past her mind's eye. To her new, unfettered way of thinking, these actions began to make her uneasy, and remorseful feelings tortured her as yet dormant conscience. The fact that she had been a willing partner in all these acts of cruelty had been shunted aside by the schizophrenic state that had been unwittingly induced by Alexander's mental contact.

Nagoth stiffened as she heard her Brood-mother's scream of rage and fury tear through the walls, when she discovered Hannah's barrier laid across the Crystal Matrix. Overtones of her mental state washed over her as her communication crystal echoed Link-soo-shan's mind in hers. She was so close that she could pick up the Tyrant's thoughts. A cesspool of hatred rose up inside her and she realised for the first time that it was not her own thoughts and feelings. All of her life she had been an echo of her Brood-mother's mind and will. For the very first time in her existence, an independent personality began to emerge. Some of it was not all of her own, but it was blending in with the new character that was beginning to form.

Shaken by her experiences, Nagoth took off her badge of office and threw the communication crystal into the mud at the side of Link-soo-shan's chambers. She held her hands against her aching head and turned away. A burgeoning hatred of her Brood-mother swelled up and dominated her thoughts and a need for revenge began to grow inside her. Nagoth's developing split personality took an increasing hold on her mind. Several times in her life, she had rebelled against the needless sacrifice of her life in Link-soo-shan's service. During the battle with Alexander's people, she had balked at the idea of uselessly dying at the Group Captain's command. There had been other occasions when she had drawn back to save her own skin instead of following Link-soo-shan's commands like the rest of the kindred. It was this independence of mind that had driven her to the Imperial Palace to steal her Brood-mother's crystal from under Trann-link-khann's nose. How she had relished the freedom of decision and thought during that escapade. Now the constant domination of her thoughts was an unrelenting pressure. She had not noticed this before and she found that she resented it fiercely.

Keeping to the walls of the settlement out of the rain's steady downfall, she found her way to San-sool's small living area.

She paused in front of the door and shouted against the rising wind, "San-sool, it is me, Nagoth. Open your door and let me in out of the rain."

San-sool rose with apprehension from his position by the comatose human and called back, "What do you want?" He pulled the door open and stared at the large rain-soaked figure towering over him, saying, "Have you not done enough damage to this poor creature?"

Nagoth's eyes were dilated because of the darkness, but they seemed to be looking into a terrible place that he could not see. She was trembling as she stood dripping onto San-sool's floor. The wind blew through the open door and caused her cape to flap to and fro. San-sool grasped her by the wrist, leading her inside, away from the rising storm's fury and closed the door.

"I say again, Nagoth-shan, what do you want here at this time of night? If you have come to vent more of your spite upon the alien being, you are wasting your time. He lies here just as you see him and I cannot wake him."

"San-sool, believe me when I say that I mean him no more harm. Is he badly damaged? Will he live?" Nagoth continued to drip unheeding upon the floor as she stared down at Alexander's unconscious figure covered by his sleeping cloak.

The healer stood back with puzzlement at his former sexual partner's uncharacteristic behaviour and asked, "Why should you care, Nagoth-shan?"

"He has been into my mind, San-sool, and I am not the creature that I was. Link-soo-shan's conditioning has been broken. All of my life I have obeyed her every command without losing my life. You do not—you cannot know what this alien male has done for me. Since I was a hatchling, I have thought her thoughts. I was nothing, just an echo of her personality. He has set me free. Through his memories, I have seen the Heretic's kindred serve with joy and without fear. There are bits and pieces of his memories entwined with mine."

San-sool watched with dawning understanding as the big female squatted down besides the alien leader's flushed and feverish body. He realised that somehow Alexander had transferred a version of the concept planted in his mind to the scarred veteran of Link's Imperial Guard. Once the deposed Ultimate Ruler got a hint of what was inside Nagoth's mind, she would not rest until any like-minded Gnathe were dead. Without Alexander's mind blocks to shield her thoughts, the female was a walking death sentence. He watched her tenderly stroke the human's cheek with her huge deadly hands and shuddered.

"What do you have in mind, Nagoth?" he asked warily.

"I am going to steal him away from her, my healing friend. Will you help me? I tell you now, I expect that she will kill, or maim him worse, in the morning. I was close by her chambers tonight when she tried to spy into the alien's home. They shut her out, San. Her scream of rage was terrifying to hear. I would bet my life that she will not be rational in the morning. This valley will not be a safe place to be."

"With Alexander gone, my life will be worthless to her. I cannot stop you, Nagoth, so I willingly join you. He has been in my mind too and I have seen much of the same as you, but he planted blocks to prevent Link-soo-shan from detecting the ideas. May I suggest that we take him to the Imperial City? Maybe the gorge is passable with care? I would not like to try the swamp. Your tales of that awful place are enough for me."

"Can you ride a Zanth, little male?" inquired Nagoth with a worried frown.

"I have never needed to. I was a city Gnathe," San-sool replied, dryly. "It looks as though I will have to learn in a hurry. Now would be the time to try. I will do my best to hang on, if you will lead my mount."

"Gather your things together then and we will go. I will carry him to the stables," the big female responded and slipped her muscular arms under Alexander's limp frame. She gave an immense effort and picked the alien leader from the floor, cradling him in her arms. His strange scent filled her mouth as her tongue flicked out to touch his face. "San-sool," she gasped in anguish, "keep a constant watch on me. I want him so badly that my soul cries out with desire."

The little healer swung round and dug his fingers into her arms with disapproval and said harshly, "If you have him again, you will kill him. It took all my skill to prevent him from bleeding to death. As it is, the bruising he has suffered will make life very difficult for him for some time. He is not made like a Gnathe. They pass their waste water through their breeding stalks. Remember all I have told you and think about it before your feelings get the better of you." The Gnathe pushed her to the door and continued, "Come now, be quick and let us get to the stables. I have all that I need. The cold wet air will bring you to your senses. Hurry or all will be lost. We must be far from here before the dawn."

Wrapping the sleeping cloak securely around Alexander, Nagoth stepped into the night, following the nimble figure of San-sool. The whole settlement was in darkness. Not a single guard was on watch as the settlement could not be approached easily from any direction. The new order holding sway over the Gnathen Empire was too busy organising itself on the new lines laid down by Trann-link-khann to even think of invading Link's stronghold.

Alexander dreamed that he was a child again, cradled in the strong arms of mother Minns. The Guardian rocked him gently, soothing his fears with her protective grasp. Somehow, he knew that he had fled from some nameless terror and now he was safe at last. Nightmare faces full of hate and spite stared down at him and he retreated further into the strange safe world that he had created. It seemed to him that he was also split into two separate Gnathen identities, complete with tails and clinging tightly to a much larger, warm, loving body. He was both Azander and Marren, partially twin mirrors of his soul, but not quite. There was also the presence of Ender-whann-soo, inter-twined with these, almost copies of himself. The two personalities were combined minds, already beginning to become separate identities in their own right. Eventually each twin would begin to differ and develop separately. A healing force swept over him, knitting him together from the fragments of insanity that chased around his mind.

"I have him, Khann. He is back again," the sweet disembodied voice spoke gently to another powerful mind. Cool bands of restful colours oozed around his torn personality and delicately soothed him.

"Hold him with care now and keep him quiet," the other mind answered, delicately weaving in and out of the bruised places. "There are memories, best repressed for a time. I will pull together the torn places and cap the dark wells of his psyche, diluting his worst experiences."

Khann skilfully repressed the worst excesses of Alexander's ordeal, allowing them to leak through slowly from his memory stores back into his conscious mind. His alien mind had altered a great deal since Ender's well-meaning experiment in telepathy had opened up the wellsprings of Alexander's un-tapped abilities. There was much that she did not fully understand about some of the new areas of power. Nevertheless, Khann had nearly a thousand years of experience to draw upon. The coming of the aliens into her world had stimulated her beyond the normal restraints of her age. All the new challenges to her keen intellect had pushed the approach of senility far away from the present. She felt younger in her mind than she had for generations of kindred. A new zest for life possessed her and she drove her aged body to its limits.

Khann searched deeply amongst the mended wounds in Alexander's mind. Her work was nearly done and she signalled her granddaughter to wake him gently and return his mind to his body.

Alexander slowly stirred into gathering awareness and was conscious of his two Gnathen friends in his mind. He felt secure and became aware of a rocking motion, with the reassuring feel of a pair of strong arms around him, holding him close. Still maintaining a tenuous contact with Ender, he opened his eyes and looked up at the face of Nagoth looking down at him.

Ender took the full impact of Alexander's fear and loathing before the contact broke. She turned to Khann and said, "Nagoth has him. She has stolen him away from Link-soo-shan somehow. Why I just cannot imagine. We can help him no more. His survival is in his own hands now. I must tell Kaameel and Asue what we know about this night's work."

Khann disagreed and replied, "No Ender. I will go and see the Guardians, as there are things I need to discuss with them. You stay here and calm the young ones."

The old scientist hurried to her personally adapted communications console and pressed the sequence of keys down necessary to call the Guardians. After a few moments the screen divided itself into three sections and she found herself looking at the featureless, silver, ovoid faces of the enigmatic beings.

"My friends," she said, "I have news of Alexander. Listen to me and I will tell you all that we have learnt." She then proceeded to tell them of Alexander's awful experiences at the hands of the deposed Tyrant and the two Brood-mothers' fight to retain his sanity.

"At least we know that he is still alive and due to your efforts, sane," Asue replied gratefully. "We can still do nothing for him yet. Maybe he will be safer with this Gnathe than held captive by Link-soo-shan. It will keep her busy searching for him and allow Kamiel to organise some resistance at the Imperial City before she mounts her attack."

"Hannah has managed to form the psychic shield, locking the Tyrant out of the Habitat and settlement," Kamiel said to the old Gnathe with relief. "She has also managed to close off many of the paths of the Matrix, making it difficult for anyone to use the crystal communications network."

"Then we are safe from her at last," Khann answered with relish.

"We will never be safe from her as long as she lives, with the powers at her command," Kamiel flatly stated. "My group will be setting out in the morning to remove her and her threat from this world. I shall be leaving you for some time, to drop from orbit again later this day. This time I go to aid Trann. We will either destroy her power there, or Alexander's rescue party will do so at the mountain stronghold. Also, when Hannah paralysed the crystal Matrix, she said that she felt Link's presence homing in onto our area before she closed her out. She will open a pathway for you to inform Trann of my imminent arrival after mid-morning. I shall want you to be ready to send that message to her via our command crystal, and then we will close down our area completely until she is defeated totally, one way or the other."

"I understand, friend Kaameel. I will be ready," Khann replied and shut down the communication console and returned to Ender-whann-soo's quarters.

Kamiel watched the first fingers of the dawn light up the sky with a sullen red glow. How like the long gone world of his creation this place was in the early morning, he thought to himself. It was only when the great orb of the giant red sun dominated the heavens that the alien landscape of the new cradle of humanity became so obvious to him. To the humans and apes it was home, even though the light was different under the domes. There at least the sun had a more golden glow, due to the efforts of Asue's construction of the roof and reflected light arrays. He had spent the remainder of the night completing the supplies and weapons ready for Frederick's war party, after helping Hannah to build her shielding device. She had linked the crystal to a random noise, pulse generator connected to a computer-generated analogue of her brainwave pattern. The results of this signal she downloaded into the nannite structure of the walls of the Habitat and settlement. A resonating effect produced the shielding waveform.

Hannah now slept soundly in her laboratory cot. Her small form was curled up in the bed, exhausted from her efforts and a soft snore carried through the room. Others of her dedicated team slept on the floor or checked circuits in the mobile systems she had constructed for the rescue party, trying fully to understand the genius of her work. Once Kamiel had been sure of the success of Hannah's work he had left them and returned to his workshop.

Now he stood waiting for the rising sun to fully illuminate the settlement. He had reviewed all the aspects of the events leading up to this moment. Until he gave the final briefing to the rescue group, there was nothing left for him to do but wait for the frail biological units of his scheme to refresh themselves with sleep. He had been awake and fully functioning for over five hundred years, ever since Asue had awakened the other Guardians on board the Nano-ship. Even after all this time, he could not be sure just what was hidden in his programming. The several virtual reality meetings with his creator, McBald, had shaken him to the core of his electronic soul.

He still did not fully understand just what had happened to him when he had nearly shut down after Link-soo-shan had so easily defeated him at the Citadel. Whatever the programme was that he had been instructed to run, it had obliterated the shut down sequence he had almost instigated. The one thing that had lodged in his mind, however, was the fact that he and the remaining Guardians were not immortal. He had never questioned his mortality before these events. Now it was a factor to be considered and taken into account in their efforts to make the new colony viable. Nothing else mattered but the continuance of this lonely outpost of humanity.

Now that they had involved themselves with the affairs of the Gnathe, the Guardians found that they felt a large measure of responsibility for the well being of the new partners. The aliens had given the human and ape race the keys to this strange world. How they would evolve together was the question of the future. The one thing that he had to do was to make sure that Link-soo-shan did not regain her Empire. Great benefits would ensue by the enlightened rule of Trann. With a new frontier to challenge the young Brood-mothers growing up in the various households, the old ways of fratricide would prove unnecessary. The two races would grow and be bound together after the Tyrant's defeat. According to Kamiel's socio-dynamic projections, tying the two cultures together made the viability of the colony go off the scale. Alexander would have to wait for whatever chance Frederick's group could give him. The Guardian had great faith in the abilities of the adventurers, particularly as they would be well armed this time.

His heat sensors picked up and became aware of the group before they entered the room. Kamiel turned and faced them.

"Good morning, my friends. I see that Joom has accompanied you," and he nodded to the large ape. "It's good to see you are at last growing back some more hair after the effect of Khann's serum. Come in and get comfortable. I have much to tell you and more to show you."

Kamiel illustrated to the group the most efficient methods of killing their Gnathen opponents, much to the interest of the two aliens, Shoo-lin and Coen-soo. There then followed a practice session with the crossbows to the delight of the bloodthirsty young Beast-master. When he was satisfied with their prowess with all the weapons he had designed, Kamiel called them to one side.

"I have one other thing to show you before we part company," Kamiel stated and walked over to a large cabinet set in the wall of his workshop. "As you know, we lost most of Minns' personality during Link-soo-shan's assault on the life lab-oratories. I have therefore adapted her body and programming to a new use. We will re-create a new Minns from what Asue managed to salvage and insert the new identity into this body of mine after I have been transmitted to one of the Nano-pods at the satellite. There was more than enough basic programming to suit my needs. This is for you, Frederick."

The big human stared in amazement as a huge skeletal being walked forwards at Kamiel's command. A pair of shovel-like flat feet supported the structure of the larger than man-sized frame. The skeleton was constructed to wrap around the wearer, with each leg encased in a double piston structure, jointed and fixed to the hip seat. A flattened spine, with extended ribs, ended in a shoulder brace, connected to a similar system as the legs. Each arm would be contained in a dou-ble rod and piston arrangement, ending in a pair of reinforced gloves. The head was a half helmet shape that terminated over the face with a visor.

"What is it Kamiel?" asked Fred in astonishment.

"As I told you, old friend, this was the nannite body of Minns. It is now an enhancer system. Call it an intelligent suit of armour. It is fitted with one of the shielding crystals cut from the one that Hannah found, as are all of your survival suits. You will wear it when you go against Link-soo-shan. It will plug into your nervous system and become an extension of your bodily actions. As you move, so it will imitate and enhance all of your actions. Do not forget however that your strength far exceeds your mass. Step into the framework and it will wrap itself around you and then you will find out what it can do," Kamiel suggested. He reached forward to assist Frederick into the construct and added, "Do not try to do too much too soon."

Frederick stepped into the silvery embrace and pulled the helmet down over his head. Immediately he felt a number of cold stings as the nannite contacts entered his nervous system through his skull and various places around his body. Within a few moments the shovel base of the feet wrapped themselves around his own feet from toes to well above his knees. They continued to creep upwards to meet the hip-seat flowing down. The shoulder brace and extended ribs closed over his upper body and the gloves fitted themselves to his fingers. This process continued until he was entirely encased in the shimmering, second skin. Reinforcing rods, like muscle extensions, spread along his limbs.

A female voice that he remembered from his long gone youth whispered in his ears, "All systems are plugged in and ready to go, Fred. You now have complete body armour mode in position, activated and at your command. Shall we go outside again?"

"Kamiel, whose voice is this I can hear in my ears?" he asked with dawning certainty.

"What you hear was the voice of Minns. I have adapted what is left of her into a battle computer and companion, my friend. She has no inhibiting programming about killing intelligent beings. Nor, I might add, is she completely self-aware. That may come as the two of you achieve an understanding. Who knows? She is unique, to my knowledge. Nothing like her has ever been made before. It is a great responsibility I am handing over to you, Frederick, old friend and pupil." The Guardian pointed to the door. "Now go outside and see what you can do. I will also add that there is a great deal of my military tactical defence and attack programming loaded into her artificial mind. She will be a second line of advice for you in times of need. Listen to her as though she were me."

Slowly Frederick turned and walked outside, following the Guardian's lead and the rest of the group. The suit was totally self-supporting and, although he felt the extra mass, there was no effort in walking.

Kamiel's voice spoke softly in his ear: "The settlement is five miles across. I suggest you try a run towards the far wall and see how you get on. Be careful of your built up inertia when you try to stop. I will remind you again, do not forget that your strength far exceeds your mass. Now let's see what you and your new companion can do."

Fred sighted himself onto a set of animal pens, situated in the far distance and started a gentle run. It was as though his body were weightless and ran without effort.

He began to pick up speed and a voice in his ear softly said, "Heart rate slightly increased, breath deeper and increase speed."

Frederick did so until he was running faster than he had ever run in his life. The outside of the suit gripped him in a firm embrace, anticipating every move he made. He was now travelling as fast as a horse could gallop. His breathing began to labour a little and his heart began to pound and he realised that the fenced area of the Zanth's compound was approaching rapidly. Frederick slowed down and felt the extra mass pulling him on. Desperately he swerved around the edge of the pens and realised that a number of Gnathe were in his way. The enhanced human increased the turn, away from the startled group, and ploughed straight into a line of posts, uprooting some and snapping others. Dazed, he tripped and fell, rolling over and over across the stony ground. He picked himself up and surveyed the damage with astonishment, feeling totally unhurt.

The voice spoke apologetically in his ear, "Sorry Fred, we were going a little too fast, but I am learning to compensate. Are you feeling all right? All bodily signs are within normal parameters."

"I'm fine, just a little bit fazed," he replied to the unseen voice. "This is incredible, Kamiel. I can scarcely believe it."

He picked up one of the broken fence posts and swung it like a club with all of his new strength against a boulder and watched it explode into fragments. There was no jarring sensation in his arm and hand. He closed the hand on the grip and observed his fingers disappearing into the wood until the post fell to bits in his hands. The only effect of the swinging club against him was to throw himself slightly off balance on impact due to the energy of the blow and he remembered Kamiel's warning about mass inertia.

Kamiel's voice spoke again in his ear: "You have done well. I think that you will master my gift to Link-soo-shan. I believe that you will be a most unwelcome surprise for the Tyrant when you meet again. Now come back and we will use you for some target practise."

"What!" exploded the large human.

"Believe me, you will not be harmed. There are several lessons you need to learn by experience. Now run gently back towards us and you will see what I mean."

Frederick did as he was instructed and the moment he was in range, felt a blow against his chest that slowed him down. The next bolt caught him on the shoulder and spun him round. Before he could straighten up another arrow took his legs from under him. This time he rolled with the blow and sprang upwards, high above their heads, snatching a bolt from out of the air with super-human speed.

The female voice spoke in his ear, "We got that one at least."

He landed right in front of them this time and held his hands outstretched.

"Enough!" he cried. "I think you have proved your point, Kamiel. I promise that I will practise and find out my limits before I attempt to destroy the tyrant."

"Good," the Guardian replied. "I have every confidence in your abilities. Listen to Minnis and take her advice when in doubt. There are a number of extra weapons included with the supplies that only Minnis knows how to use."

"I was going to ask what I was to call you," Frederick spoke softly to his companion. "You should be proud of your name. Minns was a wonderful person."

"I do not understand the feeling of proud, Frederick, but I think I know what you are trying to say," Minnis replied, gently. "Remember at all times, I am a battle computer first and an artificial intelligence in the making. There is a great deal of Kamiel's memory banks locked away in my growing awareness."

"Thank you, Kamiel," the big human said to his old friend and teacher, "this suit will give us the edge we will need when we bring that evil creature down. Are you sure that the crystal installed in this suit will protect me from her telekinetic powers?"

"It will indeed, but it will not prevent her from throwing a large rock at you. You could still be damaged inside the impervious skin of Minnis, by extreme force. Remember that before you act. Now I must go and put the other part of my plans into action. Good luck to all of you and remember, wipe out her threat forever. You do not have the inhibiting programming that prevents me from taking a more active part. I will see you again at the Imperial City perhaps, after this is all over. Do your best to bring Alexander back alive. We can do no more for him. Now listen while I tell you all that we know about what has been happening to him."

The group stood listening in stunned silence as Kamiel recounted all that Khann had told him.

Shoo-lin broke the silence and said, "Kaameel, she must be stopped. I will not rest until she is dead and all of her twisted brood are butchered. I pledge my life to this, on my beloved Trann's honour."

"And I," stated Coen-soo. "She is an abomination to our race and all of her kindred must be treated the same. It will not stop until this land of ours is cleansed of her taint."

"I am glad you feel this way," Kamiel answered. "Our two cultures have much to offer each other in the future that is to come. I must leave you now and do what I can to prevent Link-soo-shan from over-running the Imperial City. Trann needs my advice and our technology to be sure of defeating her. Frederick, I repeat, listen to the advice of Minnis as if it were me. She is a battle computer and will obey you in all things. Now I must go to Trann," and the Guardian turned and left them without a backward glance.

CHAPTER 28

▼

Nagoth stared down at Alexander's stirring body while gripping the Zanth firmly with tail and legs and watched as his eyes opened in horror. She held him tightly as he weakly struggled against her grip and tried to writhe out of her grasp. His face locked in a grimace of pain and his struggles ceased.

"Good, you are awake at last," the big female stated and brought his face closer to hers. "Be very quiet. Your life depends upon doing as I say and listening to me."

"What do you want with me, you disgusting pervert?" Alexander hissed through his clenched teeth. "Have you not damaged me enough?"

"I am taking you out of Link-soo-shan's reach, with San-sool. We are making for the Imperial city. I want to protect you, Alexander," she replied in low whisper. "Try to believe me when I tell you that I would willingly lay down my life to keep yours safe."

Alexander lay still, numbed with disbelief and asked, "Why should you do this for me and why should I trust you?"

Nagoth bowed her head and collected her whirling thoughts and replied, "During our forced mating, you reached into my mind. Somehow you cut through Link-soo-shan's conditioning. I am not the creature that I was. Most of my mind was hers. Since this afternoon I have been re-born. My thoughts are at last my own. I tell you, she will kill me if she finds me—you too—after what your people achieved this night."

Alexander lay back, conscious of the steady movement of the Zanth and the darkness surrounding them. Rain splashed into his face and ran down the inside of his cloak, making him shiver. He rapidly collected his spinning thoughts.

Moving with them was another Zanth, led by Nagoth by its halter. Hanging on for grim death was the small form of San-sool, desperately doing his best to stay curled up in the riding hollow.

He looked up at the forbidding features of his old adversary and questioned her further, "Just what have my people done to upset Link-soo-shan that makes you think she would kill her new toy?"

"In the early part of the night, my mind was confused and I could not sleep," Nagoth replied and added, "so I wandered around the settlement. After a while, I found myself outside the Ultimate Ruler's chambers. She was operating her old command crystal to spy upon your strange home. I was close enough to be able to pick up her thoughts, when somehow your people shut her out and paralysed much of the matrix. Tomorrow this will not be a safe place for you to be. That was when I decided to take you away and save you from her wrath. She is not sane. I threw my communication crystal into the mud to frustrate her seeking abilities. Her madness has driven all of her kindred since they were hatched. I have been an echo of her thoughts all of my life. Now I am free."

Alexander tentatively tried a probe into the mind of his captor and found that he could slip easily into her conscious and unconscious thoughts. He found a whirling storm of chaotic emotions settling into new pathways. The blocks and conditioning systems stamped into her mind at an early age were dissolving and breaking away. Almost all of the disciplines laid down in the distant past had eroded, leaving fresh avenues of thought and reason. Old routes of servitude and obedience had shorted out, looping away from the controlling consciousness.

There were still dark, twisted areas to this alien mind, but they were being kept under control and masked. Coiled around this seething mass of sexual hunger was a deep-seated need to make amends, fused with a naked emotion close to passion. Nagoth had never loved anyone. The closest thing to approach this was the devotion she now felt to her forced sexual partner. Raw overtones of lust flared up from her psychic depths, barely controlled. He stared thoughtfully up at the big female cradling him so protectively in her muscular arms, with dawning comprehension. Whatever had happened between them in the past, this emerging personality dominating Nagoth's body could not be held accountable for her previous actions.

Born from the liberating effect of Alexander's desperate thrust into her Brood-mother dominated mind, she was still very unstable. At the moment she represented the only island of safety for him to rely on and trust. If she ever got within mental range of Link-soo-shan, she could just as easily turn back into the perverted killer she once was. Alexander dropped back into the swirling mess and began to bring into effect some of the mental disciplines that Khann and Ender had taught him. He began by placing some blocks of his own, adding shielding over them to hide the alterations. Next he reinforced the shaky pillars of the new, emerging personality, so that a steadying influence began to take hold.

"What do you have in mind to do now, Nagoth, and what are your plans for escaping from your Brood-mother? I have to believe that you are indeed no longer my enemy, for I have been into your mind and seen the change in you for myself," Alex answered her in the swirling darkness. "The problem, however, is the fact that you have done me a great deal of damage through our sexual encounter. I will need attention for some time before I can even walk by myself."

"We must put as much distance as we can between the stronghold and our-selves," Nagoth replied and urged the Zanth onwards through the driving rain. "San-sool has joined us and will give you all the healing help he can to ease your injuries. Meanwhile I know that Link-soo-shan means to take as many of her kin-dred through the matrix gate to attack Trann's position at the Imperial City. I mean to get to her and warn her somehow."

"I thought the way back had crumbled into the Imperial River," Alex said with dismay.

"It has," Nagoth answered, shifting position slightly, "but there may be a way around, if we look carefully. I can think of no other way back into the Gnathen lands. We cannot risk the swamp—it is too dangerous to try."

"Nagoth, do you not think the Tyrant will look for us there first?" Alexander asked the big female and clenched his teeth as a spasm of pain racked his lower regions.

"I could not think of anything else," she groaned in despair. "What do you suggest? I will do anything you say."

Alexander began to think desperately while they continued to travel through the night.

"How many days will it take to get to the gorge?" Alexander asked. He added, "There is one other thing to consider. We could turn from our path and make for the high cliffs and hide at dawn. How close are we from there?"

"It will take at least three days hard travelling to reach the gorge, one day or more from here to the edge of the high cliffs if we turn soon and begin to climb. What do you suggest?" she asked, slowing the Zanth to a halt and holding Alex-ander close to her chest.

"Abandon trying for the gorge. I think she will search for us there first," Alex-ander declared, staring into the darkness. "What we must do is to make it appear as if we are making for that area and make for the high cliffs instead. Look for a hard stony area on our way and break from the trail at that point. You, Nagoth, will carry on with the Zanth and leave a plain trail for them to follow. Abandon the beasts somewhere where they can continue to wander away and confuse the Tyrant's searchers. Double back and make your own way to the edge of the cliffs and look for us there."

"How will I find you again?" Nagoth implored, unhappily.

"Now that Link-soo-shan's conditioning has been removed, I will be able to contact your mind when you are near me. When you are close enough, I will guide you to where we are hidden," Alexander replied. "Now let us put as much distance as we can between Link-soo-shan and ourselves."

Nagoth kicked her Zanth into action and set a steady pace, leaving a definite trail in the soft earth, easy to see. They carried on into the night until the sound of crunching gravel and stones told them that they were travelling over the hard ground that Alexander had hoped for. Leading away from this area, the ground once more became soft, leading off into the misty distance. The rain had eased off and now the landscape was shrouded in mist. They had a few hours before the dawn would light up the area and the sun burnt away the morning fog.

"Stop—this will have to do!" Alex shouted to Nagoth. "Leave San-sool and myself here and take the Zanth as far as you can before abandoning them. We will continue to climb towards the high cliffs as best we can and find a place to hide during the day. You must double back and find us as I explained earlier. San will keep a lookout for you while I rest. Remember, you will have the advantage of knowing roughly where we are."

Nagoth pulled the two Zanth to a halt and sat unhappily in a mood of indecision, cradling Alexander's injured body to hers. Reluctantly she dismounted and carried the alien male to a flat rock, where he carefully sat himself up with her aid.

"I don't like to leave you here, but I understand what must be done." She was reluctant to let him go and asked, "Can you walk?"

San-sool had dismounted gratefully and walked quickly over to where Alexander sat uncomfortably on the stone.

He gave the human an appraising look and said to Nagoth, "He will if he leans on me; if not, we will crawl together into some hiding place and wait for you to return. Come now, we must get moving and leave this area behind us and start climbing to the top of this cliff to the high trails."

Alex rolled over onto his hands and knees and sucked in his breath as a spasm of pain racked his lower regions. Nagoth helped him to his feet and the little male pulled Alexander's arm over his shoulder. The three of them moved unsteadily upwards along an animal trail leading away from the well-defined path that they had been following with the Zanth.

"Leave us now," grated Alexander, "and move those Zanth as far as you can from here or all this will have been for nothing."

Nagoth held the human in her embrace and flicked her tongue over his face and said, "I will do my best to find you. I will keep you safe at any costs."

She turned away to scramble back to the incurious tethered beasts and was swallowed up by the dawn mists.

Alex watched her go, turned to his male companion and said to him, "What do you make of her, San-sool? Can she be trusted, do you think?"

"I think so, my friend. She is totally different to what she was. I knew her in the city. Nagoth was one of the worst of her guards for wanton cruelty," the Gnathe replied vehemently. "I could get to like this new person that she has become. Now let us consider practical matters."

"What do you have in mind?" Alexander asked.

"I have seen the obvious distress that you are suffering. Do not forget, I have spent the best part of my life treating injuries. You must void the waste water building up in your bladder or you will soon rupture and die. Have you tried?"

"No, the pain and swelling is too much," Alexander replied with a grunt of pain as he applied some strain to his lower regions.

"You must try again while I attempt to ease open your urinal tract with the aid of my crystal and telekinetic sense."

ALEXANDER OPENED HIS CLOAK AND LOOKED DOWN AT HIMSELF FOR THE FIRST TIME. GREAT PURPLE AND BLACK BRUISES SURROUNDED HIS PENIS. SAN HAD WASHED HIM AND KNITTED TOGETHER THE LACERATIONS HE HAD SUFFERED. A PARTIAL ERECTION STOOD OUT AS THE BLOOD THAT WAS PUMPED IN FOUND DIFFICULTY IN LEAVING.

The healer gathered handfuls of cold wet moss and packed them around the worst of the damage. He held his small hand with the crystal touching both of them, closed his eyes and concentrated.

Alexander felt his flesh move gently and the pressures lessen against his urine. He pushed, wincing with the pain and was rewarded by a golden stream of relief.

"Thank you, my friend," Alex gasped gratefully.

"You will make better progress," San replied. "I have eased away much of the pooled blood. You need to rest yourself. I will help you as much as I can. Do the best that you can to follow me while I look for a better place to hide. Then we can eat."

Alexander rolled over onto his hands and knees, crawling slowly after the male Gnathe into the shelter of the rocks and undergrowth.

Nagoth pushed the Zanth as hard as she dared along the fog bound trail towards the gorge. With a lighter load the tired beasts were able to make a better turn of speed. As the sun began to burn away the morning mists she became increasingly nervous of what she had done. Soon the trail led by the side of a deep ravine. She dismounted and tied her Zanth to a bush growing from a crack in the rocks. The other Zanth she led along the edge of the ravine, keeping close to the wall of rock at her side. Nagoth waited until she was out of sight of the other beasts and drove the point of her syther into the Zanth's side, letting go of the reins. The creature reared away from the pain of the sharp stab and lost its footing. Nagoth watched the loyal beast kick and plunge as it fell through air, down into the dense undergrowth below.

The tops of the trees showed little sign of the beast's passing and hid the dying creatures' struggles from view. She hurried back to the tethered Zanth and pulled the unwilling creature to the same area. This time she deliberately led the Zanth to a more exposed, but gentler slope. She again dug the point of the syther into the side of the beast and let go of the halter. The Zanth plunged away from the sharp point and slithered down the slope, causing a great deal of the hillside to follow her down into the ravine. Nagoth observed that the beast slid on down until it came up against the first trees and bushes. The small ones snapped under her weight and she vanished into the wood with a bellow of fear.

Nagoth was satisfied with her handiwork. Anybody searching down there would take a long time before they realised that only the Zanth had fallen into the ravine. Already she felt the keen loss of her new love's presence. All she wanted was to be near him and to please him. Alexander was now the centre of her existence. She rapidly backtracked the trail that she had followed and began to climb away from it over the hard stony areas, leaving no tracks behind her.

The first red fingers of the early light began to fill the glow crystals with fresh energy and they altered their state, to store the power of the sun in the depths of the intricate matrix at their core. In this state they reflected the excess light back into their surroundings. Each crystal had been set to reflect and diffuse towards the next one deeper inside the dark interior of the living walls of the Banilik tree.

Soon all corners of the homestead were illuminated and the semi-darkness of night banished. One by one the kindred began to stir and make preparations for feeding the many workers throughout the community. Soon it would be time for them to toil in the newly won fields to plant and tend the new growth. Some would be pressed into foraging in the many wild areas of the valley for whatever could be found in this colder land. The best would be saved for their Brood-mothers' requirement as it had always been. Only the males and females of the captured homestead worked, serving the needs of the Imperial Guard as well as the three Brood-mothers. What resentment there was, was kept under iron control. Some had already paid a price for their resentment.

Bronn and Connit awoke together and stepped off their sleeping perches and flicked their tongues out to taste the air. Smells of early morning cooking filled the air as more and more of the Gnathe began to busy themselves with the tasks in hand. Connit bent down and drank from the living water bowl growing from the side of the wooden wall. She splashed the cold liquid onto her face and wiped herself clean with a wad of absorbent, fibrous material torn from a creeper inter-twined with the Banilik tree. She turned away to allow her Egg-sister to use the water and stared blankly out of the window.

"Do you think that the alien still lives, sister?" Connit asked, thoughtfully.

"Maybe he does," Bronn replied and added, "After yesterday, I would think that he would rather die than submit to another ordeal like that again. Did you hear her scream of rage during the night?"

"Yes I did," Connit answered bleakly and turned around, swishing her tail across the floor. "Something upset the Ultimate Ruler badly. I would not like to be the one to draw her wrath this morning."

"We owe her much, my sister. More than we could ever repay. To see again, after all those years of enforced darkness is beyond price. Whatever she requires of me, she can have. My pouch can remain ever full with her kindred," Bronn said fervently and patted the squirming bulge in front of her. "These new Gnathe she has designed are extremely adaptable. I am proud to carry the kindred that we have produced for her. When she takes back the Empire, we will be by her side. All will bow to us and seek to do our will. All will fear our children and beg to carry hatchlings for the Ultimate Ruler," said Connit fervently with a glazed expression.

Small feelings of disquiet lay at the back of both Brood-mother's minds, but the flares of intense loyalty planted with consummate skill by Link-soo-shan overshadowed these feelings. Awkwardly the heavily pregnant Gnathe made their way to breakfast amongst the attentive throng.

Link-soo-shan became aware of the smells of cooking on her tongue and rea-lised she was very hungry. Her face split into a feral grin as she remembered Alexander's frantic screams of pain as Nagoth had tried to remove his mating stalk with her internal organs. It had been a great disappointment to her that he had stubbornly remained unconscious after his ordeal. Maybe this morning he would have regained his senses and had awakened. The threat of a repeat encounter with her fanatically loyal daughter would loosen his mind and allow her to pick him clean of information. There was a great deal more she needed to know and understand about these strange aliens and their capabilities. It still gave her a disquieting feeling that he had screamed out at the height of his pain, insisting the silver creature she had triumphantly torn apart, still lived. She straightened up and put the matter from her mind. What she had done once, she could do again.

Link laid her hand upon her large communication crystal and sent a questing thought towards Nagoth's mind—but the customary response did not follow. Puzzled, she cast around for the position of the crystal and found that it was close by her quarters. Of the attendant mind there was no trace. She walked outside and looked down into the mud beside the door. The splits in her yellow eyes opened wide in disbelief. There, still attached to its loop of hide, was Nagoth's stone, personally given to her by Link herself. This was her most treasured possession and badge of office. Could Nagoth be dead, she wondered? She picked it up, holding it tightly and walked back to lay her hand once more upon her large communication crystal.

"Jaffin," she projected and was immediately rewarded by the bright, sharp mind of her Group Captain.

"Yes, 'Great One'," she replied. "What is it that you require?"

"Where is Nagoth? I cannot mentally find her and I have found her crystal thrown down onto the mud at the side of my chambers"—and Link projected the plan of the area where she had found the stone.

"She did not appear to sleep with us last night, Lady Link. One of our company saw her leave during the early darkness, before she fell asleep."

"After breakfast, I want you to fetch the alien leader to my presence, and find Nagoth. I need information from him if he is awake. The strain of mating seems to have taken much of his strength," Link replied, exuding amusement.

The thought of his suffering made her mood a little lighter and she made her way to the communal hall. She noted with pleasure how the new breed of Gnathe she had genetically engineered were already busy, taking their place among the captured kindred. Although very young, the difference between the two distinctive strains could easily be seen. Already, they were larger than some of the captured household and mentally, much quicker. She caught sight of her two breeding mothers, full with constant pregnancy and moved to eat beside them.

"You are both well?" she asked and looked down at their swollen pouches as she reached for a piece of roasted meat.

"Yes, great Lady, Link," they both replied in unison.

Mace added, "My time soon approaches. Are there any males suitable for mating, after my hatchlings are ready to depart?"

"San-Sool approaches maturity and should be ripe in several weeks. I will mate him to Jaffin this time," Link replied thoughtfully and began to project the genetic structures of the two individuals. She considered the blending of the characteristics that she required to keep and felt a warm pleasure spread through her. When she regained her Empire, there would be a better strain of her line in command. They would be much more adaptable to her new way of thinking. Once more, she and she alone, would shape the main gene pool. When she was secure, then would be the time to design her successors. These two compliant fools would do her bidding until they died of excessive brooding.

Till then, her mental control of them would be absolute.

She was suddenly aware of the frantically worried presence of her Group Captain standing before her table of fresh food. Jaffin stood there alone.

"Where is the being called Alexander?" Link-shoo-shan asked with a hostile hiss of increasing apprehension.

"He has gone, 'Great Lady'. Also, San-sool and Nagoth are not to be found. Two Zanth are missing from our limited stable. I fear they have made an attempt to escape from here. There are tracks leading towards the 'Great Gorge'."

"Are you sure that Nagoth travels with them and does not perhaps pursue them?" she inquired and began to weave around the table towards her message bearer.

"Two stable hands have been beaten unconscious," Jaffin replied nervously. "San-sool could not have been capable and he cannot ride a Zanth properly. He is only a city Gnathe. Nagoth must be involved with this." Jaffin stood her ground, waiting for Link's wrath to explode.

Link stopped short of her loyal guard as the various explanations passed through her mind. Why would Nagoth try to steal Alexander away from her? She thought furiously to herself. San-sool also had become an enigma to her. Why should he turn against her? She had given the clever old male great status in her community. Link hissed in sudden understanding as the only logical reason pushed itself to the front of her mind. The alien being must have interfered with the minds of her two subjects.

Her analytical mind began to chew over the possibilities and plans of action began to form.

"Jaffin," she spat in simmering anger, "gather together a number of groups led by good captains. I have a mind to try something new with my crystals. This will be good practise for the times to come when we go against Trann. You are to hunt these renegades down. Bring them to me alive. They may be bloody, but I must have them alive. Do you understand?"

Jaffin beat a hasty retreat with a grunt of assent. "I will not be long," she said as she hurriedly moved out of Link-shoo-shan's range.

The deposed Ultimate Ruler turned to Connit and Bronn. "Follow me to my chambers," she said. "We will extend your crystal training a little more. I have an idea to try."

The three Gnathe assembled at Link's crystal chamber and took positions around the new crystal assembly that she had arranged.

She looked across the table at the other two Brood-mothers and said, "Some time ago, before my assault upon the alien's city, I began to experiment with the crystals taken in our raids against the outlying settlements. I believe I can open up a doorway between selected stones. I have positioned many of the smaller communications crystal in matched pairs around the valley. What we are about to attempt to do is to open a corridor from here to each location. I will then try to transport a number of my guards through each doorway without carrying them though physically. If this works well it will be the means to assemble an army close to the Imperial City when I am ready," Link declared and gestured to the two large crystals separated by the telekinetic amplifier.

At that moment Jaffin appeared at the doorway and said fearfully, "Lady Link, we are ready. I have instructed the guards about your plan. They are in tight groups, mounted and ready for your signal. They are lined up in front of the stockade."

Link strode out of the chamber, leaving the two Brood-mothers staring thoughtfully at the crystals upon the table. She took two matching gemstones and set each one of them upon the top of the stockade gateposts. Each one was similar in size and was a shade of brown. Link made sure they were secure and not likely to move from their positions by smearing a good consistency of mud around them.

Link stood up straight and stared hard at her nervous daughters, speaking loud and clear to them. "Listen to me carefully. On Jaffin's signal you will ride through the gate. I will send you to different locations around the valley. This time you will not be travelling with me, but I will open a door for you to go though. Do not be slow, for I do not know for how long I can keep open each door."

Link left them holding their mounts securely under control and strode back through the doorway into her chambers where Connit and Bronn waited patiently. Outside, Jaffin held her crystal tightly and waited for Link's telepathic signal while the groups of apprehensive guards kept their careful eyes upon her.

Link-soo-shan settled her weight upon the perch running around the crystal table and motioned the other two to lay their hands upon the facets of the two large stones. As the crystals began to warm to their touch, Link slipped easily into the two immature minds of her assistants while she also gripped tightly the telekinetic amplifier.

With easy domination, she told them, showing them the way, "For this first time I need you to hold fast here and become my anchor as I bend space to touch the fracture lines held apart by the crystals that I placed around the valley."

Link began to recede from the area and her mind began to soar into the psychic matrix. The pathways through the labyrinth of the no-space were becoming clearer to her with every launch into this unique world. The slippery area of the aliens' home she ignored and concentrated upon the pair of beacons set at the area of the Imperial River Gorge. Each pair of matched communications crystals stood out as a distinct fracture in the space-time continuum. She was aware of her two companions holding fast, providing the anchor points that she required and reached out for the fracture points at the 'Great Gorge'. Link overlapped the distortion with the one at the stockade and held it steady until the two twists in the strange dimension of the matrix became fused together.

"Now, Jaffin," she projected with the edge of her mind.

The air shivered in a large circle between the two stockade posts and a cold draft of air began to blow through the gap. A view of the Imperial River gorge could be seen, stretching away inside the shimmering circle. An area of pathway curled away from the entrance.

Jaffin shouted, "First group, go!"

She watched the first nervous company walk their beasts quickly through the hole in space. Within a few moments everyone was through the gateway and looking back at the Group Captain, unharmed by the experience.

"All are safely through, Reverend Lady," Jaffin projected back to her Brood-mother and watched in amazement as the company of Guards abruptly disappeared from view.

Link-soo-shan cast her mind out to the focus of the fracture line and contacted the mind of the still bemused Captain of Guards.

"All is well?" she abruptly inquired and proceeded to look around through the female's eyes at the area of the gorge as she dutifully turned around.

"Yes, Lady Link, there are no ill effects that I can see or feel," the captain replied with relief.

"Good, then find my missing captive and his renegade friends. Work your way back towards the settlement and surprise them," Link retorted in good humour. "I will leave you now and send the others to cover alternative escape points."

Link removed her mind from the area and concentrated her powers onto the other twists and fracture points that she had set up, scattered around the valley. Group by group, she sent the other Gnathe on their way and finally retired from the crystal matrix triumphant.

She faced her two willing, heavily pregnant assistants, and said, "Well done, you two. Your presence made things easier for me to orientate myself inside the labyrinth. I have now the ultimate weapon against Trann and that coward Sing. Once I have Alexander back in my power, I will begin to carry over to the Imperial City area matched pairs of crystals ready for my assault. The next thing will be a dawn attack, as my loyal Guards and troops pour out of the gateways that I will open. Soon what was mine will be mine again."

"You are without doubt the greatest Gnathe that has ever lived, my Lady Link-soo-shan," Bronn answered with awe. "We are indeed fortunate and grateful that you made us part of your plans."

Link smiled to herself and thought, "Yes my two immature fools, and you will stay that way until the day you die."

All around the hidden valley, groups of diligent guards searched for clues to the whereabouts of the fugitives by slowly making their way back towards the stronghold. Bit by bit, the net began to close in over the only escape routes back to the lands of the Gnathe.

CHAPTER 29

▼

Asue sat at the controls of the auxiliary transmitter and fine-tuned the apparatus. It was located at the settlement outside of the Habitat. She was not happy with the rapid turn of events that had been forced upon her. She had agreed reluctantly that Frederick's rescue force was the only logical method of rescuing Alexander from Link-soo-shan's captivity and regaining his freedom. It was obvious that after the deposed Ultimate Ruler's triumphant strike against the human and ape colony, she would turn her attentions to regaining her old Empire. The Guardians had watched with growing misgivings the constant trickle of the egg-sister's kindred to the increasing stronghold beyond the swamp and high cliffs. The instinct to follow their surviving Brood-mother had driven the remote outposts to find her once they knew of her escape. A few had quickly been killed at some cost, but a great number had quietly disappeared from their posts around the Empire. Some were collected by Link-soo-shan and some had made their own way to her. Those with command crystals had been contacted by Link-soo-shan and had spread the word. She had survived and they were needed.

Asue was satisfied that the colony was safe and out of the Tyrant's psychic reach, due to Hannah perfecting the shielding generator. This plan of Kamiel's was the next logical step in permanently removing the insanely dangerous Brood-mother from Gnathen affairs. Nevertheless, Asue was tormented by feelings of disquiet about both ventures. She realised that a great deal of death and suffering still needed to take place and be arranged before both cultures could count themselves safe. Reluctantly she had agreed with the differently programmed mission psychologist and had begun the initiation of the transfer process for Kamiel's mind to a nano-pod's storage system high above them at the orbiting satellite.

"Are you ready to transfer, Kamiel?" she asked, pensively reaching for the transmit button.

"Quite ready, Asue," he replied on their private band and continued, "Khann has warned Trann-link-sool of my impending arrival. There is nothing left for me to do, but go and complete the next stage, and give Link-soo-shan a nasty surprise. Utilise this body for the new Minns immediately that I have left it behind. You need the extra help at Sharn's side. Do not delay in transferring the new memory patterns. I will have no further use for this shell once I have activated the nano-pod."

"Promise me that you will not confront Link-soo-shan," Asue declared grimly. "For there will be no other receptacle for your mind if she traps you with her telekinetic powers again."

"I will run if I must. My preservation is also precious to me. Have confidence in my assault team. They are well armed and advised," Kamiel assured her. "Now transmit me to the satellite above."

Without any more discussion Asue operated the equipment, causing a bridge to form between the empty, prepared nano-pod and Kamiel.

Kamiel expanded his mind to fill his new body and vacated his old one many miles beneath him. A feeling of exhilaration filled him as he extended sensors and took stock of his surroundings. The hard crispness of space spread all around him. His nannite body was superbly adapted for this environment and Kamiel thrust out feelers towards the empty space station. He began to ooze across the surface towards the airlock built at the hub of the slowly rotating wheel.

Asue's presence joined with him and projected, "Is everything perfectly functional with your new body?"

"All systems check out to perfection, old friend. It is time to re-animate my old body and give it up to the new personality of Minns. There is still a great deal of work to do at the dome next to the Citadel that will require her specialised talents."

"Very well, Kamiel, carry out your part in this next stage of the project and I will meet you again sometime in the future. Be very careful," she cautioned and withdrew.

Kamiel operated the airlock door and entered the silent vacuum world of the inside of the space station. Through the empty corridors the silver coloured globe floated, a network of cilia extended to brush the sides. In the cold vacuum no deterioration had taken place since the original crew had disappeared over six million years ago. No clues had ever been found by the Guardians as to why the perfectly habitable satellite had been sealed and abandoned. He penetrated deeper into the depths of the station, heading towards the well-stocked stores. What he needed was located in the electronics and astrophysics laboratory.

Sometime later a considerably bloated, silver globe returned from the plundered stores. The guardian quickly made his way back to the airlock on top of the space station and exited into the vast outside. The planet hung beneath him, reflecting the harsh red sunlight back into space. The satellite spun slowly in its geo-synchronised orbit and Kamiel launched himself away from its relative safety towards the world below. He exchanged mass for gas and vented enough to send him down in the direction of the lands of the Gnathen Empire.

Sensors expanded, Kamiel plotted a course across the thousands of miles of mountainous wilderness and began to enter the upper fringes of the atmosphere. He began to feel the tug of resistance and began to alter his shape, extending his sides into huge, delta wings. Now he started the long glide down and honeycombed his structure, filling it with hydrogen, effectively decreasing his density. The nucleus of his neural networks containing his mind spread themselves thinly through the structure of his new body.

He picked up speed by diving steeply down and levelled off, gaining hundreds of miles of lateral distance. Below him the ragged mountain ranges flashed by until his speed approached supersonic. As he passed the critical point, Kamiel delicately altered his shape again, pulling it in until he resembled a large needle-nosed dart. Down further into the atmosphere he sped, until the edge of the Gnathen lands came into the reach of his sensors. The Guardian tilted his wings and pulled out of the dive over the top of Link-soo-shan's valley stronghold. He hurtled over the edge of the great cliff towards the Imperial City, leaving a sonic boom echoing over the startled inhabitants. Within a few moments the City lay before him. He altered his fins to direct his trajectory upwards to kill his forward velocity and he shot into the clouds high above. Now Kamiel spun filaments out behind him into the classic thistledown pattern to brake his headlong flight. As his velocity fell, the pattern expanded further, until his forward mass swung over and he began to float gently down to the ground below.

A sea of Gnathen faces was spread out beneath him, looking upwards at the incredible shifting, silver shape drifting down towards them. The morning sun picked out Kamiel's form as he manoeuvred himself through the air to descend in the direction of the centre of the arena. Gnathen minds struggled to come to terms with what they saw, as the Guardian changed his shape finally to his humanoid form with a large hump on his back and dropped onto the sand in front of Trann-link-sool.

"Do not be afraid, friend of Khann," the silver being said as he walked towards the stunned Brood-mother. "I am the Guardian, Kamiel. The ladies Ender and Khann told you I would come to you to help defend yourselves against the Tyrant. We have a great deal of work in front of us and very little time to prepare for her coming."

Trann looked down at the much smaller figure with amazement and awe and replied, "Come with me to my chambers, great Kaameel, and tell me what we must do. We are in your hands."

Deep in the recesses of a damp, dark cave, Alexander began to take stock of the situation. After Nagoth had left them, they had climbed further up the steep hill towards the high cliffs that held this secret stronghold in its stony embrace. The rocky face had fractured after some ancient upheaval and a way deeper into the ground had opened up. Water trickled down the rock-face and had collected into a series of pools and gratefully they rested and drank. San-sool scrambled back to the entrance to keep a lookout for Nagoth while Alexander bathed himself. Already the swelling was beginning to reduce and he could relieve himself without San-sool's psychokinetic help. As he lifted his face from the pool of cold water, the faintest touch of air passed his wet cheek from deeper within the cave. Instantly, Alexander wet his hand and waved it slowly around in front of him. He was rewarded by the sensation of evaporation from the hairs from the back of his hand.

"The cave has another exit," he eagerly thought. "There is another way out. Perhaps part way down from the top of the cliffs."

From the entrance of the cave, San-sool saw the figure of Nagoth making her way up the slope towards him. He could see her carefully wiping all traces of her passage from off the stony track leading to the split in the rock face.

"Nagoth," he cried, "we are up here, in this hole in the rock face. Is there any sign of pursuit?"

The powerful female looked up and made the sign for no. She scrambled the last few steps up to where San-sool lay hidden and wriggled into the split in the cliff.

"Where is he, San? Is he recovered? Can he walk on his own yet? I left the Zanth tumbling down into the woodland below the track," she said. "They will think that we have gone into the forest to hide."

"He has gone deeper into the cave where there is water, and yes, he has recovered quite a bit since you left," the little male replied. "Come with me and you will see."

A scraping noise accompanied by a rattle of stones alerted Alexander to the return of his rescuer. He turned round to see the two Gnathe come sliding down the narrow passageway towards him.

"Nagoth, you have returned," said Alexander and sat down on a boulder. "Have you masked the trail back here? Are we safe from pursuit? Tell me all about your journey and I will tell you what I think we must do while we eat whatever food San-sool has in that sack"

Nagoth gratefully sat down with a grunt and collapsed into an untidy heap. In the gloom and safety of the cave she told Alexander and San-sool all that she had done to put their pursuers off their tracks.

When she had finished, Alexander said, "Well done, Nagoth, you should have bought us some time. If you are very careful you can just sense a tiny draft coming from deeper inside this cave's tunnels. There is another way through and we are going to find it. With luck it should come out somewhere on the cliff face surrounding the lands of the Gnathe. All we have to do then is to climb down!"

"We should ration our food or it will not last long enough," San-sool said, "and gather anything that we can use as we go along."

"Let us start and make our way down into the tunnel. Alexander had better go first as he seems to be able to sense the air movement better than I can," Nagoth replied and picked up the worryingly lighter sack of provisions.

The dark of the cave beckoned them on with only the faint breeze to guide them as they climbed deeper and deeper into the damp split through the rocks. As they moved slowly and carefully into the fracture in the rock, they were aware that the darkness was not absolute. Their eyes adjusted to the reduced light and they were aware that a faint luminescence came from off patches on the walls. Alexander put his face close to one of the areas and could just make out the shapes of tiny bugs that gave off a pale blue light. They were feeding on patches of lichen that also gave off a pale glow.

"Nagoth and San, you see these creatures," Alexander said. "Gather them up and keep them safe. These could be our salvation. We can at least see where we are going now. Scrape them off the walls and onto a flat piece of rock."

The two Gnathe began scraping the tiny creatures onto pieces of slate until they had gathered enough to produce a definite glow, good enough so that they could just see by the strange light. It was still very dark, but not absolute. The only problem was that they were now aware of being watched by many creatures that had made their home in this place.

Nagoth snatched something from off the wall and said, "It looks as if we can at least not go hungry while we are down here." She picked off the legs and scrunched the creature up and swallowed it. "Not bad either. I have eaten much worst than that out on duty!"

Alexander and San-sool quickly gathered a few of the creatures and followed suit. Alex found that he could manage them a lot easier if he cracked them open and sucked out the contents.

They continued their journey into the depths of the cave for some considerable time, following the draft of cold air that was getting more pronounced as time went on. Alexander became aware of a faint pulling sensation and vibrations similar to what he had felt before at the Citadel when Ender-whann-soo and Khann-link-sool had shown him their command crystals.

He turned and said to San-sool, "Can you feel the nearness of crystal, my friend? Somewhere close to us is a natural crystal deposit."

San-sool stiffened and reached for his small kinetic stone and nodded, "Yes Alexander, I can. It is raw and un-tuned, but I can feel it. I am sure that it is a telepathic command crystal."

"If we can find it, I am sure that with its power I can contact my people—or if not them, then someone friendly, like Trann at the Imperial City," Alexander replied and began to advance slowly towards the faint pull.

At last he could feel its presence in the rocks in front of him. There, under a heap of broken stones, was the indescribable feel of a raw command crystal with a collection of smaller shards that had shattered off the main body. Nagoth pulled the larger stones away until at last the crystal was revealed. It was much smaller than the crystal that they had found on their way home, so Alex did not feel overwhelmed by it.

Many miles away, hunched over the leathery hides of the Raptors, Fredric, Abdul, Joom, Shoo-lin and Coen-soo, wrapped in their warm insulated suits, flew ever onwards towards the hidden valley and Link-soo-shan's armed camp. Joom sat as close as he could to the female Gnathe and hung on tight as the mountainous snow-capped land slipped by underneath. They would have to make for the valley of the raptors first, to allow Munch and the other two raptors to hunt and rest.

Joom reviewed the situation as he hung on for dear life. All they knew was that Alexander was alive and badly damaged. How injured his old friend had been by the crazed Brood-mother's revenge, he could only guess. All that he knew was that both Ender and Khann had fought to retain Alex's sanity before the link was broken. This new world of enhanced psychic powers was a wonderland with pit-falls. Nothing within the Ape's experience could have prepared him for this. To actually see into another's mind and communicate with them at some distance was beyond description. No deceit was possible with mind-to-mind contact. It was impossible to lie. It was possible to shield with practise, so that you were not constantly bombarded with other people's thoughts, but when you contacted another mind you had an open door. The Gnathe had developed this ability by using their communication crystals over many centuries by selective breeding. Unlike the humans and the apes, they were not sensitive without their crystal amplifiers. Whatever Ender had changed in Alexander's mind had worked like a chain reaction amongst all the other members of the Citadel and Habitat, as soon as they were touched by anyone who had become sensitised. There was no going back, Joom thought to himself, and no one who had changed would want to.

"Fredrick," Joom projected, "this is beginning to look a bit familiar. Can we land soon before I fall off this leathery bag of bones?"

"I am not a bag of bones, just hungry," protested Claws indignantly and swooped downwards towards a break in the mountain range with Coen-soo and Joom leaning back in the harness.

Snapper drew alongside with Shoo-lin and Abdul hanging onto the straps and he added, "I too am hungry. We have flown far. We need to hunt and eat."

"I agree," replied Fredrick and directed Munch to dive down through the approaching valley walls.

The three raptors came whistling out of the ravine and straight over a hairy herd of ox-like creatures. They dropped onto the animals without a thought for their tiny riders. Claws extended and jaws agape, Munch, Snapper and Claws fell into a killing spree. Gnathe, humans and ape hung on to their harnesses with sheer strength as the raptors struck and tore chunks of warm bloody flesh from the stampeding herd.

"Stop, you crazy bastards!" Fredrick cried with all of his mind's power and the two Gnathe joined in.

The three giants folded their wings penitently and drooped their heads. Six or more of the oxen lay in bloody parts, their entrails steaming in the cold wind. Great chunks were missing where the raptors had swallowed what they had torn off. The remaining herd were now out of sight and an embarrassed silence hung in the air. The whole attack had taken just moments to carry out. The shaken rid-ers dismounted and walked unsteadily away to sit amongst the rocks.

Finally Shoo-lin approached Snapper and the other two raptors and stood looking up at the jaws of his mount and projected, "We could have been killed. What do you think you were doing?"

"Hunting, Shoo-lin. We were hungry and suddenly there was food," the great beast replied, unhappily.

"We are sorry," implored Munch.

Fredrick pulled out his knife and sliced off some fresh steak from one of the neater looking oxen and replied, "Okay, my young friend. Just be more careful when you need to hunt and let us get off first!"

"Let's gather some firewood and we can cook some of this meat," said Joom. "It will taste better than Asue's rations and we can rest awhile."

"While you three do that, I will have a look further down the valley and see whatever I can remember from the area when we were last here, just to be sure that we are in the right place," Fredrick replied and turned away.

"You do not need to do that Fred," said a small voice in his ear. "I know exactly where we are."

"Minnis!" exclaimed the startled human. "I had forgotten you were here!"

"Indeed you had, Fred. I can tell you that you are not far off the direction necessary to bring us to Link-soo-shan's armed camp. All you have to do is to continue in this general direction. I shall tell you if we are going wrong."

Fredrick walked back towards the others and the beginnings of a fire. Very little of the dead oxen could be seen, except the cooking steaks. The raptors had curled up away from the firelight and had gone to sleep to digest their meal.

At the Imperial City the Gnathe treated Kamiel with awe. When he walked among them they would stop and stare at him with disbelief. The silver sheen of his nannite covering was beyond their experience and could not be understood. The first thing he did was to request a safe place to keep the items he had brought down from the satellite orbiting high above them. Trann had quickly organised a band of helpers to do Kamiel's every command without question. He had sent them into the countryside to gather as many long hardwood lengths of timber they could find and the reeds that grew all along the irrigation ditches. He also got them to find as many old horns and long bones as they could remove from the bone pits outside of the City walls.

While the supply of materials began to grow, Kamiel began to outline his plan of defence to the lively mind of Trann-link-khann and to the fearful Sing-trow-sool.

"What I have to do is to alter your view of your culture," Kamiel said to the Brood-mothers. "The steps that you have taken to get here and the way that you fought Link-soo-shan in the arena have shown me that you are adaptable. Now you must take some more ideas into your mind's eye, so to speak."

"What do you mean, Kameel? I am eager to learn," Trann replied and settled onto her perch, listening avidly.

"For a start, the great Link-soo-shan is also adaptable. She is clever and quick to learn by experience. She is able to fold space and take a few of her guards with her to other locations. We as yet do not know how she has managed to do this, but as you have had items and Gnathe disappearing for some time, we can be sure that she intends to make you a visit. Before she comes here we must be ready for her. I will need as many of your crafters that you can find in the city. We need to alter the approaches to the city so that she cannot rush straight in through the main entrance. I have to teach you the ideas of defence and siege."

Kamiel stood and explained as much as he could to the alien ruler and watched her struggle to comprehend all that he had to instruct. Trann was also clever and adaptable and soon sent for her daughters. When they also had listened to what Kamiel had to say, they disappeared into the city to bring back as many of the male crafters as they could find.

In Link-soo-shan's new domain, a gathering of worried Gnathe began frantically to search the trails back to the central complex without a sign of the fugitives. The false trail had been followed down to where the Zanths had plunged into the deep woods. One had been found dead and the other one injured. No trace of the alien or the two Gnathe had been found.

"Great Lady," Jaffin projected through her crystal, "we can find no trace of the alien leader or Nagoth and San-sool."

"What!"

Link-soo-shan rocked back onto the stony soil and lashed her tail from side to side. She clasped her command crystal firmly and entered Jaffin's mind to see the unpleasant truth.

"He must be hiding somewhere," Link spat into her mind. "Make your way back to me while I recall all of the others. Keep looking as you return to me. He is cunning, this alien creature, but he cannot get out of this valley very easily. What was mine I will have at my mercy again. He will have to wait for I have other things to do. We will take back my Imperial City, daughter of mine, and I will amuse myself with those two usurpers. Leave some of your guards behind to look more carefully and return swiftly with the rest of them to me."

With that she withdrew her mind and began calling the others back through the doors. With each concentration of her mind it became easier until she became quite contented with her new ability.

Jaffin sat on her Zanth and called the others of the search party to her and said to them, "Three of you will stay behind and search as carefully as you can while the rest of us return quickly. Remember how pleased the 'Great One' will be if you find the alien. Three of you should be able to handle Nagoth and the little male." She pointed to the three at the back. "You will do," she said and turned her mount towards Link-soo-shan's settlement and rode swiftly away.

The three Gnathe left behind slowly urged their Zanth along the trail until they came to the area where the fugitives had turned away. The sun was going down and it was as good an area as any to make camp.

Deep under the ground, Alexander sat and examined the un-tuned crystal with his new abilities. He remembered when Khann had become shaper of crystal and had tuned the crystal at the Habitat. He wore the ring that housed San-sool's telekinetic crystal and used it to feel his way along the fault lines and exert pressure to break the bond. There was a distinct crack and a shard fell off the main piece. Again Alexander pushed along another fault line and another piece fell off. After seven shards had come away, the crystal developed a different feel of receptivity to his mind. Once more he concentrated his will along the last fracture point and pushed. The crystal hummed with power and he felt his mind expand into a strange psychic matrix that was without any dimensions. It was just there in his mind like a city full of lights glowing in the dark. There was a small one not too far away and he locked onto it.

It was Jaffin's mind! Carefully he pulled back so that he was not sensed by her and absorbed all of her recent experiences. He saw Link-soo-shan's doors through space with understanding horror and carefully withdrew.

"Nagoth, we cannot go back the way we came," Alexander said to his protector. "Jaffin has left three of her guards behind us to search more carefully. Link-soo-shan knows that we are somewhere in this area. They found the Zanth where you left them so she has recalled her forces back to her settlement." He stared at the Gnathe in the feeble light. "There is something else I must warn Trann-link-khann and Sing-trow-sool about. The Tyrant has found a way to keep open a door connected to the crystals so that she can send her army through a fold in space."

"She will be at the Imperial City with an army whenever she chooses," Nagoth replied in horror. "You must use this crystal to home in onto Trann's master crystal and warn her. Hold my hand and I will show you where it is in the Labyrinth."

Alexander reached out to take hold of Nagoth's clawed hand and was immediately aware of her altered mind dovetailed into his. The communications matrix now had direction for him and he could sense the Imperial City's master crystal in amongst all of the others. He concentrated his mind in that direction and called for Trann.

CHAPTER 30

▼

Kamiel had just finished arranging the items that he had brought from the satellite onto the flat tabletop growing out of the side of the wall, when an unfamiliar Gnathe interrupted him.

The small female skidded to an ungainly stop and said, "Great Kaameel, I have been sent to take you to Reverend Mother Trann. She has been contacted by the being that you call Alexander."

The Nannite grabbed the awestruck Gnathe by the shoulders and replied, "Take me to her now as fast as you can. Lead me to her."

The two set off through the living warren to where Trann-link-sool was perched holding her clawed hands against her communication crystal. Her eyes were closed as she concentrated her mind on the link that Alexander had forged. Kamiel gently laid his cool silver hand upon her hand and swiftly linked his neural system into hers. Conscious of the awful thing that he had done to Link's sister when he had linked to her mind, he kept his contact to a very light touch. Both Trann and Alexander were aware of his presence, but at a very unobtrusive level.

Kamiel concentrated on just picking up the images and information that Alexander was feeding Trann's mind. He was amazed at the developments that Link-soo-shan had managed with the crystals at her command. The Ultimate Ruler was indeed a complex being. If it were not for her dangerous madness, Kamiel would have felt ruled by his programming to leave her alone. As it was, he was motivated by the one major command, to save the colony at any cost. He was hindered by the overwhelming programme to defend and was powerless to take a direct offensive action. Still, he could ensure that the people here would have all the protection that he could provide and the weapons that they would be able to use and understand.

Kamiel gently put forward the information that Fredrick, Abdul, Shoo-lin, Coen-sue and Joom were on their way to rescue him, conveyed by the Raptors.

Alexander asked if they could be contacted, to be told of his present whereabouts and what he was trying to do, by penetrating deeper into the caves looking for a way out.

Kamiel withdrew before he did any lasting damage and tried contacting Minnis.

Fredrick was suddenly interrupted in his thoughts by the voice of the sentient battle suit. Munch had been aloft for some time flying along the fertile mountain-locked valleys and they were looking for a safe place to land, so that the raptors could leave their frail masters and hunt.

"Fredrick," Minnis said in his ear implant. "I have news for you. Alexander has escaped from Link-soo-shan and is hiding in a subterranean maze of caverns. He is damaged, but is with two Gnathe who are helping him to escape. He is safe for the time being, but there are other developments to consider."

Fredrick straightened up in the harness and replied, "What are they, Minnis? Do they affect our mission?"

"That will depend on events as they happen," she replied and told him about the new powers of the Ultimate Ruler and her ideas concerning the assault on the Imperial City.

Link-soo-shan brooded angrily on her perch, shifting her weight from side to side as she reviewed the situation. Alexander's escape and the turning of one of her most loyal female guards against her, made her hiss in fury. Unfortunately there was nothing that she could do about that situation. To her knowledge there was no other way out of the valley except through the swamp. She had seen the sheer cliffs that dropped down to the lands of the Gnathe and there was no way down from there. The thing to do was to concentrate on building a gate near to the Imperial City. A simple homestead would do. As long as it possessed a communication crystal she could twist space and slip through with enough crystals to form a gate. The only thing to do was to pick a location. Then it occurred to her that the old home of her subjugated Brood-mothers would be the perfect place to take over.

She summoned Connit and Bronn-mace-rann to her side, regarding them with cold appraisal and said, "I am going to return to your old home, my two obedient children. I need to know what the layout is like from whatever you can remember. In a few days I will be ready to return and form a gate, so that my loyal guards and I can pay Trann a final visit."

Great Lady Link, we can only give you a little information as we spent the majority of our lives blinded," Connit replied, unhappily.

"You may know more than you think. Join your minds with me and I will see what I can extract from your memories," Link-soo-shan answered.

The Brood-mother delved into what information she could extract concerning the size and defences of the homestead. It seemed a modest size settlement with not too many Gnathe serving the Dominant Brood-mother left without her sister. Link remembered well how easily that one had died by her hands. Considering the homestead a safe and easy target, she decided to try homing in onto the command crystal at the homestead and soon found it unprotected by the slippery feel of the human Habitat's defences.

Gently she cast around, looking for a smaller beacon of light and found it round the neck of a young female. For some time she looked through her eyes as the Gnathe busied herself in her household duties. She was very careful not to alert the mind that she was a passenger in, to her presence. She learned the mind's signature so that she would be able to find her again. The next time she would dominate her and make her wander off to a safe location. There would be no one to see her arrive, carrying her well armed guards and those 'all important' gate crystals.

Alexander sat quietly absorbing all of Trann's information. It was a relief to him that Kamiel had decided to go to the Imperial City and aid Trann-link-khann and Sing-trow-sool against the Ultimate Ruler's growing army. It was a strange feeling to be linked to Trann's mind and be aware of the Nannite's awesome intellect in the background. He had not dared to try and contact him direct. Kamiel was not a biological creature and although he had a limited experience of being linked to flesh and blood, it was not safe to try too much. It was enough that he knew that Alexander was safe for the moment. Kamiel would inform Fredrick and once he was in range, Alexander would be able to contact him telepathically.

Then he realised, Shoo-lin and Coen-soo would both be carrying a shard of crystal around their necks. Once more he reached out, closed his eyes and touched the warm face of his own command crystal. The labyrinth was all around him once more. There was no direction at first and then Alex felt a concentration of the contact points at a short distance from him and then many, many others further away. He used the Imperial City crystal as a reference point and cast his awareness in the opposite direction. There, far away, was a point of brilliance surrounded by many lesser points of light. Right next to these contacts was a slippery place that he could not understand. Try as he might he could not get through it, so he concentrated his will on the master crystal and connected to a nearby shard.

Ender-whann-soo felt the presence of a familiar alien mind questing for contact and opened up her receptivity.

"Alexander!" she projected with joy. "How are you? Where are you? Tell me all about yourself. Fredrick, Abdul, Joom, Shoo-lin and Coen-soo are on their way to rescue you by Raptor flight."

"I know, my friend, it will still take them some time to get here. I have the news by Kamiel. I have spoken to Trann at the Imperial City, so I am up to date," replied Alexander. "Thank you both for saving my sanity when I thought I would die. I still don't quite understand what happened."

"You were able to make a telepathic link with Azander from where you were! Khann and I did what we could to save you. You were very lucky that we were able to help you," she answered. "Now tell me everything. Khann is with me and is impatient to know how you have managed to make this link."

Alexander relaxed, letting the information flow out of his mind and into his alien friends. After a while he got Ender to send a contact to Shoo-lin and rode piggyback on her mind and entered his.

"Shoo-lin! It is Alexander. Connect me to Fredrick. Where are you?"

The Gnathe nearly fell off Snapper's shoulders when the contact came through and called out to the big human flying beside him: "Alexander has made contact through the crystal. Concentrate your mind to mine!"

Fredrick did so and soon found that the circumstances had changed greatly since they had started their long journey. They all took in the information and agreed a small change of plan.

Kamiel stood patiently by the side of Trann as she withdrew from the sending trance. Now he needed the co-operation of the City Gnathe to gather some more very odd materials and to direct him to the Imperial Palace's waste pit.

"Have you finished?" he said and was careful not to startle the Brood-mother by still being attached to her flesh.

"I have, Kaameel. Things are getting better and better as time goes by. I do not fear her coming as much as I once did," Trann replied and stepped off the perch by her command crystal.

"Do not be over-confident, my friend. Much still needs to be done before she gets here. We still have no real idea as to when she will strike or just where," the nannite answered grimly.

"What more do you need me to do? Just ask and it shall be done," said Trann-link-khann and stared at the silver humanoid shape before her.

"This young Gnathe will be useful to me. She can show me where your sewage goes for a start and you will instruct your followers to gather me charcoal from your roasting pits," he replied and walked out of the room.

The puzzled Gnathe did as she was bid and took Kamiel to the city outfall, where all the waste not used by the Banilik trees ended up in a large pit.

Kamiel surveyed the mucky hole with satisfaction. He then concentrated his will onto a small portion of himself and began to reprogram the ball of nannite to do a chemical conversion. Satisfied that the programming was complete with both sets of instruction, he hurled the silver ball down into the sunken basin. Immediately the contents began to fizz around the expanding ball.

"Young one," he said, placing his hands upon her shoulders, "I will leave you here to keep other nosey Gnathe away. Do not allow anyone to approach too near. It could be dangerous. The sun begins to set, but for you my young creature there will be little rest this night, or some of your friends could die. Do you understand me?"

"Yes, 'Great One', I will do your bidding. None shall be allowed to approach here. I shall not sleep. May I instruct others to assist me?" the Gnathe asked and glanced apprehensively at the now seething pit.

"Of course you may," Kamiel replied and added, "Do not worry if the pit begins to smell even worst than it does now. It will, young one, but it will be as I have willed it."

With that Kamiel made his way back to his private quarters to where he had left the parts he had brought down from the satellite far above in geo-synchronous orbit above the human habitat. Not for the first time he wondered why there was no trace of the original occupants. Not a single record had been left on the main computers. All had been shut down as if waiting for the nano-ship to find it in orbit around the surviving gas giant. The base had been left in hard vacuum and all equipment likely to be affected left in a nitrogen atmosphere. On this metal-scarce world there was nothing that he could readily make batteries from and the effort to alter the molecular substance of the material around him was not worth the time and effort.

What he had brought back from the store cupboard were solar cells and enough parts of a ruby laser to build something that would give them an advantage when Link-soo-shan attempted to storm the Imperial City. Kamiel altered his state of being to machine time and began to build the laser, capacitors and solar cells.

From time to time the silver blur would appear to freeze as Kamiel would switch from one state to another to do any frail and delicate work.

As the new dawn began, heavy rain began to fall over the lands of the Gnathe, filling the drainage ditches and irrigation channels. Kamiel walked over to the waste pit and surveyed the changed contents with satisfaction. All nannite activity had finished and two distinct materials lay around for gathering. The smell of the sulphur would have been distinct had Kamiel the ability to smell. As he did not breath it had not occurred to him to work on that biological sense. The three, tired Gnathe were feeling the effects of close proximity though and were not looking too happy.

"Right, my young friends," Kamiel said and pointed to the yellow material laying over the waste pit, "I need you to gather this material and bring it out of the rain. I will also need you to gather up the little crystals in a separate sack and bring it all to me at my workshop."

"What do you want this for, Kaameel?" asked the female that he had originally drafted into service.

"You will find out all in good time. When the rain stops, you are to take it up to the roof and dry it out, separately. Get more help if you need it and then get some sleep. Let me know when you are finished."

With that Kamiel strode quickly off to see how the male crafters had got on collecting the bones that he required for the other part of his plan. To his relief they were up and about, breakfasted and busy sorting out the bone yard gathered into one of the main halls. These Gnathe were a recent addition to the usual Gnathen profile and not designed to fight. Their claws had been kept to a minimum so that their hands were more adaptable like San-sool's. There had been no hardwood to be found so Kamiel would have to make do with what he had.

He picked up a fairly straight bone and made a nannite knife in his fist, showing them what he was going to do. He cut through the bone, a little way down from the knobbly joint at both ends. Picking up another one, he repeated the action. Next he found a smaller bone that would fit into the marrow cavity and cut it to suit, gluing it in place. The nannite picked up the other bone and fitted it over the peg sticking out and repeated the action. Kamiel now had the beginning of a lance that was light and strong. Next he trimmed down a hard piece of horn to fit in the end and glued that into place.

The males watched, fascinated, as the long spear took shape. Once Kamiel had added a third bone to the assembly, he had a sharp pointed weapon three times the length of a Gnathe. Kamiel had already engineered a number of his molecule-chained knives to hand round to his waiting apprentices.

"Right," he said to the eager crowd, "you have seen how I made these lances. Make as many as you can. Do not, I warn you, touch the sparkling line between the holding pegs or you will lose your hands. Do you understand me?"

The males all nodded to him and began work immediately with a cautious respect. They were used to taking orders without question and would not stop until they had all finished the tasks set for them so Kamiel left them to it and went to the next task. In the adjoining hall were stacked bundles of the willowy reeds that grew all along the irrigation ditches. The nannite being picked out some stems as thick as his fingers and showed the new group of crafters how to weave them into a rectangular shield. Satisfied that they were doing a competent job, he left them to it and made his way back to the royal area that Trann and Sing had taken over after Link-soo-shan had fled.

Alexander had spent a miserable night in the damp confines of the cave huddled up to the two Gnathe for warmth. He still felt very bruised and sore, but at least he could walk better now and pass his own water without San-sool's aid. He wriggled out of Nagoth's over protective grasp and felt the Gnathe awaken as he stretched out his arms. Immediately he could feel a colder draught passing over his bare flesh.

"Do you feel that cold air?" he exclaimed with excitement.

Nagoth and San-sool both extended their tongues into the darkness in front of them and slowly turned around. Suddenly they both stood very still, tasting the cooler air-flow as it moved over them.

"I feel it, Alexander," San-sool replied and moved slowly towards the faint air current.

"Me too," said Nagoth. "There is definitely a way out of this place, Alexander. Let us move towards it while the breeze is strong. First I must drink and eat something. Is there anything left in your sack, San-sool?

"Very little. I suggest that you catch some more of the creeping things that share this miserable place with us," the small male replied and snatched something off the wall by his side.

The three fugitives spent a quick hunting expedition gathering what they could, before making their way further down into the mountain. The pale light of the luminous growths led their way deeper and deeper, until the narrow way opened out into a large cavern. Water oozed down the walls and through the gravel at their feet and into a long shallow pool that wandered out of sight. There was nothing else to do but wade carefully along it to find out where it led. The cold water was up to Alexander's knees and occasionally he could feel things underfoot that wriggled away. Suddenly they were all aware that there was a lot more light than the luminescent growths on the walls could be putting out. As they carefully made their way around a sharp bend in the rocks, they could see light reflecting off the ripples in the water.

The further they splashed on, the lighter it became, until they could see actual sunlight on one of the craggy walls. The long pool came to an end and poured slowly over a stony lip in a large crack at the cave's end that went up into the roof. There was room for all three to stand side by side in the entrance to the cave. They stood there and looked over the lands of the Gnathe, far below.

Nagoth-shan looked over the edge and shivered in fright and said, "Well, that's it, Alexander, we've come to a stop. We can't get down that sheer face except to die!"

"You will be surprised," replied the human and grinned at the puzzled Gnathe. "I have a way down that will take all of your courage and your trust in me."

San-sool backed away from the sheer drop and shook his head in disbelief and gasped, "I for one will take some convincing. Gnathe were not designed to climb and I will take some convincing before I try getting out of here through there."

"When the time comes, I shall show you the way," Alexander replied. "Now what you must do is to gather as much food as you can and wait for my friends to get here. I must use the crystal and contact them again to tell them of our position."

With that Alexander sat down in the morning sun and concentrated his mind into the crystal matrix. As he had familiarised himself with Shoo-lin's crystal mind signature, it did not take long.

Shoo-lin felt the presence of the human leader enter his mind and acknowledged his connection with a warm friendly greeting.

"Hello Alexander. Are you feeling better?" he asked as he motioned to Fredrick hanging on to the back of Munch.

Fredrick signalled to Joom and Abdul that they should mentally connect to the male Gnathe and Coen-soo joined them. Alex gave them a quick update as to his and the two Gnathe's situation in the cave entrance. He quickly showed them what he had in mind to enable them to escape.

There was a stunned mental silence from the rescue party until Shoo-lin remarked, "We should ask the raptors if they think that they can do this, before we try this attempt. After all, you will only get one chance at this. I will ask Snapper if she thinks that it is possible."

Alexander replied firmly, "It will have to be tried. It is the only sensible way for us to go. Link to Snapper's mind and let me come with you and I will explain to her what I want your pets to do."

The raptor's mind was primitive and not constructed to understand complex ideas. So the human visualised what he wanted the raptors to do. Munch and Claws connected to the other raptor's mind and thought about the problem.

"We think that we can do what you want," they thought in unison and carried on the task of flying their small passengers towards the position of the escaped group.

Minnis spoke to Fredrick's ear implant, "What is going on between you? You all went very quiet. You only do that when you are talking telepathically."

"We were contacted by Alexander, using his crystal. He is safe and we are going to get him and his companions, before flying on to the Imperial City," said Fredrick and shifted about in his riding hollow.

Minnis listened carefully to what Fredrick told her about the Mayor's plan of rescue.

"Do you want to know what the odds of probability are for success with this idea?" the nannite replied.

"No, Minnis, I don't," Fredrick shuddered. "Alexander and the raptors think that it can be done and that is all there is to say on the matter. Where are we in relationship to where we think they are?"

"Another two days at least if we maintain this flying speed," the nannite answered, "but we must spend a little time surveying Link-soo-shan's settlement before we try Alexander's plan."

"All right, Minnis, I will agree to that," he replied regretfully. "I would rather make sure that Alexander is safe first, though."

"He will be hungry and cold, neither of which will kill him," Minnis dryly said and resumed her communications with Asue and Kamiel to update them on their progress.

Link-soo-shan stared at her group captain with simmering fury and spat, "What do you mean, that you could find no trace of him? He *can't* get out. I sent all of you ahead of him. All you had to do was slowly ride back and keep your eyes and hearing crest up and you should have found them!"

Jaffin's hearts pounded in fear as she cringed in front of the angry Brood-mother and replied, "We found the tracks leading to the gorge and then where the Zanth had been run off into the steep woods. We looked back along the trail as carefully as we could. The creature is nowhere to be found, Reverend Lady; nor are the two who aided him to escape. Maybe they threw themselves off the high cliffs to their deaths."

"They would not do that, Jaffin. The being called Alexander is no coward, whatever he is. No! Somewhere he is hiding from me and nursing revenge," she surmised, lashing her tail from side to side.

The powerful Gnathe strode out into the chill mountain air, held her crystal tightly and called her people to her side. Quickly the fighting females lined up in front of her, the youngest to the front with their bows and arrows and the original guards to the back. The rest of the captive Gnathe stood as close as they could, to hear what their new Brood-mother wanted from them.

Link-soo-shan stood tall and shouted to her people: "The time is close approaching the day that I take back what was taken from me. This day you will gather supplies for my army. Tomorrow I will take through a small fighting force to the old homestead of Connit and Bronn and establish a gate. I will then open the gate and bring my fighting force through and establish a base. We will rest and spy out the approaches to the Imperial City and see if anything has changed. When I am satisfied that all is quiet, we will attack and I will have the head of Trann-link-khann as a trophy in the Hall of Power."

Jaffin turned from the Brood-mother's presence, facing the apprehensive Gnathe and quickly reinforced Link-soo-shan's instructions with a bellowed, "Go!"

The crowd melted away and each Gnathe became very busy!

At the Imperial City, Kamiel was satisfied that the production of long lances and shields were going ahead without his supervision. Now it was time to show Trann's daughters how they were to be used. Jewel-khann and Natel-soo were hardened fighters forged in Trann's campaign to oust Link-soo-shan's guard in her absence. They were clever and brave females, loyal beyond any of the subjugated Gnathe.

Kamiel called them to him and said, "I must now teach you a different way of fighting against Link-soo-shan's guards that they will not understand."

They were quick to understand the new principal of shield and the long lance and made their way to the arena to practise the new manoeuvre. Kamiel had impressed on them the need for secrecy and that they must not be spied upon by any of Link-soo-shan's people. They had but a day or so to practise and no more.

Kamiel next checked on his chemical factory to see if all the ingredients were dry. To his satisfaction they had been turned to fine powder by the male crafters allotted this task. The kitchen Gnathe had hollowed out the gourds that Kamiel had asked for and dried out the insides by baking them along the edge of the fire pit. After this had been done they had been one-third filled with pebbles and sharp stones and left to dry further. The nannite had prepared the fuses himself and had mixed the raw gunpowder, not trusting the Gnathe with this task. For one thing he was not happy about the Gnathe learning too much about explosives at this point in time. It would be enough that they would see the devastating effect at first hand.

Up on the roof of the city his solar cells were soaking up power and charging the rows of capacitors placed next to the ruby laser. He had positioned this piece of equipment at the frontal approach to the city. His plan was to make this area seem undefended and this was where the main charges would be buried. It was now time to give the two Brood-mothers a demonstration. Kamiel picked up one of the primed gourds and made his way to the Imperial chambers.

He was still impressed by the way that generations of Gnathe had bent the genetic codes of almost every living thing on this new world to their advantage, this side of the central mountain ranges.

If the human's Seeder ship had not been blown out of orbit by the comet fall so many millions of years ago, none of these creatures would have evolved. Another Earth would have been formed without the Gnathe. They were the product of a life experiment without control, with a genetic makeup similar to humans, but with extra bits fitted in. Somewhere in their past, a different type of female had evolved to carry the fertilised eggs and had learnt to alter them genetically, to alter the form of the offspring. This was why the life on this world was so advanced only six million years after Jupiter had been stripped of its enormous gas mantle. The other possibility was that they had arrived on this world from somewhere else. Kamiel found that idea fascinating. Fortunately there was a molten iron core at the centre that gave off a magnetic field. The four largest moons were still in orbit, but the others had been lost when Jupiter's gravity had rapidly shrunk as it lost mass when the sun expanded. Kamiel often wondered where all the other nano-ships had ended up on their lonely journeys. None of them were expected to achieve the length of time that their ship had taken to re-awaken. It was most probable that the human beings living on this world were all of the representatives of their race in the whole of the Cosmos. This fact drove his programming and filled his mind with the overwhelming sense of purpose put there by his maker.

CHAPTER 31

▼

Shoo-lin began to recognise the outline of the valley below them in the morning light. It was the one where he had been introduced to the power of the bow. They were within a day or so from Link-soo-shan's new stronghold. He concentrated his mind to Coen-soo's and projected his awareness of the terrain below. The bitter cold wind sang along the edges of his insulated suit as the raptor glided down into a clearing in the woods below. There was a rocky ridge that stuck out from the heavily tree-covered valley. A wide plain stretched away into the distance towards the next stand of mountains. In the far distance large dark dots could be seen moving as a herd. These had been seen by the ever-hungry raptors and they were impatiently trying to let their small masters off, so that they could hunt.

The rescuer's minds were filled with the raptor's hunger and plaintive demands for release. Fredrick slid off the neck of Munch onto the stony ground and held his hand out to Abdul as he exited Snapper's riding hollow. Shoo-lin, Coen-soo and Joom rapidly followed suit. They watched as the raptors flapped into the air and made their way towards the unsuspecting herd. The three females dropped onto a group at the rear of the unsuspecting beasts and swiftly made their kills. The rest scattered in terror only to be picked off by another bigger raptor that fell onto one of them. It was a large adult male and it too was very hungry. It hissed and stared balefully at the females as it tore into the warm flesh of its kill. Nervously Munch, Snapper and Claws ripped their meals apart and quickly consumed most of them, always keeping one eye at least on their unwelcome companion.

Fed and feeling less aggressive, the male began to take an interest in the females. He sniffed the air and ascertained that these were young and not yet of breeding age. Other strange scents also began to make themselves known to his sensitive nose. The male edged closer to them to find where the unusual stinks were coming from. It was coming from something wrapped around the females' necks and bodies. He had no idea what the harnesses were. They made him nervous. These females did not smell right and he backed off, shaking his head from side to side. The inside of his head itched as the three other raptors tried to communicate with him as they did with their riders.

Finally he felt a voice in mind say, "We will share what we have killed."

Another mind said, "We have finished."

He projected a feeling of puzzlement and concentrated his mind on answering, "What are you?"

"We are as you," the answer came. "Come, finish what we have left and meet our companions."

"Are they what I smell upon you?" the male asked.

The females took to the air and projected back at the male in unison, "Yes."

The five riders had witnessed the impromptu meeting far down the valley and saw the forth raptor take to the air after he had finished what the females had left and follow the three females back towards where they had made camp.

"What do they think they are doing?" shouted Joom and built up the fire rapidly.

All of them cocked their crossbows and formed a tight group, eyeing the approach of their large companions.

"This is a wild one. To it we will just seem like morsels of food!" Coen-soo said in fear. "It's twice the size of our young females, with an appetite to match."

Fredrick frantically tried to contact the mind of his raptor.

"Munch, tell your new friend that we are not food! Stay between us and it," Fredrick ordered his giant friend.

"Not an it! He is very interested in you," replied the raptor indignantly. "We have told him you are special to us. He wants to see you and see what you are. Not food!"

The three females made a protective cordon around the companions and allowed the male raptor to approach them. Fredrick separated from the main group and waited for the big male to come closer. He could feel the arrogant power from the huge animal. This creature had never been challenged, except by others of its own kind at mating, and he bore the odd scar or two of conflict. Fred opened his mind and attempted to communicate with the massive creature. It was difficult as he had not had contact with their species before. The three females had been raised by their Gnathe and human companions and had learnt to communicate with them soon after hatching.

Minnis spoke through the ear implant, "Fred, be careful with this thing, it could swallow us whole. I do not think that I could save you from something this big. It has the advantage of mass and power."

Fredrick grunted and tried again to contact the creature's mind and felt the emotion of surprise shock through his consciousness as he made some sort of bridge.

"What you? Where from? Where you go?" the ideas spun through the human's mind as the creature regarded him closely. "What you want with females?" he asked suspiciously.

Fredrick attempted to explain how they had reared the females in a way that the wild raptor could understand. He tried to picture where they were going and explain some of their purpose and the danger they were in from Link-soo-shan if she should see them.

"Not safe, here with young females. I come too and protect against other males," he replied. "Breeding rights are mine, understand! When females are ripe!"

Fredrick hastily agreed and relayed the information to the others, who could hardly believe what the human said. They remounted their raptors and the four of them took to the air and headed towards Alexander's position, keeping an apprehensive eye on their huge companion.

Morning had arrived bright and sunny when Link-soo-shan assembled her six fighting guards around her. All had eaten and were ready to go. She had assembled the rest of her brood onto the space in front of her quarters and instructed them to be ready for the gate to open so they could quickly join her. All of them were well armed and provisioned for a prolonged stay in the Gnathen homelands. They did not want to attract attention until they were ready to take the Imperial City back into Link-soo-shan's control.

The Ultimate Ruler picked up her master crystal and concentrated her mind upon the young female she had found before. Again, she found that this pathway, along with some others, was not blocked by the slipperiness coming from the Habitat. Unobtrusively she infiltrated her mind and looked out from her eyes. The female was inside the homestead tending to the fire-pit in the kitchen. She was not alone. Other Gnathe were attending to the preparation of food close by. Link began gently to insert the idea that she needed to pass water.

The latrines were away from the kitchen and isolated from the rest of the homestead to minimise the smell. All nutrients would return to the Banilik tree that was the Gnathen home and help it to flourish. Everything was designed to re-circulate back into the living walls and feed the homestead.

Kin-loot made her way to the voiding trench and squatted over it to pass water. She was quite alone in the closed off area. The air in front of her went fuzzy and out of focus. Suddenly she found herself with company. A very large Brood-mother appeared with six well-armed Gnathe clinging to her legs and body. Before she could utter a sound, Link-soo-shan was into her mind for the location of Mace-loot-tighe and cut her throat with her syther. The female sank to the ground with a bubbling sigh and died.

"Find the resident Brood-mother while she is resting on her sleeping perch," Link commanded. "She is to be killed before she has a chance to use her command crystal. Go now and with stealth."

The six quickly made their way through the warren of the homestead towards the unsuspecting head of the household. Each had an imprint in their minds of the layout of this unfamiliar tree house. The two Gnathe with the bows were ready to pick off anyone who got in their way. Link-soo-shan followed quickly behind, carrying her all important gate crystals.

Jaffin was first into the sleeping quarters of the unsuspecting Brood-mother and swept the command crystal from off its stand with the edge of her syther. It rolled out of reach of Mace-loot-tighe's grasp and the startled Gnathe leapt from her perch towards the invading force. Two arrows buried themselves into her chest as she came towards them and brought her to a stop. One of Link-soo-shan's females thrust her syther under the Brood-mother's armpit from the side and into her lungs. They stood and watched her quietly die.

Link-soo-shan walked into the room and picked up the command crystal from the bloody ground. She replaced it on the stand and stepped onto the sleeping perch.

"Well done, my children, well done," she said, triumphantly. "Now gather together the household Gnathe while I contact Bron and Connit and action the next stage."

Kamiel primed the charge and was careful to show Jewel-khann and Natel-soo just what he was doing so that they could repeat his actions. Trann-link-khann and Sing-trow-sool were apprehensive when the nannite explained what was about to happen. He had buried twenty charges in a semi-circle in front of the main entrance some distance away from the Imperial City and a line to the nearest irrigation ditch. If all went as he expected, the explosives would create an instant moat in front of the open capital. Behind him the city was alive with curious eyes watching his every move. He had warned the Gnathe to drop their hearing crests as low as they could so as to minimise the noise. Now he unrolled the fuses back towards the city to the entrance.

"Jewel, bring the glowing embers and place it on the end of the fuse as I showed you and then run for cover," Kamiel called out to the worried Gnathe.

Jewel-khann ran swiftly over and tipped the pot of glowing embers onto the end of the fuses. Immediately they began to fizz and rapid sparkles made their way towards the buried gunpowder pots. The Gnathe covered the ground in swift leaps and swung behind the living wall of trees and dropped her crest as instructed. The line of smoke made its way across the ground until it disappeared from view into the earth.

There was a few moments of silence and then the area in front of the city erupted with a rolling explosion. Tons of earth and stones shot into the air and scattered far and wide, leaving a deep ragged trench in front of the Imperial City. Kamiel walked forwards and was very satisfied with the result. The trench was deeper than even a Brood-mother could reach and it was already filling with water from the irrigation ditches that Kamiel had breached with lesser charges. So far, his hastily thought out plans were looking favourable. He turned round to look at the wall of living trees that made the city's perimeter. Not a single Gnathe could be seen. Only a stunned silence prevailed. Slowly one by one the Gnathe emerged from their hiding places, led by Trann-link-khann, Sing-trow-sool, Jewel and Natel.

Kamiel walked back to them and said, "As I promised, we have something that Link-soo-shan has never experienced."

Trann strode over to the filling trench and looked in disbelief at the wide expanse of water rapidly covering the distance to the other side. She shook her head and covered her eyes in admiration of the silver being.

"Great Kaameel," she said in awe, "you are beyond our understanding. How can we lose! With this at our command we cannot fail."

"There is still much to do, my friend. Do not forget you have little Gnathe without any fighting skills. We have to outthink her and keep her at a distance and surprised," Kamiel replied. "I have not finished yet. Now that we have a moat in front of us we need a means of crossing it that will not aid the Tyrant, leaving her on one side and us on the other."

"How will you do that, Great Kaameel?" Sing answered, staring at the water-filled moat and back to the nannite.

"I now have to teach you about boats or, in this case, rafts," Kamiel said and made his way into the city towards where he had left the male crafters weaving shields.

He soon explained what he wanted them to do with the cut reeds that were not suitable for weaving into shields. He then organised them into dragging the bundles in front of the city walls and binding them together to make the rafts required. Satisfied that they could be left to carry on without him, he next turned to the clever young female, Natel-soo.

"Come with me to the roof top where I have your task to teach you in the coming battle," the nannite said and took her to where he had assembled the pulse laser.

Kamiel studied her hands intently. Ender's child had been genetically engineered very differently from the Tyrant's kindred. The talons had been reduced so that they were not predominant and the Gnathe had a better gripping hand than the Imperial Guards. She could manipulate the tools that Kamiel had produced far better than the city male crafters. Also, Ender-whann-soo had bred for intelligence and it showed in the quick way the female could adapt to strangeness. He explained what the device was supposed to do and Natel regarded him thoughtfully.

"Why do you not operate this weapon yourself?" she asked the silver being with surprise. "After all, you made it and you understand it."

"It will be difficult for you to understand, my young friend. I can teach you how to defend yourselves from Link-soo-shan, but I cannot attack her directly," Kamiel replied with exasperation. "I was made by beings that you could not understand, from a science beyond the human and chimpanzee people I am protecting. It was not thought safe at the time to give me that awesome power, or any of my kind. As it is, I have created a creature that is like me in many ways but without these restrictions."

"What is this thing that you have made, Kaameel, and where is it?" she asked anxiously.

"She is coming here and is controlled by a human, called Fredrick," he said. "Some of my friends are with him. They are coming on the backs of their raptors. They are the huge flying creatures that the beast-master Shoo-lin decided to rear when he was on his way to our Habitat a long way over the mountains. These are the ones who are trying to rescue my friend Alexander. They are still several days away."

Natel-soo swivelled the laser until it faced the approach to the city and looked through the telescopic sights at the terrain stretching into the distance. From here she could see over the crops in the fields and the network of roads that disappeared into the Gnathen Empire. All appeared to be quiet and at peace.

Link-soo-shan set the gate crystals in place and called to Connit and Bron with her command crystal: "Have them ready and I will open the gate."

She put forth her will and felt for the opening in the matrix. A connection was made between her mountain stronghold and the homestead around her. The area between the gate crystals shimmered and suddenly she could see her forces hurrying through as fast as they could. As they came through, they deployed to the sides so as not to block the entrance. The last creatures through were her Zanth, ridden by her elite guards. All was done quietly and with a minimum of noise and the quarrelsome beasts led round to the stock pens.

Link-soo-shan collapsed the gate and surveyed her army. The new breed she had created were all armed with the weapons built by San-sool. The young females had duplicated his arrow design. Once they had seen the pattern, it was easy to copy. The others were armed with sythers taken on raids when Link was learning to bend space. All had carried through enough provisions for several days. By the time the sun had set, the homestead had become an armed camp. All of Link-soo-shan's army had been fed and gone to their rest.

The Ultimate Ruler had left a small contingent of guards behind, just to make sure that any rebellious feelings by the captured Gnathe would not trouble Connit and Bron. They were mostly old, slow and not as fit as the troops she had taken through the gate and would do to keep order. The heavily pregnant brood-mothers would be obeyed in her absence by these guards without question, just as if the orders came from her.

In the quiet of the deserted stronghold, Bron turned to her sister and said, "Do you think she will regain her empire?"

"She is magnificent, my sister," Connit replied confidently. "With her crystal skills, I feel she can do anything. It will not be long before you and I will be seated on the royal perch in the Imperial City."

"I for one will be more than happy to get away from this cold mountainous place and back to somewhere that is warm, where the nights are not so cold. It was a great day when she released us from our blind servitude. I would follow her anywhere in gratitude for that alone." Bronn stretched herself up to allow the four young in her pouch to wriggle around.

She felt tired by the demands of the new life directed to her pouch by Link-soo-shan. Although she had been permanently pregnant since San-sool had repaired her eyelids, she did not complain. The Ultimate Ruler's mental reinforcements had seen to that. Both Brood-mothers would uncomplainingly stay pregnant until exhaustion took their lives, as it would, if they were given no rest from the constant breeding.

They were continually following Link-soo-shan's genetic patterns given to them by her overwhelmingly superior mind. All of the males and females would be born with hands and the enhanced intelligence that Ender-whann-soo's daughter, Jing-soo, had possessed. The Heretic's genetic engineering had been faithfully copied from the severed arm that Link-soo-shan had brought with her from the defeat of the Rite of Succession. The Brood-mother had studied the genetic improvements for a great deal of time before setting in motion her own breeding programme. What she had learned, she held in great respect and had taken great care to imprint the young Gnathe to her servitude. Although enhanced intelligence would have been of little use to the ruling of her old empire, she could see that it would be very necessary for the overthrow of Trann-link-khann and the Keeper, Sing-trow-sool.

Chang-soo-shan's heavy-duty guards were very good at overpowering the ordinary Gnathe, but were slow of thought and not very agile. They made good shock troops and Link had made sure that she had taken them with her through the gate. They would be in the front rows at the main attack. The captured household Gnathe were terrified of them and were quick to do their bidding. There was an atmosphere of relief that there were none left at the stronghold as night began to fall.

Asue sat at the control console, operating the satellite's telescope at the Habitat's science centre. She was worried about Alexander's condition and the way Kamiel's plans were coming together. There was so much that was completely outside of her programming. The male personality had capabilities that were beyond her comprehension. He could take risks that she would never do, particularly in the ability to accept the deaths of some of their people for the greater good. That made her mentally shudder. The new Minns was functioning as well as the old one, but she was not as the old Guardian had been. Asue mourned for her friend and regretted the loss of her personality. They had been built as a group, to function as a group and for many hundreds of years they had. Sharn and Asue had donated parts of their personality to blend with what they had salvaged from the wreck of Minns. Kamiel had added certain aspects of himself to the new personality—aspects he had remained silent about.

One thing had changed in the human and ape community. There were now two distinct groups, one living in the Citadel and one living outside, permanently genetically changed. These had integrated with the Gnathe and were building their own way of life side by side with the newcomers. Ender-whann-soo's people were willing to learn new ways of doing things, using tools created by the human and ape craftsmen. In turn, the technological people were eager to learn all they could about the fertile world outside the dome complex. Asue was content that things had turned out for the best, just as Kamiel had predicted. She still did not feel agreeable about the coming conflict. All of the lives under her care were valuable to her and she could not come to terms with Kamiel's different programming and his way of looking at the current situation.

She studied the view from the satellite's telescope again and felt uneasy about what she could see. There was something different about the stronghold that Link-soo-shan had created. Asue increased the magnification and swept the area, trying to see what it was that seemed different. It was very quiet for the end of the day. It was when she looked at the Zanth pens that it suddenly became obvious. They were empty!

"Could it be that Link-soo-shan had gone? Has she started her campaign to win back her empire?" she thought to herself.

Back and forth she studied the image of the Tyrant's realm, looking for any sign of her fighting force. She could only see a much-reduced population of Gnathe still working in the fields. There were a few larger females overseeing the work, but of the hundreds of fighting Gnathe there was no trace.

Asue did not waste any more time and concentrated her thoughts to the band that the Nannites used.

"Kamiel and Minnis," she projected urgently and felt their response. "Link-soo-shan has left the stronghold. She must have started her plans. Kamiel, be alert to her presence. Minnis, tell Fred and see what has happened before you go on to Alexander. How far are you from the stronghold?"

"We are approaching the valley as you speak, Asue," Minnis replied and relayed the information to Fredrick.

Fredrick looked down at the valley below and remembered their skirmish with Link-soo-shan and her fanatically loyal guards. Far below them he could see the hill from which they had rescued Ender, Khann and her household. It was casting a long shadow across the killing ground that Kamiel had prepared; it seemed so long ago. In the setting sun's last rays of light the stronghold could be seen, hugging the ground. A network of fields surrounded the living area. All seemed empty and quiet.

"We need to go down and spy out the area," Fredrick broadcast to his friends. "We will leave the raptors for the night. What we do not want is one of her kindred making a signal through their command crystal and warning Link-soo-shan that we are here."

"The prime objective is to obtain that crystal and prevent whoever Link has left here in charge from using it," Shoo-lin replied and added, "that seems like a job for two Gnathe!"

"Yes," Coen-soo agreed, "while we go quietly inside, the rest of you pick off any sentries that are on watch outside the stronghold."

"Remember, kill only Link's kindred. The other Gnathe are captive here and we do not want to harm them if we can," Fredrick said as they dismounted from the raptors harnesses. "Stay here, Munch," he projected to his large friend, "we will be back in the morning."

"We will stay with 'Leader of many' until you come back, Fred," the raptor replied.

"Leader! Is that what he calls himself?" Fredrick answered the female in disbelief and walked away into the dusk.

Minnis had noticed the sentries by their heat signatures and relayed the information to the others. As the two Gnathe made their way towards the entrance of the stronghold, Abdul and Joom circled round to get a clear view of the two females. They carefully sighted through the rangefinders on each crossbow and let fly together. Each bolt sped to its target and impaled the unsuspecting guard through the chest and lungs. They both died with very little noise. The ape and man retrieved their bolts and reloaded them to the reserve quiver.

Meanwhile Shoo-lin, Coen-soo and Fredrick made their way towards the stronghold. Shoo-lin noticed two pillars some lengths apart on each side of the trodden down road some way in front of the entrance. He motioned Fredrick over to them and pointed out the crystal set on top of each of them, fixed in position with clay.

"This must be the gate that she used to twist space and march her fighting force through," Shoo-lin remarked to Fred. "What shall we do?"

"I think I know," Fredrick replied and hurled both of the matching gate crystals far into the night.

A voice in his ear said quietly, "We have company, Fred. A large heat signature is approaching from the side of the stronghold to your right. Distance—ten metres."

"Thank you, Minnis," he answered and motioned Coen-soo to hug the wall to his left.

At that moment a large female Gnathe appeared around the side to stare in disbelief at the silver clad group. Before she could utter a sound, Fredrick put a bolt through her chest and leapt forward and held her mouth shut as she died, snapping her neck for good measure.

He threw her to one side and asked Minnis, "Any more to come?"

"No Fred, all other heat signatures are inside," the sentient battle-suit replied.

Fortunately all homesteads were grown to a similar pattern so the two Gnathe were fairly certain of where to go to find the other guards. They entered a communal eating hall and rapidly sent four other of Link's kindred to their deaths. The captured Gnathe stared with astonishment at the strangely dressed male and female.

"Who are you?" one of them asked, "and what is that thing with you?"

"We are here to rescue you from Link-soo-shan," Shoo-lin answered, "and this thing is called a human—he is my friend. There are two more of them outside."

"Are there any more Guards left behind?" Coen-soo asked as she retrieved her bolts from the dead females.

"No, but the two Brood-mothers are Link-soo-shan's creatures and obey her in all things," another small male replied. "They will need to be taken care of. What do you intend to do?"

"We must prevent them from using the command crystal and warning Link-soo-shan," Fredrick stated. "You must help us to do this. Someone has to go in to where they are settling down for the night and steal it from them. We will do the rest."

The first inkling that Connit and Bronn-loot-tighe had that anything was amiss was when one of the household females came into their sleeping chambers and took the command crystal from off the sending plinth. She ran out of the chamber before either of the heavily pregnant Brood-mothers could react. The next thing that happened, was two strangely dressed Gnathe entered, flanking a being that they had never seen the like of before.

Fredrick stood in front of the two larger Gnathe and said, "We are here to rescue you from Link-soo-shan and to return you to the lands of the Gnathe."

Bronn and Connit reacted with a hiss of fury, stepping off their sleeping perch and advancing towards the trio, ripping claws extended. Abdul and Joom took this moment to appear as well and stepped to the sides of the two large Gnathe. The two Brood-mothers stopped uncertainly and looked from side to side. They had seen the power of the bow and arrow unleashed by Link-soo-shan's clever crafting male, San-sool. They could not recognise the weapons trained at them as such, but they realised that they were some kind of bow. The five sharp points with barbed heads looked dangerous enough, pointed at them from each weapon.

"Back off, or we will kill you," Fredrick commanded and gestured towards the sleeping perch. "Get back onto your perch and face the other way. Shoo-lin, use the command crystal to contact Ender-whann-soo and Khann-link-sool. Ask them to contact these two and see what they can do to convince them to behave themselves."

Shoo-lin beckoned the Gnathe with the crystal forwards and took the crystal from her. He concentrated his mind into the Matrix until he was sure of the direction of the two Brood-mothers that he loved so much and sped through to make contact.

"Ender, waken," he implored with all of his strength.

The Brood-mother did so with speed and reached out for her Grand Brood-mother's mind at the same time. She listened carefully as the young male brought her up to date with all that they had done.

"We need to enter both minds at once to see what the Tyrant has done to these young creatures," Khann projected to Ender's mind, "before they try to do something stupid and get killed."

Both of the mind adepts selected a Brood-mother each and began to unravel Link-soo-shan's conditioning.

Fredrick and the rest of the group saw Bron and Connit stiffen and reach out with their arms and cradle their heads in pain, as Khann and Ender tried to undo the loyalty bonds that Link had forged. Sometimes the larger Gnathe whimpered and Bronn fell off the perch and lay on the ground in a pool of her own vomit. Connit began to shake and tremble and crouched low on the perch, swinging round to face the five invaders. Tears of pain flowed from her eyes and her breath came in gasps. Slowly she came erect and stepped down to her brood sister, helping her unsteadily to her feet. Weak and shaking with the effort, they once more stepped back onto the perch and regarded the silver clothed visitors with a different manner.

"We have been used by Link-soo-shan as her breeding pouches. Khann and Ender have undone the clouding of our minds. It is difficult to think independently again. We were blind for so many years and used then by Mace-loot-tighe. The great Lady Link gave us back our sight and our lives, such as it was," Connit gasped to Fredrick and drooped her head.

"Link-soo-shan will kill us when she comes back here," Bronn exclaimed with fear and loathing. "Against her power we are as nothing."

"We are on our way to prevent her from accomplishing what she has planned," Shoo-lin replied.

"What, five of you!" Connit exclaimed in amazement.

"There is more to us than you think," Fredrick replied with a grin. "We have to rescue our friend and leader Alexander first and his companions."

"Link-soo-shan did terrible things to him while she had him captive. How he escaped we do not know, or whether he is still alive or even where he is. He has many wounds," Bron answered and stepped off the perch to take a drink from the living bowl on the wall.

"We know where he is and in the morning we are going to fetch him to the Imperial City, hopefully before Link-soo-shan strikes," Fredrick retorted and backed out of the chamber, turned and walked away to contact Alexander.

CHAPTER 32

▼

Alexander sat wrapped in his blanket, huddled up to the warmth of the two Gnathe crouched on either side of him. The cave was dark and the wind blew relentlessly across the face of the high cliffs, filling the entrance with cold draughts. He was wondering how his friends were getting on at Link-soo-shan's stronghold when he felt the crystal's telepathic influence.

"Alexander, are you okay?" Fred's mind called to him from Shoo-lin's crystal link.

"I'll live. It's bitter cold in here, my old friend," he answered. "Bring me something warm to wear tomorrow and something to eat for me and my companions. How did you get on? Show me what happened."

Fredrick gave him all the information about their successful takeover of the mountain homestead and of Ender and Khann's turning of the two young Brood-mother's minds. Alexander concentrated his mind and broadcast to Nagoth and San the welcome news about the fall of the stronghold.

"What of the gate? Have your friends destroyed it?" Nagoth fearfully asked. "I would not like her to be able to come back with her forces."

"Fredrick threw the matching crystals far away from each other. The only way she can return is by carrying six of her fighters on her back. I do not think that she would risk that, as she will be too outnumbered. No, she will concentrate on the city," the human replied and huddled closer to the big female's warmth.

Nagoth trembled with desire for this ugly creature and had trouble controlling herself, but without the pheromone trigger of a Brood-mother's scent glands, Alexander was safe enough. She still felt it very strange to be able to think independently and not be governed by Link-soo-shan's implacable will. She wondered what the human had in mind for the morning. Going back the way they had come would be impossible as the way was too steep and slippery. Besides which, there were many twists and turns that would get them lost. It was only by following the faint breeze blowing up from here that they had found this cavern with its exit onto the world. At least they could see out and when the sun came up they would have light and some warmth. Also, Alexander had promised that there was a way to get down. Strangely, she trusted him to deliver on his guarantee.

San-sool, however, was not made of the same blind faith as the big female and crouched, worrying in the darkness, about the new morning's adventures. He was a city Gnathe, comfortable in his servitude and definitely not of an adventurous nature. His abduction by Link-soo-shan had been difficult enough to deal with, as his duties as healer to the medical centre had been uneventful. Still, if all went well, he would be back in the Imperial City again soon and that would suit him fine. It was the 'how' that bothered him, but he had been trained not to ask questions and the old habits died hard. Alexander's alteration of his mind allowed him to explore the new concepts of freedom of will and body, but he found it difficult to grasp how it would work. The threat of instant death had been part of his life for as long as he had been in service, and this had given him the habit of blind obedience. Continuance of life depended on each individual Gnathe being useful to their Brood-mother or the one allocated to them. Too many failures were rewarded by being discarded, sometimes for entertainment.

Alexander focused his mind, using his own command crystal, to try to find the Habitat science centre. All he could feel in that direction was a vast slippery area that, try as he might, he could not penetrate. Hannah had done her part well. At least there would be no more breaching of the Habitat's defences by the Ultimate Tyrant, whatever the outcome of the looming conflict. Next, he homed into the settlement outside the dome, looking for Ender-whann-soo and Khann-link-sool. This time he was successful.

"Hello, my two friends," he said. "All is well—the stronghold has been taken and the next stage is falling into place."

"That remains to be seen. Can you control that creature Nagoth?" Khann brusquely asked. "I do not trust someone that has been under Link-soo-shan's influence and mental control since she clawed herself out of her egg. What she did to you was an abomination."

"It was not something I would wish to repeat," Alexander dryly replied, "and provided she does not get a dose of your breeding pheromones I think I am safe enough. I still cannot remember all of the ordeal."

"We erased some of the experience from your mind. You nearly went insane," Ender-whann-soo answered. "How are your bodily functions and your wounded leg? Can you function alright without San-sool's help?"

"I can," the human projected to his alien friends. "I'm more than a bit sore, but past the worst. I will not rest until we have rid this world from Link-soo-shan's twisted mind. Tomorrow will be an enormous test of faith for my new friends. I have not told them yet how I intend to get them down from here."

There was a mental shudder from the two Gnathe as they thought about Alexander's risky plan for the morning. The one ability that they had bypassed when genetically designing the kindred, was the ability to climb. The fault line that straddled the super continent of the Gnathe from pole to pole had always kept them to the one side of the sheer cliff that erupted into the cloud layer. The colder atmosphere above the reaches of the Imperial gorge was another. Why explore an unproductive area when the Gnathen lands gave all that they needed? Their society was a farming community, living with a largely genetically designed landscape that they had spent thousands of years subduing. Hardly a plant or animal had not been adapted for use. The one exception was the great swamp, where the mountain reaches drained into the land. This area was just too dangerous to explore and had been ignored. Shoo-lin had been the only Gnathe to dare venture into its trackless wastes and he had only hugged the cliff face. His curiosity had driven him to explore, which is how he had found the hidden valley. Unfortunately, as the escaping household had found out, there was no way out other than the way in.

Kamiel spent the night burying the charges into the ground in a timed, scattered pattern in the approach to the moat. The city Gnathe would have to draw the over-confidant attacking force over the gunpowder loaded gourds and be in a safe place when they were detonated. This would be where the long lances and shields would come into play. Fuses would have to be laid back to the rafts floating on the moat and fired from there. Kamiel had made the fuses himself from dried animal hide and tinder dry plant material. He had tried many combinations before he had been satisfied with the results. All of the long fuses had been twisted around a ribbon of gunpowder contained in dry leaves with an oil-soaked outer layer. They burned under the sand with a swift and steadfast endurance. Kamiel hid the fuses at more than a hand's depth deep, inside a tough, thin flexible nannite pipe that had been programmed to produce oxygen at the touch of the heat generated by the burning fuse. At the far edges of the killing ground he had placed webs of nannite strands, stretched between posts to harvest any panic stricken Gnathe that attempted to escape in those directions. Everything that happened here would be the result of Link-soo-shan's aggression and not through any attack by the city Gnathe.

What Trann's people did afterwards was of no concern to him. All that was necessary was the death of the Ultimate Tyrant, combined with the extermination of her kindred and the binding of the two cultures together. Then and only then could Kamiel be sure that the colony would survive. The one thing he had to be sure of was to be out of Link-soo-shan's telekinetic reach. If she got hold of him again there would be no safe place to send his mind. His survival was of utmost importance to the human and ape colony, besides which he valued his own existence. He was pleased with the use that Fredrick had made of Minnis. The symbiotic relationship was working out exceedingly well. Minnis was gaining a definite personality from interacting with the giant human and Fredrick was learning how to control the sentient battle suit. The only thing that continually bothered him was the tagging along of the large male raptor. This was something that neither he, nor the rescue party could control. He picked up the heat signatures of a large Gnathe and escort approaching his position and turned to face Trann.

"Hello Trann," he said and looked up at the Brood-mother.

"Have you finished all of your preparations? Do you not need to sleep? I have come to find you," Trann said and crouched down to bring her face to the same level as the silver humanoid. "Do you think that she will come tomorrow?"

"To answer your questions," the nannite replied, "yes, I have finished all I need to do out here. No, I do not need sleep; and first, I think that she will spy out the approaches to the city before she comes. I think that it will be tomorrow or the next day that she will attempt to take control from your ruling council. Now go and sleep; tomorrow will come soon enough. I am going to signal my human friends at the Habitat to close down all communication through the crystal lattice so that she cannot twist space and appear in the Imperial City. She will have to come here by foot or not at all."

Trann straightened up and nodded to Kamiel. "I heed your words, Great Kaameel," she said and motioned her escort back to the safety of the Banilik tree city walls.

Kamiel sent his signal to Asue at the habitat's science centre and said, "Asue, contact Hannah and get her to increase the range of her blanket interference so that all crystal communications go silent."

"I will wake her this minute, Kamiel," the nannite replied and sent the signal to Hannah's sleeping quarters.

A sleepy face looked back at Asue's featureless silver countenance and said, "Yes, Asue. What do you want with me?"

Asue quickly told her and the petite woman quickly made her way to the experimental wing of the main laboratory, waking a few of her assistants on the way. Within a few minutes they were assembled in front of the apparatus that protected the domes and the Citadel from the attentions of Link-soo-shan.

Hannah said to her chief technician, "John, increase power and extend the field gently. Do not at any time put the crystal at risk. The rest of you keep a careful watch on the power output. Whatever you do, do not leave this equipment unattended. I will contact Asue to get feedback from Kamiel. I would think that Link-soo-shan's attack on the Imperial City must be imminent."

With that she signalled Asue at the command centre that they had hopefully put a blanket of interference completely over the Gnathen crystal communications Matrix.

Kamiel walked back into the city with Trann-link-khann and they made their way towards the sleeping quarters. The city was quiet and tense as the inhabitants attempted to get an uneasy night's rest. Sing-trow-sool looked up at the re-appearance of Trann and the nannite. The signs of stress showed on the Brood-mother's face and body and she trembled as she sat on the sleeping perch.

"What now, Trann? What new developments?" she asked, swishing her tail from side to side.

"You should take the time to see, instead of hiding in here," Trann testily replied. "The explosive devices are buried in the ground and laid ready. Great Kaameel has done all in his power to keep us safe. You had better find your courage from somewhere tomorrow and be prepared to swing a syther in your own defence."

"Now is not the time to argue," Kamiel commanded them and gestured towards the command crystal on its plinth. "Before you go to sleep, try your crystal and see if you can get through to anyone."

Trann placed her hands upon the faces of the crystal and projected her will into the familiar matrix.

"The paths are there, but closed off," she said. "I have never seen the like of this before. Every path is closed and communication is impossible."

Kamiel sent the signal back to Asue and said to Khann, "Now you can sleep a little easier, my friend. I still have things to do. I bid you and Sing-trow-sool good night."

With that the nannite turned and strode into the dimly lit corridors of the city and went to check on Jewel-khann's post at the pulse laser. He found her awake, but sleepy. She was fascinated by the night scope and had spent many hours peering through the pulse laser's telescopic sight at the approaches to the city.

"This is an amazing thing, great Kaameel. It turns night into a green day and anything alive glows!" the female said. "You are indeed strange people. I do not even know what you are. You have no smell and change shape."

"Where I come from and what I am, I cannot begin to explain to you, my young friend. All you need to know is that I am here to help you and defeat the Tyrant. She has done my people great harm and she must die. How and when, may well be in your hands tomorrow," Kamiel quietly replied and laid a silver hand on the Gnathe's shoulder. "Now I think it is time for you to sleep as well as you can. I will keep watch until morning."

Jewel-khann settled herself against the side of the roof support and closed her eyes gratefully. She was soon asleep, leaving Kamiel to think over all of his preparations for the coming bloody confrontation.

＊　　　＊　　　＊　　　＊

Jaffin watched as the first rays of the morning sun began to disperse the early morning mists that hovered over the irrigation ditches, criss-crossing the farmlands of the Gnathen Empire. It would soon be time for her scouting party to see what the situation was at the Imperial City. She was to go on ahead of the main fighting force and return to give Link-soo-shan whatever information she could. She missed Nagoth's presence at her side. They had fought together on many occasions and the big female was a reliable companion in any fight. What had changed her behaviour? The more that Jaffin thought about it, the more she found it incomprehensible. Nagoth had hated the human and after raping him under Link-soo-shan's influence, she would have been more than satisfied that old scores had been settled. Instead, she had vanished with the alien in the middle of the night, taking the healer with her.

All the old ways were changing. Jaffin was not used to change and ever since the Heretic had been rescued, her life had been turned upside down. One thing that was certain, it was good to be back home again. The Gnathen lands were much warmer than the higher regions beyond the swamp and Jaffin did not like the cooler weather that she had experienced whilst living there.

She moved out of the shelter of the captured homestead and sat in the warming rays of the sun for a few moments. It would not do to linger and waste too much time, or her new position as favourite would be soon over. Link-soo-shan had made it quite plain last night what she wanted Jaffin to do, so she sighed, turned and made her way quickly to where the younger females were stationed. She would need at least three of them who were competent with the new weapons produced by San-sool. Jaffin still marvelled at the new ability to kill over a distance. Her weapons were the syther and her talons, but she could see the advantages of the bow and arrow. Link-soo-shan would not like a pre-warning of her impending visit to the city and lose the element of surprise.

The household kindred had soon bent to the will of their new Brood-mother, particularly after Link had snapped the neck of a clumsy male who had been too slow in feeding her. As a lesson to the others, all had become much quicker in anticipating what needed to be done. Breakfast had been cooked and offered to the new occupying forces.

Jaffin ate a handful of roasted pod-vine fruit, snatched a piece of meat from off a platter and called out, "I need three of you who are good with the new weapons and I mean the best."

The group surrounding the table of food turned and faced her and three of them stepped forward in her direction.

"We are good with the bow, Group Captain. I am called Bilt, she is Frad and the male is named Morrit," the young female replied. "Where are we to go?"

"We are to get as close as we can to spy on the Imperial City," Jaffin said. "Any that see us must not live. Do you understand? You will be my eyes and ears while I see what changes have been made while the great Lady has been in exile." The Group Captain turned to make her way out of the captured homestead towards the penned up Zanth.

Alexander woke and began to wonder just how he was going to persuade his companions to trust him and blindly do as he asked. Somehow he was going to have to explain his plan to them and gain their confidence. As he moved, Nagoth and San began to stir also, stretching their cramped limbs, letting in the cold air. The two Gnathe squatted to empty their bladders while Alex stood and urinated, wincing with a little pain. At least he was able to do this for himself now and no longer needed the help of the healer with his telekinetic crystal. The arrow wound in his leg was mending faster than he had anticipated. The melding of human and Gnathe that had taken place in his body, due to Khann-link-sool's incredible piece of genetic engineering, had given him a faster healing rate than in the past, as well as a stronger skeleton. The cavern was cold and Alexander felt as if he had never been warm. The water flowing through over the edge of the cliff was bitter and the same temperature as the rocks it flowed through. As the sun began to shine into the cave, the human began to feel a bit better as he warmed up a little.

"How are we going to get out of this place, Alexander?" asked San-sool anxiously and stared out at the view over the cultivated lands far below.

"My friends are coming to take us away from here. It's a bit difficult to describe to you so I will show you telepathically." Alexander held out his hands. "Join hands and hold mine and I will show you just what we are going to do."

He concentrated his mind and showed Nagoth and San the raptors and their relationship with his human and alien friends. Next he visualised what he had in mind.

San-sool let go and stared at Alexander in horror. "You must be mad!" he shouted at him and grabbed the large rock beside him in a death grip.

Nagoth-shan just stood transfixed as she tried to get to grips with Alexander's proposal.

He let go of Nagoth's hand and said quietly, "It is the only way down from here. I will get my friends to fly past so that you can see what I have shown you is true. You will have to go first, as I will have to be in contact with Fredrick to get the timing right."

San reluctantly let go of the large rock by his side, trembling with fear and shock.

He looked Alexander in the face and replied, "Is there no other way?"

"Not unless you want to live out your life in this cold damp cavern," Alex answered. "Just try to think that you will be safe and warm soon, standing on the ground far below. Also, my friends will have brought civilised food for us to eat and we can make our way towards the Imperial City."

"We die here or we die there," Nagoth grimaced and turned to stare out of the split in the cliffs. She watched the water spill into empty space from the dark lake behind them and added, "I will chance not dying here of old age and cold. We must do as Alexander says. He will follow us, San-sool, and I believe him. Where else can he go? Besides, we may see Link-soo-shan's downfall and I for one would give a lot to see that."

"Right, my friends, I will try to contact Fredrick and see where they are," Alex replied and concentrated his mind through the crystal link.

No matter how hard he tried, he could feel nothing from the matrix. It was still there, but shut off.

"This was going to be harder than usual," he thought and let go of his newly formed command crystal.

"The crystal paths are closed," he said to his companions. "I will have to try to contact Fredrick with my own telepathic powers. I do not know how far away he is and I will have to try hard. Keep me warm, as I may go unconscious while I am doing this."

Alexander relaxed into the strong arms of Nagoth and sent his mind out towards where he felt his rescue party would be. He could feel himself wrench free from his body and soar out of the cavern. Up, and up he climbed, until he was over the top of the cliffs and making his way towards the stronghold. Down again until at last he could see the three raptors he had got to know, flapping their way towards him, carrying his friends. Close behind was the shape of something that took his breath away. It was equally as big as the raptor that had flown alongside Rescue One as the airship had made its way towards the lands of the Gnathe. He swooped down towards Munch and Fredrick and entered his friend's mind.

"Hello Fred. Good to see that all are safe this morning," Alexander projected. "Is everything planned? I have explained to my two companions what they have to do and they are terrified." He added: "All communications are down on the crystal link, so we will have to communicate this way."

"We know what we have to do, Alex," he replied and patted the scaly hide of Munch. "We will not be long now."

"Can you control that big raptor?" Alexander inquired. "What does he want?"

"None of us can quite make out, but we think it may come down to sex. Shoo-lin thinks that the species is rarer than you think and for a male to stumble onto three unmated females is an opportunity not to be missed. Shoo feels that he will stick close by until they are ripe for mating and there is nothing that we can do about it," Fredrick replied. "So far he has been quite easy to get along with. The other raptors call him 'Leader of Many,' although just how many we don't know."

"Well, as we can do nothing about it, we will just have to get on with what we are going to do. I will wait for you to fly past the opening in the high cliff face before I contact you again. Goodbye for now, my good friends," Alex said and withdrew.

He came out of the trance to find both of his new Gnathen friends bent over him with great concern as he lay in Nagoth's arms. His body was bitterly cold and his teeth were chattering. He snuggled deeper into the big female's grasp to get warmer and pulled his cloak around himself as he did so.

"Keep a lookout of the entrance of this cave and tell me when you see my friends," the human said and went to sleep.

San-sool crept to the windswept hole in the cliffs and shuddered as he surveyed the drop down to the fields and homesteads far below and said to Nagoth, "I am scared out of my wits, Nagoth. I was a city Gnathe, a healer and crafter, not made for adventure."

"Of such poor clay are heroes made!" Nagoth replied as she kept the sleeping human safe and warm. "You will live through this and gain status in the new order of things. The future that Alexander has shown us will come to pass. I was there when his people defeated the Tyrant and she lost her empire. Alexander has not told me all that they have planned against her."

"What else do you know, Nagoth, that I do not?"

"You have not met the silver being that is called Kaameel. I have. It is a made thing, not born! It does not think like us and it adapts to situations quicker than we do. It is at the city helping Trann-link-khann," Nagoth answered. "They can make things that are beyond our understanding. We did not think of the bow and never thought to grow the springy wood that it is made from. Our fighting forces were genetically engineered just to be a powerful weapon. We overwhelmed our enemies by being heavier and better clawed. These strange people can still win, although they are smaller. They fight differently. They can kill at a distance, something that we never thought of doing except short range with a Kryte. I believe that Link-soo-shan is cleverer than any Gnathe that has ever lived. Trann is no fool, however, and thinks differently. She has also two powerful telekinetic crystals and I think she can be as adaptable to the new ways as Ender and Khann have been. As I say, I would like to be there to see her downfall and if I have to throw myself off this cliff to do so, then so be it."

The two Gnathe settled down to wait for the arrival of the raptors and were lost in their own thoughts as the sun climbed higher in the sky.

Link-soo-shan sat uneasily on her captured perch and reviewed the situation. All had gone according to plan, so why was she so ill at ease? She reached for her twin command crystals to spy out the territory inside the Imperial City and concentrated her mind into the Matrix. Nothing! It was as if a slippery wall surrounded her mind. This was just like the human settlement, only now it was widespread over the whole of the familiar communication system. It was as well that she had shifted her forces when she did. She had outwitted her enemies by striking first and had got here before they had shut her out! Now she felt much better. She checked that her stolen telekinetic crystal was not influenced by this new effect and was pleased to see that it did not.

If the communications were out, that would enable her to raid any home-steads on the way to her confrontation with Trann and the coward who ruled with her. She would take great pleasure in re-acquiring all that had been hers. As for the Keeper! She would keep her alive as long as possible to torment, but Trann's head would be the first to go, just to show her power to the other ruling families. There would be no more interference to her rule, not now she had the secret of twisting space. She could come in the night to any of the ruling families and quietly kill them. With the knowledge of the bow and the genetic codes for human-like hands to wield them, a whole new world beckoned to her for the tak-ing. Power would be hers again.

This morning it felt good to be alive!

She stepped off the sleeping perch and walked to where the smells of fresh baked food wafted up the corridor. Link drank from a gourd filled with sweet Banilik sap, stuffing a handful of toasted Pod-vine nuts into her mouth and chewed them up with satisfaction. There were fresh baked fruit buns to be had and roasted meats laid out for her attention. She stared round at the attentive household kindred waiting for her every desire to be fulfilled.

"Funny how one snapped neck will get me the attention I require," she thought to herself with wry humour.

At that moment one of her new breed came to her and said, "Great Lady Link, Jaffin has departed towards the Imperial City at daybreak. She has taken Bilt, Frad and Morrit to spy out the approaches to the city."

"That is good, young one. Now fetch to me some of my older guards that came with me to the hidden valley. I need those that have the rank of captain," ordered the Brood-mother and continued her breakfast.

CHAPTER 33

▼

The three female raptors with their attentive follower soared over the edge of the high cliff and, catching the updraft, folded their wings. They stalled for a moment, then dropped down towards the fields far below. Half way down, they opened their leathery wings again and sped along the cliff-face searching for the opening that Alexander had described to them. They were looking for a thin trickle of water that gushed out of the rock-face and into the void below. This high up it would turn into mist long before it reached the bottom. As Munch went into a long glide, Fredrick saw the area that Alex had described to him. The cliff was sheer and almost featureless with hardly any cracks or bulges up or down, just the steady thin fall of water issuing from it.

Fredrick assessed the problem from his side and flew Munch as close to the face as he could. He was too far out to reach the opening and the entrance to the cavern was too small to get a toehold on the edge. There were only two possible options. The rescue attempt would have to done such that each raptor would have to fly at the cliff and twist, to glide along the face with one wing tip down. The problem with that method would be the damaging force of the sideways impact.

No, the only other way would be to soar up and snatch the Gnathe and human out of the air in front of the opening as they jumped. There would be no second chance. Either way the three of them would have to jump into the empty air, one by one, just before the raptor appeared. Indeed it would be a leap of faith.

Inside the cave the two Gnathe had momentarily seen something huge and leathery go flapping by the entrance. Nothing in their lifespans had prepared them for such a sight. What they had just seen was brief and unbelievable. Now that the opening had been found, all three raptors gave the cave a fly-pass. Fredrick coaxed Munch to hang on a thermal while he assessed the situation. The two Gnathe stared out at the new arrivals with apprehension and growing dread.

Nagoth shook Alexander awake and said, "I think your friends are here."

He stood up, walked to the entrance with the sun streaming in, and splashed some of the bitter cold water on his face from the pool as he came.

He concentrated his mind to that of his old friend: "Hello Fred, what do you think? Is it possible or do we die of old age in here?"

"Munch is confident that it can be done, but you must jump out as far as possible so that she does not scrape the cliff-face. You will have to be last, so that we can time it right for each person," replied Fredrick anxiously. "Get your people ready and let me know when the first one is to go. Coen-soo says she will go first with Claws."

Alex turned to the two Gnathe staring into the empty space outside the cavern where Munch was still hovering as she caught the thermal, now some distance away. San-sool had a death grip on the side of the entrance and had now shut his eyes, shaking his head from side to side and moaning.

Nagoth stood transfixed.

Slowly she turned to Alexander and said, "Is there no other way?"

"No," Alex replied. "Think of the city and Link-soo-shan's downfall. If you want to see both of those things, it is the only way."

"In that case I will go first," she answered quietly and turned to face the exit. "If nothing else it will show San-sool that it can be done. What do I have to do?"

"You will have to run and jump as far out as you can and Coen-soo will get Claws to catch you on my order. Keep your arms tight to your body as you jump. You will have one chance only. We will follow you. You will be safe if you do exactly as I say. San, open your eyes and watch Nagoth. Do just as she does. I promise that you will survive this. You can do it," Alexander insisted and motioned Nagoth back into the cave.

The human put his hand on Nagoth's muscular shoulder and said to her, "I need you in the struggle to come. I will not fail you. When I clap my hand on your back, you must go. Do you understand?"

Nagoth turned and popped her long tongue out and caressed Alex's cheek and whispered to him, "I am ready."

As she turned and crouched into a running stance, Alex contacted Fredrick, "Nagoth is ready. Let me know when," he said and lifted his hand.

Fred waved to Coen-soo and she started her flight towards the cave exit. She pulled the raptor into a dive towards the cave and began to pull her up.

"*Now*, Alex!" Fredrick called with all the power of his mind.

Alexander slapped the big female on her back and Nagoth took off towards the edge of the cave. She hit the edge with a bone jarring thud and leapt off into the void with her arms tucked into her sides. The wind caught her and she hung for a moment, before she began to fall screaming into the depths below. Two large, clawed and bony feet suddenly pinned her arms to her sides and she began to feel herself flying upwards. Bitter cold air rushed past her body as the raptor wheeled in the sky and turned towards the ground far below. She looked up, to catch a glance of a female Gnathe leaning out and looking down at her from around the leathery creature's neck. Coen-soo waved to her and pointed down as they began to drop.

San-sool looked down with anxious fear and turned to Alexander. "I too am ready. I must go soon, or I will never go!" he said and stood where Nagoth had just started her run.

"Next one, Fredrick. Let me know when," he projected, patting the small male on the top of his arm and giving him a friendly squeeze. "You can do it. Think of the tales you will tell when you are back in the city. You will have much status. The females will demand your attentions. Brood-mothers will be eager for your genes," he reminded the healer.

"Now again, Alex!" came the instruction from his friend.

The human clapped San-sool on his back and yelled, "Go, my brave friend!"

The small male hopped towards the exit and picked up speed. He flung himself out into the morning sunshine as far as he could. He shut his eyes and clasped his arms around his skinny body and began to fall. Snapper and Shoo-lin effortlessly flew up the cliff face to meet him with Abdul hanging on for grim death behind the beastmaster. Once more a cage of strong, well-clawed and bony feet caught the Gnathe safely in its grasp and made for the ground.

"Just you left, my old friend," projected Fredrick. "Are you ready?"

"Tell me when and I will go," replied Alexander. "The other two are okay?"

"They're fine. Now let me get you safely on the ground," he replied.

Alex made himself ready. His stomach turned to water and he felt more frightened than he had ever been as he made his way to where his two new friends had started their running jump into empty space.

"*Now* Alex!" came the command and he started his run.

Just before the edge he felt a devastating pain in his leg from the arrow wound and felt it collapse. Alexander fell to his side, felt the rough edge of the lip on his hands and shoulder as he slipped headfirst over the edge. Munch and Fredrick were split seconds too soon and the raptor's claws snapped uselessly at the empty air. The thermal filled the raptor's wings and they soared above the exit, too far away from the cliff-face to catch him as he fell. The spray of the cold waterfall drenched him as he turned over and over in the air, occasionally knocking against the granite outcrops. Faster and faster he fell towards the fields below.

A terrified telepathic and vocal scream for help erupted from Alex as he dropped further down towards his certain death.

The male raptor had watched the antics of the females with some bemusement. He could see what they had done and had watched the last small creature come sliding out of the cave in the sheer cliffs, only to be missed. He felt the creature's cry of terror and its plea for help as it fell to a certain death under the mist of the waterfall. It knew that this thing was of value to the three young females and that it would make a good mating gift, so he angled his wings to drop onto an intercept course. It would be a close thing, he could see, as the creature was too close to the surface of the cliffs to be picked up by his feet. He would have to grab him by his mouth and just hope that his sharp teeth did not do too much damage.

As Alexander hit another small outcrop he saw an enormous shape hurtling towards him. It was far too large to be one of the tame raptors. It had to be the wild male that had tagged along. He kicked out at the bulge and felt himself move out from the rock-face by several feet. Alex saw the raptor's jaws open and more teeth than he could ever count come closer to him. The hot foul breath covered the human in a wet fog. A sticky tongue curled out and wrapped itself around his body, drawing him into the immense jaws. It suddenly went dark and wet as 'Leader of Many' readjusted the wriggling morsel of food in his mouth so that he did not bite down and swallow it. He partially opened his jaws to allow the creature inside to breath and made his way down towards the others. He could sense the flood of relief and gratitude coming from the morsel of food in his mouth.

Finally he was aware of a voice in his head that said, "Thank you—you saved my life. If I can ever do anything for you, just ask! I am called Alexander."

He nearly spat out the creature in surprise, but replied, "What are you, creature with the name that says nothing? I asked the others what do you do with these females. I could not understand their reply."

"We raised them. They are our friends and help us, just as you have just done," Alex replied and tried to explain by telling their story in picture form.

It was difficult to get the ideas over to the male raptor. It was like trying to speak and teach a language to a brilliant child that had been used to talking and thinking in images. The capability was there. This creature was an intelligent being, but much more alien than the tame raptors the Beast-master had raised with Fredrick and Coen-soo. They had been amongst the people of the settlement, outside of the Habitat, since hatching from their eggs and had grown up with an adopted language of sorts. Alex knelt in the front of Leader of Many's mouth and watched the ground come closer and closer. The other three raptors were down and the human, ape and Gnathen passengers were standing, watching his approach. The wild raptor stretched out his wings, stalling over the group and dropped to the ground besides them. He lowered his great head and spat Alexander onto the dirt in front of himself in a sticky heap. The human leader stood up and tried without success to clean off some of the mess. Alex noticed an irrigation ditch and jumped straight into it and gratefully submerged himself. After a few moments he dragged himself out with the help of Fredrick and dried himself off with handfuls of leaves.

Fredrick picked Alex up and hugged him.

"I thought you were a dead man for sure," he said. "I just could not get to you in time. You fell out just underneath us and Munch missed you. What happened? Did you trip?"

"My leg gave way, where I took an arrow back at the Citadel," Alex replied and wriggled out of his friends grasp. "Now before we do anything else, can we have some cooked food? We are near starved to death!"

Joom passed over a sack of toasted pod vine nuts, fruit buns and cooked meat to Alex and said, "Eat, old friend, and you two as well. We have heard all about how you rescued my leader and friend, Nagoth. We are well aware of the risk you both took."

Nagoth looked uncomfortable and replied to the ape, "Do you know also that I fought you and what I did to your friend?"

"We know," answered Shoo-lin, "but we also know that you were under the influence of Link-soo-shan. Her mind is more powerful than any other Brood-mother I have known. You are not to blame."

"When you have finished stuffing your face, I have something else for you," said Abdul, grinning at Alexander's steady chewing and swallowing. "We brought you a suit to wear, unless you have grown over fond of those rags! Not only that, the suits are all fitted with a sliver of crystal taken from the one that Hannah found. Once activated by a small electric current supplied by the suit, it will make the wearer impervious to Link's telekinetic crystal and her crystal amplified mind."

"Things are looking better by the moment," Alex replied and stripped naked to pull on the insulated suit. "The problem we have is that there are more of us here than the raptors can carry. I do not want to leave anyone behind."

"What can we do?" asked Fredrick.

Minnis answered for him. "Alex will have to talk with the wild raptor and persuade him to carry two or more of you."

Alexander stared at the battle-suit that enveloped Fredrick's giant form and replied, "You must be Minnis, Kamiel's creation. A good idea, but I cannot guarantee that our new friend will go along with that proposal. I will try him and see."

'Leader of Many' was paying the three female raptors a great deal of attention, eagerly received, when Alex walked up to him and tried to get his awareness. The wild male saw him coming towards him and turned towards the small human. He dropped his head onto the dirt and stared at Alexander.

With some difficulty he tried to engage his mind to the intelligent creature that had ridden down in his mouth and said, "You are undamaged?"

"I am unharmed and owe you my life. If you are willing, we still have a way to go and require your assistance," replied Alexander, as he stood looking up at the great creatures eyes.

"Ask of me what you will," answered 'Leader of Many'.

Alex projected his needs to the raptor and tried to explain what they were trying to do and also the need for secrecy and the danger. He did not want the raptors to fly over Link-soo-shan's captured stronghold and alert her forces. Besides which, he was not sure of her telekinetic range and did not want to risk any of his meagre forces. They would be better used at the Imperial City.

As the immature female raptors were going in that direction anyway with their companions, the male agreed to take Alex and the two Gnathe he had seen rescued by Snapper and Claws.

Alexander made his way back to the group, smiled at Nagoth and San and said, "Your adventures have not yet finished. You get to fly again—on the back of our new friend."

San-sool drooped his head for a moment and whispered to himself, "Does this madness ever end?"

"Where you go, I will follow, Alexander," Nagoth stated and walked slowly up to the big male raptor. "Where do we sit and what do we hold onto?"

Alexander climbed upon a hind foot and wriggled onto Leader of Many's back until he gained the position at the neck and shoulders just in front of the wings. Fredrick threw a rope up to his friend and they looped it twice around the wild raptor's neck.

"We sit here and I will hold onto the first rope around the raptor's neck that Fredrick has kindly tied around. You hold onto me, San, and Nagoth can hang onto the other loop," he replied. "Come on all of you, we have much to do. We will fly low along the cliffs until we sight the Imperial River and then follow it to the City. I want to enter from the back and we can land in the arena where Trann fought Link-soo-shan. Fredrick, call Kamiel and get him to prepare the city Gnathe for our coming. Get them to kill a few Zanth or an old Carrier beast for our hungry raptors—it will help to give our flyers an incentive to know that they will be fed when we get there. Now let us go."

Shoo-lin, Joom and Snapper took the lead and the other raptors launched into the air and followed on, keeping as low as possible and making a great deal of use of the morning thermals. The working Gnathe in the fields stopped and stared in disbelief as the four great beasts and their small riders flapped through the skies.

The scouting party had put a great distance between the captured homestead and themselves when Jaffin called a halt. All of the roads that had been travelled by them had proved empty. Workers were not tending the fields close to the city and there was an eerie silence, apart from the hum of insects and the occasional chirrup of a flying creature. There was a feeling of expectancy in the air. Jaffin-shan, Group Captain and seasoned fighter that she was, was experiencing an unreasoning unease.

"You three, listen to me," she said. "We are not far from the city approaches and we must not be seen. You have never been here before and you have never seen a city. I have lived here for all of my life. It is large, ancient and has only one main entrance. The walls are immensely thick and cannot be breached or scaled. We must fight these City Gnathe outside, where we can kill many of them before the main force can storm the city. For now, what I have to do is to see what defences they have prepared for us."

"What do you want us do, Group Captain?" asked Morrit and loaded his bow with an arrow in readiness.

"Dismount, tie the Zanth to the fence posts and move on up the road on foot. We will go on each side of the road. I will go first, along the left side, keeping close to the irrigation ditch vegetation. Frad, you come with me."

The Gnathe split into two forces, edged up the road toward the city and climbed a gentle rise. At the top they stopped and melted into the reeds alongside the ditches. Jaffin strained her eyes to take in all of the changes that had taken place.

In front of the ancient Banilik trees that fronted the main entrance to the city, was a huge irrigation ditch in a semi-circular shape. On her side of the water, was an assorted collection of city Gnathe, with some of Trann's fighters amongst them. They looked a pitiful bunch. Link's disciplined troops would overwhelm them in moments. Jaffin could see no signs of the deadly bows and arrows that Link's new people carried. The Group Captain was not surprised, as the springy wood that made up the bows did not grow in the lower regions of the farmlands. All that they had, that was a bit strange to her, were a lot of rectangular shapes stacked in piles and some ridiculously long spears that were far too heavy to throw. Jaffin dismissed them from her mind. All along the edges of the centre of the large ditch were some kinds of structures made from reeds. What their purpose was she could not fathom as they did not cross the water. If it was a bridge, they had not yet finished constructing it. The forces this side of the water would be trapped against the ditch and soon annihilated by Link-soo-shan's heavy troops and archers.

The great Lady would be pleased by her observations. Jaffin felt that it would not be too long before she once more lived in this city again with servants to look after her and keep her old quarters clean. She motioned Bilt and Morrit back the way they had come and walked quickly down the road towards the tethered Zanth.

On the city roof, Jewel-khann had spent this time observing the scouting party through the pulse laser's telescope and had sent a runner to fetch Kamiel.

The nannite soon appeared at her side and said, "What have you seen, young one?"

"A scouting party, on the other side of the river, Great Kaameel. Four of them, three with the weapons you described to me, one Gnathe quite larger. They have seen our preparations and have retired. What should we do?"

"We do nothing as yet. Make the forces at the front aware that Link-soo-shan is on her way soon. My friends will soon be here. Now you will see a sight that will fill you with awe indeed. Scan the skies to the back of the Imperial City and you will see them arrive," Kamiel answered and pointed behind them. "Do not be afraid of what you are about to see. I have told Trann and Sing what to expect and they are busily telling the other city Gnathe. Keep a sharp lookout in my absence as I have someone that I need to welcome."

With that Kamiel made his way to the arena where the city butchers were busily dispatching some fat and elderly Zanth. He scanned the sky with his extended vision and could make out four dots coming their way.

"Clear the arena!" he shouted and waved the Gnathe out of the way. "My friends are coming very soon. Wait until I say, then you may come close."

Trann-link-khann made her way towards the side of Kamiel and said, "I shall be pleased to meet your leader and your other friends, Great Kaameel. I find it difficult to imagine what they look like!"

"You shall soon see. There—can you see them approach?" the nannite replied and pointed towards the rapidly visible raptors. "They are flying low over the back of the city now."

The new ruler of the Gnathen empire stood her ground, although her eyes nearly popped out of her head, as first one, then the other raptors stalled over the arena and flapped down onto the sand. There was not much room for anything else! To her increasing amazement a number of Gnathe climbed down from the neck and shoulders of the fearsome beasts. These were joined by four strange looking beings that walked the same way as Kamiel. They were covered in silver, like the guardian. One was much taller than the other two and one of the others was not quite the same build as the other three! The moment that the riders were off the backs of the flying creatures the large beasts began to noisily feed on the butchered Zanth. It was an unnerving sight. The city Gnathe watched from the safety of the arena ramparts, hardly able to believe their eyes.

Alexander walked up to Trann and looked up at the transfixed Brood-mother.

"I bid you greetings and friendship, Trann-link-khann. Where is Sing-trow-sool? I expected to meet you both," the human leader said.

"She is close by," Trann replied and beckoned the nervous co-leader out from one of the arena entrances. "See, she comes now."

Sing slowly made her way towards the group, never once taking her eyes off the feeding raptors for a moment. Finally she stood by Trann's side and looked down on the much smaller form of the human leader.

"You are Alexander," she said. "I have been in your mind and Ender-whann-soo owes her life to you and your people. Now we will owe ours to you also."

Trann suddenly caught sight of Nagoth, trying not to draw attention to herself and said, "You were Link-soo-shan's creature! You are the reason she still lives and is a threat to us all. Why should I let you live?"

Nagoth hung her head and replied, "My life is yours to take, Great Trann, if you feel that it is the only debt that I can pay. I am guilty of many crimes, I know, but that was when I was indeed the Tyrant's creature. Alexander set me free from her influence and I will willingly give my life in the struggle to defeat her."

"This is true, my Brood-mother," Shoo-lin called out in defence of his old adversary. "She saved Alexander's life."

"I know, but I still distrust her," Trann answered.

"Enough!" Kamiel exclaimed impatiently and walked swiftly up to the group and gripped Alex by the shoulders. "We need to talk, you and I. Link-soo-shan has sent a scouting group to spy on the city's defences no more than an hour ago on the main approach road."

Alex turned to Fredrick and said, "Find them, Fred, and spy out her advance to the city. When you have seen all that you can, report back to Kamiel and myself. Try to avoid any conflict if you can. We will achieve more by the Tyrant coming here with over-confidence than full of suspicion."

"Okay boss. I will tell Munch to stay here before I go," he replied and walked over to the group of raptors before he left.

San-sool hopped over to Alex and Trann and said, "I would like to go to the medical centre, where I will be of the most use when the conflict starts."

"Go, my friend," said Alex. "You have done enough. I told you that I would get you home. Tell your tales to the other Gnathe and get some more food into your skinny frame. Thank you for all your help."

"It's not over yet, Alexander," San-sool dourly replied and walked away.

Kamiel took Alexander firmly by the arm and made his way to the position of the pulse laser mounted on the roof of the Imperial Palace, leaving the others to keep an eye on the raptors. On the way he updated his friend on the preparations he had made for the coming attack by Link-soo-shan's forces. They made their way across the springy roof of tightly interlocked branches to the higher vantage point of where Kamiel had mounted the laser. A group of Gnathe were taking turns to look through the laser's telescopic, infrared scope.

"How did you manage to get that thing down out of orbit, Kamiel?" asked Alex in amazement.

"In bits and with some difficulty," the nannite wryly replied. "I carried all of that inside me in a 'flat pack'. It was not an elegant landing, but nothing was damaged."

"If only we could get access to the store of parts on that orbiting space station," Alex mused, thoughtfully.

"There are only a few more nano-pods left up there and that is where they must stay, or I will not be able to do the necessary maintenance from time to time. Dropping out of orbit again is not an option. We must sort out this problem once and for all with what we have. I think we have enough tools to do the job in hand. Fredrick and Minnis are a formidable combination. Bye-the-way, this is Jewel-khann operating the telescopic scope."

"You are the one who helped mount the telekinetic attack on Link-soo-shan during the rite of succession," Alexander said. "You are Trann's daughter."

"I am," she replied. "You are the alien leader that the Great Kaameel has told me about. You were in my mind when the co-ordination was broken. I remember you. You were the one who directed me to build sand around the Tyrant's feet. We nearly had her then. A pity that we failed."

"We will not fail this time," Alex said with confidence. "You are trained in the use of the telekinetic crystal and I think you may be of more use with that than this machine. I shall be the one using the pulse laser. How far can you throw a load, say the size of my head? I am thinking about Kamiel's home-made bombs."

"I do not know, Alexander. That is something we have never tried," Jewel answered.

"See Trann, find Natel-soo, borrow two of the crystals and both of you find out," ordered the human. "Do it now! Both of you are to return to here. Kamiel, make as many more of your explosive gourds as you can and stack them up here by the pulse laser. You there, locate two or three fire-pots and have them up here and sheltered from the wind. Come on, what are you waiting for?"

"Yes, I go," said the Gnathe and disappeared from sight.

Alexander turned to Kamiel and added, "I need to talk to the others down at the arena and explain the situation to them. I have things that I want them to do, also. So while this Gnathe guides me to them, I will leave you to do as I ask."

"It's good to have you back in control, McBald," the nannite answered and jumped over the edge of the roof to make the swiftest way back to his chemical store.

Alexander caught hold of one of the remaining Gnathe and said, "You will be my guide while I am here and show me where to go when I need you. Understand!"

She nodded and began to take Alex back to the arena.

CHAPTER 34

▼

Fredrick made his way to the main entrance and stood looking out at the formidable moat and the hive of activity on the other side. At each side of the water an area of dry ground had been left in front of the Banilik tree walls of the city that was easily defendable. In the distance beyond that was the fast flowing Imperial River, where the repaired bridge had been deliberately left standing. Kamiel wanted the army of Link-soo-shan to gain easy access to the area in front of the city walls. He proceeded around the edge of the moat towards the approach road. Here, tribute and supplies had been hauled along this hardened surface for untold centuries to the Imperial City.

"Right Minnis, you have the satellite map of this area in your memory banks. Find me the original homestead of those two Brood-mothers in the valley that Link-soo-shan has taken," Fredrick instructed.

Minnis projected the map in front of the human's eyes, red-lined the quickest approach along the main road and across the fields and said, "Time to run, Fred."

Fredrick started off with a steady jog, picked up the pace and disappeared from the watching Gnathe in a blur of dust over the bridge and away. The terrain flashed by at a steady rate until it was time to cut across the fields and pick up the road again. He checked the map to see how far he was from Link-soo-shan's forces and estimated that he was less than half a day from them, when he spotted four Zanth being rode at a furious pace. It was the scouting party.

"What do you think, Minnis? Shall we slow down or take them out?"

"Alexander's orders were quite explicit, Fred. We are to observe only and not be seen," replied the battle-suit. "So we slow down and spy out the size of her forces. Alexander could not be specific, as he was never allowed to see all of her people."

Fredrick ground his teeth in frustration but agreed and slowed right down to a steady jog. He kept them in sight and angled across the deserted fields of pod-vines to intercept the hurrying Gnathe. At last he made his way into the cover of an overgrown, dry roadside ditch and waited for the party to pass.

As the scouting party reached Fredrick's position, Jaffin slowed her Zanth down to a brisk walk and spoke to the two females: "Bilt and Frad, I want you two to ride back and observe the defences until we reach you with the main force. You may see something more that could help the Great Lady Link in the coming battle. Do not be seen. Do you understand?"

"Yes Group Captain," Bilt answered. "We will stay in the position that we occupied until you rejoin us. Come Frad, back the way we came."

Jaffin urged her tired beast back into a swifter gait and motioned Morrit to keep up. Fredrick watched and listened to this from his viewpoint in the ditch. Soon the two females were out of sight with Jaffin and the male Gnathe, making their way towards Link-soo-shan's forces.

Minnis said in Fredrick's earpiece, "We should follow those two back to Link's stronghold. The other two, we will collect on the way back."

The human grunted his acceptance and began to jog in the same direction the Group Captain took.

Inside the captured homestead, Link-soo-shan's forces were busily collecting whatever stores they could lay their hands on, piling them into the back cavity of a carrier beast. The original guards, who had been with the Ultimate Ruler before being trapped in the valley, were quietly confidant of the result of the coming conflict. They kept the edges of their sythers sharp by running the coarse hide of a specially bred lizard's skin along the blade. Many of them had killed before in Link's service. It was what they were born to do and they were good at it.

The younger Gnathe that were born in the valley were smaller than their elder cousins and were not battle tested. They constantly asked questions of the elder guards about what they should do. Tempers were getting edgy.

Link-soo-shan had called her captains to her. She had five of the older Gnathe trained in the old ways, to control the action of the infantry and Zanth mounted forces. The other two were of the younger variety and would command the long-range bow and arrow forces.

"Listen carefully to me, all of you. With the matrix blocked, I will not be able to instruct you with my mind," said Link-soo-shan and turned her head to fix each of them with a baleful glare. "That being the case, I will impress upon you a battle plan. We cannot win this fight easily inside the city. If we can, we will have to draw them out without them seeing our mounted forces too soon. Much will be dependant on the information gathered by Jaffin-shan and the others with her. I will adapt what I am about to tell you when she comes here with that knowledge."

All hearing crests were fully erect and all eyes centred on the towering form of the Brood-mother.

"We will be fighting in a new formation. The foot troops will edge forwards with archers behind them. A volley of arrows will be directed at the enemy and the infantry will pull aside to let the mounted forces assault in a 'vee' formation. As they break down the ranks of the enemy in front, they will split into two forces and veer to the sides. Infantry and archers will then kill as many as they can, until we have the clear advantage. Leave no wounded. Then advance into the city and find Trann and Sing if they are not with their forces in front of my city. I would expect little resistance from the city Gnathe, as they have been bred to serve, not fight. Remember, they do not have the bow. Archers, gather your arrows from the dead. Remember, what you carry with you are all the weapons that you have, apart from your sythers. Now gather your forces and let us make our way towards my old home."

Link-soo-shan selected the largest Zanth she could find and mounted the beast. She faced towards the city and motioned her forces along the road at an easy gait. It would not do to get there tired. The following morning would be the best time to attack, but first she wanted the news from Jaffin. The morning sun began to climb higher into the sky and the heat began to build up.

At last she could see two mounted Gnathe approaching from the direction of the city road. It was Jaffin and one other. She gave the order to stop and waited for them to move towards her.

"My Lady," Jaffin called out as she reined her mount to a stop, "it could not be better for us. The fools have dug a great ditch in front of the main entrance and have their main defensive force camped in front of that. We can drive them into the water. They have started to build a bridge of sorts, but are nowhere near finishing it. It will be easy to go around it once the forces in front are dead. I could see some of Trann's fighters amongst the defending forces. They are a disorganised rabble!"

"What were they doing? Trann is no fool," Link said suspiciously and fixed Jaffin with an appraising look. "Think hard and remember everything while I hold your hand. I will go into your mind and see for myself."

With that the Brood-mother clasped Jaffin's wrist and swiftly entered her daughter's mind. She marvelled at the size of the water-filled barrier in front of the main entrance. Trann had been busy to achieve that scale of work in such a short time. As Jaffin said, the bridge had not yet been finished. They would be trapped the wrong side of the defences. There seemed to be a great deal of parts of partially finished pieces of bridge left in neat piles. The other thing she noticed was the pitiful amount of fighting Gnathe that Trann seemed to have at her command. It looked very favourable and the odds seemed stacked in her direction as Link let go of the loyal female and loosened her mind's grip.

From a safe position in amongst a heavy stand of pod-vines, Frederick took stock of the forces massed against the Imperial City. Link-soo-shan must have spent a great deal of her time collecting her sister's and her own daughters from the far-flung reaches of her old empire. There were far more Gnathe here than Alexander had been allowed to see during his long days of capture. Everywhere a command crystal existed, Link had found a doorway and had slipped through on a collecting expedition. Considering that she had collected them in five and sixes, the effort involved had been tremendous. She had been also lucky that Bronn and Connit's brood-mother had been a breeder of Zanth for the city. Many of them were young, however, and were not quite as well broken to service as they could be and were more likely to panic. Fred had seen an out of control Zanth at the settlement when one of the raptors had got too close and the beast had picked up her scent. That gave him an idea. He retreated through the vines and began to jog back towards the city. Once free of the clinging vines he let Minnis pick up speed until his legs became a blur.

"When we get within range of where those other two spies are hidden, find them with your heat sensing equipment. Contact Kamiel and let him know what we have seen. Find a clean irrigation ditch along our way and pause to allow me to drink."

"I do carry water, Fredrick," Minnis answered and a pipe inserted itself into his mouth and cool water dribbled down the human's throat. "Everything else is being taken care of as we run."

"You still surprise me, Minnis," Fred replied in amazement and spat out the tube when he had finished.

"I re-circulate and purify your body fluids as you lose them. Nothing is lost," the nannite answered with pride.

"I wish you hadn't told me that, Minnis," the human said with a shudder and carried on running without a pause.

Although Fredrick was extremely fit, the toll of moving with the battle-suit was proving to begin to sap his energy reserves. They had put many miles between Link-soo-shan's forces and themselves, so Minnis slowed down when she monitored the human's fatigue.

"I could do with something to eat, but I'm afraid to ask where you got it from!" Fredrick wryly commented.

"I carry concentrated rations," Minnis replied tartly, "but you will have to mix it with water!"

Fred sat down on the side of an irrigation ditch and mixed himself a quick meal of vitamins and concentrates. To his disappointment it tasted very bland, but he noticed a melon plant growing along the water's edge and helped himself to one of the brightly coloured fruits.

"Will this kill me?" he asked.

"Stick your finger into the flesh and I will tell you," Minnis answered and Fred did so. "My analysis is that it has a high sugar content and will do you no lasting harm," the nannite continued.

Fredrick broke open the fruit and sank his teeth into the sweet pulpy flesh.

When he had finished he said to Minnis, "Contact Kamiel again. I have something to tell him."

A familiar voice spoke into his ear: "I am here Fred, what do you want?"

Fredrick chuckled and told the guardian his idea.

Nagoth avoided Sing-trow-sool as much as possible and tried to find Alexander. The Brood-mother had not forgotten her previous encounter with the scarred fighter and was unforgiving. The city Gnathe did not trust her and no matter how many times San-sool spoke out in her defence, old humiliations and cruelties were not easily forgotten. She was still not allowed to carry a weapon and this made her feel useless. What use would she be in the coming conflict if she could not fight? Then she heard that her new master was at the arena and hurried there as fast as she could.

She found him organising a clean-up squad around the sleeping raptors. The city Gnathe were collecting the dung left by the great beasts and carrying it out of the arena. To her puzzlement, she could see them scattering the excrement some distance in front of the moat and over the ground ahead of the fighting force.

Nagoth eyed the raptors with great respect and warily walked around them to confront Shoo-lin and Coen-soo.

"What are they doing?" she asked.

Shoo-lin laughed and said, "This is another weapon, my new friend. The Zanth go mad if they smell the raptors. I wouldn't give a shit for the chances of controlling a newly broken Zanth when they march through that stink!"

"It was Fredrick's idea," Coen-soo added and turned to face the big female. "He has seen that Link-soo-shan has mounted a great deal of her people on young Zanth and some of the riders are having difficulty controlling them. Anyway, what do you want?"

"I am weapon-less," Nagoth replied. "I need to see Alexander to intercede for me, as no-one will trust me."

"Come with me and we will see him together," said the Beast-master and led the way across the arena to where the human stood talking with Jewel and Natel.

"You have seen the destructive power of Kamiel's explosive devices," Alex was telling the two telekinetic trained Gnathe. "What I want you to do, is to show me how far you can throw them with the power of your mind. I need you to be able to project them beyond our fighting force to land in amongst the enemy. We will go to the roof where the pulse laser has been placed and try from there."

Nagoth called out, "Alexander! I need to speak with you."

"What is it, Nagoth," the human asked. "What can I do for you?"

"I wish to fight for you out there, but they have taken away all of my weapons. Can you make them understand that I am not Link-soo-shan's creature anymore?" she said in desperation.

"Let me into your mind. First I need to know for certain that this is really true and if so, I will need to show you what we are going to do. Remember, we do not fight the same as you. Everyone out there has been schooled by Kamiel with our battle plan," Alex replied and seized the big female by the arm.

He instantly sank into Nagoth's mind and searched for traces of the old conditioning, put there by the ruthless tyrant. It had been some while since he had altered the female's allegiances. To his surprise, the Gnathe's mind had healed from the rigorous remoulding he had achieved during their perverted sexual union. There was now a steadfast purpose to bring down her Brood-mother at any cost and she would defend Alexander to the death. Her love for him was unshakable. So now he filled her mind with Kamiel's plan of battle and explained what he would like her to do with her powerful bow and arrows.

He withdrew from her mind and said to Shoo-lin, "See Trann and make sure Nagoth is armed once more. I have work for her to do out there in the battlefield. That powerful bow will be most useful."

Shoo-lin hurried off with a grateful Nagoth close behind him and Alex transferred his attention back to the two Gnathe.

"Right, you two, onto the roof to try your talents. Joom and Abdul, come with me and look for the best vantage points to use your crossbows. Coen-soo, stay with the raptors and keep them calm. From what Fredrick has told Kamiel it would be likely that she will try her luck tomorrow. We will be ready."

As Fredrick slowly approached the rise where the two Gnathe spies were hiding, Minnis whispered in his ear, "Two heat sources to the right, hidden in the ditch, two hundred yards. What do you want to do?"

"Capture them alive if we can," replied the giant and dropped to the ground out of sight.

He wriggled and crawled the intervening distance, until he could see the backs of their heads with hearing crests held tautly erect. Both Gnathe were engrossed in the comings and goings in front of the main entrance over the river. They were watching the attempts of Jewel and Natel hurling gourds from the roof by telekinetic power without a great deal of success. This was indeed a puzzle to them, as a gourd was hardly a weapon of any use.

These two females were smaller than the guards that Fredrick had fought, it seemed, so long ago, when they had rescued Ender-whann-soo and the old scientist Khann. He studied them carefully and paid special attention to their hands. They were uncannily like a human's hand and without the ripping claws that had characterised the usual Gnathe. As Fredrick was well over six and a half feet tall, they would come up to his shoulders only. These were more like city Gnathe, just a bit smaller than the only human being they had ever seen.

Fredrick decided on the element of surprise and stood erect on the edge of the dry ditch and jumped in with them. He snapped his extended fingers around the heads of the two females and, holding them fast, he brought them together with an audible crack. They slumped in total unconsciousness and he walked out of the ditch and laid them side-by-side on the ground. He collected their bows and arrows and admired the workmanship as he did so.

"Hello, Kamiel," he said as he picked up both of the females and slung them over his shoulders, "I'm bringing company. I have two spies that were left here to tell more to Link-soo-shan. They won't be here when she comes."

Minnis lifted the load without effort and allowed Fredrick to walk easily through the fields, around the moat and through the main entrance into the arena.

Many miles away Asue had been discussing the situation with the two Brood-mothers and looking for flaws in Kamiel and Alexander's plans for the coming dawn. Ender and Khann had pointed out something in favour that had not been considered by the defenders. Link-soo-shan's new breed were much more intelligent than the Gnathe that she had bred for centuries. Unlike the guards, whose thoughts had been shaped by the two ruling sisters since birth, they had been bred in the pouches of Connit and Bronn. They did not have the blind obedience of the older Gnathe and Link-soo-shan's efforts at controlling their minds were perfunctory at most, because of the time factor involved.

Khann faced the silver being and said, "Trann's people will have to exterminate all of Link's old guard, as they will never fit in with the new order. Now that Fredrick has captured two of the new strain, perhaps Alexander could take a little time to study them and check their minds. These new kindred should be harvested if possible. If the city will not take them, then we will take them here, as long as they are not too brain damaged by their creator."

"Yes, Asue," exclaimed Ender as she proudly regarded her young, Azander and Marren, attentively listening. "I for one would like to study their genetic makeup. We should inform Alexander and Trann about how we feel."

Asue regarded the two tall forms perched before her and replied, "I will speak to Kamiel and see how Alexander feels about this idea. The less that have to be killed the better, as I see it. I was programmed to heal and build, not to destroy, but even so, I can understand that there will be indiscriminate killing. It is the destruction of Link-soo-shan that is all-important. I know that we will never be safe here as long as she lives."

Asue sent a signal to the command centre and activated the satellite's communication system to contact her nannite partner.

On top of the roof, Alex watched with dismay as the best efforts of each female hurling the homemade bombs fell short. The telekinetic power diminished over distance due to the inverse law of energy. Close up, the power of lift was impressive, but once beyond the walls of the city and over the moat, the gourds fell into the water.

"Rest yourselves for the moment, while I think about this problem," the human said as Kamiel came into sight carrying more of the gunpowder-filled gourds.

"Asue has been communicating with me," the nannite said. "Ender and Khann have made the point that the younger kindred that Link designed will not be so mind controlled as the older ones. If we can avoid killing these, they can be absorbed by our own settlement. I think that finding out their genetic makeup obsesses Khann, but she has a point."

"I can promise nothing," replied Alex tersely. "At the moment my idea of launching these bombs telekinetically has failed. Neither Jewel nor Natel can hurl the gourds further than the moat! It has been just a waste of time. It is a pity that I cannot get past your programming block."

"It's there for a very good purpose, Alexander McBald," the Guardian flatly said. "Use your brains and think. This psychokinetic mental world that you have opened up is beyond my memory banks. You are the one that must blend it together."

Alex swung round and grasped the silver figure by his upper arms and kissed the nannite on his featureless forehead.

"That's it, Kamiel—you have just given me an idea!" he gleefully exclaimed and turned to the shocked Gnathe. "Listen to me. I will mentally join the two of you together. Next, you will catch hold of one of Kamiel's bombs and then we will see just how far you can throw one, linked together."

Alex caught hold of both Gnathe and concentrated on blending their minds together. The others watched as one of Kamiel's freshly made dummy bombs lifted off the floor and sailed up into the air and flew out of sight, to land hundreds of yards past the armed camp set up in front of the moat.

He let go of them and said, "Now join your minds together on your own and try again. You have grown up with telepathy and even without a crystal you are capable of making contact with each other's minds at short range."

Jewel-khann and Natel-soo held hands and concentrated once more. This time, with precision, they dropped the next dummy bomb exactly on top of the other one.

"Right," ordered Alexander, "both of you will stay up here and never be further away from each other than you need to be. Food, water and anything else will be brought to you. Here you will sleep. I will join you tomorrow before dawn and operate the pulse laser. Understand?"

"Yes Alexander," they replied in unison and found a comfortable place to rest.

"One more thing," the human ordered, "keep the fire-pots alight and make sure that the real bomb's fuses are lit before you throw them at the enemy!"

Kamiel caught hold of Alexander's arm and said, "Fredrick is back here with two prisoners. I think we should go and see them. They are in the arena."

"I'm coming, my old friend. I'll tell you what—this means of delivery beats rockets every time. We can drop the bombs exactly where we want them." He followed the nannite off the roof and down to the city level.

In the arena, Fredrick had dumped the two unconscious Gnathe onto the sand and waved to Coen-soo. She came over with a water bag for the big human to drink from and handed it to him.

"These are the new kindred. I like their hands. They are much like yours, Fred. I am pleased that you have brought their weapons. You can never have enough killing sticks." She said pointing at the bows and arrows on the sand.

"Coen-soo, your way of looking at the world still surprises me from time to time. Keep an eye on these two if you would and I will see to Munch," he replied and drank gratefully from the water-skin and passed it back.

Coen-soo emptied some of the water over the faces of the two Gnathe lying on the ground. With a great deal of spluttering and coughing they awoke and looked around the arena. When they saw the four raptors sleeping quietly at the far end of the sandy amphitheatre they went ridged with fear. The next thing they saw was Fredrick wake one of the smaller ones with a hearty kick to the hind claws. It opened its eyes and seized the human delicately in its jaws and swung him onto its back.

"Sit very still or that thing will eat you," Coen-soo cruelly said. "You are in the Imperial City and our prisoners. If you make no trouble you will live. There is someone here that wants to see you. You know him. He is Alexander and a good friend to all the Gnathe in this city."

"How can he be here? He escaped in the valley!" Bilt-shan exclaimed in disbelief.

"He came here on the back of one of those great beasts," Coen-soo replied and pointed in the opposite direction of the raptors. "There he is now with the Great Kaameel and he is coming over here. Stand up."

Alex walked over to the two terrified females and said to them, "I need to find out if your conditioning by Link-soo-shan is easily breakable. You, what is your name?"

"Frad-shan. What are you going to do?" she asked nervously.

"This," replied the human and reached out to the Gnathe's arm and held it tightly.

Alexander entered her mind with ease. Unlike Nagoth's mind there was little conditioning to break. Love and respect for Link-soo-shan was in evidence, but the blind obedience that had dominated the Group Captain's mind was not in place. Alex quickly altered the allegiance to himself and the others of his group and let go of the females arm.

Coen-soo caught hold of the dazed archer and propelled the other female towards Alexander's waiting grasp.

He quickly assessed the young creature and reversed her loyalties as well, leaving her to slowly recover her wits.

"That's two more Gnathe that will no longer want to kill us," the human retorted. "Ender and Khann would be proud of me. Now let us see if there is anything they can tell us that we do not know."

Kamiel regarded Alexander with some concern. "You are becoming very ruthless, old friend. I knew the man from whom you were cloned, Dr. McBald. He taught me and directed my programming after I was created. He too, let nothing get in his way. The Alexander that I knew, that ran the Genesis project, would have thought that you were a mirror of his soul."

"Don't get metaphysical on me, Kamiel. You know as well as I do, that I will do what has to be done to protect the colony. Besides which, Link and I have a score to settle," Alexander grated and shuddered as old repressed memories resurfaced.

He turned away and confronted the two young Gnathe. "What is Link-soo-shan's plan of action? Will she attack at dawn or will she wait awhile? Who will she send first against us?"

"She will attack just after dawn, by first sending in infantry covered by archers," replied Bilt-shan and added, "This is a feint so that masses of Zanth riders will crash through the centre as her infantry makes a hole for them to go through. They will then follow and destroy all on foot. When that is done they will storm the city to find Trann-link-khann and Sing-trow-sool. They are to be captured alive so that the Lady Link can kill them herself."

"She still thinks of the overwhelming rush," commented Alex and chuckled darkly. "Wait until she gets a taste of warfare, human style! So the older guards go first, do they? Good! The more that we can rid this world of them the better I shall feel. I'm glad that the new breeds are being kept back. After seeing these two I'm sure we can find a use for them at the settlement once the Tyrant is out of the way."

Shoo-lin had returned from his brief interview with Trann-link-khann and a disbelieving Sing-trow-sool with a fully armed and jubilant Nagoth.

The big female squatted down in front of Alexander and bowed her head submissively and said, "Thank you for what you have done for me. I ask just one more thing of you before I go to my position."

"What is it, Nagoth," he replied and fixed her with a steely gaze.

"If it is within my power to capture Jaffin-shan, will you do for her what you did for me? She was my friend. I will kill her if I must, but if I can keep her alive, she will be a useful addition to any dangerous situation in the future. Shoo-lin has told me of the wild lands beyond your settlement. If I live, I want to go there with you and I would be happy to have Jaffin with me."

"Nagoth, you amaze me," Alex said, taking the female by the upper arms and holding her tightly. "If you can do this thing, then I agree. Just do not get killed doing it. I mean it when I say that your safety is important to me. What is in our past is done with. I have not forgotten that you saved my life by taking my help-less body away from Link-soo-shan's tortures. You have proved yourself to me. Now go and be lucky and keep well away from the telekinetic reach of that foul creature or she will kill you without mercy."

Nagoth straightened up and, looking Alexander in the eyes, she quickly caressed his face with her tongue. She then walked away towards the moat and the defending forces.

Alexander turned to the two young females that still stood bemused by their de-conditioning and said, "You two will be my personal bodyguards. Where I go, you go. Tomorrow, our position will be on the roof and you will pick off any of Link-soo-shan's old guards that come anywhere near our position. Understand!"

"Yes, Alexander," they both answered.

Frad-shan added, "It will not be hard to kill any of the old ones. They hated us anyway, because we are different to them."

"That's another factor that Link-soo-shan seems to have overlooked," Alex thoughtfully mused and, motioning them to stay where they were, he walked over to the raptors and their riders.

Shoo-lin, Coen-soo and Fredrick watched him approach across the early evening sunlit sands of the arena. All the raptors were fully awake and alert.

The Beast-master left Snapper and greeted his friend, "What do you want us to do, Alexander?"

"I need you to be behind them, once things get nasty. You will need to be some distance away to begin with. The sound of the explosions will be too much for your large friends. Even they could panic! It will be difficult enough to keep our own people in order and Kamiel tells me that they at least have experienced the excavation of the moat. You will be shielded from her telekinetic power by the circuits in these suits. The raptors will not. Keep them away from her."

"Agreed," said Fredrick. "We had best be going now and circle well around the back of her. Signal Minnis when you have run out of explosive charges and we will start our attack from behind. Everything willing, we will meet again tomorrow after this is finished."

"We will, my friends, we will, and then we can go home!" Alexander exclaimed and hugged each of his friends in turn and walked over to the big male.

He pressed his hands against the great beast's head and tried to explain in pictures what would happen the next day.

"Leader of Many," he projected, "do you understand me?"

"Creature whose name means nothing, I do not understand the reason for this fight, only that it is not mine. If my females are in danger than I will take part."

Alex withdrew and hoped that the maverick attitudes of the wild male would not be brought into play during the struggle on the next day. With that, he watched the four raptors take flight over the back of the city and the Imperial River and out of sight. He made his way with Kamiel back to his new bodyguards and the vantage point of the roof.

CHAPTER 35

▼

The spring melt had long since caused the Imperial River to assume a dull grey hue. It foamed and tossed itself against the sharp and rocky sides of the riverbed as it made its way to the sea. Link-soo-shan knew that the only way to get over this obstacle would be to cross the great bridge near the city. Jaffin's mind had shown that the bridge was as yet unguarded, with the pitifully small armed camp set up in front of the huge ditch dug in front of the Imperial City's main entrance. Trann had repaired Shoo-lin's damage to this bridge after his escape with the Heretic and her accursed grand Brood-mother, Khann. What other work she had carried out, Link could only guess at. The numbers of Gnathe at her disposal must be small to leave the bridge so undefended. The fields from there to the city would take about an hour's crossing. At last, the army had reached the rise from where Jaffin's party had spied upon the city defences that very morning. Link motioned them to stop and disappear into the vegetation on each side of the ditches. She dismounted and beckoned Jaffin to her side.

"Where are the two you left here to watch the city?" she asked. "They must have seen us arrive."

"I cannot see them, great Lady. I fear they may be taken captive or dead. They were told to stay out of sight and just observe," Jaffin nervously replied.

"Scout the area around the bridge and see if there is any sign of them while you do so. We will cross over at nightfall and assemble in battle formation with the river at our side," she answered and flexed her ripping claws. "Tomorrow, I will get my city back or die trying, Jaffin-shan. Now go and report back to me with some good news."

The group captain turned and made her way on foot towards the bridge beckoning Morrit to her side. They took advantage of every bit of cover as they did so, unaware that they stood out plainly on the pulse laser's infrared scope being operated by Alexander.

"Well, she's here, Kamiel," Alexander observed and turned away from the scope. "Our front line troops are still making sure that they look like a disorganised rabble. She will be feeling over-confidant this night if she has seen them. What she can't see are the extra fighters we have behind the walls."

Trann-link-khann stood next to the human and confidently said, "I have called in all the personal guards of every one of the new ruling families that will rejoice at her demise. She thinks that all she has to do is defeat my people and the city Gnathe. I'm sorry that we could not warn Mace-loot-tighe, but she was a nasty piece of work. One of the old types! Blinding your own young Brood-mothers to keep them pliable!"

She shuddered in disgust.

"The old ways will go, my friend," Alex retorted and squeezed her arm, "and you will be the main driving force. We have a great deal to offer each other when this is done."

Kamiel mused on his loss of invulnerability due to Link-soo-shan's telekinetic reach and said to his friend, "I do not know what to do for the best. I must stay here, to at least tend to the wounded and oversee our plans, but she must not see me until I am sure she is separated from that crystal. Each of the suits has a small piece from the one that Hannah found, connected to a resonating circuit. For the good of the future I must play the part of coward!"

"You will never be seen by me as a coward, my old friend," Alexander replied, looking directly at the featureless face of the nannite. "You must be prudent above all else. To the colony and the new settlement you are beyond price. We humans and ape are at the last resort expendable; you are not. All have their part to play in this struggle. Now go and check that Joom and Abdul are settled and that their weapons are fully functional."

Kamiel withdrew and made his way along the leafy roof of the outer walls towards where Joom had stationed himself. The ape was comfortable in the tree-tops and had removed his shoes to enable a better grip on the branches. He was trimming the twigs and small branches from a formidable club.

"Hello Kamiel," the ape smiled. "Come to check up on me, have you? I have a fine view from here. The first fifteen Gnathe to come this way around the moat will be fifteen dead! After that, me and my friend here will see what we can do about the rest."

"I sense that you will do all that you can, old friend," Kamiel answered and picked up Joom's crossbow. "I'll just check this over while I am here and make sure no grit has got into the mechanism. She is here, Joom, just beyond the river with her loyal guards and her new breed."

"I'll not be sorry to meet up with her again. If I can avenge Jo-Jo's death and those of my friends caught in the Citadel, I will die fulfilled," Joom stated as he carried on shaping his club.

"I would like to see you safely home," replied Kamiel as he handed back the cleaned weapon.

"We shall see. I have lived a long life and with luck I shall live a little longer," the ape said flatly. "Go and check on Abdul. He decided to keep a watch at the other end of the moat. Give him all my luck for the morning."

Kamiel left the big ape to his thoughts and the small company of Gnathe tucked up in the roof with him and started for the other end of the moat to check with Abdul.

Fredrick coerced the raptors to fly away from the city and circle round until they were some distance from the rear of Link-soo-shan's army. He recognised the road that he had travelled earlier in the day.

"Down, Munch. This is as far as you go. Wait here for me to come back," the human ordered the female.

"You hide your mind from me!" the raptor exclaimed. "What you do? Fred in danger?"

"You must stay here unless I call you," he replied. "Do you understand? All of you must stay here or you may be in danger."

Shoo-lin and Coen-soo were having the same kind of mental conversation with their devoted raptors. It was proving difficult until a forth voice echoed in all their minds.

"You will stay with me," Leader of Many projected on a telepathic broadband. "I will listen and we will come when called. After that?"

The two Gnathe and the big human turned away and made their way along the road towards the rear of the Tyrant's army.

Jaffin and Morrit watched the empty bridge for some time. It remained unguarded and the road to the city was empty of Gnathe. Everything was unnaturally quiet. The only activity they could see was in front of the water-filled ditch where Trann's meagre defences were busily settling down for the night. They were too far off for Jaffin to be able to see clearly what they were doing. There was some activity along the roof of the city that the Group captain dismissed from her mind. The fighting would be on the ground and hand to hand, except for Link's archers who would give long-range cover. Jaffin liked the idea of being able to strike down your enemies from a distance. The young male Gnathe at her side had proved the power of the bow to her with target practice at the hidden valley. The first thing they would do would be to pick off as many of Trann's fighting force amongst the city Gnathe that they could, leaving what was left a disorganised rabble.

"I think we have seen enough," said the seasoned killer. "I think that we can return to the great Lady Link and cross this bridge during cover of darkness."

"I have never killed before, Group Captain," exclaimed Morrit worriedly and wriggled away from the vicinity of the bridge. "Do you remember your first time? Did you find it easy?"

The older female slid down the bank towards Morrit and replied, "I remember the first time. It is something that you do not easily forget, but that was hand-to-hand combat. When you kill for the first time it will just be a target that falls. When you run out of arrows, then will be the time to find out. Now enough talking! Let us get back to our own people and tell Link-soo-shan what we have seen."

They hopped and bounded the distance back to the hidden armed camp with the news of their scouting expedition, where Jaffin made her way straight to Link-soo-shan.

"My Lady," she gasped as she stopped in front of her Brood-mother, "I have been to the bridge and there is no-one there! They are not ready for us. They cannot know that we are so close. All we have to do is cross it quietly and make our way across the fields and wait for the dawn. There is no trace of the two that I left here; they must have been killed."

"If they have them alive, we will not have the element of surprise, but we do outnumber them," Link mused and studied the sinking sun over the distant city. "Right, collect the other captains and make your way slowly towards the bridge, infantry first. I want quiet and that means the Zanth as well, so walk them gently."

Jaffin called over to the other Group Captains and passed on Link-soo-shan's orders. Chang-soo-shan's heavy guard went first in good order towards the bridge. A line of archers on each side with bows strung and ready came with them. Next came the Zanth, led carefully by Link's daughters with the larger form of the Brood-mother amongst them. Behind them came the rest of her ground troops and hand-to-hand fighters. As the sun began to set, the first of the army began to cross over and melt away into the fields.

At last the Ultimate Ruler stood on the bridge and dug her claws into the road with a feeling of triumph and said to Jaffin, "I'm coming home at last. What was mine will again be mine. I will not lose my grip again on what Chang and I built here. I will have Trann's head polished and set in my royal chambers for me to gaze at every night before I sleep!"

She led her Zanth across the bridge and into the fields of young grain that stretched up to the city walls in places, except for the area of the 'Killing Stones.' Quietly the rest of the army made their way behind her and moved through the crops until they reached a hollow where they gratefully sank to the ground to sleep.

Before Jaffin settled down she rounded up six of Chang's heavy guards and instructed them to go back to the bridge and keep guard in case there were any other fighters in the vicinity. Slow of thought and used to blind obedience, they made their way back towards the bridge in the failing light.

Across the river Shoo-lin, Coen-soo and Fredrick were carefully approaching the ramparts of the bridge. The non-reflective nature of Kamiel's insulated suits made them almost invisible in the encroaching darkness. Fredrick motioned Shoo-lin and Coen-soo to the right while he kept to the left. They hid behind the stone pillars, waiting for the unsuspecting guards to make their way towards the middle of the bridge and a clear shot.

As the six Gnathe grumbled amongst themselves about drawing guard duty, they began to spread out.

Fredrick softly said into his communicator, "Shoo, two on the right. Coen, two centre. Me, the two on the left. Now!"

Shoo-lin sighted through the scope and saw a red spot appear on the chest of his first target. He let fly and picked off the next one in seconds. The male was delighted with the weapon that Kamiel had designed for him. It was so more accurate than the ordinary bow!

The three moved swiftly across the bridge and quickly made sure that the six heavy-set guards were dead by cutting their throats. They carefully removed the bolts from the bodies and Fredrick rolled them over the parapet of the bridge into the river below.

"Release the tension on the bows and reload. You may need all five bolts the next time you use your crossbows," the human commanded and beckoned the two Gnathe into the shadows.

"It will not be difficult to find them," Coen observed, pointing to the tracks across the fields of young grain.

"We will make our way back along the river bank and get well behind them. Remember to be quiet. If we are seen we will lose that element of surprise. They must be tempted into that overwhelming rush that Link-soo-shan has been so over-fond of. Minnis, tell Kamiel that we are here and going into hiding and waiting for the dawn."

On the roof of the Imperial City overlooking the new moat, Alexander received the news from Kamiel with a feral grin.

"It's all coming together, my inscrutable friend. Have we missed anything?"

"I don't think so, Alexander. It all depends on our people at the front line. Once she charges them, then we will see," the Guardian replied. "It is time you got some sleep if you can. I will do the rounds and make sure that all is in order. Trann and Sing may need some reassurance—at least Sing-trow-sool will. I think that Trann is afraid of nothing. She reminds me of Khann-link-sool a great deal. Her intelligence and mind is so like the old scientist's it's uncanny. Tomorrow I will be where I am most needed, but out of the telekinetic range of Link-soo-shan, I promise!"

With that the nannite made his way down into the sleeping city and the royal quarters to find the two unlikely ruling companions.

The two Brood-mothers were settling down for the night in the royal chambers and Trann was trying to reassure her partner about the coming day when Kamiel entered.

He paused as he walked up to the two large forms and said, "All is in place. Fredrick, Shoo-lin and Coen-soo are behind Link-soo-shan's forces. They have freed the bridge of her guards. Six less will be on the field tomorrow."

"What of the rest of them?" Sing asked anxiously. "Tell me, Great Kaameel, what do you think about tomorrow? How do you feel about the battle to be fought by us and not you?"

"Sing-trow-sool, I have done all in my power to aid you," Kamiel retorted. "My people are ready to die in your defence. All you have to do is to be prepared to do as much!"

Trann turned to her frightened co-ruler and declared, "It is as Kaameel says. All is ready for tomorrow. He can do no more than he has. This very moment his leader Alexander sleeps upon the roof, waiting for the dawn. Two more of his race are hidden at each side of the moat, ready to die if need be. There is another, with my own-bred male and Ender's prime female behind them. We owe a debt to these people that will echo down the generations. They are our friends and ask nothing of us except to remain so."

"I am happy that you feel that way, Trann," Kamiel said and bowed to her. "Sing, I told you that I cannot fight in battle. I cannot explain it to you in any way that you could understand. You must just believe me when I say that I have done all that I can to defend you. Now I must go and continue my rounds while you sleep. Fear not, I will waken you before the dawn."

The Guardian walked away from the two Brood-mothers and followed the winding corridors until he once more stood in the open air of the arena. Around the walls and tucked into the cover of the Banilik tree roots, were the huddled forms of loyal Brood-mothers and their personal guards. Any of Link-soo-shan's troops who got this far would get a nasty surprise. They had elected to sleep out in the open and under the starlight rather than get caught inside the city's winding corridors and dormitories. He walked through the main entrance towards the moat and stood looking out over the water barrier that he had produced in a few moments. There was no movement over the water as the advance section, acting as bait, laid themselves down to sleep before the coming day. Kamiel opened his receptors and communication systems, tuning in to the nannite band.

"Hello Kamiel," projected the other three Guardians together, "is all prepared?"

"Everything is ready. I have set the trap. All Link-soo-shan has to do is step into it and her power base will be gone forever."

"There will be much death when the dawn comes," said Sharn sadly. "Take care of our people Kamiel, as much as you can."

"Do not allow her to do what was done to me," added the new Minns. "I can just remember the Minns that was. You have all managed to recreate me as far as possible, but I know that a great deal of the original me is gone. There are holes in my mind that I cannot unravel. We are not the immortal beings that we thought we were. I am thankful that I still have my purpose, but I will be more than happy to put all of this behind me," the reconstructed nannite urged. "Be careful out there, Kamiel. That's all I ask. Now I must go and be about my duties in the nursery. Dawn is breaking here and there are hungry mouths to feed!"

"Well, Kamiel," said Asue, "once more we are to witness conflict and bloodshed to enable the grand plan to mature."

"If we don't tie these two cultures together, we will lose ours. Without a frontier to push against and Khann's serum to open up this world, our people will die out. We need them to survive here," Kamiel flatly stated. "You've seen my projections and the changes since Ender, Khann and their kindred have come to live amongst us. Although we have lost thousands of our people to Link-soo-shan's raid, we have got over it. The colony must and will survive when this is finished. We are probably all that are left in the universe after this length of time. The 'Genesis Project' will be successful; our people will not die out."

"I know," Asue unhappily replied, "but so much death, Kamiel. So much death."

She withdrew, leaving the mission psychologist alone and apprehensive.

Above the new science labs at the settlement, outside of the domed world of the Habitat, the dawn was breaking. Hannah sat alone amongst the selection of crystals that she had brought back from her expedition into the mountains. Her staff had long since gone to their beds. She could not sleep and her thoughts were with Fredrick and the others far across the mountains. The apparatus holding the blanketing crystal hummed continuously as it sent its fluctuating signal out and into the communication matrix. It was enough that it also shut down the ability of the Tyrant to warp space and make it possible to teleport her people from one place to another.

Hannah had no chance to evaluate what its range could be before putting it into operation. She had endlessly experimented with the number of telekinetic crystals and found that different ones had different ranges. Some were more powerful than others and in amongst the collection were some that could do something different, if only she could find the key. What kept nagging at her mind was trying to think whatever Link-soo-shan had managed to do to open doors in space. If they could only learn to do what she had discovered, then this whole world would open up. It might even be possible to reach the space station orbiting high above in geo-synchronous orbit. There were metal rich stores on board that would be so useful if they could only get them down to the colony. Finally the scientist fell asleep in the chair with her head pillowed on her arms. She began to dream.

As the night drew to a close and the dawn sun began to pierce the morning mists at the Imperial City, Kamiel began his rounds, making sure that all were awake.

The armed camp in front of the city gave every indication to the unpractised eye that everything was still in disarray. In fact every member of Trann's senior females had made sure that all were awake, fed and watered some time before the first early light. They had all quietly lain down again in formation with the shields underneath them and the pikes by their sides, keeping a wary eye on the approaches. The smaller city Gnathe situated at the back were making the rafts ready and keeping the fire pots alight. Several were in charge of the fuses, in case Link-soo-shan's archers should take any of them out.

Nagoth marvelled at the efficiency that Trann had instilled in these non-fighting city dwellers. She had always treated them with contempt before Alexander had changed her way of looking at the world. Bred for fighting, she had known no other life in the service of her Brood-mother. When Alexander had explained to her that none of the human and ape population had been bred or trained as fighters, she had reacted with disbelief. To her it was unthinkable what Kamiel had achieved with the help of Trann. Ordinary Gnathe without any skills at fighting had been trained to obey Trann's trusted elite members of her household. The way that they were going to fight this bloody encounter was so beyond her experience that all she could do was to obey meekly. Trann had expressly ordered her not to attempt to lead any of the defenders in case it altered Kamiel's plans. She was to kill as many Group Captains and her old comrades as she could, when it came-to-hand to hand fighting, but up until then she was to do exactly as she was told. The only concession was if she could take Jaffin-shan prisoner during the fight, she could keep her safe. She had been warned about the weapons hidden under the earth. Alexander had even taken the trouble to show her in her mind what to expect, by telepathy. It shook her to the core and she wondered how she would react when it happened.

On the roof, Alexander was checking over the capacitors fuelling the pulse laser and estimating the amount of power at his disposal when Kamiel appeared at his side.

"How much energy do these capacitors hold, Kamiel?" the human leader asked.

"They have been charging since I got here and set everything up, my old friend," the nannite replied. "They have been tested and they do work. The first burst of light will be the strongest, so direct it to where it will do most good. After that the charge will diminish, so pick your targets with care. It will make a significant difference on that first charge. It should affect about twenty or more in the front rows. Sweep the beam along the infantry and then pick off the Zanth as soon as they get within the smell of the raptor dung. That should prove interesting!"

Jewel-khann and Natel-soo arrived, still chewing a hasty breakfast snatched from the ever-busy kitchens. With them were the two new members of Alexander's bodyguard, Built and Frad, wide eyed from their experience of the size of the Imperial City. They were checking their arrows for damage and stringing their bows.

"Alexander, we have met San-sool and he has told us all about your escape," said Built-shan. "He asked if he could be by your side when the conflict begins, in case he is needed."

"He has come with us," added Frad and moved away to show the small male that stood behind her.

"San! I did not think that you would want to be up here," exclaimed Alexander. "I quite thought that you would have had enough adventure to last you the rest of your life!"

The Gnathe stiffly replied, "If the new ways are to be, then I want to be part of them. You have shown me a different path to tread and I would earn my place and that place is by your side. My medical skill may be needed. I should be here!"

"Thank you, my friend. I will not forget this whatever happens this day," the human replied and stared out towards the fields of new crops disappearing into the distance. "Kamiel, contact Fredrick and tell him that we are ready. Can he see any movement from where he is?"

Kamiel contacted Minnis and Fredrick replied, "Morning, Alex. Things are starting to happen here. I do not think it will be long before she starts coming at you. They are finishing eating and gathering up their weapons. The Zanth are being un-hobbled and harnessed. They are being pulled into formation as we speak."

Alexander caught the rising sun on the polished mirror that Kamiel had brought down from the satellite and signalled the waiting defences.

An answering waving flag told him that the signal had been seen.

"Tell Hannah to drop the barrier and monitor events. The moment she senses any movement from Link-soo-shan she is to seal it off again," Alex commanded the guardian. "We may need the crystal matrix at some time to direct information to each other. I think that we can gambol that Link will be reluctant to try teleporting while we can shut down the system at any time."

At the science laboratories, Hannah heard the news as Asue awaked her. She immediately cut the power to the oscillating circuit that was blanketing the crystal matrix. She sat staring at the collection of crystals scattered over the table and tried to recall the dream she had experienced. It was something that Alex had said when he was telling her about his awful period of captivity. She had dreamt about Link-soo-shan and her taunts and torture of her lifelong friend. The room that Link-soo-shan had made her own was full of her trophies. On the table where the skulls of the humans and apes were kept, was also her collection of crystals. Why did she value them so much that her command crystals were kept together? They were practically indestructible. So why not keep the spare one somewhere else for safekeeping?

She decided to ask Ender-whann-soo and Khann-link-sool a few questions, held her crystal tightly and concentrated her mind.

"Ender, are you awake?" she asked.

"Of course, Hannah, and so is Khann. What can we do for you?" the Gnathe answered.

"Have you ever possessed two command crystals at the same time? I have an idea that I would like to try," the scientist projected to the two Brood-mothers. "I would like you to bring yours to me as quickly as you can. In amongst my mixed haul of crystals that I collected is one that I judge is a command crystal. We need to tune it so that we have two."

In a very short time, the two large forms of the Gnathe were standing by her side. Khann at once began to tune the raw crystal to resonate with the one they had brought back in the airship. At last she was finished and studied her handiwork carefully. Taking the crystal in her hands she concentrated and nodded to Hannah.

"This is as good as the other one," Khann said and handed it to the human. "What are you going to do?"

"Pick up both," she said, "and see what difference it will make."

Immediately she was aware of a sense of perspective unlike anything she had experienced before. Every crystal had a direction and she could sense a fold in space around it, as if each crystal was a door. She also knew where they were. It did not matter that thousands of miles remained between them. They all remained firmly shut, however. What had the Tyrant done to open them? What else did Link possess to enable her to twist space? Hanna opened her eyes and stared at the telekinetic crystals scattered in a platter. Keeping hold of the two command crystals, she put the largest one between them. Instantly, the matrix changed again. Now the folds in space around each crystal had a solid feel to them. All she had to do was push and they would open. Wherever two matching shards of a communication crystal were close together a wider door could be opened.

"I know how she did it! Come into my mind and see what I can see," Hannah triumphantly said and the two Gnathe did so.

"I see," Khann's mind projected into the gestalt. "Do you also see how it is possible to open other folds even where there are no crystals! It takes more than one mind to do this. Let us try a small experiment."

The corporate mind of Hannah and the two Gnathe began to concentrate on their new powers.

CHAPTER 36

▼

Link-soo-shan gathered her Group captains around her in the dawning light. Jaffin had reported back that the disorganised defences were showing some movement although many were still asleep. The Zanth had been made ready for the attack and had been fed lightly. Her own mount was harnessed and stood ready. It was the largest of the beasts at her command and had an evil temper, as it was a breeding male. Link had soon taught it to respect her and take her extra weight. She regarded it as a good trampling weapon. It would not be long now before the puny city Gnathe were scattered under its clawed feet. She stood tall before her kindred and opened her arms to show her crystals firmly bound into place.

"Do you all know what you have to do? Are there any questions? Right then, my proud kindred, let us take back what was taken from me!" shouted the Ultimate Ruler and drew her syther. "In the future, you will be served by all who live in these lands. Once we have control, I will bring Connit and Bronn-mace-ran back here to rule and breed in my name. All will bow to me and in my name shall bow to you!"

Jaffin raised her syther, took her mount by the reins and swung herself up into the riding position.

"Let us go," she ordered, "as the great Lady Link has commanded! Leave none alive that oppose us!"

The dead Chang-soo-shan's heavy-duty guards formed up first and began to move out across the young crops towards the defending opposition. They began to walk slowly up and out of the hollow where they had camped for the night, closely followed by the archers. Next came the light infantry and the mounted Zanth. The rising sun was burning off the morning mists and visibility was increasing at every moment. The morning sun was at their backs, giving them the advantage. Everything was as perfect as Link-soo-shan had planned. They gained the rise and could now see the city walls in the distance and the water of the great ditch dug in front. The defenders were standing waiting for them in a box formation of five rows spread along the front of the ditch. They looked ill prepared for the coming battle and very puny up against the power of Chang's guards.

Link-soo-shan's forces began to take up their battle formation and continued to advance.

To their surprise, the defenders began to come forward to meet them and displayed an unusual pattern amongst the ranks. They marched in staggered rows towards the heavy-set daughters of Chang-soo-shan and stopped in formation, just standing quietly. They did not appear to be armed with any weapons that the attackers could see.

Closer and closer, the front ranks made their way towards the defending ranks of seemingly empty-handed city Gnathe and Trann's fighting guards. The dull-minded ranks of Link's old enforcers began to smile at the prospect of an easy killing spree and picked up speed. They flexed their ripping claws into the attack position and hopped with ground-devouring leaps straight at the front row. Behind them, the first line of archers came into range.

"Archers, let fly! Front row charge!" Jaffin shouted to the front rows.

As the bowstrings sent their cargo of death towards the waiting defenders, the front row quickly knelt, picked up the shields and the front of the long lances, keeping them hidden. All had been laid out the previous day and had been placed there for them to use. Next they brought the rectangular shields into play. Smoothly, as they had been trained to do, a roof of tightly woven reeds covered with tanned leather were held over their heads. These were held in place by every second Gnathe while the front row held their shields steady in a long fence before them. Not one arrow got through!

The charging heavy guards kept coming with ripping claws extended.

Alexander flicked off the safety switch on the pulse laser, aimed at the front rank and swivelled the projector to shine into the eyes of the first wave. A bright light, set to be about two foot in diameter at that distance, blazed down from the laser's diffuser. Twenty times brighter than the sun, the glare would blind permanently at this power.

At the same time the front row of shields backed away, leaving a row of spikes sticking forwards. Each pike-wielding Gnathe picked an adversary and dug the heel of the lance into the ground, held there by a backstop prepared the previous day.

Without pause, with most of the first wave impaled on the hardened bone tips of the long lances, the front ranks backed away, leaving the second rank. They were busy directing another row of sharp-ended poles for the next row to charge upon.

As the second row hurled forwards, climbing over their dying or blinded comrades, Alex repeated a sweep of brilliance across the eyes of the next wave and noted the remaining charge left in the capacitors was adequate for two more diminished actions. He reset the laser to single pulse and began to pick his targets individually while his two bodyguards picked off as many of the old guards that they could.

San-sool watched incredulously as the first and second wave slaughtered themselves by impalement. The archers continued to waste their arrows on the shields of the small defending force that were still working to Kamiel's master plan.

"This is terrible, Alexander," he gasped. "They have no chance!"

"This is execution, my friend. We are building a world without fear. To do that we have to utterly destroy that evil creature's power-base. I warn you now, it will get worse. Look there, I see a familiar figure. Where the shields have made a small hole. Its Nagoth with her bow."

Link-soo-shan's former number one had worked out a good strategy, tucked away as she was behind the shields. Whenever she spotted a likely target she ordered the shield bearer with her to tilt her shield and she bobbed up. Nagoth took her chances and began to pick off the Group Captains that she easily recognised. Her powerful bow was a good match for the use she put it to. Desperately she searched for her old friend, but of Jaffin, so far, there was no sign. She reasoned that she would probably be at the back with Link-soo-shan.

Once more the defenders pulled back and saw that the heavy infantry had pulled away in the front, leaving a hole. From the far back of the field Nagoth could see a mass of Zanth racing towards them ridden by Link-soo-shan's elite troops. It looked as if nothing could stop them and they would be trampled underfoot. Then some of the young Zanth trod in the raptor dung that had been left in heaps around the area that they would have to charge over. Once the smell of the raptors' excrement reached the Zanth's nostrils, those that were nearest went crazy and began to rear up in an attempt to get away. The wicked horns caught the flanks of the next beast and the riders were tossed from their seats. The half-trained and rider-less Zanth tried to get as far as they could from the smell of the predators and managed to trample underfoot some of Link-soo-shan's elite infantry in their haste to escape. More of them became uncontrollable as the smell began to permeate the area and were abandoned by their riders.

Link pulled hard on the reins and controlled her rearing mount with savage skill.

"Forward, you cowards! Get inside their defences and trample your way to victory!" she shouted and pointed to the retreating defenders.

Indeed, to the amazement of the attacking forces, while the Zanth were going out of control, the defenders were retreating onto the half finished bridges, still with their shields held over themselves. Desperately, the remaining foot soldiers pressed forwards to gain an advantage. As the charging Gnathe once more assailed the trapped fighters, the defenders did a very strange thing. All of them dropped flat to the structure and the un-finished bridge began to float back to the city out of reach.

Before the well-drilled city dwellers left the ramp in the front of the moat, the ones entrusted with the fire-pots lit the fuses.

Alexander watched the well-executed plan unfold from his vantage point on the roof. Two rows of the heavy guards lay impaled on the long lances that Kamiel had made the crafting males produce. Some had made it through and killed some of the city Gnathe, before being impaled from the side. He had picked off some of the charging Zanth and left them frenzied and blind. Link-soo-shan was too far to the back for him to be able to get a clear shot at her or her mount. She was desperately trying to gain order from her surrounding troops. When he saw the rafts pulled back towards the city he knew that the next stage was underway. All the defending Gnathe were huddled down on the rafts with the shield roof over them, hearing crests down as far as possible.

Alexander turned to the Gnathe on the roof with him and said, "Now would be a good time to drop your hearing crest, as you could be deafened when the charges go off!"

Not knowing what to expect, all the Gnathe dived to the floor and put their hands over their crests holding them flat. Alex stood by the laser and waited, not quite knowing just how powerful Kamiel's laid charges were. The Guardian stood impassively with him and watched.

The first charges went off, hurling sections of Link's imperial guard high in the air. Pebbles acting like shrapnel scattered from each explosion, wounding more. The charges close to the front of the moat peppered the defenders' shields with pieces of Link-soo-shan's heavy guards. As the fuses wound their way underneath and further towards the back of the Tyrant's forces, another set of explosions rocked the air, terrifying the elite guards. Foul smelling smoke and dust filled the air combined with Gnathen blood and body parts. Disorientated, blinded and terrified, Link-soo-shan's finest troops did not know what to do.

Those that made a break to the side found themselves running into the nan-nite strands that Kamiel had again stretched from post to post. As soon as Link-soo-shan saw that happen she knew her nemesis was here. This was the moment when Jewel and Natel joined forces and began to lob with terrible accuracy Kamiel's homemade bombs into the rest of her troops. San-sool was lighting the fuses as Jewel and Natel fused their minds and lifted each pebble-loaded gourd into the air in front of him, pausing for a moment. As each fuse started to burn, the dual mind of the Gnathe took hold and hurled it towards the back of the battlefield. Some they timed just right so that they exploded in the air above the cowering undefended troops. Others hit the ground first and tore apart any unlucky Gnathe close by.

Link-soo-shan had lost control of her mount and watched it madly bolt away from the noise and smoke. Frantically she concentrated her mind on the teleki-netic crystal, bound to her arm. She was able to deflect the nearer stones raining down and prevent the shrapnel from hitting herself and Jaffin. Her newly bred fighters were busily trying to dig themselves into the ground and were in no state to do anything but hide. In the middle of all this she felt her communication crystal warm and someone was attempting to enter her mind.

"I warned you," Alexander projected grimly. "I told you that we would come for you and you would be destroyed."

"Where are you? How can you be here?" The vanquished Tyrant frantically searched the bloody battlefield for her hated foe. "I will kill you. Come to me!"

"I am at the city, on the roof. So is my friend Kamiel. How do you like my kind of warfare? Someone else is coming for you, not me," rang Alexander's thoughts in her mind and he withdrew.

Behind her, Fredrick and his two friends watched as the earth shook and Link's forces went to pieces. Shoo-lin and Coen-soo were enthusiastically picking off any of the elite guards that came into their sights and dodging the fleeing Zanth. Fredrick had received the news that the bombardment had finished and he started his promised reckoning with the Tyrant.

Joom had watched the carnage on the battlefield and decided that as the attacking Gnathe were not coming to him, he would go to them. He contacted Abdul and the two of them dropped over the edge of the leafy roof and made their way around the moat's edge. They were quickly followed by the bands of Brood-mothers and their personal guards that had hidden behind the city walls in the arena.

The ape raised his crossbow and proceeded to put nine able-bodied, heavy-duty guards to their deaths who were still trying to get round to the city.

Abdul was working his way around the other side doing much the same. Joom brought his club down onto the head of one of the Group Captains that happened to try to get to her feet in front of him. He was steadily making for the back of the field where the majority of the survivors huddled together.

The rafts had made their way back to the explosion-torn bank and the shield-bearing defenders were fanning out. They were busily collecting sythers from the dead and dying. These they used to deadly effect, remorselessly cutting the throats of any still living guards that they came across.

In the centre of the carnage, leaping over the bodies came Nagoth, searching for Jaffin-shan. She hardly paused to dispatch any of Link-soo-shan's forces that she came across. Trann's fighting staff were organising the collection of the new breed and the ruthless destruction of the rest. At last she could see the larger figure of her once Brood-mother and by her side stood the loyal Jaffin.

Making sure that she was well out of range of Link's telekinetic abilities, Nagoth called out, "Jaffin, it is I, Nagoth. Leave her! She is finished. They will kill her soon and you will be alone."

"What can you do for me, Nagoth?" Jaffin edged slowly away from the dazed Brood-mother whose mind was connected to Alexander's at that moment.

"I can keep you safe. All of the others are deemed too untrustworthy and will be killed. Alexander has given me his word that you will live if you stay with me," and Nagoth frantically beckoned to her.

Jaffin took a last look at the expression of fury flushing over Link-soo-shan's face and took off like someone possessed. She dropped her syther in the trampled crops and leaped and hopped as fast as she could towards the pleading form of her old friend and companion. As she moved out of the Tyrant's reach, a tall silver form leapt forward over the ranks of the fallen, placing himself in-between the Brood-mother and terrified daughter. Two more humanoid figures and two Gnathen ones clad in silver joined it.

Link-soo-shan stopped short and stared with disbelief at the thing in front of her. It was much bigger than Kamiel and a human face looked out at her from under a helmet. She instinctively reached for it with her mind and encountered a slippery something that she could not grasp.

"What are you?" She extended her ripping claws on one hand and dropped back into a defensive pose, with her syther pointing at Fredrick's head.

"Death," said Fredrick, and using Minnis's power, jumped over Link's head and kicked her hard on the side of her jaw.

The Gnathe reacted quickly and spun with the blow, swinging her tail into the space that Fredrick was dropping into. The human had expected this and drew his knees up to his chest so that her tail passed just under his feet. As he landed, Fred dived to the side and rolled over, springing back to a standing position.

He stood in front of her and looked up at the face twisted in hate and said, "I am one of those humans that you met before, when we left you in exile in the valley. You came to my home and killed thousands. Now, it's time for you to die!"

Link retaliated by picking up a wad of dirt and hurling it at Fredrick's eyes with her mind. She also picked up Jaffin's abandoned syther and sent it spinning towards Joom's head. He raised his wooden club to ward off the blow, dropping to his knees with the force of impact and losing his grip on his homemade weapon. Link now took hold of both and sent the club swinging round at the two Gnathe, catching both crossbows as they were aiming them at her. There was an audible crunch as Shoo-lin's arm shattered and Coen-soo was sent spinning round with him unconscious. The two high-tech weapons were smashed beyond use. Abdul saw the sharp syther coming at him and picked up a dead guard, holding it in front as a shield. The point of the sharp weapon sliced through the chest of the guard and out through her back. Four inches of crystallised tail penetrated Abdul's right shoulder, just missing his lung and snapped off. He dropped the crossbow and dropped to the ground with the dead Gnathe on top of him, unable to move.

Fredrick cleared the dirt from his eyes and sprang at the enraged Brood-mother and went for the crystal strapped to her arm, making a clenched fist as he did so. Minnis concentrated her nannite material into a hammer around the human's fist and grew a row of spikes along the inside of Fredrick's arms. Link dropped the double handed syther in front of her and grasped at the silver form flying towards her. She got a hold on one arm with her powerful right hand, but not before Fredrick had brought the hammer down on the crystal.

She felt it shatter and all sense of telekinesis was gone. The spikes inside the silver coated human began to dig into her body, so she swung the human round by the captive arm and wrenched it as she let go. Fredrick spun through the air and hit the ground with a bone-jarring crunch twenty feet away.

"Minnis, my shoulder has dislocated. Put it back in," he grated and the battle-suit twisted the arm back into place.

Fredrick screamed as the bone popped back into the socket and the sweat poured out of him. He rose to his feet to see Joom run at the maddened Tyrant, who was twice his size and leap at the arm that he had hammered.

He shouted at her, "You slaughtered my daughter, Jo-jo, you filthy killer. Now you will pay."

The ape snatched hold of her weakened arm and sunk his canine teeth deep into her arm as she turned to fend him off. She shook him off, leaving a deep bloody gash and caught him with a backhanded slap that turned the ape in the air, spinning him round. As he hit the ground, dazed, and stood up, Link turned to the side and sent the bony end of her tail straight through his stomach. Joom hung in the air screaming with the wound filling the insides of his insulation suit with his own blood. Link-soo-shan shook him off the bony point and left him to bleed.

"No, you unnatural creature, it is you that will pay. I will see all of you die, friends of Alexander, no matter what happens to me on this day! I will die content, knowing that he will bear the loss!" she screamed at Fredrick and advanced towards him, ripping claws extended.

On her way she pulled the dead Gnathe from off Abdul, stared down at him and threw him aside to bleed, picking up her abandoned syther. She began slowly to advance towards Fredrick's position, swinging her weapon from side to side. The human watched in frozen fascination as the brood-mother walked over her dead and kicked them out of her way. Fred began to back away, desperately looking for an advantage. He was weapon-less, having used all of his bolts in situations that had decided the issue for him.

Minnis had flooded his body with as much painkiller drugs at her disposal so that he could use the injured arm. She formed a short sword in front of the right hand and grew a shield over the left with sharp points.

The raptors had all heard the anguished mental screams of pain coming from the small beings that had formed the strange alliance with them. From the first transmitted feelings of pain, the raptors had taken to the air, heading for the battlefield. When Minnis put Fredrick's shoulder back into place, Munch dropped from the skies hissing death and fury. Snapper and Claws followed close behind with the wild male in close attendance.

As Link-soo-shan closed in on the weakened Fredrick she noticed that her enemy was not watching her but the sky above her back. He was grinning.

"Here comes something else you never knew anything about, Link-soo-shan!" Fredrick shouted at the towering creature and pointed.

The Ultimate Ruler turned, looked up into the late morning sun and saw four impossible shapes dropping fast. At the last moment they opened their wings and the crack as they filled with air shook the area. The three female raptors made for their small companions while the larger one took up station some way away. Munch put herself between Fredrick and Link-soo-shan, hissed angrily at the Brood-mother and began to advance towards her.

The Tyrant screamed her anger and rushed at the raptor, swinging her sword as she came. The raptor reared up in surprise and the Gnathe's syther bit deep into the leg of Fredrick's large companion. She screamed in pain and turned away, bleeding over the Gnathe as she pulled her syther from the wound. Link attempted to get at the human down the side of the retreating raptor. The other two raptors were too busy searching for Shoo-lin and the still unconscious Coen-soo amongst the dead Gnathe to notice what was going on. Link had forgotten about the other raptor.

'Leader of Many' had watched the drama without comprehension. He could not understand what was going on in front of his eyes. A raptor killed for food or to win a mate and for no other reason. This action in front of him was unnatural, but this vicious thing had hurt a female. He began to stalk forward.

Fredrick saw Link-soo-shan coming for him, swinging her sword in a scything motion aimed at his legs. Munch had limped to the side of him and was turned away, favouring her wounded leg. He dropped the shield and squatted down to deflect the blow to the legs as Link's syther hurtled towards them.

Nagoth had waited her chance and let fly with her last remaining arrow at her Brood-mother as Fredrick ducked down. The arrow sped over his head and buried itself deep into her groin. Link-soo-shan screamed with pain and smelt a moist foul breath from behind her as 'Leader of Many' leant forward, mouth open. She swung round clutching at the arrow protruding from her groin and dropped her syther in terror as she looked into the tooth-encrusted jaws of her death. The male raptor snapped his teeth together and one half of the Tyrant's body fell to the ground while the other half slid down his throat. 'Leader of Many' dipped his head down and broke off the arrow from the lower section before swallowing that piece as well.

Fredrick lent against his raptor friend's side and just stared at the large beast in relief. His body ached in every muscle and bone, but his thoughts were at peace.

He used the communication crystal around his neck and projected his thoughts to Alexander at the city and said, "She is gone, old friend. It is over. See in my mind what we have done and what we need to do."

Alexander put his arms around Kamiel and said, "She is gone, Kamiel. The blood price has been paid. Tell Asue and the others at the Citadel and Habitat that it is all over."

Kamiel stiffened and said, "You can tell them yourself. Hannah has discovered Link-soo-shan's secret."

The air next to them shimmered and Hannah and Ender-whann-soo appeared.

"Where is my Fredrick? We have much to tell you, but first there are the wounded to take back and heal," the scientist cried.

Alexander showed Hannah the position with his mind and there was a pop as the air rushed in to where she had been.

Fredrick couldn't believe his eyes as first Hannah, then Sharn and the new Minns appeared in front of him with a group of paramedics in attendance. The first to go were Abdul and Joom, who was just hanging onto life. Sharn was already busily putting him back together as she vanished with him.

"How did you get here, little flower?" Fredrick asked.

"I solved her secret of twisting space, after Alexander told me to shut down the blanket," Hannah replied. "That's not all I found out either, but Alexander needs to know before anyone else."

The new version of Minns took a few moments to stop the bleeding from the leg of Munch and knitted it together so that it would heal before she left.

On the roof of the Imperial City two old friends were busily getting together again as Ender-whann-soo and Alexander looked out over the carnage beyond the moat. The Brood-mothers and their personal guards were methodically checking that all of Link-soo-shan's kindred except for the new breed were dead. Those that showed any signs of life were executed on the spot. There would be no more armies in the future for anyone. The only survivors allowed were Nagoth, with her prisoner and friend Jaffin, who were making their way back to the city.

"We have come a long way since the rescue of you and your kindred," Alexander remarked to the towering form beside him.

"There is still much that we can teach each other, my alien friend. Do you know that the two Brood-mothers that I shaped in my pouch carry a great deal of your mind? They will grow up thinking in a completely different way. You were right when you said to Trann that the old ways are finished. We are a new people, the Gnathe and the Humankind."

"What did Hannah mean, when she said that she had something else to tell me?" The human looked appraisingly at his alien friend and added, "I have a feeling that it was quite important."

"Some of the crystals that Hannah discovered at the bottom of that pool do something different to all the others, according to Khann," she said excitedly and turned to fix him with a wide-eyed stare.

"Well, what do they do Ender?" Alex asked.

"Khann says that they seem to co-exist throughout time," Ender answered. "The matrix exists outside of just space. She thinks that it may be possible to open doors in time!"

END

About the Author

Barry Woodham spent his working life as a design engineer/draughtsman and has been an avid reader of science fiction for over fifty years. When he worked on the nuclear fusion project some years ago, he found himself with nothing to read one lunchtime. He began to write the saga of the Gnathe and after many of his colleagues began to read his efforts, as quickly as he could finish the chapters, he continued on and finished the first half of the book. He was persuaded to carry on and was halfway through the final section when, as the project drew to a close, he was able to take early retirement before redundancy, through a legacy. He promised his friends he would finish the story and let them know when he had finished. The joys of early retirement followed—fishing and walking the dogs, and the separation from his old reading colleagues meant the story remained unfinished. He lost the text through changing computers and it took some effort to retrieve the full story. He knew how *Genesis 2* would end, but could never seem to be able to get round to finishing it. This has now changed.

Barry's wife typed most of the first part of the story until he got the hang of doing it himself. And so the story unfolded as he typed and he could tell the rest of the tale. Unfortunately his three sons have no interest in science fiction, so it is unlikely they will ever read it, although they have lent it to enough of their friends to read. "I hope you will enjoy reading this book," Barry says, "as much as all the others and as much as I have enjoyed writing it!"

0-595-33560-8

www.ingramcontent.com/pod-product-compliance
Lightning Source LLC
Chambersburg PA
CBHW051939020726
47501CB00001B/188